POW WOW

POW WOW

CHARTING THE FAULT LINES
IN THE AMERICAN EXPERIENCE—
SHORT FICTION FROM THEN TO NOW

EDITED BY

Ishmael Reed

WITH

Carla Blank

DA CAPO PRESS
A Member of the Perseus Books Group

Library of Congress Cataloging-in-Publication Data

Pow Wow : charting the fault lines in the American experience : short fiction from then to now / edited by Ishmael Reed with Carla Blank.
    p. cm.
ISBN 978-1-56858-340-2 (hardcover : alk. paper)—ISBN 978-1-56858-342-6 (pbk. : alk. paper) 1. Short stories, American. 2. American fiction—Minority authors. I. Reed, Ishmael, 1938-II. Blank, Carla.
PS647.E85P68 2009
813'.01083552—dc22

2008044571

Set in 10.5 point Adobe Garamond by Wordstop Technologies Pvt Ltd. Chennai, India

HC ISBN 978-1-56858-340-2
PB ISBN 978-1-56858-342-6
Published by Da Capo Press
A Member of the Perseus Books Group
www.dacapopress.com

Da Capo Press books are available at special discounts for bulk purchases in the U.S. by corporations, institutions, and other organizations. For more information, please contact the Special Markets Department at the Perseus Books Group, 2300 Chestnut Street, Suite 200, Philadelphia, PA 19103, or call (800) 810-4145, extension 5000, or e-mail special.markets@perseusbooks.com.

10 9 8 7 6 5 4 3 2 1

This book is dedicated to
Sister Goodwin,
Bob Callahan,
Lorenzo Thomas,
Andrew Hope III,
Danny Cassidy,
Paula Gunn Allen,
and
Ron Sukenick

"One must arrive
with a story to tell"
Qanemcikarluni
Tekitnarqelartuq

—a traditional greeting
among the Yup'ik people of the village of Tununak, Alaska
for returning hunters

CONTENTS

FOREWORD

by Ishmael Reed

The late Robert Maynard, former publisher of the *Oakland Tribune*, challenged the media to diversify by the year 2000. They have failed to meet this challenge. An April 2 article in the *New York Times* reported: "The most prominent positions on television remain overwhelmingly with those who are white and male." The same can be said of newspapers. Each day one may read at Richard Prince's media site, sponsored by the Maynard Institute, of the firing, buyouts, and resignations of African American, Native American, Asian American, and Hispanic journalists. Most of the books reviewed are written by white males, whether the publication be the *New York Review of Books*, the *American Book Review,* or the *Nation*, even though the editor of the last magazine is a feminist. This is not the fault of those white male writers who continue to produce quality literature and among whom are those who struggle to have their talent recognized. Rather, it is the fault of the middle persons—reviewers, academics, and publishers—who require that all writers belonging to a particular ethnic group or race write like the acceptable tokens whose sales at Bookscan are muscular. These middle persons are depriving American readers of the variety of perspectives available to them.

Deprived of or excluded from the normal channels of communication by media increasingly monopolized by a few companies, people from diverse backgrounds and from different time periods may have no other means but writing to engage in a cross-cultural or a cross-time dialogue with one another. No other means to comment on the important issues both historical and current: war, slavery, race, anti-Semitism, gender, class, dysfunctional family life, and the like. Writing is a way by which minority thinkers can offer fresh perspectives and by which white thinkers can offer portraits of European Americans that are missing from the world as depicted by the corporate media, where all the men look like Tom Cruise and all the women look like Farah Fawcett.

So what are the views of those not required to file copy overnight for news stories or op-eds? Those not constricted by the pressure-cooker demands of 24/7 cable news programs in which, like championship wrestling matches, the outcome of debates is preordained by ratings-minded producers? What are the points of view of those who are not inhibited from expressing their true beliefs?

Such viewpoints were not to be found in coverage of the 2008 Democratic primary, which showed that the media, no matter how well equipped with modern special effects and the ability to transmit information from across the globe instantaneously, haven't abandoned their role as the village gossip who turns neighbor against neighbor. Unlike those wags, though, the media hire well-dressed, well-educated commentators to sell The Wedge for money. They flood the public's consciousness with what 2008 Democratic presidential candidate Barack Obama called "distractions." At crucial moments during the 2008 Democratic primary, the media pitted blacks against women, even though a large percentage of black women voted for Obama, and pitted Asians and Latinos against blacks, even though, as Latino journalists pointed out, Latinos have voted for black candidates in the past. Their caveat was ignored.

As usual, it took the artist to go a step further. To cite the African heritage of Mexico, something even many Mexican American journalists have failed to mention, an exhibit held in Los Angeles was entitled "The African Presence in México: From Yanga to the Present" (January 31–June 1, 2008). According to the exhibit catalog:

> The existence of Afro-Mexicans was officially affirmed in the 1990s when the Mexican government acknowledged Africa as Mexico's 'Third Root.' For nearly 500 years, the existence and contributions of African descendants in Mexico have been overlooked, although they have continued to contribute their cultural, musical, and culinary traditions to Mexican society through the present day. This groundbreaking exhibition provides an important opportunity to revisit and embrace the African legacy in Mexico and the Americas while creating significant occasions for cross-cultural dialogue.

Pow Wow offers a gathering of writers from different backgrounds, ethnicities, and eras including the present. As only a small percentage of writers earn a living from their craft, the majority who do not are able to address the issues of the day without stockholders peering over their shoulders or being held to the bottom line. They can tell the truth as they see it. They can tell the truth about, for example, the original sin of American history, practiced when the most dominant actors were European settlers: slavery. The periodic demands for reparations to descendants of slaves indicate that the forced enslavement of Africans remains a topic over four hundred years after the landing of those ships with their human cargo in 1619.

In what might be considered a call-and-response, a form later made popular by the great storyteller Duke Ellington, Victor Séjour, a nineteenth-century black author, writes about a slave auction in "The Mulatto." The title character in Stanley Elkins's "I Look Out for Ed Wolfe" participates in a contemporary mock slave auction. Benjamin Franklin's last letter and satire, "Sidi Mehemet Ibrahim on the Slave Trade," written in 1790, shows that some of the arguments supporting slavery sound quite contemporary. He attributes the arguments to a fictional Sidi Mehemet Ibrahim, who tries to justify the enslavement of white Christians by Arabs. With this device, Franklin, who used the pen name Historicus, lampoons the southern justification for the enslavement of Africans, a feature of which defense was that they were better off here—in captivity—than they were in their homelands.

Over two hundred years later, one hears the same argument. Replying to Barack Obama's speech on race, Pat Buchanan said, on March 21, 2008: "America has been the best country on earth for black folks. It was here that 600,000 black people, brought from Africa in slave ships, grew into a community of 40 million, were introduced to Christian salvation."

The late Ralph Ellison doubted sociologists' ability to capture the feel of human relationships. He might have had the same opinion of the yellow press, which offers commentators such as Pat Buchanan unlimited time to comment on race despite controversial statements of a racist nature that he has made in the past. Ellison believed that the writer was better at the task. Sociologists have their graphs, charts, statistics, and jargon, while fiction writers flesh out the way in which characters of different backgrounds—racial, ethnic, class—interact. If Harriet Beecher Stowe and Richard Wright had written sociological tracts rather than novels, they would not have had as powerful an impact upon the public. *Uncle Tom's Cabin* is credited with having started the Civil War, and *Native Son*, in the words of critic Irving Howe, changed how white Americans viewed black Americans. Wright's character Bigger Thomas is not the kindly, subservient uncle staring out at shoppers from the box of rice.

Excluded from media power, American Indian, Hispanic, Asian American, and African American writers often use fiction to tell their side of the American story and to explore the fault lines that separate groups from one another. In the media it is left to outsiders to define members of ethnic groups, often with disastrous results like *Birth of a Nation* and the television series *The Wire*. Cecil Brown, a contributor to this anthology, remarked that he welcomed the recent Hollywood writers' strike because it meant that less demeaning portraits of African Americans would appear in the media. Black representation in the screenwriters' union is a paltry 2 percent.

The main character in John A. Williams's "Son in the Afternoon" is a scriptwriter whose task is to weed out passages in movie scripts that might seem offensive to African Americans. He tussles with a white "hippie" writer who depicts African Americans in a stereotypical manner, an issue that "liberal" Hollywood has chosen to ignore. Film scholars have written about how films have damaged race relations. Black, Latino, and Native Americans complain about their lack of participation in the producing, directing, and writing of films having to do with their cultures. Hollywood has often stirred tensions between people of different groups. With all of its glitz, Hollywood, like television, is like those ancient village wags who engaged in scapegoating. Indeed, some of the most damaging portraits of blacks, the ones that influence public perceptions, are created by those who view themselves as members of the liberal and progressive left. They offer the scapegoaters red meat, while they dine on fish and white wine.

Lamed Shapiro writes about scapegoating in "White Challah," included in *The Cross and Other Jewish Stories* published by Yale University Press. In this classic story, it's the Jews who are blamed. "Someone said that all this was the fault of the Jews. Again the Jews! They sold Christ, they eat white challah and on top of it all they are to blame for everything."

Writers can portray conflicts between city dwellers and country dwellers, or between Hispanics and Anglos, a tension rarely expressed in media that see everything in black and white. Nash Candelaria's "The Day the Cisco Kid Shot John Wayne" opens with an argument between members of a Mexican American family over whether country or city life is more desirable. In the midst of "a family uproar," Uncle Luis shouts to the narrator's father, "You think you're too good for us . . . just because you finished high school and have a job in town! My God! We grew up in the country. Our parents and grandparents grew up in the country."

Just like Elizabeth Nunez's main character Sara Edgehill in *Beyond the Limbo Silence*, who is ripped from the tropics of Trinidad and moves to the cold climate of Wisconsin after she receives a scholarship from a Catholic school, the narrator, suddenly set down in the city, experiences cultural shock. "All the pale-faced Anglos were the vanilla ice cream, while we brown Hispanos were the sauce. The nun, with her starched white headdress under her cowl, could have been the whipped cream except that I figured she was too sour for that." Later Sara observes, "I had never been among so many Anglo children before; they outnumbered us two to one. In the country church on Sundays it was rare to see an Anglo."

The character in Jimmy Santiago Baca's "Imagine My Life" also has problems with Anglos:

> The Anglo boys mocked me and hurled insults at me. I felt ashamed and lowered my head, trying to hide my face. When they beat me up they were heroes; but when I struck back, defending myself and knocking them down, I got the name of troublemaker. Their blows boosted their self-esteem, while, for a time, my defenseless silence assured my survival.

Writers are also able to challenge the official history, the feel-good legends embraced by a knee-jerk patriotism. While the country still engages in a victory lap in the movies and in books over its conquest of Nazi fascism, the experience of the black soldier was quite different. Willie, the soldier in Frank Yerby's "The Homecoming," is one of those soldiers. After fighting valiantly in a segregated army, black soldiers thought that things would change when they returned home; that the Jim Crow laws and racist southern codes would disappear. Because Willie breaks the unwritten laws that define the proper attitude of a black man toward southern white people, Willie is considered wounded in the head, a "crazy nigger." In this story, Yerby tackles a question that has, to this day, remained unanswered. How can a generation be called "great" when its claim to greatness is based upon a lie, when its members, while fighting an enemy whose racial theories plunged the world into war, practiced racism themselves? A generation that rewarded black soldiers by lynching them and depriving them of the GI Bill, which brought millions of white ethnics into the middle class? The treatment of black soldiers after World War II is among the most shameful episodes in American history.

Nancy Mercado, in her story "The Day They Went Shopping," reminds us that the army is drawn disproportionately from among the poor—people not eligible for deferments. The "she" in the story muses, "[I]f she only had money, she could get her parents and brothers out of that apartment situated in a crippled house that made weird noises and swayed with the ocean winds." One brother curses "his meager living conditions to himself night after night." He quits high school "only to find himself drafted into the Vietnam War."

War also breaks up the home of a Native American family in Mary TallMountain's "Naaholooyah." The mother is dying, and the children wonder why they can't live with their father in the barracks.

Many of the stories in this anthology enter into a kind of dialogue with each other that one doesn't often find on the screen, where the side we're on is virtuous while the other side is part of an Axis of Evil. The writer knows that human relations are more nuanced.

Ignored in the hoopla and flag-in-the-lapel rejoicing over the anniversary of the Allied triumph over another Axis is the ambiguity of African Americans' attitude toward the war. Indeed, some were reluctant to fight against "colored" nations. Gerald Horne, in his work *Race War: White Supremacy and the Japanese Attack on the British Empire*, reports that more African Americans belonged to pro-Japanese fronts than to Communist fronts. Nation of Islam leader Elijah Muhammad was arrested for sedition during World War II and charged with making pro-Japanese speeches. John O. Killens never received a Pulitzer Prize because he wrote about this sentiment among black Americans. In his story "God Bless America," as Cleo's husband prepares to join his unit to fight in the Korean War, she says, "I don't understand what colored soldiers have to fight for—especially against other colored people." The war this time is fought in Korea. Instead of invading American forces finding faceless collateral damage or cartoon enemies like those portrayed in the classic *Faces of the Enemy*, fiction affords a gifted writer like Ty Pak opportunity to tell us how it feels to be on the receiving end. It's Sunday, June 25, 1950, and South Korea is under attack:

> With the intensifying American air raids, which did not distinguish between military and civilian targets, it wasn't too uncommon to be reported missing, unless there were witnesses to the contrary. There was no food in the house, and Yoomi had to drag her heavy body laden with clothes, utensils, and other valuables for barter to the nearest open market, until we had nothing left. Even the bedding was gone, and we shivered at night.

Frank Yerby, John A. Williams, and John O. Killens wrote about World War II so that a future generation—one that isn't burdened by racism, the monkey on the back of American history—would be exposed to an argument different from Tom Brokaw and Steven Spielberg's view of the war. The latter's version of World War II has been criticized by black servicemen for eliminating their contribution.

Propaganda books that cast black men as the chief impediment to African American progress are widely reviewed and praised, while books by Williams and Killens struggle to remain in print. They challenge the public lies. Again, the writer can tell the truth. Unlike other media, he or she is not burdened with the demand to fill mall movie houses with bodies, or required to compete about who can best cannibalize eyeballs—the mission of network and cable television.

"Take off that uniform and start behaving like a nigger" was how some white southerners greeted black soldiers who risked their lives to protect them. And soldiers who returned from Vietnam think *they* had it bad. Not one of them was lynched. Yerby's character Willie even had his leg shot off during the war. Willie returns from World War II no longer bowing and scraping before the master race. A few lines of dialogue tell the story. Willie approaches the town square, replete with Confederate regalia including a sign that reads: "No nation rose so white and pure, none fell so free of stain." He is taunted by one of the white townsmen:

"What do it say, boy?" he asked.
Willie looked past him at the dusty, unpaved streets straggling out from the Monument.
"I ask you a question, boy." The white man's voice was very quiet.
"You talking to me?" Willie said softly.
"You know Goddamn well I'm talking to you. You got ears, ain't you?"
"You said boy," Willie said. "I didn't know you was talking to me."
"Who else could I been talking to, nigger?" the white man demanded.
"I don't know," Willie said. "I didn't see no boys around."

Even an old Colonel Bob, Willie's mentor before the war, is shocked at the insolence of the returning veteran. "'Do you think it's right,' Colonel Bob asked evenly, 'for you to talk to a white man like this—any white man—even me?'"

With "Manny," Floyd Salas has written one of the best stories about city life during World War II. It's about a Hispanic soldier, Manny, and the younger brother who admires him. The scene is downtown Oakland, just as white flight was beginning and before people, drawn by television, disappeared into their homes. The dance halls were full and celebrants were entertained by big bands.

War has been a theme covered by American storytellers for hundreds of years. In the ancient Tlingit story told by Anna Nelson Harry, "Giant Rat," combatants fight over rat skin. Reasons for modern warfare aren't all that different from what they were in ancient times. In "The War Prayer," Mark Twain mocks the standard jingoistic appeal that demagogues continue to use to mobilize the public for war. With the creation of bombing from the air, powerful nations have been able to subdue weaker populations with little opposition. But Vietnam and Afghanistan have shown that the mighty United States and Russian fighting forces can be humbled by those who in a former time would have been dismissed as "tribesmen."

Terrorism, including suicide bombing and kidnapping, has become a common feature of modern warfare. Terrorists targeted the La Belle Disco in Berlin on April 5, 1986. Cecil Brown's character Jimmy in "Berlin Disco Inferno" was there: "On the grass where he is standing now, with the rain still slightly falling, he remembers that night when people were walking around with their clothes hanging on them like rags, not far from where he is standing. Another fifty or sixty people lay scattered all over the streets."

In the United States, the spread of privately owned modern weapons into urban, suburban, and rural areas has led to carnage, but so powerful and so armed with cash is the gun lobby that politicians are too timid to challenge its influence. In a series of movies—*American Gangster*, *Street Kings*, and *Training Day*—white heroes use black, Latino, and Asian gang members as target practice. Left entirely unaddressed are the social conditions that create gang members, the focus of Danny Romero's "Mice." In this story a dissolute Hispanic apartment dweller is harassed by some black children with a number of sometimes dangerous pranks. Given that one of the children has an alcoholic mother and a convict father, we know that the pranks might lead to more serious antisocial activities. A character who did do prison time in Jimmy Santiago Baca's story "Imagine My Life" speaks about the importance of listening to wise elders from whom one can learn to avoid falling in with bad company. Of his grandmother, the character reflects: "I could have learned from her; I could have been a better man than I am today. My life seemed to me a fool's jig of drunken jesters dancing for the deaf and blind."

Lucha Corpi presents a Hispanic gang member in her story "Insidious Disease," in which she shows that a good writer can award hero status to those shunned by a mainstream whose heroes tend to be white and male. Her story mentions Rubén Salazar, the crusading Hispanic journalist in Los Angeles who was murdered by the Los Angeles police while reporting on an anti–Vietnam War demonstration. Blacks, Latinos, and Native Americans have complained about their brutal treatment at the hands of the white police since the days of the "patarollers," whites who monitored the movements of slaves found off the plantations. During the O.J. Simpson trial, detective Mark Furhman, caught on tape, boasted about police stations whose walls were "caked with the blood" of black suspects.

Before there were urban black, Hispanic, and Asian American gangs, Jewish, Italian, and Irish American gangs left the streets littered with their murder victims. In James T. Farrell's "For White Men Only," a white gang beats up two black swimmers whose aim is to integrate a public swimming pool in Chicago. The black main character, Alfred, says as he sets out on his mission, "[I]f the Negro was to go on being afraid of the white man, he was never going to get anywhere, and if the Negro wanted more space to swim in, he just had to go and take it." The white gang, led by Buddy Coen, justifies "pounding a few black bastards full of lumps" as a way of protecting "all these white girls bathing around here."

But lest you think whites have a monopoly on bigotry, check out the black racists in Walter K. Lew's "Black Korea 2"; or Harold Ball, E. Donald Two-Rivers' black bus driver in "Harold's Ball," a character one rarely finds in contemporary fiction: a black man seen through the eyes of a Native American writer as he engages in a conflict with bus passengers. Harold's most serious confrontation involves two white gay men. Unlike politicians and the cable guys and girls, he just doesn't have the power to do anything about his homophobia. Two-Rivers uses the omniscient narrator to get into the head of a lovable black bigot. We travel with Harold Ball as he drives his bus through some hazardous urban zones. "He claimed to hate his job," Two-Rivers writes. "He hated noisy teenagers, especially black girls and Mexicans. . . . He hated the *Chicago Sun-Times* because of its conservative writing, yet he read it every day without fail." Harold looks forward to retirement: "'Once I retire, I'm getting my ass out of Chicago, I can tell you that much.'" But we know from an earlier description of his ambivalent attitude toward the Chicago newspaper that he doesn't mean it. Unlike those scriptwriters and novelists who present a monochromatic view of people classified arbitrarily as "minorities," Two-Rivers provides us with the full scope of his character's personality. After he has an encounter with some gay passengers, Harold changes his mind about Chicago. Of these passengers, he muses:

> Character. That's where it's at. The Indian got character and the young white girl too. If that ain't character, I don't know what is, he thought. Respect your elders. Now that's character, he thought, . . . despite the baggy pants and her daddy's underwear. Even those two gay guys. They was willing to stand up for what they believed in and get their gay asses whipped if they had to or, maybe, whip some old foolish ass.

The "old foolish ass" is Harold.

Whereas Harold Ball criticizes the style of the younger generation, young people in stories by Hillel Heinstein, Corie Rosen, Mitch Berman, and Robert Hass observe the customs and styles of an older generation. While the relationship that the sister and brother have to the nation of Israel in Hillel Heinstein's "Let's Go, Israel" is problematic, their parents, now elderly, plan to expatriate to that country. The youngster in Corie Rosen's "The Funeral" observes how his parents deal with the grief caused by the death of his sister. In Mitch Berman's "The Poorest Boy in Chicago," the curmudgeonly grandfather hides his affection for his grandson with a brusque exterior caused by growing up during the Depression. In "Moses Mama," William Melvin Kelley provides us with the portrait of Nanny Eva Dunford, who claims that she was once a slave. Her feminism is based on Scripture. Rosie Lieber was a liberated woman before it was fashionable. In the great Grace Paley's "Goodbye and Good Luck," which exhibits the poetic beauty that Yiddish speakers brought to English, she tells her niece, Lillie, about her on-again off-again affair with the married Yiddish actor Volodya Vlashkin, the Valentino of Second Avenue.

Unlike the fifty-inch plasma screen, these writers, like E. Donald Two-Rivers, offer three-dimensional portraits of people of different ethnic groups. Two-Rivers's black man is different from the 24/7 parade of black men shuffling across our TV screens in handcuffs and jumpsuits. And James T. Farrell—in contrast to many contemporary white authors, who seem to get all their information about blacks from hip-hop CDs and the news—knew enough about the black struggle to create convincing black characters.

But, again, Gerald Vizenor shows that bigoted attitudes are not the monopoly of any one group. In "Panic Portage," Vizenor comments with characteristic dry wit on Native Americans' ownership of casinos. An urbane Indian who has gone from flannel shirts to Armani explains to a visitor to The Good Cheer Casino about expulsion of Afro-Cherokees from the Cherokee Nation.

> The Cherokee, as you know, were slavers, and then, five or six generations later they voted to deny the rights to almost three thousand freedman, but racial separatism is never an exoneration for the shame of slavery. Now we hear the blues of the native slavers, once we had some color. The Cherokee benefited from the labor, culture, and color of their slaves. The recent plebiscite of racist separatism was motivated by greed, dominance, and racial hatred.

When Andrew Jackson expelled the Cherokee from their traditional homelands, the Indians took their black slaves with them on the Trail of Tears. Vizenor also takes shots at hunters "in designer camouflage, snowmobilers in noisy insulated suits, men and women of sport and mockery. . . . They loudly toast and boast, and propagate the cruel separation of humans and animals." Humans not only treat each other cruelly, but also animals.

Writers can challenge gender stereotypes, as well as unexamined notions about people who engage in antisocial behavior. A recent issue of a slick magazine featured photos of some of Hollywood's leading women actors posed in skimpy attire as though they were auditioning before the Mayflower Madam. When these women lose their looks, or grow older, they will not be as much in demand. Without stockholders looking over their shoulders, good writers can present a variety of women, including some who would never pass a screen test or recline on a director's casting couch. In the movies, whites with no visible means of employment live in co-op apartment buildings like New York's beautiful Ansonia, where the Tom Cruise character lives in *Vanilla Sky*.

In "The Guinea Pig Lady," Russell Banks writes of his character Flora Pease: "You often hear in these small towns of a woman no one will deal with anymore, except to sell her something she wants or needs—food, clothing, or shelter. In other words, you don't have a social relationship with a woman like Flora, you have an economic one, and that's it." Flora lives in a trailer park. "She was about forty or forty-five, kind of flat-faced and plain, a red-colored person, with short red hair and a reddish tint to her skin. Even her eyes, which happened to be pale blue, looked red, as if she smoked too much and slept too little, which, as it later turned out, happened to be true." Her body is "blocky and square-shaped." Flora Pease is a character whom writers have the freedom to write about, a woman who will never be played by Nicole Kidman. Banks writes, "Magicians, wise men, and fools are supposed to be able to recognize each other instantly, but so, too, are poor women who raise children alone."

A writer with Banks's talent can also shatter accepted myths. The face of domestic violence, not only in the media but even on a stamp issued by the Post Office, is a black face. Through the character Doreen, an abused wife, Banks shows that white men are capable of injuring women as well. Unlike the trailer park white woman in Banks's story, the Puerto Rican couple in "The Last Dream," by Edgardo Vega Yunqué, has tasted success, but the nagging issue of assimilation dogs the two in their "spacious, high-ceilinged Upper West Side apartment on Riverside Drive," evidence that they have escaped their Puerto Ricanness. They live in a world in which the familiar icons of white culture are honored, lest they be reminded of their roots. Of the wife, Yunqué writes:

> [S]he had grown up in the shadow of La Marqueta, and both of them had been raised speaking "Puertorican," as most of their friends said; her insides screaming with the rage of wanting to announce that she was one of those dreaded Puerto Ricans; cringing whenever the papers or television made the distinctions between Blacks, Whites, and Puerto Ricans; wanting to state

that there were white Puerto Ricans and instead keeping to safe ground and always announcing that they were Spanish.

Isn't it refreshing to encounter Puerto Rican characters different from those we encounter in popular culture, where they are framed by those who aren't Puerto Rican?

Just as Russell Banks and Edgardo Vega Yunqué acquaint us with characters whom we rarely see on television or on the movie screen, Paule Marshall presents Reena, a black woman unlike those who've become pop culture mainstays—prostitutes, or models for Michelin tires. Among other things, she's a reader. Her library is located in "a cold-water railroad flat above a kosher butcher on Belmont Avenue in Brownsville" in Brooklyn. "For Reena, as early as the age of twelve, had had a quality that was unique, superior, and therefore dangerous."

At thirteen, for instance, she was reading Zola, Hauptmann, Steinbeck, while I was still in the thrall of the Little Minister and Lorna Doone. When I could barely conceive of the world beyond Brooklyn, she was talking of the Civil War in Spain, lynchings in the South, Hitler in Poland—and talking with the outrage and passion of a revolutionary.

The narrator and Reena meet as adults. The occasion is the wake for Reena's Aunt Vi, who "never really got to enjoy her bed of roses what with only Thursdays and every other Sunday off. All that hard work. All her life. . . . Our lives have got to make more sense, if only for her."

Like Nanny Eva Dunford in William Melvin Kelley's story, the black women characters drawn by Paule Marshall and Kristin Hunter are fully realized. But while Aunt Vi's generation—the last of the domestic workers, who in 1900 made up 80 percent of employed black women—was beset by economic hardships, the generation to which Marshall's narrator and Reena belong are educated. Their problems are with relationships. Reena's affairs with both white and black men have ended in breakups. The white man uses her to visit revenge upon his father. Her marriage to her black husband disintegrates when his fragile ego cannot withstand his being married to a woman who has a life that doesn't depend on his. In Marshall's story, we are reminded again of the color hierarchy that exists among some minority groups, for not only within African American communities but also within Mexican American, Puerto Rican American, Cuban American, and South Asian ones, the lighter you are the better the breaks you are likely to receive. Reena says,

Because I was dark I was always being plastered with Vaseline so I wouldn't look ashy. Whenever I had my picture taken they would pile a whitish powder on my face and make the lights so bright I always came out looking ghostly. My mother stopped speaking to any number of people because they said I would have been pretty if I hadn't been so dark. Like nearly every little black girl, I had my share of dreams of waking up to find myself with long, blond curls, blue eyes, and skin like milk.

Marshall thus offers a glimpse into the color divide that still exists in ethnic communities. Many minority women are indoctrinated from an early age to believe that the standard of beauty must be that of the white woman icon of the time. They play with dolls that don't resemble them. In "Shirley Temple, Hotcha-cha," Wakako Yamauchi writes: "My Shirley doll sits on my dresser now. I bought her a new wig and made a fancy nylon dress for her. She smiles at me. Her lips are cracked, she's a bit sallow, the luster is gone from her blue eyes. She's not what she used to be. But she's been around a long time now."

Ntozake Shange and her generation are not as reserved in their complaints about the conventional standard of beauty that diminishes their beauty. "Anyway," says the narrator in "aw, babee, you so pretty," "the whole world knows, european & non-european alike, the whole world knows that nobody loves the black woman like they love farrah fawcett-majors. the whole world don't turn out for a dead black woman like they did for marilyn monroe."

Some of those whose appearance is not compatible with a particular country's standard of beauty undergo painful physical alterations to appear beautiful. In a country where straight hair is desirable, those with hair that is not straight use chemicals to make it so. Others' appearance fit the standard well enough that no alteration is necessary. George Schuyler in his great 1931 satire, *Black No More*, made a wager with white readers that they could not trace their ancestry without uncovering black relations. Millions of Americans have black ancestry, though their outward appearance is Caucasian. Authors such as Charles Chesnutt and Walter White were so externally "white," they had the option of passing in the white world, an option exercised by millions. Many black families have relatives who have disappeared into the shadows of white America.

Most American critics concentrate on literature authored by whites, regardless of right-wing propaganda that falsely claims that in American universities and colleges Toni Morrison has replaced Shakespeare. These conservative critics, ignorant of other storytelling traditions, credit William Faulkner and Philip Roth for inventing and keeping alive passing stories. But passing stories are like magical realist stories, which in North America are actually centuries old. In early American stories, animals transform themselves into humans in order to obtain human mates, sometimes by kidnapping.

Of course, Roth didn't have to go to blacks to find a contemporary example of passing. Members of his ethnic group, Jewish Americans, changed their names, as the Irish did, in order to fit in. Some of them, like some Mexican Americans, straightened their hair to avoid being identified as black. From the time of Séjour to today's literature featuring biracial characters, a number of writers have tackled the issue. Sometimes the passing and denial of one's roots leads to tragic results, as in Alice Dunbar-Nelson's "The Stones of the Village." But at other times, as in Langston Hughes's "Who's Passing for Who?" about mistaken identity, passing can often be a source of amusement. Hughes used the phrase "laughing to keep from crying" to describe the comic possibilities of harrowing situations that blacks encounter in everyday life.

In Ray Smith's "Decoy," the experience of blacks being watched by store personnel while shopping in department stores is given a comic twist when two con artists deceive a store detective. In Chester Himes's "The Clochard," published here for the first time, it is an American tourist who is duped, in this case by French hustlers.

Although some characters might attempt to shed their identity by disappearing into a sea of whiteness, others search for a cultural or ethnic anchor. The main character in "Tales Left Untold," by Aphrodite Désirée Navab, says: "I am Iranian, Greek, American. Not just one, but all of them. How I've tried for consistency, to be one of them, complete! Just one of them, please. Just to make things neat."

Mistaken identity can have tragic results. In Paul Laurence Dunbar's "The Lynching of Jube Benson," the lynchers murder the wrong black. There must be thousands of blacks and Hispanics who've been imprisoned and even lynched or executed as a result of witnesses' inability to distinguish one black or Hispanic from another. George S. Schuyler, one of the country's great satirists, began on the left but spent his later years writing for conservative publications. In his sardonic story "Lynching for Profit," he predicted that cable networks and the press would commercialize the hi-tech pillorying of black celebrities for their customers' entertainment. Schuyler, who didn't suffer fools, would have scoffed at recent media discussions about who can use the N-word. Here again, while the public intellectual or academic opportunist might generate book sales by weighing in on the discussion, Charles Wright gets into the viscera of the topic with his "A New Day," about the character Lee Mosely's response to the charged word.

Some assume identities willfully, while others have identities imposed on them. For more than one hundred years, writers have addressed the European heritage of most African Americans, a subject that rarely arises in public discussion. But this unscientific designation has been imposed on blacks to this day. And they are not the only ones who have been subjected to mistaken identity. In Leo Surmelian's "The Sombrero," an Armenian is mistaken for a Mexican. Many immigrants who are not considered white in their country discover that in North America, they can achieve a whiteness upgrade. Undergoing interrogation before entering Canada, a character in Sholeh Wolpé's story "My Brother at the Canadian Border" is asked the ethnicity of his parents. He answers that his father is from Iran and his mother from Russia. The interrogator tells him,

"You are white."
My brother stumbled back. . . . "O my God! All these years and I did not know. I am white. I can go anywhere. Do anything."

Before the recent arrival of immigrants from Southeast Asia and Central and South America, the Irish, the Germans, and the Italians were caught between abiding by the customs of the old country and the tug of assimilation—another subject treated by American writers. In Judith Ortiz Cofer's "Silent Dancing," the title piece from her 1990 collection of essays and poems, available from Arte Publico Press, the father is the central character. His name is mostly in upper case letters. He and his family live in El Building, an apartment building formerly occupied by Jews who, with the Italian Americans, were among the last "white groups" to flee the inner city. The second generation mixes the customs of the old country with those of the new, celebrating both Christmas and Día de Reyes, just as some Jewish Americans celebrate both Hanukkah and Christmas, and some Muslim families enjoy Ramadan and Christmas, and many black Americans Kwanzaa and Christmas. As the young member of a Jewish family says, "Not forgetting we were Jewish did not, however, mean forgetting Christmas."

The tensions between the mother and father in Cofer's story are those of the first generation, those born in one country only to settle in a new one. The father discourages his children from mingling with the Puerto Rican families in El Building; with his navy pension separating him and his neighbors economically, he wants to leave the physical barrio. His daughter seeks another way out by passing, another ancient theme in American storytelling. "I can pass for an American girl anywhere—I've tried it—at least for Italian, anyway. I never speak Spanish in public. . . . I have an American boyfriend." The key tensions in this story exist between the Father, the Patriarch, capitalized, and the mother, presented in lowercase most of the time. The Father, the Patriarch, wants to get away from the barrio. The mother wishes to remain with her own kind.

The United States might be the place where shape changers are required to make a pilgrimage before they die. It may be the center of reinventing oneself. By surveying stories by writers from different cultural, economic, racial, class, and gender points of view, we are able to draw contrasts. In many older tales shape changing is taken quite literally, such as in the magical realist story "A Black Mare," from the Southwest, in which a horse and a woman exchange shapes. Compare that to the contemporary story "Thin" found here, in which Minjon LeNoir-Irwin also refers to literal shape changing, but in a far different context, satirizing one's body shape as an American obsession. Americans paying billions of dollars to lose weight only to regain the pounds might be the ultimate expression of shape changing.

Class issues are addressed in Kristin Hunter's "Debut." The mother has plans for moving her daughter into a higher social station—class shifting.

> It was her mother who had ingratiated her way into the Gay Charmers two years ago, taking all sorts of humiliation from the better-dressed, better-off, lighter-skinned women, humbly making and mending their dresses, fixing food for their meetings. . . . The club had put it off as long as they could, but finally they had to admit Mrs. Simmons to membership because she worked so hard. And that meant, of course, that Judy would be on the list for this year's Ball.

Gender issues have been treated by American storytellers since those told by early Native Americans. Try "Condor Steals Falcon's Wife," told by Ross Ellis, of the Yowlumni Yokuts of California, collected in *Surviving Through the Days: Translations of Native California Stories and Songs* edited by Herbert W. Luthin and available from University of California Press. Also see Washington Irving's classic "The Devil and Tom Walker," which would by today's standards be considered misogynistic because of the portrayal of Tom Walker's wife as a shrew. Poet Ann Bradstreet complains about the restrictions that Puritan society placed on women.

Although blueprints have been imposed on American writers—disproportionately so on minority writers—few have submitted. Mike Gold, a Marxist writer who captures his times and deserves more readers, criticized black writer Claude McKay for writing about cabarets and gin. The feminist blueprint seems to require that women characters be positive, that they dwell in a world where they are always the victims. Gloria Steinem drew the ire of black feminists when she claimed that gender is more restrictive in American life than race. Nicholas Kristof said, following Steinem's lead, that racism will be easier to overcome than sexism. Both seem to have equated the conditions of black, yellow, brown, and red women and men with that of white women.

Longevity rates would seem to refute such an assessment. White women on average survive to the age of eighty-one, while the average life span of black men is sixty-seven years. This is not to say that patriarchs can't be stupidly cruel. The family in Yuri Kageyama's "The Father and the Son" has a higher income than Russell Banks's trailer park dwellers. The father worked at NASA and helped "send people to the moon," but in the story's beginning scene he is lying in a hospital after suffering a stroke. The NASA scientist is now "a lump of meat." This father has often been brutal with his daughter, who recalls: "He reached out and smacked me across the cheek. I would get thrown off my chair. I would see yellow stars circle in my head just like the Saturday morning cartoons."

Unlike Kristin Hunter's character Mrs. Simmons in "Debut," most mothers don't have the time to enhance the social standing of their children. I am one of millions of children, black, Hispanic, and Asian, who often had to fend for themselves while their mothers were away taking care of other families. Both my grandmother and mother did day work until my mother made a fuss at a department store and obtained a white-collar job. "Why are all the black women stock girls?" she complained to management.

The mother in Alejandro Murguía's "Boy on a Wooden Horse" also leaves her son with others—not because she is cleaning the homes of the well-off but because she is an aspiring actress. Murguía writes: "As Mother becomes ever more busy with her career, La Guela [the boy's grandmother] takes over the task of raising me. She demands devotion to her saints, but her endless praying bores me. When I'm forced to kneel with her, I mix up the prayers so she becomes confused."

The mother in Al Young's "Going for the Moon" is estranged from her family, which consists of two brothers, one of whom is the other brother's guardian. "Even though Edrick wasn't but twenty-two, that was old enough for him to be my legal guardian." While the brothers try to make ends meet in a San Francisco apartment, located above a bar, their mother is drying out in Texas. "And as much as Moms and me fought and didn't get along, especially when she was juicing and smoking that stuff, I still missed her something terrible. Sometime in the middle of the afternoon, while I'd be working at the bookstore or in the middle of some class, I'd remember how Moms'd spoken to me inside a dream I'd forgot I had the night before. I worried about her, and wondered how long she was gonna stay down in Texas, drying out."

In John A. Williams's "Son in the Afternoon," the narrator reflects the resentment of those children of color whose mothers doubled as mothers for white families. Of his mother, Nora, the narrator says:

> But somehow when the six of us, her own children, were growing up we never had her. She was gone, out scuffling to get those crumbs to put into our mouths and shoes for our feet and praying for something to happen so that all the space in between would be taken care of. Nora's affection for us took the form of rushing out into the morning's five o'clock blackness to wake some silly bitch and get her coffee.

Of the attention that Nora gives to Ronnie, the child of the white family, the narrator says, bitterly, "We never had the physical affection, the pat on the head, the quick, smiling kiss, the 'gimmie a hug' routine. All of this Ronnie was getting." And a few paragraphs later: "[Ronnie's] head bobbed gently on Nora's shoulder. The only time I ever got that close to her was when she trapped me with a bear hug so she could whale the daylights out of me after I put a snowball through Mrs. Grant's window."

The mother in Williams's story challenges the feminist blueprint for fiction: that all women must be good, and all men bad. Is violence in the DNA only of men, or do women commit domestic violence too? In Bharati Mukherjee's "A Wife's Story," the narrator's mother "was beaten by her mother-in-law, my grandmother, when she registered for French lessons."

I still don't know why the feminist movement has adopted Zora Neale Hurston as an icon. In her literature, women can be just as duplicitous as men, while in standard feminist literature all the women are good and all the men are louts. Unlike the Greenwich Village comfort women that Fielding Dawson and others write about, Delia in Hurston's "Sweat" reaches the breaking point in her relationship with her abusive and clownish husband, Sykes: "Delia's habitual meekness seemed to slip from her shoulders like a blown scarf. She was on her feet; her poor little body, her bare knuckly hands bravely defying the strapping hulk before her." But in Hurston's story "The Gilded Six Bits," it's the woman who is messed up.

Like the women in Katherine Mansfield's "Leves Amores," men are the furthest things from the minds of the title characters in Gertrude Stein's "Miss Furr and Miss Skeene" (fur and skin?). But it seems that here and elsewhere, Stein is more interested in rhythm and lulling the reader into a trance than in telling a story. Stein reminds the reader that at one time writers were prohibited from writing about gay sex explicitly. Susanne Lee's characters Kari and Alex show how much progress has been made. The two make the chic Hong Kong scene in Lee's "Vol de Nuit." Alex, of the "'never leave home without mascara and lipstick' school," services older men for money. How does she handle the "ugly fogies?" Her answer: "Close your eyes, count and think of God or any man you desire." Though Kari has an "emperor" in London, the two women seem to be more interested in each other than men. And if one compares Stein's heavily coded story about women lovers to Russell Charles Leong's story "Geography One," one can gauge how assertive, like the gay passengers on Harold Ball's bus, gay fiction has become.

At one time, the same stigma was applied to couples from different races. In fact, in some states, prohibitions against "interracial" marriage existed until the 1960s, even though millions of blacks were biracial. A stigma still seems to be attached to such couplings, but not as much as in former times. Many whites are still opposed to such arrangements, and some blacks, even those with PhDs, sound like Klansmen and Klanswomen when speaking of such pairings. All that separates them from a Grand Dragon or somebody else in a white sheet are their designer clothes. In Roberta Hill's story "Cables," a "black guy" who is "French, Irish, African-American, and Cherokee," and a woman—"Mohawk, Dakota, and French"—are attracted to each other.

Moses and Alva in Stanley Crouch's "Dream a Dream of Me," also seem to enjoy each other's company. Like Conyus Calhoun's narrator in "Wormwood," an endearing portrait of North Beach denizens that spotlights the social diversity of that San Francisco district, the reader travels with the couple as they hit the New York landmarks—the Apollo Theater, the Savoy, the Modern Art and Metropolitan museums, Carnegie Hall. The time is the 1940s when avant-garde jazz artists were blossoming on 52nd Street. One of their friends is Charlie Parker. Lester Young, the great tenor man, also makes a cameo appearance, and Moses is put off by his bad manners. Unlike the stick figures that we see in the movies and on television, Crouch presents blacks who have culture. Like Crouch's couple, the characters in Ellen Geist's "Big Bug" shows that some cultures resist being vacuumed up by "the Anglo Saxon mainstream," as one writer in the *New York Review of Books* wishes it to be. He said that blacks were the only ones holding up complete assimilation—that they were a drag on the process of our becoming all alike.

In "Big Bug" the couple consists of a patient who awaits the results of a biopsy and her doctor, who at a crucial moment shows his humanity—a comment on the impersonal and sometimes begrudging services one receives from HMOs, for whom profit is the goal.

Family members are alienated not only from one another but also from government. Vivian Demuth, in "Night of the FEMA Trailers," makes government incompetence the object of her stinging satire.

On the tube and in the movies, stereotypes about different religions are looped endlessly. The old stereotype of the sinister Oriental "Fu Man Chu" has been replaced by the sinister Islamofacsist. Just as many Americans during World War II could not distinguish between Japanese who'd been American citizens for generations and the enemy, Island Japanese, many today cannot distinguish between American-born Muslims and those who bombed the World Trade Center. While movies and television commentators have whipped up hysteria against Muslim Americans, the brilliant young writer Wajahat Ali succeeds in his story "Ramadan Blues" not only to teach readers about some of the customs of Islam but also to introduce us to a young Muslim who has the same obsessions as members of his generation. He struggles to fast during the Muslim holy holidays. He makes a vow to his father: "'I promise not to eat during my fast. I will only eat at *maghrib*, after the sun sets, with every other fasting Muslim.'" Ali reminds us: "This previous promise fell victim to a delectable and treacherous 'M&M.' Like Eve and her apple, the young boy discovered his 'fall from grace' stuck to the inner linings of his Husky pants' pocket covered with a still edible chocolate-y goodness. His first attempt at fasting was hijacked by a stale, melted candy."

Most interactions between different ethnic and racial groups are mediated by outsiders. An anthology such as this one provides an unrefereed, one-to-one encounter between divergent social interests. In "Gold Coast," James Alan McPherson examines a relationship between a black student and an apprentice to an Irish American building manager. Fielding Dawson looks at a legendary black tavern owner in "Pirate One." In "Backcity Transit by Day," Wanda Coleman views a Hispanic woman through the eyes of a black woman.

When people ask, Does writing change things or affect events, they should look at this anthology, where they will learn and even be entertained by points of view unavailable elsewhere. In Hollywood and television, it's a 24/7, 99-cent fast-food intellectual diet. When I compare these fiction writers' contributions to what is called the marketplace of ideas, with its bought-and-paid-for points of view that monopolize the attention of average members of the public, who get all their information about the world from television and have their opinions of other groups influenced by Hollywood, I regret that there are no antitrust laws that apply to art.

In assembling this anthology, I have read over four hundred short stories written by American writers of all backgrounds. It is a journey I recommend for all readers who want to know where American civilization has been and where it is going. It is a pow wow, a gathering of voices from the different American tribes.

IshmaeL Reed
Rockefeller Center
New York
Cinco de Mayo 2008

POW WOW

RAMADAN BLUES
Wajahat Ali

"I promise."

The young boy—ashamed, dishonored, and fearing the wrath of a vengeful, omnipotent Allah—promised his Pakistani immigrant father with conviction and resolve.

"I promise not to eat during my fast. I will only eat at *maghrib*, after the sun sets, with every other fasting Muslim."

This previous promise fell victim to a delectable and treacherous "M&M." Like Eve and her apple, the young boy discovered his "fall from grace" stuck to the inner linings of his Husky pants' pocket covered with a still edible chocolate-y goodness. His first attempt at fasting was hijacked by a stale, melted candy.

But, that was 2 days ago on the 27th of Ramadan. The blessed month—the young boy was taught—in which Muslims fast from eating, drinking, and being bad people, so Allah would be happy with them and forgive their sins and let them enter heaven and not go to Hell, where they would burn forever and ever and ever.

During the month of Ramadan, fasting Muslims were also forbidden from engaging in "adult activity" and "fornication" until sunset. The young boy asked his parents, "What does adult activity and *for-nee-katyon* mean? Is that what happens when men and women go to their rooms, lock the doors and it sounds like they're hurting each other?"

The parents, flushed with concerned, grave looks blindsided by a question they hoped to avoid till the boy was a teenager, sharply answered, "We'll tell you when you're older! Who taught you this word?"

"It's in the book you gave me about Ramadan."

The mother's eagle eyes honed in on the father, whose lowered head conceded a confession.

"Just—don't worry about that now. Tomorrow is the last day of Ramadan, and you will *inshallah*—God willing—do your first *roza*, right?" coached his mother.

"First *successful roza*," added his father both proud and hopeful. "*Mashallah*—what a big boy doing your first fast. So much sooner and younger than all the other boys! Everyone at the community *iftar* will be so proud of you."

"Be sure to tell the uncles and aunties you fasted," reminded his mother. "Then, they will give you more *eidi* money and presents on *Eid*. Except of course for Shabnam Aunty and Abdullah uncle—they are *kanjoose makhi choos* [Literal translation: Misers who suck more than a bee]. Never once have they given you *eidi*. We've given their 4 children *eidi* money on every *Eid* year after year . . ." and the young boy, accustomed to his mother's rants, stopped paying attention and ran upstairs to play his Nintendo.

Later that night, the boy's father quietly entered the boy's room as the boy violently mashed his thumbs against the plastic game controller. The father smiled looking at the son. "What's so funny?" inquired the young boy. "Nothing," remarked the father.

"*Beta*, I want to give you this," said the father as he placed two crisp George Washingtons in his son's pudgy hands. "Is this my *eidi* already? But it's not even *Eid* yet! And last year, you gave me $10." The father smiled and calmly replied, "It's not your *eidi*, relax. *Inshallah*, you'll get more on *Eid*. Don't be greedy! I'm giving you $2 now on one condition and one condition only: you promise me *again* not to eat during your fast tomorrow. After the sun sets, then you can eat *iftar* with all the other Muslims only *after* sunset. If you complete the fast, I'll give you $5 at *iftar*."

"Whoa!" exclaimed the boy.

"Yes. 5 whole dollars just for you on top of this 2 dollar down payment. Ok? But, if you break your promise and eat like you did before, then, well, I will be very disappointed, *beta*. So, do you think you can do it? *Think* before promising. Remember, Allah knows all our intentions and thoughts. Can you make an honest promise?" questioned the father, still holding on to the green.

"I-I promise—this time I'll do it. I swear."

The father released the money, kissed the boy on the cheek—which prompted the boy to wipe the disgusting wetness off his face with left palm as per custom of all young boys. The father made his way for the door having successfully completed the contract. Just before leaving, the father put his hands in his *khameez* and remembered—

"Wait, *beta*. Here, I want you to have something." The father looked down at the furry item, and his eyes—if only for a moment—recalled a youth long since passed but not entirely forgotten.

"My father gave this to me when I was a boy your age—many, many years ago, *beta*. It reminds me of you. So, now it is yours." The father gave the young boy a small plush toy that looked like a white cow with two small horns.

"Why are you giving me a cow?" asked the boy.

"It's a *bakra*—a goat. It's *zidee* like you."

"What does *zidee* mean?"

"It means stubborn."

"What does stubborn mean?"

The father smiled, and, before leaving, answered, "I'll tell you when you're older."

The boy examined the plush toy that wiggled around in his hands making a "whish" squishy sound when he pressed it. He tossed it aside and thought to himself, "Why do I get so hungry when I fast? I get *so* hungry especially towards the end. I'm always hungry" the young boy mused to himself, fearing tomorrow's impending dietary discipline. This piety exercise seemed unfair and almost cruel to the portly seven year old boy, whose famished innards played a vigorous game of pinball with his organs and growled like Chewbacca only 2 days ago during his initial aborted fasting attempt.

Praying to Allah as he nuzzled, comfortably, in bed underneath his Batman blankets, wearing his Spiderman pajamas and Incredible Hulk t-shirt, the boy earnestly pleaded:

"Dear *Allah-mia*, please let me not eat tomorrow until *maghrib*. I will try very hard, but you made me so hungry the last time I tried. So, please, *Allah-mia*, please help me fast so *Ami* and *Abu* don't get sad and mad at me. And, also, please give me lots of *eidi* and, also Tecmo Super Bowl for Nintendo on *Eid*. I promise, promise, promise I'll be a better person and Muslim—so please don't let me go to hell. *Ameen*."

And so, on the last day of Ramadan, the young boy sat by himself swinging on the *masjid*'s lopsided, downtrodden swing-set, that was independently constructed by the community's Muslim uncles for their American-born "youth." Across the street, a large ice cream cone was lit in front of Briar's Ice Creamery, which sold fudge twirl with "M & M" toppings on a sugar cone—the young boy's favorite.

The community's *masjid*, which in actuality was a rented senior center recreational facility, served as a "temporary" mosque until the "real" *masjid* was completed. The "mosque" smelled like Ben-gay curry and Vic's Vapor chai. The young boy's clogged sinuses and allergies always miraculously cleared up after a *masjid* visit.

The center's staff repeatedly asked the Muslim leaders, "Why are there pools of water by the sink in the restroom?" however, they never received an adequate answer. How could the uncles confess, let alone explain, the Islamic ritual of *ablution*, a quick water cleansing ritual where Muslims washed their face, arms, and feet three times before offering their daily prayers?

Instead, when asked this question week after week, *Ganja* uncle, aptly named for his shiny, bald head that a resembled a brown Mr. Clean, simply pointed to *Mota* uncle, nodded his head, and said no more.

The scapegoat and martyr for the community's religious idiosyncrasies was *Mota* uncle: a morbidly obese, middle aged, nearly invalid Pakistani uncle who barely spoke English and always sat in the corner eating his wife's sweet, homemade *halwa*. When the young boy would grow older he would fondly recall *Mota* uncle's bright colored suspenders attached to his corduroy pants that he wore up to his chest like a *Desi* Santa Claus. His bellowing laugh consumed all other noises and sounds and reddened his face like the strawberry syrupy color of a *Rooh Afza* bottle. *Mota* uncle used to feed the young boy *halwa*, and then bless the boy by grazing the boy's head with his hands and saying, "*Allah khush rakeh*"—May Allah keep you content. The young boy always thought that *Mota* Uncle was much smarter than he appeared and secretly knew all along of *Ganja* uncle's deception; but, since he was a nice man, he kept quiet, played dumb, and ate his *halwa*. The young boy always liked *Mota* Uncle for that. This was to be his last Ramadan.

"Brothers, brothers. Sisters, please. Please. Please stop talking. Please—" begged the thick, accented South Asian voice cracking the audio on the homemade speaker system. The young boy could recognize this distinctive voice even if he was deaf, blind and mute. Pakistani *dari-wala* uncle, aptly titled for his lengthy and scraggly beard that looked like curly Velcro stuck on his face with a Glue-stick, dominated the mosque's only megaphone pleading members to give "funds" and "donations" for "the unfinished community mosque project." *Dari-wala* uncle also always complained about "the brothers and sisters" who parked their cars illegally on the road or pavement and never in the rented parking lot. As the years eventually passed, the young boy never recalled seeing any cars parked in the lot—ever.

However, today, the *dari-wala* uncle kept requesting, in fact begging, that the shoes, *jootas* and *chapals* be placed outside the center, next to the door. The young boy saw nearly one hundred shoes inside the center—in front of the door.

The young boy, naturally shy and bored by the *iftar* preparations inside the hall, awkwardly sat on the deformed swing chair, uncomfortably squeezing his above average "healthy" rear in the seat, and casually swinging back and forth waiting for *maghrib*. He could smell the *kheema samosas* made with ground beef, the deep fried, potato *pakoras* and the chicken tikka—no—wait—no. Ah yes, sorry, the lamb curry. Mmmm. The young boy's stomach started to jab and shimmy.

Meanwhile, the other boys played a make shift game of tag football, in which the bigger and older kids would always play the fun positions of QB, Running back and Wide receiver, forcing the younger kids to play the lame position of offensive line. Normally, the young boy would try to play—he was, naturally, the "center" on account of his "healthy" size—but today he recalled yet *another* promise he made earlier to his mother.

"*Beta*, for the last day of Ramadan, I want my *shehzada* to look like a handsome prince. Here, wear this brand new cream-colored *shalwar khameez* your aunt bought you. It's from Pakistan and is 100% cotton! It is extra large on the account of your healthy size. Promise me you won't get this dirty or spill *khana* on it like you always do! Promise, ok?"

The young boy's daily meals could easily be ascertained by observing his t-shirt at the end of the day. Yesterday, the evidence alluded to a smudge of purple (peanut butter and jelly), a blotch of dark brown (chocolate milk), a yellow spot (mustard indicating a *halal* turkey sandwich), and some turmeric powder on his collar indicating a nourishing, authentic Pakistani *salan* or curry for dinner.

To honor this second promise, the young boy quietly swung on the set by his lonesome avoiding the dirt, grass and mud stains that could potentially be acquired by a harmless game of football.

The other Muslim boys had already made fun of him on account of his costume and called him "hella gay" for not wearing t-shirt and pants. The young boy retaliated, "I only wore this because my mom made me!"

This comment borne from ignorance and honesty, the young boy later learned, was a grave mistake—as it fueled the other boys' laughter and ridicule. In addition to being "hella gay," he was now also affectionately known as "mamma's boy" and "Jabba the Hut" on account of his "healthy size." His stomach now started throwing counters and hooks.

He fumbled around his *shalwar khameez's* one pocket and found the two crumpled and wrinkled George Washingtons. His plush toy goat, completely concealed in his pocket as to avoid mockery, served as his only companion. With one hand squeezing the goat, the young boy's other hand unraveled the green paper. He turned around and saw the ice cream cone across the street—illuminated. The sun prepared for its daily retirement as the moon began rising for its nightly comeback. Within ten minutes, the sun would set, the last fast of Ramadan would be complete, and the community would eat *iftar* together, joyously awaiting the next day's *Eid* festivities.

The young boy shamefully entertained a wicked thought. His stomach threw a knockout combo and went down for the count.

The *Adhan* could be heard across the street—even at the ice cream store. The call to prayer announced *maghrib*, the daily prayer at sunset, commencing *iftar*—the opening of the fast. Throughout the day, Muslims practiced a spiritual discipline of moderation and restraint. That discipline died the moment the aluminum foil was removed from the *pakora* and *samosa* trays and the sweet dates were placed on the fasting tongues. Chaos, screaming children, garrulous women, hungry uncles, nonstop commotion, the hustle and bustle for food, the laying of mats preparing for prayer: another typical *iftar* thought the father spying the crowd for the young boy.

As the grease ridden plastic plates and date seeds accumulated in the black garbage bags, the father stepped out to find the young boy. His first inclination was to look on the field and ask the older boys who were playing football if they had seen a young boy in a *shalwar khameez*. The boys, upon remembering, again laughed. The father looked around, called the boy's name, and then saw the swing set that barely moved as if someone had recently abandoned it in haste.

The father approached the swing, saw no one, but heard a quiet whimpering from behind the tree. Nearing the tree, the father heard the whimper transformed into small sobbing noises reminding the father of his son's voice. Hiding, the father found a young boy, with his back turned, quietly crying. The father spun the boy around and saw his son.

The young boy, with tears streaming down his cheeks, held a half eaten, fudge twirl ice cream on a dripping sugar cone in his left hand while squeezing the plush toy in his right. Most of his mouth and chin, like his t-shirts, resembled a Pollock painting smeared with melted chocolate and vanilla ice cream, including pieces of "M&M" sugar coated shells stuck on his lips.

At that moment, it appeared the boy had only broken one of his promises.

And then—a drop of ice cream from the sugar cone fell on his *khameez*.

IMAGINE MY LIFE

Jimmy Santiago Baca

One afternoon, as I was editing video footage shot in the village where I spent part of my childhood, my grandmother's face appeared on the monitor, and shock waves of hurt erupted in me. Her image revived the unbearable pain of leaving her when I was a child. I always thought my childhood was savage, beautiful in parts, but mostly full of hurt. Seeing her face, ravaged leather cracked and burned by the sun, her silver, squash-blossom eyes, it came back to me how much she had loved me and how warm and nurturing my childhood had been because of her love.

On the film, her mouth pursed into wrinkles as she said in Spanish, "You ran every day to the railroad, and no matter how we spanked and scolded you, you would run to play on the tracks. You spent so many afternoons there. You loved waving to the caboose engineers, and throwing rocks at the cattle cars to see if you could hit them between the slats. You had a fascination for things that went away, that traveled and came by in a whoosh and then were gone. You wanted to go with them, and it was hard to bring you back, to bring you home, especially after you had seen a train. You wanted to go after those trains, and I was scared when you ran alongside them. Once you threw your rosary on top of one of those flatcars and waved it good-bye. Yes, how you loved things that ran and went on and on."

I didn't remember any of that. It hurt to have forgotten so much, and I wondered why I had imagined my life so destitute and deprived.

My grandmother had an old-world decency. She would offer food first to the guest, offer the best chair, offer whatever the guest lacked: comfort, a bed, change from her penny purse. She would share anything she had, listen in consoling silence for hours, give of herself unstintingly, and pray every night for those less fortunate than she. I would fall asleep to that mumbling drone of prayers, like a Buddhist monastery chant. They calmed me and I fell into tranquil dreams.

My grandmother's face has a powerful dignity, like that of an old female eagle on a craggy peak, whose world is eternal. Her gestures are restrained, tentative and soft, as if the world around her, the innocent earth and flowers, were a child easily bruised. Her silence is sunlight sparkling in a freshwater snowmelt stream.

The memories of her suffering, evoked by those film images, were too much for me. I stopped the monitor, pulled on my oilskin jacket, and left the house. As I walked, a dark remorse brimmed in me. If I had not left our village, if I had stayed all these years with her, I could have learned from her; I could have been a better man than I am today. My life seemed to me a fool's jig of drunken jesters dancing for the deaf and blind. I fled from her face because it was too strong a telling of undeserved suffering. As I thought these things, my rage burst out in savage sounds of grief.

Those who cannot see might take my grandmother's kindness and caring for weakness. She has lived with hunger—beans, tortillas, and chile her daily bread; worn frayed and faded clothes, mended a thousand times over. Yet never has she extended her hands for help, those hands always reaching to help others. For more than eighty-five years she has risen before daybreak to prepare the breakfast for her family. Her meals are offerings of the highest graces from her heart—food like spring flowers, to those who know how to savor the fragrant scents of fermenting earth and the magic of dew and sunlight. Her aged body is bent as if in perpetual homage to the earth. Those aspects of goodness that she embodies—truth, kindness, giving, and compassion—are virtues of high wisdom that the hurrying world derides.

I wish I had sat with her longer to listen to the stories of the history of our people that she carried inside her frail rib cage as a morning dove carries the song that awakens dreamers to the dawn. On rare visits after I left home, we would sit in her kitchen, happy to be together, and I would make her laugh, so hard she would cry, at my *vato loco* jokes, pulling her handkerchief from her sleeve and dabbing her wrinkled cheeks. She loved my wordplay. To her I was still the little boy who obeyed no one, who after getting spanked would rush to a grown-up's knees and hug them, who needed to be loved and was afraid to love. I was still the angel who tripped over his wings and loved running more than being still—and good, who loved laughter and men's conversations in bars more than prayers in church.

When I would tell her how difficult it was to pay my bills, she would smile gently and say, "Poverty in the pockets brims riches in the imagination, that's why you are a poet."

Those images of my grandmother's anguished face impacted the deepest reserves of my feelings and made me understand the misery of her life as something criminal. How distant she is from my world, how much truer and more sustained is her world in grounded work of the spirit. As I mourned the distance, it seemed as if my life, a boat halfway across the lake, was capsizing.

Yet as a child I had lived in her world and drawn from her spirit, the mirror that gave me my face. When I was near her, I too was gentle and caring, and raucous with joy as a yearling colt cavorting on canyon slab rocks, outrunning the wind. With gusto and reverence, I lapped up hot chile and bean soup, slurped the goat's milk that fed my young strength. Leaping up from the table, I would roll on the ground, intoxicated with laughter.

In those early days, I used to watch the men of our barrio build adobe and clapboard houses for neighbors, how their hands worked the earth with love, with such dignified attention to their tasks. The rigors of life were themselves occasions of praise for the sustaining life force that allowed us to breathe and wake and work. Work became a celebration of hands, of fingers that could move and bend, grip and push. Intelligence, wood, mud, voice, eye, were all precious, all gifts, but laughter was the highest gift, and courage and endurance. When the men worked there was much laughter, but long spells of silence, too, before the talk would start up again, so quietly. They did with words what Bach could do with musical notes: they composed the most beautiful improvised poems from everyday talk. And, as I listened, the red seed of my young heart took root and blossomed under the prairie moon.

These men always followed careful pathways through their days, following ways where they would not be obstructed, avoiding foreigners who might question them or block their passage. They refused promotions that would compromise their cultural values, preferring to work with friends and earn less than to work with strangers at a higher status and wage. Work of the hands, with the earth, was to them holy work, good for the spirit, that allowed a man to feel his life lived on earth was shared with others. And there is much good to say about leaving your house at dawn, in your trusty jacket, and breathing in the cold air, walking down a familiar path to meet friends who wait for you, noticing the changes in the fields around you, and feeling the rising sun on your cheeks and brow.

It was a mythic life they lived. Yet these gentle heroes were regarded as ignorant and vicious by those who did not know their hearts. Outsiders provoked them to fight to enhance their own machismo. They treated these kind men as if they were knife-carrying savages, every one, against whom you had to strike the first blow. When they came around looking for trouble, or arrogant tourists snooped around our yard, my uncles would ask them politely to leave. But then, if they still hung around, treating the place as if it was their own, my uncles would get angry. Without a word they would lift these intruders off the ground and toss them into the pickup bed, or drag them out of the yard by the collar and throw them in the dirt road.

The time came for me to leave the pueblo and go to school. There I learned hard lessons not to be found in books. The Anglo boys mocked me and hurled insults at me. I felt ashamed and lowered my head, trying to hide my face. When they beat me up they were heroes; but when I struck back, defending myself and knocking them down, I got the name of troublemaker. Their blows boosted their self-esteem, while, for a time, my defenseless silence assured my survival.

Looking at the monitor, hearing my grandmother talk and seeing her gestures, brought back to me what I had lost. Because I was too fragile and sensitive to endure the abuse, eventually I struck back. And, in so doing, I lost the inner balance of my elders, rejecting their wisdom and becoming lost to their ways.

At first I withdrew into silence, searching out others like me, brown children from rural towns whose confidence had been crushed; outsiders, unwanted, scorned, and condemned to lives of servitude. But later I rebelled, refusing to do anything I was told to do. Yet fighting was against my deepest instincts. When I raised a fist, my other hand stretched out, pleading for peace. I was caught in a conflict not of my making that squeezed from me every drop of my childhood's sweetness.

I soon realized that, to many, I was just a *mestizo* boy destined for a life of hard work in the fields or mines, and nothing more. But that was a judgment I couldn't accept. Knowing no other way to refuse, I found myself falling into the dark worlds where the winos and ex-cons live, a gypsy child in the urban wasteland, hanging under neon lights and on hopeless street corners. I began to drink and take drugs.

I was becoming what society told me I was—prone to drugs and alcohol, unable to control my own life, needing a master to order my affairs, unworthy of opportunity and justice—a senseless beast of labor. I drugged my pain and drowned my self-hatred in drink, seeking oblivion. I had no future, no plans, no destiny, no regard for my life; I was free-falling into bottomless despair. Death seemed the only way out.

Finally, I found myself hoping for death in a fight with the police or the Anglos; or that a security guard would shoot me when I tried to rob his building. Or that one night while driving my car I'd be so high I would sail off a cliff and explode in a rage, of bursting petroleum and gnarled iron, my misery ending in a smoldering, lifeless mound of pulverized bone and burning flesh at the bottom of a canyon.

Now I had become the coauthor, with society, of my own oppression. The system that wanted to destroy me had taught me self-destruction. I had become my own jailer and racist judge, my own brutal policeman. I was ruthless to myself and murdered all my hopes and dreams. I was in hell.

They told me I was violent and I became violent, they told me I was ignorant and I feigned ignorance. It was taken for granted I would work for slave rations at the most foul and filthy jobs, and I did. It was taken for granted I could not resolve my own problems, and I relinquished control of my life to society's masters.

I was still young, a teenager, tormented because none of what I did was who I was. I was screaming for release, I was afraid. My dreams for a good life, a life I would make for myself, had been strangled at birth or were stillborn.

They sent me to prison for drug possession. And there, out of suffering, I found a reprieve from my chaos, found language, and it led me back to the teachings and conduct of my elders. I discovered a reason for living, for breathing, and I could love myself again, trust again what my heart dreamed and find the strength to pursue those dreams.

Language has the power to transform, to strip you of what is not truly yourself. In language I have burned my old selves and improvised myself into a new being. Language has fertilized the womb of my soul with embryos of new being.

When I left prison, I went to see my sister, who showed me photographs of a teenager leaning against a Studebaker, his foot on the bumper, a bottle of wine in his hand. In the background a park, mildly subdued in afternoon sunlight. It was me, my sister said, at Highland Park. I remember my amazement and pain that I had no recollection of ever being this person I was looking at.

The minstrel singer I am, whose hand-clapping, heel-kicking love dances celebrate every living moment, has always found it hard to go back home. The place of humble origins exposes the illusions of my life. My loss thunders with fountains of memories, and I want to reach out to the paths, the alleys, the leaning fences, the adobe bricks, the ground, and kiss them all, rub my face in the grass and inhale the sweet earth and mesquite fragrance of my innocence.

Going back, there is so much hurt to overcome.

Recently, I visited our village again. My grandmother's house there is a very lonely house, filled with spirit shadows, spiritual presences, lingering echoes of ancient drumbeats. In the yard, the golden yield of spring in all its millions of shoots is evocations of the returning dead, breaking dirt to smell and taste and bathe again in the warm sunlight.

My grandmother is hunchbacked and disfigured now with age, a bronzed anchor, her hooked fingers refusing to loosen their grip on the *llano*. Her wrinkles are encrusted watermarks on canyon walls, telling of almost a century of living. So many years after her birth, she still stands in her back doorway to welcome friends.

Pools of silence float in the rooms where her children, my uncles and aunts, once lived. People were born and grew up there and went away, leaving their spirit prints on the air. There is something in quiet rooms where old grandfathers and grandmothers have lived and died that vibrates with sanctity. Some of these presences do not want something to be touched or revealed. Others want something to be remembered. These spirits mourn lives filled with struggle, pain, solitude, and love, mourn the moments when they felt truly one with all earth and all people. And now there is empty space, the great vertigo of nothingness, of chairs and beds, rugs and old photos, and curtains and wood and windows falling into a meaningless abyss of motionless silence.

So few things make sense to me. I have lived on the dark side of life so long, nosing my way into patches of rotting life to find my answers; the side of life where I wear my coat without sleeves, where sometimes I wake up in the morning and shave only one side of my face, where I wear a hat with a brim and no crown. I furnish my life with what I can find on the road or in trash cans—books, chairs, and shoes that have known other lives, picked up by the waysides on my journey. I am fool and king, genius and imbecile, for this is what it is to be a poet. In my poems, whatever has been crippled in me, my hope and love and trust and endurance, rises again in spume of fire, unleashing bird wings and jungle howls. My poems beckon those who are dry into the rain, those without love into lovers' beds, call those who are silent to cry out and moan in revery.

Who can say why one day I take my shotgun and shoot the newspaper, bits of paper floating on the air as the little dog whines and scampers for cover? The poor telephone rings, and it, too, goes up in an explosion of black plastic pieces, and I am howling and laughing. The next thing I know, I am sitting cross-legged in a tepee under a pine tree in the forest off South 14, fasting and meditating. This to me is normal.

How can I contain this violent bursting of canoes that white-water in my blood and vault into the world laden with songs and flowers? Such joy will not be confined in prisons of nine-to-five. There is too much life and too much flint in my blood, and the crazy and wild light in a boy's eyes, the innocence in a small girl's whisper need all my life to tell and to praise.

And so my grandmother. How her image hit me with a jolt of lightning, and how her way of living, so different from mine, makes so much sense to me now, and I understand her gift to me. In her presence I can be anyone. I am a scuttling lizard scurrying from tin can to tin can, under boards, into weeds; then I jerk my praying mantis head and my right eyeball stares in one direction while my left eyeball swivels askance. My heart is a cow's tongue slowly licking a block of ice. My legs want to catch the train the way a cat catches a mouse in the cupboards. I flick on the light in the midnight of my life, and cockroaches skitter everywhere on these pages, on the fingers of the reader, along the woman's dress, up the man's arm and neck and into his nose, to nest in his heart that touches the life around him with cockroach antennae, testing the floors in filthy housing projects. In the French Quarter, I am that woman at the table by a window drinking her cappuccino, her suffering concentrated in her ankles like cold iron anvils pounded with sledgehammers, her life a red-hot iron sizzling in a bucket of black water.

And on the Lower East Side, down a dingy street, in crack dealer alleys, I howl and mutter in unknown sacred tongues. In a small mountain town in Arkansas, I am the woman screaming because her parakeet got stuck under the refrigerator and died, green shit smearing his once-sleek feathers. I am the field-worker in south Texas whose showered-off dirt forms the image of Christ's face on the floor of the stall. Thousands of people arrive to pay homage to the miracle, kneeling with candles and rosaries, cripples crowding the bathroom with their crutches and braces and bottles of pills, it's a sanctuary; while the president's son in the Rose Garden snares a butterfly into his net and rips off its wings. Some day he will command great armies.

A poet in the forests of the Sangre de Cristo Mountains stares at a placid pond frozen over with crust ice, where a bluebird flits across the steamy, cold fog simmering off the surface. And I walk out and take off my clothes and start to sing and flowers appear on the air, blue and red and green and yellow flowers, and the ice cracks and fish spin in glittering swirls and catch the flowers. And in other places millions of things are happening, equally absurd, equally heartbreaking and marvelous. How incredible our life is! How much there is that we do not understand. How honorable and full of heart has been my grandmother's life.

My grandmother does not understand what a Chicano is. She does not read newspapers, listen to radios, watch TV. Her life is lived elsewhere: thirty years meditating on the pebbles in her yard, fifty years smelling the dawn, eighty years listening to the silence at dusk, ninety years waiting for the two hummingbirds that come each spring to her unpainted picket fence—if they arrive she will live another year to await their arrival again. Forgiveness rises in her heart as she watches them whirr around the yard and hum at her screen door. She understands how they are truly flowers given wings and a beak, and how she is truly an old female turtle lumbering on wide, wrinkled footpads, raising her head with the millennial slowness of a diamond forming in the coal mines of dark years, ocean moaning in her blood vessels, returning home. While the image of a young boy chasing a train visits her, a boy as new as a just-hatched baby turtle, stumbling toward the ocean for the very first time.

THE GUINEA PIG LADY

Russell Banks

The story of Flora Pease, how she got to be the way she is now, isn't all that uncommon a story, except maybe in the particulars. You often hear in these small towns of a woman no one will deal with anymore, except to sell her something she wants or needs—food, clothing, or shelter. In other words, you don't have a social relationship with a woman like Flora, you have an economic one, and that's it. But that's important, because it's what keeps women like Flora alive, and, after all, no matter what you might think of her, you don't want to let her die, because, if you're not related to her somehow, you're likely to have a friend who is, or your friend will have a friend who is, which is almost the same thing in a small town. And not only in a small town, either—these things are true for any group of people that knows its limits and plans to keep them.

When Flora Pease first came to the trailerpark and rented number 11, which is the second trailer on your left as you come in from Old Road, no one in the park thought much about her one way or the other. She was about forty or forty-five, kind of flat-faced and plain, a red-colored person, with short red hair and a reddish tint to her skin. Even her eyes, which happened to be pale blue, looked red, as if she smoked too much and slept too little, which, as it later turned out, happened to be true. Her body was a little strange, however, and people remarked on that. It was blocky and square-shaped, not exactly feminine and not exactly masculine, so that while she could almost pass for either man or woman, she was generally regarded as neither. She wore mostly men's work shirts and ankle-high work boots, which, except for the overcoat, was not all that unusual among certain women who work outside a lot and don't do much socializing. But with Flora, because of the shape of her body, or rather, its shapelessness, her clothing only contributed to the vagueness of her sexual identity. Privately, there was probably no vagueness at all, but publicly there was. People elbowed one another and winked and made not quite kindly remarks about her when she passed by them on the streets of Catamount or when she passed along the trailerpark road on her way to or from town. The story, which came from Marcelle Chagnon, who rented her the trailer, was that Flora was retired military and lived off a small pension, and that made sense in one way, given people's prejudices about women in the military, and in another way, too, because at that time Captain Dewey Knox (U.S. Army, ret.) was already living at number 6, and people at the park had got used to the idea of someone living off a military pension instead of working for a living.

What didn't make sense was how someone who seemed slightly cracked, as Flora came quickly to seem, could have stayed in the military long enough to end up collecting a pension for it. Here's how she first came to seem cracked. She sang out loud, in public. She supposedly was raised here in Catamount, and though she had moved away when she was a girl, she still knew a lot of the old-timers in town, and she would walk into town every day or two for groceries and beer, singing in a loud voice all the way, as if she were the only person who could hear her. But by the time she had got out to Old Road, she naturally would have passed someone in the park who knew her, so she had to be aware that she wasn't the only person who could hear her. Regardless, she'd just go right on singing in a huge voice, singing songs from old Broadway musicals, mostly. She knew all the songs from *Oklahoma* and *West Side Story* and a few others as well, and she sang them, one after the other, all the way into town, then up and down the streets of town, as she stopped off at the A&P, Brown's Drug Store, maybe Hayward's Hardware, finally ending up at the Hawthorne House for a beer, before she headed back to the trailerpark. Everywhere she went, she sang those songs in a loud voice that was puffed up with feeling, if it was a happy song, or thick with melancholy, if it was sad. You don't mind a person whistling or humming or maybe even singing to herself under her breath while she does something else, sort of singing absentmindedly. But you do have to wonder about someone who forces you to listen to her the way Flora Pease forced everyone within hearing range to listen to her Broadway songs. Her voice wasn't half-bad, actually, and if she had been singing for the annual talent show at the high school, say, and you were sitting in the audience, you might have been pleased to listen, but at midday in June on Main Street, when you're coming out of the bank and about to step into your car, it can be a slightly jarring experience to see and hear a person who looks like Flora Pease come striding down the sidewalk singing in full voice about how the corn is as high as an elephant's eye.

The second thing that made Flora seem cracked early on was the way she never greeted you the same way twice, or at least twice in a row, so you could never work out exactly how to act toward her. You'd see her stepping out of her trailer early, on a summer day—it was summer when she first moved into the park, so everyone's remembered first impressions naturally put her into summertime scenes—and you'd give a friendly nod, the kind of nod you offer people you live among but aren't exactly friends with, just a quick, downward tip of the face, followed by a long, upsweeping lift of the whole head, with the eyes closed for a second as the head reaches its farthest point back. Afterwards, resuming your earlier expression and posture, you'd continue walking, wholly under the impression that, when your eyes were closed and your head tilted back, Flora had given you the appropriate answering nod. But no, or apparently no, because she'd call out, as you walked off, "Good *morn*-ing!" and she'd wave her hands at you as if brushing cobwebs away. "*Wonderful* morning for a walk!" she'd bellow (her voice was a loud one), and caught off guard like that, you'd agree and hurry away. The next time you saw her, however, the next morning, for instance, when once again you walked out to the row of mailboxes for your mail and passed her as, mail in hand, she headed back in from Old Road, you'd recall her greeting of the day before and how it had caught you off guard, and you'd say, "Morning," to her and maybe smile a bit and give her a friendly and more or less direct gaze. But what you'd get back would be a glare, a harsh, silent stare, as if you'd just made an improper advance on her. So you'd naturally say to yourself, "The hell with it," and that would be fine until the following morning, when you'd try to ignore her, and she wouldn't let you. She'd holler the second she saw you, "Hey! A scorcher! Right? Goin' to be a scorcher today, eh?" It was the sort of thing you had to answer, even if only with a word, "Yup," which you did, wondering as you said it what the hell was going on with that woman.

Everyone in the park that summer was scratching his or her head and asking what the hell was going on with the woman in number 11. Doreen Tiede, who lived with her five-year-old daughter, Maureen, in number 4, which was diagonally across the park road from Flora Pease's trailer, put Marcelle on the spot, so to speak, something Doreen could get away with more easily than most of the other residents of the park. Marcelle Chagnon intimidated most people. She was a large, hawk-faced woman, and that helped, and she was French Canadian, which also helped, because it meant that she could talk fast and loud without seeming to think about it first, and most people who were not French Canadians could not, so most people tended to remain silent and let Marcelle have her way. In a sense Marcelle was a little like Flora Pease—she was sudden and unpredictable and said what she wanted to, or so it seemed, regardless of what you might have said first. She didn't exactly ignore you, but she made it clear that it didn't matter to her what you thought of her or anything else. She always had business to take care of. She was the resident manager of the Granite State Trailerpark, which was owned by the Granite State Realty Development Corporation down in Nashua, and she had certain responsibilities toward the park and the people who lived there that no one else had. Beyond collecting everyone's monthly rent on time, she had to be sure no one in the park caused any trouble that would hurt the reputation of the park; she had to keep people from infringing on other people's rights, which wasn't all that simple, since in a trailerpark people live within ten or fifteen feet of each other and yet still feel they have their own private dwelling place and thus have control over their own destiny; and she also had to assert the rights of the people in the park whenever those rights got stepped on by outsiders, by Catamount police without a warrant, say, or by strangers who wanted to put their boats into the lake from the trailerpark dock, or by ex-husbands who might want to hassle ex-wives and make their kids cry. These things happened, and Marcelle was always able to handle them efficiently, with force and intelligence, and with no sentimentality, which, in the end, is probably the real reason she intimidated most people. She seemed to be without sentimentality.

Except when dealing with Doreen Tiede, that is. Which is why Doreen was able to put Marcelle on the spot and say to her late one afternoon in Marcelle's trailer at number 1, "What's with that woman, Flora Pease? Is she a fruitcake, or what? And if she is, how come you let her move in? And if she isn't a fruitcake, how come she looks the way she does and acts the way she does?" There were in the park, besides Doreen, Marcelle, and Flora, three additional women, but none of them could make Marcelle look at herself and give a straight answer to a direct question. None of them could make her forget her work and stop, even for a second. Only Doreen could get away with embarrassing Marcelle, or at least with demanding a straight answer from her, and getting it, too, probably because both Doreen and Marcelle looked tired in the same way, and each woman understood the nature of the fatigue and respected it in the other. They didn't feel sorry for it in each other; they respected it. There were twenty or more years between them, and Marcelle's children had long ago gone off and left her—one was a computer programmer in Billerica, Massachusetts, another was in the Navy and making a career of it, a third was running a McDonald's in Seattle, Washington, and a fourth had died. Because she had raised them herself, while at the same time fending off the attacks of the man who had fathered them on her, she thought of her life as work and her work as feeding, housing, and clothing her three surviving children and teaching them to be kindly, strong people, despite the fact that their father happened to have been a cruel, weak person. A life like that, or rather, twenty-five years of it, can permanently mark your face and make it instantly recognizable to anyone who happens to be engaged in similar work. Magicians, wise men, and fools are supposed to be able to recognize each other instantly, but so, too, are poor women who raise children alone.

They were sitting in Marcelle's trailer, having a beer. It was five-thirty, Doreen was on her way home from her job at the tannery, where she was a bookkeeper in the office. Her daughter, Maureen, was with her, having spent the afternoon with a baby-sitter in town next door to the kindergarten she attended in the mornings, and was whining for supper. Doreen had stopped in to pay her June rent, a week late, and Marcelle had accepted her apology for the lateness and had offered her a beer. Because of the lateness of the payment and Marcelle's graciousness, Doreen felt obliged to accept it, even though she preferred to get home and start supper so Maureen would stop whining.

Flora's name had come up when Maureen had stopped whining and had suddenly said, "Look, Momma, at the funny lady!" and had pointed out the window at Flora, wearing a heavy, ankle-length coat in the heat, sweeping her yard with a broom. She was working her way across the packed dirt yard toward the road that ran through the center of the park, raising a cloud of dust as she swept, singing in a loud voice something from *Fiddler on the Roof*—"If I were a rich man . . ."—and the two women and the child watched her, amazed. That's when Doreen had demanded to know what Marcelle had been thinking when she agreed to rent a trailer to Flora Pease.

Marcelle sighed, sat heavily back down at the kitchen table, and said, "Naw, I knew she was a little crazy. But not like this." She lit a cigarette and took a quick drag. "I guess I felt sorry for her. And I needed the money. We got two vacancies now out of twelve trailers, and I get paid by how many trailers have tenants, you know. When Flora came by that day, we got three vacancies, and I'm broke and need the money, so I look the other way a little and I say, sure, you can have number eleven, which is always the hardest to rent anyhow, because its on the backside away from the lake, and it's got number twelve and number ten right next to it and the swamp behind. Number five I'll rent easy, it's on the lake, and nine should be easy too, soon's people forget about Tom Smith's suicide. It's the end of the row and has a nice yard on one side, plus the toolshed in back. But eleven has always been a bitch to rent. So here's this lady, if you want to call her that, and she's got a regular income from the Air Force, and she seems friendly enough, lives alone, she says, has relations around here, she says, so what the hell, even though I can already see she's a little off I figure it was because of her being maybe not interested in men, one of those women. And I figure, what the hell, that's her business, not mine, I don't give a damn what she does or who she does it with, so long as she keeps to herself. So I say, sure, take number eleven, thinking maybe she won't. But she did."

Marcelle sipped at her can of beer, and Doreen went for hers. The radio was tuned quietly in the background to the country-and-western station from Dover. Doreen reached across the counter to the radio and turned up the volume, saying to no one in particular, "I like this song."

"That's 'cause you're not thirty yet, honey. You'll get to be thirty, and then you'll like a different kind of song. Wait."

Doreen smiled from somewhere behind the fatigue that covered her face. It was a veil she had taken several years ago, and she'd probably wear it until she died or lost her memory, whichever came first. She looked at her red-painted fingernails. "What happens when you're forty, and then fifty? You like a different kind of song then too?"

"Can't say for fifty yet, but, yes, for forty. Thirty, then forty, and probably fifty, too. Sixty, now, that's the question. That's when you decide you don't like any of the songs they play, and so you go and sit in front of the TV and watch game shows," she laughed.

"Well, I'll tell you," Doreen said, finishing her beer off and standing to leave, "that Flora Pease over there, she's going to be trouble, Marcelle. You made a big mistake letting her in the park. Mark my words."

"Naw. She's harmless. A little fruity, that's all. We're all a little fruity, if you want to think about it," she said. "Some are just more able to cover it up than others, that's all."

Doreen shook her head and hurried her daughter out the screened door and along the road to number 4. When she had left, Marcelle stood up and from the window over the sink watched Flora, who swept and sang her way back from the road across her dirt yard to the door, then stepped daintily up the cinder blocks and entered her home.

Then, in August that summer, a quarrel between Terry Constant and his older sister, Carol, who lived in number 10 next door to Flora, caused young Terry to fly out the door one night around midnight and bang fiercely against the metal wall of their trailer. It was the outer wall of the bedroom where his sister slept, and he was doubtless pounding that particular wall to impress his sister with his anger. No one in the park knew what the quarrel was about, and at that hour no one much cared, but when Terry commenced his banging on the wall of the trailer, several people were obliged to involve themselves with the fight. Lights went on across the road at number 6, where Captain Knox lived alone, and 7, where Noni Hubner and her mother, Nancy, lived. It wasn't unusual for Terry to be making a lot of noise at night, but it was unusual for him to be making it this late and outside the privacy of his own home.

It was easy to be frightened of Terry if you didn't know him—he was about twenty-five, tall and muscular and very dark, and he had an expressive face and a loud voice—but if you knew him, he was, at worst, irritating. To his sister Carol, though, he must often have been a pure burden, and that was why they quarreled. She had come up from Boston a few years ago to work as a nurse for a dying real estate man who had died shortly after, leaving her sort of stuck in this white world, insofar as she was immediately offered a good job in town as Doctor Wickshaw's nurse and had no other job to go to anywhere else and no money to live on while she looked. So she took it. Then her mother down in Boston died, and Terry moved in with his sister for a spell and stayed on, working here and there and now and then for what he called monkey money as a carpenter's helper or stacking hides in the tannery. Sometimes he and Carol would have an argument, caused, everyone was sure, by Terry, since he was so loud and insecure and she was so quiet and sure of herself, and then Terry would be gone for a month or so, only to return one night all smiles and compliments. He was skillful with tools and usually free to fix broken appliances or plumbing in the trailerpark, so Marcelle never objected to Carol's taking him back in—not that Marcelle actually had a right to object, but if she had fussed about it, Carol would have sent Terry packing. People liked Carol Constant, and because she put up with Terry, they put up with him, too. Besides, he was good-humored and often full of compliments and, when he wasn't angry, good to look at.

Captain Knox was the first to leave his trailer and try to quiet Terry. In his fatherly way, embellished somewhat by his white hair and plaid bathrobe and bedroom slippers, he informed Terry that he was waking up working people. He stood across the road in the light from his window, tall and straight, arms crossed over his chest, one bushy black eyebrow raised in disapproval, and said, "Not everybody in this place can sleep till noon, young man."

Terry stopped banging for a second, peered over his shoulder at the man, and said, "Fuck you, Knox!" and went back to banging on the tin wall, as if he were hammering nails with his bare fists. Captain Knox turned and marched back inside his trailer, and, after a few seconds, his lights went out.

Then the girl, Noni Hubner, in her nightgown, appeared at the open door of number 7. Her long, silky blond hair hung loosely over her shoulders, circling her like a halo lit from behind. A woman's voice, her mother's, called from inside the trailer, "Noni, *don't*! Don't go out there!"

The girl waved the voice away and stepped out to the landing, barefoot, delicately exposing the silhouette of her body against the light of the living room behind her.

Now the mother shrieked, "Noni! Come back! He may be on drugs!"

Terry ceased hammering and turned to stare at the girl across the road. He was wearing a T-shirt and khaki work pants and blue tennis shoes, and his arms hung loosely at his sides, his chest heaving from the exertion of his noisemaking and his anger, and he smiled over at the girl and said, "Hey, honey, you want to come beat on my drum?"

"You're waking everyone up," she said politely.

"Please come back inside, Noni! *Please*!"

The black man took a step toward the girl, and she whirled and disappeared inside, slamming the door and locking it, switching off the lights and dumping the trailer back into darkness.

Terry stood by the side of the road looking after her. "Fuck," he said. Then he noticed Flora Pease standing next to him, a blocky figure in a long overcoat, barefoot, and carrying in her arms, as if it were a baby, a small, furry animal.

"What you got there?" Terry demanded.

"Elbourne." Flora smiled down at the chocolate-colored animal and made a quiet, clucking noise with her mouth.

"What the hell's an Elbourne?"

"Guinea pig. Elbourne's his name."

"Why'd you name him Elbourne?"

"After my grandfather. How come you're making such a racket out here?"

Terry took a step closer, trying to see the guinea pig more clearly, and Flora wrapped the animal in her coat sleeve, as if to protect it from his gaze.

"I won't hurt ol' Elbourne. I just want to see him. I never seen a guinea pig before."

"He's a lot quieter than you are, mister, I'll tell you that much. Now, how come you're making such a racket out here banging on the side of your house?"

"That ain't my house. That's my *sister's* house!"

"Oh," Flora said, as if she now understood everything, and she extended the animal toward Terry so he could see it entirely. It was long-haired, shaped like a football, with circular, dark eyes on the sides of its head and small ears and tiny legs tucked beneath its body. It seemed terrified and trembled in Flora's outstretched hands.

Terry took the animal and held it up to examine its paws and involuted tail, then brought it close to his chest and, holding it in one large hand, tickled it under the chin with his forefinger. The animal made a tiny cluttering noise that gradually subsided to a light *drr-r-r*, and Terry chuckled. "Nice little thing," he said. "How many you got, or is this the only one?"

"Lots."

"Lots? You got a bunch of these guinea pigs in there?"

"I said so, didn't I?"

"I suppose you did."

"Give him back," she said and brusquely reached out for the animal.

Terry placed Elbourne into Flora's hands, and she turned and walked swiftly on her short legs around the front of her trailer. After a few seconds, her door slammed shut, and the lights went out, and Terry was once again standing alone in darkness in the middle of the trailerpark. Tiptoeing across the narrow belt of knee-high weeds and grass that ran between the trailers, he came up close to Flora's bedroom window. "No pets allowed in the trailerpark, honey!" he called out, and he turned and strolled off to get some sleep, so he could leave this place behind him early in the morning.

Either Terry didn't find the opportunity to tell anyone about Flora Pease having "lots" of guinea pigs in her trailer or he simply chose not to mention it, because it wasn't until after he returned to the trailerpark, two months later, in early October, that anyone other than he had a clue to the fact that, indeed, there were living in number 11, besides Flora, a total of seventeen guinea pigs, five of which were male. Of the twelve females, eight were pregnant, and since guinea pigs produce an average of 2.5 piglets per litter, in a matter of days there would be an additional twenty guinea pigs in Flora's trailer, making a total of thirty-seven. About two months after birth, these newcomers would be sexually mature, with a two-month gestation period, so that if half the newborns were females, and if the other mothers continued to be fertile, along with the four original females, then sometime late in December there would be approximately one hundred fifteen guinea pigs residing in Flora's trailer, of which fifty-four would be male and sixty-one female. These calculations were made by Leon LaRoche, who lived at number 2, the second trailer on your right as you entered the park. Leon worked as a teller for the Catamount Savings and Loan, so calculations of this sort came more or less naturally to him.

"That's a *minimum!*" he told Marcelle. "One hundred fifteen guinea pigs, fifty-four males and sixty-one females. Minimum. And you don't have to be a genius to calculate how many of those filthy little animals will be living in her trailer with her by March. Want me to compute it for you?" he asked, drawing his calculator from his jacket pocket again.

"No, I get the picture." Marcelle scowled. It was a bright, sunny Sunday morning in early October, and the two were standing in Marcelle's kitchen, Marcelle, in flannel shirt and jeans, taller by half a hand than Leon, who, in sport coat, slacks, shirt and tie, was dressed for mass, which he regularly attended at St, Joseph's Catholic Church in Catamount. It was a conversation last night with Captain Knox that had led young Leon to bring his figures to the attention of the manager, for it was he, the Captain, who had made the discovery that there were precisely seventeen guinea pigs in Flora's trailer, rather than merely "lots," as Terry had discovered, and the Captain was alarmed.

It hadn't taken much imagination for the Captain to conclude that something funny was going on in number 11. When you are one of the three or four people who happen to be around the park all day because you are either retired or unemployed, and when you live across the road from a woman who announces her comings and goings with loud singing, which in turn draws your attention to her numerous expeditions to town for more food than one person can possibly consume, and when you notice her carting into her trailer an entire bale of hay and daily emptying buckets of what appears to be animal feces, tiny pellets rapidly becoming a conical heap behind the trailer, then before long you can conclude that the woman is doing something that requires an explanation. And when you are a retired captain of the United States Army, you feel entitled to require that explanation, which is precisely what Captain Dewey Knox did.

He waited by his window until he saw Flora one morning carrying out the daily bucket of droppings, and he strode out his door, crossed the road, and passed her trailer to the back, where he stood silently behind her, hands clasped behind his back, briar pipe stuck between healthy teeth, one dark, bushy eyebrow raised, so that when the woman turned with her empty bucket, she met him face to face.

Switching the bucket from her right hand to her left, she saluted smartly. "Captain," she said. "Good morning, sir."

The Captain casually returned the salute, as befitted his rank. "What was your rank at retirement, Pease?"

"Airman Third Class, sir." She stood not exactly at attention, but not exactly at ease, either. It's difficult when retired military personnel meet each other as civilians: their bodies have enormous resistance to accepting the new modes of acknowledging each other, with the result that they don't quite operate as either military or civilian bodies, but as something uncomfortably neither.

"Airman Third, eh?" The Captain scratched his cleanly shaved chin. "I would have thought after twenty years you'd have risen a little higher."

"No reason to, sir. I was a steward in the officers' clubs, sir, mostly in Lackland, and for a while, because of my name, I guess," she said, smiling broadly, "at Pease down in Portsmouth. Pease Air Force Base," she added.

"I know that. You were happy being a steward, then?"

"Yes, sir. Very happy. That's good duty, sir. People treat you right, especially officers. I once kept house for General Curtis LeMay, a very fine man who could have been vice president of the United States. Once I was watching a quiz show on TV and that question came up, 'Who was George Wallace's running mate?' and I knew the answer. But that was after General LeMay had retired—"

"Yes, yes, I know," the Captain interrupted. "I thought the Air Force used male stewards in the officers' clubs."

"Not always, sir. Some of us like that duty, and some don't, so if you like it, you have an advantage, if you know what I mean, and most of the men don't much like it, especially when it comes to the housekeeping, though the men don't mind being waiters and so forth. . . ."

The Captain turned aside to let Flora pass and walked along beside her toward the door of her trailer. At the door they paused, unsure of how to depart from one another, and the Captain glanced back at the pyramid of pellets and straw. "I've been meaning to ask you about that, Pease," he said, pointing with his pipe stem.

"Sir?"

"What is it?"

"Shit, sir."

"I surmised that. I mean, what kind of shit?"

"Guinea pig shit, sir."

"And that implies you are keeping guinea pigs."

Flora smiled tolerantly. "Yes, sir, it does."

"You know the rule about pets in the trailerpark, don't you, Pease?"

"Oh, sure I do."

"Well, then," he said, "what do you call guinea pigs?"

"I don't call them pets, sir. Dogs and cats I call pets. But not guinea pigs. I just call them guinea pigs. They're sort of like plants, sir," she explained patiently. "You don't call plants pets, do you?"

"But guinea pigs are alive, for heaven's sake!"

"There's some would say plants are alive, too, if you don't mind my saying so, sir."

"That's different! These are animals!" The Captain sucked on his cold pipe, drew ash and spit into his mouth, and coughed.

"Animals, vegetables, minerals, all that matters is that they're not like dogs and cats, which are pets, because they can cause trouble for people. They're more like babies. That's why they have rules against pets in places like this, sir," she explained. "But not babies."

"How many guinea pigs have you?" the Captain coldly inquired.

"Seventeen."

"Males and females alike, I suppose."

"Yes, sir," she said, smiling broadly. "Twelve females, and eight of them is pregnant at this very moment. If you take good care of them, they thrive," she said with pride. "Like plants," she added, suddenly serious.

"But they're not plants! They're animals, and they produce . . . waste materials," he said, again pointing with the stem of his pipe at the pile behind the trailer. "And they're dirty."

Flora stepped onto her cinder-block stairs, bringing herself to the same height as the Captain. "Sir, guinea pigs are not dirty. They're cleaner than most people I know, and I know how most people can be. Don't forget, I was a steward for twenty years almost. And as for producing 'waste materials,' even plants produce waste materials. It's called oxygen, sir, which we human people find pretty useful, if you don't mind my saying so, sir. And, as a matter of fact, come next spring you might want me to let you take some of that pile of waste material I got going over to your place." She shoved her chin in the direction of Captain Knox's trailer, where there was a now-dormant ten-foot-by-ten-foot garden plot on the slope facing the lake. Then she turned and abruptly entered her home.

That same evening, the Captain, in number 6, telephoned Leon LaRoche, in number 2, to explain the situation. "I'd take it to her myself," he said, meaning to Marcelle Chagnon, "but she's got it into her head that I'm trying to take over her job of running this place, so every time I ask her to do something, she does the opposite."

LaRoche understood. "I'll put a little data together first," he said. "Guinea pigs are like rats, aren't they?"

"Very much."

LaRoche was eager to please the older man, as he admired and even envied him a little. He had once confessed to Doreen, after her ex-husband had made one of his brutal, unexpected visits and had been hauled away by the Catamount Police Department, that he was open-minded about the idea of marriage, assuming he met the right person and all, but if it turned out that he remained a bachelor all his life, he hoped he would be able to achieve the dignity and force, by the time he reached sixty or sixty-five, of a Captain Dewey Knox, say.

That night LaRoche researched guinea pigs in volume 7 of his complete *Cooper's World Encyclopedia*, which he had obtained, volume by volume, by shopping every week at the A&P, and learned that guinea pigs, or cavies (*Rodentia caviidae*), a descendant of the Peruvian *Cavia aperea porcellus*, which were kept by the Indians for food and even today are sold as a delicacy in many South American marketplaces, have a life expectancy of eight years maximum, an average litter size of 2.5, a gestation period of sixty-three days, and reach reproductive maturity in five to six weeks. He further learned that the female goes through estrus every sixteen days for fifty hours, during which time the female will accept the male continuously, but only between the hours of 5:00 P.M. and 5:00 A.M. He also discovered that 8 percent of all guinea pig pregnancies end in abortion, a variable that made his calculations somewhat complicated but also somewhat more interesting to perform. He learned many other things about guinea pigs that night, but it was the numbers that he decided to present to Marcelle. He thought of telling her that guinea pigs are coprophagists, eaters of feces, a habit necessitated by their innate difficulty in digesting cellulose tissue, creating thereby a need for bacteria as an aid to digestion, but thought better of it. The numbers, he decided, would be sufficient to make her aware of the gravity of the situation.

The next morning, a crisp, early fall day, with the birches near the lake already gone to gold and shimmering in the clear air, LaRoche walked next door to Marcelle's trailer fifteen minutes before his usual departure time for Sunday mass and presented her with the evidence and the mathematical implications of the evidence. Captain Dewey Knox's testimony was unimpeachable, and Leon LaRoche's logic and calculations were irrefutable. Marcelle's course of action, therefore, was inescapable. The guinea pigs would have to go, or Flora Pease would have to go.

"I need this like I need a hole in the head," Marcelle griped, when LaRoche had left her alone with her cup of coffee and cigarette. Winter was coming on fast, and she had to be sure all the trailers were winterized, storm windows repaired and in place, exposed water pipes insulated, heating units all cleaned and operating at maximum efficiency to avoid unnecessary breakdowns and expensive service calls, contracts for fuel oil and snowplowing made with local contractors and approved by the Granite State Realty Development Corporation, leaky roofs patched, picnic tables and waterfront equipment and docks stored away until spring, and on and on—a long list of things to do before the first snowfall in November. Not only that, she had to collect rents, not always a simple job, and sometime this month she had to testify in court in the case involving Doreen's ex-husband, since Marcelle had been the one to control him with her shotgun when Doreen called the police, and Terry Constant had taken off again for parts unknown, so she had no one to help her, no one (since Terry had a deal with his sister whereby his work for Marcelle helped pay her rent) she could afford. And now in the middle of all this she had to cope with a fruitcake who had a passion for raising guinea pigs and didn't seem to realize that they were going to breed her out of her own home right into the street. No sense treating the woman like a child. Rules were rules, and it wasn't up to Flora Pease to say whether her guinea pigs were pets, it was up to management, and Marcelle was management. The pigs would have to go, or else the woman would have to go.

Days went by, however, and, for one reason or another, Marcelle left Flora alone, let her come and go as usual without bothering to stop her and inform her that guinea pigs were pets and pets were not allowed in the trailerpark. Terry came back, evidently from New York City, where he'd gone to hear some music, he said, and she put him to work winterizing the trailers, which, for another week, as she laid out Terry's work and checked after him to be sure he actually did it, allowed Marcelle to continue to ignore the problem. Leon LaRoche thought better of the idea of bringing up the topic again and generally avoided her, although he did get together several times with Captain Knox to discuss Marcelle's obvious unwillingness to deal forthrightly with what would very soon turn into a sanitation problem. Something for the health department, Captain Knox pointed out.

Finally, one morning late in the month, Marcelle went looking for Terry. It was a Saturday, and ordinarily she didn't hire him on Saturdays, because it brought forward speeches about exploitation of the minorities and complaints about not getting paid time and a half, which is what anyone else would have to pay a man to work on Saturdays, unless, of course, that man happens to be a black man in a white world. Marcelle more or less accepted the truth of Terry's argument, but that didn't make it any easier for her to hire him on Saturdays, since she couldn't afford to pay him the six dollars an hour it would have required. On this day, however, she had no choice in the matter—the weather prediction was for a heavy freeze that night and Sunday, and half the trailers had water pipes that would surely burst if Terry didn't spend the day nailing homosote skirting to the undersides.

He wasn't home, and his sister, Carol, didn't know where he'd gone, unless it was next door to visit that woman, Flora Pease, where he seemed to spend a considerable amount of his time lately, Carol observed cautiously. Yes, well, Marcelle didn't know anything about that, nor did she much care where Terry spent his spare time, so long as he stayed out of her hair (Carol said she could certainly understand that), but right now she needed him to help her finish winterizing the trailerpark by nightfall or they would have to spend the next two weeks finding and fixing water pipe leaks. Carol excused herself, as she had to get dressed for work, and Marcelle left in a hurry for Flora's trailer.

At first when she knocked on the door there was no answer. A single crow called from the sedgy swamp out back, a leafless and desolate-looking place, with a skin of ice over the reedy water. The skeletal, low trees and bushes clattered lightly in the breeze, and Marcelle pulled the collar of her denim jacket tightly against her face. The swamp, which was more of a muskeg than an actual swamp, lay at the southern end of about three thousand acres of state forest—most of the land between the northwest shore of Skitter Lake and the Turnpike, Route 28, which ran from the White Mountains, fifty miles to the north, to Boston, ninety miles to the south. The trailerpark had been placed there as a temporary measure (before local zoning restrictions could be voted into action) to hold and initiate development on the only large plot of land available between the town of Catamount and the Skitter Lake State Forest. That was right after the Korean War, when the Granite State Realty Development Corporation, anticipating a coming statewide need for low-income housing, had gone all over the state purchasing large tracts of land that also happened to lie close to cities and towns where low income people were employed, usually mill towns like Catamount, whose tannery kept between seventy and eighty families marginally poor. As it turned out, the trailerpark was all the Granite State Realty Development Corporation could finance in Catamount, for it soon became apparent that no one in the area would be able to purchase houses, if the Corporation built single-family dwellings, or pay high enough rents to justify the expense of constructing a town house apartment complex. Soon it became clear that the best use the Corporation could make of the land and trailers was as collateral for financing projects elsewhere in the state, in the larger towns and cities where there were people who could afford to buy single-family dwellings or rent duplex apartments. In the meantime, the Corporation maintained the twelve trailers just adequately, paid the relatively low taxes, and came close to breaking even on its investment. Marcelle had been the first tenant in the trailerpark, moving out of a shabby, wood-frame tenement building in town because of her kids, who, she believed, needed more space, and she had immediately become the manager—when the company representative recognized her tough-mindedness, made evident, as soon as there were no more vacancies, by her ability to organize a rent strike to protest the open sewage and contaminated water. They had installed septic tanks and leach fields, and she had continued as resident manager ever since.

Flora's door opened a dark inch, and Marcelle saw a bit of cheek, blond hair, and an eye looking through the inch. She shoved against the door with the flat of one hand, pushing it back against the face behind it, and stepped up the cinder blocks and in, where she discovered the owner of the cheek, blond hair, and eye—Bruce Severance, the college kid who lived in number 3, between LaRoche and Doreen.

"Hold it a minute, man," he said uselessly, rubbing his nose from the blow it had received from the door and stepping back into the room to make space for the large, gray-haired woman. The room, though dark from the venetian blinds being drawn, was filled with at least two other people than Bruce and Marcelle, batches of oddly arranged furniture, and what looked like merchandise counters from a department store.

"Don't you have any lights in here, for Christ's sake?" Marcelle demanded. She stood inside the room in front of the open door, blinking as she tried to accustom herself to the gloom and see who else was there. "Why are all the blinds drawn? What the hell are you doing here, Severance?" Then she smelled it. "Grass! You smoking your goddamned hippie pot in here with Flora?"

"Hey, man, it's cool."

"Don't 'man' me. And it isn't cool. I don't let nothing illegal go on here. Something illegal goes on, and I happen to find out about it, I call in the goddamned cops. Let them sort out the problems. I don't need problems, I got enough of them already to keep me busy."

"That's right, baby, you don't want no more problems," came a soft voice from a particularly dark corner.

"Terry! What the hell are you doing here?" She could make out a lumpy shape next to him on what appeared to be a mattress on the floor. "Is that Flora over there?" Marcelle asked, her voice suddenly a bit shaky. Things were changing a little too fast for her to keep track of. You don't mind the long-haired hippie kid smoking a little grass and maybe yakking stupidly, the way they do when they're stoned, with probably the only person in the trailerpark who didn't need to get stoned herself in order to understand him. You don't really mind that. A kid like Bruce Severance, you knew he smoked marijuana, but it was harmless, because he did it for ideological reasons, the same reasons behind his vegetarian diet and his T'ai Chi exercises and his way of getting a little rest, Transcendental Meditation—he did all these things, not because they were fun, but because he believed they were good for him, and good for you, too, if only you were able to come up with the wisdom, self-discipline, and money so that you, too, could smoke marijuana instead of drink beer and rye whiskey, eat organic vegetables instead of supermarket junk, study and practice exotic, ancient Oriental forms of exercise instead of sitting around at night watching TV. You, too, could learn how to spend a half hour in the morning and a half hour in the evening meditating, instead of sleeping to the last minute before getting up and making breakfast for yourself and the kid and rushing off to work and in the evening dragging yourself home just in time to make supper for the kid. And if you could accomplish these things, you would be like Bruce Severance, a much improved person. That was one of Bruce's favorite phrases, "much improved person," and he believed that it ought to be a universal goal and that only ignorance (fostered by the military-industrial complex), sheer laziness, and/or purely malicious ideological opposition (that is to say, a "fascist mentality") kept the people he lived among from participating with him in his several rites. So, unless you happened to share his ideology, you could easily view his several rites as harmless, mainly because you could also trust the good sense of the poor people he lived among, and also their self-discipline and the day-to-day realities they were forced to struggle against. A fool surrounded by sensible poor people remains a fool and is, therefore, seldom troublesome. But when it starts to occur to you that some of the poor people are not sensible—which is what occurred to Marcelle when she peered into the dingy, dim clutter of the trailer and saw Terry sprawled out on a mattress on the floor with Flora Pease clumped next to him, both with marijuana cigarettes dangling from their lips—that's when you start to view the fool as troublesome.

"Listen, Bruce," she said, wagging a finger at the boy, "I don't give a good goddamn about you wearing all them signs about legalizing pot and plastering bumper stickers against nuclear energy and so on all over your trailer, just so long as you take 'em down and clean the place up the way you found it when you leave here. And I don't mind you putting that kind of stuff on your clothes," she said, pointing with her forefinger at the image of a cannabis plant on the chest of Bruce's tie-dyed T-shirt. "Because what you do behind your own closed door and how you decorate your trailer or your van or your clothes is all your own private business. But when you start mixing all this stuff up together like this," she said, waving a hand contemptuously in the direction of Terry and Flora, "well, that's a little different."

"Like what, man?" Bruce asked. "C'mon, will you? And hey, calm down a little, man. No big thing. We're just having us a little morning toke, then I'm headin' out of here. No big thing."

"Yeah, it's cool," Terry said lightly from the corner.

Marcelle shot a scowl in his direction. "I don't want no dope dens in this park. I got my job to look out for. You do anything to make my job risky, I'll come down on you," she said to Terry. "And you, too," she said to Bruce. "And you, too, sister," she said to Flora. "Like a goddamned ton of bricks!"

"No big thing, man," Bruce said, closing the door behind her, wrapping them all in the gray light of the room. Now Marcelle noticed the sharp, acidic smell of animal life, not human animals, but small, furred animals—urine and fecal matter and straw and warm fur. It was the smell of a nest. It was both irritating and at the same time comforting, that smell, because she was both unused to the smell and immediately familiar with it. Then she heard it, a chattering, sometimes clucking noise that rose and ran off to a purr, then rose again like a shudder, diminishing after a few seconds to a quiet, sustained hum. She looked closely at what she had thought at first were counters and saw that they were cages, large waist-high cages, a half dozen of them, placed in no clear order around the shabby furniture of the room, a mattress on the floor, a rocker, a pole lamp, a Formica-topped kitchen table, and, without the easy chair, a hassock. Beyond the living room, she could make out the kitchen area, where she could see two more of the large cages.

"You want a hit, man?" Terry asked, holding his breath as he talked, so that his words came out in high-pitched, breathless clicks. He extended the joint toward her, a relaxed smile on his lips. Next to him, Flora, who lay slumped against his muscular frame like a sack of grain dropped from several feet above, seemed to be dozing.

"That's what *she* looks like, like she got hit."

"Ah, no, Flora's happy. Ain't you, Flora honey?" Terry asked, chucking her under the chin.

She rolled her head and came gradually to attention, saw Marcelle, and grinned. "Hi, Mrs. Chagnon!" she cried, just this side of panic. "Have you ever smoked marijuana?"

"No."

"Well, I have. I love to smoke marijuana!"

"That right?"

"Yep. I can't drink, it makes me crazy, and I start to cry and hit people and everything . . ."

"Right on," Bruce said.

". . . so I drink marijuana, I mean, I smoke marijuana, and then I feel real fine and everything's a joke, just the way its s'posed to be. The trouble is, I can't get the knack of rolling these little cigarettes, so I need to have someone roll them for me, which is why I asked these boys here to come in and help me out this morning. You want a seat? Why don't you sit down, Mrs. Chagnon? I been meaning to ask you over to visit sometime, but I been so busy, you know?" She waved toward the hassock for Marcelle to sit down.

"You sure you don't want a hit, Marcelle baby?" Terry offered again. "This's some dynamite shit. Flora's got herself some dynamite grass, right, man?" he said to Bruce.

"Oh, wow, man. Dynamite shit. Really dynamite shit."

"No, thanks," Marcelle sat gingerly on the hassock in the middle of the room. Bruce strolled loosely over and dropped himself on the mattress, plucked the joint from Terry's hand, and sucked noisily on it. "So *you're* the one who smokes the marijuana," Marcelle said to Flora. "I mean, these boys didn't . . ."

"Corrupt her?" Bruce interrupted. "Oh, wow, man, no way! She corrupted us!" he said, laughing and rolling back on the mattress. "Dynamite shit, man! What fucking dynamite grass!"

"He's just being silly," Flora explained. "It makes you a little silly sometimes, Mrs. Chagnon. Nothing to worry about."

"But it's illegal."

"These days, Mrs. Chagnon, what isn't? I mean, honestly."

"Yeah, well, I suppose it's okay, so long as you do it in the privacy of your own home, I mean."

"Really, Mrs. Chagnon! I would never be so foolish as to risk being arrested by the police!" Flora was now sitting pertly, her legs crossed at the ankles, gesturing limp-wristedly as she talked.

Marcelle sighed heavily. "I came over here looking for Terry to help me finish winterizing, because we got a cold snap coming. But I can see he won't be any good today, all doped up like he is . . ."

"Hey, man!" Terry said and sat up straight, his feelings hurt. "You paying time and a half, you got yourself a man. In fact, you pay time and a half, you might getcha self two men," he said, waving toward Bruce. "You need a few bucks, man?"

"No, no, not today. I gotta study for a quiz on Monday, and I haven't even looked at the stuff . . ."

"Right, right," Terry said. "College boys gotta study for quizzes and stuff. But that's okay. More for me, as I always say." His voice was crisp and loud again, which to Marcelle was cheering, for she had been made anxious by his slurred, quiet, speech as if his voice had an edge she couldn't see—if he was going to say things that cut, she wanted to be able to see them coming, and usually, with Terry, she could do that, so she was relieved to hear him yammering away again, snapping and slashing with his sarcasm and bravado.

"Hey, Flora," Terry suddenly said, "now that you got the boss lady here, whyn't you show her all your little furry friends! C'mon, baby, show the boss lady all your furry little friends!" He jumped up and urged Marcelle to follow. "C'mere and take a peek at these beasties. She's got a whole heap of 'em."

"Not so many," Flora said shyly from the mattress.

"I gotta go," Bruce said. "I gotta study," he added and quickly let himself out the door.

Marcelle said not now and told Terry that he could start work by putting the winter skirting around Merle Ring's trailer, which was the most exposed in the park, located as it was out there on the point facing the lake. She reminded him where the sheets of homosote were stored, and he took off, not before, as usual, synchronizing watches with her, so that, as he put it, she wouldn't be able later on to say he didn't work as long as he did. "I've been screwed that way too many times," he reminded her.

Then he was gone, and Marcelle was alone in the trailer with Flora—alone with Flora and her animals, which to Marcelle seemed to number in the hundreds. Their scurrying and rustling in the cages and the chittering noises they made filled the silence, and the smell of the animals thickened the air. Flora moved about the room with a grace and lightness that Marcelle had never seen in her before. She seemed almost to be dancing, and Marcelle wondered if it was the effect of the marijuana, an effect caused by inhaling the smoke-filled air, because, after all, Flora was a heavy, awkward woman who moved slowly and deliberately, not in this floating, delicate, improvisational way, as if she were underwater.

"Flora! You can't keep these animals in here anymore!"

Flora ignored the words and waved for Marcelle to follow her into the kitchen area, where the babies were. "The babies and the new mommies, actually," she went on with obvious pride. As soon as they were weaned, she would place the mommies back with the daddies in the living room. Soon, she pointed out, she was going to have to build some more cages, because these babies would need to be moved to make room for more. She repeated what she had told Captain Knox: "When you take care of them, they thrive. Just like plants."

Marcelle Chagnon said it again, this time almost pleading. "You can't keep these animals in here anymore!"

Flora stopped fluttering. "It's getting colder, winter's coming in. I must keep them inside, or they'll freeze to death. Just like plants."

Marcelle Chagnon crossed her arms over her chest and for the third time informed Flora that she would not be able to keep her guinea pigs inside the trailer.

Finally, the words seemed to have been understood. Flora stood still, hands extended as if for alms, and cried, "What will I do with them, then? I can't put them outside. They're weak little animals, not made for this climate. You want me to *kill* them? Is that what you're telling me? That I have to *kill* my babies?"

"I don't know what the hell you're going to do with them!" Marcelle was angry now. Her head had cleared somewhat, and she knew again that this was Flora's problem, not hers. "It's your problem, not mine. I'm not God. What you do with the damned things is your business . . ."

"But I'm not God, either!" Flora cried. "All I can do is take care of them and try to keep them from dying unnaturally," she explained. That was all anyone could do and, therefore, it was what one had to do. "You do what you can. When you can take care of things, you do it. Because when you take care of things, they thrive." She said it as if it were a motto.

"Then I'll have to call the health board and have them take the guinea pigs out. I don't want the scandal, it'll make it hard to rent, and it's hard enough already, but if I can't get you to take care of these animals by getting rid of them, I'll have some-one else do it."

"You wouldn't do that!" Flora said, shocked.

"Yes."

"Then you'll have to get rid of me first," she said. "You'll have to toss *me* into the cold first, let me freeze or starve to death first, before I'll let you do that to my babies." She pushed her square chin defiantly out and glared at Marcelle.

"Oh, Jesus, what did I do to deserve this?"

Quickly, as if she knew she had won, Flora started reassuring Marcelle, telling her not to worry, no one would be bothered by the animals, their shit was almost odorless and would make fertilizer for the several vegetable and flower gardens in the park, and she, Flora, took good care of them and kept their cages clean, so there was no possible health hazard, and except for their relatively quiet chitchat, the animals made no noise that would bother anyone. "People just don't like the *idea* of my having guinea pigs, that's all," she explained. "The *reality* of it don't bother anyone, not even Captain Knox. If people were willing to change their ideas, then everyone could be happy together," she said brightly.

In a final attempt to convince her to give up the guinea pigs, Marcelle tried using some of Leon LaRoche's calculations. She couldn't remember the specific numbers, but she understood the principle behind them. "You realize you're going to have twice as many of these things by spring. And how many have you got now, seventy-five or a hundred, right?"

Flora told her not to worry herself over it, she already had plenty to worry about with the trailerpark and winter coming and all. She should forget all about the guinea pigs, Flora told her with sympathy, and look after the people in the trailerpark, just as she always had. "Life is hard enough, Mrs. Chagnon, without us going around worrying about things we can't do anything about. You let me worry about taking care of the guinea pigs. That's something I can do something about, and you can't, so therefore it's something I *should* do something about, and you shouldn't even try." Her voice had a consoling, almost motherly tone, and for a second Marcelle wanted to thank her.

"All right," Marcelle said brusquely, gathering herself up to her full height. "Just make sure these bastards don't cause any trouble around here, and make sure there isn't any health hazard from . . . whatever, bugs, garbage, I don't know, anything . . . and you can keep them here. Till the weather gets warm, though. Only till spring."

Marcelle moved toward the door, and Flora smiled broadly. She modestly thanked Marcelle, who answered that, if Flora was going to smoke pot here, she'd better do it alone and not with those two big-mouthed jerks, Terry and Bruce. "Those jerks, one or the other of 'em, will get you in trouble. Smoke it alone, if you have to smoke it."

"But I don't know how to make those little cigarettes. My fingers are too fat, and I spill it all over."

"Buy yourself a corncob pipe," Marcelle advised. "Where do you buy the stuff from, anyway?" she suddenly asked, as she opened the door to leave and felt the raw chill from outside.

"Oh, I don't *buy* it!" Flora exclaimed. "It grows wild all over the place, especially along the Old Road where there used to be a farm, between the river and the state forest." There were, as part of the land owned by the Corporation, ten or fifteen acres of old, unused farmland now grown over with brush and weeds. "They used to grow hemp all over this area when I was a little girl," Flora told her. "During the War, for rope. But after the War, when they had to compete with the Filipinos and all, they couldn't make any money at it anymore, so it just kind of went wild."

"That sure is interesting," Marcelle said, shaking her head. "And I don't believe you. But it's okay, I don't need to know who you buy your pot from. I don't *want* to know. I already know too much," she said, and she stepped out and closed the door behind her.

The trailerpark was located three and a half miles northwest of the center of the town of Catamount, a mill town of about five thousand people situated and more or less organized around a dam and millpond first established on the Catamount River some two hundred years ago. The mill had originally been set up as a gristmill, then a lumber mill, then a shoe factory, and, in modern times, a tannery that processed hides from New Zealand cattle and sent the leather to Colombia for the manufacture of shoes.

To get to the trailerpark from the town, you drove north out of town past the Hawthorne House (named for the author Nathaniel Hawthorne, who stopped there overnight in May of 1864 with the then ex-president Franklin Pierce on the way to the White Mountains for a holiday; the author died the following night in a rooming house and tavern not unlike the present Hawthorne House, located in Plymouth, New Hampshire, but the legend had grown up in the region that he had died in his bed in Catamount), then along Main Street, past the half dozen or so blocks of local businesses and the large white Victorian houses that once were the residences of the gentry and the owners of the mill or shoe factory or tannery, whichever it happened to be at the time, and that were now the residences and offices of the local physician (for whom Terry's sister, Carol Constant, worked), dentist, lawyer, certified public accountant, and mortician. A ways beyond the town, you came to an intersection. To your right, Mountain Road sloped crookedly toward the hill that gave the town its name, Catamount Mountain, so named by the dark presence in colonial times of mountain lions and the rocky top of the hill. Turning left, however, you drove along Old Road, called that only recently and for the purpose of distinguishing between it and New Road, or the Turnpike that ran north and south between the White Mountains and Boston. When, three and a half miles from town, you crossed the Catamount River, you turned right at the tipped, flaking sign, GRANITE STATE TRAILERPARK, posted off the road behind a bank of mailboxes standing like sentries at the intersection. Passing through some old, brush-filled fields and a pinewoods that grew on both sides of the narrow, paved lane, you emerged into a clearing, with a sedge-thickened swamp on your left, the Catamount River on your right, and, beyond, a cluster of somewhat battered and aging house trailers. Some were in better repair than others, and some, situated in obviously more attractive locations than others, were alongside the lake, where they exhibited small lawns and flower gardens and other signs of domestic tidiness and care. The lake itself stretched beyond the trailerpark, four and a half miles long and in the approximate shape of a turkey. For that reason, for over a hundred years it had been called Turkey Pond until Ephraim Skitter, who owned the shoe factory, left the town a large endowment for its library and bandstand, and in gratitude the town fathers changed the name of the lake. That, in turn, gave the name Skitter to the large parcel of land that bordered the north and west sides of the lake, becoming by 1950, when the Turnpike was built, the Skitter Lake State Forest. All in all, it was a pretty piece of land and water. If you stood out on the point of land where the trailerpark was situated, with the swamp and pinewoods behind you, you could see, out beyond the deep blue water of the lake, spruce-covered hills that lumped their way northward all the way to the mauve-colored wedges at the horizon, the world-famous White Mountains.

In the trailerpark itself were an even dozen trailers, pastel-colored blocks, some with slightly canted roofs, some with low eaves, but most of them simply rectangular cubes sitting on cinder blocks, with dirt or gravel driveways beside them, usually an old car or pickup truck parked there, with some pathetic, feeble attempt at a lawn or garden evident, but evident mainly in a failure to succeed as such. Some of the trailers, Leon LaRoche's, for example, looked to be in better repair than others, and a few even indicated that the tenants were practically affluent and could afford embellishments such as glassed-in porches, wrought-iron railings at the doorstep, toolsheds, picnic tables and lawn furniture by the shore, and a new or nearly new car in the driveway. The trailer rented to Noni Hubner's mother, Nancy, was one of these—Nancy Hubner was a widow whose late husband had owned the Catamount Insurance Company and was rumored to have had a small interest in the tannery—and Captain Dewey Knox's was another. Captain Knox, like Nancy Hubner, was from an old and relatively well off family in town, as suggested by the name of Knox Island, located out at the northern end of Skitter Lake, where the turkey's eye was. Captain Knox enjoyed recalling childhood summer picnics on "the family island" with his mother and his father, a man who had been one of the successful hemp growers before and during the war, or "War Two," as Captain Knox called it. Prior to that, his father had been a dairy farmer, but after the War decided to sell his land and moved to Maryland, where he died within six months and where Captain Knox's mother, a woman in her eighties, still lived. Captain Knox's return to Catamount after his retirement, he said, had been an act of love. "For this region, this climate, this people, and the principles and values that have prospered here." He talked that way sometimes.

Two of the twelve trailers, numbers 5 and 9, were vacant at this time, number 9 having been vacated only last February as the result of the suicide of a man who had lived in the park as long as Marcelle Chagnon and who had been extremely popular among his neighbors. Tom Smith was his name, and he had raised his son alone in the park, and when his son, at the age of twenty-one or so, had gone away, Tom had withdrawn into himself, and one gray afternoon in February he shot himself in the mouth. He had been a nice man, everyone insisted, though no one had known him very well. In fact, people seemed to think he was a nice man mainly because his son Buddy was so troublesome, always drunk and fighting at the Hawthorne House and, according to the people in the park, guilty of stealing and selling in Boston their TV sets, stereos, radios, jewelry, and so forth. Tom Smith's trailer, number 9, wasn't a particularly fancy one, but it was well located at the end of the land side of the park, right next to Terry and Carol Constant and with a view of the lake. But even so, Marcelle hadn't yet been able to rent it, possibly because of the association with Tom's suicide, but also possibly because of there being black people living next door, which irritated Marcelle whenever it came up, bringing her to announce right to the prospective tenant's face, "Good, I'm glad you don't want to rent that trailer, because we don't want people like you living around here." That would be the end of the tour, and even though Marcelle felt just fine about losing that particular kind of tenant, her attitude certainly did not help her fill number 9, which cost her money. But you had to admire Marcelle Chagnon—she was like an old Indian chief, the way she came forward to protect her people, even if with nothing but her pride, and even at her own expense.

Number 5, the other vacancy, was located between Doreen Tiede, the divorcee who lived with her little girl, and Captain Knox, and was on the lake side of the park, facing the stones and sticks where the lake flowed into the Catamount River and where the Abenaki Indians, back before the whites came north from Massachusetts and drove the Indians away to Canada, had built their fishing weirs. Number 5 was a sleek, sixty-eight-foot-long Marlette with a mansard roof, very fancy, a replacement for the one that burned to the ground a few years ago. A young, newly married couple, Ginnie and Claudel Bing, had moved in, and only three months later, returning home from a weekend down on the Maine coast, found it leveled and still smoldering in the ground, the result of Ginnie's having left the kitchen stove on. They had bought the trailer, financed through the Granite State Realty Development Corporation, and were renting only the lot and services, and their insurance on the place hadn't covered half of what they owed (as newlyweds, they were counting on a long and increasingly rewarding future, so they had purchased a new car and five rooms of new furniture, all on time). Afterwards, they broke up, Claudel lost his job, became something of a drunk, and ended up living alone in a room at the Hawthorne House and working down at the tannery. It was a sad story, and most people in the park knew it and remembered it whenever they passed the shining new trailer that the Corporation moved in to replace the one the Bings had burned down. Because the new trailer was expensive, the rent was high, which made it difficult for Marcelle to find a tenant for it, but the Corporation didn't mind, since it was being paid for anyhow by Claudel Bing's monthly checks. Corporations have a way of making things come out even in the end.

There was in the park one trailer, an old Skyline, that was situated more favorably than any other in the park, number 8, and it was out at the end of the shoreline side, where the road became a cul-de-sac and the shore curved back around toward the swamp and state forest. It was a plain, dark gray trailer, with the grass untended, uncut, growing naturally all around, as if no one lived there. A rowboat lay tilted on one side where someone had drawn it up from the lake behind the trailer, and there was an ice-fishing shanty on a sledge waiting by the shore for winter, but there were no other signs of life around the yard, no automobile, none of the usual junk and tools lying around, no piles of gravel, crushed stone, or loam to indicate projects under way and forsaken for lack of funds, no old and broken toys or tricycles or wagons, nothing out back but a single clothesline stretching from one corner of the trailer back to a pole that looked like a small chokecherry tree cut from the swamp. This was where Merle Ring lived.

Merle Ring was a retired carpenter, retired by virtue of his arthritis, though he could still do a bit of finish work in warm weather, cabinet-making and such, to supplement his monthly social security check. He lived alone and modestly and in that way managed to get by all right. He had outlived and divorced numerous wives, the number varied from three to seven, depending on who Merle happened to be talking to, and he had fathered on these three to seven women at least a dozen children, most of whom lived within twenty miles of him, but none of them wanted Merle to live with him or her because Merle would only live with him or her if, as he put it, he could be the boss of the house. No grown child would accept a condition like that, naturally, and so Merle lived alone, where he was in fact and indisputably the boss of the house.

Merle, in certain respects, was controversial in the park, though he did have the respect of Marcelle Chagnon, which helped keep the controversy from coming to a head. He was mouthy, much given to offering his opinions on subjects that involved him not at all, which would not have been so bad, however irritating it might have been, had he not been so perverse and contradictory with his opinions. He never seemed to mean what he said, but he said it so cleverly that you felt compelled to take him seriously. Then, later, when you brought his opinion back to him and tried to make him own up to it and take responsibility for its consequences, he would laugh at you for ever having taken him seriously in the first place. He caused no little friction in the lives of many of the people in the park. When one night Doreen Tiede's ex-husband arrived at the park drunk and threatening violence, Merle, just coming in from a long night of hornpout fishing on the lake, stopped and watched with obvious amusement, as if he were watching a movie and not a real man cockeyed drunk and shouting through a locked door at a terrorized woman and child that he was going to kill them both. Buck Tiede caught sight of old Merle standing there at the edge of the road, where the light just reached him, his string of hornpout dangling next to the ground.

"You old fart!" Buck, a large and disheveled man, roared at Merle. "What the hell you lookin' at! G'wan, get the hell outa here!" He made a swiping gesture at Merle, as if chasing a dog.

Then, according to Marcelle, who had come up in the darkness carrying her shotgun, Merle said to the man, "Once you kill her, Buck, it's done. Dead is dead. If I was you and wanted that woman dead as you seem to, I'd just get me some dynamite and blow the place all to hell. Or better yet, just catch her someday coming out of work down to the tannery, and snipe her with a high-powered rifle from a window on the third floor of the Hawthorne House. Then she'd be dead, and you could stop all this hollering and banging on doors and stuff."

Buck stared at him in amazement. "What the hell are you saying?"

"I'm saying you ought to get yourself a window up in the Hawthorne House that looks down the hill to the tannery, and when she comes out the door after work, plug her. Get her in the head, to be sure. Just bang, and that'd be that. You could do your daughter the same way. Dead is dead, and you wouldn't have to go around like this all the time. If you was cute about it, you'd get away with it all right. I could help you arrange it. Give you an alibi, even." He held up the string of whiskered fish. "I'd tell 'em you was out hornpouting with me."

"What are you telling me to do?" Buck took a step away from the door toward Merle. "You're crazy."

"Step aside, Merle, I'll take care of this," Marcelle ordered, shouldering the tiny man out of the way and bringing her shotgun to bear on Buck Tiede. "Doreen!" she called out. "You hear me?"

Buck made a move toward Marcelle.

"Stay right where you are, mister, or I'll splash you all over the wall. You know what a mess a twelve-gauge can make?"

Buck stood still.

A thin, frightened voice came from inside. "Marcelle, I'm all right! Oh God, I'm sorry for all this! I'm so sorry!" Then there was weeping, a woman's and a child's.

"Forget sorry. Just call the cops. I'll hold Mister Bigshot here until they come."

And she did hold him, frozen and silent at the top of the steps, while Doreen called the police, who came in less than five minutes and hauled Buck off to spend the night in jail. Merle, once Marcelle and her shotgun had taken charge of the situation, had strolled on with his fish. The cops came and went, blue lights flashing, and later Marcelle returned home, her shotgun slung over her thick arm, and when she entered her kitchen, she found Merle sitting at the kitchen table over a can of Budweiser, reading her copy of *People* magazine.

"You're crazy, dealing with Buck Tiede that way," she said angrily.

"What way?"

"Telling him to shoot Doreen from a room in the Hawthorne House! He's just liable to do that, he's a madman when he's drinking!" She cracked open a can of beer and sat down across from the old man.

He closed the magazine. "I never told him to kill her. I just said how he might do it, if he wanted to kill her. The way he was going about it seemed all wrong to me." He smiled and showed his brown teeth through his beard.

"What if he actually went and did it, shot her from the Hawthorne House some afternoon as she came out of work? How would you feel then?"

"Good."

"Good! Why, in the name of Jesus, Mary, and Joseph, would you feel good?"

"Because we'd know who did it."

"But you said you'd give him an alibi!"

"That was just a trick. I wouldn't, and that way he'd be trapped. He'd say he was with me all afternoon fishing, and then I'd come out and say no, he wasn't. I'd fix it so there'd be no way he could prove he was with me, because I'd make sure someone else saw me fishing alone, and that way he'd be trapped, and they'd take him over to Concord and hang him by the neck until dead."

"Why do you fool around like that with people?" she asked, genuinely curious. "I don't understand you, old man."

He got up, smiled, and flipped the copy of *People* magazine across the table. "It's more interesting than reading this kind of stuff," he said and started for the door. "I put an even dozen hornpouts in your freezer."

"Thanks. Thanks a lot," she said absently, and he went out.

Merle heard about Flora's guinea pigs from Nancy Hubner, the widow in number 7, who heard about them from her daughter, Noni, who was having a love affair with the college boy, Bruce Severance. He told her one night in his trailer, after they had made love and were lying in darkness on the huge water bed he'd built, smoking a joint while the stereo played the songs of the humpback whale quietly around them. Noni had been a college girl in Northern California before her nervous breakdown, so she understood and appreciated Bruce more than anyone else in the park could. Most everyone tolerated Bruce good-humoredly—he believed in knowledge and seemed to be earnest in his quest for it, and what little knowledge he had already acquired, or believed he had acquired, he dispensed liberally to anyone who would listen. He was somberly trying to explain to Noni how yogic birth control worked, and how "basically feminist" it was, because the responsibility was the man's, not the woman's.

"I wondered how come you never asked me if I was protected," she said.

"No need to, man. It's all in the breathing and certain motions with the belly, so the sperm gets separated from the ejaculatory fluid prior to emission. It's really quite simple."

"Amazing."

"Yeah."

"Overpopulation is an incredible problem."

"Yeah. It is."

"I believe that if we could just solve the overpopulation problem, all the rest of the world's problems would be solved, too. Like wars."

"Ecological balance, man. The destruction of the earth."

"The energy crisis. Everything."

"Yeah, man. It's like those guinea pigs of Flora Pease's. Flora, she's got these guinea pigs, hundreds of them by now. And they just keep on making new guinea pigs, doubling their numbers every couple of months. It's incredible, man."

Noni rolled over on her belly and stretched out her legs and wiggled her toes. "Do you have the record of Dylan's, the one where he sings all those country-and-western songs, way before anyone even *heard* of country and western? What's it called? *Nashville Skyline?*"

"Yeah, that's it. Isn't it incredible, how he was singing country and western way before anyone even heard of it?"

"Yeah, he's really incredible, Dylan. Anyhow . . ."

"Do you have it, the record?" she interrupted.

"No, man. Listen, I was telling you something."

"Sorry."

"That's okay, man. Anyhow, Flora's guinea pigs, it's like they're a *metaphor*. I mean, it's like Flora is some kind of god, and the first two guinea pigs, the ones she bought from the five-and-dime in town, were Adam and Eve, and that trailer of hers is the world. Be fruitful and multiply, Flora told them, and, fine, they go out and do what they're programmed to do, and pretty soon they're like taking over the world, which is the trailer, so that Flora, who's like God, can't take care of them anymore. No matter how hard she works, they eat too much, they shit too much, they take up too much room. So what happens?"

Silence.

"What happens?" Bruce repeated.

"A flood, maybe?"

"No, man, it's not that literal, it's a metaphor. What happens is, Flora moves out. She leaves the trailer to the guinea pigs. Twilight of the gods, man. God is dead!"

"That's really incredible."

"Yeah," Bruce said, drifting into still deeper pools of thought.

After a few moments, Noni got up from the bed and drew on her clothes. "I better get home, my mother'll kill me. She thinks I'm at the movies with you."

"Naw, man, she knows where you are. All she's got to do is walk three doors down and see my van's still here. C'mon, she *knows* we're making it together. She's not that out of it."

Noni shrugged. "She believes what she wants to believe. Sometimes I think she still doesn't believe Daddy's dead, and it's been over four years now. There's no point in forcing things on people. You know what I mean?"

Bruce understood, but he didn't agree. People needed to face reality, it was good for them and good for humanity as a whole, he felt. He was about to tell her why it was good for them, but Noni was already dressed and heading for the door, so he said good night instead and waved from the bed as she slipped out the door.

When later that same evening she told her mother that Flora Pease was raising hundreds of guinea pigs in her trailer, it was not so much because Noni was interested in Flora or the guinea pigs, as because her mother, Nancy, was quizzing her about the movie she was supposed to have seen with Bruce.

"That's not true," the woman said.

"What's not?" Noni switched on the TV set and sat down cross-legged on the floor.

"About the guinea pigs. Where'd you hear such a thing?"

"Bruce. Do you think I could study yoga somewhere around here?"

"Of course not. Don't be silly." Nancy lit a cigarette and sat down on the sofa, where she'd been reading this month's Book-of-the-Month Club selection, a novel that gently satirized the morals and mores of Westchester County's smart set. "Bruce.

I don't know about that boy. How can he be a college student when the nearest college is the state university in Durham, which is over forty miles from here?"

"I don't know." Noni was sliding into the plot intricacies of a situation comedy about two young women who worked on an assembly line in Milwaukee and made comically stupid errors of judgment and perception. "It's a correspondence school or something, in Vermont. He has to go there and see his teachers for a couple of weeks twice a year or something. It's the new thing in education."

Nancy didn't know how it could be much of an education, and it certainly didn't explain why Bruce lived where he did and not at his college or even at his parents' home, as Noni did.

"I don't know," Noni said.

"Don't you ever ask, for heaven's sake?"

"No."

That was their conversation for the night. At eleven, Nancy yawned and went to bed in her room at the far end of the trailer, the rooms of which were carpeted and furnished lavishly and resembled the rooms of a fine apartment. Around midnight, Noni rolled a joint and went to her room, next to her mother's, and smoked it, and fell asleep with her light on. She bought her marijuana from Bruce. So did Terry. Also Leon LaRoche, who had never tried smoking grass before, but certainly did not reveal that to Bruce, who knew it anyhow and charged him twice the going rate. Doreen Tiede bought grass from Bruce, too. Not often, however; about once every two or three months. She liked to smoke it in her trailer with men she went out with and came home with, so she called herself a social smoker, but Bruce knew what that meant. Over the years, Bruce had bought his grass from several people, most recently from a Jamaican named Keppie who lived in the West Roxbury area of Boston, but who did business from a motel room in Revere. Next year, Bruce had decided, he would harvest the hemp crop Flora Pease had discovered, and he could sell the grass back, running it the other direction, to Keppie and his Boston friends. He figured there must be five hundred pounds of the stuff growing wild out there, just waiting for a smart guy like him to cut, dry, chop, and pack. He might have to cut Terry Constant in, but that would be fine, because in this business you often needed a partner who happened to be black.

The next morning, on her way to town to have her hair cut and curled, Nancy Hubner picked up Merle Ring. Merle was walking out from the trailerpark and had almost reached Old Road, when he heard the high-pitched whirr of Nancy's powerful Japanese sedan and without turning around stepped off the road into the light, leafless brush. There had been an early snow in late October that winter, and then no snow throughout November and well into December, which had made it an excellent year for ice fishing; After the first October snow, there was a brief melt and then a cold snap that lasted for five weeks now, so that the ice had thickened daily, swiftly becoming iron-hard and black and smooth. All over the lake, fishing shanties had appeared, and all day and long into the night men and sometimes women sat inside the shanties, keeping warm from tiny kerosene or coal-burning heaters, sipping from bottles of whiskey, watching their lines, and yakking slowly to friends or meditating alone and outside of time and space, until the flag went up and the line got yanked and the fisherman would come crashing back into that reality from the other. The ice had hardened sufficiently to bear even the weight of motor vehicles, and now and then you could look out from the shore and see a car or pickup truck creeping across the slick ice and stopping at one of the shanties, bringing society and a fresh six-pack or pint of rye. No one visited Merle's shanty, though he certainly had plenty of friends of various ages and sexes. He had made it known that, when he went ice fishing, it was as if he were going into religious withdrawal and meditation, a journey into the wilderness, as it were, and if you were foolish or ignorant enough to visit him out there on the ice in his tiny, windowless shack with the stovepipe chimney sticking up and puffing smoke, you would be greeted by a man who seemed determined to be left alone. He would be cold, detached, abstracted, unable or unwilling to connect to the person standing self-consciously before him, and after a few moments you would leave, your good-bye hanging unanswered in the air, and Merle would take a sip from his fifth of Canadian Club and drift back into his trance.

Nancy braked her car to a quick stop next to Merle, lowered the window and asked if he wanted a lift into town. She liked the old man, or perhaps it would be more accurate to say that the old man intrigued her, as if she believed he knew something about the world they lived in together that she did not know and that would profit her greatly if she did know. So she courted him, fussed over him, seemed to be looking after his comfort and welfare, behaving the way, as she once said to Noni, his daughters ought to behave.

Merle apparently knew all this, and more, though you could never be sure with him. He got inside the low, sleek car, slammed the door shut, and surrounded himself with the smell of leather and the pressure of fan-driven heat. "Morning, Mrs. Hubner. A fine, crispy morning, isn't it?"

She agreed and asked him where she could drop him. A fast, urgent driver, she was already flying past the intersection of Old Road and Main Street and was approaching the center of town. She drove so as to endanger, but didn't seem to know it. It was as if her relation to the physical act of driving was the same as her relation to poverty—abstract, wholly theoretical, and sentimental— which, from Merle's perspective, made her as dangerous a driver as she was a citizen.

Merle and Nancy exchanged brief remarks, mostly solicitous on her part as to the present condition of Merle's arthritis and mostly whining on his part as to the same thing. Merle knew that by whining he could put Nancy at her ease, and in encounters as brief as this he, like most people, enjoyed being able to put people at their ease. It made things more interesting for him later on. Stopping in front of Hayward's Hardware and Sporting Goods Store, where Merle was headed for traps, she suddenly asked him a direct question (since she was now sufficiently at her ease to trust that he would answer directly and honestly and in that way might be brought to reveal more than he wished to): "Tell me, Mr. Ring, is it true that that woman, Flora in number eleven, you know the one, is raising hundreds of guinea pigs in her trailer?"

"Yes," he said, lying, for he had heard nothing of it. "Though I'm not sure of the numbers. It's hard to count 'em after a certain point, sixty, say."

"Don't you think that's a little . . . disgusting? I mean, the *filth*! I think the woman ought to be put away, don't you?" she asked, still trying to get information.

"What would you do with all those guinea pigs then?"

"Let the SPCA take them, I suppose. They know how to handle these things, when things like this get out of hand. Imagine, all those tiny animals crowded into a trailer, and remember, number eleven is not one of the larger trailers in the park, you know."

"I guess you're right, the SPCA could kill 'em for us, once we'd got Flora locked up someplace. The whole thing would probably drive her right over the edge, anyhow, taking away her animals and killing 'em like that, tossing 'em into that incinerator they got. That'd push ol' Flora right over the edge. She'd be booby-hatch material for sure then, whether she is now or not."

"You're making fun of me, Mr. Ring. Aren't you?"

"No, no, no, I'm not making fun of you, Mrs. Hubner," he said, opening the door and stepping out, not without difficulty, because of the shape of the car and his stiff back. "I'll check into it for you, ma'am. Get the facts of the situation, so to speak. Because you're probably right. I mean, something will have to be done, eventually, by someone. Because those kinds of animals, rodents and such, they breed fast, and before you know it, one hundred is two hundred, two hundred is four, four is eight, and so on."

"Thank you so much, Mr. Ring," she said with clear relief. He was such a nice man. She wondered if there was some way she could make his life a little easier. At his age, to be alone like that, it was simply awful.

Merle closed the door, waved, and walked into Hayward's and Nancy drove on to Ginnie's Beauty Nook on Green Street across from Knight's Paint Store, where Ginnie and her husband, Claudel, had rented the upstairs apartment after their trailer burned down. That was over three years ago, or maybe four. Nancy couldn't remember, until it came back to her that it had happened the summer Noni turned fifteen and started having migraines and saying she hated her, and then Nancy remembered that was the summer her husband died. So it must be over four years now since Ginnie and Claudel moved into town and rented that apartment over Knight's Paint Store. Isn't it amazing how time flies when you're not paying attention, she reflected.

A week later, Merle woke late, after having spent most of the night out on the lake in his ice house, and because the sun was shining, casting a raw light that somehow pleased him, he decided to visit Flora Pease and determine if all this fuss over her guinea pigs was justified. Since talking with Nancy Hubner, he had spoken only to Marcelle Chagnon about the guinea pigs, and her response had been to look heavenward, as if for help or possibly mere solace, and   to say, "Just don't talk to me about that crazy woman, Merle, don't start in about her. As long as she doesn't cause any troubles for me, I won't cause any troubles for her. But if *you* start in on this, there'll be troubles. For me. And that means for her, too, remember that."

"Makes sense," Merle said, and for several days he went strictly about his business—ice fishing, eating, cleaning, reading the Manchester *Union Leader*, puttering with his tools and equipment—slow, solitary activities that he seemed to savor. He was the kind of person who, by the slowness of his pace and the hard quality of his attention, appeared to take sensual pleasure from the most ordinary activity. He was a small, lightly framed man and wore a short, white beard, which he kept neatly trimmed. His clothing was simple and functional, flannel shirts, khaki pants, steel-toed work shoes—the same style of clothing he had worn since his youth, when he first became a carpenter's apprentice and determined what sort of clothing was appropriate for that kind of life. His teeth were brown, stained from a lifetime of smoking a cob pipe, and his weathered skin was still taut, indicating that he had always been a small, trim man. There was something effeminate about him that, at least in old age, made him physically attractive, especially to women, but to men as well. Generally, his manner with people was odd and somewhat disconcerting, for he was both involved with their lives and not involved, both serious and not serious, both present and absent. For example, a compliment from Merle somehow had the effect of reminding the recipient of his or her vanity, while an uninvited criticism came out sounding like praise for having possessed qualities that got you singled out in the first place.

Though seasonably cold (fifteen degrees below freezing), the day was pleasant and dry, the light falling on the rock ground directly, so that the edges of objects took on an unusual sharpness and clarity. Merle knocked briskly on Flora's door, and after a moment, she swung it open. She was wrapped in a wool bathrobe that must have been several decades old and belonged originally to a very large man, for it flowed around her blocky body like a carpet. Her short hair stuck out in a corolla of dark red spikes, and her eyes were red-rimmed and watery-looking, as, grumpily, she asked Merle what he wanted from her.

"A look," he chirped, smiling.

"A look. At what?"

"At your animals. The guinea pigs I been hearing about."

"You heard about them? What did you hear?" She stood before the door, obstructing his view into the darkened room beyond. An odor of fur and straw, however, seeped past and merged warmly with the cold, almost sterile air outdoors.

Merle sniffed with interest at the odor, apparently relishing it. "Heard you got a passel of 'em. I never seen one of these guinea pigs before and was wondering what in hell they look like. Pigs?"

"No. More like fat, furry chipmunks," Flora said, easing away from the door. She still had not smiled, however, and was not ready to invite Merle inside. "Mrs. Chagnon send you over here?" she demanded. "That woman is putting me on the spot. I can't have any friends anymore to visit or to talk to me here, or else I'll get into trouble with that woman."

"No, Marcelle didn't send me, she didn't even want to talk about your guinea pigs with me. She just said as long as they don't cause her any trouble, she won't cause you any trouble."

"That's what I mean," Flora said, defiantly crossing her short, thick arms over her chest. "People come around here and see my guinea pigs, and then I get into trouble. If they don't come around here and don't see nothing, then it's like the guinea pigs, for them, don't exist. That kid, Terry, the black one, he started it, when all I was doing was trying to be friendly, and then he went and dragged the other kid, the white one, in here, and they got to smoking my hemp, and then pretty soon here comes Mrs. Chagnon, and I get in trouble. All

I want is to be left alone," she said with great clarity, as if she said it to herself many times a day.

Merle nodded sympathetically. "I understand how you feel. It's like when I won the lottery, that was back a ways before you come here, and everybody thought I had a whole heap more money than I had, so everyone was after me for some."

That interested Flora. She had never met anyone who had won the lottery. In fact, she was starting to believe that it was all faked, that no one ever won, that those people jumping up and down hysterically in the TV ads were just actors. Now, because of Merle's having won, her faith in the basic goodness of the world was magically restored. "This means they probably went to the moon, too!" she said with clear relief.

"Who?"

"The astronauts."

"You didn't believe that, the rocket to the moon? I thought you used to be in the Air Force."

"That's why I had so much trouble believing it," she said and stood aside and waved him in.

Inside, when his eyes had grown accustomed to the dim light of the room, this is what Merle saw: large, waist-high, wood-framed, chicken-wire pens that were divided into cubicles about two feet square. The pens were placed throughout the room in no apparent order or pattern, which gave the room, despite the absence of furniture, the effect of being incredibly cluttered, as if someone were either just moving in or all packed to move out. As far as Merle could see, the rooms adjacent to this one were similarly jammed with pens, and he surmised that the rooms he couldn't see, the bedroom at the back and the bathroom, were also filled with pens like these. In each cubicle there was a pair of grown or nearly grown guinea pigs or else one grown (presumably female) pig and a litter of two or three piglets. Merle could see and hear the animals in the nearby cubicles scurrying nervously in their cages, but the animals closest to him were crouched and still, their large round eyes rolling frantically and their noses twitching as, somehow, Merle's own odor penetrated the heavy odor of the room.

Flora reached down and plucked a black and white spotted pig from the cage it shared with a tan, long-haired mate. Cradling it in her arm and stroking its nose with her free hand, she walked cooing and clucking over to Merle and showed him the animal. "This here's Ferdinand," she said. "After the bull."

"Ah. May I?" he said, reaching out to take Ferdinand.

Merle held the animal as Flora had and studied its trembling, limp body. It seemed to offer no defense and showed no response except stark terror. When Merle placed it back into its cubicle, it remained exactly where he had placed it, as if waiting for a sudden, wholly deserved execution.

"How come you like these animals, Flora?"

"Don't *you* like them?" she bristled.

"I don't feel one way or the other about them. I was wondering about you."

She was silent for a moment and moved nervously around the cages, checking into the cubicles as she moved. "Well, somebody's got to take care of them. Especially in this climate. They're really not built for the ice and snow."

"So you don't do it because you like them?"

"No. I mean, I like looking at them and all, the colors are pretty, and their little faces are cute and all. But I'm just taking care of them so they won't die, that's all."

There was a silence, and Merle said, "I hate to ask it, but how come you let them breed together? You know where that'll lead?"

"Do you know where it'll lead if I *don't* let them breed together?" she asked, facing him with her hands fisted on her hips.

"Yup."

"Where?"

"They'll die out."

"Right. That answer your question?"

"Yup."

Merle stayed with her for the next half hour, as she showed him her elaborate watering system—a series of interconnected hoses that ran from the cold water spigot in the kitchen sink around and through all the cages, ending back in the bathroom sink—and her cleverly designed system of trays beneath the cages for removing from the cages the feces and spilled food, and her gravity-fed system of grain troughs, so that all she had to do was dump a quart a day into each cage and the small trough in each individual cubicle would be automatically filled. She designed and built the cages herself, she explained, and, because she was no carpenter, they weren't very fancy or pretty to look at. But the basic idea was a good one, she insisted, so that, despite her lack of skill, the system worked, and consequently every one of her animals was clean, well-fed, and watered at all times. "You can't ask for much more in this life, can you?" she said proudly as she led Merle to the door.

He guessed no, you couldn't. "But I still think you're headed for troubles," he told her, and he opened the door to leave.

"What do you mean? What's going on?" Suddenly she was suspicious of him and frightened of Marcelle Chagnon again, with her suspicion of the one and fear of the other swiftly merging and becoming anger at everyone.

"No, no, no. Not troubles with Marcelle or any of the rest of the folks in the park. Just with the breeding and all. In time, there will be too many of them. They breed new ones faster than the old ones die off. It's simple. There will come a day when you won't have any more room left in there. What will you do then?"

"Move out."

"What about the animals?"

"I'll take care of them. They can have the whole trailer. They'll have lots of room if I move out."

"But you don't understand," Merle said calmly. "It goes on forever. It's numbers, and it doesn't change or level off or get better. It gets worse and worse, faster and faster."

"*You* don't understand," she said to him. "Everything depends on how you look at it. And what looks worse and worse to you might look better and better to me."

Merle smiled, and his blue eyes gleamed. He stepped down to the ground and waved pleasantly at the grim woman. "You are right, Flora Pease. Absolutely right. And I thank you for straightening me out this fine morning!" he exclaimed, and, whistling softly, he walked off for Marcelle's trailer, where he would sit down at her table and drink a cup of coffee with her and recommend to her that, in the matter of Flora and her guinea pigs, the best policy was no policy, because Flora was more than capable of handling any problem that the proliferation of the guinea pigs might create.

Marcelle was not happy with Merle's advice. She was a woman of action and it pained her to sit still and let things happen. But, she told Merle, she had no choice in this matter of the guinea pigs. If she tried to evict Flora and the animals, there would be a ruckus and possibly a scandal; if she brought in the health department, there was bound to be a scandal; if she evicted Flora and not the guinea pigs, then she'd have the problem of disposing of the damn things herself. "It's just gone too far," she said, scowling.

"But everything's fine right now, at this very moment, isn't it?" Merle asked, stirring his coffee.

"I suppose you could say that."

"Then it hasn't gone too far. It's gone just far enough."

At this stage, just before Christmas, everyone had an opinion as to what ought to be done with regard to the question of the guinea pigs.

FLORA PEASE: Keep the animals warm, well-fed, clean, and breeding. Naturally, as their numbers increase, their universe will expand. (Flora didn't express herself that way, for she would have been speaking to people who would have been confused by language like that coming from her. She said it this way: "When you take care of things, they thrive. Animals, vegetables, minerals, same with all of them. And that makes you a better person, since it's the taking care that makes *people* thrive. Feeling good is good, and feeling better is better. No two ways about it. All people ever argue about anyhow is how to go about feeling good and then better.")

DOREEN TIEDE: Evict Flora (she could always rent a room at the Hawthorne House, Claudel Bing had and, God knows, he was barely able to tie his own shoes for a while, he was so drunk, though of course he's much better now and may actually move out of the Hawthorne House one of these days, and in fact the man was starting to look like his old self again, which was not half bad), and then call in the SPCA to find homes for the animals (the ones that couldn't be placed in foster homes would have to be destroyed but, really, all they are is animals, rodents, rats, almost).

TERRY CONSTANT: Sneak into her trailer one day when she's in town buying grain, and, one by one, liberate the animals. Maybe you ought to wait till spring and then just set them free to live in the swamp and the piney woods and fields between Old Road and the trailerpark. By the time winter came rolling around again, they'd have figured out how to tunnel into the ground and hibernate like the rest of the warm-blooded animals. The ones that didn't learn how to survive, well, too bad for them. Survival of the fittest.

BRUCE SEVERANCE: The profit motive, man. That's what needs to be invoked here. Explain to Flora that laboratories pay well for clean, well-fed guinea pigs, especially those bred and housed under such controlled conditions as

Flora has established. Explain this, pointing out how it'll enable her to breed guinea pigs for both fun and profit for an indefinite period of time, for as long as she wants, when you get right down to it. Show her that this is not only socially useful but it'll provide her with enough money to take even better care of her animals than now.

NONI HUBNER: Bruce's idea is a good one, and so is Leon LaRoche's, and Captain Knox has a good idea too. Maybe we ought to try one first, Captain Knox's, say, since he's the oldest and has the most experience of the world, and if that doesn't work, we could try Leon LaRoche's, and then if that fails, we can try Bruce's. That would be the democratic way.

LEON LAROCHE: Captain Knox's idea, of course, is the logical one, but it runs certain risks and depends on his being able to keep Flora, by the sheer force of his will, from reacting hysterically or somehow "causing a scene" that would embarrass the trailerpark and we who live in it. If the *Suncook Valley Sun* learned that we had this sort of thing going on here, that we had a village eccentric living here among us at the trailerpark, we would all suffer deep embarrassment. I agree, therefore, with Doreen Tiede's plan. But my admiration, of course, is for Captain Knox's plan.

CAROL CONSTANT: I don't care what you do with the damned things, just do something. The world's got enough problems, real problems, without people going out and inventing new ones. The main thing is to keep the poor woman happy, and if having a lot of little rodents around is what makes her happy, and they aren't bothering anyone else yet, then, for God's sake, leave her alone. She'll end up taking care of them herself, getting rid of them or whatever, if and when they start to bother her—and they'll bother her a lot sooner than they bother us, once we stop thinking about them all the time. Her ideas will change as soon as the guinea pigs get to the point where they're causing more trouble than they're giving pleasure. Everybody's that way, and Flora Pease is no different. You have to trust the fact that we're all human beings.

NANCY HUBNER: Obviously, the guinea pigs are Flora's substitutes for a family and friends. She's trying to tell us something, and we're not listening. If we, and I mean all of us, associated more with Flora on a social level, if we befriended her, then her need for these filthy animals would diminish and probably disappear. It would be something that in the future we could all laugh about, Flora laughing right along with us. We should drop by for coffee, invite her over for drinks, offer to help redecorate her trailer, and so on. We should be more charitable. It's as simple as that. Christian charity. I know it won't be easy—Flora's not exactly socially "flexible," if you know what I mean, but we are, at least most of us are, and therefore it's our responsibility to initiate contact, not hers, poor thing.

CAPTAIN DEWEY KNOX: It's her choice, no one else's. Either she goes, or the animals go. She decides which it's to be, we don't. If she decides to go, fine, she can take the animals with her or leave them behind, in which case I'm sure some more or less humane way can be found to dispose of them. If she stays, also fine, but she stays without the animals. Those are the rules—no pets. They're the same rules for all of us, no exceptions. All one has to do is apply the rules, and that forces onto the woman a decision that, however painful it may be for her, she must make. No one can make that decision for her.

MARCELLE CHAGNON: If she'd stop the damned things from breeding, the whole problem would be solved. At least it would not bother me anymore, which is important. The only way to get her to stop breeding them, without bringing the Corporation or the health board or the SPCA or any other outsiders into it, is to go in there and separate the males from the females ourselves, and when she comes back from town, say to her, okay, Flora, this is a compromise. Sometimes people don't understand what a compromise is until you force it on them. It's either that or we sit around waiting for this thing to explode, and then it'll be too late to compromise, because the outsiders will be in charge.

MERLE RING: Let Flora continue to keep the animals warm, well-fed, clean, and breeding. Naturally, as their numbers increase, their universe will expand. And as a result, all the people in the trailerpark, insofar as they observe this phenomenon, will find their universe expanding also. (It's understood that Merle did not express himself this way, for he would have been expressing himself to people who would have been offended by language like that. Here's how he put it: "It'll be interesting to see what the woman does with her problem—if it ever actually becomes a problem. And if it never becomes a problem, that should be interesting, too.")

Flora's life up to now ought to have prepared her for what eventually happened with the guinea pigs. It had been a hard life, beginning with the death of her mother when Flora was barely a year old. Flora's father was what in these parts is often called a rough carpenter, meaning that he could use a hammer and saw well enough to work as a helper to a bona fide carpenter. Usually he was the one who nailed together the plywood forms for making cellar walls and then, when the cement had set, tore the forms apart. During the fall and winter months, when it was too cold for cement to pour, the bona fide carpenters moved to interior work, which required a certain skill and a basic fluency with numbers, and Flora's father was always among the first in the fall unemployment line.

There were three older children, older by one, two, and three years, and after the mother died, the children more or less took care of themselves. They lived out beyond Shackford Corners in a dilapidated house that appeared to be falling into its own cellar hole, an unpainted, leaky, abandoned house heated in winter by a kerosene stove, with no running water and only rudimentary wiring. The father's way of raising his children was to stay drunk when he was not working, to beat them if they cried or intruded on his particular misery, and, when he was working, to leave them to their own devices, which were not especially healthful devices. When Flora's older brother was six, he set off one of the blasting caps that he found near the lumber camp a half mile behind the house in the woods and blew one of his arms off and almost died. When Flora's only sister was eleven, she was raped by an uncle visiting from Saskatchewan and after that could only gaze blankly past your head when you tried to talk to her or get her to talk to you. Flora's older brother, when he was fourteen and she thirteen, sickened and died of what was determined by the local health authorities to have been malnutrition, at which point the remaining three children were taken away from the father and placed into the care of the state, which meant, at that time, the New Hampshire State Hospital over in Concord, where they had a wing for juveniles who could not be placed in foster homes or who were drug addicts or had committed crimes of violence but were too young to be tried as adults. Four years later, Flora was allowed to leave the mental hospital (for that is what it was) on the condition that she join the United States Air Force, where she spent the next twenty years working in the main as a maid, or steward, in officers' clubs and quarters at various bases around the country. She was not badly treated by the Air Force itself, but numerous individual servicemen, enlisted men as well as officers, treated her unspeakably.

Despite her life, Flora remained good-naturedly ambitious for her spirit. She believed in self-improvement, believed that it was possible, and that not to seek it was reprehensible, was, in fact, a sin. And sinners she viewed the way most people view the stupid or the poor—as if their stupidity or poverty were their own fault, the direct result of sheer laziness and a calculated desire to exploit the rest of humankind, who, of course, are intelligent or well-off as a direct result of their willingness to work and not ask for help from others. This might not seem a particularly enlightened way to view sinners, and it certainly was not a Christian way to view sinners; but it did preserve a kind of chastity for Flora. It also, of course, made it difficult for her to learn much, in moral terms, from the behavior of others. There was probably a wisdom in that, however, a trade-off that made it possible for her to survive into something like middle age without falling into madness and despair.

Within a week of having moved into the trailerpark, Flora had purchased her first pair of guinea pigs. She went into the Catamount five-and-dime looking for goldfish, but when she saw the pair of scrawny, matted animals in their tiny, filthy cages at the back of the store, she forgot the goldfish, which by comparison looked relatively healthy, despite the cloudiness of the water in their tank. She built her cages herself, mostly from cast-off boards and chicken wire she found at the town dump and carried home. The skills required were not great, were, in fact, about the same as had been required of her father in the construction of cement forms. At the dump she also found pieces of garden hose she needed to make her watering system and the old gutters she hooked up as grain troughs.

Day and night, she worked for her guinea pigs, walking to town and hauling back fifty-pound bags of grain, dragging back from the dump more old boards, sheets of tin, gutters, and so on. As the guinea pigs multiplied and more cages became necessary, Flora soon found herself working long hours into the night alone in her trailer, feeding, watering, and cleaning the animals, while out behind the trailer the pyramid of mixed straw, feces, urine, and grain gradually rose to waist height, then to shoulder height, finally reaching to head height, when she had to start a second pyramid, and then, a few months later, a third. And as the space requirements of the guinea pigs increased, her own living space decreased, until finally she was sleeping on a cot in a corner of the back bedroom, eating standing up at the kitchen sink, stashing her clothing and personal belongings under her cot, so that all the remaining space could be devoted to the care, housing, and feeding of the guinea pigs.

By the start of her third summer at the trailerpark, she had begun to lose weight noticeably, and her usually pinkish skin had taken on a gray pallor. Never particularly fastidious anyhow, her personal hygiene now could be said not to exist at all, and the odor she bore with her was the same odor given off by the guinea pigs, so that, in time, to call Flora Pease the Guinea Pig Lady was not to misrepresent her. Her eyes grew dull, as if the light behind them were slowly going out, and her hair was tangled and stiff with dirt, and her clothing seemed increasingly to be hidden behind stains, smears, spills, drips, and dust.

"Here comes the Guinea Pig Lady!" You'd hear the call from the loafers outside McCallister's News & Variety leaning against the glass front, and a tall, angular teenager with shoulder-length hair and acne, wearing torn jeans and a Mothers of Invention T-shirt, would stick his long head inside and call your name, "C'mere, take a look at this, man!"

You'd be picking up your paper, maybe, or because McCallister's was the only place that sold it, the racing form with yesterday's Rockingham results and today's odds. The kid might irritate you slightly—his gawky, witless pleasure, his slightly pornographic acne, the affectation of his T-shirt and long hair—but still, your curiosity up, you'd pay for your paper and stroll to the door to see what had got the kid so excited.

In a low, conspiratorial voice, the kid would say, "The Guinea Pig Lady."

She'd be on the other side of the street, shuffling rapidly along the sidewalk in the direction of Merrimack Farmers' Exchange, wearing her blue, U.S. Air Force, wool, ankle-length coat, even though this was May and an unusually warm day even for May, and her boot lacings were undone and trailing behind her, her arms chopping away at the air as if she were a boxer working out with the heavy bag, and she was singing in a voice moderately loud, loud enough to be heard easily across the street, "My Boy Bill" from *Carousel.*

"Hey, honey!" the kid wailed, and the Guinea Pig Lady, though she ignored his call, stopped singing at once. "Hey, honey, how about a little nookie, sweets!" The Guinea Pig Lady sped up a bit, her arms churning faster against the air. "Got something for ya, honey! Got me a licking stick, sweet lips!"

If you already knew who the woman was, Flora Pease, of the Granite State Trailerpark out at Skitter Lake, and knew about the guinea pigs and, thereby, could guess why she was headed for the grain store, you'd ease past the kid and away. But if you didn't know who she was, you might ask the kid, and he'd say, "The Guinea Pig Lady, man. She lives with these hundreds of guinea pigs in the trailerpark out at Skitter Lake. Just her and all these animals. Everybody in town knows about it, but she won't let anyone inside her trailer to see 'em, man. She's got these huge piles of shit out behind her trailer, and she comes into town all the time to buy feed for 'em. She's a fuckin' freak, man! A freak! And nobody in town can do anything about 'em, the guinea pigs, I mean, because so far nobody out at the trailerpark will make a formal complaint about 'em. You can bet your ass if I lived out there I'd sure as shit make a complaint. I'd burn the fucking trailer to the ground, man. I mean, that's disgusting, all them animals. Somebody ought to go out there some night and pull her outa there and burn the place down. It's a health hazard, man! You can get a disease from them things!"

One September morning, after about a week of not having seen Flora leave her trailer once, even to empty the trays of feces out back, Marcelle decided to make sure the woman was all right, so she stepped across the roadway and knocked on Flora's door. The lake, below a cloudless sky, was deep blue, and the leaves of the birches along the shore were yellowing. There had already been a hard frost, and the grass and weeds and low scrub shone dully gold in the sunlight.

There was no answer. Marcelle knocked again, firmly this time, and called Flora's name.

A moment later she heard a low, muffled voice from inside. "Go away." Then silence, except for the breeze off the lake.

"Are you all right? It's me, Marcelle!"

Silence.

Marcelle tried the door. Locked. She called again, "Flora, let me in!" and stood with her fists jammed against her hips. She breathed in and out rapidly, her large brow pulled down in alarm. A few seconds passed, and she called out, "Flora, I'm coming inside!"

Moving quickly to the top step, she pitched her shoulder against the door just above the latch, which immediately gave way and let the door blow open, causing Marcelle to stagger inside, off-balance, blinking in the darkness and floundering in the odor of the animals as if she'd fallen in a huge tub of warm water. "Flora!" she yelled. "Flora, where are you?" Bumping against the cages, she made her way around them and into the kitchen area, shouting Flora's name and peering in vain into the darkness. In several minutes, she had made her way to the bedroom in back, and there in a corner she found Flora on her cot, wrapped in a blanket, looking almost unconscious, limp, bulky, gray. Her hands were near her throat, clutching the top of the blanket like the hands of a frightened, beaten child, and she had her head turned toward the wall, with her eyes closed. She looked like a sick child to Marcelle, like her own child, Joel, who had died when he was twelve—the fever had risen, and the hallucinations had come until he was out of his head with them, and then, suddenly, while she was mopping his body with damp washcloths, the wildness had gone out of him, and he had turned on his side, drawn his skinny legs up to his belly, and died.

Flora was feverish, though not with as high a fever as the boy, Joel, had endured, and she had drawn her legs up to her, bulking her body into a lumpy heap beneath the filthy blanket. "You're sick," Marcelle announced to the woman, who seemed not to hear her. Marcelle straightened the blanket, brushed the woman's matted hair away from her face, and looked around the room to see if there wasn't some way she could make her more comfortable. The room was jammed with the large, odd-shaped cages, and Marcelle could hear the animals rustling back and forth on the wire flooring, now and then chittering in what she supposed was protest against hunger and thirst.

Taking a backward step, Marcelle yanked the cord and opened the venetian blind, and sunlight tumbled into the room. Suddenly Flora was shouting, "Shut it! Shut it! Don't let them see! No one can see me!"

Marcelle closed the blind, and the room once again filled with the gloom and shadow that Flora believed hid the shape of the life being lived here. "I got to get you to a doctor," Marcelle said quietly. "Doctor Wickshaw's got office hours today. You know Carol Constant, his nurse, that nice colored lady who lives next door? You got to see a doctor, missy."

"No. I'll be all right soon," she said in a weak voice. "Just the flu, that's all." She pulled the blanket up higher, covering most of her face, but exposing her dirty bare feet.

Marcelle persisted, and soon Flora began to curse the woman, her voice rising in fear and anger, the force of it pushing Marcelle away from the cot, "You leave me alone, you bitch! I know your tricks, I know what you're trying to do! You just want to get me out of here so you can take my babies away from me! I'm fine, I can take care of my babies fine, just fine! Now you get out of my house! Go on, get!"

Marcelle backed slowly away, then turned and walked to the open door and outside to the sunshine and the clean fall air.

Doctor Wickshaw, Carol told her, doesn't make house calls. Marcelle sat at her kitchen table, looked out the window, and talked on the telephone. She was watching Flora's trailer, number 11, as if watching a bomb about to explode.

"I know that," Marcelle said, holding the receiver between her shoulder and cheek so both hands could be free to light a cigarette. "Listen, Carol, this is Flora Pease we're talking about, and there's no way I'm going to be able to get her into that office. But she's real sick, and it could be just the flu, but it could be meningitis, for all I know. My boy died of that, you know, and you have to do tests and everything before you can tell if it's meningitis." There was silence for a few seconds. "Maybe I should call the ambulance and get her over to the Concord Hospital. I need somebody who knows something to come here and look at her," she said, her voice rising.

"Maybe on my lunch hour I'll be able to come by and take a look," Carol said. "At least I should be capable of saying if she should be got to a hospital or not."

Marcelle thanked her and hung up the phone. Nervously tapping her fingers against the table, she thought to call in Merle Ring or maybe Captain Knox, to get their opinions of Flora's condition, and then decided against it. That damned Dewey Knox, he'd just take over, one way or the other, and after reducing the situation to a choice between two courses, probably between leaving her alone in the trailer and calling the ambulance, he'd insist that someone other than he do the choosing, probably Flora herself, who, of course, would choose to be left alone. Then he'd walk off believing he'd done the right thing, the only right thing. Merle would be just as bad, she figured, with all his smart-ass comments about illness and death and leaving things alone until they have something to say to you that's completely clear. Some illnesses lead to death, he'd say, and some lead to health, and we'll know before long which it is, and when we do, we'll know how to act. Men. Either they take responsibility for everything, or they take responsibility for nothing.

Around one, Carol Constant arrived in her little blue sedan, dressed in a white nurse's uniform and looking, to Marcelle, very much like a medical authority. Marcelle led her into Flora's trailer, after warning her about the clutter and the smell— "It's like some kinda burrow in there," she said as they stepped through the door—and Carol, placing a plastic tape against Flora's forehead, determined that

Flora was indeed quite ill, her temperature was 105 degrees. She turned to Marcelle and told her to call the ambulance.

Immediately, Flora went wild, bellowing and moaning about her babies and how she couldn't leave them, they needed her. She thrashed against Carol's strong grip for a moment and then gave up and fell weakly back into the cot.

"Go ahead and call," Carol told Marcelle. "I'll hold on to things here until they come." When Marcelle had gone, Carol commenced talking to the ill woman in a low, soothing voice, stroking her forehead with one hand and holding her by the shoulder with the other, until, after a few moments, Flora began to whimper and then to weep, and finally, as if her heart were broken, to sob. Marcelle had returned from calling the ambulance and stood in the background almost out of sight, while Carol soothed the woman and crooned, "Poor thing, you poor thing."

"My babies, who'll take care of my babies?" she wailed.

"I'll get my brother Terry to take care of them," Carol promised, and for a second that seemed to placate the woman.

Then she began to wail again, because she knew it was a lie and when she came back her babies would be gone.

No, no, no, no, both Carol and Marcelle insisted. When she got back, the guinea pigs would be here, all of them, every last one. Terry would water and feed them, and he'd clean out the cages every day, just as she did.

"I'll make sure he does," Marcelle promised, "or he'll have his ass in a sling."

That calmed the woman, but just then two young men dressed in white, the ambulance attendants, stepped into the room, and when Flora saw them, their large, grim faces and, from her vantage point, their enormous, uniformed bodies, her eyes rolled back, and she began to wail, "No, no, no! I'm not going! I'm not going!"

The force of her thrashing movements tossed Carol off the cot onto the floor. Moving swiftly, the two young men reached down and pinned Flora against her cot. One of them, the larger one, told the other to bring his bag, and the smaller man rushed out of the trailer to the ambulance parked outside.

"I'm just going to give you something to calm yourself, ma'am," the big man said in a mechanical way. The other man was back, and Carol and Marcelle, regarding one another with slight regret and apprehension, stepped out of his way.

In seconds, Flora had been injected with a tranquilizer, and while the two hard-faced men in white strapped her body into a four-wheeled, chromium and canvas stretcher, she descended swiftly into slumber. They wheeled her efficiently out of the trailer as if she were a piece of furniture and slid her into the back of the ambulance and were gone, with Marcelle following in her car.

Alone by the roadway outside Flora's trailer, Carol watched the ambulance and Marcelle's battered old Ford head out toward Old Road and away. After a moment or two, drifting from their trailers one by one, came Nancy Hubner, her face stricken with concern, and Captain Dewey Knox, his face firmed to hear the grim news, and Merle Ring, his face smiling benignly.

"Where's my brother Terry?" Carol asked the three as they drew near.

It was near midnight that same night. Most of the trailers were dark, except for Bruce Severance's, where Terry, after having fed, watered, and cleaned the ravenous, thirsty, and dirty guinea pigs, was considering a business proposition from Bruce that would not demand humiliating labor for mere monkey-money, and Doreen Tiede's trailer, where Claudel Bing's naked, muscular arm was reaching over Doreen's head to snap off the lamp next to the bed—when, out by Old Road, the Guinea Pig Lady came shuffling along the lane between the pinewoods. She moved quickly and purposefully, just as she always moved, but silently now. She wore the clothes she'd worn in the morning when the men had taken her from her cot and strapped her onto the stretcher—old bib overalls and a faded, stained, plaid flannel shirt. Her face was ablaze with fever. Her red hair ringed her head in a stiff, wet halo that made her look like an especially blessed peasant figure in a medieval fresco, a shepherd or stonemason rushing to see the Divine Child.

When she neared the trailerpark, sufficiently close to glimpse the few remaining lights and the dully shining, geometric shapes of the trailers through the trees and, here and there, a dark strip of the lake beyond, she cut to her left and departed from the road and made for the swamp. Without hesitation, she darted into the swamp, locating even in darkness the pathways and patches of dry ground, moving slowly through the mushy, brush-covered muskeg, emerging from the deep shadows of the swamp after a while at the edge of the clearing directly behind her own trailer. Soundlessly, she crossed her backyard, passed the head-high pyramids standing like dolmens in the dim light, and stepped through the broken door of the trailer.

The trailer was in pitch darkness, and the only sound was that of the animals as they chirped, bred, and scuffled in their cages through the nighttime. With the same familiarity she had shown cutting across the swamp, Flora moved in darkness to the kitchen area, where she opened a cupboard and drew from a clutter of cans and bottles a red one-gallon can of kerosene. Then, starting at the farthest corner of the trailer, she dribbled the kerosene through every room, looping through and around every one of the cages, until she arrived at the door. She placed the can on the floor next to the broken door, then stepped nimbly outside, where she took a single step toward the ground, lit a wooden match against her thumbnail, tossed it into the trailer, and ran.

Instantly, the trailer was a box of flame, roaring and snapping and sending a dark cloud and poisonous fumes into the night sky as the paneling and walls ignited and burst into flame. Next door, wakened by the first explosion and terrified by the sight of the flames and the roar of the fire, Carol Constant rushed from her bed to the road, where everyone else in the park was gathering, wide-eyed, confused, struck with wonder and fear.

Marcelle hollered at Terry and Bruce, ordering them to hook up garden hoses and wash down the trailers next to Flora's. Then she yelled to Doreen. Dressed in a filmy nightgown, with the naked Claudel Bing standing in darkness behind her, the woman peered through her half-open door at the long, flame-filled coffin across the lane. "Call the fire department, for Christ's sake! And tell Bing to get his clothes on and get out here and help us!" Captain Knox gave orders to people who were already doing what he ordered them to do, and Nancy Hubner, in nightgown, dressing gown, and slippers, hauled her garden hose from under the trailer and dragged it toward the front, screeching as she passed each window along the way for Noni to wake up, wake up and get out here and help, while inside, Noni slid along a stoned slope of sleep—dreamless, and genuinely happy. Leon LaRoche appeared fully dressed in clean and pressed khaki work clothes with gloves and silver-colored hard hat, looking like an ad agency's version of a construction worker. He asked the Captain what he should do, and the Captain pointed him toward Bruce and Terry, who were hosing down the steaming sides of the trailers next to the fire, At the far end of the row of trailers, in darkness at the edge of the glow cast by the flames, stood Merle Ring, uniquely somber, his arms limply at his sides, in one hand a fishing rod, in the other a string of hornpout.

A few moments later, the fire engines arrived, but it was already too late to save Flora's trailer or anything that had been inside it. All they could accomplish, they realized immediately, was to attempt to save the rest of the trailers, which they instantly set about doing, washing down the metal sides and sending huge, billowing columns of steam into the air. Gradually, as the flames subsided, the firemen turned their hoses and doused the dying fire completely. An hour before daylight, they left, and behind them, where Flora's trailer had been, was a cold, charred, shapeless mass of indistinguishable materials—melted plastic, crumbled wood and ash, blackened, bent sheet metal, and charred flesh and fur.

By the pink light of dawn, Flora emerged from the swamp and came to stand before the remains of the pyre. She was alone, for the others, as soon as the fire engines left, had trudged heavily and exhausted to bed. Around nine, Marcelle Chagnon was stirred from her sleep by the telephone—it was the Concord Hospital, informing her that the woman she had signed in the day before, Flora Pease, had left sometime during the night without permission, and they did not know her whereabouts.

Marcelle wearily peered out the window next to the bed and saw Flora standing before the long, black heap across the lane. She told the woman from the hospital that Flora was here. She must have heard last night that her trailer burned down, over the radio, maybe, and hitch-hiked back to Catamount. She assured the woman that she would look after her, but the woman said not to bother, she only had the flu and probably would be fine in a few days, unless, of course, she caught pneumonia hitchhiking last night without a hat or coat on.

Marcelle hung up the phone and continued to watch Flora, who stood as if before a grave. The others in the park, as they rose from their beds, looked out at the wreckage, and, seeing Flora there, stayed inside, and left her alone. Eventually, around midday, she slowly turned and walked back to the swamp.

Marcelle saw her leaving and ran out to stop her. "Flora!" she cried, and the woman turned back and waited in the middle of the clearing.

Marcelle trotted heavily across the open space, and when she came up to her, said to Flora, "I'm sorry."

Flora stared at her blankly, as if she didn't understand.

"Flora, I'm sorry . . . about your babies." Marcelle put one arm around the woman's shoulders, and they stood side by side, facing away from the trailerpark.

Flora said nothing for a few moments. "They wasn't my babies. Babies make me nervous," she said, shrugging the arm away. Then, when she looked up into Marcelle's big face, she must have seen that she had hurt her, for her tone softened.

"I'm sorry, Mrs. Chagnon. But they wasn't my babies. I know the difference, and babies make me nervous."

That was in September. The fire was determined to have been "of suspicious origin," and everyone concluded that some drunken kids from town had set it. The several young men suspected of the crime, however, came up with alibis, and no further investigation seemed reasonable.

By the middle of October, Flora Pease had built an awkwardly pitched shanty on the land where the swamp behind the trailerpark rose slightly and met the pinewoods, land that might have belonged to the Corporation and might have been New Hampshire state property. But it was going to take a judge, a battery of lawyers, and a pair of surveyors before anyone could say for sure. As long as neither the Corporation nor the state fussed about it, no one was willing to make Flora tear down her shanty and move.

She built it herself from stuff she dragged from the town dump down the road and into the woods to the swamp—old boards, galvanized sheet metal, strips of tar paper, cast-off shingles—and furnished it the same way, with a discolored, torn mattress, a three-legged card table, an easy chair with the stuffing blossoming at the seams, and a moldy rug that had been in a children's playhouse. It was a single room, with a tin woodstove for cooking and heat, a privy out back, and a kerosene lantern for light.

For a while, a few people from the trailerpark went on occasion to the edge of the swamp and visited with her. You could see her shack easily from the park, as she had situated it on a low rise where she had the clearest view of the charred wreckage of old number 11. Bruce Severance, the college kid, dropped by fairly often, especially in early summer, when he was busily locating the feral hemp plants in the area and needed her expert help, and Terry Constant went out there, "just for laughs," he said. He used to sit peacefully on a stump in the sun and get stoned on hemp and rap with her about his childhood and dead mother. Whether Flora talked about her childhood and her dead mother Terry never said. It got hard to talk about Flora. She was just there, the Guinea Pig Lady, even though she didn't have any guinea pigs, and there wasn't much anyone could say about it anymore, since everyone more or less knew how she had got to be who she was, and everyone more or less knew who she was going to be from here on out.

Merle used to walk out there in warm weather, and he continued to visit Flora long after everyone else had ceased doing it. The reason he went out, he said, was because you got a different perspective on the trailerpark from out there, practically the same perspective he said he got in winter from the lake when he was in his ice house. And though Marcelle never visited Flora's shack herself, every time she passed it with her gaze, she stopped her gaze and for a long time looked at the place and Flora sitting outside on an old metal folding chair, smoking her cob pipe and staring back at the trailerpark. She gazed at Flora mournfully and with an anger longing for a shape, for Marcelle believed that she alone knew the woman's secret.

THE POOREST BOY IN CHICAGO

Mitch Berman

I was allowed, until I was much too old, to punch my grandfather as hard as I wanted, provided I didn't hit him in the stomach. I used to climb him like a mountain, pummeling as he laughed. His head was enormous, its leading feature the family nose, broad and bulbous and quite equal to the task of holding dominion over a wide, powerful face. His hair, though thin, never went completely gray; he Brylcreemed it straight back, the comb tracks visible, in the way of men of his generation. He bore a striking resemblance to Babe Ruth.

Grandpa drove a succession of new white Cadillacs with white leather upholstery. Parked in one of those Cadillacs in front of our tract home in the Los Angeles suburb of Buena Park, Grandpa opened his wallet to show me twelve hundred-dollar bills. He was my idea of a high roller.

When I was seven, Grandpa outfitted me with my first blazer—bright red with embossed brass buttons—and drove to Las Vegas so fast the wind from the window hurt my face.

A highway cop pulled us over near the Nevada border. Somehow Grandpa got him talking about the Dodgers, and was on the verge of charming his way out of a ticket, when I piped up shrilly from the back seat: "I told you you were driving too fast, Grandpa!"

Grandpa put the inevitable ticket next to the millions of dollars in his wallet and pulled back onto Interstate 15, grumbling, "I'll give you a slap."

At the Golden Nugget Casino, Grandpa and I had Shirley Temples while Grandma drank something that made her expansive enough to laugh at everything Jimmy Durante said and invite me on their upcoming trip to Hawaii. Grandpa raised the back of his hand to his mouth and told me confidentially, "Your Grandma's soused."

When Grandma told me he had been elected president, I took for granted she meant of the United States. Actually, Grandpa had been elected president of the Sanitary Suppliers' Association of Southern California. He was a founding father of that organization, having started his factory, Captain Kleenzit, Inc., in 1936. Our home was full of Captain Kleenzit paraphernalia: not just the all-purpose household cleaner, pink and perfumy, but playing cards, pens and pads, and the calendar, all bearing the art-deco Kleenzit logo Grandpa had never changed. One of his company's two annual calendars depicted a different vintage car each month, the other the semi-nude frolickings of a plump and rather over-aged nymph named Hilda. The family always got the version with the cars.

There were two Grandpas as well. Mine never swore and rebuked me for doing so ("You've got a filthy mouth, like your father"); the Other Grandpa, I learned after his death, when it fell to Grandma to run the factory, had been the source of innumerable off-color jokes that a Kleenzit trucker would repeat only after issuing warnings to the ladies. I was astonished to discover a massive collage of explicit pornography splayed out across the wall above the urinals where my Grandpa had peed every weekday of his adult life.

In his last years Grandpa had developed a mysterious blood disease that doctors called a precursor to leukemia. Though he required increasingly frequent transfusions, his life went on more or less as usual, except that he was forced to relinquish his vice presidency of the liberal California Democratic Committee.

On a visit from college, I drove up to my grandparents' home in Laurel Canyon as Grandpa and Beau-beau, the miniature poodle he spoiled rotten, jogged across the road. I embraced Grandpa while he put up a mild struggle and his customary protest: "C'mon c'mon c'mon c'mon."

Physical contact made him uncomfortable now that I had grown up, a fact in which I took a perverse delight. I kissed his fat cheeks until he said, as always, "I'll give you a slap."

Only then did I release him. "You look like you're in good shape, Grandpa."

"What do you mean?"

I had pressed a nerve. "Well," I fumbled, "running across the street and everything."

"Big deal!" he snapped. "I'm only seventy-one-and-a-half."

And a half. He had begun again to count his years in fractions, as a child does.

Long, long before, when the notion of achieving such an age would have seemed preposterous, the *Chicago Mirror* had announced a search for "The Poorest Boy in Chicago," upon whose waifish head would descend "Eight Dollars and Forty Cents, in Silver." My grandfather, then six years of age—six-and-a-half, he would have said—was the fruit of that search. "Little Joseph," as the *Mirror* dubbed him, "supports his mother and two infant sisters on his odd-job pittance of seventeen cents per day." In a sepia-toned photograph on the front page of the December 19, 1915, *Mirror*, Grandpa was wearing clean knickerbockers and a saucy, pugnacious expression, as if challenging the reader to repeat an unkind remark about a female member of his family.

Grandpa never spoke about his origins, perhaps because he did not like their memory, or perhaps because he scoffed at the notion that anything could have held him back. He was fond, however, of telling the story of how he had quit his four-pack-a-day smoking habit. It was a remarkably short story. "One day I said, 'Who's the boss? Me or these cigarettes?' I never smoked another. Never missed it." He would give a quick sharp stare to each of his listeners, daring someone to deny it, to deny the lesson in it.

The lesson was that Grandpa had, through clean living and indomitable force of will, rendered himself invulnerable to the weaknesses of ordinary men. And so it dumbfounded us all when a minor piece of oral surgery went sour, Grandpa's red-blood-cell count plunged, and he was taken by ambulance to Cedars-Sinai Hospital.

I flew in from New York, and spent the next month with Grandma. Every morning she stuffed me full of eggs—scrambled with green peppers, with fried salami, easy over, in omelettes—and then we were off to Cedars-Sinai, where I listened to my grandparents debate about finances and the factory. "You shut up!" he'd tell her, when things had reached a certain point.

"No, *you* shut up!" she'd tell him.

Maggie, my youngest aunt, came daily to the hospital, and together we giggled as her parents carped. When we became too much for Grandpa, we found ourselves—politely but firmly, Grandma being his ambassador in matters requiting tact—expelled from his room. We would wander to Beverly Center, the six-floor shopping mall newly opened on the grounds where, as a child, my grandparents had taken me for pony rides in the middle of Los Angeles. Maggie and I would anesthetize ourselves for hours by popping chocolate-coated coffee beans and touching things we could not afford. Finally we would sink into the Star Trek lobby furniture and look at each other's haggard faces.

After visiting hours, Grandma would take me for a run on Fairfax Avenue, it being imperative that her only grandson be constantly supplied with his favorite foods—strawberries, T-bone steaks, Canter Delicatessen's onion bagels and lox—all the foods she called my favorites turning out to be her own. I stalked her with my new Minolta in the open-air produce markets; "Oh no, I look awful," she would say, patting her hair like a forties film queen.

We returned to watch old movies on TV as she crocheted throw rugs to cover up the spots on the white wool carpet that were Beau-beau's legacy. ("Beau-beau," she would murmur, "was a pisher.") Grandma loved Paul Muni and Charles Laughton, hated sex scenes and subtitles. One night we made Droste's cocoa with fresh whipped cream and watched *Pygmalion*. It was her opinion that Leslie Howard had beautiful eyes.

Specialists were swirling around Grandpa at Cedars-Sinai, but I considered myself the only doctor assigned to Grandma. I blanketed her with good intentions, insisting that she eat when she wasn't hungry, setting her alarm an hour forward while she slept. She puttered endlessly in the kitchen and bore my ministrations with a girlish resistance that she usually allowed me to beat down.

There were many reasons why Grandma's yellow-tiled kitchen had always been my favorite room in their home—the laughter of my aunts, the smells of chicken soup and kasha varnishkes—but perhaps the best was that it was not the living room, where Grandpa sat at his card table doing jigsaw puzzles under a goose-necked lamp and occasionally peering over his half-framed glasses and giving the TV's remote control a dour pump. Only Beau-beau could violate this sanctuary with impunity; Grandpa would buffet the dog with big blunt hands until he elicited his phony snarl, pluck out any ribbons his daughters had tied into Beau's black curls, and dispense Chips Ahoy cookies from a glass jar kept close by for that purpose.

I once calculated that the number of Chips Ahoys the tiny poodle devoured would be equivalent, for an adult human, to fifty-four chocolate-chip cookies per day. Grandma laughed at me, "Try telling that to Grandpa!"

I never did, and Beau-beau lived to be seventeen. When Maggie came home for family dinners, Beau-beau jumped all over her; Grandpa could say only, "The dog's happy to see you, Margaret."

My grandparents had put five years between each of their three daughters. Though Maggie was thirteen years older than me, she had always seemed of my own generation. She had introduced me, in my teens, to rock music and marijuana, taken me to Fellini films with her friends. Now, until such time as Grandpa got better, both our lives were on hold.

Grandpa would get better; that was our common coin. Maggie clung to a form of hope that I couldn't abide: not only would her father live, but the hospital was the best in the world, and the nurses were nice, and in fact everyone was very nice, and no one was ugly. I rubbed her raw with constant arguments that the only realistic thing to believe was that Grandpa would recover: though the doctors now said that Grandpa had crossed the border into leukemia, and the odds were ten to one against him, the odds did not take into account Grandpa's extraordinary constitution, his iron will; the odds, when viewed rightly, were all in his favor. In one picture snapped by a stranger in Beverly Center, Maggie and I were leaning against each other like adjacent buildings slowly collapsing together.

It was as if the entire family had smoked marijuana and the high was lasting a month: if something was good, it was very very good, if bad, it was unbearable; and in either event we immediately forgot it. Grandpa had reached the point where he had good days and bad days; and we had all become Grandpas.

Grandpa had taken his chemotherapy with no vomiting or hair loss, seeming to prove my childish theory that he was more than human. The initial blood and bone-marrow tests were clean, but soon a few cancer cells were discovered.

The second round of chemotherapy was as hard as the first had been easy. Grandpa's hair fell out in bunches, and solid food became an impossibility. A second intravenous unit appeared beside his bed, dispensing clear foodstuff while the other dripped noxious chemicals into his bloodstream. The doctors told us he was vulnerable to infection and asked us to wear surgical masks in his room. Grandpa insisted on his daily shower more adamantly now that strangers were regularly inspecting his body, and the intravenous units had to be disconnected every morning, reconnected when he finished.

Grandpa had always been something of a dandy. My mother had recalled to me her amazement, long before Captain Kleenzit became successful, at seeing her father bring home silken boxer shorts. All his socks were Egyptian cotton, their colors fastidiously coordinated with the loud, expensive Italian slip-on shoes he favored. Now Grandpa lay naked in his bed at Cedars-Sinai, waiting to be exposed by anyone who cared to lift his sheet.

Judge Jimmy Eisenberg, an alert, narrow man in a tailored brown suit, came to reminisce with Grandpa about their lives in California politics. I listened, encouraged by Grandpa's energy. When he dozed off suddenly, the judge, waiting for him to awaken, talked with me for a while about New York, rents, and crime. He said he'd heard I was a writer.

Before I could answer, Grandpa awoke and roared, and not only awoke and roared but actually sat up to do it, "Ask him how much money he's made on his writing!"

Grandpa had always had a knack for the killing interpolation. When I called from college to talk to Grandma, chattering for half an hour about her daughters, my professors, her latest short story and the letter she'd had in Tuesday's *Times*, Grandpa would seize the phone and say, "Listen to me: Don't ever forget you're Jewish!"

Not forgetting we were Jewish did not, however, mean forgetting Christmas, but we displayed no holiday decoration that bore the likeness of any figure from the New Testament, and when my first grade sang "O Come All Ye Faithful" at the year-end assembly, I silently mouthed the words "Christ the Lord," feeling it inappropriate to give an enemy deity my personal endorsement. We had to neuter the holiday in order to claim it.

On Christmas Eve, my grandparents' living room—and the baby grand piano, with gifts piled high, spilling off, stacked on the floor—became the center of the family. And at the center of the center sat Grandpa, playing the piano both well and badly. More particularly, his right hand played well while his left played badly; he could read the treble clef but not the bass, and as he unerringly picked out the melody of "Tea for Two" or "Begin the Beguine," his left hand crashed and bumbled randomly among the deep notes. We saved Grandpa's gifts, always the most lavish, for last; his card always insisted, *Happy Hanukkah.*

As Grandpa grew more prosperous and more irascible, it became increasingly hard to find presents that pleased him. Finally we began giving him intentionally foolish objects, like a horribly large plastic leprechaun with a grinning head mounted on a spring. You hit the leprechaun's head, and, after a preliminary *werrrrrrr*, it began to laugh—"HahahahahaHEEHEHEEHEHEEHAHAHEEEEH HAAAHAAAHAAA"—and just when it was winding down, could not possibly have another breath in it, would start all over again with renewed vigor. There was no way to stop it short of the great violence that it inspired.

We had little reason to believe Grandpa liked these things any better than the chromatic harmonica that was instantly recycled back into my own family, or the neckties that never made it to his electrical tie rack (two people had, in desperation, given him electrical tie racks); but Grandma swore he loved them, which only meant that she did.

The room at Cedars-Sinai contained nothing to hint at how difficult it had become to get anything, do anything for this man. Suspended between beige walls and beige linoleum, between the odors of human illness and the false denials of sweet antiseptic, between intervals of darkness and fluorescent light, between intervals of silence and soft trebly Muzak, between artificial night and artificial day, lay a fully insured elderly white male patient, waiting for blood tests and medications, waiting for puncture and palpation, waiting for change, simply waiting, waiting and wearing the plastic ID bracelet that hospitals affix impartially to old men, babies, teenagers, and corpses.

In an ongoing attempt to infect that no-man's-land with a few germs of personality, we were exporting Grandpa's household effects to the hospital. Like gift-giving, it was a hit-and-miss proposition, with the misses coming considerably more often than the hits. One morning we put the mechanical leprechaun in a brown Ralph's supermarket bag and smuggled it in.

The large elevator car was already crowded with nurses and interns when several patients' families got on with us in the lobby. Everybody in this elevator was headed toward a cancer case—lung and lymph on the third floor, leukemia on the fourth— and no one spoke above a whisper. In the quiet, the hospital's Muzak became foreground. It always seemed to be playing something from *Fiddler on the Roof.*

A platoon of nurses and orderlies boarded on the second floor. I moved toward the rear, slid sideways, hunched my shoulders, flattening myself to the wall, compressing myself, when somebody elbowed the package in my hands. There was an ominous *werrrrrrr*. Grandma and I exchanged a look of horror.

"*Hahahaha!*" began the paper bag. Conversation stopped as every eye stared at me. Like all hospital elevators, this one was torturously slow, and while we inched upward to the leukemia ward the paper bag howled and screamed in irrepressible hilarity.

"Get that goddamn thing out of here!" Grandpa barked as soon as he saw it. We took the leprechaun back that night in the trunk of the car, and when we bumped over the old trolley tracks on La Cienega we could hear the muffled hooting of its interminable laughter.

Unless I am forgetting a perfunctory goodbye that evening, "Get that goddamn thing out of here!" was the last thing Grandpa ever said to me. A little after midnight the hospital called to tell us that Grandpa had taken a turn for the worse. He'd been moved to the Intensive Care Unit.

Our family reunited from its diaspora that morning at Cedars-Sinai: Grandma and me, my mother and her sisters Maggie and Evelyn, Grandpa's younger brother Charlie and his wife; from Laurel Canyon and New York, from Seattle and Venice and Marina Del Ray and the San Fernando Valley, all of us embracing and reassembling the lobby furniture until, armchairs and sofas and love seats and end-tables, we were in a circle like an embattled wagon train.

Uncle Charlie was the first to go in. When my grandparents had been courting, Charlie had introduced himself to Grandma by riding a horse into her mother's Brooklyn candy shop to deliver a love letter from his big brother. Over the years Charlie had developed the embarrassing habit of falling asleep after dinner when company was present. Because I had always visited with my grandparents, I had never seen him do it; Charlie could listen to Grandpa for hours.

Charlie spent only a few minutes in Intensive Care. When he emerged, his arms rigid at his sides, his face utterly composed, we converged on him. Charlie gave a hoarse bark and collapsed into a chair. Looking around at us, as if our hopeful faces would contradict what he had seen in there, he cried, gasping and choking like a man who had not cried since childhood and thought he had forgotten how. With his bulk and his thick nervous fingers, now drumming on his knees, now barring his broad face, he seemed more than ever before a slightly smaller, slightly younger version of Grandpa.

"Joe!" Grandma was up and halfway across the lobby, striding to Intensive Care and throwing the door open and demanding to see her husband. Maggie and my mother and I followed. Evelyn remained, paralyzed, in her chair, watching us and shaking her head slightly.

Grandpa writhed. He was naked to the waist, very white and still fat, although he'd lost thirty pounds. Under the respirator, strapped into restraints, completely unconscious, he tossed his great wild bald head from side to side as an electronic monitor implacably flashed readings of heartbeat and blood pressure. We asked questions, as if the readouts proved that this heaving figure was still Grandpa, using loud voices as if he was merely hard of hearing: "Are you warm enough? . . . Can you hear us? Squeeze my hand once for 'yes.'" The nurses assured us he was very comfortable. His yellow nails protruded half an inch beyond his toes.

Grandma knelt beside the bed and buried her face in the huge white hand that lolled, upturned and passive, over the metal railing. "Don't leave me!" she sobbed. "Don't leave me, Joe!"

For fifty-two years Grandma had not only remained married to this man, but had remained happy with him. Now, at her signal, the rest of us lost control at once: me telling Grandma in a sober, masterly voice not to upset Grandpa; Maggie telling me to leave Grandma alone; and my mother imploring generally for peace: all of us bawling and shouting advice at one another as Grandpa began to die.

After a while we retreated to the lobby, where we stayed for hours, waiting for news and trying to sleep on furniture that seemed continually to change form, usually for the worse, beneath us. I kept seeing the whiteness of his body, under the respirator, the harsh lights, under restraint: I knew I'd never easily dislodge that image and hang any other picture of Grandpa in its place.

A week later, on the flight back to New York, I sat in the shaft of the overhead light, flipping through the photographs I'd taken in Los Angeles, while a movie caused the other passengers, under their headphones, to laugh in response to stimuli I did not hear. The family had dispersed: my mother to Seattle, Uncle Charlie to the Valley, my aunts to Venice and Marina Del Rey. I always returned to one photograph, the way you will, if you turn over each card in a deck, keep coming back to the ace of spades. I had taken it two nights after Grandpa died, following Grandma out into her garden as she went to cut a rose for the kitchen table. I'd used a flash and it had illuminated Grandma while failing to penetrate the blackness of the night around her.

BERLIN DISCO INFERNO

Cecil Brown

Author's Note: The La Belle Bombing in Berlin, Germany on April 5, 1986, inspired the events that form "Berlin Disco Inferno." I have drawn upon published accounts of the bombing and the trial of the suspected terrorists, but the characters in the story are the products of my imagination and are not intended to represent real people.

> The space of the foreigner is a moving train, a plane in flight,
> the very transition that precludes stopping. . . . As to landmarks,
> there are none.
>
> —JULIA KRISTEVA, *Strangers to Ourselves*

He takes bus 186 to Radhaus Stieglitz. He gets off, and stands for a moment admiring the red brick monument, remembering how his girlfriend had shown it to him years ago. He stands there, not minding the light rain falling on his face. It is a reddish-orange cathedral with three steeples. Then he gets on bus 148. On the bus, he tells the driver he wants to go to Rheinstrasse. The driver tells him that to get to Rheinstrasse, he had to get off at Belzigerstrasse.

From Belzigerstrasse, he would walk one block to Rheinstrasse. These were the same directions that Jimmy had been given that morning when he was leaving the house.

When Jimmy says, "Danke," the driver says, "Blieben," (stay here) "and when the street comes, I'll tell you!"

Jimmy stands there next to the driver as people get on and off. He is thankful for the special treatment. He is not sure of his German. When he speaks, he keeps his voice low so that nobody would laugh at him. He probably doesn't have much to worry about, because most of his fellow travelers seem indifferent to him.

"Here!" the driver says suddenly, and slams the bus to a stop. It feels like the driver has suddenly decided to put him off. There is a loud screeching sound as the doors open. "Da," he hears the driver call over his shoulder as he descends from the bus onto the wet pavement. He turns and watches the back of the bus disappear as he crosses the street, looking for Belzigerstrasse.

The next street is Eienacherstrasse, so he keeps walking. Then, he sees the street sign: "Rheinstrasse." He realizes that he must not be far from Hauptstrasse, because Rheinstrasse is supposed to turn into Hauptstrasse. There it is; he was right. Jimmy stands in the street, the rain soaking his face, his coat, and the top of his backpack.

There are so many people on the street! He sees a young man holding a guitar case walking together with an old woman who carries a red purse. Is she his mother? Directly across from him, he sees a large billboard. Rudolph Steiner Schuler. He keeps walking, looking for the place where the disco club had been, and where he wants to go.

He looks up at the street sign again. Rheinstrasse has turned into Hauptstrasse. So, he is there.

He looks around to see if he can recognize any of the surroundings. He is looking for the place where he had been twenty years before. Nothing. No, he recognizes nothing. No, wait. Wait . . . WAIT.

He keeps walking. Then he stops again. Wait, he says to himself. He looks around. Where is he standing? He is in the middle of the two broad streets, standing on the grass divide, the median. This was where the victims were brought, he remembers. As the club blew up, and the red awning collapsed, the victims stumbled over here where he is now standing and lay down. The ambulances stopped on both sides of the street to load the injured.

On the grass where he is standing now, with the rain still slightly falling, he remembers that night when people were walking around with their clothes hanging on them like rags, not far from where he is standing.

Another fifty or sixty people lay scattered all over the streets. There had been two hundred and fifty people, probably more, packed into that disco the night the bomb went off.

Overwhelmed by memory, Jimmy lets his backpack find rest near his foot and kneels down as if to pray. He now remembers all of it.

He looks at the small tree in front of him, its branches reaching to both sides of the street. Beneath this tree is green grass.

That night, right after the explosion, this grass was filled with bloody bodies. He recalls looking at his own face in the reflection of a glass window as he stumbled out of the burning building and fell onto the grass. His black skin had peeled off, revealing white layers on his face. He heard the screaming people, and the muffled painful cries of "Hilfe, hilfe!" He stands there, remembering the white-jacketed men who loaded the bleeding people onto stretchers.

One stretcher had passed close to him, bearing a badly burnt man. Now, he remembers how he had only recognized his brother Tony's body by the green Italian suit he wore that night. Tony's whole right side was burnt black, and blood poured from his busted legs. Jimmy remembers how he saw his eyes staring open, and he knew he was dead.

Now looking across the street, Jimmy sees a sign that reads GOTA. It was a sign over a carpet store. They had told them that the disco was now a carpet store, when he arrived yesterday. So that must be the place, he reasons, as he starts across the street.

At the entrance to the store, he notices a brown square on the wall. Going closer he sees that it is a plaque. "Here on April 5, some young people were murdered." There is no doubt now that he is at the right place. They were young, it said, and that gives him a jolt. He had been young then too, even though he had a good ten years on his younger brother.

Jimmy takes his camera out of his backpack and snaps a picture of the plaque. He decides to look around, maybe talk to the people who ran the GOTA carpet store. He didn't have to go far.

Just as he turns, he has a moment of reflection. Next to the carpet store is a window with a row of high heels on display. He remembers something that he had forgotten until just now: he had seen a woman reach in and grab a pair of shoes even as the explosion was going off. Somebody had broken the glass of a shoe shop next door, and a blonde woman reached in and took a pair of shoes. Everybody on the street was in shock—nobody else noticed her or said a word.

He looks back at the plaque: [IN DIESEM HAUS WURDEN AM 5 AVRIL 1986 JUNGE MENSCHEN DURCH EINEN VERBRECHERISCHEN BOMBENANSLAC ERMORDET] Avril 5, it said. April 5, 1986 had changed his life forever. On that cool, spring morning around 1:15, his life turned around forever. Two hundred and fifty young people in a disco had their lives shattered forever when that bomb exploded near the bar where he had been sitting. His brother, who had just left him at the bar to dance with a girl who had caught his eye, was one of the three people who were killed.

He had been watching his brother and the girl with amusement, when everything went dark. He saw a blaze of glaring light and felt himself flying backwards. And as he was flying backwards, he heard a distant thunderclap. His body suddenly felt ice cold and he had thought, *something has grabbed my leg*—it felt like a linebacker's hard tackle. He kept hearing something, far away. *An electric cable has fallen from the roof,* he remembers thinking. Somebody was calling for help in German. "Hilfe! Hilfe!" He became aware of other voices screaming. There seemed plenty of time to think. They were going to die. *Any second there will be another explosion!* He had been very aware of the richness of life and death—something, everything, was clear to him: death and life are equal.

Then lights came back on for an instant, and in that brief flash, he saw someone's arm bleeding where it was pinned beneath the bar, and a green slipper. He gasped for air and smelled something burning, like rubber or human flesh or hair.

He kept pulling his leg again and realized it was stuck. He pushed something off it and freed himself. The blast had blown the back wall of the club wide open, and there was a light, and he made his way to that light. Somebody pushed at the wall and it fell open and he saw that it was a window. A woman was screaming. He pushed through the hole in the wall and was outside. As he stumbled out, other people came out behind him and there were others already outside. He felt something wet on his leg and reached down and touched something hot and then he looked at his fingers and saw they were red.

Somebody else—a black man—was coming through the window. Jimmy reached down and pulled him out. "Help me get some others out," he said. Jimmy went back in through the blown out window and started dragging people. "Help me," he heard somebody call, and a hand gripped his. He took it and pulled hard. "No! No! My leg!" a woman howled. It was the Duchess. A few minutes earlier she'd been sitting by herself, sipping Dom Perignon, looking unavailable. (They called her "Duchess" because she always sat alone and never left with anybody.) He moved a chair that held her leg down, and pulled her free.

He helped her out through the window. Others had kicked open the front door and from the reflection of the street light he could see that people were pulling each other out of the building.

When he got outside again, he heard fire engines down the street. A girl was bleeding badly. He had seen her yellow blouse before in the club. She had been dancing. Now she lay down, her blouse blown off of her and her bloody breast exposed and bleeding.

"Get the ambulance here!" a man shouted and ran off to the street. Jimmy realized then that he had been shouting at him. He followed after the man.

There, he saw about fifty people lying scattered all over the street.

There was a black gaping hole where the disco used to be. The red awning had caved in. Shoes and clothes and people were scattered all over the street. He glimpsed a piece of an arm laying on the pavement.

The door of the ambulance was open and white-jacketed men were putting a woman on a stretcher. From behind them came another stretcher and as it passed close to Jimmy, he saw his brother's mangled body.

Somebody put a blanket over Jimmy's shoulders—the kindest thing anybody ever did for him. He was so cold, but when the blanket got thrown over him, he stopped shivering and kept thinking, "Thank God! Thank God! I won't freeze to death."

Now thinking about how cold he had been that night, he stands in the rain looking at the store across the street. He decided to go over there. Was that where it happened? Yes, he would go over there.

After walking over to the store, he enters it, and sees a large warehouse of carpets rolled and stacked with aisles between them. Three men dressed in yellow vests come up to him, but only one of them asks if he could help him. In German, Jimmy asks if he knew about the La Belle bombing. Yes, he knew about it. Did he know about it in 1986 when it happened? No, he was not in Berlin at that time. Where was he? He was in school in Stuttgart. He had only recently come to Berlin. How did he know about it?

People told him. And every year a woman comes and puts a dozen roses at the site, he said. As he is talking to the man, Jimmy notices how the other men drift closer to hear what they are saying. They are coming purely out of curiosity, Jimmy thinks. Just to check him out.

"Jeder Avril 5," he informs the foreigner. "A woman comes and puts a dozen roses there." He is pointing to the meridian of grass across the street. Jimmy thanks them and leaves. Who could that woman be? Then he stands in the doorway and cries. It seems so sad, all of it.

He sees that the next place of business is a bookstore, and over his shoulder he has a glimpse of the interior of the bookstore. There is an attractive woman behind the counter. Very classy looking, even by German standards. The woman who is buying a book is a good-looking woman too. What kind of bookstore is it anyway? He looks again at the window display. Faulkner. Bellows. Baldwin. They sell bestsellers, a poster claims in red letters. American Best sellers translated into German. He decides to go inside, to check it out. Yes, he would go inside.

Now he is inside, he has a look at the book titles. Just as he is standing there, the very classy looking woman behind the desk finishes her conversation and turns to him. She greets him in German, but as soon as he opens his mouth to reply in German, she switches to English. He tells her that he had been in the La Belle bombing.

She says, "Every spring, you know, a limousine drives up and someone leaves a dozen roses."

He nods. "How touching."

WORMWOOD

Conyus

The last time I saw Wormwood was at Vesuvio's Bar in San Francisco, one cold foggy summer night in August.

It was around 12:30 a.m. and I was sitting at the front table near the window where all the regulars sat most every night, drinking wine and beer, getting high, and talking shit.

The whole crowd was there: Big Jim Bell, Little JJ, Wanda, Big JJ, Little Andre, Benny the Bat, Bernie the Dip, Red Pat, Bitter Bob, Smiling Joan, Hammering Hank, Gino, Sexy Sarah, Billy the Mechanic, Scooby, Little Cal, Rene, and myself.

We were all joking and laughing about something that had happened earlier in the day, which had been precipitated at the next table the night before.

Billy and Bernie had been discussing cars and boats. Their love for them, the joy of driving, and the thrill of travel.

Billy had worked for European Auto Repair, and Bernie, with his ol' lady Red Pat, was building a sailboat in the backyard of their flat in the Upper Haight on Downey Street.

Billy was talking about how he would love to have a sailboat. Move to Sausalito, learn to sail, dock at Pier 9 with the other smugglers and scoundrels, and maybe smuggle some weed up from Mexico, if he could get a decent connection. A minor problem, it seemed, at Pier 9 in Sausalito.

Bernie agreed with him. Sailing was indeed the way to go. In drug smuggling or water recreation as well. Sailing on a boat gave you an incredible sense of freedom, an opportunity to bond with nature, and most certainly lessened your chance of getting arrested. It was so Gestalt. If he could be of any help, in sailing or smuggling, please, let him know. (Bernie had never sailed a boat, but he had been on one once, when he and Pat caught the ferry from San Francisco to Sausalito one Sunday afternoon for the Art Fair. That's when he got the sailing fever, while standing on the top deck of the ferry, throwing the sea gulls stale bread and cigarette butts, while watching the sailboats on the bay glide by the ferryboat like ice skaters in love, even though the ferryboat had a motor.)

Scooby, who was eavesdropping from our table, moved over to sit with them and got in on the discussion. He told Billy that he had a 22-foot sailboat for sale, and that he would exchange it for the car, he had heard Billy had for sale.

Billy asked Scooby, what kind of condition the boat was in and where was it docked?

Scooby said the boat was in good condition, ready for sailing, and was anchored at the foot of Van Ness Boulevard at Aquatic Park.

"What about the car?" Scooby said. "What condition is it in? What make is it? Where is it? And when can I see it?"

"The car is in good shape. It's a Black Citroën. Runs like a top. Good rubber all the way around. AM/FM radio. Leather interior. Mint. You'll like it. Let's meet at Aquatic Park, tomorrow at noon, and exchange them," Billy said.

"Cool," said Scooby. "Be there or be square." He slapped five with Billy and got up from the table, grinned like he had stole something and bopped out the door into the wet fog and cold San Francisco night.

Bernie slid on over next to Billy and said almost in a whisper, "Need somebody to handle that boat for you?"

Billy looked at Bernie. Saw the twinkle in his eyes, the enthusiasm in his gold tooth smile and the excitement in his voice. "You qualified?"

"Absolutely!"

In San Francisco a sexual revolution was occurring that would have ramifications so far and wide that it would affect the mores and lives of women forever in the United States and around the world. A revolution with slogans like: "Make love, not war: If you can't be with the one you love, then love the one you're with: Burn your bra, if you're against the war: You'll get no leg here, if you're fighting over there," and the slogan that became the anthem for the woman's sexual revolution, "This pussy ain't going to war!" This last slogan sold over a million t-shirts around the world in 35 different languages with a picture of a domestic house cat sitting in the lap of a naked hippie girl.

Across the bay in Oakland a revolution of another kind was also taking place and it would reverberate across the country like a brush fire. In October of 1966 Bobby Seale and Huey P. Newton founded the Black Panther Party for Self-Defense in Oakland, California. It was a militant organization that practiced self-defense and self-determination in the minority community against police brutality, capitalist exploitation, racism, and human rights violations.

The original six members of the Black Panther Party were Huey P. Newton, Bobby Seale, Bobby Hutton, Elbert "Big Man" Howard, Sherman Forte and Reggie Forte. These young men dressed in their black berets, with a white button of a black panther pinned to its side, black leather 3/4 length jackets, black pants, short black boots, and either a black or white turtleneck, cut an imposing look in the black community and within a year, a chapter of their organization was formed in every major city in America. At one time the membership reached over 6,000 and every young black man in America secretly wanted to join, but very few had the courage to.

A young man arrived from East St. Louis who was extremely impressed with the Panthers, their Ten Point Program, their Feed the Children Program, and their uncompromising stand against the Oakland Police Department and their brutality in the community. His name was Willie T. Range and he couldn't wait to become a Panther. Nothing like this was happening in East St. Louis. Yet.

He went to a couple of inauguration meetings where the recruits were interviewed and introduced to the rules of The Black Panther Party, the Chain of Command, the Ten Point Program, and the Neighbor Watch. The last meeting he went to was in

West Oakland at the home of Little Robert Johnson. More then 20 potential recruits arrived within an hour of each other and a snitch watching from a parked car across the street called the police and notified them that an unlawful assembly was being held in the house by the Panthers, with weapons. Within minutes the Oakland PD arrived with agents from the ATF and FBI. They surrounded the house and demanded on loud speakers that everyone come out with their hands up. They gave them five minutes then began to fire tear gas canisters into the house. Ten minutes later they began to fire automatic rifles at the house in such volume that people across the freeway at a Warrior's game thought it was a fireworks display going off in the parking lot next door.

Nobody knows why the young recruits didn't come out with their hands up. Nobody knows why Little Robert Johnson ran out the front door with one hand in his pockets screaming, "You muthafuckers, you muthafucking pigs!" They do know that they shot him down before he reached the sidewalk. Later the coroner said he had been shot over 20 times and had died instantly. Six other young recruits were shot, none seriously, but all were jailed and hospitalized. The other 13 were jailed and held over on resisting arrest and weapons charges. After an extensive search no weapons were found in the house or on the premises. The police said there must have been some mistake; they were told weapons were in the house by a very credible informant. They think shots were fired. They returned fire in self defense. Their lives were in danger. Two months later the charges were dropped on all the defendants. They were set free at midnight on a Monday and most disappeared into the night never to be heard from again. Willie T. caught the next bus to San Francisco across the bay. Within three months he had hooked up with some hippies in the Haight Ashbury and had changed his name to Wormwood. Robert Johnson was buried in a close coffin.

Aquatic Park sits at the foot of both Van Ness Boulevard and Polk Street. Formerly known as "Black Point Cove," it has a tiny 1/4-mile-long sandy beach with gentle water, protected by a half-moon shape fishing pier.

The people of San Francisco after the Great Earthquake and Fire, in 1906, unanimously agreed that a site for water sports was needed. It was the perfect location on the waterfront for that recreation.

Dedicated in January, 1939, the stonework to build the seawall was taken from the "Odd Fellows Cemetery," which was moved to Colma.

The park made international news in 1937, when Harry Houdini escaped from locked chains underwater in 57 seconds. It has never been the same since.

The next day we all met at Aquatic Park. Most of us were there with the exception of Hammering Hank, who had to meet with his parole officer, and Bitter Bob, who said, he didn't have time for such foolishness.

It was a sunny day. The San Joaquin Valley had heated up early and the high pressure zone had pushed the fog far out to sea. At the beach you could see as far as the Farallon Islands which set on the horizon, and in back of them, the fog, sitting like a gray picket fence all up and down the California Coast.

The park had its usual assortment of characters and flim flam men in and around its border. There were the sun worshipers lying on the tanning decks coated with baby oil and iodine: Old Italian men playing bocce ball with short cigars stuck in the corner of their mouths and racing forms in their back pockets; bongo and conga players naked to their waist, sitting high up in the bleachers against the back wall wailing away with saxophone players in tow; longshoremen fresh off the docks, standing along the seawall playing cards and gambling with pockets full of money; muscle bound men fresh out of prison lifting weights in the hot sun and watching all the young boys surreptitiously; aspiring young pimps from the Fillmore parading back and forth along the beach front like hawks looking for chickens; hippies from the Haight Ashbury, tripping on acid, smoking weed and playing guitars on the lawn; tourists walking around with maps, funny hats and paper cups full of sweet drinks; members of the Dolphin Club swimming in the cold waters of the cove with bright orange swimming caps that look like pumpkin heads; Sea Scouts on small boats practicing rescue maneuvers; Chinese men throwing crab nets full of rotten meat into the bay off the fishing pier; old men and women sitting on park benches feeding pigeons and nodding in the warm sun; junkies straight out of the Tenderloin scratching with their pant legs rolled up to get some sun on the track marks that cover their legs like a road map. It was a typical summer day at Aquatic Park.

Billy arrived in the Citroën and found a parking space up front. We all walked around it, kicking the tires and sitting in the back seat.

It was a four door. The seats were real leather and smelled liked new. Each arm rest had a small cigarette lighter with an ashtray. The car was from France. A French car. Billy said the French smoked a lot, and everyone needed their own ashtray. They smoked Gauloises, a strong and unfiltered cigarette like a Camel. It came in the same size package. We were all impressed. We thought all the French did was make love and wine. Make cars? Unbelievable. Detroit better wake up. The French might be on to something.

Scooby, who was wearing a watchman's cap with dark sun glasses, a Navy pea coat with denim bellbottoms and workmen boots, sat behind the wheel smiling.

"How do I look, man?" he asked.

"Like a Frenchman," we all said in unison.

"Where's the boat?" Billy asked.

Scooby pointed out to the middle of the cove, where a small single mast red sailboat with a white stripe was anchored. It looked like a postcard with the backdrop of Angel Island and Alcatraz in the distance.

"You've got to take the dinghy out to it. It's tied up over there."

We all looked down to the water's edge, where a tiny row boat had suddenly appeared. It was pulled up on the sand and sat there unattended.

"Let's go," we all said.

"Naw. Let's wait a minute. Bernie is going to sail it over for me and he's not here yet. I don't know anything about sailing."

At just about that time Bernie came walking down the sidewalk from North Point Street. He was wearing a World War II tank helmet complete with goggles, a dark brown leather bomber's jacket with a white fur collar, navy blue sailors pants tucked into a pair of dark brown knee-length riding boots, a red satin shirt with a white silk scarf wrapped around his neck, and a pair of aviator sunglasses.

"Scooby, Billy, my man," Bernie said, and slapped five with Billy. "Looks like a fine day for sailing." And he smiled a big gold tooth smile that looked like a ray of sunshine.

We all followed them down to the beach. Scooby and Billy leading the way. Followed by Bernie, charts under his arms, Red Pat, Little JJ, Big JJ, Andre, Smiling Joan, Sexy Sarah, Benny the Bat, Big Jim, and myself. A couple of winos drinking under a eucalyptus tree joined us, thinking it was a party, and some Native Americans thinking we were sailing to Alcatraz to join the Indian protest, also got in line with bags full of avocadoes and oranges.

We were really something to see. With Billy in his greasy overalls and timing chain in his back pocket. Scooby dressed in his longshoremans' black pea coat and steel toe boots. Bernie in his get-up. Red Pat dressed like she had been cast in "Gone with the Wind." Little JJ, and Big JJ, looking like convention waiters (which they were) without the napkins. Little Andre, spectacular as always in his "North Beach" black beatnik assemble of beret, sandals, and dark sunglasses. Joan and Sarah dressed slovenly in Goodwill chic. Benny, clean as "the board of health" in a Brooks Brother navy blue three-piece pinstriped suit with a light yellow silk shirt and a deep solid maroon silk tie. Big Jim in a black leather cowboy hat with a small beaded Navajo band and chaparajos worn over faded jeans with imitation python skin cowboy boots. And I, looking a little bit like all of them, with the winos and Indians bring up the rear. We made quite an impression on the tourists and the narcs hiding in the bushes waiting to pop someone.

At the water's edge, where the dinghy was anchored, Billy and Scooby exchanged some papers, shook hands and departed.

Scooby immediately turned and walked back past us to the parked cars. We all turned and watched him get into the Black Citroën parked next to the railroad tracks going through the tunnel into Fort Mason. The engine started right up and purred like a cat in its owners lap. We heard Billy say, "Right on," in back of us, and saw Scooby back up the Citroën and head south on Van Ness Boulevard. At the light he stopped and waved and we all waved back. All we had left was the sailing.

Billy and Bernie got into the dinghy and begin to row out to the small sailboat. Billy did the rowing, and Bernie stood in the front, looking at some charts and putting his hand into the water every now and then, like he was checking the temperature in a bathtub or some thing. When they got to the sailboat, it was difficult for them to board, but with some effort, they managed, amidst the oohs and aahs from all of us on the shore, including the Indians, who were miffed that they weren't included on this "maiden voyage."

"Bro, can't an Indian get a break? We came all the way from Yuma to join the protest. Can't we get a ride to the island with them dudes? You know we can't swim. Ain't got no ocean in Arizona. They do know what they doing don't they? They sort of look like they don't."

At that moment Billy was hoisting the single sail, and Bernie was standing on the bow looking at charts and barking out instructions to Billy. Billy pulled up the anchor, and the boat actually started to move. It headed slowly out the cove toward the entrance and that's when a shout rang out from the shore. The winos got to slapping five and passing around the jug, the Indians got to drinking and forgot about the protest, Red Pat did a little dance in a circle and kept saying, "That's my baby, that's my baby!" Little JJ pulled out a joint of some dynamite shit and passed it around. Big JJ started to hand out some sugar cubes of fresh Owsley acid he had copped that morning in the Haight. Big Jim said he had some peyote, but everyone passed except Sexy Sarah, who threw-up later in Jim's truck. Joan who was already high on valium, refused all offers, but did take a couple of tokes of "Thai Stick" that JJ had. From out of nowhere a bottle of cheap bourbon appeared and got passed around the crowd. A couple of GIQ's popped up, a quart of Tokay, a handful of bennies, some strong cough syrup, a couple of Quaaludes and the party was on.

Meanwhile, Billy and Bernie had just about reached the entrance to the bay from the cove when we noticed that Billy was at the stern of the boat with a yellow plastic bucket dipping water and throwing it overboard as fast as he could.

Bernie was in the front throwing water out as well with something that looked like a beer can, and he was hollering out something to Billy about "I think we're sinking! Man, I know we're sinking!" Neither of them had on a life vest, nor had they brought one. We all stood helpless on the shore, passing around a joint and a jug, while watching the boat sink slowly into the cold waters of the San Francisco Bay.

Billy was bailing out water as fast as he could. He was bent over and all we could see was his ass and a yellow bucket. Bernie, who had stopped bailing water, was now yelling at the top of his lungs, "Help! Help! We're sinking! We're sinking! S.O.S., S.O.S.!"

The aft of the boat was now dipping into the water, and you knew the water was now up to Billy's knees. Bernie, who had climbed up on the front of the bow, was now waving his white silk scarf in the air, like a flag and howling like a banshee.

The Sea Scouts, who were practicing rescue maneuvers in the cove, spotted them, and beelined to the boat. It was an opportunity of a lifetime for them. A real-life rescue. Most of the time all they did was tie knots and goose each other in the club house. Whenever they did go out into the bay, most of them got sea sick and threw up. That's why they stayed in the cove. The water was calm and they didn't have to do much sailing. When they saw the boat going down, they couldn't believe their eyes. It was too good to be true. A gift from the gods. The sailboat started to sink so fast it scared them. Nobody sunk in the cove. At least none that they knew of. It was always calm and the perfect place to train. But when the white scarf came out, they knew it was for real.

Billy Johnson was the senior scout in charge of Sea Scouts No. 9 stationed at Aquatic Park. He was 16 years old, had big blue eyes, buck teeth, freckles, and a mop of blond hair that looked like a straw broom. When he saw the sailboat going down he couldn't believe his luck. This rescue might enhance his career, move him up to Eagle Scout, or at the least put him in one of the suburban-based chapters he so desperately wanted to belong, even though he was overweight, flat-footed and couldn't tie the anchor knot for shit.

The rescue took less then one minute. When they pulled up next to the sinking boat and before they could get their gear out and begin rescuing, Billy and Bernie jumped onboard like Olympic long jumpers. It was really amazing. They both jumped from the sinking boat onto "The Pimple" in one hop. It had to be a record. (One of the winos agreed it was. He had had a track scholarship to Wayne State University, and knew his stuff. The long jump was his thing.) Jesse Owens would have been proud. Billy Johnson was really bummed.

We were totally gassed. High as a kite, and rolling around in the sand with laughter and surprise. Nobody could believe what they had seen or understand what had happened, it had happened so fast. It was like Murphy's Law had just jumped up and bit Billy and Bernie in the ass: Anything that can go wrong will go wrong. The same could be said for Scooby.

The Sea Scouts dropped off Billy and Bernie on shore and they proceeded to partake of some herb, sweet Tokay and a bit of peyote. Even though Bernie hadn't sailed an inch on the bay, people came up to him and shook his hand, patted him on the back. Congratulated him on a job well done and a masterful escape from a bad situation.

Billy, high now and hallucinating from the peyote on an empty stomach, started to cry and thank Bernie for saving his life. He kept on saying over and over, "Thank you God. Thank you Bernie. Thank you God! Bernie show knows his shit! Thank you God!" (Billy we found out later couldn't swim.)

The Indians standing around with bags of oranges and avocados in each hand hollered out "How in the hell are we suppose to get to Alcatraz?"

A wino taking another chug of cheap Tokay shouted out, "Walk on water brother, walk on water." And just like that the entire group started to walk up from the beach holding hands and chanting "Walk on water brother, walk on water, walk on water."

The bongo and conga players, sensing something was happening, came down from the stands thinking it was a party and joined us. Tourists passing by thought it was a calypso line and fell in step. Soon a procession of people was snaking their way up from the beach to the parking area. The old folks on the benches woke up and begin to pat their feet; the narcs stood up in the bushes to get a better look. The sailboat flipped over, sunk and vanished. That's when the legend of Bernie the Dip disappeared and Bernie the Sailor begin.

Bernie The Dip was from Chicago. He was about 5'8" and 155 lbs. His skin was the color of burnt butterscotch and as smooth as a newborn baby's ass. He had high cheekbones, a narrow nose and thin lips. His hair was jet black, straight on top, but a little nappy at the kitchen. He kept it combed to the back and in a ponytail. His teeth were large like piano keys, except for one in the front, which was half gold top. He always wore a Red Fez, and quoted from the Koran. He was a flashy dresser and walked with a sincere hipness that suggested he came from the "South Side." He had game and a swagger about him that came from the street. He carried a pair of dice in his breast pocket and a racing form in his back. He didn't eat "no pork" and professed to be a "race man." (Even though he dated white women, and was living with one in the Upper Haight.) Some said he spoke fluent Arabic and could decipher hieroglyphics, backward. Rumor was he was running from the mob because he had stolen the bank from a numbers man.

He got the nick name "The Dip" from when he drove a taxi in San Francisco. He worked the night shift and cruised North Beach or the Castro where there was a heavy nightlife on weekends when the amateurs came in from the suburbs to look at the topless girls in North Beach, or the pretty young boys in the Castro.

He only picked up drunks (or those who had puked on their shoes). If you were sober, he never gave you a second look when hailing down a cab and drove right on by. He had a good eye for the mark and never failed.

The first thing he would do after the mark got into his cab and told him their destination was to turn the heat up. High. So high the windows would usually steam up and the passenger would fall off into a slobbering sleep.

The second thing he would do was to find a dark and secluded area to stop en route to the mark's destination. He would then lean over the front seat of the cab and "dip" into the pockets of the drunken man lying on the back seat, taking all of his cash, travelers' checks, and food stamps, but never his watch, ring, credit cards or wallet. When he arrived at the location requested, he would awaken the slobbering passenger on the back seat and asks for the registered fare.

When the drunk awoke and went through his pockets and found them empty, he would start to question what happened to his money. "Where is my money? I know that I had some money. What happened to it? I'm so sorry. Really. I thought I had about 40 dollars when I left the bar. Shit! If I could just go inside, I'll get the fare. Seriously."

Bernie would then slam the taxi door, muttering out loud about calling the "damn police," and take off cussing into the night. On a good night, he would clear about two to three hundred in four hours. He never had a paying fare on any of his shifts. He never got caught, and he always made the first race at the track the next day.

The traffic along Van Ness Boulevard was fairly light for this time of day. The commuters had already come in from the suburbs and the tour buses had long since headed north, across the Golden Gate Bridge into Muir Woods or further Northeast into Napa or Sonoma.

Scooby was cruising along slowly in the right lane. He passed Lombard Street and watched the tourists in cars turn right onto Lombard and head east toward the "crookedest street in the world." They started to line up here at Van Ness Boulevard early in the morning, reading maps that did not tell them that the portion of the street they wanted to drive down was 12 blocks away and about 2 hours in traffic, when all they had to do was drive up Hyde Street south, turn left on Lombard at the entrance to the "crookedest street," and save an hour and forty-five minutes. It was a tourist thing.

He passed Lombard and headed south toward Union Street. When he crossed at Green and headed slightly uphill, he shifted from third to second gear. That's when he heard the noise. It sounded like something metal had hit the pavement. It had. When he saw the sparks from his rearview mirror flying out from the back of the car, and heard this sound that sounded like he was pulling an aluminum boat, he knew he had a problem. He did. His transmission fell from his car directly onto the pavement and was dragged about 20 feet before it flew out from under his car like a cat in heat and landed directly in the back of Jamaican George McCorkle's salvage truck, which was headed south for the junkyard in South City. He never saw his transmission again.

Scooby abandoned his car and hitchhiked over Union Street with some hippies in a beat-up, psychedelic painted Volkswagen van, to North Beach. He walked down Grant Street past coffee houses and old beatnik bohemian bars filled with faces peering behind smoky windows with Benzedrine eyes, to Mike's Pool Hall. Mike's was a combination café and pool hall. It had the best hamburgers with greasy grilled onions on a sourdough roll in North Beach. It was located on Broadway, across from Finochio's, the famous female impersonators revue, which sat atop Enrico's, the sidewalk café, where anyone that was famous and not so famous sat at curbside tables, drinking espresso and red wine while watching the characters of North Beach's little Bohemia walk by.

He copped a bag of weed from "Pool Shooting" Johnny, the reigning king of the pool hall who pimped on the side when his money got low. In the dingy restroom at the rear of the club, he snorted a couple of lines of good blow with a female impersonator from Finochio's, who was taking a piss at the stall next to him. He also had recently bought a car from Billy that had broken down on the Golden Gate Bridge while on his way to his connection's house in Sausalito.

He sympathized with Scooby over his recent mishap, and asked him would he like to stop by his apartment, which was nearby at the top of Kearney Street, with a good view of the Bay Bridge, for some lunch and a hit of acid, to console him. Scooby passed. (Although a home-cooked meal was inviting, and this dude looked really good.)

* * *

Scooby was a longshoreman from Texas who moved to San Francisco from Corpus Christi where he had worked on the docks in the Gulf of Mexico. He had gotten tired of the smell of rotten shrimp and killer hurricanes during the winter along the coast, so he moved to San Francisco after hearing the song "Sitting on the Dock of the Bay" by Otis Redding in a juke joint. Within a year on the docks he had gotten on the A list and was working steadily with the longshoremen in San Francisco and Oakland. Most times he worked the most dangerous job on a ship during its unloading, "the deep hole," with a Paiute Indian from Northern Nevada named Small Time Coming. Small Time was from a reservation just outside Reno that was so impoverished it made East St. Louis look like Hawaii. He was thin, the color of burnt copper, with long jet black hair streaked with silver, and hands so large that they caught a 12 pack of Black Label thrown from the upper dock to the deep hole with one hand.

He was having a drink with Small Time at a biker bar on Townsend Street at the Embarcadero called Hellhounds when Small Time mentioned that his cousin, Blues for Mr. Charlie (his mother read a lot of James Baldwin while she was pregnant), knew a Miwok Indian near San Jose who had a 22-foot sailboat for sale. He had mentioned to Small Time not too long ago, that he was thinking about acquiring a small boat to sail around the bay on weekends. Anchor it at Aquatic Park and just walk around the waterfront offering boating excursions to all the honeys on a sunny Sunday. Wouldn't go far, just stay inside the break wall and look good piddling around.

The Miwok couldn't be trusted with their reed boats, Small Time said, because for hundreds of years they had made a number of faulty and inferior boats that had sunk in and around the bay with Spanish explorers and soldiers on board. Some California Indian historians from the University of California, Los Angeles, speculate that this could have been one of the earliest forms of guerrilla activity in California against foreign invaders in the United States, or just bad craftsmanship. So this boat might be suspect. They should check it out.

Small Time found out from Blues for Mr. Charlie that the boat was in a barn just south of San Jose in an old cherry orchard. The fields in and around San Jose at one time had been used for farming prior to the housing boom that had been generated by the growth of the Silicon Valley, just North of San Jose. The area South of San Jose had once been apple and cherry orchards, artichoke and garlic fields, strawberry farms, and walnut groves. As the Silicon Valley computer industry grew, so did the need for housing the employees that worked in the industry. The agriculture land east and south of San Jose was doomed. The developers moved in like locust, overnight it seemed, and the new housing developments stretched over the fields like quilts as far as Gilroy. A few old timers held onto their land, with great difficulty considering the amount of money being offered, so it wasn't unusual to see a cherry orchard, or an artichoke field, surrounded by a new urban housing complex, or a shopping mall of chain outlet stores. That's where they found the sloop. On a cherry orchard, in a barn outback covered with chicken shit and rotting cherries. The farm was bordered on all four sides by manicured green lawns and computerized sprinkler systems. It looked like a Southern outhouse on a sleek golf course in Hawaii.

The boat was a 22-foot open single mast sloop that had been used by the Coast Guard to train new recruits in the treacherous waters of the San Francisco Bay. It was purchased at an auction at Moffett Field Naval Air Station that was held in one of the huge hangers that housed zeppelins who patrolled the California Coast during World War II. Surplus equipment from all the U.S. Armed Services were on sale at the auction which was held over the Columbus Day Weekend. The sloop was bought by an old Portuguese farmer who owned a cherry orchard in the San Jacinto Valley and hoped to use it one day to fish for crappie on Lake Anderson just out of Morgan Hill. Lake Anderson was a man-made reservoir known for its crappie, blue gill and small-mouth bass. It covered 1,000 acres in the Gavilan Mountains of Santa Clara County and was the main water supply for all the new housing developments being built.

Luis Miguel Jobim was a small Portuguese man whose parents had immigrated to the United States in 1922. His father, Don Miguel Jobim and his mother, Maria Velasquez Jobim, moved to the Santa Clara Valley in 1924, and had a son, Luis Miguel, one year later. His father worked hard for walnut farmer Armando Baptista and saved his money until he could buy a piece of property for his family. It was a small farm, about 75 acres with a cherry orchard and enough land to grow vegetables for sale at a roadside stand. It sat south of San Jose by about forty-five minutes and west of highway 101 in the San Jacinto Valley.

His father barely eked out a living, but they met ends and when he died some thirty years later, he left Luis Miguel the farm with an added addition of twenty-five more acres, a small barn and a chicken coop outback with about 50 laying chickens.

Luis worked the farm with black Bing cherries his biggest crop. In between cherry season he sold tomatoes, okra, garlic, basil, fresh eggs and homemade Portuguese sausage that his mother had taught him to make when he was a young boy. (His mother passed exactly one year and a day after his father.) During cherry harvest he hired migratory workers to help work in the field, the rest of the year he worked the farm with a Miwok Indian named John Smith from Berkeley.

Luis, like his father, never fished the boat on Lake Anderson. He never had time because of constant work on the farm, and because in his sixty years of life, he hit the Iris Sweepstakes for 25 million dollars on a $1.00 ticket that he had bought from a friend who owned a garlic farm in Gilroy. It was a single ticket hit against millions of odds. It changed his life. He moved to Portugal and married a 62-year-old widow with a little mustache and great legs. He bought a penthouse in downtown Lisbon overlooking the Tagus River on the east, and a view of the Atlantic Ocean in the distance on the west.

In the evening he and his lovely wife often sat on their balcony sipping aged Port or drinking Pink Ladies while watching the sunset over the Atlantic. He installed a rooftop garden of potted lemon trees, tomatoes, primrose, flowering gardenia, avocado, rose bushes, garlic, young Bing cherries, red apple, olive, orange, Southern magnolia, Sweet William and honeysuckle entwined with bougainvillea all along the rooftop. He had his California farm on his rooftop in Lisbon. All he was missing was his boat and chicken coop. He had left that to Shikadoan.

John Smith was a Miwok Indian from Clear Lake whose ancestors had lived around the lake for hundreds of years. His Indian name was Shikadoan Ladosicah and his family had lived on the shores of Clear Lake for over 200 years. He left home when he graduated from Upper Clear Lake High School and earned a scholarship in mathematics to the University of California, Berkeley. He changed his name to John Smith in his sophomore year because it was much easier for people to remember, and he plain got tired of white folks' laziness.

One year while hitchhiking down the coast from Berkeley to Monterey to catch the Monterey Blues Festival featuring "Big Mama" Willie Mae Thornton, "Magic" Sam, and Jimmy Witherspoon, he saw a sign on Highway 101 South just out of San Jose that said, "Cherry pickers wanted. Paid daily." On his way back from the festival, he stopped at San Jacinto Road and walked back the two miles to the cherry farm. He picked cherries for two days, got paid a little money, and fell in love with the San Jacinto Valley. The next year he came back to work and stayed. He loved the cherries too.

He worked the farm side by side with Luis Miguel for many years until Luis hit the Iris sweepstakes. (The odds of winning the Iris sweepstakes are 1 in 26 million. Luis did it with one single $1.00 ticket.)

After Luis gave the farm to him and moved to Portugal, he invited some of his hippie friends from Mendocino County to come and help him work the farm. It became some what of a commune to hitchhiking hippies traveling up and down the coast between Mendocino and Big Sur. He converted the farm to organic gardening and released the chickens to roam free range around the property. That's when he decided to sell the boat, and convert the barn into more living space for his friends and fellow workers. When he heard from a Paiute friend of his living in Berkeley that he knew someone who was looking for a small boat to buy, he said, "Oh yea." He had one.

Small Time Coming, the cousin of his friend Blues for Mr. Charlie, who lived in Berkeley, came down to the farm over Fourth of July weekend with his friend and co-worker, Scooby, to look over the boat. They pulled it out of the barn, smoked a dubie, kicked the tires, washed the chicken shit off of it, and found out it had a few leaks when they filled up the inside with water on a hunch. No problem. They smoked another dubie, mixed up some plaster of Paris, and patched the small leaks with chicken wire, tar paper, plastic bags and plaster of Paris. After it dried, it didn't leak at all. Looked pretty good too, and with a little red paint that he found in the barn, looked liked new. Neither of them knew much about sailing, but they all agreed on one thing, the boat should stay in shallow water. It might not be able to handle the pressure of the deep end, was the way they figured it, and the patches might be suspect in salt water. Scooby nodded in agreement and said, "No problem. I intend to moor inside the breaker wall at Aquatic Park and only sail over to the dock to pick up girls. This baby won't be doing much sailing at all. It'll be a babe magnet. That's all. Just for show, gentleman. For sure." That was the last he saw of the boat, Scooby, and Small Time Coming.

Billy the Mechanic operated a car repair in a red brick building on the corner of Grove and Buchanan in the Western Addition. The bricks were salvaged from the 1906 earthquake and fire and had a burnt color to them. He worked primarily on British imports, but would fix Italian, French, German, Japanese, and Fords. His charges were cheap and his work was shady; sometimes you left your car for a tune-up and picked it up without one. Most times it was a minor error that he had forgot and could be repaired immediately, once you had your car towed in. He also dealt a little herb on the side to augment his income, thus his acquisition of the Black Citroën.

He had middled a deal for a kilo of "Panama Red" for Fast Walking Jack, a small time hustler from North Beach, and Jack had come up short at the buy. Billy wasn't that tight with Jack so he wasn't going to front him the difference for the buy. Jack asked him if he could make up the bread with a trade.

"What do you have to trade?" Billy asked.

"How about that Black Citroën outside?"

"How does it run?"

"The car is in good shape. Runs like a top. Black leather interior. Good rubber all the way around. AM/FM radio. Mint. Could be a little trouble with the title though, but no big thing."

"Deal." Billy could feel the hairs rise on his back. Fast Walking Jack wasn't called "Fast Walking" because he drove a car. Something wasn't right, but a Citroën was a hard deal to pass. And he was a mechanic.

Jack was copping the weed for Henry Ho, a Chinese guy who owned an import-export shop in San Francisco's Chinatown. He had purchased the Citroën from a friend who worked at a repo agency that had been given the car as a bonus by a local bank for a number of exemplary jobs throughout the year. Henry had lent Jack the Citroën to get over to the Western Addition and cop. When he returned without the car, but with a dynamite kilo of "Red" that he could triple his money with, he didn't bat an eye, he just started to bag it up.

The car had once been in the ownership of Paul Julian, a flim flam man that worked the San Joaquin Valley between Sacramento and Bakersfield. In one year he had driven the car over 10,000 miles and made only one payment. The main branch of the Bank of America in San Francisco had put out a repo for the car and the agency had found it in a rear parking lot of a revival meeting in Lodi. The car looked mint, but below the hood it was spent like a salmon swimming up stream to spawn. Paul didn't believe in maintenance, and it became the legacy of the car.

Prior to Paul the car was owned by a little old lady from the Pacific Heights neighborhood in San Francisco. She was quite active in community affairs for Glide Memorial Church and drove her car up and down virtually every hill in San Francisco at one time or another in first gear. She never learned how to shift gears properly and thought that one gear was enough, the rest were a waste of time. Nobody ever told Evelyn Felicity the car needed an oil change, either, so she never got one. In fact she never changed the oil at all in the four years she owned the car, just put in a quart of the cheap stuff every now and then when she was at the 7 Eleven getting a strawberry slurpee. It ran fine as far as she was concerned, although it did smoke a bit. She sold it when she couldn't pass the DMV eye exam at 75.

The original owner of the car was a Moroccan who had a wholesale concrete and sand business in New Jersey. He had the car shipped over from Rabat in the late 60's with a trunk lined with hashish. He had an exclusive contract with the Mafia to provide material for their construction projects and midnight burial service; sometimes he delivered hundreds of pounds of concrete at midnight to his clients from the trunk of his car to meet their special needs. (Heavy springs were installed to meet that need.) On occasions he moved things, from one place to another. Then dumped them. No questions asked. Nobody knew how the car got from New Jersey to California, but they did know it had a transmission problem and the trunk stunk.

A bizarre set of circumstances had to happen for the Black Citroën and the red sailboat with a white stripe to come together that day. It did. It started earlier in the day in Mill Valley, a town north of San Francisco in Marin County across the Golden Gate Bridge and in the redwoods. A man was burning leaves in his front yard when his wife started screaming hysterically from inside the house. He dropped what he was doing immediately and ran inside to see what all the commotion was about. She was standing on a stool in one corner of the kitchen with a spoon in one hand and a lemon in the other. On the floor in the middle of the kitchen a mouse was going around in circles like a chicken with his head cut off. His wife was making a howling sound like a banshee and wheeling the spoon around like a baseball bat. He grabbed a broom from the corner and whacked the mouse against the floor.

The mouse stopped moving and lay still on the checkerboard tile floor. He swept it into a paper bag, took it outside and threw it into the fire. The bag burned quickly and the mouse on fire ran from the bag and under the house. In a matter of minutes the house caught on fire, and within an hour it burned to the ground. This incident was the first in a series of strange and bizarre occurrences that happen that day. The boat and car came later.

We all planned to gather that evening at Vesuvio's to see what was going to transpire between Billy and Scooby about the fiasco that happen earlier in the day.

I got there first, around 7:00 p.m. The rest of the gang arrived around 8:00 p.m. and we sat at the front window joking and laughing. Billy came in around 8:30 p.m. and Scooby came in about 9:00 p.m. Scooby sat down at the end of the table across from Billy and grinned.

"Billy my man," Scooby said, and reached out to slap five with Billy over a lacquered table with old postcards of nude French women glued to it.

"Scooby my man," Billy returned, and grinned right back at him.

We all dropped the volume level of our conversations and eavesdropped to hear what was happening.

Billy and Scooby talked all night about many things and never once mentioned the sailboat or the car. They talked about jazz, art, philosophy, women, and life. But not once did they ever bring up what had happen earlier that day or reacted like anything had ever happen at all. They acted as if they were at a church picnic eating chilled watermelon and fried chicken beneath a shaded oak tree next to a still pond. Somewhere around midnight Billy got up, excused his self, and split. Scooby, after a couple more pops, left shortly after and he never once mentioned to any of us in conversation the series of events that had occurred that day. It was one of two very strange things that happen that evening.

At Vesuvio's "English" Ron was tending bar, and "pretty" Maya was waiting tables. Henri, the owner, was standing at the end of the bar, near the door, in a pinstriped seersucker suit, black turtleneck, his patent black beret, and expensive Italian loafers. He was French, about 5'6," had a heavy accent, and smoked Gauloises with a long silver cigarette holder. He let people into Vesuvio's according to his select texture for the evening. If you didn't meet his discriminating eye, then you weren't allowed to enter. No excuse necessary. See you later. He thought of himself as a painter (which he was) and each evening he created a different scene for Vesuvio's canvas. Every evening changed the crowd to fit his mood which depended on how much he had been drinking; who you were and who you were with (especially if they were beautiful women); if he was in love or falling in love; if he was going to get laid, or not; what time of night it was and what day; how much hashish he had smoked; and especially if it was raining. He got real bitchy on cold rainy nights.

The regulars of North Beach just came and went. But if you were new to the scene, or a tourist, and didn't know anyone, your chances of getting in on a Friday or Saturday night were slim and none. Mostly none.

There were two things he didn't allow in the bar, no matter what his mood might have been: (1) sex in the restrooms, on weekends, and (2) cops. No cops at any time. In uniform, or undercover, it didn't matter. (Reminded him of France, during the Second World War when the Nazis occupied Paris and he was a young man fighting with the Resistance. Everywhere you looked, he said, there were soldiers in uniform or the secret police known as the SS, lurking in bars or coffee houses dressed in trench coats and black fedoras. Young blond anorexic men peeking in your bedroom window at night, in your closet, or through your dirty underwear. No privacy for the artisan or novice. Despicable.) Everything else was a go.

The major problem with the cops was that they were always trying to buy drugs off of us and set us up for a bust. (Charlie Gums had just got popped for a matchbox of weed that he had sold some narc in the restroom of the Coffee Gallery last month. He was on his way to Vacaville to do a stint of from 5 to life for a $5.00 buy!) They always tried to pose as a hipster from out of town just looking for a good time with the locals, but most times they stood out like a fire hydrant in your kitchen. (Charlie Gums knew better, but he was high on pure crank, had been up for three days talking to himself, and his judgment was impaired.)

And the thing about sex in the restroom was that both the men and women's restrooms were extremely small. On the weekends when the bar was crowded, the line from the men's room snaked up the stairs from the cellar where the restroom was located, and into the bar and the line from the women's room, which was on the balcony, flowed down the stairs and into the bar. When they both met on the main floor at the rear of the bar, it created a huge traffic jam that was impassable and of course unacceptable to Henri, not to mention a violation of the fire code. If it was a slow night, say during the week perhaps, then sex was ok in the restroom, as long as you didn't have someone waiting to pee or throw up. Most of the time if we were really horny and needed some sex, we went next door to City Lights Bookstore, and fucked in the poetry section. There was usually no one there late at night except Neeli Cherkovski with a couple of young Jewish boys in scraggy beards and braces standing against the rear brick wall reading "Howl" by Allen Ginsberg and hoping to get a glimpse of Bob Kaufman in passing outside on Columbus Street.

"Hey Tukos, lemme borrow $5.00." The voice came from in back of me. With all the conversation from the bar, our table, and the sound system, I could hardly hear it.

"Hey Tukos, lemme borrow, $5.00."

I turned around and there was Wormwood, standing in the aisle in back of me, across from Henri, who was smoking a cigarette and smiling.

He must have come in the bar from in back of me, the Pacific Street side, because I was facing the Broadway entrance, and had not seen him enter.

He was dressed in a classical light pink soiled tutu, with dingy gray white tights with holes in the knees and a short dark brown Army dress jacket. He had on a pair of white spiked 2" pumps that were run over and scuffed at the heel and toe.

Around his neck was a red scarf of some sort, and on his head a white turban made from a bath towel that had "Property of the Golden Eagle Hotel" printed on it. (A fleabag for hourly whores, two bit thieves, alcoholics, drug addicts, psychotics, and aging Beatniks, on lower Broadway near the waterfront.) He was carrying a secondhand beaded bag in his left hand, and a lit Camel cigarette in his right. His beard had set in, and his eyes looked at me from someplace far away. He didn't look healthy and appeared to be down on his luck. Nobody gave him a second glance, except the tourist, who thought he might have been a poet, or at least a painter, soon to be discovered after he died. Some thought he might have been the legendary poet Bob Kaufman and began to stare.

Henri looked at me and moved to the back of the bar with a cocktail in one hand and a Gauloise in the other. He was smiling and loving every bit of this theater. It was what he painted, orchestrated at the bar and lived for, each and every night.

"Let me borrow $5.00 man!"

"Sure no problem. What's up Worm?"

"Oh I don't know man. I'm just hanging. I'm thinking about joining the space program and cutting out of here."

"Oh yea. The space program. That's cool. That's some deep shit ain't it? Don't you have to have some kind of special training or something? Join the Air Force, or NASA, go to MIT, Cal. Tech, or Cape Canaveral?"

"Not really. A whole lotta cats been in the space program and they didn't know NASA from the NAACP. I'm not talking about being an astronaut, outer space, the space shuttle, or walking on the moon, muthafucker. I'm talking about space. The blue light star. Way out like Skippy. You know what I'm talking about? Not outer space. Space! Some place far beyond that safe house you all go home to."

"Oh yea. I know exactly what you mean."

"Yea, I thought you would. You're almost there but not quite. All you got to do is lose some of that gangster in your walk, that Detroit bop, and change your diet. Eat more vegetables and brown rice. More yin, less yang. You're almost there brother. Almost."

"Oh yea? I thought I was a lot farther away then that. You know I'm still eating pork and smoking weed, don't you?"

"Don't be silly! You know what the fuck I'm talking about. This shit is deep and it's getting deeper everyday. It's out there man."

"Oh yea? Way out there?"

"Hu huh. A lotta cats went into space and never came back."

"Is that right? A whole lotta cats? Or just a few that we thought was a whole lot. You know numbers can be tricky. Depends on who is preparing the chart."

"Don't play with me. A whole lot, boo koo. Cats like Bud Powell, Bobby Fisher, Phineas Newborn Jr., Sun Ra, Paul Murphy, Albert Ayler, King Pleasure (Clarence Beeks), Eric Satie, Buddy Bolden, Thelonious Monk, Vincent van Gogh, and of course the greatest space traveler of them all, Charlie Parker. That's just to name a few. Believe it or not. Muthafuckers are dropping like flies as we speak, and I don't feel too good myself."

"Oh yea. I see what you mean. Are you sure $5.00 is enough. I could loan you $10.00 if it will help you get closer."

"Solid."

That was the last time I saw Wormwood. He walked out the door into the foggy San Francisco night and disappeared like an apparition. I never saw him again. Over the years rumors came back to me about him. He was squatting in the old Hamm's Brewery at Bryant and 12th Street in an empty beer vat on the 9th floor with a view of the East Bay and Hunters Point. He was collecting bottles and cans at night on the street with other homeless in shopping carts; he had been committed to Napa State Hospital for acute schizophrenia and was locked in a padded cell all day staring into infinity; he had disappeared in the jungle of Guyana with Jim Jones and finally got to space after drinking kool aid spiked with cyanide and goodbye. Whatever the truth may be, one thing is for certain. Wormwood disappeared into the foggy San Francisco night like a shooting star running from hell and reappeared in the lore and mystery of the City like Weldon Kees, Andre Lewis, Lew Welch and so many before and all those that followed.

THE DAY THE CISCO KID SHOT JOHN WAYNE

Nash Candelaria

Just before I started the first grade we moved from Los Rafas into town. It created a family uproar that left hard feelings for a long time.

"You think you're too good for us," Uncle Luis shouted at Papa in Spanish, "just because you finished high school and have a job in town! My God! We grew up in the country. Our parents and grandparents grew up in the country. If New Mexico country was good enough for them—"

Papa stood with his cup and saucer held tightly in his hands, his knuckles bleached by the vicious grip as if all the blood had been squeezed up to his bright red face. But even when angry, he was polite to his older brother.

"I'll be much closer to work, and Josie can have the car to shop once in a while. We'll still come out on weekends. It's only five miles."

Uncle Luis looked around in disbelief. My aunt tried not to look at either him or Papa, while Grandma sat on her rocking chair smoking a hand-rolled cigarette. She was blind and couldn't see the anger on the men's faces, but she wasn't deaf. Her chair started to rock faster, and I knew that in a moment she was going to scream at them both.

"It's much closer to work," Papa repeated.

Before Uncle Luis could shout again, Grandma blew out a puff of cigarette smoke in exasperation. "He's a grown man, Luis. With a wife and children. He can live anywhere he wants."

"But what about the—"

He was going to say orchard next to Grandma's house. It belonged to Papa and everyone expected him to build a house there someday. Grandma cut Uncle short: "Enough!"

As we bumped along the dirt of Rafas Road toward home in the slightly used Ford we were all so proud of, Papa and Mama talked some more. It wasn't just being nearer to work, Papa said, but he couldn't tell the family because they wouldn't understand. It was time for Junior—that was me—to use English as his main language. He would get much better schooling in town than in the little country school where all the grades were in just two rooms.

"Times have changed," Papa said. "He'll have to live in the English-speaking world."

It surprised me. I was, it turned out, the real reason we were moving into town, and I felt a little unworthy. I also felt apprehensive about a new house, a new neighborhood, and my first year in school. Nevertheless, the third week in August we moved into the small house on Fruit Avenue, not far from Immaculate Heart Parochial School.

I barely had time to acquaint myself with the neighborhood before school began. It was just as well. It was not like the country. Sidewalks were new to me, and I vowed to ask Santa Claus for roller skates at Christmas like those that city kids had. All of the streets were paved, not just the main highway like in the country. At night streetlights blazed into life so you could see what was happening outside. It wasn't much. And the lights bothered me. I missed the secret warm darkness with its silence punctuated only by the night sounds of owls and crickets and frogs and distant dogs barking. Somehow the country dark had always been a friend, like a warm bed and being tucked in and being hugged and kissed good night.

There were no neighbors my age. The most interesting parts of the neighborhood were the vacant house next door and the vacant lot across the street. But then the rush to school left me no time to think or worry about neighbors.

I suppose I was a little smug, a little superior, marching off that first day. My little sister and brother stood beside Aunt Tillie and watched anxiously through the front window, blocking their wide-eyed views with their steaming hot breaths. I shook off Mama's hand and shifted my new metal lunchbox to that side so she wouldn't try again.

Mama wanted to walk me into the classroom, but I wouldn't let her, even though I was frightened. On the steps in front of the old brick school building a melee of high voices said goodbye to mothers, interrupted by the occasional tearful face or clinging hand that refused to let go. At the corner of the entrance, leaning jauntily against the bricks, leered a brown-faced tough whose half-closed eyes singled me out. Even his wet, combed hair, scrubbed face, and neatly patched clothes did not disguise his true nature.

He stuck out a foot to trip me as I walked past. Like with my boy cousins in the country, I stepped on it good and hard without giving him even so much as a glance.

Sister Mary Margaret welcomed us to class. "You are here," she said, "as good Catholic children to learn your lessons well so you can better worship and glorify God." Ominous words in Anglo that I understood too well. I knew that cleanliness was next to godliness, but I never knew that learning your school lessons was—until then.

The students stirred restlessly, and during the turmoil I took a quick look around. It reminded me of a chocolate sundae. All the pale-faced Anglos were the vanilla ice cream, while we brown Hispanos were the sauce. The nun, with her starched white headdress under her cowl, could have been the whipped cream except that I figured she was too sour for that.

I had never been among so many Anglo children before; they outnumbered us two to one. In the country church on Sundays it was rare to see an Anglo. The only time I saw many of these foreigners—except for a few friends of my father's—was when my parents took me into town shopping.

"One thing more," Sister Mary Margaret said. She stiffened, and her face turned to granite. It was the look that I later learned meant the ruler for some sinner's outstretched hands. Her hard eyes focused directly on me. "The language of this classroom is English. This is America. We will only speak English in class and on the school grounds." The warning hung ominously in the silent, crackling air. She didn't need to say what we brownfaces knew: If I hear Spanish, you're in trouble.

As we burst from the confines of the room for our first recess, I searched for that tough whose foot I had stomped on the way in. But surprise! He was not in our class. This puzzled me, because I had thought there was only one first grade.

I found him out on the school grounds, though. Or rather, he found me. When he saw me, he swaggered across the playground tailed by a ragtag bunch of boys like odds and ends of torn cloth tied to a kite. One of the boys from my class whispered to me in English with an accent that sounded normal—only Anglos really had accents. "Oh, oh! Chango, the third grader. Don't let his size fool you. He can beat up guys twice as big." With which my classmate suddenly remembered something he had to do across the way by the water fountain.

"¡Ojos largos!" Chango shouted at me. I looked up in surprise. Not so much for the meaning of the words, which was "big eyes," but for his audacity in not only speaking Spanish against the nun's orders, but shouting it in complete disregard of our jailers in black robes.

"Yes?" I said in English like an obedient student. I was afraid he would see my pounding heart bumping the cloth of my shirt.

Chango and his friends formed a semicircle in front of me. He placed his hands on his hips and thrust his challenging face at me, his words in the forbidden language. "Let's see you do that again."

"What?" I said in English, even though I knew what.

"And talk in Spanish," he hissed at me. "None of your highfalutin Anglo."

Warily I looked around to see if any of the nuns were nearby.

"¿Qué?" I repeated when I saw that the coast was clear.

"You stepped on my foot, big eyes. And your big eyes are going to get it for that."

I shook my head urgently. "Not me," I said in all innocence. "It must have been somebody else."

But he knew better. In answer, he thrust a foot out and flicked his head at it in invitation. I stood my ground as if I didn't understand, and one of his orderlies laughed and hissed, "¡Gallina!"

The accusation angered me. I didn't like being called chicken, but a glance at the five of them waiting for me to do something did wonders for my self-restraint.

Then Chango swaggered forward, his arms out low like a wrestler's. He figured I was going to be easy, but I hadn't grown up with older cousins for nothing. When he feinted an arm at me, I stood my ground. At the next feint, I grabbed him with both hands, one on his wrist, the other at his elbow, and tripped him over my leg that snapped out like a jackknife. He landed flat on his behind, his face changing from surprise to anger and then to caution, all in an instant.

His cronies looked down at him for the order to jump me, but he ignored them. He bounced up immediately to show that it hadn't hurt or perhaps had been an accident and snarled, "Do that again."

I did. This time his look of surprise shaded into one of respect. His subordinates looked at each other in wonder and bewilderment. "He's only a first grader," one of them said. "Just think how tough he's going to be when he's older."

Meanwhile I was praying that Chango wouldn't ask me to do it a third time. I had a premonition that I had used up all of my luck. Somebody heard my prayer, because Chango looked up from the dirt and extended a hand. Was it an offer of friendship, or did he just want me to pull him to his feet?

To show that I was a good sport, I reached down. Instead of a shake or a tug up, he pulled me down so I sprawled alongside him. Everybody laughed.

"That's showing him, Chango," somebody said.

Then Chango grinned, and I could see why the nickname. With his brown face, small size, and simian smile there could be no other. "You wanna join our gang?" he asked. "I think you'll do." What if I say no? I thought. But the bell saved me, because they started to amble back to class. "Meet us on the steps after school," Chango shouted. I nodded, brushing the dust from my cords as I hurried off.

That was how I became one of Los Indios, which was what we called ourselves. It was all pretty innocent, not at all what people think of when they see brown faces, hear Spanish words, and are told about gangs. It was a club really, like any kid club. It made us more than nonentities. It was a recognition, like the medal for bravery given to the cowardly lion in *The Wizard of Oz*.

What we mostly did was walk home together through enemy territory. Since we were Los Indios, it was the cowboys and the settlers we had to watch out for. The Anglo ones. *Vaqueros y paisanos* were okay. Also, it was a relief to slip into Spanish again after guarding my tongue all day so it wouldn't incite Sister Mary Margaret. It got so I even began to dream in English, and that made me feel very uncomfortable, as if I were betraying something very deep and ancient and basic.

Some of the times, too, there were fights. As I said before, we were outnumbered two to one, and the sound of words in another language sometimes outraged other students, although they didn't seem to think about that when we all prayed in Latin. In our parish it was a twist on the old cliche: the students that pray together fight together—against each other.

But there was more to Los Indios than that. Most important were the movies. I forget the name of the theater. I think it was the Rio. But no matter. We called it the Rat House. When it was very quiet during the scary part of the movie, just before the villain was going to pounce on the heroine, you could hear the scamper of little feet across the floor. We sat with our smelly tennis shoes up on the torn seats—we couldn't have done any more harm to those uncomfortable lumps. And one day someone swore he saw a large, gray furry something slither through the cold, stale popcorn in the machine in the lobby. None of us would ever have bought popcorn after that, even if we'd had the money.

For a dime, though, you still couldn't beat the Rat House. Saturday matinees were their specialty, although at night during the week they showed Spanish-language movies that parents and aunts and uncles went to see. Saturdays, though, were for American westerns, monster movies, and serials.

Since I was one of the few who ever had money, I was initiated into a special assignment that first Saturday. I was the front man, paying hard cash for a ticket that allowed me to hurry past the candy counter—no point in being tempted by what you couldn't get. I slipped down the left aisle near the screen, where behind a half-drawn curtain was a door on which was painted "Exit." No one could see the sign because the light bulb was burned out, and they never replaced it in all the years we went there. I guess they figured if the lights were too strong, the patrons would see what a terrible wreck the theater was and not come back.

The owner was a short, round, excitable man with the wrinkles and quavering voice of a person in his seventies but with black, black hair. We kept trying to figure out whether it was a toupee or not, and if it was, how we could snatch it off.

For all his wrinkles, though, he could rush up and down the aisles and grab an unruly kid by the collar and march him out like nothing you ever saw. So fast that we nicknamed him Flash Gordo. We would explode into fits of laughter when one of us saw him zoom down the aisle and whispered "Flash Gordo" to the rest of us. He gave us almost as many laughs as Chris-Pin Martin of the movies.

I counted out my money that first Saturday. I was nervous, knowing what I had to do, and the pennies kept sticking to my sweaty fingers. Finally, in exasperation, Flash Gordo's long-nosed wife counted them herself, watching me like a hawk so I wouldn't try to sneak in until she got to ten, and then she growled, "All right!"

Zoom! Past the candy counter and down the aisle like I said, looking for Flash. I didn't see him until I got right up front, my heart pounding, and started to move toward the door. That's when this circular shadow loomed in the semidark, and I looked up in fright to see him standing at the edge of the stage looking at the screen. Then he turned abruptly and scowled at me as if he could read my mind. I slipped into an aisle seat and pretended I was testing it by bouncing up and down a couple of times and then sliding over to try the next one.

I thought Flash was going to say something as he walked in my direction. But he suddenly bobbed down and picked something off the floor—a dead rat?— when a yell came from the back of the theater. "Lupe and Carlos are doing it again! Back in the last row!"

Flash bolted upright so quickly my mouth fell open. Before I could close it, he rushed up the aisle out of sight, toward those sex maniacs in the last row. Of all the things Flash Gordo could not tolerate, this was the worst. And every Saturday some clown would tattle on Lupe and Carlos, and Flash would rush across the theater. Only later did I learn that there never was any Lupe or Carlos. If there had been, I'm sure Los Indios would have kept very quiet and watched whatever it was they were doing back there.

"Oh, Carlos!" someone yelled in a falsetto. "Stop that this minute!"

I jumped out of my seat and rushed to the door to let Los Indios in. By the time Flash Gordo had shined his flashlight over and under the seats in the back, we were all across the theater at the edge of the crowd where we wouldn't be conspicuous. Later we moved to our favorite spot in the front row, where we craned our necks to look up at the giant figures acting out their adventures.

While the movies were fantastic—the highlight of our week—sometimes I think we had almost as much fun talking about them afterwards and acting them out. It was like much later when I went to high school; rehashing the Saturday night dance or party was sometimes better than the actual event.

We all had our favorites and our definite point of view about Hollywood movies. We barely tolerated those cowboy movies with actors like Johnny Mack Brown and Wild Bill Elliot and Gene Autry and even Hopalong Cassidy. Gringos!

we'd sniff with disdain. But we'd watch them in preference to roaming the streets, and we'd cheer for the Indians and sometimes for the bad guys if they were swarthy and Mexican.

They showed the Zorro movies several times each, including the serials, with one chapter each Saturday. Zorro drew mixed reviews and was the subject of endless argument. "Spanish dandy!" one would scoff. "¿Dónde están los mejicanos?" Over in the background hanging on to their straw sombreros and smiling fearfully as they bowed to the tax collector, I remember.

"But at least Zorro speaks the right language."

Then somebody would hoot, "Yeah. Hollywood inglés. Look at the actors who play Zorro. Gringos every one. John Carroll. Reed Handley. Tyrone Power. ¡Mierda!"

That was what Zorro did to us. Better than Gene Autry but still a phony Spaniard, while all the *indios y mestizos* were bit players.

That was no doubt the reason why our favorite was the Cisco Kid. Even the one gringo who played the role, Warner Baxter, could have passed for a Mexican. More than one kid said he looked like my old man, so I was one of those who accepted Warner Baxter. Somebody even thought that he was Mexican but had changed his name so he could get parts in Hollywood—you know how Hollywood is. But we conveniently leaped from that to cheering for the "real" Cisco Kids without wondering how *they* ever got parts in that Hollywood: Gilbert Roland, César Romero, Duncan Renaldo. With the arch-sidekick of all time, Chris-Pin Martin, who was better any day than Fuzzy Knight, Smiley Burnette, or Gabby Hayes.

"Sí, Ceesco," we'd lisp to each other and laugh, trying to sound like Chris-Pin.

We'd leave the theater laughing and chattering, bumping and elbowing each other past the lobby. There Flash Gordo would stare at us as if trying to remember whether or not we had bought tickets, thoughtfully clicking his false teeth like castanets. We'd quiet down as we filed past, looking at that toupee of his that was, on closer inspection, old hair blackened with shoe polish that looked like dyed rat fur. Hasta la vista, Flash, I'd think. See you again next week.

One Saturday afternoon when I returned home there was a beat-up old truck parked in front of the empty house next door and a slow parade in and out. In the distance I saw the curious stare of a towhead about my age.

When I rushed into the house, my three-year-old brother ran up to me and excitedly told me in baby talk, "La huera. La huera, huera."

"Hush," Mama said.

Uncle Tito, who was Mama's unmarried younger brother, winked at me.

"Blondie's wearing a halter top and shorts," he said. "In the backyard next door."

"Hush," Mama said to him, scowling, and he winked at me again.

That night when I was supposed to be sleeping, I heard Mama and Papa arguing. "Well," Mama said, "what do you think about that? They swept up the gutters of Oklahoma City. What was too lightweight to settle got blown across the panhandle to New Mexico. Right next door."

"Now, Josefa," Papa said, "you have to give people a chance."

"Halter top and shorts," Mama snipped. "What will the children think?"

"The only child who's going to notice is Tito, and he's old enough, although sometimes he doesn't act it."

But then my eyelids started to get heavy, and the words turned into a fuzzy murmur.

One day after school that next week, Chango decided that we needed some new adventures. We took the long way home all the way past Fourth Street Elementary School, where all the pagan Protestants went. "Only Catholics go to heaven," Sister Mary Margaret warned us. "Good Catholics." While her cold eye sought out a few of us and chilled our hearts with her stare.

But after school the thaw set in. We wanted to see what those candidates for hell looked like—those condemned souls who attended public school. And I wondered: if God had only one spot left in heaven, and He had to choose between a bad Catholic who spoke Spanish and a good Protestant who spoke English, which one he would let in. A fearful possibility crossed my mind, but I quickly dismissed it.

We rambled along, picking up rocks and throwing them at tree trunks, looking for lizards or maybe even a lost coin dulled by weather and dirt but still very spendable. What we found was nothing. The schoolyard was empty, so we turned back toward home. It was then, in the large empty field across from the Rio Valley Creamery, that we saw this laggard, my new neighbor, the undesirable Okie.

Chango gave a shout of joy. There he was. The enemy. Let's go get him! We saddled our imaginary horses and galloped into the sunset. Meanwhile, John Wayne, which was the name I called him then, turned his flour-white face and blinked his watery pale eyes at us in fear. Then he took off across the field in a dead run, which only increased our excitement, as if it were an admission that he truly was the enemy and deserved thrashing.

He escaped that day, but not before he got a good look at us. I forgot what we called him besides Okie *gabacho gringo cabrón*. In my memory he was John Wayne to our Cisco Kid, maybe because of the movie about the Alamo.

That then became our favorite after-school pastime. We'd make our way toward the Fourth Street Elementary School looking for our enemy, John Wayne. As cunning as enemies usually are, we figured that he'd be on the lookout, so we stalked him Indian-style. We missed him the next day, but the day after that when we were still a long block away, he suddenly stopped and lifted his head like a wild deer and seemed to feel or scent alien vibrations in the air, because he set off at a dogtrot toward home.

"Head him off at the pass!" Chango Cisco shouted, and we headed across toward Fifth Street. But John Wayne ran too fast, so we finally stopped and cut across to Lomas Park to work out a better plan.

We ambushed him the next day. Four of us came around the way he'd expect us to, while the other two of us sneaked the back way to intercept him between home and the elementary school. At the first sight of the stalkers he ran through the open field that was too big to be called a city lot. Chango and I waited for him behind the tamaracks. When he came near, breathing so heavily we could hear his wheeze, and casting quick glances over his shoulder, we stepped out from behind the trees.

He stopped dead. I couldn't believe anyone could stop that fast. No slow down, no gradual transition. One instant he was running full speed; the next instant he was absolutely immobile, staring at us with fright.

"You!" he said breathlessly, staring straight into my eyes.

"You!" I answered.

"¿Que hablas español?" Chango asked.

His look of fear deepened, swept now with perplexity like a ripple across the surface of water. When he didn't answer, Chango whooped out a laugh of joy and charged with clenched fists. It wasn't much of a fight. A couple of punches and a bloody nose and John Wayne was down. When we heard the shouts from the others, Chango turned and yelled to them. That was when John Wayne made his escape. We didn't follow this time. It wasn't worth it. There was no fight in him, and we didn't beat up on sissies or girls.

On the way home it suddenly struck me that since he lived next door, he would tell his mother, who might tell my mother, who would unquestionably tell my father. I entered the house with apprehension. Whether it was fear or conscience didn't matter.

But luck was with me. That night, although I watched my father's piercing looks across the dinner table with foreboding (or was it my conscience that saw his looks as piercing?), nothing came of it. Not a word. Only questions about school. What were they teaching us to read and write in English? Were we already preparing for our First Communion? Wouldn't Grandma be proud when we went to the country next Sunday. I could read for her from my schoolbook, *Bible Stories for Children*. Only my overambitious father forgot that *Bible Stories for Children* was a third-grade book that he had bought for me at a church rummage sale. I was barely at the reading level of "Run, Spot. Run." Hardly exciting fare even for my blind grandmother, who spoke no English and read nothing at all.

Before Sunday, though, there was Saturday. In order to do my share of the family chores and "earn" movie money instead of accepting charity, my father had me pick up in the backyard. I gathered toys that belonged to my little sister and brother, carried a bag of garbage to the heavy galvanized can out back by the shed, even helped pull a few weeds in the vegetable garden. This last was the "country" that my father carried with him to every house we lived in until I grew up and left home. You can take the boy out of the country, as the old saying goes. And in his case it was true.

I dragged my feet reluctantly out to the tiny patch of yard behind the doll's house in which we lived, ignoring my mother's scolding about not wearing out the toes of my shoes.

I must have been staring at the rubber tips of my tennis shoes to watch them wear down, so I didn't see my arch-enemy across the low fence. I heard him first. A kind of cowardly snivel that jolted me like an electric shock. Without looking I knew who it was.

"You!" he said as I looked across the fence.

"You!" I answered back with hostility.

Then his eyes watered up and his lips twitched in readiness for the blubbering that, in disgust, I anticipated.

"You hate me," he accused. I squatted down to pick up a rock, not taking my eyes off him. "Because I don't speak Spanish and I have yellow hair."

No, I thought, I don't like you because you're a sniveler. I wanted to leap the fence and punch him on those twitching lips, but I sensed my father behind me watching. Or was it my conscience again? I didn't dare turn and look.

"I hate Okies," I said. To my delight it was as if my itching fist had connected. He all but yelped in pain, though what I heard was a sharp expulsion of air.

"Denver?" The soft, feminine voice startled me, and I looked toward the back stoop of their house. I didn't see what Tito had made such a fuss about. She was blond and pale as her son and kind of lumpy, I thought, even in the everyday housedress she wore. She tried to smile—a weak, sniveling motion of her mouth that told me how Denver had come by that same expression. Then she stepped into the yard where we boys stared at each other like tomcats at bay.

"Howdy," she said in a soft funny accent that I figured must be Oklahoma. "I was telling your mother that you boys ought to get together, being neighbors and all. Denver's in the second grade at the public school."

Denver backed away from the fence and nestled against his mother's side. Before I could answer that Immaculate Heart boys didn't play with sniveling heathens, I heard our back door squeak open, then slam shut.

"I understand there's a nice movie in town where the boys go Saturday afternoons," she went on. But she was looking over my head toward whoever had come out of the house.

I looked back and saw Mama. Through the window over the kitchen sink I saw Papa. He's making sure she and I behave, I thought.

"It would be nice for the boys to go together," Mama said. She came down the steps and across the yard.

You didn't ask me! my silent angry self screamed. It's not fair! You didn't ask me! But Mama didn't even look at me; she addressed herself to Mrs. Oklahoma as if Snivel Nose and I weren't even there.

Then an unbelievable thought occurred to me. For some reason Denver had not told his mama about being chased home from school. Or if he did, he hadn't mentioned me. He was too afraid, I decided. He knew what would happen if he squealed. But even that left me with an uneasy feeling. I looked at him to see if the answer was on his face. All I got was a weak twitch of a smile and a blink of his pleading eyes.

I was struck dumb by the entire negotiation. It was settled without my comment or consent, like watching someone bargain away my life. When I went back into the house, all of my pent-up anger exploded. I screamed and kicked my heels and even cried—but to no avail.

"You have two choices, young man," my father warned. "Go to the matinee with Denver or stay in your room." But his ominous tone of voice told me that there was another choice: a good belting on the rear end.

Of course, this Saturday the Rat House was showing a movie about one of our favorite subjects where the mejicanos whipped the gringos: the Alamo. I had to go. Los Indios were counting on me to let them in.

I walked the few blocks to town, a boy torn apart. One of me hurried eagerly toward the Saturday afternoon adventure. The other dragged his feet, scuffing the toes of his shoes to spite his parents, all the while conscious of this hated stranger walking silently beside him.

When we came within sight of the theater, I felt Denver tense and slow his pace even more than mine. "Your gang is waiting," he said, and I swear he started to tremble.

What a chicken, I thought. "You're with me," I said. But then he had reminded me. What would I tell Chango and the rest of Los Indios?

They came at us with a rush. "What's he doing here?" Chango snarled.

I tried to explain. They deflected my words and listened instead to the silent fear they heard as they scrutinized Denver. My explanation did not wash, so I tried something in desperation.

"He's not what you think," I said. Skepticism and disbelief. "Just because he doesn't understand Spanish doesn't mean he can't be one of us." Show me! Chango's expression said. "He's—he's—" My voice was so loud that a passer-by turned and stared. "He's an Indian from Oklahoma," I lied.

"A blond Indian?" They all laughed.

My capacity for lying ballooned in proportion to their disbelief. I grew indignant, angry, self-righteous. "Yes!" I shouted. "An albino Indian!"

The laughs froze in their throats, and they looked at each other, seeing their own doubts mirrored in their friends' eyes. "Honest to God?" Chango asked.

"Honest to God!"

"Does he have money?"

Denver unfolded a sweaty fist to show the dime in his palm. Chango took it quickly, like a rooster pecking a kernel of corn. "Run to the dime store," he commanded the fastest of his lackeys. "Get that hard candy that lasts a long time. And hurry. We'll meet you in the back."

Denver's mouth fell open but not a sound emerged. "When we see him running back," Chango said to me, "you buy the ticket and let us in." Then he riveted his suspicious eyes on Denver and said, "Talk Indian."

I don't remember what kind of gibberish Denver faked. It didn't have to be much, because our runner had dashed across the street and down the block and was already sprinting back.

Our seven-for-the-price-of-one worked as always. When the theater was dark, we moved to our favorite seats. In the meantime, I had drawn Denver aside and maliciously told him he had better learn some Spanish. When we came to the crucial part of the movie, he had to shout what I told him.

It was a memorable Saturday. The hard sugar candy lasted through two cartoons and half of the first feature. We relived the story of the Alamo again—we had seen this movie at least twice before, and we had seen other versions more times than I can remember. When the crucial, climactic attack began, we started our chant. I elbowed Denver to shout what I had taught him.

"Maten los gringos!" Kill the gringos! Then others in the audience took up the chant, while Flash Gordo ran around in circles trying to shush us up.

I sat in secret pleasure, a conqueror of two worlds. To my left was this blond Indian shouting heresies he little dreamed of, while I was already at least as proficient in English as he. On my right were my fellow tribesmen, who had accepted my audacious lie and welcomed this albino redskin into our group.

But memory plays its little tricks. Years later, when I couldn't think of Denver's name, I would always remember the Alamo and John Wayne. There were probably three or four movies about that infamous mission, but John Wayne's was the one that stuck in my mind. Imagine my shock when I learned that his movie had not been made until 1960, by which time I was already through high school, had two years of college, and had gone to work. There was no way we could have seen the John Wayne version when I was in the first grade.

Looking back, I realized that Wayne, as America's gringo hero, was forever to me the bigoted Indian hater of *The Searchers* fused with the deserving victim of the attacking Mexican forces at the Alamo—the natural enemy of the Cisco Kid.

Another of my illusions shattered hard when I later learned that in real life Wayne had married a woman named Pilar or Chata or maybe both. That separated the man, the actor, from the characters he portrayed and left me in total confusion.

But then life was never guaranteed to be simple. For I saw the beak of the chick I was at six years old pecking through the hard shell of my own preconceptions. Moving into an alien land. First hating, then becoming friends with aliens like my blond Indian Okie friend, Denver, and finally becoming almost an alien myself.

BACKCITY TRANSIT BY DAY

Wanda Coleman

I guess I wandered senselessly from the platform, near as I can figure. But my memory has returned. Vividly. Following the dictates of habit, I must have boarded this city bus, which will, in the next five minutes, deposit me on the corner of the block where I rent my modest apartment. As soon as I enter my front room door, I will seize the remote control unit, turn on the television, and watch the early afternoon newscasts. I'm certain this horrible incident that has caused my temporary blank-out will be the special report on every local station.

I knew I was in trouble when the alarm went off this morning. I could not get up. I hit the snooze button five times before I finally drug myself from beneath the queen-sized comforter. It was tough facing the morning's chill, tough forcing my recalcitrant feet across the icy bathroom tiles, tough ridding my head of the residue of interrupted dreams.

Nevertheless, the demands of body and wallet prevailed, I had to be at work on time, and the bus would not wait. Riders are scarce in those frosty hours before the rush. Mine is a professional-class residential area where only the maids, the decrepit, and the adolescent ride the bus during peak hours. Odd worker out, I usually find myself rattling around in it alone, except for the driver, until we reach the tiny mall at the heart of this little bedroom enclave hidden sedately within the sprawling anus of Los Angeles.

Standing in the cool, early morning drizzle, I'm pleased to lower my umbrella and climb aboard, my fare buried in the palm of my gloved left hand so that I don't have to go into my purse. The conk-haired, mocha-skinned driver stares hard at me as I nervously slip the bill into the vacuum slot and drop in the necessary coins. I hear his question, but it's none of his business what I'm doing in the neighborhood, why I'm wearing such expensive sunglasses on a rainy day, that he didn't know Black people lived in this area, and otherwise I'm not in the mood to talk to strangers.

"Blue line, green line," I sing.

He gives me a transfer and I slip it neatly into my glove. I have a right to be eccentric. I take the seat directly behind the driver's cubby so that I don't have to be bothered by his nose. I make a mental note to buy that monthly boarding pass as soon as possible so I can give up my evening ritual of organizing loose change and singles.

Tada! In minutes, I exit the familiar bus, feeling the driver's eyes on my behind. But my thoughts are on my next connection, the city's first real tramway. It's been open for well over a year but still feels new. My first trip on the metro rail was better than expected. The Nippon-style trams zip along quietly compared to a bus.

Like those sci-fi comic book tramways. All metal and Plexiglas as translucent as clean dishwater. Not at all like the old red cars of my childhood, smelling of oil, smoke, and axle grease. There's no smell these days, except what drifts in on the air from outside, the sweaty stink of other passengers or the artificial lemony twinge of industrial cleaning solvents. As I ride, it's difficult to remain awake. All noises are dull except for the distant clang of the warning lights, the strangely correct honk of the train itself as a station is approached, and the electronic buzzer that signals the openings and closings of passenger doors. Everything is diffuse, spotless and hushed, all silvery grays, muted whites, and unobtrusive blues.

(Someone is staring at me. I do not allow them to draw my eyes. Having a young face is not always a blessing.)

I find it so easy to lose consciousness, nodding with the gentle shimmy of the over-ground people mover. Mercifully, none of that tepid pop-rock brood music is piped into the cars. One is left to one's thoughts, provided one is not seated sideways so that one's ear is assaulted by the loud smacking of insensitive bitchy jaws on a monstrous wad of chewing gum, the intramural sports babblings of macho enthusiasts of "the game," the rantings of a deranged street hustler, or a colic-and-scream spewing mink-haired infant raging to escape from the stroller that has just rolled over one's foot.

The majority of the passengers all seem to be undergoing the same process of being lulled into mild catatonic pose: the breath becomes shallow, the posture frozen, the eyes introspective, the jaw relaxed, the arms limp and sinewless as one is whizzed work-ward, schoolward, to whatever destiny unreels. Getting there incrementally.

And this, too, infects me as I stare without focus at the passing landscape which, with the exception of a shopping mall or two, is a depressing spectacle of dilapidated pastel A-frames and gritty-gray public housing projects with shabby roofs, junk-filled lawns, unmendable fences, and dented primer-splatted jalopies blooming on the blacktop. These are neighborhoods I once knew and cannot forget. Watching carefully, I can almost taste the mornings as they were then: the resonant repetitions of engines marginally turning over; the fresh drizzle settled on windshields and windows, evaporating with the sun's easterly warming; the aromas of hot cereals, cheap coffee, greasy sausages, and burnt Nucoaed toast; the broad avenues dotted with meandering clumps of dark children, reluctantly headed schoolward; the solitary, elderly churchwomen with their heavy-handled totes on their ways to tend the sick and shut-ins or the preschoolers of young working class couples.

I knew such a woman. She cared for me as a child.

What I remember most about her was how the yellows of her ancient Honduran eyes lit up when she was surprised. And how I delighted in causing that expression by making mischief. Her pressed red-brown hair was always perfect-kept in a fine brown hair net. And now that I think of it, I enjoyed how, when she got especially angry, she'd forget herself and curse in a mix of Spanish and an Africanized native dialect I loved and laughed to hear. I remember my fascination with her ringless fingers as she quick-iced the high layers of her home-baked butter cakes. I remember the bronze, red, and gold silk shawl she prized with its elegantly fine fringe. She wore it over her shoulder—on brisk, fall mornings or wrapped around her broad, high hips on special occasions. And I remember that she kept her man when most women her age always seemed to be alone, in mourning.

A stop is called and my reverie snaps. The ghost dispelled is replaced by a vision of cement structures rising and falling across a palm-dotted distance.

My stop always comes up too soon.

Now my workday has ended, as has the return trip on the crowded bus that jerked to a slam at the intersection before the metropolitan blue line station, causing me to brace myself by jamming the tip of my damp umbrella into a gap between a neighboring seat and a Latino student's booted foot. Everyone rushes the exit, knowing the northbound tram is due. I'm exhausted and barely able to follow them as they wade against traffic, ignoring the red stoplight, forcing eager automobile drivers to slam on brakes. The tram arrives as I waddle up the access ramp, my feet aching, protesting with every step of my pricey wedgies as I join the late-day swarm.

No seats are available except the ones that make the rider face backward, in the direction from which they've just come. I wonder what idiot bureaucrat on antidepressants approved this design.

Invariably, the train crosses the awesomely engineered cement river, the slight flow of water indistinguishable except on sunny days when the light catches it proper or when heavy rains send it brimming high, choppy and wide. On certain walls, on underpasses, and in some daringly remarkable spots, taggers have spray-painted defiant graffiti on all available space. Without my specs, I'm unable to interpret any of it. But the steady clip of the tram causes the images to flow together in a momentary visual dance.

As my mid-transit stop approaches, I force myself out of the narrow seat designed to marginally contain my mass, shift my purse so that it's snug under my left arm, grip my umbrella, and follow the crowd out, down, and around to the escalator rising toward the intersecting green line. There's a deputy uniformed in matching pants and jacket, brass star radiant on his chest. He asks to see my ticket. I extend my left palm forward and peel back the glove. He peeps, nods, and I move on.

I envision myself standing on the westbound side, as I grasp the rail and mount the step rising skyward. In two blinks it seems I'm there, wading through the crowd, looking for a place to sit. But it's late afternoon. The few precious green and blue benches and those clunky immobile stone chairs are fully occupied. I find a pale green post to lean against for the five minutes I know it will take before the train arrives.

It is at this moment that I'm overpowered by the urge for a drink of coffee, tea, or chocolate—a wet hotness steaming upward toward my brow, fogging my tinted lenses. A futile search for anything resembling a vending machine reveals signs stating that no food or drinks are allowed on the platform, that everyone must have a ticket, and that the Country Sheriff's department is now responsible for security on the platform. My thirst is awful, and I struggle to moisten my throat, imagining the cool sweet high-caloric contents of my little refrigerator. I have a flask in my purse, but to risk a swig might prove embarrassing if not illegal.

To distract myself from the wait and my thirst, I survey my surroundings. I recognize several double life-size sculptures, designed on the old pickaninny theme. I'd seen them earlier, placed in strategic spots, some of the figures mounted high on the cement walls, most of them placed playfully as if potential passengers themselves. I know the work of this Californian artist, a Black man who has fused his Legba-like sensibility with the expressionism of Dubuffet and a clever overlay of Chagall. I'm struck by the irony of my observation, doubt any of the passengers appreciate the decades of thought underscoring these artworks, let alone the monumental confluences of history that have created the very platform on which we stand and have brought us to this stepping-off point.

As I inwardly pursue the convolutions of my knowing, my eyes focus on one particular pickaninny whose head is shaped to suggest it has thick braided hair echoed in the shapes of the cartoon-like hands that hide its grotesquely cute face-lessness. Two children, the color of paper bags, with that sandy gray-colored hair suggestive of a White grandparent, step into my line of vision. They are darling, the boy about seven, the girl about six and nearly his twin. The boy holds their tickets in his left hand, wondrously touches and strokes the giant female pick-aninny with his right hand. His sister is also enthralled by the figure. They circle it, smile at it and each other. Then they turn abruptly and resume their horseplay, darting in and out between the other passengers. Peripherally, I look around. Isn't there an adult keeping an eye on them? A mother who might be preoccupied with a teething infant or distracted by a travel-sick toddler? Perhaps an unemployed father, the day's involuntary babysitter. Or an older brother or sister. It is a cool sunny day despite the periodic fall rain. These children should have coats on over their thin blue polyester rags to protect their skinny little limbs.

How fast does it take to have such thoughts? To internally chide the absent parent for allowing their children to travel alone under such dangerous conditions? I notice that like the subways in Manhattan, there's nothing but common sense and sure footing between the platform and the rail below.

Suddenly, I hear the clang that accompanies the warning lights as the eastbound train on the other side of the platform arrives, passengers exit and enter, and in seconds it's gone. I go back to my own preoccupation with nothing, notice two warning signs painted on the concrete, one in Spanish and, a few feet away, in English. I amuse myself by silently sounding out the Spanish. Now, I hear the clang that accompanies the arrival of the westbound tram. I see its shadowy form through the mesh of the freeway divider as it rounds the curb and that halogen cyclops eye shimmers like a beacon. But my eyes are drawn quickly to my right, not more than two yards away.

Those same two children are at the platform ledge. The boy has lifted his sister by her waist and is dangling her over the edge. I am not the only one who sees this. A tall sepia man in a leather tam, matching trousers, and a white long-sleeved shirt, races toward them, his arms outstretched, his mouth opened in a shout. From another angle, a yelling blond White man in his thirties rushes toward them, his arms likewise outstretched.

The boy is on tiptoes, his gray-tinged head resting against the small of his sister's back just as his grip fails. She drops through the chute of his arms. And his arms fly skyward and dangle there, clawing heaven, high above his head, which is jerked downward, his mouth gaped as wide as the smile on that faceless pickaninny.

The swoosh of the approaching tram is a roar between my ears above the moans and screams of shocked witnesses. People are rushing about the tram, on and off it. Someone jostles me backward and I recognize the contorted face of the deputy as he wades through the knot of onlookers. I turn away. An old Mexican woman faints in front of me. Someone kicks her purse open as he stumbles over her.

It's all blank after that.

I estimate that nearly an hour of my day was lost. Up until that moment ago when I awoke on the bus, jarred back into my skin by the hydraulic hiss of doors snapping open then shut in mid-traffic. The ribs of my umbrella were fairly embedded in my right hand. There was the annoying awareness that my purse strap was strangling my left shoulder. Its bulk was uncomfortable in my lap. I open it now to see if I lost anything in my confusion. My doeskin eyeglass case is open and empty. I plow fruitlessly for my sunglasses until I remember I'm still wearing them. No, all the contents are here. Lucky me, nothing is missing. Nothing was lost in the panic.

Nothing at all.

QUENBY AND OLA, SWEDE AND CARL

Robert Coover

Night on the lake. A low cloud cover. The boat bobs silently, its motor for some reason dead. There's enough light in the far sky to see the obscure humps of islands a mile or two distant, but up close: nothing. There are islands in the intermediate distance, but their uncertain contours are more felt than seen. The same might be said, in fact, for the boat itself. From either end, the opposite end seems to melt into the blackness of the lake. It feels like it might rain.

Imagine Quenby and Ola at the barbecue pit. Their faces pale in the gathering dusk. The silence after the sudden report broken only by the whine of mosquitos in the damp grass, a distant whistle. Quenby has apparently tried to turn Ola away, back toward the house, but Ola is staring back over her shoulder. What is she looking at, Swede or the cat? Can she even see either?

In the bow sat Carl. Carl was from the city. He came north to the lake every summer for a week or two of fishing. Sometimes he came along with other guys, this year he came alone.

He always told himself he liked it up on the lake, liked to get away, that's what he told the fellows he worked with, too: get out of the old harness, he'd say. But he wasn't sure. Maybe he didn't like it. Just now, on a pitchblack lake with a stalled motor, miles from nowhere, cold and hungry and no fish to show for the long day, he was pretty sure he didn't like it.

You know the islands are out there, not more than a couple hundred yards proba- bly, because you've seen them in the daylight. All you can make out now is here and there the pale stroke of what is probably a birch trunk, but you know there are spruce and jack pines as well, and balsam firs and white cedars and Norway pines and even maples and tamaracks. Forests have collapsed upon forests on these islands.

The old springs crush and grate like crashing limbs, exhausted trees, rocks tumbling into the bay, like the lake wind rattling through dry branches and pine needles. She is hot, wet, rich, softly spread. Needful. "Oh yes!" she whispers.

Walking on the islands, you've noticed saxifrage and bellwort, clintonia, shinleaf, and stemless lady's slippers. Sioux country once upon a time, you've heard tell, and Algonquin, mostly Cree and Ojibwa. Such things you know. Or the names of the birds up here: like spruce grouse and whiskey jack and American three-toed woodpecker. Blue-headed vireo. Scarlet tanager. Useless information. Just now, anyway. You don't even know what makes that strange whistle that pierces the stillness now.

"Say, what's that whistling sound, Swede? Sounds like a goddamn traffic whistle!" That was pretty funny, but Swede didn't laugh. Didn't say anything. "Some bird, I guess. Eh, Swede? Some goddamn bird."

"Squirrels," Swede said finally.

"Squirrels!" Carl was glad Swede had said something. At least he knew he was still back there. My Jesus, it was dark! He waited hopefully for another response from Swede, but it didn't come. "Learn something new every day."

Ola, telling the story, laughed brightly. The others laughed with her. What had she seen that night? It didn't matter, it was long ago. There were more lemon pies and there were more cats. She enjoyed being at the center of attention and she told the story well, imitating her father's laconic ways delightfully. She strode longleggedly across the livingroom floor at the main house, gripping an imaginary cat, her face puckered in a comic scowl. Only her flowering breasts under the orange shirt, her young hips packed snugly in last year's bright white shorts, her soft girlish thighs, slender calves: these were not Swede's.

She is an obscure teasing shape, now shattering the sheen of moonlight on the bay, now blending with it. Is she moving toward the shore, toward the house? No, she is in by the boats near the end of the docks, dipping in among shadows. You follow.

By day, there is a heavy greenness, mostly the deep dense greens of pines and shadowed undergrowth, and glazed blues and the whiteness of rocks and driftwood. At night, there is only darkness. Branches scrape gently on the roof of the guests' lodge; sometimes squirrels scamper across it. There are bird calls, the burping of frogs, the rustle of porcupines and muskrats, and now and then what sounds like the crushing footfalls of deer. At times, there is the sound of wind or rain, waves snapping in the bay. But essentially a deep stillness prevails, a stillness and darkness unknown to the city. And often, from far out on the lake, miles out perhaps, yet clearly ringing as though just outside the door: the conversation of men in fishing boats.

"Well, I guess you know your way around this lake pretty well. Eh, Swede?"

"Oh yah."

"Like the back of your hand, I guess." Carl felt somehow encouraged that Swede had answered him. That "oh yah" was Swede's trademark. He almost never talked, and when he did, it was usually just "oh yah." Up on the "oh," down on the "yah." Swede was bent down over the motor, but what was he looking at? Was he looking at the motor or was he looking back this way? It was hard to tell. "It all looks the same to me, just a lot of trees and water and sky, and now you can't even see that much. Those goddamn squirrels sure make a lot of noise, don't they?" Actually, they were probably miles away.

Carl sighed and cracked his knuckles. "Can you hunt ducks up here?" Maybe it was better up here in the fall or winter. Maybe he could get a group interested. Probably cold, though. It was cold enough right now. "Well, I suppose you can. Sure, hell, why not?"

Quenby at the barbecue pit, grilling steaks. Thick T-bones, because he's back after two long weeks away. He has poured a glass of whiskey for himself, splashed a little water in it, mixed a more diluted one for Quenby. He hands her her drink and spreads himself into a lawnchair. Flames lick and snap at the steaks, and smoke from the burning fat billows up from the pit. Quenby wears pants, those relaxed faded bluejeans probably, and a soft leather jacket. The late evening sun gives a gentle rich glow to the leather. There is something solid and good about Quenby. Most women complain about hunting trips. Quenby bakes lemon pies to celebrate returns. Her full buttocks flex in the soft blue denim as, with tongs, she flips the steaks over. Imagine.

Her hips jammed against the gunwales, your wet bodies sliding together, shivering, astonished, your lips meeting—you wonder at your madness, what an island can do to a man, what an island girl can do. Later, having crossed the bay again, returning to the rocks, you find your underwear is gone. Yes, here's the path, here's the very tree—but gone. A childish prank? But she was with you all the time. Down by the kennels, the dogs begin to yelp.

Swede was a native of sorts. He and his wife Quenby lived year-round on an island up here on the lake. They operated a kind of small rustic lodge for men from the city who came up to fish and hunt. Swede took them out to the best places, Quenby cooked and kept the cabin up. They could take care of as many as eight at a time. They moved here years ago, shortly after marrying. Real natives, folks born and bred on the lake, are pretty rare; their 14-year-old daughter Ola is one of the few.

How far was it to Swede's island? This is a better question maybe than "Who is Swede?" but you are even less sure of the answer. You've been fishing all day and you haven't been paying much attention. No lights to be seen anywhere, and Swede always keeps a dock light burning, but you may be on the luck side of his island, cut off from the light by the thick pines, only yards away from home, so to speak. Or maybe miles away. Most likely miles.

Yes, goddamn it, it was going to rain. Carl sucked on a beer in the bow. Swede tinkered quietly with the motor in the stern.

What made a guy move up into these parts? Carl wondered. It was okay for maybe a week or two, but he couldn't see living up here all the time. Well, of course, if a man really loved to fish. Fish and hunt. If he didn't like the rat race in the city, and so on. Must be a bitch for Swede's wife and kid, though. Carl knew his own wife would never stand still for the idea. And Swede was probably pretty hard on old Quenby. With Swede there were never two ways about it. That's the idea Carl got.

Carl tipped the can of beer back, drained it. Stale and warm. It disgusted him. He heaved the empty tin out into the darkness, heard it plunk somewhere on the black water. He couldn't see if it sank or not. It probably didn't sink. He'd have to piss again soon. Probably he should do it before they got moving again. He didn't mind pissing from the boat, in a way he even enjoyed it, he felt like part of things up here when he was pissing from a boat, but right now it seemed too quiet or something.

Then he got to worrying that maybe he shouldn't have thrown it out there on the water, that beer can, probably there was some law about it, and anyway you could get things like that caught in boat motors, couldn't you? Hell, maybe that was what was wrong with the goddamn motor now. He'd just shown his ignorance again probably. That was what he hated most about coming up here, showing his ignorance. In groups it wasn't so bad, they were all green and could joke about it, but Carl was all alone this trip. Never again.

The Coleman lantern is lit. Her flesh glows in its eery light and the starched white linens are ominously alive with their thrashing shadows. She has brought clean towels; or perhaps some coffee, a book. Wouldn't look right to put out the lantern while she's down here, but its fierce gleam is disquieting. Pine boughs scratch the roof. The springs clatter and something scurries under the cabin. "Hurry!" she whispers.

"Listen, Swede, you need some help?" Swede didn't reply, so Carl stood up in a kind of crouch and made a motion as though he were going to step back and give a hand. He could barely make Swede out back there. He stayed carefully in the middle of the boat. He wasn't completely stupid.

Swede grunted. Carl took it to mean he didn't want any help, so he sat down again. There was one more can of beer under his seat, but he didn't much care to drink it. His pants, he had noticed on rising and sitting, were damp, and he felt stiff and sore. It was late. The truth was, he didn't know the first goddamn thing about outboard motors anyway.

There's this story about Swede. Ola liked to tell it and she told it well. About three years ago, when Ola was eleven, Swede had come back from a two-week hunting trip up north. For ducks. Ola, telling the story, would make a big thing about the beard he came back with and the jokes her mother made about it.

Quenby had welcomed Swede home with a big steak supper: thick T-bones, potatoes wrapped in foil and baked in the coals, a heaped green salad. And lemon pie. Nothing in the world like Quenby's homemade lemon pie, and she'd baked it just for Swede. It was a great supper. Ola skipped most of the details, but one could imagine them. After supper, Swede said he'd bring in the pie and coffee.

In the kitchen, he discovered that Ola's cat had tracked through the pie. Right through the middle of it. It was riddled with cat tracks, and there was lemon pie all over the bench and floor. Daddy had been looking forward to that lemon pie for two weeks, Ola would say, and now it was full of cat tracks.

He picked up his gun from beside the back door, pulled some shells out of his jacket pocket, and loaded it. He found the cat in the laundryroom with lemon pie still stuck to its paws and whiskers. He picked it up by the nape and carried it outside. It was getting dark, but you could still see plainly enough. At least against the sky.

He walked out past the barbecue pit. It was dark enough that the coals seemed to glow now. Just past the pit, he stopped. He swung his arm in a lazy arc and pitched the cat high in the air. Its four paws scrambled in space. He lifted the gun to his shoulder and blew the cat's head off. Her daddy was a good shot.

Her mock pout, as she strides across the room, clutching the imaginary cat, makes you laugh. She needs a new pair of shorts. Last year they were loose on her, wrinkled where bunched at the waist, gaping around her small thighs. But she's grown, filled out a lot, as young girls her age do. When her shirt rides up over her waist, you notice that the zipper gapes in an open V above her hip bone. The white cloth is taut and glossy over her firm bottom; the only wrinkle is the almost painful crease between her legs.

Carl scrubbed his beard. It was pretty bristly, but that was because it was still new. He could imagine what his wife would say. He'd kid his face into a serious frown and tell her, hell, he was figuring on keeping the beard permanently now.

Well, he wouldn't, of course, he'd feel like an ass at the office with it on, he'd just say that to rile his wife a little. Though, damn it, he did enjoy the beard. He wished more guys where he worked wore beards. He liked to scratch the back of his hand and wrist with it.

"You want this last beer, Swede?" he asked. He didn't get an answer. Swede was awful quiet. He was a quiet type of guy. Reticent, that's how he is, thought Carl. "Maybe Quenby's baked a pie," he said, hoping he wasn't being too obvious. Sure was taking one helluva long time.

He lifts the hem of his teeshirt off his hairy belly, up his chest, but she can't seem to wait for that—her thighs jerk up, her ankles lock behind his buttocks, and they crash to the bed, the old springs shrieking and thumping like a speeding subway, traffic at noon, arriving trains. His legs and buttocks, though pale and flabby, seem dark against the pure white spectacle of the starched sheets, the flushed glow of her full heaving body, there in the harsh blaze of the Coleman lantern. Strange, they should keep it burning. His short stiff beard scrubs the hollow of her throat, his broad hands knead her trembling flesh. She sighs, whimpers, pleads, as her body slaps rhythmically against his. "Yes!" she cries hoarsely.

You turn silently from the window. At the house, when you arrive, you find Ola washing dishes.

What did Quenby talk about? Her garden probably, pie baking, the neighbors. About the wind that had come up one night while he'd been gone, and how she'd had to move some of the boats around. His two-week beard: looked like a darned broom, she said. He'd have to sleep down with the dogs if he didn't cut it off. Ola would giggle, imagining her daddy sleeping with the dogs. And, yes, Quenby would probably talk about Ola, about the things she'd done or said while he was away, what she was doing in sixth grade, about her pets and her friends and the ways she'd helped around the place.

Quenby at the barbecue pit, her full backside to him, turning the steaks, sipping the whiskey, talking about life on the island. Or maybe not talking at all. Just watching the steaks maybe. Ola inside setting the table. Or swimming down by the docks. A good thing here. The sun now an orangish ball over behind the pines. Water lapping at the dock and the boats, curling up on the shore, some minutes after a boat passes distantly. The flames and the smoke. Down at the kennels, the dogs were maybe making a ruckus. Maybe Ola's cat had wandered down there. The cat had a habit of teasing them outside their pen. The dogs had worked hard, they deserved a rest. Mentally, he gave the cat a boot in the ribs. He had already fed the dogs, but later he would take the steak bones down.

Quenby's thighs brush together when she walks. In denim, they whistle; bare, they whisper. Not so, Ola's. Even with her knees together (they rarely are), there is space between her thighs. A pressure there, not of opening, but of awkwardness.

Perhaps, too, island born, her walk is different. Her mother's weight is settled solidly beneath her buttocks; she moves out from there, easily, calmly, weightlessly. Ola's center is still between her narrow shoulders, somewhere in the midst of her fine new breasts, and her quick astonished stride is guided by the tips of her hipbones, her knees, her toes. Quenby's thick black cushion is a rich locus of movement; her daughter still arches uneasily out and away from the strange outcropping of pale fur that peeks out now at the inner edges of the white shorts.

It is difficult for a man to be alone on a green island.

Carl wished he had a cigarette. He'd started out with cigarettes, but he'd got all excited once when he hooked a goddamn fish, and they had all spilled out on the wet bottom of the boat. What was worse, the damn fish—a great northern, Swede had said—had broke his line and got away. My Jesus, the only strike he'd got all day, and he'd messed it up! Swede had caught two. Both bass. A poor day, all in all. Swede didn't smoke.

To tell the truth, even more than a cigarette, he wished he had a good stiff drink. A hot supper. A bed. Even that breezy empty lodge at Swede's with its stale piney smell and cold damp sheets and peculiar noises filled him with a terrific longing. Not to mention home, real home, the TV, friends over for bridge or poker, his own electric blanket.

"Sure is awful dark, ain't it?" Carl said "ain't" out of deference to Swede. Swede always said "ain't" and Carl liked to talk that way when he was up here. He liked to drink beer and say "ain't" and "he don't" and stomp heavily around with big boots on. He even found himself saying "oh yah!" sometimes, just like Swede did. Up on the "oh," down on the "yah." Carl wondered how it would go over back at the office. They might even get to know him by it. When he was dead, they'd say: "Well, just like good old Carl used to say: oh yah!"

In his mind, he watched the ducks fall. He drank the whiskey and watched the steaks and listened to Quenby and watched the ducks fall. They didn't just plummet, they fluttered and flopped. Sometimes they did seem to plummet, but in his mind he saw the ones that kept trying to fly, kept trying to understand what the hell was happening. It was the rough flutter sound and the soft loose splash of the fall that made him like to hunt ducks.

Swede, Quenby, Ola, Carl . . . Having a drink after supper, in the livingroom around the fireplace, though there's no fire in it. Ola's not drinking, of course. She's telling a story about her daddy and a cat. It is easy to laugh. She's a cute girl. Carl stretches. "Well, off to the sack, folks. Thanks for the terrific supper. See you in the morning, Swede." Quenby: "Swede or I'll bring you fresh towels, Carl. I forgot to put any this morning."

You know what's going on out here, don't you? You're not that stupid. You know why the motor's gone dead, way out here, miles from nowhere. You know the reason for the silence. For the wait. Dragging it out. Making you feel it. After all, there was the missing underwear. Couldn't find it in the morning sunlight either.

But what could a man do? You remember the teasing buttocks as she dogpaddled away, the taste of her wet belly on the gunwales of the launch, the terrible splash when you fell. Awhile ago, you gave a tug on the stringer. You were hungry and you were half-tempted to paddle the boat to the nearest shore and cook up the two bass. The stringer felt oddly weighted. You had a sudden vision of a long cold body at the end of it, hooked through a cheek, eyes glazed over, childish limbs adrift. What do you do with a vision like that? You forget it. You try to.

They go in to supper. He mixes a couple more drinks on the way. The whiskey plup-plup-plups out of the bottle. Outside, the sun is setting. Ola's cat rubs up against his leg. Probably contemplating the big feed when the ducks get cleaned. Brownnoser. He lifts one foot and scrubs the cat's ears with the toe of his boot. Deep-throated purr. He grins, carries the drinks in and sits down at the diningroom table.

Quenby talks about town gossip, Ola talks about school and Scouts, and he talks about shooting ducks. A pretty happy situation. He eats with enthusiasm. He tells how he got the first bird, and Ola explains about the Golden Gate Bridge, cross-pollination, and Tom Sawyer, things she's been reading in school.

He cleans his plate and piles on seconds and thirds of everything. Quenby smiles to see him eat. She warns him to save room for the pie, and he replies that he could put away a herd of elephants and still have space for ten pies. Ola laughs gaily at that. She sure has a nice laugh. Ungainly as she is just now, she's going to be a pretty girl, he decides. He drinks his whiskey off, announces he'll bring in the pie and coffee.

How good it had felt! In spite of the musty odors, the rawness of the stiff sheets, the gaudy brilliance of the Coleman lantern, the anxious haste, the cool air teasing the hairs on your buttocks, the scamper of squirrels across the roof, the hurried by-passing of preliminaries (one astonishing kiss, then shirt and jacket and pants had dropped away in one nervous gesture, and down you'd gone, you in teeshirt and socks still): once it began, it was wonderful! Lunging recklessly into that steaming softness, your lonely hands hungering over her flesh, her heavy thighs kicking up and up, then slamming down behind your knees, hips rearing up off the sheets, her voice rasping: "Hurry!"—everything else forgotten, how good, how good!

And then she was gone. And you lay in your teeshirt and socks, staring half-dazed at the Coleman lantern, smoking a cigarette, thinking about tomorrow's fishing trip, idly sponging away your groin's dampness with your shorts. You stubbed out the cigarette, pulled on your khaki pants, scratchy on your bare and agitated skin, slipped out the door to urinate. The light leaking out your shuttered window caught your eye. You went to stand there, and through the broken shutter, you stared at the bed, the roughed-up sheets, watched yourself there. Well. Well. You pissed on the wall, staring up toward the main house, through the pines. Dimly, you could see Ola's head in the kitchen window. You know. You know.

"Listen, uh, Swede . . ."

"Yah?"

"Oh, nothing. I mean, well, what I started to say was, maybe I better start putting my shoulder to, you know, one of the paddles or whatever the hell you call them. I—well, unless you're sure you can get it—"

"Oh yah. I'm sure."

"Well . . ."

Swede, Carl, Ola, Quenby . . . One or more may soon be dead. Swede or Carl, for example, in revenge or lust or self-defense. And if one or both of them do return to the island, what will they find there? Or perhaps Swede is long since dead, and Carl only imagines his presence. A man can imagine a lot of things, alone on a strange lake in a dark night.

Carl, Quenby, Swede, Ola . . . Drinks in the livingroom. An after-dinner sleepiness on all of them. Except Ola. Wonderful supper. Nothing like fresh lake bass. And Quenby's lemon pie. "Did you ever hear about Daddy and the cat?" Ola asks. "No!" All smile. Ola perches forward on the hassock. "Well, Daddy had been away for two weeks . . ."

Listen: alone, far from your wife, nobody even to play poker with, a man does foolish things sometimes. You're stretched out in your underwear on an uncomfortable bed in the middle of the night; for example, awakened perhaps by the footfalls of deer outside the cabin, or the whistle of squirrels, the cry of loons, unable now to sleep. You step out, barefoot, to urinate by the front wall of the lodge. There seems to be someone swimming down in the bay, over near the docks, across from the point here. No lights up at the main house, just the single dull bulb glittering as usual out on the far end of the dock, casting no light. A bright moon.

You pad quietly down toward the bay, away from the kennels, hoping the dogs don't wake. She is swimming this way. She reaches the docks near the point here, pulls herself up on them, then stands shivering, her slender back to you, gazing out on the way she's come, out toward the boats and docks, heavy structures crouched in the moonglazed water. Pinpricks of bright moonlight sparkle on the crown of her head, her narrow shoulders and shoulderblades, the crest of her buttocks, her calves and heels.

Hardly thinking, you slip off your underwear, glance once at the house, then creep out on the rock beside her. "How's the water?" you whisper.

She huddles over her breasts, a little surprised, but smiles up at you. "It's better in than out," she says, her teeth chattering a little with the chill.

You stoop to conceal, in part, your burgeoning excitement, which you'd hoped against, and dip your fingers in the water. Is it cold? You hardly notice, for you are glancing back up now, past the hard cleft nub where fine droplets of water, catching the moonlight, bejewel the soft down, past the flat gleaming tummy and clutched elbows, at the young girl's dark shivering lips. She, too, seems self-conscious, for like you, she squats now, presenting you only her bony knees and shoulders, trembling, and her smile. "It's okay," you say, "I have a daughter just your age." Which is pretty stupid.

They were drifting between two black islands. Carl squinted and concentrated, but he couldn't see the shores, couldn't guess how far away the islands were. Didn't matter anyway. Nobody on them. "Hey, listen, Swede, you need a light? I think I still got some matches here if they're not wet—"

"No, sit down. Just be a moment . . ."

Well, hell, stop and think, goddamn it, you can't stick a lighted match around a gasoline motor. "Well, I just thought . . ." Carl wondered why Swede didn't carry a flashlight. My Jesus, a man live up here on a lake all these years and doesn't know enough to take along a goddamn flashlight. Maybe he wasn't so bright, after all.

He wondered if Swede's wife wasn't worrying about them by now. Well, she was probably used to it. A nice woman, friendly, a good cook, probably pretty well built in her day, though not Carl's type really. A little too slack in the britches. Skinny little daughter, looked more like Swede. Filling out, though. Probably be a cute girl in a couple years. Carl got the idea vaguely that Quenby, Swede's wife, didn't really like it up here. Too lonely or something. Couldn't blame her.

He knew it was a screwy notion, but he kept wishing there was a goddamn neon light or something around. He fumbled under the seat for the other beer.

"I asked Daddy why he shot my cat," she said. She stood at the opposite end of the livingroom, facing them, in her orange shirt and bright white shorts, thin legs apart. It was a sad question, but her lips were smiling, her small white teeth glittering gaily. She'd just imitated her daddy lobbing the cat up in the air and blowing its head off. "'Well, honey, I gave it a sporting chance,' he said. 'I threw it up in the air, and if it'd flown away, I wouldn't have shot it!'" She joined in the general laughter, skipping awkwardly, girlishly, back to the group. It was a good story.

She slips into the water without a word, and dogpaddles away, her narrow bottom bobbing in and out of sight. What the hell, the house is dark, the dogs silent: you drop into the water—wow! sudden breathtaking impact of the icy envelope! whoopee!—and follow her, a dark teasing shape rippling the moonlit surface.

You expect her to bend her course in toward the shore, toward the house, and, feeling suddenly exposed and naked and foolish in the middle of the bright bay, in spite of your hunger to see her again, out of the water, you pause, prepare to return to the point. But, no, she is in by the boats, near the end of the docks, disappearing into the wrap of shadows. You sink out of sight, swim underwater to the docks—a long stretch for a man your age—and find her there, holding onto the rope ladder of the launch her father uses for guiding large groups. The house is out of sight, caution out of mind.

She pulls herself up the ladder and you follow close behind, her legs brushing your face and shoulders. At the gunwales, she emerges into full moonlight, and as she bends forward to crawl into the launch, drugged by the fantasy of the moment, you lean up to kiss her glistening buttocks. In your throbbing mind is the foolish idea that, if she protests, you will make some joke about your beard.

He punched the can and the beer exploded out. He ducked just in time, but got part of it in his ear. "Hey! Did I get you, Swede?" he laughed. Swede didn't say anything. Hell, it was silly even to ask. The beer had shot off over his shoulder, past the bow, the opposite direction from Swede. He had asked only out of habit. Because he didn't like the silence. He punched a second hole and put the can to his lips. All he got at first was foam. But by tipping the can almost straight up, he managed a couple swallows of beer. At first, he thought it tasted good, but a moment later, the flat warm yeasty taste sliming his mouth, he wondered why the hell he had opened it up. He considered dumping the rest of it in the lake. But, damn it, Swede would hear him and wonder why he was doing it. This time, though, he would remember and not throw the empty can away.

Swede, Quenby, Carl, Ola . . . The story and the laughter and off to bed. The girl has omitted one detail from her story. After her daddy's shot, the cat had plummeted to the earth. But afterwards, there was a fluttering sound on the ground where it hit. Still, late at night, it caused her wonder. Branches scrape softly on the roof. Squirrels whistle and scamper. There is a rustling of beavers, foxes, skunks, and porcupines. A profound stillness, soon to be broken surely by rain. And, from far out on the lake, men in fishing boats, arguing, chattering, opening beercans. Telling stories.

INSIDIOUS DISEASE

Lucha Corpi

Little Michael David Cisneros had been identified by his mother and father, Lillian and Michael Cisneros, about six hours after Luisa and I found him. His maternal grandmother, Otilia Juarez who had reported him missing at 2:45 that afternoon, claimed that he'd been taken from the porch of her house on Alma Avenue, about three blocks from Laguna Park.

We had found him less than two miles from Otilia Juarez's house, approximately the length of the area swept by the police during the riot, as they forced the crowd from the park back toward Atlantic Park where the march had originated.

Joel had insisted on going back with me to that spot. Michael David's body was there, still with no more company than Luisa and the flies. I knelt down to fan them away so that Joel could take pictures of the scene. He didn't seem to have the same reaction I'd had when I first looked at the body, but his hands shook as he snapped photo after photo.

Luisa assured me that nothing had been disturbed. No one had passed by, for the area was quite isolated. A building rose to a height of about three floors, on the side of the street where we stood, one of those windowless low-budget plaster fortresses where unwanted memories are stored and sometimes forgotten. Across the street, a number of small neighborhood stores had been closed because of the disturbance. Even under ordinary circumstances this was an out-of-the-way street, a good ten blocks from the main thoroughfare.

Suddenly I saw a Chicano teenager standing at the corner, smoking a cigarette and glancing furtively in our direction. He was wearing a red bandana, folded twice and tied around his head, a black leather vest, no shirt, and black pants. Just then, he turned around and I noticed a haloed skull and the word "*Santos*" painted on the back of his vest. He seemed no older than 18, most likely a "home boy"—a member of a youth gang. What was he doing there, I wondered.

Luisa told us she'd seen him cross that intersection twice since she'd been there. It was obvious the young man didn't seem disturbed by our surveillance, and after a few minutes he began to walk in our direction. Luisa instinctively retreated behind me, and I, behind Joel. Finding himself suddenly cast in the role of defender, Joel put his camera in its case, and began searching in his pockets for something to use as a weapon.

Two years before, after a couple of attempted rapes of students at Cal State Bayward, Luisa and I had taken a self-defense course for women, and as a reward for our good performance, we had received a small container of mace, a permit to carry it, and a whistle. I reached for the whistle and Luisa grabbed her mace from her purse. Joel gave out a sigh of relief, but his eyes didn't show fear. Instead, he frowned.

"Is this guy someone you know?" I asked Joel. He shook his head.

With a slow stride, the young man approached, then stopped a few feet away from us.

"*Soy Mando,*" he said and looked straight at Joel, but his eyes took in everything between the wall and the opposite sidewalk. He threw a quick glance at the body, then at me. "*El chavalito este. Es tuyo?*"

"No," I replied, "it's not my child." This Mando was much younger than he'd seemed from a distance, not quite 15. Not a bad young man I sensed, and relaxed a little.

"The dude who brought the *chavalito* here dropped this." Mando handed me a folded newspaper clipping, which had turned yellow and was already showing signs of wear at the creases. No doubt it had been kept for a long time in a wallet.

My heart beat wildly and my hands shook as I reached for the clipping. Almost automatically, I closed my eyes. I suddenly sensed the presence of a man, saw his shadow, then a small house surrounded by tall trees. Somewhere in the area children were laughing. The scene passed and I felt nauseous, but I managed to overcome the desire to vomit. Still I had to hold on to Luisa.

My strange behavior disconcerted her, but Mando didn't seem to notice it at all. Perhaps he had witnessed stranger things, seen a lot of pain or wanton cruelty in his short life. I doubted there was much left in this world that would shake him, except perhaps the death of the child. Why had he decided to give us the clipping? And why did I trust him? Instinctively I had felt that he had nothing to do with the death of the child.

"Did you see the person who did this? Can you tell us what he looked like?" Joel took a small memo pad and pencil from his shirt pocket, flipping for a blank page. Like my husband, who was also left-handed, Joel held the memo pad in the hollow of his right hand, across his chest.

"I didn't see nothing. Understand? *Nada.*" Mando looked at Joel's hand, put his palms out, and took a couple of steps back.

"How do we know it wasn't you who killed this *chicanito?*" There was a double edge of contempt and defiance in Joel's voice, which surprised both Luisa and me.

Mando stood his ground. His eyes moved rapidly from Joel's face to his torso and arms, locking on the camera hanging from his neck. A wry smile began to form on Mando's lips. He spat on the ground, wiped his mouth with the back of his hand. "Later, *vato,*" he said, waving a finger at Joel.

"*Cuando quieras,*" Joel answered back, accepting the challenge. "Any time," he repeated.

Irritated with their childish confrontation, Luisa commanded, "Stop it! Both of you!" She looked at Joel, then added, "A child is dead. That's why we're here." Joel's face flushed with anger, but he remained quiet. Mando turned slightly to the left, cocking his head. The only noise was the distant clattering of the waning riot. Mando jumped over little Michael's body and stood beside me.

With his face close to mine, he whispered in my ear, "The dude—the one who brought the *chavalito*? He wasn't a *Santo*. I know 'cause he was wearing a wig. *Era gabacho*. He had a scar—a *media luna*—a half-moon, and a birthmark under his right arm."

Looking over his right shoulder, Mando began moving swiftly down the street, every muscle in his body ready for either attack or defense. I was fascinated, yet sad. A mother would be crying for him sooner than later, I thought. Not many gang members live long enough to bury their mothers.

"I'll see if I can get some more information from him," Joel said. He ran off in pursuit of Mando, who was already turning the corner when Matthew Kenyon's unmarked car stopped with a screech beside us.

Why is it that cops and tough men—young or old—have to brake or start up a car with a screech, I wondered. Do they think they are establishing turf, like moose or sea elephants?

I looked toward the corner. How had Mando known the cops were on their way? I had a feeling I would never have a chance to ask him.

So I gave my full attention to Kenyon. He was a lanky man, six feet tall, with very short red hair already graying and a pallid, freckled face. Everything seems to be fading in this man, I thought, as I focused on his Roman nose, his only feature that seemed atypical.

With Kenyon was another man who answered to the name of Todd, obviously from the crime lab since he was already marking the place where the body lay. A third man, driving a car marked with the seal of the Los Angeles County Coroner's Office, pulled up behind Kenyon's car. He, too, got out and began to examine the body.

Before questioning us, Kenyon helped Todd cordon off the area. Actually, he hardly paid any attention to us at all until Todd referred to the vomit on the sidewalk and I claimed it as mine.

"Ah, yes. Gloria Damasco?" Kenyon said. It amazed me that anyone besides Marlon Brando and Humphrey Bogart could speak without moving his upper lip in the slightest. True, it is easier to do that in English than in Spanish, because of the closeness in quality of English vowels; but Kenyon's case, next to Brando's and Bogie's, was definitely one for the books. He had soulful, expressive eyes, and perhaps because of that I expected his voice to reveal much more emotion.

"Yes," I said, "I'm Gloria Damasco." I asked Luisa for the clipping Mando had given us and was about to hand it to Kenyon when I was seized by the same kind of fear I had felt when I had tried to take it from Mando. Again, I saw the house, but this time I saw the word "park" carved into a board next to it. In my haste to get rid of the clipping before I became nauseated again, I threw it at the policeman. "Here. I think the murderer might have dropped this."

"So much for fingerprints," Todd muttered, shaking his head.

"I told you not to disturb anything." Despite his perfectly controlled tone, Kenyon's eyes showed anger, but I didn't care since I was more preoccupied with the realization that I was experiencing something out of the ordinary every time I touched that clipping. Perhaps it was only the product of what my grandmother called my "impressionable mind," her term for an imagination that could easily develop a morbid curiosity for the forbidden or the dark side of nature. Even a liking for death. These possibilities distressed me.

I must have looked pretty distraught, because Kenyon invited Luisa and me to wait in his car. Since he had already taken note of our names and addresses, perhaps he simply wanted us out of the way until he had time to question us, I thought.

We got into the back seat and I lowered the window so I could hear what Todd and the coroner were telling Kenyon, who was now putting Michael David's body on the stretcher and covering him with a cloth. "Well, Dr. D., was he strangled?"

Dr. D.—whose full name, according to his tag, was Donald Dewey—nodded, then shook his head, making the detective raise an eyebrow. "Whoever did this wanted to be extra sure that the boy would die. So the boy was drugged. I'm almost sure. This is all preliminary, you understand. I'll have more for you in the morning."

"That soon?" Kenyon smiled. "They're putting the others in the deep freeze, huh?" He flipped the pages in his notebook and read aloud: "Ruben Salazar, Angel Diaz and Lynn Ward."

"Looks that way." Donald Dewey picked up his equipment and headed toward the coroner's wagon. "Just buying time, I suppose. They got themselves into a real jug of jalapeno this time." I wondered if "they" referred to the police or to the demonstrators. Dr. Dewey came back after putting everything in the vehicle, then called Kenyon aside.

Trying not to be too conspicuous, I stuck my head out the window, but I could hear only fragments of the conversation because both men were speaking in a low voice. ". . . Second opinion. You never know. You'll have to tell them . . . soon."

Dewey patted Kenyon on the shoulder.

"Maybe Joel was right," I concluded. "Maybe it was a mistake to call the cops."

"Someone was going to do it anyway," Luisa said in a reassuring tone.

Todd and Kenyon picked up the stretcher and headed toward the wagon.

"Before I forget," Kenyon said to the coroner. "Will you find out as much as you can about the fecal matter?"

"Try my best," Dewey answered. "Need about two weeks though." He shook his head. "Real backlog and two lab boys just went on vacation."

Kenyon nodded and waved at the coroner.

I made the sign of the cross, closed my eyes and said a silent prayer for little Michael. My eyes were burning inside my lids. I opened them again and looked at my watch. It was now 5:15. The sun was still beating down on the streets and the sirens of ambulances and patrol cars were still wailing in the distance.

I had aged years in ten hours. By sundown, I would be as old as Mando.

For Ruben Salazar, Angel Gilberto Diaz, and Lynn Ward there was no going home, and the horror that would make the living toss and turn for many nights was of little consequence to them now. They were lying on autopsy slabs, side by side, waiting for their bodies to be opened and drained of blood, their insides emptied, then studied and tested to determine the exact cause of their deaths.

In time, perhaps someone would admit to the *real* cause of what happened that day. But perhaps we already knew the name of the insidious disease that had claimed three—perhaps four—more lives that late August afternoon.

More than ever before, I wanted to go home, to hold my daughter and seek the comfort of Dario's arms. But the spirit of little Michael had taken hold of me and I would not again be able to go about my life without my feeling his presence in me.

DREAM A DREAM OF ME

Stanley Crouch

Alva and Charlie shared birthdays, same day, same year, in fact. The last time she and Moses saw him, he had a party for her, for himself, and for Lester Young, who was also a Virgo, as was his mother and Buster Smith, an alto saxophonist and a first influence from Kansas City whom Charlie fondly talked of as a father figure. Charlie said Smith had skin the color of an eggplant and was known to smoke cigars when writing music. He was a welcoming mentor who took him in when Charlie first came to New York, his feet swollen and his clothes stinking, after hoboing across the country from Kansas City and arriving in front of the Savoy Ballroom with a nickel and a nail in his pocket. Though he spoke of hopping trains and living in hobo jungles with a jaunty tone, Alva felt a brutal and disruptive set of memories residing somewhere down in his voice. No one she knew had ever really hopped trains but there were plenty of train hopping stories in the blues numbers she heard coming through the windows of homes back down in South Carolina. The singer made you hear the racket of the train's metal wheels against the track and feel the wind and experience that emotion of escape or loss or adventure. None of that was in Charlie's sound. He made her feel like those pictures she had seen of Manolete in *Life* Magazine as he was dressing to meet his death in the ring. She shuddered inside and felt sad for him but did not know what, exactly, was breaking her heart. He was like that.

By the time of that birthday celebration Alva and Moses were living in the nation's capital but they had sublet a little place in Harlem and were spending the summer in that favorite city of theirs. You couldn't have kept them out of Central Park or out of the Apollo Theater or the Savoy or the Museum of Modern Art or the Metropolitan Museum or out of Carnegie Hall or off of 52nd Street. They wanted it all, every bit of anything that was good in New York, from uptown to downtown, which meant that they even strolled around in Greenwich Village and looked at the place where Richard Wright had lived before packing up and heading for Paris. They even strolled all the way to the end of the island, where they could stare across at the Statue of Liberty and joke about the cramp that must have been in her green arm from holding up that symbol of freedom year in and year out, even though few paid attention to the meaning of liberty or were concerned with setting things so right that justice for all might become some kind of a norm. She was green cheese. She was gangrene. She was not an edifice of liberty. But she would do until the real thing came along.

Walking down from where they were subletting in Harlem to where Charlie now hung his hat, they recalled how it had been a few years before, when the war was winding to a finish and 52nd Street had been their home away from home. It was so exciting to be there just that little bit younger and seeing it all. They could not forget the little shotgun clubs and the street full of people just west of where the wealthy had their fun at "21" and might just step up into that block where so much jazz was playing and a couple of Negro graduate students were there to hear their buddy Charlie Parker. That music took some listening to get used to but there was a quality so dazzling about his playing. It was bold and full of virtuosic flourishes. His tone was as hard as a diamond but rather elegant in the way it had been cut, with the pitiless edges wrought by a master jeweler who had heard the hopeless sobs of the damned, both in the flesh and in his dreams. The music was just as rich in that back home blues ache for something good, but not anything in particular.

When he stood up there as still as a cigar store Indian with sweat flooding off of him, Charlie could seem like a religious statue bleeding the pure clear blood of a determined and no less than saintly compassion. Or he could squeal like a thief caught in the act who tried to back out of his guilt with a laugh as full of fright as menace and cynicism. Somewhere down in the rumbles of his soul were brilliant details almost equal in their brightness to the romantic fantasy of a mythical knight's dreams as he rode into danger or in quest of his lady love, burdening his horse by wearing a polished suit of armor that shone for miles but would surely doom him if he was unseated and incapable of rising under its weight. Getting his soul to somehow float up from the things that held him down seemed to be the ultimate theme at the center of Charlie's music and it was the finesse with which he both begged and prayed for the strength to do it that made his music so bracing. He could make you dream, he could make you remember, he could break your heart, he could force you to pat your foot and grin as if it had just been proven that you had the best luck in the world.

After they had listened to him or had crisscrossed the street throughout the night spending time in the presence of different kinds of entertainers and jokers and geniuses, they might find themselves walking. No, not really walking. Wandering, actually. That they knew where they were didn't remove the feeling of wandering because they were never paying much attention to anything outside of each other, almost sensing the end of a block or stopping when there was a light and the danger of passing night traffic was only a few feet away. Someone looking at the two might think they were dancing or that one of them had just returned from a long visit or assignment some place far away from New York, where there were no telephones, no telegraphs, no mail service. They seemed too grateful to be seeing each other to make much of the night, the weather, the time. The feeling they gave off had a paradoxical quality of the mellow and the fervent: Yaz, yaz, yaz. They moved at a slow stride that was almost woozy, her leaning against, him almost trying to lean against her so gently that he might bring off the sweet trick of actually slipping under her skin, which was obviously impossible but that fantasy gave him a taste of the poetic magic that transforms a dream into a spiritual reality. They usually traveled along what became a familiar path—or an usual one that took them to the usual place, Grand Central Station, where they would sit and talk and drink coffee. There they would find themselves looking at the powder blue of the ceiling design for a while as they held hands. Or, if those other two were there, they might inspire the tall light-skinned guy and the petite black gal to start wondering aloud to each other about what Miles Davis and J.J. Johnson were talking about as they sat not far from the college couple, looking at sheets of music paper and nodding to one another as they pointed to different parts of the score.

Alva thought those young men were fitting themselves for the future, just as she and Moses were. The look in their eyes said that they were filling their minds with the kinds of things that would carry them through a world they knew did not necessarily welcome them but would not be given the chance to discourage the two princely young men from pursuing those things they had promised themselves they would get. There was no doubt in Alva's mind that her man Moses was going to do or write or innovate a very important and presently unnamed something or other. She felt the same way about herself as she walked with him uptown on those special nights, taking in the rich summer air of Manhattan and wondering when Moses was going to think of taking her riding in a carriage through Central Park rather than walking alongside it either down Fifth Avenue or up Central Park West. It was something she wanted to do but something she didn't want to ask for. Alva wasn't the asking kind but she was the kind whose heart suffered from a small fissure when a thing she wanted wasn't given, even a thing she could have gotten easily had she ever mentioned it. What she never knew was that Moses assumed she loved those long walks and actually would have loved to ride in a carriage with her but thought that since she never mentioned it or even kind of implied that she wanted one of those rides that she might have thought them stupid and wasteful.

Charlie had a bigger apartment by that summer when they were less kids than when they had met him. He also had a long tall white woman whose mouth was full of huge teeth, whose manner was awkward and sweet with more than a streak or two of optimistic anticipation and great sadness. She seemed, finally, as though the only thing in the world she knew worth knowing was her Charlie. She could have learned a few other things if Alva had had anything to say about it. The woman, though nice as pie, cooked horribly. Everything was either over or underdone or nearly burned. On that special birthday as she was leaving her twenties, Alva wished she could have gotten there early enough to save Charlie's wife and herself and the other guests from the terrible meal they were served. You could tell nothing about the taste of it from looking at Charlie. Too gallant for words, he ate the food with the same gusto that he did what Alva put on the table when he so regularly found himself in their old apartment around dinner time.

Moses and Alva left their home pondering how odd a person Lester Young was and in awe of how much gin he could drink, sitting there yellow and handsome and so lazy seeming, the weirdest combination of the gentle and the profane, the raucous and the unhappy. Alva prided herself on kicking Moses under the table every time he was beginning to show anger at the way Young talked, when it was obvious he was just trying to shock everyone with a casual dirty mouth. Something was wrong in the world to him—deep down dirty and wrong—and the only way he could get it out, off of a bandstand, was by upsetting any expectations of grace and cleaniness in conversation. So what? They had danced to too many of his records. He had paid the price to be a bad boy by providing joy to the anonymous ones listening to the radio or sitting somewhere with his records turning and telling them things they wanted to hear. Only a burdened few had to endure his personality, which still had no strain of malice, something that Alva was particularly good at picking up on even faster than immediately. She told Moses she thought he was just a guy who wanted to be babied and was never babied enough to settle him down.

As she turned her head in the heat of the evening, Alva knew then for the first time that someday, somewhere, sitting at some writing desk, she would put that feeling she got from Lester Young into a character who was not a musician and whose life had nothing remotely going on in the way his had but who shared with him that same sweet blueness, heartbreak, anger, rage to shock, and the longing to be coddled once again, perhaps as he had when his mother blocked out the blows of the world, turning every wound into something wonderful and deceiving him into believing all was well with life, when that was as far from the truth as the earth was from the moon.

Moses was glad that Alva, who was so dedicated to grace, had gotten him to control himself. There was no doubt about that. She had saved everyone a big flood of trouble and embarrassment. He could easily have put that drunken Lester Young on his back. It was very evident. He could feel his color changing and he did feel like standing up and telling that Negro to either shut up talking that way in front of these women or put down his drink and step out into the hall where he would soon wish he had never learned even one curse word. It was all right, baby, she had told him as the late, late August moon sat in an imperial position on that hot New York night, discouraging all but the most determined from coupling up and making the marvelous creature of two sweating backs. They were not discouraged and realized—as they lay there afterwards, moaning and whining and wishing the fan was bigger—that the only person more in love with somebody than Charlie's wife was each of them. I would say, Moses almost crooned to her, that you might love me more than I love you but I know that's not possible. Yes it is, she answered, yes it is.

PIRATE ONE

Fielding Dawson

I'm writing this on Mozart's birthday—January 27th; a Wednesday morning, just a few minutes after nine a.m.

It all came clear last night. I don't know how. Through talking, I guess.

Last night Nixon announced the war was over and the day before yesterday Johnson died, and George Foreman TKO'd Joe Frazier in not quite two rounds, as reported in yesterday's papers. Also, the Supreme Court ruled that abortions are legal in the first three months. So, a lot of news, and most of it good, and though my heart's been with it, especially the war and abortion news—I've secretly been thinking about something else. And talking with a lovely young dancer last night at the bar, I realized what it's been; running around in my head there. These last two or three weeks since he died, and being with her last night, talking, and drinking, the memory of last fall, after sixteen years of an unanswered question, at least that part came clear, a big part, when the question was answered.

About the place where I'd met him. Not really met him, but I'd stood beside him, and, well, that was enough, I mean.

All along I've been thinking—so I thought—about him, but what's really been on my mind is Jackson Pollock and Johnny Romero. Then him.

Do you remember Johnny Romero? I remember Pollock yelling and being angry when strangers didn't know who he was.

Well. I came to New York in May of 1956 because I had to, it was where my future was, and it was also where Julie Eastman was, in her wonderful apartment on Spring Street. I was so completely in love with her my life was hardly real, and it was only later—too late by then—that she realized how much in love with me she was. Because, in spite of all the famous guys who loved her, she loved me most of all. I knew it, too, but she didn't. Not then. I was—really crazy about her. It didn't take much. Christ she was beautiful.

Anyway, it was very brief, and after we broke up, I moped around New York for a few months, and around September or October of that year, I was walking along a street in the Village and I passed a little place with one door, which was open, and I stopped, because Chris Conner, who got all she knew about singing from June Christy, was on the jukebox and Stan Kenton was behind her and it was All About Ronnie, and I was standing on a side street in New York City, just come from my home town Kirkwood, Missouri, and I was inside a dive outside U.S. Army Headquarters Germany, with a couple of lean bleached Lesbians, who hummed along with Chris and stared through smoke, boy Hesse caught that, and the name in neon in the window to the right of the open door said *Johnny Romero's*.

I went in.

The jukebox was to the left of the door, and beyond it was a small rectangular wooden table, which fit into a small corner, fitted with an L-shaped bench, and beyond that on the left still, were a lot of posters mostly of Negro guys and women, and just beyond that, along the wall there, were the bathrooms, and as they marked the rear of the place, the door (curtains, actually) that was there, led, I assumed, to the kitchen. And following around, the bar ran the length of the place, opposite the jukebox and wall of posters. Underneath the window up front, was a cigarette machine.

The young colored guy behind the bar looked at me, and I sat on a barstool and asked for a draft, which he gave me and I paid for, I looked around the place, it was small, clean, and had a nice feeling, I played a couple of songs, took a leak, finished another draft, and left.

I began to go there when I was in the neighborhood, and occasionally when I wasn't, and it was quite a while later that I discovered the kitchen wasn't behind the curtains, it was a small, lovely and secluded garden, with three or four tables and some chairs. So, often if it was a nice day, and I had a couple of dollars, I'd go to Johnny Romero's and sit out in the garden, and think the grave thoughts serious romantics think, drinking at three o'clock in the afternoon in New York. On a beautiful day. The beer was so cold, and good. Julie Eastman sure made a blunder when she let me go, I'll say.

I also went at night. Thirsty for experience, and frustrated and angry because I couldn't seem to bring my life into focus, and somehow use it in my art. So the knowledge that I had a lot of living yet to do, while thrilling me, yet made me angry and impatient.

The slang was different then, of course; the word was spade, and in more proper circles, colored, or Negro. But the city was simply alive with jazz, and everyone spoke hipster lingo. Yeah man, well, I'm like cool.

Johnny Romero's was the first all-black downtown bar in the city; very few white people went, though no one was actually unwelcome in a racial sense, but there were so many other places to go, and drink and hear jazz, why go to Romero's, where there was, actually, not much happening and people stood around and talked, drank, and listened to the jukebox. Why listen to a jukebox, when two or three blocks away the man on the record was alive before your eyes?

Tea (grass) was still a fairly inside thing, and the hipster jokes, some of which were really funny, were spade jokes about grass, until suddenly they weren't, which like grass, slows reality down. Most white cats including myself spoke a spade musician's lingo and it was (embarrassing) strange, me talking to some spade cat imitating his jive. Hi man, gimme some skin!

Heeyyy baby, what's happenin'?

But I—and I cooled it—so I never experienced much hostility; and I enjoyed Romero's because I was in a world I hardly knew—hey, let me put it like this (you dig):

New York, in 1956, was the wildest, greatest city anywhere; American painting had just been taken seriously for a first in history, and the city was the art center of the world. Europe was as jealous as all hell, and it was wonderful. You could walk along 10th Street and stop and say a few words with Philip Guston, go into the Colony on the corner there, at 4th Avenue, have a beer with deKooning, walk over to the Cedar and have a few with Creeley, Dan Rice, or Kline, and that night fall by the Riviera or Romero's and then cross up to the Vanguard on 7th Avenue, dig Getz and Brookmeyer, and then walk down to the Cafe Bohemia, and get your head torn off by Miles, and around one, fall by the Cedar, and pick up some friends and go over to the 5 Spot and completely flip over Cecil Taylor, then afterwards go to Riker's for breakfast, and around dawn head home, maybe with a chick. It was really great. You could feel the exuberance, you could see and hear the dedication. I did, and I miss the way musicians talked. Things were opening out. I'd made friends with a few spade cats overseas so I had an idea how to behave, a little, I mean, I tended to get carried away. It was easy enough. I'd slip into Romero's, get a beer and stand around for an hour or two and then split to hear Sonny. Or Monk. Or Miles. What not many people knew was Romero's was an essentially middle-class place. Black guys and their chicks drove downtown in their big cars, or their sports cars, and went to Johnny Romero's.

Especially on weekends. It was the downtown place to go. I guess there were black gangsters and black detectives, too, but it didn't matter to me, as I stood by the door, watching, because what the place was all about, which you could feel, I mean even when it was crowded there was a nice quality, and people were friendly, and that's what I learned. It was Johnny's effect. He was a popular guy. Everybody liked him; he was very friendly, and in a very real sense, though odd-seeming, there wasn't any reason for violence, and then, sensibly perhaps, the black guys that went there were *big*, big guys, and some of them must have been prize fighters. Also, the customers were cool. To themselves. Yes, baby, tonight I am very cool. It was a bright, warm, classy little joint, and those big dark skinned guys dressed in dark blue and white silk and their chicks looking like twenty million in furs and perfumes, and as I stood there, learning Johnny's effect, I caught a sense of friendship that was to me at the end of a long and far flung thread, which yet seemed, for these people, the beginning of every day.

Happily, there were precious few of the white guys who hang around only with black people because they don't know what to do with their lives, and they figure black cats will understand because they don't either—it's a loser's fantasy and rationale—white guys feeling black guys will understand because black guys are born losers; how can they handle life, being black, and the double irony is lost in the misunderstanding that the loss is in being black! a natural fact you dig, and the implication in the audacity of that white fantasy, is also lost. And if, following the definition of irony in a textbook of rhetoric published about 1872, irony consists in ridiculing an object under a pretense of praising it (with the true meaning indicated by the tone of voice), you can see the rather horrible meaning of that loss. Which, of course, black people were, and are, supposed to understand. Literally.

Those white guys would be called spade freaks today. Then they said he digs spades. Chicks, too. She digs spades. But you could tell in the tone of the voice. In the beginning, like when she hit on him, the spade stud was flattered, but when he discovered she dug him because he was—uhn, well, and she couldn't dig herself anyway, he—it was a pretty bitter discovery. There was a lot of that in the Fifties.

You can spot chicks and cats who only dig spades; they have a sleepy look, a somnambulant look, eyes wide open. And a sharp kind of hysterical glitter along the edges. Somebody else is holding them up; guess who.

Anyway, my involvement with writing and painting made my life hectic enough, and lonely enough, so that Romero's was so different from me, though I might want somebody to hold me up, the effect of Johnny Romero's persona wouldn't have it, so I enjoyed his bar, and the obvious tone of relaxation. In fact that effect rejected the cats and chicks who dug spades. And kept me just different enough to constantly realize something I had learned in the Army: when black people are together the circumstance is of people being together in that way.

And that success was because of Johnny—hands down. Without a *doubt*. He was a very nice guy—he was the kind of guy when he saw you on the street he'd wave or call to you just as you did him, and then when he suddenly saw you, and remembered you from his bar, the warmth in his greeting deepened. Really, everybody liked him.

He was about six feet two, had a lithe walk, dressed casually, and stayed calm; but of course there was something behind his eyes, that something the response-structure to his making it in the white world. Every black musician in America and maybe Europe had that look; some guys were more outspoken than others, but it was tough, because the guys who owned the clubs where you played were Italian gangsters, and they held you in contempt for the obvious reasons, and they told you what to do, and they took your money, and there wasn't anything you could do about it. I'm certain drugs were a way out of that humiliation, rage and anxiety, and then a way into the music. I often saw Miles take breaks between sets, and walk outside for a smoke so tightlipped and angry he was literally speechless—or couldn't speak what was on his mind.

But Johnny Romero seemed to take it all pretty well; he had a good thing going, and the sacrifices he made were at least conscious. One of the nicest things about him was he tended bar, and I don't know if he needed to, but I think he enjoyed it, because he was an active man, and he enjoyed work, and the company of people, and especially people he liked. He was very handsome, and given his size, and his casual open friendly style, and his attractive light brown skin, warm smile and grin, it was obviously a pleasant thing to drop by for a drink, sit at the bar, and say Hi Johnny, how about a nice cold beer! And in that spirit, one day about a year later, I was in the neighborhood, so I walked over for a quick one, and to dig Billie on the jukebox and when I got there, the door was closed, locked, the lights were out inside, and the sign on the door said Closed. What the hell I thought.

So I walked away, and that night and a few days later I asked around—what had happened? I asked a couple of black guys I thought might know, they didn't, and I asked a couple of bar owners, and they spoke in low tones, mumbling something about Johnny and trouble. Trouble, in that usage, meant the Mafia, and until last fall—for sixteen years—all I knew was something about Johnny and trouble.

It was after a game, in very early October—1972—I'd pitched a two hit shutout, and our team had won 7–0. We were happily getting our gear together, most of us half drunk from the beer we'd had during the game, we always have fun, we have a good softball team, and in the car heading across town to our bar, I was in the back seat, fat and forty-two, and somebody was talking about the Pirates, and remarked that Clemente couldn't do it *all* by himself, and for some reason, maybe the warm afternoon, and the motion of the car and the breeze, and our victory and therefore our good spirits and certainly my relaxed pleasure—I'd gotten a double and single, driven in a run and scored once—I lit a smoke, and in a rather wistful way remembered Johnny Romero's bar, and the night I had stood beside him at that bar, and I asked my pal Joe, who was in the front seat,

Do you remember Johnny Romero's?

Yes, he said, adding, that spade joint in the Village.

I nodded, and asked, right out, What ever happened to him? I heard he'd gotten into some tr—

Trouble! Listen man, that guy was balling a Mafia guy's chick!

Holy Christ! I cried, horrified. But, why—why I mean they didn't but why didn't they kill him? How *awful!*

Joe laughed because they liked him, and added—he was a nice guy!

I made a peculiar smile, and shook my head, remembering Johnny, saying, Boy, how close can you get. What did they do? I asked, did they do anything? What did they do to her?

Joe shrugged. They didn't do anything to him, they told him to get out of the country or else.

Man, I whispered, he must have moved fast. No wonder I'd been surprised, seeing the *Closed* sign on the door. I'd stopped in the night before.

Fast! Who wouldn't—

After a minute or two I told Joe, and the other guys in the car, what had happened one night, around one in the morning, at Johnny Romero's bar, when I had been standing at the bar near the door, having a bottle of beer; Ballantine, it was. Ballantine was good in the Fifties.

There were a few customers in the place, I was thinking my thoughts and Johnny was serving people and talking, and the lights were low. The mixture of perfume scent and cigars breezed around the vision of dark-skinned couples, talking, as Miles and Sonny played Paper Moon, and as I faced the bar, on the wall in back and above the bar, just opposite me and up a little, I looked at the advertisement that never ceased to amuse and fascinate me: slick photo in color of a handsome black guy beautifully dressed, and his chick, a knockout, in low cut gown, enjoying the drink Smirnoff was advertising and it was the White Cadillac—flashy and funny: vodka and milk, and a guy moved in and stood next to me, on my left, and I moved to my right as the guy stood there and got comfortable, both hands on the bar in a relaxed manner as Johnny walked up the duckboards to him, and I saw the guy, who was about six three, was wearing a baseball cap, and it looked professional. Johnny and I exchanged glances, and I made a thin smile.

So did Johnny.

The guy to my left was muscular, and extremely handsome; skin very dark, but of a rich hue, and his features were chiseled, and his eyes dark, but very bright, and he pointed at Johnny, and then at his ball cap, and said,

You know who I be?

Johnny shook his head.

The guy was hurt, and he tapped his own chest, and then his ball cap, and asked, surprised: You no know who I be?

Johnny smiled, and said no, and that he was sorry, but—

Well, the guy got a little angry. He took off the cap, and pointed to the large curved P on the front, and glaring at Johnny, he said, angrily,

You *know* who I be!

Johnny lifted his big shoulders, and turned a hand palm up, and was about to say something, when the guy slammed the cap on his own head, jabbed himself in the chest, and yelled,

I BE ROBERTO CLEMENTE!

Hey, great! Johnny grinned, but the Pittsburgh outfielder sensed it hadn't really worked, and glancing at me—I was poker face O.K. because this guy Clemente was a powerful cat, man, and he was very bugged, and as he was calling the shots, I was just there, Period. So he looked at Johnny, again, tapped himself on the chest again, and yelled,

I BE RO-BER-TO CLE-MEN-TE! He looked at Johnny and, searching for words, stammered, I—I be—he cursed in Spanish—PITTSBURG!

He looked at Johnny to see if he had said it right, knowing somehow he hadn't. I said, Right field.

Clemente nodded, yelled, Si, laughed, and cried, I—RO-BER-TO—I Ro-ber-to CLE-MEN-TE!

And Johnny laughed, reached across the bar and put a big hand on Clemente's shoulder, and laughing right out, said,

That's great, baby, and what is it you want to drink?

They laughed, I had imitated the voices, and the car pulled up outside the bar and we got out with our bats and gloves, and as we went inside, I said, in a deep soft swirl of emotion, to no one in particular,

He reminded me of Pollock.

Pollock had died in an automobile accident. August 10th, 1956; last night, when I had remembered Clemente, too.

NIGHT OF THE FEMA TRAILERS
Vivian Demuth

One evening, a month after the last hurricane, Rosie Lupin sat on her legless couch by the side of Shrimpers Highway watching a full moon illuminate the mist on the Chitimaucha bayou, when a convoy of fifty FEMA trailers and motor homes rolled quietly down the road towards her like an ivory colonial mansion or a giant Catholic tomb, shinier than any of the damp, fungal Chitimaucha homes and much longer than the shrimp boats still belly-up on the sides of the roads. The trailers and motor homes rolled by beneath a rising moon towards the old bridge to New Orleans, with its dark hotel skyscrapers and daily jazz funerals. The moon's iridescent light transformed the flooded Native land and cabins into a magnetic glow of flapping rooftop tarps and dying live oaks, abandoned wooden stilts and solitary pelicans.

Rosie who had been appointed chairperson of the Chitimaucha band, but who had not been given a chief's office nor Federal cultural grants, waited alone daily in front of the remains of her dilapidated cabin for her people's promised trailers and she listened for the caterpillar engines of Army Corps engineers. She often walked on the damaged levees and prayed for government trucks, and sometimes while she sat on her couch at midnight she watched the winter shrimp jump in the starlight. On this night Rosie witnessed, as the moon's skull waxed full, the convoy of giant FEMA trailers appear, then disappear, towards the towering hotels of New Orleans, searching like zombies for Voodoo signs of hungry contractors and random inspectors. But something happened as the convoy approached the Homa Bridge and Rosie heard the squealing of tires and smelled the burning of rubber as the trailers plunged one by one into the murky Mississippi. Standing on her couch, she watched a waiting oil barge tow the trailers out to the sea where they disappeared silently, without disturbing the Native elders and children sleeping in family cars, nor the few remaining alligators.

Rosie felt bewildered in the dawn's hazy light. But when she saw her people washing flood-water marks off their homes, when she noticed the nearby oil flares of prosperous companies with their monstrous shipping tanks that widened freshwater bayous with deadly saltwater streams, when she saw the fingers of eroding and sinking coastal land and the rainbow-colored shorebirds that flew farther and farther north and the duck hunters in their fashionable camouflage scanning the shallow shores, she thought that clearly the disappearing FEMA trailers must have been some sort of mirage.

Rosie completely forgot about the ominous event until the next full moon when she was watching for the odd tourists in their *Wilderness* motor homes driving along Shrimpers Highway, and once again she saw the shrimp jump in the moonlit bayou and a solemn convoy of FEMA trailers and motor homes rolling down the highway towards her. She momentarily wondered if these were same trailers that she had seen before, or a brand new shipment, until she saw them swerve away from the Homa Bridge again and fall into the dammed Mississippi where they were hauled away by an oil barge out to sea. But this time, Rosie bolted to a neighboring Episcopal church where a team of born-again Christians, who had come to help fix a few houses and perhaps recruit a few members, lay sleeping inside the church.

Elroy, the head Christian, groaned as he opened the church door because they had dined on pasta and cakes late into the night. When Rosie finished recounting her sighting of the FEMA trailers, Elroy told her to go back to bed, that she'd had too much drink, and to come to one of their meetings in the morning. Rosie yelled to the door as it closed, "I don't drink." Then she drove to the home of her French friend Cecil, who had married Albert, a Chitimaucha whom everyone knew would someday make a fine chief when the band got Federal recognition.

Cecil and Albert were sleeping in their backyard tent, tired from re-tiling their damaged floor and from sorting through clothing donated by a grassroots organization for all the poor people of Homa. They rubbed the sleep from their eyes and agreed to go and take a look for the FEMA convoy so that they could see what was really there in the snaking Mississippi. All they found were the shadows of dying cypress trees quivering along the moonlit water's surface, while plywood and shingles bounced in and out of the eddies. They even saw the broken bones of victims from a tearful Cajun trail but there was no trace of the giant FEMA convoy. Yet Rosie was so determined that Cecil and Albert agreed to watch with her during the next full moon because they had already visited the FEMA appeals office in New Orleans, where an inspector had said, "No trailers without sites that have electrical hookups and septic tanks," and he left them with appeal forms and a FEMA handbook. Afterwards, Cecil and Albert found only one contractor in the whole parish and his rates had dix-drupled. They gave Rosie the appeal forms and the FEMA handbook, which they couldn't understand, and she tossed the useless book into the mud of a destroyed drainage levee.

Soon after that, Rosie had to get used to some of the band members looking away when she walked by because FEMA had messed up their minds with broken promises. As Rosie's voice began to jambalaya inside and her memory started to waver with community needs, she continued seeking donations from all over the world and researching green sustainable building. A few weeks later, as she ate some kumquats late one evening on her legless couch by the side of the highway and watched a brown pelican waiting for shrimp and perch to jump in the moonlight, Rosie looked around into the gleaming frames of the FEMA trailer convoy, which went rolling quietly past her once again. This time, Rosie quickly gave chase in her old Toyota, flicking her headlights and leaning on the horn until a band of coyotes howled and some Native elders rose from their tents and their cars wondering if some Federal department had decided to relocate them again. But no one else saw the giant convoy of FEMA trailers that repeated its moonlit plunge into the ancient Mississippi, and the police pulled up behind Rosie and searched with their flashlights in the back of her car for liquor bottles. She told them that she didn't drink. She just thought she saw a caravan of lost FEMA trailers. The officers shook their heads and laughed as she pulled away from the Homa Bridge, her black hair and her dashboard owl feathers fluttering in the wind. Then, as her thin hands gripped the steering wheel, Rosie said to herself, "My people need proper shelter before the next storms come." And all night, while she sat by the side of the highway on her legless couch, she thought of what she would do.

On the eve of the following full moon, she borrowed the biggest state patrol boat which was waiting on a trailer for a fresh coat of paint in a corner of Homa Wharf. With her old Toyota, she pulled the boat home, where she parked by the bridge on the side of the road, her body trembling across from the Episcopal church. She realized while she waited that she had forgotten to distribute the care kits and clothing that were piled in the back of her truck, and she had forgotten to call the Homa Clinic to see if the doctors needed more high-blood-pressure pills. She had also forgotten to talk to the elders about their dwindling food stamp supply. And she had neglected to check on the boundaries of the new condo site for foreign anglers that encroached on an ancient burial mound for the Chitimaucha and had once been a refuge for now-extinct species of snakes. She hadn't so much as glanced at all the damaged grocers still closed from the hurricane, because she was focused on that night with the frowning, full moon and the wind humming like a million mosquitoes through the tall, bayou grasses and the next ghostly appearance of the FEMA trailer convoy. While she continued waiting by the side of the rickety, wooden bridge, she heard the sound of rooftop tarps flapping, wild coyotes and dogs, and the restrained murmuring of the Mississippi river, until the sound of wheels pierced the cool winter air.

Rosie stirred while lightning whipped out across the New Orleans skyline, and she prayed by the side of the bridge. By the great Creator, there was the convoy of trailers winding along the highway, heading towards her, while she blocked its path to the tamed river with the big patrol boat whose anchor clung to the bridge. With her truck headlights aimed at the dented highway, she felt the strength of her determination to stop the convoy from disappearing into the whispering waters, waiting alone, not having told anyone. She briefly wondered if it was all a hallucination because patches of the night sky were dark with low clouds from Washington that obscured the moon, and the convoy disappeared behind a flaring sour gas plant whose foul odor Rosie had occasionally smelled. But she again heard the sound of fortune's wheels on the pavement and the convoy reappeared, glistening at the end of the road and entranced like Mardi Gras revelers. This time a voice buried inside Rosie said, We will not wait any longer, and she blasted the truck horn at the approaching giant convoy, while brown pelicans watched safely from the swing sets of the decaying church playground nearby. On the large FEMA trailers, signs shone in the dark. "Government Property," they said, and the trailers continued towards her as she revved the big truck's engine and blasted the bloody horn and screamed at the shiny window shields of motor homes and trailers until they screeched back, crashing right into the giant patrol boat and pushing her struggling truck towards the rocky cliff. The boat skidded and lurched with the force of the convoy, swerving out of control for hundreds of feet until it butted against the frame of the decrepit Mississippi bridge.

Rosie touched her swaying owl feather and took a deep breath that was answered by a sigh from the long line of FEMA trailers and motor homes. As she slowly opened the door of the first jumbo-sized motor home, the Government Property sign slid off its side. Inside, glowing on the dashboard by the steering wheel, sat a flashing remote control device that Rosie immediately switched off. She sat in the plush driver's seat and turned the lead motor home around in front of the mangled state patrol boat. All the other motor homes and trailers followed, as she drove back grinning and honking the motor home horn at some Chitimaucha people who cheered by the side of the road and who spread the word that Rosie had delivered a convoy of fifty new FEMA trailers and motor homes.

When she finally parked the immense convoy along the side of Shrimpers Highway in front of her legless couch, Cecil and Albert were there to help Rosie dispatch a trailer or motor home to fifty families that arrived in need. Rosie began to feel pleased as a red dawn glowed on the horizon. The new scent of the trailers and the hum of the motor homes dispersed throughout the community. No one worried about the government reclaiming their property because not even the Red Cross had visited Homa in months. But soon, fifty more families in need came, and then fifty more. There were no more saved trailers and motor homes left to distribute. Only the haunting memory of them floating under the bridge remained, and the hope that more would somehow escape the slippery hands of FEMA.

And after breakfast which she cooked on her new stove, Rosie began to clean up the hurricane debris of clothing and torn photographs scattered over her lawn and watched as a speckled king snake made its home underneath the lead motor home sparkling in her driveway.

THE LYNCHING OF JUBE BENSON

Paul Laurence Dunbar

Gordon Fairfax's library held but three men, but the air was dense with clouds of smoke. The talk had drifted from one topic to another much as the smoke wreaths had puffed, floated, and thinned away. Then Handon Gay, who was an ambitious young reporter, spoke of a lynching story in a recent magazine, and the matter of punishment without trial put new life into the conversation.

"I should like to see a real lynching," said Gay rather callously.

"Well, I should hardly express it that way," said Fairfax, "but if a real, live lynching were to come my way, I should not avoid it."

"I should," spoke the other from the depths of his chair, where he had been puffing in moody silence. Judged by his hair, which was freely sprinkled with gray, the speaker might have been a man of forty-five or fifty, but his face, though lined and serious, was youthful, the face of a man hardly past thirty.

"What! you, Dr. Melville? Why, I thought that you physicians wouldn't weaken at anything."

"I have seen one such affair," said the doctor gravely; "in fact, I took a prominent part in it."

"Tell us about it," said the reporter, feeling for his pencil and notebook, which he was, nevertheless, careful to hide from the speaker.

The men drew their chairs eagerly up to the doctor's, but for a minute he did not seem to see them, but sat gazing abstractedly into the fire; then he took a long draw upon his cigar and began:

"I can see it all very vividly now. It was in the summertime and about seven years ago. I was practicing at the time down in the little town of Bradford. It was a small and primitive place, just the location for an impecunious medical man, recently out of college.

"In lieu of a regular office, I attended to business in the first of two rooms which I rented from Hiram Daly, one of the more prosperous of the townsmen. Here I boarded and here also came my patients—white and black—whites from every section, and blacks from 'nigger town,' as the west portion of the place was called.

"The people about me were most of them coarse and rough, but they were simple and generous, and as time passed on I had about abandoned my intention of seeking distinction in wider fields and determined to settle into the place of a modest country doctor. This was rather a strange conclusion for a young man to arrive at, and I will not deny that the presence in the house of my host's beautiful young daughter, Annie, had something to do with my decision. She was a girl of seventeen or eighteen, and very far superior to her surroundings. She had a native grace and a pleasing way about her that made everybody that came under her spell her abject slave. White and black who knew her loved her, and none, I thought, more deeply and respectfully than Jube Benson, the black man of all work about the place.

"He was a fellow whom everybody trusted—an apparently steady-going, grinning sort, as we used to call him. Well, he was completely under Miss Annie's thumb, and as soon as he saw that I began to care for Annie, and anybody could see that, he transferred some of his allegiance to me and became my faithful servitor also. Never did a man have a more devoted adherent in his wooing than did I, and many a one of Annie's tasks which he volunteered to do gave her an extra hour with me. You can imagine that I liked the boy, and you need not wonder any more that, as both wooing and my practice waxed apace, I was content to give up my great ambitions and stay just where I was.

"It wasn't a very pleasant thing, then, to have an epidemic of typhoid break out in the town that kept me going so that I hardly had time for the courting that a fellow wants to carry on with his sweetheart while he is still young enough to call her his girl. I fumed, but duty was duty, and I kept to my work night and day. It was now that Jube proved how invaluable he was as coadjutor. He not only took messages to Annie, but brought sometimes little ones from her to me, and he would tell me little secret things that he had overheard her say that made me throb with joy and swear at him for repeating his mistress's conversation. But, best of all, Jube was a perfect Cerberus, and no one on earth could have been more effective in keeping away or deluding the other young fellows who visited the Dalys. He would tell me of it afterwards, chuckling softly to himself, 'An', Doctah, I say to Mistah Hemp Stevens, "'Scuse us, Mistah Stevens, but Miss Annie, she des gone out," an' den he go outer de gate lookin' moughty lonesome. When Sam Elkins come, I say, "Sh, Mistah Elkins, Miss Annie, she done tuk down," an' he say, "What, Jube, you don' reckon hit de—" Den he stop an' look skeert, an' I say, "I feared hit is, Mistah Elkins," an' sheks my haid ez solemn. He goes outer de gate lookin' lak his bes' frien' done daid, an' all de time Miss Annie behine de cu'tain ovah de po'ch des a-laffin' fit to kill.'

"Jube was a most admirable liar, but what could I do? He knew that I was a young fool of a hypocrite, and when I would rebuke him for these deceptions, he would give way and roll on the floor in an excess of delighted laughter until from very contagion I had to join him—and, well, there was no need of my preaching when there had been no beginning to his repentance and when there must ensue a continuance of his wrong-doing.

"This thing went on for over three months, and then, pouf! I was down like a shot. My patients were nearly all up, but the reaction from overwork made me an easy victim of the lurking germs. Then Jube loomed up as a nurse. He put everyone else aside, and with the doctor, a friend of mine from a neighboring town, took entire charge of me. Even Annie herself was put aside, and I was cared for as tenderly as a baby. Tom, that was my physician and friend, told me all about it afterward with tears in his eyes. Only he was a big, blunt man, and his expressions did not convey all that he meant. He told me how Jube had nursed me as if I were a sick kitten and he my mother. Of how fiercely he guarded his right to be the sole one to 'do' for me, as he called it, and how, when the crisis came, he hovered, weeping but hopeful, at my bedside until it was safely passed, when they drove him, weak and exhausted, from the room. As for me, I knew little about it at the time, and cared less. I was too busy in my fight with death. To my chimerical vision there was only a black but gentle demon that came and went, alternating with a white fairy, who would insist on coming in on her head, growing larger and larger and then dissolving. But the pathos and devotion in the story lost nothing in my blunt friend's telling.

"It was during the period of a long convalescence, however, that I came to know my humble ally as he really was, devoted to the point of abjectness. There were times when, for very shame at his goodness to me, I would beg him to go away, to do something else. He would go, but before I had time to realize that I was not being ministered to, he would be back at my side, grinning and puttering just the same. He manufactured duties for the joy of performing them. He pretended to see desires in me that I never had, because he liked to pander to them, and when I became entirely exasperated and ripped out a good round oath, he chuckled with the remark, 'Dah, now, you sholy is gittin' well. Nevah did hyeah a man anywhaih nigh Jo'dan's sho' cuss lak dat.'

"Why, I grew to love him, love him, oh, yes, I loved him as well—oh, what am I saying? All human love and gratitude are damned poor things; excuse me, gentlemen, this isn't a pleasant story. The truth is usually a nasty thing to stand.

"It was not six months after that that my friendship to Jube, which he had been at such great pains to win, was put to too severe a test.

"It was in the summertime again, and, as business was slack, I had ridden over to see my friend, Dr. Tom. I had spent a good part of the day there, and it was past four o'clock when I rode leisurely into Bradford. I was in a particularly joyous mood and no premonition of the impending catastrophe oppressed me. No sense of sorrow, present or to come, forced itself upon me, even when I saw men hurrying through the almost deserted streets. When I got within sight of my home and saw a crowd surrounding it, I was only interested sufficiently to spur my horse into a jog trot, which brought me up to the throng, when something in the sullen, settled horror in the men's faces gave me a sudden, sick thrill. They whispered a word to me, and without a thought save for Annie, the girl who had been so surely growing into my heart, I leaped from the saddle and tore my way through the people to the house.

"It was Annie, poor girl, bruised and bleeding, her face and dress torn from struggling. They were gathered round her with white faces, and oh! with what terrible patience they were trying to gain from her fluttering lips the name of her murderer. They made way for me and I knelt at her side. She was beyond my skill, and my will merged with theirs. One thought was in our minds.

"'Who?' I asked.

"Her eyes half opened. 'That black—' She fell back into my arms dead.

"We turned and looked at each other. The mother had broken down and was weeping, but the face of the father was like iron.

"'It is enough,' he said; 'Jube has disappeared.' He went to the door and said to the expectant crowd, 'She is dead.'

"I heard the angry roar without swelling up like the noise of a flood, and then I heard the sudden movement of many feet as the men separated into searching parties, and laying the dead girl back upon her couch, I took my rifle and went out to join them.

"As if by intuition the knowledge had passed among the men that Jube Benson had disappeared, and he, by common consent, was to be the object of our search. Fully a dozen of the citizens had seen him hastening toward the woods and noted his skulking air, but as he had grinned in his old good-natured way, they had, at the time, thought nothing of it. Now, however, the diabolical reason of his slyness was apparent. He had been shrewd enough to disarm suspicion, and by now was far away. Even Mrs. Daly, who was visiting with a neighbor, had seen him stepping out by a back way, and had said with a laugh, 'I reckon that black rascal's a-running off somewhere.' Oh, if she had only known!

"'To the woods! To the woods!' that was the cry; and away we went, each with the determination not to shoot, but to bring the culprit alive into town, and then to deal with him as his crime deserved.

"I cannot describe the feelings I experienced as I went out that night to beat the woods for this human tiger. My heart smoldered within me like a coal, and I went forward under the impulse of a will that was half my own, half some more malignant power's. My throat throbbed drily, but water or whisky would not have quenched my thirst. The thought has come to me since, that now I could interpret the panther's desire for blood and sympathize with it, but then I thought nothing. I simply went forward and watched, watched with burning eyes for a familiar form that I had looked for as often before with such different emotions.

"Luck or ill-luck, which you will, was with our party, and just as dawn was graying the sky, we came upon our quarry crouched in the corner of a fence. It was only half light, and we might have passed, but my eyes caught sight of him, and I raised the cry. We leveled our guns and he rose and came toward us.

"'I t'ought you wa'n't gwine see me,' he said sullenly; 'I didn't mean no harm.'

"'Harm!'

"Some of the men took the word up with oaths, others were ominously silent.

"We gathered around him like hungry beasts, and I began to see terror dawning in his eyes. He turned to me, 'I's moughty glad you's hyeah, Doc,' he said; 'you ain't gwine let 'em whup me.'

"'Whip you, you hound,' I said, 'I'm going to see you hanged,' and in the excess of my passion I struck him full on the mouth. He made a motion as if to resent the blow against such great odds, but controlled himself.

"'W'y, Doctah,' he exclaimed in the saddest voice I have ever heard, 'w'y, Doctah! I ain't stole nuffin' o' yo'n, an' I was comin' back. I only run off to see my gal, Lucy, ovah to de Centah.'

"'You lie!' I said, and my hands were busy helping others bind him upon a horse. Why did I do it? I don't know. A false education, I reckon, one false from the beginning. I saw his black face glooming there in the half light, and I could only think of him as a monster. It's tradition. At first I was told that the black man would catch me, and when I got over that, they taught me that the devil was black, and when I recovered from the sickness of that belief, here were Jube and his fellows with faces of menacing blackness. There was only one conclusion: This black man stood for all the powers of evil, the result of whose machinations had been gathering in my mind from childhood up. But this has nothing to do with what happened.

"After firing a few shots to announce our capture, we rode back into town with Jube. The ingathering parties from all directions met us as we made our way up to the house. All was very quiet and orderly. There was no doubt that it was, as the papers would have said, a gathering of the best citizens. It was a gathering of stern, determined men, bent on a terrible vengeance.

"We took Jube into the house, into the room where the corpse lay. At the sight of it he gave a scream like an animal's, and his face went the color of storm-blown water. This was enough to condemn him. We divined rather than heard his cry of 'Miss Ann, Miss Ann; oh, my God! Doc, you don't t'ink I done it?'

"Hungry hands were ready. We hurried him out into the yard. A rope was ready. A tree was at hand. Well, that part was the least of it, save that Hiram Daly stepped aside to let me be the first to pull upon the rope. It was lax at first. Then it tightened, and I felt the quivering soft weight resist my muscles. Other hands joined and Jube swung off his feet.

"No one was masked. We knew each other. Not even the culprit's face was covered, and the last I remember of him as he went into the air was a look of sad reproach that will remain with me until I meet him face to face again.

"We were tying the end of the rope to a tree, where the dead man might hang as a warning to his fellows, when a terrible cry chilled us to the marrow.

"'Cut 'im down, cut 'im down; he ain't guilty. We got de one. Cut him down, fu' Gawd's sake. Here's de man; we foun' him hidin' in de barn!'

"Jube's brother, Ben, and another Negro came rushing toward us, half dragging, half carrying a miserable-looking wretch between them. Someone cut the rope and Jube dropped lifeless to the ground.

"'Oh, my Gawd, he's daid, he's daid!' wailed the brother, but with blazing eyes he brought his captive into the center of the group, and we saw in the full light the scratched face of Tom Skinner, the worst white ruffian in town; but the face we saw was not as we were accustomed to see it, merely smeared with dirt. It was blackened to imitate a Negro's.

"God forgive me; I could not wait to try to resuscitate Jube: I knew he was already past help; so I rushed into the house and to the dead girl's side. In the excitement they had not yet washed or laid her out. Carefully, carefully, I searched underneath her broken fingernails. There was skin there. I took it out, the little curled pieces, and went with it into my office.

"There, determinedly, I examined it under a powerful glass, and read my own doom. It was the skin of a white man, and in it were embedded strands of short brown hair or beard.

"How I went out to tell the waiting crowd I do not know, for something kept crying in my ears, 'Blood guilty! Blood guilty!'

"The men went away stricken into silence and awe. The new prisoner attempted neither denial nor plea. When they were gone, I would have helped Ben carry his brother in, but he waved me away fiercely. 'You he'ped murder my brothah, you dat was his frien'; go 'way, go 'way! I'll tek him home myse'f.' I could only respect his wish, and he and his comrade took up the dead man and between them bore him up the street on which the sun was now shining full.

"I saw the few men who had not skulked indoors uncover as they passed, and I—I—stood there between the two murdered ones, while all the while something in my ears kept crying, 'Blood guilty! Blood guilty!'"

The doctor's head dropped into his hands and he sat for some time in silence, which was broken by neither of the men; then he rose, saying, "Gentlemen, that was my last lynching."

THE STONES OF THE VILLAGE

Alice Dunbar-Nelson

Victor Grabert strode down the one wide, tree-shaded street of the village, his heart throbbing with a bitterness and anger that seemed too great to bear. So often had he gone home in the same spirit, however, that it had grown nearly second nature to him—this dull, sullen resentment, flaming out now and then into almost murderous vindictiveness. Behind him there floated derisive laughs and shouts, the taunts of little brutes, boys of his own age.

He reached the tumbledown cottage at the farther end of the street and flung himself on the battered step. Grandmère Grabert sat rocking herself to and fro, crooning a bit of song brought over from the West Indies years ago; but when the boy sat silent, his head bowed in his hands, she paused in the midst of a line and regarded him with keen, piercing eyes.

"Eh, Victor?" she asked. That was all, but he understood. He raised his head and waved a hand angrily down the street towards the lighted square that marked the village center.

"Dose boy," he gulped.

Grandmère Grabert laid a sympathetic hand on his black curls, but withdrew it the next instant.

"*Bien,*" she said angrily. "Fo' what you go by dem, eh? W'y not keep to yo'self? Dey don' want you, dey don' care fo' you. H'ain' you got no sense?"

"Oh, but Grandmère," he wailed piteously, "I wan' fo' to play."

The old woman stood up in the doorway, her tall, spare form towering menacingly over him.

"You wan' fo' to play, eh? Fo' w'y? You don' need no play. Dose boy"—she swept a magnificent gesture down the street—"dey fools!"

"Eef I could play wid—" began Victor, but his grandmother caught him by the wrist, and held him as in a vise.

"Hush," she cried. "You mus' be goin' crazy," and still holding him by the wrist, she pulled him indoors.

It was a two-room house, bare and poor and miserable, but never had it seemed so meagre before to Victor as it did this night. The supper was frugal almost to the starvation point. They ate in silence, and afterwards Victor threw himself on his cot in the corner of the kitchen and closed his eyes. Grandmère Grabert thought him asleep, and closed the door noiselessly as she went into her own room. But he was awake, and his mind was like a shifting kaleidoscope of miserable incidents and heartaches. He had lived fourteen years and he could remember most of them as years of misery. He had never known a mother's love, for his mother had died, so he was told, when he was but a few months old. No one ever spoke to him of a father, and Grandmère Grabert had been all to him. She was kind, after a stern, unloving fashion, and she provided for him as best she could. He had picked up some sort of an education at the parish school. It was a good one after its way, but his life there had been such a succession of miseries, that he rebelled one day and refused to go any more.

His earliest memories were clustered about this poor little cottage. He could see himself toddling about its broken steps, playing alone with a few broken pieces of china which his fancy magnified into glorious toys. He remembered his first whipping too. Tired one day of the loneliness, which even the broken china could not mitigate, he had toddled out the side gate after a merry group of little black and yellow boys of his own age. When Grandmère Grabert, missing him from his accustomed garden corner, came to look for him, she found him sitting contentedly in the center of the group in the dusty street, all of them gravely scooping up handsful of the gravelly dirt and trickling it down their chubby bare legs. Grandmère snatched at him fiercely, and he whimpered, for he was learning for the first time what fear was.

"What you mean?" she hissed at him. "What you mean playin' in de strit wid dose niggers?" And she struck at him wildly with her open hand.

He looked up into her brown face surmounted by a wealth of curly black hair faintly streaked with gray, but he was too frightened to question.

It had been loneliness ever since. For the parents of the little black and yellow boys, resenting the insult Grandmère had offered their offspring, sternly bade them have nothing more to do with Victor. Then when he toddled after some other little boys, whose faces were white like his own, they ran away with derisive hoots of "Nigger! Nigger!" And again, he could not understand.

Hardest of all, though, was when Grandmère sternly bade him cease speaking the soft, Creole patois that they chattered together, and forced him to learn English. The result was a confused jumble which was no language at all; that when he spoke it in the streets or in the school, all the boys, white and black and yellow, hooted at him and called him "White nigger! White nigger!"

He writhed on his cot that night and lived over all the anguish of his years until hot tears scalded their way down a burning face, and he fell into a troubled sleep wherein he sobbed over some dreamland miseries.

The next morning, Grandmère eyed his heavy, swollen eyes sharply, and a momentary thrill of compassion passed over her and found expression in a new tenderness of manner towards him as she served his breakfast. She too, had thought over the matter in the night, and it bore fruit in an unexpected way.

Some few weeks after, Victor found himself timidly ringing the doorbell of a house on Hospital Street in New Orleans. His heart throbbed in painful unison to the jangle of the bell. How was he to know that old Madame Guichard, Grandmère's one friend in the city, to whom she had confided him, would be kind? He had walked from the river landing to the house, timidly inquiring the way of busy pedestrians. He was hungry and frightened. Never in all his life had he seen so many people before, and in all the busy streets there was not one eye which would light up with recognition when it met his own. Moreover, it had been a weary journey down the Red River, thence into the Mississippi, and finally here. Perhaps it had not been devoid of interest, after its fashion, but Victor did not know. He was too heartsick at leaving home.

However, Mme. Guichard was kind. She welcomed him with a volubility and overflow of tenderness that acted like balm to the boy's sore spirit. Thence they were firm friends, even confidants.

Victor must find work to do. Grandmère Grabert's idea in sending him to New Orleans was that he might "mek one man of himse'f" as she phrased it. And Victor, grown suddenly old in the sense that he had a responsibility to bear, set about his search valiantly.

It chanced one day that he saw a sign in an old bookstore on Royal Street that stated in both French and English the need of a boy. Almost before he knew it, he had entered the shop and was gasping out some choked words to the little old man who sat behind the counter.

The old man looked keenly over his glasses at the boy and rubbed his bald head reflectively. In order to do this, he had to take off an old black silk cap which he looked at with apparent regret.

"Eh, what you say?" he asked sharply, when Victor had finished.

"I—I—want a place to work," stammered the boy again.

"Eh, you do? Well, can you read?"

"Yes, sir," replied Victor.

The old man got down from his stool, came from behind the counter, and, putting his finger under the boy's chin, stared hard into his eyes. They met his own unflinchingly, though there was the suspicion of pathos and timidity in their brown depths.

"Do you know where you live, eh?"

"On Hospital Street," said Victor. It did not occur to him to give the number, and the old man did not ask.

"*Trés bien,*" grunted the bookseller, and his interest relaxed. He gave a few curt directions about the manner of work Victor was to do, and settled himself again upon his stool, poring into his dingy book with renewed ardor.

Thus began Victor's commercial life. It was an easy one. At seven, he opened the shutters of the little shop and swept and dusted. At eight, the bookseller came downstairs, and passed out to get his coffee at the restaurant across the street. At eight in the evening, the shop was closed again. That was all.

Occasionally, there came a customer, but not often, for there were only odd books and rare ones in the shop, and those who came were usually old, yellow, querulous bookworms, who nosed about for hours, and went away leaving many bank notes behind them. Sometimes there was an errand to do, and sometimes there came a customer when the proprietor was out. It was an easy matter to wait on them. He had but to point to the shelves and say, "Monsieur will be in directly," and all was settled, for those who came here to buy had plenty of leisure and did not mind waiting.

So a year went by, then two and three, and the stream of Victor's life flowed smoothly on its uneventful way. He had grown tall and thin, and often Mme. Guichard would look at him and chuckle to herself, "Ha, he is lak one beanpole, yaas, *mais*—" and there would be a world of unfinished reflection in that last word.

Victor had grown pale from much reading. Like a shadow of the old bookseller, he sat day after day poring into some dusty yellow paged book, and his mind was a queer jumble of ideas. History and philosophy and old-fashioned social economy were tangled with French romance and classic mythology and astrology and mysticism. He had made few friends, for his experience in the village had made him chary of strangers. Every week, he wrote to Grandmère Grabert and sent her part of his earnings. In his way he was happy, and if he was lonely, he had ceased to care about it, for his world was peopled with images of his own fancying.

Then all at once, the world he had built about him tumbled down, and he was left staring helplessly at its ruins. The little bookseller died one day, and his shop and its books were sold by an unscrupulous nephew who cared not for bindings or precious yellowed pages, but only for the grossly material things that money can buy. Victor ground his teeth as the auctioneer's strident voice sounded through the shop where all once had been hushed quiet, and wept as he saw some of his favorite books carried away by men and women, whom he was sure could not appreciate their value.

He dried his tears, however, the next day when a grave-faced lawyer came to the little house on Hospital Street, and informed him that he had been left a sum of money by the bookseller.

Victor sat staring at him helplessly. Money meant little to him. He never needed it, never used it. After he had sent Grandmère her sum each week, Mme. Guichard kept the rest and doled it out to him as he needed it for carfare and clothes.

"The interest of the money," continued the lawyer, clearing his throat, "is sufficient to keep you very handsomely, without touching the principal. It was my client's wish that you should enter Tulane College, and there fit yourself for your profession. He had great confidence in your ability."

"Tulane College!" cried Victor. "Why—why—why—" Then he stopped suddenly, and the hot blood mounted to his face. He glanced furtively about the room. Mme. Guichard was not near; the lawyer had seen no one but him. Then why tell him? His heart leaped wildly at the thought. Well, Grandmère would have willed it so.

The lawyer was waiting politely for him to finish his sentence.

"Why—why—I should have to study in order to enter there," finished Victor lamely.

"Exactly so," said Mr. Buckley, "and as I have, in a way, been appointed your guardian, I will see to that."

Victor found himself murmuring confused thanks and good-byes to Buckley. After he had gone, the boy sat down and gazed blankly at the wall. Then he wrote a long letter to Grandmère.

A week later, he changed boarding places at Mr. Buckley's advice, and entered a preparatory school for Tulane. And still, Mme. Guichard and Mr. Buckley had not met.

It was a handsomely furnished office on Carondelet Street in which Lawyer Grabert sat some years later. His day's work done, he was leaning back in his chair and smiling pleasantly out of the window. Within was warmth and light and cheer; without, the wind howled and gusty rains beat against the windowpane. Lawyer Grabert smiled again as he looked about at the comfort, and found himself half pitying those without who were forced to buffet the storm afoot. He rose finally and, donning his overcoat, called a cab and was driven to his rooms in the most fashionable part of the city. There he found his old-time college friend, awaiting him with some impatience.

"Thought you never were coming, old man" was his greeting.

Grabert smiled pleasantly. "Well, I was a bit tired, you know," he answered, "and I have been sitting idle for an hour or more, just relaxing, as it were."

Vannier laid his hand affectionately on the other's shoulder. "That was a mighty effort you made today," he said earnestly. "I, for one, am proud of you."

"Thank you," replied Grabert simply, and the two sat silent for a minute.

"Going to the Charles' dance tonight?" asked Vannier finally.

"I don't believe I am. I am tired and lazy."

"It will do you good. Come on."

"No, I want to read and ruminate."

"Ruminate over your good fortune of today?"

"If you will have it so, yes."

But it was not simply his good fortune of that day over which Grabert pondered. It was over the good fortune of the past fifteen years. From school to college and from college to law school he had gone, and thence into practice, and he was now accredited a successful young lawyer. His small fortune, which Mr. Buckley, with generous kindness, had invested wisely, had almost doubled, and his school career, while not of the brilliant, meteoric kind, had been pleasant and profitable. He had made friends, at first, with the boys he met, and they in turn had taken him into their homes. Now and then, the Buckleys asked him to dinner, and he was seen occasionally in their box at the opera. He was rapidly becoming a social favorite, and girls vied with each other to dance with him. No one had asked any questions, and he had volunteered no information concerning himself. Vannier, who had known him in preparatory school days, had said that he was a young country fellow with some money, no connections, and a ward of Mr. Buckley's, and somehow, contrary to the usual social custom of the South, this meagre account had passed muster. But Vannier's family had been a social arbiter for many years, and Grabert's personality was pleasing, without being aggressive, so he had passed through the portals of the social world and was in the inner circle.

One year, when he and Vannier were in Switzerland, pretending to climb impossible mountains and in reality smoking many cigars a day on hotel porches, a letter came to Grabert from the priest of his old-time town, telling him that Grandmère Grabert had been laid away in the parish churchyard. There was no more to tell. The little old hut had been sold to pay funeral expenses.

"Poor Grandmère," sighed Victor. "She did care for me after her fashion. I'll go take a look at her grave when I go back."

But he did not go, for when he returned to Louisiana, he was too busy, then he decided that it would be useless, sentimental folly. Moreover, he had no love for the old village. Its very name suggested things that made him turn and look about him nervously. He had long since eliminated Mme. Guichard from his list of acquaintances.

And yet, as he sat there in his cosy study that night, and smiled as he went over in his mind triumph after triumph which he had made since the old bookstore days in Royal Street, he was conscious of a subtle undercurrent of annoyance; a sort of mental reservation that placed itself on every pleasant memory.

"I wonder what's the matter with me?" he asked himself as he rose and paced the floor impatiently. Then he tried to recall his other triumph, the one of the day. The case of Tate vs. Tate, a famous will contest, had been dragging through the courts for seven years and his speech had decided it that day. He could hear the applause of the courtroom as he sat down, but it rang hollow in his ears, for he remembered another scene. The day before he had been in another court, and found himself interested in the prisoner before the bar. The offense was a slight one, a mere technicality. Grabert was conscious of something pleasant in the man's face; a scrupulous neatness in his dress, an unostentatious conforming to the prevailing style. The Recorder, however, was short and brusque.

"Wilson—Wilson—" he growled. "Oh, yes, I know you, always kicking up some sort of a row about theatre seats and cars. Hum-um: What do you mean by coming before me with a flower in your buttonhole?"

The prisoner looked down indifferently at the bud on his coat, and made no reply.

"Hey?" growled the Recorder. "You niggers are putting yourselves up too much for me."

At the forbidden word, the blood rushed to Grabert's face, and he started from his seat angrily. The next instant, he had recovered himself and buried his face in a paper. After Wilson had paid his fine, Grabert looked at him furtively as he passed out. His face was perfectly impassive, but his eyes flashed defiantly. The lawyer was tingling with rage and indignation, although the affront had not been given him.

"If Recorder Grant had any reason to think that I was in any way like Wilson, I would stand no better show," he mused bitterly.

However, as he thought it over tonight, he decided that he was a sentimental fool. "What have I to do with them?" he asked himself. "I must be careful."

The next week, he discharged the man who cared for his office. He was a Negro, and Grabert had no fault to find with him generally, but he found himself with a growing sympathy towards the man, and since the episode in the courtroom, he was morbidly nervous lest something in his manner betray him. Thereafter, a round-eyed Irish boy cared for his rooms.

The Vanniers were wont to smile indulgently at his every move. Elise Vannier, particularly, was more than interested in his work. He had a way of dropping in of evenings and talking over his cases and speeches with her in a cosy corner of the library. She had a gracious sympathetic manner that was soothing and a cheery fund of repartee to whet her conversation. Victor found himself drifting into sentimental bits of talk now and then. He found himself carrying around in his pocketbook a faded rose which she had once worn, and when he laughed at it one day and started to throw it in the wastebasket, he suddenly kissed it instead, and replaced it in the pocketbook. That Elise was not indifferent to him he could easily see. She had not learned yet how to veil her eyes and mask her face under a cool assumption of superiority. She would give him her hand when they met with a girlish impulsiveness, and her color came and went under his gaze. Sometimes, when he held her hand a bit longer than necessary, he could feel it flutter in his own, and she would sigh a quick little gasp that made his heart leap and choked his utterance.

They were tucked away in their usual cosy corner one evening, and the conversation had drifted to the problem of where they would spend the summer.

"Papa wants to go to the country-house," pouted Elise, "and Mama and I don't want to go. It isn't fair, of course, because when we go so far away, Papa can be with us only for a few weeks when he can get away from his office, while if we go to the country place, he can run up every few days. But it is so dull there, don't you think so?"

Victor recalled some pleasant vacation days at the plantation home and laughed. "Not if you are there."

"Yes, but you see, I can't take myself for a companion. Now if you'll promise to come up sometimes, it will be better."

"If I may, I shall be delighted to come."

Elise laughed intimately. "If you 'may'" she replied, "as if such a word had to enter into our plans. Oh, but Victor, haven't you some sort of plantation somewhere? It seems to me that I heard Steven years ago speak of your home in the country, and I wondered sometimes that you never spoke of it, or ever mentioned having visited it."

The girl's artless words were bringing cold sweat to Victor's brow, his tongue felt heavy and useless, but he managed to answer quietly, "I have no home in the country."

"Well, didn't you ever own one, or your family?"

"It was old quite a good many years ago," he replied, and a vision of the little old hut with its tumbledown steps and weed-grown garden came into his mind.

"Where was it?" pursued Elise innocently.

"Oh, away up in St. Landry parish, too far away from civilization to mention." He tried to laugh, but it was a hollow, forced attempt that rang false. But Elise was too absorbed in her own thoughts of the summer to notice.

"And you haven't a relative living?" she continued.

"Not one."

"How strange. Why it seems to me if I did not have half a hundred cousins and uncles and aunts that I should feel somehow out of touch with the world."

He did not reply, and she chattered away on another topic.

When he was alone in his room that night, he paced the floor again, chewing wildly at a cigar that he had forgotten to light.

"What did she mean? What did she mean?" he asked himself over and over. Could she have heard or suspected anything that she was trying to find out about? Could any action, any unguarded expression of his have set the family thinking? But he soon dismissed the thought as unworthy of him. Elise was too frank and transparent a girl to stoop to subterfuge. If she wished to know anything, she was wont to ask out at once, and if she had once thought anyone was sailing under false colors, she would say so frankly, and dismiss them from her presence.

Well, he must be prepared to answer questions if he were going to marry her. The family would want to know all about him, and Elise herself would be curious for more than her brother, Steven Vannier's meagre account. But was he going to marry Elise? That was the question.

He sat down and buried his head in his hands. Would it be right for him to take a wife, especially such a woman as Elise, and from such a family as the Vanniers? Would it be fair? Would it be just? If they knew and were willing, it would be different. But they did not know, and they would not consent if they did. In fancy, he saw the dainty girl, whom he loved, shrinking from him as he told her of Grandmère Grabert and the village boys. This last thought made him set his teeth hard, and the hot blood rushed to his face.

Well, why not, after all, why not? What was the difference between him and the hosts of other suitors who hovered about Elise? They had money; so had he. They had education, polite training, culture, social position; so had he. But they had family traditions, and he had none. Most of them could point to a long line of family portraits with justifiable pride; while if he had had a picture of Grandmère Grabert, he would have destroyed it fearfully, lest it fall into the hands of some too curious person. This was the subtle barrier that separated them. He recalled with a sting how often he had had to sit silent and constrained when the conversation turned to ancestors and family traditions. He might be one with his companions and friends in everything but this. He must ever be on the outside, hovering at the gates, as it were. Into the inner life of his social world, he might never enter. The charming impoliteness of an intercourse begun by their fathers and grandfathers was not for him. There must always be a certain formality with him, even though they were his most intimate friends. He had not fifty cousins; therefore, as Elise phrased it, he was "out of touch with the world."

"If ever I have a son or a daughter," he found himself saying unconsciously, "I would try to save him from this."

Then he laughed bitterly as he realized the irony of the thought. Well, anyway, Elise loved him. There was a sweet consolation in that. He had but to look into her frank eyes and read her soul. Perhaps she wondered why he had not spoken. Should he speak? There he was back at the old question again.

"According to the standard of the world," he mused reflectively, "my blood is tainted in two ways. Who knows it? No one but myself, and I shall not tell. Otherwise, I am quite as good as the rest, and Elise loves me."

But even this thought failed of its sweetness in a moment. Elise loved him because she did not know. He found a sickening anger and disgust rising in himself at a people whose prejudices made him live a life of deception. He would cater to their traditions no longer; he would be honest. Then he found himself shrinking from the alternative with a dread that made him wonder. It was the old problem of his life in the village; and the boys, both white and black and yellow, stood as before, with stones in their hands to hurl at him.

He went to bed worn out with the struggle, but still with no definite idea what to do. Sleep was impossible. He rolled and tossed miserably, and cursed the fate that had thrown him in such a position. He had never thought very seriously over the subject before. He had rather drifted with the tide and accepted what came to him as a sort of recompense the world owed him for his unhappy childhood. He had known fear, yes, and qualms now and then, and a hot resentment occasionally when the outsideness of his situation was inborn to him; but that was all. Elise had awakened a disagreeable conscientiousness within him, which he decided was as unpleasant as it was unnecessary.

He could not sleep, so he arose and, dressing, walked out and stood on the banquette. The low hum of the city came to him like the droning of some sleepy insect, and ever and anon the quick flash and fire of the gashouses, like a huge winking fiery eye, lit up the south of the city. It was inexpressibly soothing to Victor—the great unknowing city, teeming with life and with lives whose sadness mocked his own teacup tempest. He smiled and shook himself as a dog shakes off the water from his coat.

"I think a walk will help me out," he said absently, and presently he was striding down St. Charles Avenue, around Lee Circle and down to Canal Street, where the lights and glare absorbed him for a while. He walked out the wide boulevard towards Claiborne Street, hardly thinking, hardly realizing that he was walking. When he was thoroughly worn out, he retraced his steps and dropped wearily into a restaurant near Bourbon Street.

"Hullo!" said a familiar voice from a table as he entered. Victor turned and recognized Frank Ward, a little oculist, whose office was in the same building as his own.

"Another night owl besides myself," laughed Ward, making room for him at his table. "Can't you sleep too, old fellow?"

"Not very well," said Victor, taking the proffered seat. "I believe I'm getting nerves. Think I need toning up."

"Well, you'd have been toned up if you had been in here a few minutes ago. Why—why—" And Ward went off into peals of laughter at the memory of the scene.

"What was it?" asked Victor.

"Why—a fellow came in here, nice sort of fellow, apparently, and wanted to have supper. Well, would you believe it, when they wouldn't serve him, he wanted to fight everything in sight. It was positively exciting for a time."

"Why wouldn't the waiter serve him?" Victor tried to make his tone indifferent, but he felt the quaver in his voice.

"Why? Why, he was a darky, you know."

"Well, what of it?" demanded Grabert fiercely. "Wasn't he quiet, well-dressed, polite? Didn't he have money?"

"My dear fellow," began Ward mockingly. "Upon my word, I believe you are losing your mind. You do need toning up or something. Would you—could you—?"

"Oh, pshaw," broke in Grabert. "I—I—believe I am losing my mind. Really, Ward, I need something to make me sleep. My head aches."

Ward was at once all sympathy and advice, and chiding to the waiter for his slowness in filling their order. Victor toyed with his food, and made an excuse to leave the restaurant as soon as he could decently.

"Good heavens," he said when he was alone. "What will I do next?" His outburst of indignation at Ward's narrative had come from his lips almost before he knew it, and he was frightened, frightened at his own unguardedness. He did not know what had come over him.

"I must be careful, I must be careful," he muttered to himself. "I must go to the other extreme, if necessary." He was pacing his rooms again, and, suddenly, he faced the mirror.

"You wouldn't fare any better than the rest, if they knew," he told the reflection. "You poor wretch, what are you?"

When he thought of Elise, he smiled. He loved her, but he hated the traditions which she represented. He was conscious of a blind fury which bade him wreak vengeance on those traditions, and of a cowardly fear which cried out to him to retain his position in the world's and Elise's eyes at any cost.

Mrs. Grabert was delighted to have visiting her old school friend from Virginia, and the two spent hours laughing over their girlish escapades, and comparing notes about their little ones. Each was confident that her darling had said the cutest things, and their polite deference to each other's opinions on the matter was a sham through which each saw without resentment.

"But, Elise," remonstrated Mrs. Allen, "I think it so strange you don't have a mammy for Baby Vannier. He would be so much better cared for than by that harum-scarum young white girl you have."

"I think so too, Adelaide," sighed Mrs. Grabert. "It seems strange for me not to have a darky maid about, but Victor can't bear them. I cried and cried for my old mammy, but he was stern. He doesn't like darkies, you know, and he says old mammies just frighten children, and ruin their childhood. I don't see how he could say that, do you?" She looked wistfully to Mrs. Allen for sympathy.

"I don't know," mused that lady. "We were all looked after by our mammies, and I think they are the best kind of nurses."

"And Victor won't have any kind of darky servant either here or at the office. He says they're shiftless and worthless and generally no-account. Of course, he knows, he's had lots of experience with them in his business."

Mrs. Allen folded her hands behind her head and stared hard at the ceiling. "Oh, well, men don't know everything," she said, "and Victor may come around to our way of thinking after all."

It was late that evening when the lawyer came in for dinner. His eyes had acquired a habit of veiling themselves under their lashes, as if they were constantly concealing something which they feared might be wrenched from them by a stare. He was nervous and restless, with a habit of glancing about him furtively, and a twitching compressing of his lips when he had finished a sentence, which somehow reminded you of a kindhearted judge, who is forced to give a death sentence.

Elise met him at the door as was her wont, and she knew from the first glance into his eyes that something had disturbed him more than usual that day, but she forbore asking questions, for she knew he would tell her when the time had come.

They were in their room that night when the rest of the household lay in slumber. He sat for a long while gazing at the open fire, then he passed his hand over his forehead wearily.

"I have had a rather unpleasant experience today," he began.

"Yes."

"Pavageau, again."

His wife was brushing her hair before the mirror. At the name she turned hastily with the brush in her uplifted hand.

"I can't understand, Victor, why you must have dealings with that man. He is constantly irritating you. I simply wouldn't associate with him."

"I don't," and he laughed at her feminine argument. "It isn't a question of association, cherie, it's a purely business and unsocial relation, if relation it may be called, that throws us together."

She threw down the brush petulantly, and came to his side. "Victor," she began hesitatingly, her arms about his neck, her face close to his, "won't you—won't you give up politics for me? It was ever so much nicer when you were just a lawyer and wanted only to be the best lawyer in the state, without all this worry about corruption and votes and such things. You've changed, oh, Victor, you've changed so. Baby and I won't know you after a while."

He put her gently on his knee. "You mustn't blame the poor politics, darling. Don't you think, perhaps, it's the inevitable hardening and embittering that must come to us all as we grow older?"

"No, I don't," she replied emphatically. "Why do you go into this struggle, anyhow? You have nothing to gain but an empty honor. It won't bring you more money, or make you more loved or respected. Why must you be mixed up with such—such—awful people?"

"I don't know," he said wearily.

And in truth, he did not know. He had gone on after his marriage with Elise making one success after another. It seemed that a beneficent Providence had singled him out as the one man in the state upon whom to heap the most lavish attentions. He was popular after the fashion, of those who are high in the esteem of the world; and this very fact made him tremble the more, for he feared that should some disclosure come, he could not stand the shock of public opinion that must overwhelm him.

"What disclosure?" he would say impatiently when such a thought would come to him. "Where could it come from, and then, what is there to disclose?"

Thus he would deceive himself for as much as a month at a time.

He was surprised to find awaiting him in his office one day the man Wilson, whom he remembered in the courtroom before Recorder Grant. He was surprised and annoyed. Why had the man come to his office? Had he seen the telltale flush on his face that day?

But it was soon evident that Wilson did not even remember having seen him before.

"I came to see if I could retain you in a case of mine," he began, after the usual formalities of greeting were over.

"I am afraid, my good man," said Grabert brusquely, "that you have mistaken the office."

Wilson's face flushed at the appellation, but he went on bravely. "I have not mistaken the office. I know you are the best civil lawyer in the city, and I want your services."

"An impossible thing."

"Why? Are you too busy? My case is a simple thing, a mere point in law, but I want the best authority and the best opinion brought to bear on it."

"I could not give you any help—and—I fear, we—do not understand each other—I do not wish to." He turned to his desk abruptly.

"What could he have meant by coming to me?" he questioned himself fearfully, as Wilson left the office. "Do I look like a man likely to take up his impossible contentions?"

He did not look like it, nor was he. When it came to a question involving the Negro, Victor Grabert was noted for his stern, unrelenting attitude; it was simply impossible to convince him that there was anything but sheerest incapacity in that race. For him, no good could come out of this Nazareth. He was liked and respected by men of his political belief, because, even when he was a candidate for a judgeship, neither money nor the possible chance of a deluge of votes from the First and Fourth Wards could cause him to swerve one hair's breadth from his opinion of the black inhabitants of those wards.

Pavageau, however, was his *bête noire*. Pavageau was a lawyer, a coolheaded, calculating man with steely eyes set in a grim brown face. They had first met in the courtroom in a case which involved the question whether a man may set aside the will of his father, who, disregarding the legal offspring of another race than himself, chooses to leave his property to educational institutions which would not have granted admission to that son. Pavageau represented the son. He lost, of course. The judge, the jury, the people and Grabert were against him; but he fought his fight with a grim determination which commanded Victor's admiration and respect.

"Fools," he said between his teeth to himself, when they were crowding about him with congratulations. "Fools, can't they see who is the abler man of the two?"

He wanted to go up to Pavageau and give him his hand; to tell him that he was proud of him and that he had really won the case, but public opinion was against him; but he dared not. Another one of his colleagues might; but he was afraid. Pavageau and the world might misunderstand, or would it be understanding?

Thereafter they met often. Either by some freak of nature, or because there was a shrewd sense of the possibilities in his position, Pavageau was of the same political side of the fence as Grabert. Secretly, Grabert admired the man; he respected him; he liked him; and because of this Grabert was always ready with sneer and invective for him. He fought him bitterly when there was no occasion for fighting, and Pavageau became his enemy, and his name a very synonym of horror to Elise, who learned to trace her husband's fits of moodiness and depression to the one source.

Meanwhile, Vannier Grabert was growing up, a handsome lad, with his father's and mother's physical beauty, and a strength and force of character that belonged to neither. In him, Grabert saw the reparation of all his childhood's wrongs and sufferings. The boy realized all his own longings. He had family traditions, and a social position which was his from birth and an inalienable right to hold up his head without an unknown fear gripping at his heart. Grabert felt that he could forgive all—the village boys of long ago, and the imaginary village boys of today— when he looked at his son. He had bought and paid for Vannier's freedom and happiness. The coins may have been each a drop of his heart's blood, but he had reckoned the cost before he had given it.

It was a source of great pride for Grabert, now that he was a judge, to take the boy to court with him, and one Saturday morning when he was starting out, Vannier asked if he might go.

"There is nothing that would interest you today, *mon fils*," he said tenderly, "but you may go."

In fact, there was nothing interesting that day; merely a troublesome old woman, who instead of taking her fair-skinned grandchild out of the school where it had been found it did not belong, had preferred to bring the matter to court. She was represented by Pavageau. Of course, there was not the ghost of a show for her. Pavageau had told her that. The law was very explicit about the matter. The only question lay in proving the child's affinity to the Negro race, which was not such a difficult matter to do, so the case was quickly settled, since the child's grandmother accompanied him. The judge, however, was irritated. It was a hot day and he was provoked that such a trivial matter should have taken up his time. He lost his temper as he looked at his watch.

"I don't see why these people want to force their children into the white schools," he declared. "There should be a rigid inspection to prevent it, and all the suspected children put out and made to go where they belong."

Pavageau, too, was irritated that day. He looked up from some papers which he was folding, and his gaze met Grabert's with a keen, cold, penetrating flash.

"Perhaps Your Honor would like to set the example by taking your son from the schools."

There was an instant silence in the courtroom, a hush intense and eager. Every eye turned upon the judge, who sat still, a figure carven in stone with livid face and fear-stricken eyes. After the first flash of his eyes, Pavageau had gone on cooly sorting the papers.

The courtroom waited, waited, for the judge to rise and thunder forth a fine against the daring Negro lawyer for contempt. A minute passed, which seemed like an hour. Why did not Grabert speak? Pavageau's implied accusation was too absurd for denial; but he should be punished. Was His Honor ill, or did he merely hold the man in too much contempt to notice him or his remark?

Finally Grabert spoke; he moistened his lips, for they were dry and parched, and his voice was weak and sounded far away in his own ears. "My son—does—not—attend the public schools."

Someone in the rear of the room laughed, and the atmosphere lightened at once. Plainly Pavageau was an idiot, and His Honor too far above him; too much of a gentleman to notice him. Grabert continued calmly: "The gentleman"—there was an unmistakable sneer in this word, habit if nothing else, and not even fear could restrain him—"the gentleman doubtless intended a little pleasantry, but I shall have to fine him for contempt of court."

"As you will," replied Pavageau, and he flashed another look at Grabert. It was a look of insolent triumph and derision. His Honor's eyes dropped beneath it.

"What did that man mean, Father, by saying you should take me out of school?" asked Vannier on his way home.

"He was provoked, my son, because he had lost his case, and when a man is provoked he is likely to say silly things. By the way, Vannier, I hope you won't say anything to your mother about the incident. It would only annoy her."

For the public, the incident was forgotten as soon as it had closed, but for Grabert, it was indelibly stamped on his memory; a scene that shrieked in his mind and stood out before him at every footstep he took. Again and again as he tossed on a sleepless bed did he see the cold flash of Pavageau's eyes, and hear his quiet accusation. How did he know? Where had he gotten his information? For he spoke, not as one who makes a random shot in anger, but as one who knows, who has known a long while, and who is betrayed by irritation into playing his trump card too early in the game.

He passed a wretched week, wherein it seemed that his every footstep was dogged, his every gesture watched and recorded. He fancied that Elise, even, was suspecting him. When he took his judicial seat each morning, it seemed that every eye in the courtroom was fastened upon him in derision; everyone who spoke, it seemed, was but biding his time to shout the old village street refrain which had haunted him all his life, "Nigger!—Nigger!—White nigger!"

Finally, he could stand it no longer; and with leaden feet and furtive glances to the right and left for fear he might be seen, he went up a flight of dusty stairs in an Exchange Alley building, which led to Pavageau's office.

The latter was frankly surprised to see him. He made a polite attempt to conceal it, however. It was the first time in his legal life that Grabert had ever sought out a Negro; the first time that he had ever voluntarily opened conversation with one.

He mopped his forehead nervously as he took the chair Pavageau offered him; he stared about the room for an instant; then with a sudden, almost brutal directness, he turned on the lawyer.

"See here, what did you mean by that remark you made in court the other day?"

"I meant just what I said" was the cool reply. Grabert paused.

"Why did you say it?" he asked slowly.

"Because I was a fool. I should have kept my mouth shut until another time, should I not?"

"Pavageau," said Grabert softly, "let's not fence. Where did you get your information?"

Pavageau paused for an instant. He put his fingertips together and closed his eyes as one who meditates. Then he said with provoking calmness, "You seem anxious—well, I don't mind letting you know. It doesn't really matter."

"Yes, yes," broke in Grabert impatiently.

"Did you ever hear of a Mme. Guichard of Hospital Street?" The sweat broke out on the judge's brow as he replied weakly, "Yes."

"Well, I am her nephew."

"And she?"

"Is dead. She told me about you once—with pride, let me say. No one else knows."

Grabert sat dazed. He had forgotten about Mme. Guichard. She had never entered into his calculations at all. Pavageau turned to his desk with a sigh, as if he wished the interview were ended. Grabert rose.

"If—if—this were known—to—to—my—my wife," he said thickly, "it would hurt her very much."

His head was swimming. He had had to appeal to this man, and to appeal to his wife's name. His wife, whose name he scarcely spoke to men whom he considered his social equals.

Pavageau looked up quickly. "It happens that I often have cases in your court," he spoke deliberately. "I am willing, if I lose fairly, to give up; but I do not like to have a decision made against me because my opponent is of a different complexion from mine, or because the decision against me would please a certain class of people. I only ask what I have never had from you—fair play."

"I understand," said Grabert.

He admired Pavageau more than ever as he went out of his office, yet this admiration was tempered by the knowledge that this man was the only person in the whole world who possessed positive knowledge of his secret. He groveled in a self-abasement at his position; and yet he could not but feel a certain relief that the vague, formless fear which had hitherto dogged his life and haunted it had taken on a definite shape. He knew where it was now; he could lay his hands on it, and fight it.

But with what weapons? There were none offered him save a substantial backing down from his position on certain questions; the position that had been his for so long that he was almost known by it. For in the quiet deliberate sentence of Pavageau's, he read that he must cease all the oppression, all the little injustices which he had offered Pavageau's clientele. He must act now as his convictions and secret sympathies and affiliations had bidden him act, not as prudence and fear and cowardice had made him act.

Then what would be the result? he asked himself. Would not the suspicions of the people be aroused by this sudden change in his manner? Would not they begin to question and to wonder? Would not someone remember Pavageau's remark that morning and, putting two and two together, start some rumor flying? His heart sickened again at the thought.

There was a banquet that night. It was in his honor, and he was to speak, and the thought was distasteful to him beyond measure. He knew how it all would be. He would be hailed with shouts and acclamations, as the finest flower of civilization. He would be listened to deferentially, and younger men would go away holding him in their hearts as a truly worthy model. When all the while—

He threw back his head and laughed. Oh, what a glorious revenge he had on those little white village boys! How he had made a race atone for Wilson's insult in the courtroom; for the man in the restaurant at whom Ward had laughed so uproariously; for all the affronts seen and unseen given these people of his own whom he had denied. He had taken a diploma from their most exclusive college; he had broken down the barriers of their social world; he had taken the highest possible position among them and, aping their own ways, had shown them that he, too, could despise this inferior race they despised. Nay, he had taken for his wife the best woman among them all, and she had borne him a son. Ha, ha! What a joke on them all!

And he had not forgotten the black and yellow boys either. They had stoned him too, and he had lived to spurn them; to look down upon them, and to crush them at every possible turn from his seat on the bench. Truly, his life had not been wasted.

He had lived forty-nine years now, and the zenith of his power was not yet reached. There was much more to do, much more, and he was going to do it. He owed it to Elise and the boy. For their sake he must go on and on and keep his tongue still, and truckle to Pavageau and suffer alone. Someday, perhaps, he would have a grandson, who would point with pride to "My grandfather, the famous Judge Grabert!" Ah, that in itself, was a reward. To have founded a dynasty; to bequeath to others that which he had never possessed himself, and the lack of which had made his life a misery.

It was a banquet with a political significance; one that meant a virtual triumph for Judge Grabert in the next contest for the District Judge. He smiled around at the eager faces which were turned up to his as he arose to speak. The tumult of applause which had greeted his rising had died away, and an expectant hush fell on the room.

"What a sensation I could make now," he thought. He had but to open his mouth and cry out, "Fools! Fools! I whom you are honoring, I am one of the despised ones. Yes, I'm a nigger—do you hear, a nigger!" What a temptation it was to end the whole miserable farce. If he were alone in the world, if it were not for Elise and the boy, he would, just to see their horror and wonder. How they would shrink from him! But what could they do? They could take away his office; but his wealth, and his former successes, and his learning, they could not touch. Well, he must speak, and he must remember Elise and the boy.

Every eye was fastened on him in eager expectancy. Judge Grabert's speech was expected to outline the policy of their faction in the coming campaign. He turned to the chairman at the head of the table.

"Mr. Chairman," he began, and paused again. How peculiar it was that in the place of the chairman there sat Grandmère Grabert, as she had been wont to sit on the steps of the tumbledown cottage in the village. She was looking at him sternly and bidding him give an account of his life since she had kissed him good-bye ere he had sailed down the river to New Orleans. He was surprised, and not a little annoyed. He had expected to address the chairman, not Grandmère Grabert. He cleared his throat and frowned.

"Mr. Chairman," he said again. Well, what was the use of addressing her that way? She would not understand him. He would call her Grandmère, of course. Were they not alone again on the cottage steps at twilight with the cries of the little brutish boys ringing derisively from the distant village square?

"Grandmère," he said softly, "you don't understand—" And then he was sitting down in his seat pointing one finger angrily at her because the other words would not come. They stuck in his throat, and he choked and beat the air with his hands. When the men crowded around him with water and hastily improvised fans, he fought them away wildly and desperately with furious curses that came from his blackened lips. For were they not all boys with stones to pelt him because he wanted to play with them? He would run away to Grandmère who would soothe him and comfort him. So he arose and, stumbling, shrieking and beating them back from him, ran the length of the hall, and fell across the threshold of the door.

The secret died with him, for Pavageau's lips were ever sealed.

I LOOK OUT FOR ED WOLFE

Stanley Elkin

He was an orphan, and, to himself, he seemed like one, looked like one. His orphan's features were as true of himself as are their pale, pinched faces to the blind. At twenty-seven he was a neat, thin young man in white shirts and light suits with lintless pockets. Something about him suggested the ruthless isolation, the hard self-sufficiency of the orphaned, the peculiar dignity of men seen eating alone in restaurants on national holidays. Yet it was this perhaps which shamed him chiefly, for there was a suggestion, too, that his impregnability was a myth, a smell not of the furnished room which he did not inhabit, but of the three-room apartment on a good street which he did. The very excellence of his taste, conditioned by need and lack, lent to him the odd, maidenly primness of the lonely.

He saved the photographs of strangers and imprisoned them behind clear plastic windows in his wallet. In the sound of his own voice he detected the accent of the night school and the correspondence course, and nothing of the fat, sunny ring of the word's casually afternooned. He strove against himself, a supererogatory enemy, and sought by a kind of helpless abrasion, as one rubs wood, the gleaming self beneath. An orphan's thinness, he thought, was no accident.

Returning from lunch, he entered the office building where he worked. It was an old building, squat and gargoyled, brightly patched where sandblasters had once worked and then, for some reason, quit before they had finished. He entered the lobby, which smelled always of disinfectant, and walked past the wide, dirty glass of the cigarette-and-candy counter to the single elevator, as thickly barred as a cell.

The building was an outlaw. Low rents and a downtown address and the landlord's indifference had brought together from the peripheries of business and professionalism a strange band of entrepreneurs and visionaries, men desperately but imaginatively failing: an eye doctor who corrected vision by massage; a radio evangelist; a black-belt judo champion; a self-help organization for crippled veterans; dealers in pornographic books, in paper flowers, in fireworks, in plastic jewelry, in the artificial, in the artfully made, in the imitated, in the copied, in the stolen, the unreal, the perversion, the plastic, the *schlak*.

On the third floor the elevator opened and the young man, Ed Wolfe, stepped out.

He passed the Association for the Indians, passed Plasti-Pens, passed *Coffin & Tombstone*, passed Soldier Toys, passed Prayer-a-Day. He walked by the open door of C. Morris Brut, Chiropractor, and saw him, alone, standing at a mad attention, framed in the arching golden nimbus of his inverted name on the window, squeezing handballs.

He looked quickly away, but Dr. Brut saw him and came toward him, putting the handballs in his shirt pocket, where they bulged awkwardly. He held him by the elbow. Ed Wolfe looked down at the yellowing tile, infinitely diamonded, chipped, the floor of a public toilet, and saw Dr. Brut's dusty shoes. He stared sadly at the jagged, broken glass of the mail chute.

"Ed Wolfe, take care of yourself," Dr. Brut said.

"Right."

"Regard your position in life. A tall man like yourself looks terrible when he slumps. Don't be a *schlump*. It's no good for the organs."

"I'll watch it."

"When the organs get out of line the man begins to die."

"I know."

"You say so. How many guys make promises. Brains in the brainpan. Balls in the strap. The bastards downtown." Dr. Brut meant doctors in hospitals, in clinics, on boards, non-orphans with M.D. degrees and special license plates and respectable patients who had Blue Cross, charts, died in clean hospital rooms. They were the bastards downtown, his personal New Deal, his neighborhood Wall Street banker. A disease cartel. "They won't tell you. The white bread kills you. The cigarettes. The whiskey. The sneakers. The high heels. They won't tell you. Me, *I'll* tell you."

"I appreciate it."

"Wise guy. Punk. I'm a friend. I give a father's advice."

"I'm an orphan."

"I'll adopt you."

"I'm late to work."

"We'll open a clinic. 'C. Morris Brut and Adopted Son.'"

"It's something to think about."

"Poetry," Dr. Brut said and walked back to his office, his posture stiff, awkward, a man in a million who knew how to hold himself.

Ed Wolfe went on to his own office. The sad-faced telephone girl was saying, "Cornucopia Finance Corporation." She pulled the wire out of the board and slipped her headset around her neck, where it hung like a delicate horse collar. "Mr. La Meck wants to see you. But don't go in yet. He's talking to somebody."

He went toward his desk at one end of the big main office. Standing, fists on the desk, he turned to the girl. "What happened to my call cards?"

"Mr. La Meck took them," she said.

"Give me the carbons," Ed Wolfe said. "I've got to make some calls."

The girl looked embarrassed. Her face went through a weird change, the sadness taking on an impossible burden of shame, so that she seemed massively tragic, like a hit-and-run driver. "I'll get them," she said, moving out of the chair heavily. Ed Wolfe thought of Dr. Brut.

He took the carbons and fanned them out on the desk, then picked one in an intense, random gesture like someone drawing a number on a public stage. He dialed rapidly.

As the phone buzzed brokenly in his ear he felt the old excitement. Someone at the other end greeted him sleepily.

"Mr. Flay? This is Ed Wolfe at Cornucopia Finance." (Can you cope, can you cope? he hummed to himself.)

"Who?"

"Ed Wolfe. I've got an unpleasant duty," he began pleasantly. "You've skipped two payments."

"I didn't skip nothing. I called the girl. She said it was okay."

"That was three months ago. She meant it was all right to miss a few days. Listen, Mr. Flay, we've got that call recorded, too. Nothing gets by."

"I'm a little short."

"Grow."

"I couldn't help it," the man said. Ed Wolfe didn't like the cringing tone. Petulance and anger he could meet with his own petulance, his own anger. But guilt would have to be met with his own guilt, and that, here, was irrelevant.

"Don't con me, Flay. You're a troublemaker. What are you, Flay, a Polish person? Flay isn't a Polish name, but your address . . ."

"What's that?"

"What are you? Are you Polish?"

"What's that to you? What difference does it make?" That's more like it, Ed Wolfe thought warmly.

"That's what you are, Flay. You're a Pole. It's guys like you who give your race a bad name. Half our bugouts are Polish persons."

"Listen. You can't . . ."

He began to shout. "*You* listen. You wanted the car. The refrigerator. The chintzy furniture. The sectional you saw in the funny papers. And we paid for it, right?"

"Listen. The money I owe is one thing, the way . . ."

"We paid for it, right?"

"That doesn't . . ."

"Right? *Right?*"

"Yes, you . . ."

"*Okay*. You're in trouble, Warsaw. You're in terrible trouble. It means a lien. A judgment. We've got lawyers. You've got nothing. We'll pull the furniture the hell out of there. The car. Everything."

"Wait," he said. "Listen, my brother-in-law . . ."

Ed Wolfe broke in sharply. "He's got money?"

"I don't know. A little. I don't know."

"Get it. If you're short, grow. This is America."

"I don't know if he'll let me have it."

"Steal it. This is America. Good-by."

"Wait a minute. Please."

"That's it. There are other Polish persons on my list. This time it was just a friendly warning. Cornucopia wants its money. Cornucopia. Can you cope? Can you cope? Just a friendly warning, Polish-American. Next time we come with the lawyers and the machine guns. Am I making myself clear?"

"I'll try to get it to you."

Ed Wolfe hung up. He pulled a handkerchief from his drawer and wiped his face. His chest was heaving. He took another call card. The girl came by and stood beside his desk. "Mr. La Meck can see you now," she mourned.

"Later. I'm calling." The number was already ringing.

"Please, Mr. Wolfe."

"Later, I said. In a minute." The girl went away. "Hello. Let me speak with your husband, madam. I am Ed Wolfe of Cornucopia Finance. He can't cope. Your husband can't cope."

The woman made an excuse. "Put him on, goddamn it. We know he's out of work. Nothing gets by. Nothing."

There was a hand on the receiver beside his own, the wide male fingers pink and vaguely perfumed, the nails manicured. For a moment he struggled with it fitfully, as though the hand itself were all he had to contend with. Then he recognized La Meck and let go. La Meck pulled the phone quickly toward his mouth and spoke softly into it, words of apology, some ingenious excuse Ed Wolfe couldn't hear. He put the receiver down beside the phone itself and Ed Wolfe picked it up and returned it to its cradle.

"Ed," La Meck said, "come into the office with me."

Ed Wolfe followed La Meck, his eyes on La Meck's behind.

La Meck stopped at his office door. Looking around, he shook his head sadly, and Ed Wolfe nodded in agreement. La Meck let him enter first. While La Meck stood, Ed Wolfe could discern a kind of sadness in his slouch, but once the man was seated behind his desk he seemed restored, once again certain of the world's soundness. "All right," La Meck began, "I won't lie to you."

Lie to me. Lie to me, Ed Wolfe prayed silently.

"You're in here for me to fire you. You're not being laid off. I'm not going to tell you that I think you'd be happier some place else, that the collection business isn't your game, that profits don't justify our keeping you around. Profits are terrific, and if collection isn't your game it's because you haven't got a game. As far as your being happier some place else, that's bullshit. You're not supposed to be happy. It isn't in the cards for you. You're a fall guy type, God bless you, and though I like you personally I've got no use for you in my office."

I'd like to get you on the other end of a telephone some day, Ed Wolfe thought miserably.

"Don't ask me for a reference," La Meck said. "I couldn't give you one."

"No, no," Ed Wolfe said. "I wouldn't ask you for a reference." A helpless civility was all he was capable of. If you're going to suffer, *suffer*, he told himself.

"Look," La Meck said, his tone changing, shifting from brutality to compassion as though there were no difference between the two, "you've got a kind of quality, a real feeling for collection. I'm frank to tell you, when you first came to work for us I figured you wouldn't last. I put you on the phones because I wanted you to see the toughest part first. A lot of people can't do it. You take a guy who's already down and bury him deeper. It's heart-wringing work. But you, you were amazing. An artist. You had a real thing for the deadbeat soul, I thought. But we started to get complaints, and I had to warn you. Didn't I warn you? I should have suspected something when the delinquent accounts started to turn over again. It was like rancid butter turning sweet. So I don't say this to knock your technique. Your technique's terrific. With you around we could have laid off the lawyers. But Ed, you're a gangster. A gangster."

That's it. Ed Wolfe thought. I'm a gangster. Babyface Wolfe at nobody's door.

"Well," La Meck said, "I guess we owe you some money."

"Two weeks' pay," Ed Wolfe said.

"And two weeks in lieu of notice," La Meck said grandly.

"And a week's pay for my vacation."

"You haven't been here a year," La Meck said.

"It would have been a year in another month. I've earned the vacation."

"What the hell," La Meck said. "A week's pay for vacation."

La Meck figured on a pad, and tearing off a sheet, handed it to Ed Wolfe. "Does that check with your figures?" he asked.

Ed Wolfe, who had no figures, was amazed to see that his check was so large. After the deductions he made $92.73 a week. Five $92.73's was evidently $463.65. It was a lot of money. "That seems to be right," he told La Meck.

La Meck gave him a check and Ed Wolfe got up. Already it was as though he had never worked there. When La Meck handed him the check he almost couldn't think what it was for. There should have been a photographer there to record the ceremony: ORPHAN AWARDED CHECK BY BUSINESSMAN.

"Good-by, Mr. La Meck," he said. "It has been an interesting association," he added foolishly.

"Good-by, Ed," La Meck answered, putting his arm around Ed Wolfe's shoulders and leading him to the door. "I'm sorry it had to end this way." He shook Ed Wolfe's hand seriously and looked into his eyes. He had a hard grip.

Quantity and quality, Ed Wolfe thought.

"One thing, Ed. Watch yourself. Your mistake here was that you took the job too seriously. You hated the chiselers."

No, no, I loved them, he thought.

"You've got to watch it. Don't love. Don't hate. That's the secret. Detachment and caution. Look out for Ed Wolfe."

"I'll watch out for him," he said giddily, and in a moment he was out of La Meck's office, and the main office, and the elevator, and the building itself, loose in the world, as cautious and as detached as La Meck could want him.

He took the car from the parking lot, handing the attendant the two dollars. The man gave him back fifty cents. "That's right," Ed Wolfe said, "it's only two o'clock." He put the half-dollar in his pocket, and, on an impulse, took out his wallet. He had twelve dollars. He counted his change. Eighty-two cents. With his finger, on the dusty dashboard, he added $12.82 to $463.65. He had $476.47. Does that check with your figures? he asked himself and drove in the crowded traffic.

Proceeding slowly, past his old building, past garages, past bar-and-grills, past second-rate hotels, he followed the traffic further downtown. He drove into the deepest part of the city, down and downtown to the bottom, the foundation, the city's navel. He watched the shoppers and tourists and messengers and men with appointments. He was tranquil, serene. It was something he could be content to do forever. He could use his check to buy gas, to take his meals at drive-in restaurants, to pay tolls. It would be a pleasant life, a great life, and he contemplated it thoughtfully. To drive at fifteen or twenty miles an hour through eternity, stopping at stoplights and signs, pulling over to the curb at the sound of sirens and the sight of funerals, obeying all traffic laws, making obedience to them his very code. Ed Wolfe, the Flying Dutchman, the Wandering Jew, the Off and Running Orphan, "Look Out for Ed Wolfe," a ghostly wailing down the city's corridors. What would be bad? he thought.

In the morning, out of habit, he dressed himself in a white shirt and light suit. Before he went downstairs he saw that his check and his twelve dollars were still in his wallet. Carefully he counted the eighty-two cents that he had placed on the dresser the night before, put the coins in his pocket, and went downstairs to his car.

Something green had been shoved under the wiper blade on the driver's side. YOUR CAR WILL NEVER BE WORTH MORE THAN IT IS WORTH RIGHT NOW! WHY WAIT FOR DEPRECIATION TO MAKE YOU AUTOMATICALLY BANKRUPT? I WILL BUY THIS CAR AND PAY YOU CASH! I WILL NOT CHEAT YOU!

Ed Wolfe considered his car thoughtfully a moment and then got in. That day he drove through the city, playing the car radio softly. He heard the news on the hour and half-hour. He listened to Art Linkletter, far away and in another world. He heard Bing Crosby's ancient voice, and thought sadly, Depreciation. When his tank was almost empty he thought wearily of having it filled and could see himself, bored and discontented behind the bug-stained glass, forced into a patience he did not feel, having to decide whether to take the Green Stamps the attendant tried to extend. Put money in your purse, Ed Wolfe, he thought. Cash! he thought with passion.

He went to the address on the circular.

He drove up onto the gravel lot but remained in his car. In a moment a man came out of a small wooden shack and walked toward Ed Wolfe's car. If he was appraising it he gave no sign. He stood at the side of the automobile and waited while Ed Wolfe got out.

"Look around," the man said. "No pennants, no strings of electric lights." He saw the advertisement in Ed Wolfe's hand. "I ran the ad off on my brother-in-law's mimeograph. My kid stole the paper from his school."

Ed Wolfe looked at him.

"The place looks like a goddamn parking lot. When the snow starts falling I get rid of the cars and move the Christmas trees in. No overhead. That's the beauty of a volume business."

Ed Wolfe looked pointedly at the nearly empty lot.

"That's right," the man said. "It's slow. I'm giving the policy one more chance. Then I cheat the public just like everybody else. You're just in time. Come on, I'll show you a beautiful car."

"I want to sell my car," Ed Wolfe said.

"Sure, sure," the man said. "You want to trade with me. I give top allowances. I play fair."

"I want you to buy my car."

The man looked at him closely. "What do you want? You want me to go into the office and put on the ten-gallon hat? It's my only overhead, so I guess you're entitled to see it. You're paying for it. I put on this big frigging hat, see, and I become Texas Willie Waxelman, the Mad Cowboy. If that's what you want, I can get it in a minute."

It's incredible, Ed Wolfe thought. There are bastards everywhere who hate other bastards downtown everywhere. "I don't want to trade my car in," he said. "I want to sell it. I, too, want to reduce my inventory."

The man smiled sadly. "You want me to *buy* your car. You run in and put on the hat. I'm an automobile *salesman*, kid."

"No, you're not," Ed Wolfe said. "I was with Cornucopia Finance. We handled your paper. You're an automobile *buyer*. Your business is in buying up four-and five-year-old cars like mine from people who need dough fast and then auctioning them off to the trade."

The man turned away and Ed Wolfe followed him. Inside the shack the man said, "I'll give you two hundred."

"I need six hundred," Ed Wolfe said.

"I'll lend you the hat. Hold up a goddamn stagecoach."

"Give me five."

"I'll give you two-fifty and we'll part friends."

"Four hundred and fifty."

"Three hundred. Here," the man said, reaching his hand into an opened safe and taking out three sheaves of thick, banded bills. He held the money out to Ed Wolfe. "Go ahead, count it."

Absently Ed Wolfe took the money. The bills were stiff, like money in a teller's drawer, their value as decorous and untapped as a sheet of postage stamps. He held the money, pleased by its weight. "Tens and fives," he said, grinning.

"You bet," the man said, taking the money back. "You want to sell your car?"

"Yes," Ed Wolfe said. "Give me the money," he said hoarsely.

He had been to the bank, had stood in the patient, slow, money-conscious line, had presented his formidable check to the impassive teller, hoping the four hundred and sixty-three dollars and sixty-five cents she counted out would seem his week's salary to the man who waited behind him. Fool, he thought, it will seem two weeks' pay and two weeks in lieu of notice and a week for vacation for the hell of it, the three-week margin of an orphan.

"Thank you," the teller said, already looking beyond Ed Wolfe to the man behind him.

"Wait," Ed Wolfe said. "Here." He handed her a white withdrawal slip.

She took it impatiently and walked to a file. "You're closing your savings account?" she asked loudly.

"Yes," Ed Wolfe answered, embarrassed.

"I'll have a cashier's check made out for this."

"No, no," Ed Wolfe said desperately. "Give me cash."

"Sir, we make out a cashier's check and cash it for you," the teller explained.

"Oh," Ed Wolfe said. "I see."

When the teller had given him the two hundred fourteen dollars and twenty-three cents, he went to the next window, where he made out a check for $38.91. It was what he had in his checking account.

On Ed Wolfe's kitchen table was a thousand dollars. That day he had spent one dollar and ninety cents. He had twenty-seven dollars and seventy-one cents in his pocket. For expenses. "For attrition," he said aloud. "The cost of living. For street-cars and newspapers and half-gallons of milk and loaves of white bread. For the movies. For a cup of coffee." He went to his pantry. He counted the cans and packages, the boxes and bottles. "The three weeks again," he said. "The orphan's nutritional margin." He looked in his icebox. In the freezer he poked around among white packages of frozen meat. He looked brightly into the vegetable tray. A whole lettuce. Five tomatoes. Several slices of cucumber. Browning celery. On another shelf four bananas. Three and a half apples. A cut pineapple. Some grapes, loose and collapsing darkly in a white bowl. A quarter-pound of butter. A few eggs. Another egg, broken last week, congealing in a blue dish. Things in plastic bowls, in jars, forgotten, faintly mysterious left overs, faintly rotten, vaguely futured, equivocal garbage. He closed the door, feeling a draft. "Really," he said, "it's quite cozy." He looked at the thousand dollars on the kitchen table. "It's not enough," he said. "It's not enough," he shouted. "It's not enough to be cautious on. La Meck, you bastard, detachment comes higher, what do you think? You think it's cheap?" He raged against himself. It was the way he used to speak to people on the telephone. "Wake up. Orphan! Jerk! Wake up. It costs to be detached."

He moved solidly through the small apartment and lay down on his bed with his shoes still on, putting his hands behind his head luxuriously. It's marvelous, he thought. Tomorrow I'll buy a trench coat. I'll take my meals in piano bars. He lit a cigarette. *"I'll never smile again,"* he sang, smiling. "All right, Eddie, play it again," he said. "Mistuh Wuf, you don' wan' to heah dat ol' song no maw. You know whut it do to you. She ain' wuth it, Mistuh Wuf." He nodded. "Again, Eddie." Eddie played his black ass off. "The way I see it, Eddie," he said, taking a long, sad drink of warm Scotch, "there are orphans and there are orphans." The overhead fan chuffed slowly, stirring the potted palmetto leaves.

He sat up in the bed, grinding his heels across the sheets. "There are orphans and there are orphans," he said. "I'll move. I'll liquidate. I'll sell out."

He went to the phone, called his landlady and made an appointment to see her.

It was a time of ruthless parting from his things, but there was no bitterness in it. He was a born salesman, he told himself. A disposer, a natural dumper. He administered severance. As detached as a funeral director, what he had learned was to say good-by. It was a talent of a sort. And he had never felt quite so interested. He supposed he was doing what he had been meant for—what, perhaps, everyone was meant for. He sold and he sold, each day spinning off little pieces of himself, like controlled explosions of the sun. Now his life was a series of speeches, of nearly earnest pitches. What he remembered of the day was what he had said. What others said to him, or even whether they spoke at all, he was unsure of.

Tuesday he told his landlady, "Buy my furniture. It's new. It's good stuff. It's expensive. You can forget about that. Put it out of your mind. I want to sell it. I'll show you bills for over seven hundred dollars. Forget the bills. Consider my character. Consider the man. Only the man. That's how to get your bargains. Examine. Examine. I could tell you about inner springs; I could talk to you of leather. But I won't. I don't. I smoke, but I'm careful. I can show you the ashtrays. You won't find cigarette holes in *my* tables. Examine. I drink. I'm a drinker. I drink. But I hold it. You won't find alcohol stains. May I be frank? I make love. Again, I could show you the bills. But I'm cautious. My sheets are virginal, white.

"Two hundred fifty dollars, landlady. Sit on that sofa. That chair. Buy my furniture. Rent the apartment furnished. Deduct what you pay from your taxes. Collect additional rents. Realize enormous profits. Wallow in gravy. Get it, landlady? Get it, landlady! Two hundred fifty dollars. Don't disclose the figure or my name. I want to remain anonymous."

He took her into his bedroom. "The piece of resistance, landlady. What you're really buying is the bedroom stuff. This is where I do all my dreaming. What do you think? Elegance. *Elegance!* I throw in the living-room rug. That I throw in. You have to take that or it's no deal. Give me cash and I move tomorrow."

Wednesday he said, "I heard you buy books. That must be interesting. And sad. It must be very sad. A man who loves books doesn't like to sell them. It would be the last thing. Excuse me. I've got no right to talk to you this way. You buy books and I've got books to sell. There. It's business now. As it should be. My library—" He smiled helplessly. "Excuse me. Such a grand name. Library." He began again slowly. "My books, my books are in there. Look them over. I'm afraid my taste has been rather eclectic. You see, my education has not been formal. There are over eleven hundred. Of course, many are paperbacks. Well, you can see that. I feel as if I'm selling my mind."

The book buyer gave Ed Wolfe one hundred twenty dollars for his mind.

On Thursday he wrote a letter:

American Annuity & Life Insurance Company,
Suite 410,
Lipton-Hill Building,
2007 Beverly Street, S.W.,
Boston 19, Massachusetts

Dear Sirs,

I am writing in regard to Policy Number 593–000–34–78, a $5,000, twenty-year annuity held by Edward Wolfe of the address below.

Although only four payments have been made, and sixteen years remain before the policy matures, I find I must make application for the immediate return of my payments and cancel the policy.

I have read the "In event of cancellation" clause in my policy, and realize that I am entitled to only a flat three percent interest on the "total paid-in amount of the partial amortizement." Your records will show that I have made four payments of $198.45 each. If your figures check with mine this would come to $793.80. Adding three percent interest to this amount ($23.81), your company owes me $817.61.

Your prompt attention to my request would be gratefully appreciated, although I feel, frankly, as though I were selling my future.

On Monday someone came to buy his record collection. "What do you want to hear? I'll put something comfortable on while we talk. What do you like? Here, try this. Go ahead, put it on the machine. By the edges, man. By the edges! I feel as if I'm selling my throat. Never mind about that. Dig the sounds. Orphans up from Orleans singing the news of chain gangs to café society. You can smell the freight trains, man. Recorded during actual performance. You can hear the ice cubes clinkin' in the glasses, the waiters picking up their tips. I have jazz. Folk. Classical. Broadway. Spoken word. Spoken word, man! I feel as though I'm selling my ears. The stuff lives in my heart or I wouldn't sell. I have a one-price throat, one-price ears. Sixty dollars for the noise the world makes, man. But remember, I'll be watching. By the edges. *Only by the edges!*"

On Friday he went to a pawnshop in a Checker cab.

"*You?* You buy gold? You buy clothes? You buy Hawaiian guitars? You buy pistols for resale to suicides? I wouldn't have recognized you. Where's the skull cap, the garters around the sleeves? The cigar I wouldn't ask you about. You look like anybody. You look like everybody. I don't know what to say. I'm stuck. I don't know how to deal with you. I was going to tell you something sordid, you know? You know what I mean? Okay, I'll give you facts.

"The fact is, I'm the average man. That's what the fact is. Eleven shirts, 15 neck, 34 sleeve. Six slacks, 32 waist. Five suits at 38 long. Shoes 10-C. A 7½ hat. You know something? Those marginal restaurants where you can never remember whether they'll let you in without a jacket? Well, the jackets they lend you in those places always fit me. That's the kind of guy you're dealing with. You can have confidence. Look at the clothes. Feel the material. And there's one thing about me. I'm fastidious. Fastidious. Immaculate. You think I'd be clumsy. A fall guy falls down, right? There's not a mark on the clothes. Inside? Inside it's another story. I don't speak of inside. Inside it's all Band-Aids, plaster, iodine, sticky stuff for burns. But outside—fastidiousness, immaculation, reality! My clothes will fly off your racks. I promise, I feel as if I'm selling my skin. Does that check with your figures?

"So now you know. It's me, Ed Wolfe. Ed Wolfe, the orphan? I lived in the orphanage for sixteen years. They gave me a name. It was a Jewish orphanage, so they gave me a Jewish name. Almost. That is, they couldn't know for sure themselves, so they kept it deliberately vague. I'm a foundling. A lostling. Who needs it, right? Who the hell needs it? I'm at loose ends, pawnbroker. I'm at loose ends out of looser beginnings. I need the money to stay alive. All you can give me.

"Here's a good watch. Here's a bad one. For good times and bad. That's life, right? You can sell them as a package deal. Here are radios. You like Art Linkletter? A phonograph. Automatic. Three speeds. Two speakers. One thing and another thing, see? And a pressure cooker. It's valueless to me, frankly. No pressure. I can live only on cold meals. Spartan. Spartan.

"I feel as if I'm selling—this is the last of it, I have no more things—I feel as if I'm selling my things."

On Saturday he called the phone company: "Operator? Let me speak to your supervisor, please.

"Supervisor? Supervisor, I am Ed Wolfe, your subscriber at TErrace 7–3572. There is nothing wrong with the service. The service has been excellent. No one calls, but you have nothing to do with that. However, I must cancel. I find that I no longer have any need of a telephone. Please connect me with the business office.

"Business office? Business office, this is Ed Wolfe. My telephone number is TErrace 7–3572. I am closing my account with you. When the service was first installed I had to surrender a twenty-five dollar deposit to your company. It was understood that the deposit was to be refunded when our connection with each other had been terminated. Disconnect me. Deduct what I owe on my current account from my deposit and refund the rest immediately. Business office, I feel as if I'm selling my mouth."

When he had nothing left to sell, when that was finally that, he stayed until he had finished all the food and then moved from his old apartment into a small, thinly furnished room. He took with him a single carton of clothing—the suit, the few shirts, the socks, the pajamas, the underwear and overcoat he did not sell. It was in preparing this carton that he discovered the hangers. There were hundreds of them. His own, previous tenants'. Hundreds. In each closet, on rods, in dark, dark corners, was this anonymous residue of all their lives. He unpacked his carton and put the hangers inside. They made a weight. He took them to the pawnshop and demanded a dollar for them. They were worth more, he argued. In an A&P he got another carton for nothing and went back to repack his clothes.

At the new place the landlord gave him his key.

"You got anything else?" the landlord asked. "I could give you a hand."

"No," he said. "Nothing."

Following the landlord up the deep stairs he was conscious of the $2,479.03 he had packed into the pockets of the suit and shirts and pajamas and overcoat inside the carton. It was like carrying a community of economically viable dolls.

When the landlord left him he opened the carton and gathered all his money together. In fading light he reviewed the figures he had entered in the pages of an old spiral notebook:

Pay	Pawned: $463.65
Cash	12.82
Car	300.00
Savings	214.23
Checking	38.91
Furniture (& bedding)	250.00
Books	120.00

Insurance	817.61
Records	60.00
Clothes	110.00
2 watches	18.00
2 radios	12.00
Phonograph	35.00
Pressure cooker	6.00
Phone deposit (less bill)	19.81
Hangers	1.00
Total	$2,479.03

So, he thought, that was what he was worth. That was the going rate for orphans in a wicked world. Something under $2,500. He took his pencil and crossed out all the nouns on his list. He tore the list carefully from top to bottom and crumpled the half which inventoried his expossessions. Then he crumpled the other half.

He went to the window and pushed aside the loose, broken shade. He opened the window and set both lists on the ledge. He made a ring of his forefinger and thumb and flicked the paper balls into the street. "Look out for Ed Wolfe," he said softly.

In six weeks the season changed. The afternoons failed. The steam failed. He was as unafraid of the dark as he had been of the sunlight. He longed for a special grief, to be touched by anguish or terror, but when he saw the others in the street, in the cafeteria, in the theater, in the hallway, on the stairs, at the newsstand, in the basement rushing their fouled linen from basket to machine, he stood as indifferent to their errand, their appetite, their joy, their greeting, their effort, their curiosity, their grime, as he was to his own. No envy wrenched him, no despair unhoped him, but, gradually, he became restless.

He began to spend, not recklessly so much as indifferently. At first he was able to recall for weeks what he spent on a given day. It was his way of telling time. Now he had difficulty remembering, and could tell how much his life was costing only by subtracting what he had left from his original two thousand four hundred seventy-nine dollars and three cents. In eleven weeks he had spent six hundred and seventy-seven dollars and thirty-four cents. It was almost three times more than he had planned. He became panicky. He had come to think of his money as his life. Spending it was the abrasion again, the old habit of self-buffing to come to the thing beneath. He could not draw infinitely on his credit. It was limited. Limited. He checked his figures. He had eighteen hundred and one dollars, sixty-nine cents. He warned himself, "Rothschild, child. Rockefeller, feller. Look out, Ed Wolfe. Look out."

He argued with his landlord and won a five-dollar reduction in his rent. He was constantly hungry, wore clothes stingily, realized an odd reassurance in his thin pain, his vague fetidness. He surrendered his dimes, his quarters, his half-dollars in a kind of sober anger. In seven more weeks he spent only one hundred and thirty dollars and fifty-one cents. He checked his figures. He had sixteen hundred seventy-one dollars, eighteen cents. He had spent almost twice what he had anticipated. "It's all right," he said. "I've reversed the trend. I can catch up." He held the money in his hand. He could smell his soiled underwear, "Nah, nah," he said. "It's not enough."

It was not enough, it was not enough, it was not enough. He had painted himself into a corner. Death by *cul-de-sac*. He had nothing left to sell, the born salesman. The born champion, long-distance, Ed Wolfe of a salesman lay in his room, winded, wounded, wondering where his next pitch was coming from, at one with the ages.

He put on his suit, took his sixteen hundred seventy-one dollars and eighteen cents and went down into the street. It was a warm night. He would walk downtown. The ice which just days before had covered the sidewalk was dissolved to slush. In darkness he walked through a thawing, melting world. There was something on the edge of the air, the warm, moist odor of the change of the season. He was touched despite himself. "I'll take a bus," he threatened. "I'll take a bus and close the windows and ride over the wheel."

He had dinner and some drinks in a hotel. When he finished he was feeling pretty good. He didn't want to go back. He looked at the bills thick in his wallet and went over to the desk clerk. "Where's the action?" he whispered. The clerk looked at him, startled. He went over to the bell captain. "Where's the action?" he asked and gave the man a dollar. He winked. The man stared at him helplessly.

"Sir?" the bell captain said, looking at the dollar.

Ed Wolfe nudged him in his gold buttons. He winked again. "Nice town you got here," he said expansively. "I'm a salesman, you understand, and this is new territory for me. Now if I were in Beantown or Philly or L.A. or Vegas or Big D or Frisco or Cincy—why, I'd know what was what. I'd be okay, know what I mean?" He winked once more. "Keep the buck, kid," he said. "Keep it, keep it," he said, walking off.

In the lobby a man sat in a deep chair, *The Wall Street Journal* opened wide across his face. "Where's the action?" Ed Wolfe said, peering over the top of the paper into the crown of the man's hat.

"What's that?" the man asked.

Ed Wolfe, surprised, saw that the man was a Negro.

"What's that?" the man repeated, vaguely nervous. Embarrassed, Ed Wolfe watched him guiltily, as though he had been caught in an act of bigotry.

"I thought you were someone else," he said lamely. The man smiled and lifted the paper to his face. Ed Wolfe stood before the opened paper, conscious of mildly teetering. He felt lousy, awkward, complicatedly irritated and ashamed, the mere act of hurting someone's feelings suddenly the most that could be held against him. It came to him how completely he had failed to make himself felt. "Look out for Ed Wolfe, indeed," he said aloud. The man lowered his paper. "Some of my best friends are Comanches," Ed Wolfe said. "Can I buy you a drink?"

"No," the man said.

"Resistance, eh?" Ed Wolfe said. "That's good. Resistance is good. A deal closed without resistance is no deal. Let me introduce myself. I'm Ed Wolfe. What's your name?"

"Please, I'm not bothering anybody. Leave me alone."

"Why?" Ed Wolfe asked.

The man stared at him and Ed Wolfe sat suddenly down beside him. "I won't press it," he said generously. "Where's the action? Where is it? Fold the paper, man. You're playing somebody else's gig." He leaned across the space between them and took the man by the arm. He pulled at him gently, awed by his own boldness. It was the first time since he had shaken hands with La Meck that he had touched anyone physically. What he was risking surprised and puzzled him. In all those months to have touched only two people, to have touched *even* two people! To feel their life, even, as now, through the unyielding wool of clothing, was disturbing. He was unused to it, frightened and oddly moved. Bewildered, the man looked at Ed Wolfe timidly and allowed himself to be taken toward the cocktail lounge.

They took a table near the bar. There, in the alcoholic dark, within earshot of the easy banter of the regulars, Ed Wolfe seated the Negro and then himself. He looked around the room and listened for a moment, then turned back to the Negro. Smoothly boozy, he pledged the man's health when the girl brought their drinks. He drank stolidly, abstractedly. Coming to life briefly, he indicated the men and women around them, their suntans apparent even in the dark. "Pilots," he said. "All of them. Airline pilots. The girls are all stewardesses and the pilots lay them." He ordered more drinks. He did not like liquor, and liberally poured ginger ale into his bourbon. He ordered more drinks and forgot the ginger ale. "*Goyim*," he said. "White *goyim*. American *goyim*." He stared at the Negro. He leaned across the table. "Little Orphan Annie, what the hell kind of an orphan is that with all her millions and her white American *goyim* friends to bail her out?"

He watched them narrowly, drunkenly. He had seen them before—in good motels, in airports, in bars—and he wondered about them, seeing them, he supposed, as Negroes or children of the poor must have seen him when he had sometimes driven his car through slums. They were removed, aloof—he meant it—a different breed. He turned and saw the Negro, and could not think for a moment what the man was doing there. The Negro slouched in his chair, his great white eyes hooded. "You want to hang around here?" Ed Wolfe asked him.

"It's your party," the man said.

"Then let's go some place else," Ed Wolfe said. "I get nervous here."

"I know a place," the Negro said.

"*You* know a place. You're a stranger here."

"No, man," the Negro said. "This is my home town. I come down here sometimes just to sit in the lobby and read the newspapers. It looks good, you know what I mean? It looks good for the race."

"*The Wall Street Journal*? You're kidding Ed Wolfe. Watch that."

"No," the Negro said. "Honest."

"I'll be damned," Ed Wolfe said. "I come for the same reasons."

"Yeah," the Negro said. "No shit?"

"Sure, the same reasons." He laughed. "Let's get out of here." He tried to stand, but fell back again in his chair. "Hey, help me up," he said loudly. The Negro got up and came around to Ed Wolfe's side of the table. Leaning over, he raised him to his feet. Some of the others in the room looked at them curiously. "It's all right," Ed Wolfe said. "He's my man. I take him with me everywhere. It looks good for the race." With their arms around each other's shoulders they stumbled out of the bar and through the lobby.

In the street Ed Wolfe leaned against the building, and the Negro hailed a cab, the dark left hand shooting up boldly, the long black body stretching forward, raised on tiptoes, the head turned sharply along the left shoulder. Ed Wolfe knew that he had never done it before. The Negro came up beside him and guided Ed Wolfe toward the curb. Holding the door open, he shoved him into the cab with his left hand. Ed Wolfe lurched against the cushioned seat awkwardly. The Negro gave the driver an address and the cab moved off. Ed Wolfe reached for the window handle and rolled it down rapidly. He shoved his head out the window of the taxi and smiled and waved at the people along the curb.

"Hey, man, close the window," the Negro said after a moment. "Close the window. The cops, the cops."

Ed Wolfe laid his head on the edge of the taxi window and looked up at the Negro, who was leaning over him, smiling; he seemed to be trying to tell him something.

"Where we going, man?" Ed Wolfe asked.

"We're there," the Negro said, sliding along the seat toward the door.

"One ninety-five," the driver said.

"It's your party," Ed Wolfe told the Negro, waving away responsibility.

The Negro looked disappointed, but reached into his pocket.

Did he see what I had on me? Ed Wolfe wondered anxiously. Jerk, drunk, you'll be rolled. They'll cut your throat and leave your skin in an alley. Be careful.

"Come on, Ed," the Negro said. He took Ed Wolfe by the arm and got him out of the taxi.

Fake. Fake, Ed Wolfe thought. Murderer. Nigger. Razor man.

The Negro pulled him toward a doorway. "You'll meet my friends," he said.

"Yeah, yeah," Ed Wolfe said. "I've heard so much about them."

"Hold it a second," the Negro said. He went up to the window and pressed his ear against the opaque glass.

Ed Wolfe watched him without making a move.

"Here's the place," the Negro said proudly.

"Sure," Ed Wolfe said. "Sure it is."

"Come on, man," the Negro urged him.

"I'm coming, I'm coming," Ed Wolfe said. "But my head is bending low," he mumbled.

The Negro took out a ring of keys, selected one and put it in the door. Ed Wolfe followed him through.

"Hey, Oliver," somebody called. "Hey, baby, it's Oliver. Oliver looks good. He looks *good*."

"Hello, Mopiani," the Negro said to a short black man.

"How is stuff, Oliver?" Mopiani said to him.

"How's the market?" a man next to Mopiani asked, with a laugh.

"Ain't no mahket, baby. It's a *sto'*," somebody else said.

A woman stopped, looked at Ed Wolfe for a moment, and asked, "Who's the ofay, Oliver?"

"That's Oliver's broker, baby."

"Oliver's broker looks good," Mopiani said. "He looks *good.*"

"This is my friend, Mr. Ed Wolfe," Oliver told them.

"Hey there," Mopiani said.

"Charmed," Ed Wolfe said.

"How's it going, man," a Negro said indifferently.

"Delighted," Ed Wolfe said.

He let Oliver lead him to a table.

"I'll get the drinks, Ed," Oliver said, leaving him.

Ed Wolfe looked at the room glumly. People were drinking steadily, gaily. They kept their bottles under their chairs in paper bags. He watched a man take a bag from beneath his chair, raise it and twist the open end of the bag carefully around the neck of the bottle so that it resembled a bottle of champagne swaddled in its toweling. The man poured liquor into his glass grandly. At the dark far end of the room some musicians were playing and three or four couples danced dreamily in front of them. He watched the musicians closely and was vaguely reminded of the airline pilots.

In a few minutes Oliver returned with a paper bag and some glasses. A girl was with him. "Mary Roberta, Ed Wolfe," he said, very pleased. Ed Wolfe stood up clumsily and the girl nodded.

"No more ice," Oliver explained.

"What the hell," Ed Wolfe said.

Mary Roberta sat down and Oliver pushed her chair up to the table. She sat with her hands in her lap and Oliver pushed her as though she were a cripple.

"Real nice little place here, Ollie," Ed Wolfe said.

"Oh, it's just the club," Oliver said.

"Real nice," Ed Wolfe said.

Oliver opened the bottle, then poured liquor into their glasses and put the paper bag under his chair. Oliver raised his glass. Ed Wolfe touched it lamely with his own and leaned back, drinking. When he put it down empty, Oliver filled it again from the paper bag. Ed Wolfe drank sluggishly, like one falling asleep, and listened, numbed, to Oliver and the girl. His glass never seemed to be empty any more. He drank steadily, but the liquor seemed to remain at the same level in the glass. He was conscious that someone else had joined them at the table. "Oliver's broker looks good," he heard somebody say. Mopiani. Warm and drowsy and gently detached, he listened, feeling as he had in barbershops, having his hair cut, conscious of the barber, unseen behind him, touching his hair and scalp with his warm fingers. "You see, Bert? He looks good," Mopiani was saying.

With great effort Ed Wolfe shifted in his chair, turning to the girl.

"Thought you were giving out on us, Ed," Oliver said. "That's it. That's it." The girl sat with her hands folded in her lap.

"Mary Roberta," Ed Wolfe said.

"Uh huh," the girl said.

"Mary Roberta."

"Yes," the girl said. "That's right."

"You want to dance?" Ed Wolfe asked.

"All right," she said. "I guess so."

"That's it, that's it," Oliver said. "Stir yourself."

Ed Wolfe rose clumsily, cautiously, like one standing in a stalled Ferris wheel, and went around behind her chair, pulling it far back from the table with the girl in it. He took her warm, bare arm and moved toward the dancers. Mopiani passed them with a bottle. "Looks good, looks good," Mopiani said approvingly. He pulled her against him to let Mopiani pass, tightening the grip of his pale hand on her brown arm. A muscle leaped beneath the girl's smooth skin, filling his palm. At the edge of the dance floor he leaned forward into the girl's arms and they moved slowly, thickly across the floor. He held the girl close, conscious of her weight, the life beneath her body, just under her skin. Sick, he remembered a jumping bean he had held once in his palm, awed and frightened by the invisible life, jerking and hysterical, inside the stony shell. The girl moved with him in the music, Ed Wolfe astonished by the burden of her life. He stumbled away from her deliberately. Grinning, he moved ungently back against her. "Look out for Ed Wolfe," he crooned.

The girl stiffened and held him away from her, dancing self-consciously. Brooding, Ed Wolfe tried to concentrate on the lost rhythm. They danced in silence for a while.

"What do you do?" she asked him finally.

"I'm a salesman," he told her gloomily.

"Door to door?"

"Floor to ceiling. Wall to wall."

"Too much," she said.

"I'm a pusher," he said, suddenly angry. She looked frightened. "But I'm not hooked myself. It's a weakness in my character. I can't get hooked. Ach, what would you *goyim* know about it?"

"Take it easy," she said. "What's the matter with you? Do you want to sit down?"

"I can't push sitting down," he said.

"Hey," she said, "don't talk so loud."

"Boy," he said, "you black Protestants. What's the song you people sing?"

"Come on," she said.

"*Sometimes I feel like a motherless child,*" he sang roughly. The other dancers watched him nervously. "That's our national anthem, man," he said to a couple that had stopped dancing to look at him. "That's our song, sweethearts," he said, looking around him. "All right, *mine* then. I'm an orphan."

"Oh, come on," the girl said, exasperated, "an orphan. A grown man."

He pulled away from her. The band stopped playing. "Hell," he said loudly, "from the beginning. Orphan. Bachelor. Widower. Only child. All my names scorn me. I'm a survivor. I'm a goddamned survivor, that's what." The other couples crowded around him now. People got up from their tables. He could see them, on tiptoes, stretching their necks over the heads of the dancers. No, he thought. No, no. Detachment and caution. The La Meck Plan. They'll kill you. They'll kill you and kill you. He edged away from them, moving carefully backward against the bandstand. People pushed forward onto the dance floor to watch him. He could hear their questions, could see heads darting from behind backs and suddenly appearing over shoulders as they strained to get a look at him.

He grabbed Mary Roberta's hand, pulling her to him fiercely. He pulled and pushed her up onto the bandstand and then climbed up beside her. The trumpet player, bewildered, made room for him. "Tell you what I'm going to do," he shouted over their heads. "Tell you what I'm going to do."

Everyone was listening to him now.

"Tell you what I'm going to do," he began again.

Quietly they waited for him to go on.

"I don't *know* what I'm going to do," he shouted. "I don't *know* what I'm going to do. Isn't that a hell of a note?"

"Isn't it?" he demanded.

"Brothers and sisters," he shouted, "and as an only child bachelor orphan I use the term playfully, you understand. Brothers and sisters, I tell you what I'm *not* going to do. I'm no consumer. Nobody's death can make me that. I won't consume. I mean, it's a question of identity, right? Closer, come up closer, buddies. You don't want to miss any of this."

"Oliver's broker looks good up there. Mary Roberta looks good. She looks good," Mopiani said below him.

"Right, Mopiani. She looks good, she looks *good*," Ed Wolfe called loudly. "So I tell you what I'm going to do. What am I bid? What am I bid for this fine strong wench? Daughter of a chief, masters. Dear dark daughter of a dead dinge chief. Look at those arms. Those arms, those arms. What am I bid?"

They looked at him, astonished.

"What am I bid?" he demanded. "Reluctant, masters? Reluctant masters, masters? Say, what's the matter with you darkies? Come on, what am I bid?" He turned to the girl. "No one wants you, honey," he said. "Folks, folks, I'd buy her myself, but I've already told you. I'm not a consumer. Please forgive me, miss."

He heard them shifting uncomfortably.

"Look," he said patiently, "the management has asked me to remind you that this is a living human being. This is the real thing, the genuine article, the goods. Oh, I told them I wasn't the right man for this job. As an orphan I have no conviction about the product. Now, you should have seen me in my old job. I could be rough. *Rough!* I hurt people. Can you imagine? I actually caused them pain. I mean, what the hell, I was an orphan. I *could* hurt people. An orphan doesn't have to bother with love. An orphan's like a nigger in that respect. Emancipated. But you people are another problem entirely. That's why I came here tonight. There are parents among you. I can feel it. There's even a sense of parents behind those parents. My God, don't any of you folks ever die? So what's holding us up? We're not making any money. Come on, what am I bid?"

"Shut up, mister." The voice was raised hollowly some place in the back of the crowd.

Ed Wolfe could not see the owner of the voice.

"He's not in," Ed Wolfe said.

"Shut up. What right you got to come down here and speak to us like that?"

"He's not in, I tell you. I'm his brother."

"You're a guest. A guest got no call to talk like that."

"He's out. I'm his father. He didn't tell me and I don't know when he'll be back."

"You can't make fun of us," the voice said.

"He isn't here. I'm his son."

"Bring that girl down off that stage!"

"Speaking," Ed Wolfe said brightly.

"Let go of that girl!" someone called angrily.

The girl moved closer to him.

"She's mine," Ed Wolfe said. "I danced with her."

"Get her down from there!"

"Okay," he said giddily. "Okay. All right." He let go of the girl's hand and pulled out his wallet. The girl did not move. He took out the bills and dropped the wallet to the floor.

"Damned drunk!" someone shouted.

"That whitey's crazy," someone else said.

"Here," Ed Wolfe said. "There's over sixteen hundred dollars here," he yelled, waving the money. It was, for him, like holding so much paper. "I'll start the bidding. I hear over sixteen hundred dollars once. I hear over sixteen hundred dollars twice. I hear it three times. Sold! A deal's a deal," he cried, flinging the money high over their heads. He saw them reach helplessly, noiselessly toward the bills, heard distinctly the sound of paper tearing.

He faced the girl. "Good-by," he said.

She reached forward, taking his hand.

"Good-by," he said again, "I'm leaving."

She held his hand, squeezing it. He looked down at the luxuriant brown hand, seeing beneath it the fine articulation of bones, the rich sudden rush of muscle. Inside her own he saw, indifferently, his own pale hand, lifeless and serene, still and infinitely free.

FOR WHITE MEN ONLY

James T. Farrell

I

"Boy, I tell you, don' you go there," Booker Jones, a small and yellowish Negro, said.

"Booker, there is no white man alive who's gonna tell me where I is to go swimming, and where I isn't. If I wants to go swimming this lake here at Jackson Park, that's where I'm going swimming," Alfred, a tall and handsome broad-shouldered and coppery Negro, replied.

They were shirtless, wearing blue swimming suits and old trousers, and they walked eastward along Fifty-seventh Street.

"Oh, come on, Alfred, let's go to Thirty-ninth Street," Booker said with intended persuasiveness as they passed across Dorchester after they had ambled on for a block in silence.

"You go! Me, I'm going swimming over in Jackson Park, whether there's white men there or not," Alfred said, his face hardening, his voice determined.

"Alfred, you is always courtin' trouble, and just because you want to show off before that no-account mulatto gal . . ."

"What you say, nigger?"

"Well, no, I'm sorry, Alfred," Booker cringed. "But some day, you'll go courtin' trouble, and trouble is just gonna catch right on up with you, and it's gonna say, 'Well, Alfred, you been courtin' me, so here I is with my mind made up to give you plenty of me'."

"Shut up, black boy!" Alfred said curtly.

Booker shook his head with disconsolate wonder. As they passed under the Illinois Central viaduct, Booker again suggested that they go down to the Thirty-ninth Street beach, and Alfred testily told him that Thirty-ninth Street wasn't a beach at all, just a measly, over-crowded pile of stones. The black man had no beach. But he was aiming to go swimming where he had some space without so many people all around him. He added that if the Negro was to go on being afraid of the white man, he was never going to get anywhere, and if the Negro wanted more space to swim in, he just had to go and take it. And he had told that to Melinda, and she had laughed at him, but she was not going to laugh at him again. Booker just shook his head sadly from side to side.

They entered Jackson Park where the grass and shrubbery and tree leaves shimmered and gleamed with sunlight. The walks were crowded with people, and along the drive, a succession of automobiles hummed by. Alfred walked along with unconcerned and even challenging pride. Booker glanced nervously about him, feeling that the white men were thrusting contemptuous looks at him. He looked up at Alfred, admiring his friend's courage, and he wished that he were unafraid like Alfred.

Turning by the lake, they passed along the sidewalk which paralleled the waters. Sandy beach ran down from the sidewalk to the shore line, and many were scattered along it in bathing suits. Down several blocks from them, they could see that the regular beach was crowded. More white people frowned at them, and both of them could sense hate and fear in these furtive, hasty glances. Alfred's lips curled into a surly expression.

Halfway along toward the regular beach Alfred jumped down into the sand, tagged by Booker. He gazed around him, nonchalant, and then removed his trousers. He stood in his bathing suit, tall and impressively strong, graceful. Booker jittered beside him, hesitating until Alfred, without turning his head, taunted him into haste. Booker removed his trousers, and stood skinny beside Alfred whose arms were folded and whose gaze was sphinx-like on the waters. They heard a gentle and steady rippling against the shore line.

Nearby, white bathers stared with apprehension. A group of three fellows and two young girls who had been splashing and ducking close to the shore saw them, and immediately left the water and walked down a hundred yards to re-enter it. Alfred seemed to wince, and then his face again became hard and intent. Booker saw various white bathers picking up their bundles and moving away from them, and still afraid of these white men, he hated them.

Alfred trotted gracefully to the shore line, again plunged into the water, followed by Booker. They cut outward, and Alfred suddenly paddled around and playfully ducked Booker. They again hit outward. Catching his breath and plunging beside his companion, Booker told Alfred that they had made a mistake coming out here where they were two against a mob. Alfred retorted that he was not going to whine and beg the white man for anything. Some black men had to be the first to come, if they wanted to have the right of a place to swim. And he wasn't scared anyway. Booker shook a pained head, caught a mouthful of water, and splashed to keep himself up. Alfred dove under water and reappeared a number of yards away, laughing, snorting, glorying in the use of his body. After they had swum around, Booker again chattered that he was afraid.

"Here is one black boy that's not going to be mobbed," Alfred said.

II

Buddy Coen and his friends emerged from the water laughing, shaking their wet bodies and heads. They found a space of sand within the enclosure of the regular beach and dropped down, hunting for the cigarettes they had hidden.

"Well, boys, I was just going to say, if you lads want to provide the bottle, I'm all set for a bender tonight," Buddy said after lighting a cigarette.

"If you'd go back driving a hack, you'd have dough enough for your own liquor," fat Marty Mulligan said.

"What the hell have I got a wife working as a waitress for? So that I can drive a taxi all night. See any holes in my head, Irish?" Buddy said tauntingly.

"After the fight Buddy started last Saturday night with two dicks, I should think he'd stay sober once in a while and see how it feels," Morris said.

"Say, there's plenty of neat pickups around here, even if most of them are Polacks," the big Swede said.

"Boys, my girl is out of town tonight, and I'm dated up with a married woman I met out on my territory. Her husband works nights, and brother, she's the stuff," Marty bragged, following his statement with an anatomical description of her contours, charms and sexual technique.

The big Swede began talking about the old days, and Marty told anecdotes of how he used to get drunk when he was going to Saint Stanislaus high school. They talked on until suddenly from a group close to them they heard a lad say:

"There's niggers down a way on the beach."

They became tense, and Buddy asked was that straight stuff.

"Bad enough having Polacks dirtying up the lake without diseased shines," the big Swede said in hate.

"A few weeks ago, a coal-black bastard tried to get into the lockers here, but he was told that there weren't any free. Then a couple of us boys just talked to him outside, you know, we talked, and used a little persuasion, and he's one black bastard that knows his place, and knows that this is a white man's park and a white man's beach," Buddy said.

"Say, I just need to sock somebody to make the day exciting and put me in good spirits for my date tonight," Marty Mulligan said.

"Well, then, what the hell are you guys waiting for?" Buddy said, jumping to his feet.

They followed Buddy to the water, swam out around the fencing that extended along the formal beach limits and walked along the shore line in search of the Negroes.

"I know I don't mind pounding a few black bastards full of lumps," Norton said.

"Me now, I ain't sloughed anybody since Christ knows when, and I need a little practice," Morris said.

III

"Alfred, I'm tired," Booker said.

"Nigger, shut up! Nobody's going to hurt you," Alfred said.

"Well, I is, just the same," Booker said, his voice breaking into a whine.

Ignoring Booker, Alfred turned over on his back and floated with the sun boiling down upon his coppery limbs. Booker paddled after him, afraid to go in alone. He turned and looked back along the avenue of sand, filled with so many white people. Blocks and blocks of sand, populated with all these whites. The fears of a mob assailed him. He wished that he had never come. He thought of Negroes lynched in the South, of many who had been beaten and mobbed in the Chicago race riots of 1919. He remembered as a boy in those times how he had seen one of his race, dead, hanging livid from a telephone post in an alley. He was afraid, and with his fear was hate, hatred of the white man, hatred because of the injustices to him, to his race, hatred because he was afraid of the white man. Again he glanced along the avenue of sand filled with white men, and each small figure along it was a potential member of a mob to beat him and Alfred. He turned and again looked at his friend who was floating, unconcerned. He wished that he had Alfred's courage. With chattering teeth, he shook his head slowly and sadly, feeling, sensing, knowing that they were going to pay dearly for this venture. He trod water waiting for Alfred, wishing that he was out of it. He saw a group of white bathers stand at the shore and look out over the water. He had a premonition.

IV

"There they are," Buddy said, curtly nodding his head toward the water, and they saw two kinky heads and two Negro faces, diminished by distance.

"Let's drown the bastards!" Morris said.

Buddy said that they would walk off a little ways and wait until the two shines came in. They moved a few yards away, and waited, keen and eager. Buddy lashed out contemptuous remarks, keeping them on edge, and Marty remarked that they had driven the white man out of Washington Park, and that if things went on, soon the whole South Side would be black.

"If they want Jackson Park, they got to fight for it!" Buddy sneered.

"Just think! Look at all these white girls bathing around here. With niggers on the beach, it ain't safe for them," Morris said.

"And do you fellows know, my sister nearly came out here swimming today?" Morris said.

They saw the two Negroes coming in and heard the smaller one trying to convince the big one about something, but they could not catch enough of what he said. The two Negroes walked slowly toward their small bundles of clothing, their wet bodies glistening in the sunlight. After they had sat down, Buddy arose and led the group toward them. Seeing the white fellows approaching, Booker grabbed his clothes and ran. Four of the white lads pursued him, yelling to stop that nigger.

With a sulky expression on his face, Alfred arose at the approach of Buddy and Morris.

"The water nice?" Buddy asked, his voice constrained and threatening.

"Passable," Alfred answered, his fists clenched.

"Been out here before?" Buddy continued.

"No. . . .Why?" Alfred said with unmistakable fearlessness.

A crowd gathered around, and excitement cut through the beach like an electric current because of the shouts and chase after Booker. A white bather tripped him as he ran and joined the four other pursuers in cursing and punching him, mercilessly disregarding his pleas to be let alone. They dragged him to his feet, knocked him down, kicked him, dragged him up, knocked him over again while he continued to emit shrill and helpless cries.

"Anybody ever tell you that this is a white man's beach?" Morris asked Alfred.

"You know we don't want niggers here!" Buddy said.

Buddy went down from a quick and surprising punch on the jaw, and Alfred countered Morris' left swing with a thudding right that snapped the white lad's head back. Buddy sat down, rubbed his jaw, shook his dazed head, leaped to his feet, and went into Alfred swinging both hands. While the Negro fought off the two of them, others dragged back the howling Booker to the fight scene. The big Swede broke through the crowd of spectators and clipped Alfred viciously on the side of the head. Two other white bathers smashed into the attack. Defending himself, Alfred crashed Morris to the sand and was then battered off his feet. A heel was brought against his jaw, and as he struggled to arise, five white bodies piled onto him, punching, scratching, kneeing him. Spectators shouted, females screamed and encouraged the white lads, and Alfred was quickly and severely punished. Booker opened his mouth to beg for mercy, and a smashing fist brought blood from his lips, and another wallop between the eyes toppled him over backward.

A bald-headed Jewish man with a paunchy stomach protested, and a small, pretty blonde girl screamed that he must be a nigger lover. A middle-aged woman with a reddish bovine face called in an Irish brogue for them to hit the black skunks, while a child strained at her waist and shouted.

A park policeman hurriedly shoved through the spectators, and the slugging ceased. The two Negroes sat in the sand, their faces cut and bleeding.

"You fellows better go home!" the policeman said roughly, sneering as he spoke.

They slowly got up, and Booker tried to explain that they had done nothing.

"Don't be giving me any lip," the policeman said. "I said you better go home or do your swimming down at Thirty-ninth if you don't want to be starting riots. Now move along!"

He shoved Booker.

"And you, too," he said to Alfred who had not moved.

Booker hurriedly put his trousers on and Alfred did likewise slowly, as if with endless patience. They wiped their bleeding faces with dirty handkerchiefs, and Booker sniffled.

"Go ahead now!" the policeman roughly repeated.

"We will, but we'll come back!" Alfred said challengingly.

The crowd slowly dispersed, and the six fellows stood there near the policeman.

"Shall we follow them?" asked Marty.

"They ain't worth hitting, the skunks, and the dirty fighting they do, kicking me that way," said Collins, limping.

They turned and walked heroically back toward the enclosed beach.

"That black bastard had the nerve to hit me," Buddy said, pointing to his puffed eye.

"Like all niggers, they were yellow," said Morris.

"Well, we did a neat job with them," Norton bragged.

"Boy, I caught that big one between his teeth. Look at my hand," Marty said, showing his swollen knuckles.

"Look at that, fellows! There's somethin'. I say there, sisters!" the Swede said to three girls who were coquetting on the sand.

Looking covertly at legs and breasts, they leered.

SIDI MEHEMET IBRAHIM
ON THE SLAVE TRADE

Benjamin Franklin

Benjamin Franklin to the Federal Gazette
(unpublished)

To the Editor of the Federal Gazette.
March 23.

Sir,

Reading last night in your excellent paper the speech of Mr. Jackson in Congress, against meddling with the affair of slavery, or attempting to mend the condition of slaves, it put me in mind of a similar one made about one hundred years since, by Sidi Mehemet Ibrahim, a member of the Divan of Algiers, which may be seen in Martin's account of his consulship, anno 1687. It was against granting the petition of the Sect called Erika or Purists, who prayed for the abolition of piracy and slavery, as being unjust. Mr. Jackson does not quote it; perhaps he has not seen it. If therefore some of its reasonings are to be found in his eloquent speech, it may only show that men's interests and intellects operate and are operated on with surprising similarity in all countries and climates, whenever they are under similar circumstances. The African's speech, as translated, is as follows:
"Allah Bismillah, &c. God is great, and Mahomet is his Prophet.
"Have these Erika considered the consequences of granting their petition? If we cease our cruises against the christians, how shall we be furnished with the commodities their countries produce, and which are so necessary for us? If we forbear to make slaves of their people, who, in this hot climate, are to cultivate our lands? Who are to perform the common labours of our city, and in our families? Must we not then be our own slaves? And is there not more compassion and more favour due to us Mussulmen, than to these christian dogs? We have now above 50,000 slaves in and near Algiers. This number, if not kept up by fresh supplies, will soon diminish, and be gradually annihilated. If then we cease taking and plundering the Infidel ships, and making slaves of the seamen and passengers, our lands will become of no value for want of cultivation; the rents of houses in the city will sink one half? and the revenues of government arising from its share of prizes must be totally destroyed. And for what? to gratify the whim of a whimsical sect! who

would have us not only forbear making more slaves, but even to manumit those we have. But who is to indemnify their masters for the loss? Will the state do it? Is our treasury sufficient? Will the Erika do it? Can they do it? Or would they, to do what they think justice to the slaves, do a greater injustice to the owners? And if we set our slaves free, what is to be done with them? Few of them will return to their countries, they know too well the greater hardships they must there be subject to: they will not embrace our holy religion: they will not adopt our manners: our people will not pollute themselves by intermarying with them: must we maintain them as beggars in our streets; or suffer our properties to be the prey of their pillage: for men accostomed to slavery, will not work for a livelihood when not compelled. And what is there so pitiable in their present condition? Were they not slaves in their own countries? Are not Spain, Portugal, France and the Italian states, governed by despots, who hold all their subjects in slavery, without exception? Even England treats its sailors as slaves, for they are, whenever the government pleases, seized and confined in ships of war, condemned not only to work but to fight for small wages or a mere subsistance, not better than our slaves are allowed by us. Is their condition then made worse by their falling into our hands? No, they have only exchanged one slavery for another: and I may say a better: for here they are brought into a land where the sun of Islamism gives forth its light, and shines in full splendor, and they have an opportunity of making themselves acquainted with the true doctrine, and thereby saving their immortal souls. Those who remain at home have not that happiness. Sending the slaves home then, would be sending them out of light into darkness. I repeat the question, what is to be done with them? I have heard it suggested, that they may be planted in the wilderness, where there is plenty of land for them to subsist on, and where they may flourish as a free state; but they are, I doubt, too little disposed to labour without compulsion, as well as too ignorant to establish a good government, and the wild Arabs would soon molest and destroy or again enslave them. While serving us, we take care to provide them with every thing; and they are treated with humanity. The labourers in their own countries, are, as I am well informed, worse fed, lodged and cloathed. The condition of most of them is therefore already mended, and requires no farther improvement. Here their lives are in safety. They are not liable to be impressed for soldiers, and forced to cut one another's christian throats, as in the wars of their own countries. If some of the religious mad bigots who now teaze us with their silly petitions, have in a fit of blind zeal freed their slaves, it was not generosity, it was not humanity that moved then to the action; it was from the conscious burthen of a load of sins, and hope from the supposed merits of so good a work to be excused from damnation. How grosly are they mistaken in imagining slavery to be disallowed by the Alcoran! Are not the two precepts, to quote no more, Masters treat your slaves with kindness: Slaves serve your masters with cheerfulness and fidelity, clear proofs to the contrary? Nor can the plundering of infidels be in that sacred book forbidden, since it is well known from it, that God has given the world and all that it contains to his faithful Mussulmen, who are to enjoy it of right as fast as they can conquer it. Let us then hear no more of this detestable proposition, the manumission of christian slaves, the adoption of which would, by depreciating our lands and houses, and thereby depriving so many good citizens of their properties, create universal discontent, and provoke insurrections, to the endangering of government, and producing general confusion. I have therefore no doubt, but this wise Council will prefer the comfort and happiness of a whole nation of true believers, to the whim of a few Erika, and dismiss their petition."

The result was, as Martin tells us, that the Divan came to this resolution.

"The doctrine that plundering and enslaving the Christians is unjust, is at best problematical; but that it is the interest of this state to continue the practice, is clear, therefore let the petition be rejected."

And it was rejected accordingly.

And since like motives are apt to produce in the minds of men like opinions and resolutions, may we not, Mr. Brown, venture to predict, from this account, that the petitions to the parliament of England for abolishing the slave trade, to say nothing of other legislatures, and the debates upon them, will have a similar conclusion. I am, Sir, Your constant reader and humble servant.

Historicus.

BIG BUG

Ellen Geist

"My hair looks exactly like these dear rice noodles," I announce to my friend Janice. We are eating in a Japanese restaurant with my daughter Sophie. Janice smiles and ignores me. She has dragged me all the way across the bridge to her neighborhood in Brooklyn Heights to consume what she insists is the freshest sushi in New York, and she refuses to be deterred from her mission.

"Are we going to talk about your hair again?" Sophie says. Sophie has been my beauty consultant during my course of chemotherapy and although she's done a remarkably good job for a nine-year-old, she is becoming understandably weary.

In the middle of eating an inside-out tuna roll, I feel a searing pain in my back. I try to appear nonchalant and order more green tea. Janice, however, has noticed me wriggling around in my seat.

"It's probably a little touch of pleurisy, is all," I explain. "I got this once years ago. Sounds bad, but it's just an inflammation around your lungs. Though I do think I should go home and take a bath." I am doing my best to sound casual, but have risen to leave. I need to move quickly to avoid Sophie's scrutiny. She already has that strange wide-open-eyed look I've seen too often this past year.

The waitresses in a pile-up by the cash register take the money I throw in their direction and offer kind murmurs, for which I am grateful. In moments I have stumbled out to the street with Sophie and Janice scurrying after me. Court Street is deserted and freezing cold.

"You go back inside and I'll get you a cab," Janice says. "No, no," I insist, not from any courage but because I feel I can't actually move. There are no cabs, or, that is, there are only cabs with people in them. Finally I spot one with a light on. It slows down so as not to hit me, but there is someone in the car. "Liar, liar," I yell at the driver and attempt to kick the door as he goes by.

"Mom, don't," Sophie says, giving me her most disapproving look. It upsets her when I behave like this.

"We *must* get you a cab," Janice gently insists as if that will make it happen. Just then one comes around the corner, not a real cab but a gypsy. It's making a terrible racket that seems to emanate from underneath the car. But it stops. "Do you think it's OK?" Janice asks, a worried look on her face.

"Sure," I say. "It's probably just the muffler." Sophie dutifully jumps in first; I follow behind, waving goodbye to Janice, who stands in the wind and watches us lurch past. Inside the noise is louder. I wonder if the problem is in fact the muffler or might not be a far more important appendage. I lean into a bulging spring of the rear seat and try not to moan.

Apparently I've not been successful. "Mom, are you really OK?" Sophie asks.

"I'm fine," I tell her. I don't mind kvetching about minor inconveniences but I don't want to truly alarm her.

We are now on the Brooklyn Bridge. It appears to me as a vast expanse of metal that cannot possibly be crossed in this ramshackle vehicle. "I wonder if we're going to make it over the bridge," I make the mistake of saying.

"Mommy, Mommy, is everything all right?" Sophie has that little girl tone that appears only on those occasions when nothing is all right.

"Fine, fine," I say with much less conviction than before. I am holding her hand tightly, and now I have to lean into her so as not to fall out the door, something that appears to be a real possibility since the hinge doesn't look particularly stationary.

"Dear God," I pray. "Just let us make it over the bridge." I've never gone in much for religion. Lately, though, given recent events, I've wandered into a couple of synagogues. This is one of my most successful spiritual experiences so far as we do indeed make it across the bridge and beyond that up the FDR.

When we get home I take my bath and two aspirin to no avail. Then I decide to take my temperature. It's 104. I call the oncology floor at Mount Carmel and ask to speak to the resident on call. This is a technique one only learns from experience, and it applies to nearly all aspects of life. It's all a matter of knowing the exact lingo. In this case "on call" is the key word.

"I'm Dr. Kaminetzky's patient, breast CA." I explain. I find it also helps to say CA instead of cancer.

"You have to come in tonight," the resident tells me. "I can't tell anything over the phone." Before going to the hospital, I drop a too-sleepy-to-protest Sophie off at the neighbors.

The resident is young and dapper. He's dressed in a crisp white shirt, a bow tie, and I hate him. How could he ever know me the way Kaminetzky does? I am inordinately attached to my doctor because he dresses in schlumpy pale green shirts that invariably have an oil spot above the pocket and ties with unsightly patterns, that he takes obvious delight in for their garishness. I love my doctor because he says things like "Where the hell have you been?" when I'm late, which I usually am. Most of all I adore my doctor because he is inappropriately fond of me, maybe more than of the rest of his patients, although he is unprofessionally caring and compassionate toward all of them and doesn't know any proper boundaries.

"Everyone says he's wonderful." The head nurse is trying to reassure me about the resident. "His wife is a survivor, too."

The resident looks about twenty-four. How could his wife have survived the concentration camps? Although I'm dyslexic with numbers, I can do the math on this one. Even if she were one of the babies born in Bergen-Belsen or Dachau, she would be way too old for him. Then suddenly it hits me: breast cancer survivor, of course. I'm embarrassed to be included in this term.

The resident looks in my eyes with intent interest while he talks. I learned that trick of pretending to pay attention long ago in high school, and I'm not falling for it.

178 | ELLEN GEIST

"You have pneumonia," he says, handing me a prescription for antibiotics. "You know your blood count is still down and you have to be careful." He pauses. "Dr. Kaminetzky is out of town until Thursday. Why don't you take these antibiotics and come in then for a follow-up?" Perhaps he senses my hostility.

"Where the hell were you?" I ask Kaminetzky on Thursday.

"Puerto Rico," he tells me.

"You doctors always go to places like Puerto Rico for conferences." I picture cobalt ocean, white sand.

"Next time," Kaminetzky says, "Why don't you come with me?"

I sigh as I refuse him. My only shot at the beach lately has been Jacob Riis Park, which my friend Janice has dubbed "the people's beach" and where the sand is dark grey, although Janice has tried to convince me this is due to minerals.

"The problem is that you lack courage," Kaminetzky tells me.

"The problem," I answer, "is that you lack a divorce."

We've been waiting for my chest X-rays to appear. "Get out of here, kiddo," he says. "All you have is a little pneumonia." I'm surprised to see relief on his face. But then he clarifies. "You don't have mets to the lung." He means metastatic cancer, not the baseball team.

Oncologists, I tell myself. That's all they think about.

I can't stand staying in bed doing nothing, so in a few days I'm up and running around. I do seem to be coughing less.

On my way home from my job at Scepter Books where I share a cube with Janice, next to the usual plastic surgeon ads on the subway, I see a billboard for a progressive Jewish organization called Chesed. Its purpose: to instate "Radical Kindness" in our society. We are separated, alienated, lack community. That's me, I think, alienated—although generally it's a status I prefer. I despise group activities. I once went to Parents Without Partners and wanted to jump out the window. I attended one cancer support group: the facilitator asked me how I thought I'd gotten cancer. Did I know it could be caused by stress?

"Broccoli," I told her. "I think I got it from eating too much Broccoli." But I scribble the Chesed number down on my bank receipt. And when I get home I do something uncharacteristic. I call.

At the Chesed meeting that Wednesday I look entirely out of place in my blue jean jacket with silver spangles and long flowered skirt. There are only five of us in one of those dismal upper west side apartments, the kind with lots of wall molding and not one single painting: an older man, a very young woman, Sophie, whom I dragged there under duress, Aaron, and myself. Aaron is the leader of the "Radical Kindness" movement and author of the previously cited billboard. At the end of the meeting I saunter up and introduce myself. "I have cancer," I tell him. He seems to find this a sexy opening line.

"Call me later tonight. As late as you like," he says.

Sophie is glaring at me that she wants to go. She is at the other end of the room picking at the few desserts provided: a grocery store bag of rugelach, some Entenmann's cookies. Then, though, Aaron reveals the coup de grace of the evening. He brings out a plate of blueberry blintzes from the oven. "We can stay for a while if you want," Sophie calls out to me.

Although I think it's weird to call someone I hardly know at 11 p.m., which is when we get home after two half-hour subway delays, I don't want to blow this opportunity. Aaron and I talk for hours on the phone. He asks me about my life—my hardships and travails—all of which I'm only too happy to reveal. I find his re-interpretation of the Old Testament God very original, although how would I know? When he asks me to bring Sophie for a Shabbes lunch that Saturday, I eagerly agree. "Will there be blintzes?" I remember to ask.

The lunch, though, does not go as well as I'd hoped. To begin with, Aaron, upset that my kitchen isn't kosher, has directed me to bring something vegetarian. I try "Rocket Soup," a recipe I have from my sister-in-law's gourmet restaurant in Seattle. It's made with Arugula and tasted delicious there, only with my rendering it becomes a strange lumpy substance much like sea algae. It is leaking from the sides of the bowl as Sophie and I arrive.

This time Aaron's apartment is packed with people and a kind of study session appears to be in progress. I try unobtrusively to find some edge of a sofa for us, but Aaron interrupts himself to walk over and put his arm around me. "Karen," he announces, "and Sophie." He holds his hand out to Sophie and she backs away. She hates being touched by strangers, or for that matter, close relatives.

I feel as if I'm in school and behind on my homework, an all-too-familiar sensation. I try to catch up quickly by reading the photocopied page that has been handed out.

It is the story of the four who entered Paradise: Ben Azzai, Ben Zoma, Aher and Akiva. "Rabbi Akiva said to them: When you reach near the stones of pure marble, do not say 'Water, water.' Ben Azzai glanced at it and died. Ben Zoma glanced and became demented. Aher cut down seedlings. Rabbi Akiva came out in peace." I am crazy about this story although I couldn't explain why.

Apparently, though, one is expected to make comments. A number of people have their hands up. A woman with long black curls and intense grey eyes is speaking. "So I think the story all has to do with studying Torah. Wisdom is like the pure marble."

Aaron nods approvingly. He glances in my direction, but I can think of nothing to say except "water, water," and this I have to truly struggle to restrain myself from doing. I lower my head and continue reading. "There are those who walk around the house always searching for its gate, and about whom it is said: *Ben Zoma is still outside.*" That Ben Zoma, I think, that's my kind of guy.

All of a sudden I spot my second cousin Benjy wedged into an embroidered high back wooden chair on the other side of the room. I haven't seen him since my father last dragged me to a family seder about twenty years ago. He's from the orthodox side of the family, but he doesn't look it in his blue jeans and suspenders. He immediately runs over and starts jabbering about something to do with past lives and the Kabbalah. Talking so quickly, and with his black handlebar mustache and long greyish hair, he reminds me of Albert Einstein on Methamphetamines, but still he's always been my cutest cousin.

The lunch or meeting or class, I'm not sure what to call it, is breaking up. "Stay" Aaron comes over to tell me. Benjy looks disappointed for a moment but scatters off as quickly as if he'd been a Kabalistic vision.

Sophie and I dutifully sit down at Aaron's flip-up wooden table. "That woman with the grey eyes seems very smart," I say, "Who is she?"

"My former girlfriend," he announces. "She is brilliant, and very imaginative, especially in bed."

I'm not happy with the picture this forces into my head. It's his charisma I'm attracted to, not his looks. And I hope Sophie hasn't understood, but if she has, she isn't giving any indication. Instead she has her lips pressed together tightly while he tries to talk to her.

"Why is your daughter so hostile to me? We've only just met. I think we should discuss it."

I shake my head to stave him off this path. I don't believe in children expressing anger at the dinner table. I made Sophie repeat after me at an early age, "Parenthood is a dictatorship. A benevolent dictatorship, yes, but still a dictatorship."

Suddenly Sophie decides to engage in the conversation. "Where are the blintzes?" she asks brightly.

Aaron rummages through the freezer. "It looks like we're out."

Within seconds of receiving this information, Sophie has risen from the table, landed on the staircase, and plunged her head down in her hands. She raises her head briefly to shout in my direction, "I came here for one reason and one reason only and that was blintzes. And now you tell me—NO BLINTZES!"

I walk over and try to console her. I'm still hoping to salvage this outing. After all, Aaron seemed so insightful on the phone and clearly many people respect him; we must be bringing out the worst in him. We are faced off in different corners of the room when someone bangs on the door.

"Who's that?" Aaron asks with irritation.

"I was thinking you might want to walk down to my place for Havdalah." My cousin Benjy enters with endearing obliviousness to anything wrong in his breaking up our little gathering. He smiles broadly at the three of us.

I'm not sure what Havdalah is, but it seems to be my cue to exit. "We should really go," I tell Aaron. He touches my hand and looks in my eyes intently. Although I now see this is a routine of his, at the moment I appreciate the gesture. This time he knows better than to come near Sophie.

As we head down West End Avenue, Benjy fires off a rapid string of joke lines to Sophie, accompanied by some sort of song-and-dance routine she finds immensely entertaining.

"So are you orthodox?" I interrupt to ask.

"I'm *shomer shabbes*," he says. I have no idea what this means but am reluctant to appear ignorant.

"Ignore the mess," he urges as we enter his apartment, decorated with a collection of twentieth century newspapers and empty boxes from a variety of digital music equipment.

Havdalah, I find out, is a ceremony marking the end of the Sabbath. As we step into his darkened kitchen, Benjy lights a braided candle and hands it to me. "They say how high you hold it is the height of your future husband's eyes."

I hold the candle up until I see the flames flash across his irises. It's too dark in the room for me to see his expression as he takes the candle from me and sizzles it out in a glass of wine. Then he sings a song, Eliahu Hanavi. He has a clear, absolutely pitched, sweet voice.

"Thanks for coming over. You made my *Shabbes*," he says.

"You made my *Shabbes*, too," I reply.

"You know it is an old world tradition—second cousins. Joke," he adds. Then he quickly turns on the light. "Th, th, that's all folks," he says in an Elmer Fudd impersonation. Before we go, though, he insists on showing Sophie his repertoire of magic tricks involving coins and a salt-shaker that disappears.

"Can we come back here a lot?" she says.

On the subway home we see the Chesed ad again, which Sophie decides to read aloud. She has been learning to read with "expression" in school and her performance is flawless. "Many people have grown weary of this competitive dog-eat-dog society that robs people of their dignity. That's why our founder, Aaron Stanley, started the 'Radical Kindness' movement." Sophie has put just the right sardonic spin on "our founder."

"It's not good to be so sarcastic about my potential boyfriends," I tell her, suppressing my delight.

I think about becoming *shomer shabbes* myself. I do some research on what's involved. There are many complicated rules for observing the Sabbath, none of which I learned in the reform synagogue of my childhood. I decide to start with something manageable: not tearing toilet paper. The next Friday afternoon in preparation I stack up piles of pre-torn paper.

Unfortunately my Sabbath plans are interrupted by a coughing fit. When I call Kaminetzky, he sadly concedes, "You're going to have to see a pulmonologist." He never likes me going to other doctors.

The pulmonologist orders a CT-scan. I decide to head up to the Cancer Clinic to wait for the results. When I see Kaminetzky, I wave wildly in his direction, but he ignores me. I watch as he walks back and forth several times bringing in patients. Suddenly he comes over. "What the hell are you staring at?" he barks.

"Nothing," I answer meekly. "I was looking at you—maybe."

He turns in a huff and storms off. Tears well up in my eyes. No matter how weird he's been, he's never yelled at me like this before.

A few minutes later he waves me into one of the examining rooms. He's prominently holding a folder with film in his hand. "I had them send the CT up here— I just got the report. It's good. Definitely not cancer."

"I thought you told me it was definitely not cancer before."

"Look, I'm sorry I snapped at you. It's just that I was really scared."

I'm surprised at the frankness of his apology, but even more taken aback that he'd worried. Until then I'd bought that definitely-not-lung-cancer line.

"The pulmonologist said this might be some side effect of the chemo," I say for revenge.

"It's not from the chemo," he says.

"Methetrexate, specifically. Look, I know it saved my life," I add.

"Remember it was your choice."

It's true; he had handed me stacks of photocopied articles from the *New England Journal of Medicine*. I found my type of tumor in there, the bad kind. I saw the difference chemo would make, lowering my chance of recurrence from thirty-five per cent to thirty—a mere five per cent.

"Really, it was Sophie's choice," I counter, thinking myself remarkably funny. Ever since my diagnosis, Sophie has become very involved in statistics.

"What is the percentage of your dying from chemo?" she asked me at the time.

"None, I guess." I hadn't read of any measurable risk.

"And what about without?" she wanted to know.

Three weeks later, though, the coughing still hasn't gone away. This time the pulmonologist says he has to schedule a bronchoscopy. "We are going to insert a tube and take tiny samples of your lung," he explains as if that's reassuring.

When I go to his secretary to schedule the procedure, I'm in a state of terror. Her name is Lu Ann and she has a large puff of teased orangish hair.

"You need someone to pick you up afterwards," she says. "Any family?"

"I have Sophie, but she's nine," I reply.

Lu Ann is very sympathetic. As I'm apt to do without warning, I tell her my life story, at least the illness part.

"I might know someone who can help you," she interrupts. "He knows all about the future. He's a remarkable man. He reads palms and everything. I met him when I worked for Orthodox Jews in Borough Park. They treated me like a member of the family," she adds proudly. "I even sat *Shiva* with them." She pronounced *Shiva* so it sounded like the name of an exotic Indian goddess.

I wonder if she thinks that I'm not Jewish. "You don't *look* Jewish," everyone told me when I was young. In Torrance, California, a town without Jews, I was supposed to take this as a compliment. "You killed Christ," the kids would say on the playground.

"Jesus was a Jew, a rabbi," I would reply as my father had instructed, but this historically accurate information did nothing to repel the bullies.

This is why I appreciate living in New York City. You can purchase Yahrzeit candles in the Spanish grocery on the corner. I'm thrilled to see the tacky menorahs with yellow electric lightbulbs in hotel lobbys. I am ecstatic about the suspension of alternate side parking on even the most obscure Jewish holidays.

"His name is Zev Essen," Lu Ann says. "I'll call first to smooth the way and give him your phone number. I can tell you are nervous about making phone calls. I've been told I have real insight into people."

That night Zev Essen phones, my second in a series of late night phone calls. His Yiddish accent has an eerie familial quality. He gives me elaborate directions to his house in Borough Park.

The next day Sophie and I take the J train, one I'd always wondered where it goes. But I can't follow his directions to a street called Tehama somewhere off 13th Avenue. Sophie tries to help but complains she can't read my handwriting.

We walk in circles until finally the street appears along with the green two-story house he described so completely. Zev Essen awaits us at the top of a set of rickety side stairs. As we follow him up, I try to spot the peyes I thought all orthodox men had. He looks quite modern with his close-cropped beard, wearing an ordinary businessman's hat. I notice a curl tucked in around one ear and feel more confident of his authenticity.

At the door, his wife greets us in a white sort of housedress/gown. She has a white turban wrapped around her head, giving her the appearance of someone from a Buddhist sect. Everything in the apartment matches her. The wool sofa is bright white, as is the long shag rug, the walls, and the shelving. The chairs are white leather. Even the silver candles and prayer goblets gleam a whitish glow. I've never seen more white concentrated in one location.

"Come in," Zev Essen urges. "Don't be nervous." His wife merely nods in a way that doesn't seem quite as hospitable.

"Your daughter looks tired. Would she like to lie down on the sofa while we talk?" The white couch is so inviting. Who wouldn't want to try it? Sophie immediately stretches out and turns her head to the ceiling, signaling she will be asleep within moments.

Zev Essen and I retire to his study, lined with Hebrew books in leather bindings. "For the first time in my life I'm worried about dying," I announce.

He instructs me to hold out my palm and moves a pencil across it. I recall hearing that Orthodox men are not supposed to touch women or look at them. Zev Essen, though, is definitely looking at me.

"You are not going to die right now, but you are going through many trials. Our fortunes have to with the explicable and the inexplicable."

"What's the explicable part?" I want to know.

"In the Talmud, the Sayings of the Fathers, Rabbi Yannai said, 'It is not in our power to explain either the prosperity of the wicked or the afflictions of the righteous.' However in your case—"

I hear a bloodcurdling scream from the other room: Sophie. We rush in as Sophie hurtles toward me. Smack in the middle of her white T-shirt is the biggest, blackest beetle I'd ever seen in my life, with giant hard wings, massive legs, crawling up toward her throat. I'm terrified. Sophie is frantically trying to brush it off, but it clings tenaciously.

Zev Essen merely smiles and hurriedly swats it to the floor. Then he steps on it, and with some embarrassment, drops it into the garbage pail. "An uninvited visitor," he comments.

Sophie clings to me, sobbing. "Do call me," Zev Essen says. "And come again." His wife, emerging from the kitchen in her turban, silently hands Sophie a few pieces of gaily Hebrew-wrapped chewing gum.

"I never want to go back there," Sophie says when we are safely on the subway.

"I don't think I want to either," I concur.

"What did he say anyway?"

"He told me some quote from the Talmud, you know this book of Jewish wisdom. Something about no way to explain the good luck of evil people or the bad luck of the righteous."

"It's supposed to be the smartest book and that's the best they can come up with?" Sophie says.

In the third of my late night calls, I phone my cousin Benjy. "What do you know about big bugs and Kabbalah?"

"In Shamanistic terms they're a sign of mystical power. The Egyptians used them to travel safely through the underworld."

"And what about Judaism?"

"No idea," he says.

I mention my upcoming bronchoscopy.

"Call me on my 800 number when you get out and let me know how it goes," he offers. I don't know how an itinerant musician gets an 800 number, but I'm glad to have someone to call.

Before the procedure I meet with the anesthesiologist. I can't take valium, Demoral, or anything with "zine" as the final suffix. It seems I have a paradoxical reaction to nearly everything. In fact my whole life could be summed up as a paradoxical effect. "You have to be awake and breathe," he says. "What about morphine?"

"Give me lots of it," I tell him.

As far as twilight sleep goes, I feel more awake than I ever have in my life. "More morphine," I call out continually, trying to give it some cadence like that old cereal commercial, hoping that might evoke nostalgia from the anesthesiologist.

"We've given you 10 CC's," the anesthesiologist says. "It's enough to kill a horse."

Afterwards when I am wheeled into recovery, finally the morphine takes effect; I am pain free and delirious. "You see this," I tell myself, grabbing a blue piece of terry beside my head. "This is a towel. Say it." "Towel," I dutifully obey. In this way I name all the objects around me. Then I ask and give correct answers to my name and address.

Despite my valiant and impressive efforts, I'm panicking "Kaminetzky," I cry out as I somehow get myself out of bed and hurl myself toward the nearest nurse. "Page Dr. Kaminetzky." I am quite proud of myself for having remembered his name and the paging part.

"Why do you want to see him?" the nurse asks me suspiciously. "He's not the attending on this case."

Because he's the only one I can think of around here who loves me, I want to tell her, but I don't. I decide to try the docile approach instead. "Do you think you could beep Dr. Kaminetzky for me?" I say in what I hope is my sweetest, most passive voice. "I promised I would come see him before I go."

"Hmm," she answers.

I inch past her desk toward the door. "Where are you going?" she shouts.

"To see Dr. Kaminetzky," I yell as I duck out. "Ben Zoma is still outside," I call back to her, an inside joke that I no longer know why I find this funny.

I know the way to Kaminetzky's office by heart: the circular passageway, the wall of doors, then tucked away, the almost hidden staircase. As I go up the stairs, I have a sudden realization: *What about Rabbi Akiva?* I wonder. *How did he get inside?*

I head down the long hall lined with stones I've been told are just markers for the big donors, but I think they could have thought of something less funereal. Then I go through the double doors and into Kaminetzky's paneled office. Behind the comforting beige desk sits Kaminetzky in half-glasses for reading I've never seen him in before.

"Oh, there you are," he says as if he's been expecting me.

"Did they beep you? I asked them about a million times."

"Nah. They're all a bunch of losers around here. Have a seat and let's get the results."

"Like that?"

"Just like that." He relishes this role of being someone who gives meaning to the phrase "instant results."

While we wait for the call back from the pulmonologist, for once we have nothing to say to each other. He shuffles papers fitfully while I study the pattern of the carpet pile. I'm about to break the silence with my latest doctor joke when the phone rings. I try to decipher his murmurs but can't make them out. He's beaming as he hangs up.

"It's something called bronchiectosis. Some messed up bronchia, a little fluid. It's really not lung cancer."

"I thought you told me all along you knew it wasn't lung cancer."

"I lied," he says.

I'm surprised the relief brings tears to my eyes. Following the tradition of my Eastern European ancestors, I know well what rewards there are in suffering, but what kind of punishment can good fortune bring? Can I handle this? Or am I stuck like Aher pulling up the seedlings, or my former soul brother, Ben Zoma? How *did* Rabbi Akiva glimpse Paradise and manage to come out in peace?

"They called from Recovery." His secretary is standing in the doorway. "Apparently she escaped and we are supposed to order a wheel chair and have someone to take her downstairs. They won't let her go by herself."

"I'll wheel you down," says Kaminetzky.

First I borrow the secretary's phone and call Benjy. "I'm fine," I tell him. "According to Kaminetzky I'm going to be like my grandmother and die at the age of 102 on the toilet. You remember we all thought she was a hundred and one? I just found out from the Ellis Island records she lied about her age."

"That's really great about the bronchoscopy results," he says. "I'm really glad you called me."

"Yeah," I agree, and quickly get off the phone. I see Kaminetzky peering around at me, and besides, that's about as much private or public display of affection as I can manage at the present moment.

My wheelchair arrives; and as promised, Kaminetzky wheels me down. I glide easily through the salmon-colored halls, not even disgusted, as I usually am, by their color. "You must be very special," a nurse stops to comment, "being taken downstairs by the Chairman of Oncology."

Kaminetzky wheels me up to the exit. "You're free," he says and holds his hand out to help me stand. Then I step through the glass doors into the chill winter sunlight, and I am on my own.

GIANT RAT

Anna Nelson Harry
(Translated and Edited by Michael Krauss)

A man and woman and their child were boating along, looking for berries, when they came upon the cliff where the monster reputedly had its hole.

"I wish we might see it," said the woman.

The man said, "Shhh! Don't ask for trouble!" And just as he spoke the rat emerged behind them, capsizing their canoe. The woman was lost. The man grabbed the child and jumped onto the back of the big rat.

It took them into its hole, where they jumped off. The man held the child. She was afraid of the monster. Nevertheless, they lived a long time with this giant monster rat.

When it got dark the rat would go out hunting. It would bring home seals and ducks for the man and his child. Then it would lie down on top of them to cook them. When the food was cooked, the rat gave it to the man and his child and they ate it. They were living this way for some time. The man would try climbing the spruce-roots which hung from above, while the rat was gone. He got out. But he knew the rat would look for them as soon as it came back, so he hurried back in. When the rat returned, they were sitting there. It lay in under itself what it had killed and gave it to the man and his child to eat.

His child was a little girl.

When it was pitch-dark the rat would leave, returning as it began to get light out. One day just before it got light the man put the girl on his back and climbed out of the rat-hole. He was going along, and had not yet gotten very far, when the rat returned. He immediately missed them and began banging its tail around, knocking everything down.

The man and his daughter returned to their people safely. He told them, "Go get some young ravens. Snare them. Snare lots of them." They did as he asked.

When the moon was full, they went there. (The rat would stay in and never go out when the moon was full.)

They sharpened their knives and axes, packed the young ravens on their backs, and headed for the rat-hole. "Now dump the ravens down into the rat-hole to see if they'll be quiet." (If the birds remained quiet, that would mean the hole was empty.) Immediately they clamored. The rat jerked his tail partway down but the people chopped it off, thus killing the monster.

The rat moved forward as it died, but only about halfway out. They were going to tow it down to shore but it was too big. They had to leave it there, until a big tide came and carried it down to the shore.

The monster rat was more massive than a very big whale, and had enormously long upper teeth. Its hair was longer than a black bear's fur.

The corpse of the giant rat floated out and as it washed around, they towed it ashore. They butchered it to get to the skin. When they cut it open, they found all sorts of things in its stomach. People who had been disappearing mysteriously, they now found, had been killed and eaten by this big rat. They found people's skulls in its stomach. The people butchered it for its skin. The hair was already going in some places, but where it was good they dried it.

After this, they called a potlatch and exhibited before the people's eyes what had been killing their relatives. Now, not just anyone could use that rat-skin, only a chief could sit on the monster rat-skin. At the potlatch the people kept saying, "No cheapskate will sit on it. Only chiefs. Too many people have fallen victim to this rat. Those poor wretches, all killed. That's why only chiefs will sit on it."

Word spread of the giant rat-skin and a tribe from some distant land wanted it for themselves. These people from another land came and made war over it. Many people died, but the rat-skin was not wrested from them. The chief who used to sit on it was the first to be killed in the war for that rat-skin. Therefore it could not be abandoned. It was of no concern to them how many would perish on its account, or how many would die in the pursuit of that skin. They fought to a finish.

When the battle ended, they took the chief's corpse from among the other dead people and put it inside the rat's tail. Then they wrapped it in the rat-skin and burned it.

(In the old days people didn't bury one another. Whoever died was cremated and his charred remains were gathered in a box.)

Thus they did to their chief's bones. But then the other tribe found out about the box and stole it and packed it up the mountain and threw it in the water.

Then there was another battle, between that other tribe and those whose chief's bones had been thrown into the water. They were all wiped out, except for old men and women and children. They killed all the young men. That's what happened in those whose chief's bones were thrown in the water.

Their children grew up and wanted revenge, but never got revenge. They got wiped out, those whose chief's bones were thrown in the water.

These people were just like each other, though living in a different land. There are people from Sitka living here at Yakutat just like we do. Though they are foreigners, they live harmoniously with us. But these people waged war over that rat-skin, people just like each other. What good is a rat-skin? They did that, though, and nothing more could happen to them, no more wars with anyone. They were wiped out completely.

That's all.

THE DRY MOUNTAIN AIR

Robert Hass

Our Grandma Dahling arrived from the train station
In a limousine: an old Lincoln touring car
With immense, black, shiny, rounded fenders
And a silver ornament of Nike on the hood.
She wore a long black coat and pearl-grey gloves.
White hair, very soft white, and carefully curled.
Also rimless glasses with thin gold frames.
Once in the house, having presented ourselves
To be hugged completely, the important thing
Was to watch her take off her large, black,
Squarish, thatched, and feathered confection of a hat.
She raised both hands above her head, elbows akimbo,
Lifting the black scrim of a veil in the process,
Removed a pin from either side, and lifted it,
Gingerly, straight up, as if it were a saucer of water
That I must not spill, and then she set it down,
Carefully, solicitously even, as if it were a nest
Of fledgling birds (which it somewhat resembled),
And then there arrived, after she had looked at the hat
For a moment to see that it wasn't going to move,
The important thing. Well, she would say, well, now,
In a musical German-inflected English, touching together
Her two soft, white, ungloved hands from which emanated
The slightly spiced, floral scent of some hand lotion
That made the hands of great-grandmothers singularly soft,
And regard us, and shake her head just a little, but for a while,
To express her wonder at our palpable bodies before her,
And then turn to her suitcase on the sea-chest in the hall,
Not having been transferred yet to her bedroom by my father
Who had hauled it up the long, precipitous front stairs;
She flipped open the brass clasps and the shield-shaped lock
She had not locked and opened the case to a lavender interior
From which rose the scent of chocolate, mingled faintly
With the smell of anise from the Christmas cookies
That she always baked. But first were the paper mats
From the dining car of the California Zephyr, adorned
With soft pastel images of what you might see

from the Vista Car: Grand Canyon, Mount Shasta,
a slightly wrinkled Bridal Veil Falls, and, serene, contemplative
Almost, a view of Lake Louise, intimate to me because,
Although it was Canadian, it bore my mother's name.
My brother and I each got two views. He, being the eldest,
Always took Grand Canyon, which I found obscurely terrifying
And so being second was always a relief. I took Lake Louise
And he took Half Dome and the waterfall, and she looked surprised
That we were down to one and handed me the brooding angel,
Shasta. And then from under layers of shimmery print dresses,
she produced, as if relieved that it wasn't lost, the largest chocolate bar
That either of us had ever seen. Wrapped in dignified brown paper,
On which ceremonial, silvery capital letters must have announced—
I couldn't read—the sort of thing it was. These were the war years.
Chocolate was rationed. The winy, dark scent rose like manna
in the air and filled the room. My brother, four years older,
Says this never happened. Not once. She never visited the house
On Jackson Street with its sea air and the sound of fog horns
At the Gate. I thought it might help to write it down here,
That the truth of things might be easier to come to
On a quiet evening in the clear, dry, mountain air.

LET'S GO, ISRAEL

Hillel Heinstein

When I enter the store called *Luxury* the owner is on the phone, absorbed in negotiations.

"No no no no no. It is very good.—Yes.—Yes.—Of course.—No.—No.—Yes. What do you think?"

Above the counter I see the upper slope of a proud paunch, neither hidden nor accentuated by an untucked silky shirt, which is exposed at the throat where rings of hair escape like puffs of a cigar. The head is tanned in dreary November, the face newly shaven, the hair like silver flames from ears to crown. A gold chain swims in black forests on one wrist. I have something in common with this man, though I'm not sure exactly what. I toss him a nod.

I pass appraising eyes over stained-glass wrought-iron lanterns, enormous inlaid chests, mirrors framed by turquoise and tangerine stones, tiles with painted peacocks, fish, and strange crossbreeds of dog and goat, bronze samovars and tiny tea glasses, and carpets hung like posters in a college necessities store. I see the Moroccan serving platter I bought for my mother.

"My friend, you let me know you need any help, OK, my friend?"

"OK," I say, pitching my voice low. I notice the thick digits of his hands strangely cradling the receiver.

There are some scarves hanging above the counter. I spread the most colorful one out before me, and study the sophisticated lengthwise orange, brown, and purplish-gray bands, and the intricate needlework of two sets of exuberant perpendicular stripes. The beating yellow redness of these stripes excites me, like the suddenly unmuted sound of table drumming and cymbals.

"We just get these in, my friend. Very beautiful. From Kashmir," I hear. "In a minute I bring you many more."

"Thanks," I say politely without lowering the scarf that veils me. Briefly, I wish away the lackluster shades of the lengthwise bands. An unwelcome energy churns within me as the storeowner hangs up the phone.

"You know how it is, some people," he says. "I be right back." He starts from behind the counter.

"No no, don't worry about it," I say. "I'll take this one."

"That one is very beautiful. You have a good eye. But I have many more. No worry. I be right back." He moves towards a shiny curtain in the wall.

"It's OK. Really. I'll take this one. It's for my sister."

"It is Kashmiri," he says, coming back to me. "How old is your sister?" He lays crepe paper on the counter.

"Twenty-three," I say and take out my wallet.

"Yes, she like this very much. You are very close to your sister, I see. That is very good. Very good to have close family." He places my package in an unmarked gold bag.

"Are you," I begin. "Do you have a big family?" I put my credit card on the counter.

"Yes. Yes. Very big family. We are eleven brothers and sisters. Myself, I have four children."

"Are any of them in Canada?" I hear the morse-code buzz of the printing receipt.

"No no, all in Morocco. It is only me," he says. "My wife, she has a brother." He hands me a pen.

My mother was born in Casablanca, I think, but do not speak, knowing that if I do I will also have to explain that she grew up in Israel. I wonder if he will read this history in the features of my face.

I silently sign the receipt and hand it back to him. "How do you like it here?"

"Canada?" he says, considering his response with receipt in hand. "Canada is a very good country."

"It seems very nice. I just got here last month . . . from the U.S."

"America is very nice. Canada, too, is very nice. Only too much work. Too much work. It is not so good."

He hands me the bag over the counter as the doorbell rings.

"You will show me the other scarves next time I come?" I ask, and point at the curtain.

"You wish to see more?" he says, and starts around the counter. "Come with me."

"Yes, but next time. Next time."

"Any time, my friend."

I consider extending my hand, but decide not to. On my way out I hear something, and stop to finger the stained glass of a lantern by the door.

"In Morocco I buy this bowl for five dollar."

"No no no no. Look here. Let me show you."

"I can see. What? Do I not have eyes?"

"You have, but I show you the difference." Something less precious than crystal is struck. "Copper."

"What do you want, ten dollar? OK. Ten Dollar." The crinkle of a banknote. Then the sound of feet moving away, then coming in my direction. Meanwhile I see my miniature reflection in one facet of the lantern, a little shrunken thumb of clay with a popsicle stick stuck in.

"If you want fair price, you come back. Or you stay away. You waste my time."

Something is said, I'm not sure what, nor in which language. As I reach out to touch my aspect in the mirror and blot out my head, a form passes behind me and out the door. The bell tinkles.

"Stupid!" the owner says. "Stupid!" He comes to the door, peers out, and then circles back inside.

"What can I do with such people? What? Tell me!" he says with his back to me.

I am uncertain whether I am being called upon to respond. My nerves stand poised as I watch him stalk away. Then suddenly, unconsciously, with a feeling of horrible contraction, I turn and slink through the door. It jingles happily. I shuffle down the street, looking back into the store at my own reflection and the reflection of a streetcar behind me, unsure if I am being watched.

A week later my sister calls from Israel.

"I just got the scarf. It's beautiful! I love it."

* * *

A month after leaving Berkeley for Toronto my family's dog dies prematurely of cancer. She had been a stray in Puerto Rico where a friend had rescued her. Perhaps that's why she liked all humans, and most creatures too. She did something strange to the neighbor's Rottweiler, penned in by an eight-foot fence he never stopped trying to scale. He would whimper when he saw her. She seemed to have him bewitched.

"She didn't want to be left behind," my mother sobs on the phone.

My parents hadn't planned on taking her with them to Israel when they move next year. After thirty years in the States, two children, and three careers, my mother never relinquished the idea of going back.

"It was her time," I say.

"Your father says he never believed in reincarnation until he met her," she continues. "Yesterday we were sitting in the backyard and we saw the most beautiful yellow bird. I never saw a bird like that before. It sat on the bush where BB dug her holes." I am afraid to divulge that my new Ontario license plates begin with BB plus my father's initials.

When I speak to my father his voice cracks repeatedly. I am deeply impressed. After a minute he begs off the phone.

I feel like a distant relative unable to make it for the Shiva. When my mother's mother died, I came home to stay with my parents. The Shiva was in Israel, but my mother did not go, the distance being too far, her health a concern. When the mourners recited Kaddish at the burial, a cousin held a phone over the open grave so my mother could listen in California. At three in the morning, in her bed in the dark, my mother wailed for her mother and her country.

I struggle against the feeling of having betrayed my origins, and needing to make reparations. I have moved and must achieve something new.

* * *

Israel isn't the easiest place in the world to live—not for me, not for my sister. We chat about once a week across the ocean. This time the connection is awful.

"How are negotiations?" I say. Last semester the students struck. This semester it's the professors' turn.

"Oh, they're the same. They won't exist," she says.

"How do you *know* they won't exist?" I say.

No answer at first. "Huh?" she says.

"How do you *know*? You said negotiations *won't* exist. How do you know?"

"I said they *don't* exist, not *won't* exist."

"Oh," I say. "The connection's bad. You sound like you're under water."

"Anyway, the way things are going the strike might never end."

"How many weeks is it now?"

"Seven."

"Unbelievable. How can they not be talking seven weeks into the semester? Are the high school teachers still striking too?"

"Uh-huh. Apparently *they're* talking, at least, so I guess there is some hope."

"It makes you wonder how anything gets done in that country."

"It doesn't. Or it does, but you have to struggle first. It used to get me so down." I pause momentarily. "Not any more?"

"No, not so much. I'm doing my best to be Men about it," I hear.

"You're doing your best to be *what* about it?"

"*Zen* about it. *Zen* about it. I decided that I just can't let it get to me anymore. Whatever happens, happens."

Whenever the connection improves her voice comes through as light, scratchy, broken, like the sound of a mouse sniffing for food in a pile of leaves. Her rhythmic melodies have passed through an Autumn of bureaucracy, labor disputes, burglaries, boys, and war. I try to recall how she sounded on her first visit home during freshman year at NYU, boasting about Bleeker St., the Park, and cockroaches. Lying in bed, I straighten up, and screw the receiver against my ear.

"I understand how you feel," I say. "But two strikes in two semesters is totally fucked up. I would understand if you just felt angry."

"I know. I am angry. But it's out of my control, so it doesn't do me any good to be upset about it," she says. "It's not good for me, either."

"So you're *not* upset?"

"Not as long as I don't get my emotions tied up in the outcome."

I delay my response, thinking about the futility of encouragement. I feel like an aid worker planning the departure of a convoy of supplies into alien territory, into an ambush of shame.

"Israel is a tough place to live. I know I couldn't live there," I say.

"It is tough, but—" she says.

"And I hope you don't feel bad that you want to return to the States."

"No I don't feel bad."

"Cause I know Israel can make you feel like a failure, like you can't hack it. Take Mom for example. She felt—"

"But Mom can hack it."

"Maybe she can hack it. All right, she can hack it. So what. You can hack it too." No answer.

"I don't see any of your friends making Aliyah by themselves, getting an education *in Hebrew*, trying to immerse themselves in Israeli society. Excuse my language, but—"

"Excuse my language? That's Mom's phrase."

"It is her phrase, but—"

"Mom is moving back to Israel. And Dad too."

"Dad *left* Israel when he was your age. He didn't spend much longer there than you have."

"But now he's moving back."

"Yeah but he's almost sixty!"

No answer. I get out of bed, walk to the window, and look out on the first snow of the year. A black squirrel, head down at the base of a tree, sniffs the white stuff and seems to ponder its meaning.

"I mean, Naomi, Jesus, you've got to cut yourself some slack. How can you feel guilty that you don't want to live in a war zone, with robbers who rob you for a second time on the anniversary of the first burglary, with an education system that's falling apart, where you can't get anything done without a second or a third trip, where it's Gaza this and Lebanon that and separation fence and checkpoint and suicide bomber and 'the Jews are devils' and the 'Arabs are animals' and everyone 'only understands force.' What do you want from yourself?"

"You know what?" she says.

"What?"

"You said it yourself once. You feel like such a *frier* here."

"I said it? Oh, I guess I did . . . which should tell you something too. If you get taken advantage of in Israel, it's your own fault!"

No answer.

"Listen, I don't know what's got into me today. I'm talking like Mom all of a sudden."

"You totally are! You totally are!"

"Yeah, well . . ."

No answer. Instead I hear what sounds like a coin being tossed into a fountain, followed by footsteps, and the scraping of a broom. I don't interrupt, and instead idly scan the titles on a bookshelf. I stop when I see *Let's Go Israel*, which is Becca's, not mine.

"Naomi?" I say finally.

"Yeah I'm here. What did you say?"

"I didn't say anything."

"Hey bro-man, I should probably get going cause we have company coming soon. I hope I didn't bring you down. I'm feeling better now."

I don't know what to say. I take the guidebook off the shelf

"And we didn't even talk about you," she continues. "Next time I want to hear how the teaching is going."

"OK," I say, while I replay in my head the tone of her answers (I am always listening to the tone of her answers). I want to say something like: "Keep in mind what I said," but am afraid that sounding out the gravity of my seven extra years will invalidate them. So I say instead:

"I was just looking at Becca's copy of *Let's Go Israel*."

"I've got it too, I think. Not that I can remember ever looking through it."

"Well, I'll let you go. Say hi to Mark for me."

"Sounds good. Good night, bro."

I take the guidebook with me to the living room. Becca is reading on the couch.

"It's pretty funny that we have this book," I say, and fling it onto the coffee table.

"How come?" she says, peering over the spine of her book.

I pour myself a glass of water, and stare at the colossal head of the CN Tower peeking through the neighbor's rooftop antennae like a turkey baster.

"So you don't feel it's weird?" I say.

"No, not at all."

"Why not? You were born there, you spent a year there after college, you've got family there."

"I've got some second cousins, and I can't always remember all their names. Both my parents are Canadian. They happened to be in Israel when my mother's water broke."

"I haven't spent any more time in that country than you have."

"I guess it's spent more time in you."

* * *

Becca and I arrive at the traditional egalitarian synagogue just as the Torah service concludes. We stand against the rear wall until her parents arrive. Together we sit and the next reading begins. The reader does what rates as an adequate perform-ance, betraying the foreignness of Hebrew by mispronouncing a handful of theo-logically important words. Instead of "rebuild you" she says "your sons"; instead of "supplications" a fortuitous vowel saves her from saying "underwear."

The man giving the sermon has a baby face. He reminds me of a tennis coach I once had.

"On the second day of Rosh Hashanah we read the story of the Akeidah, the binding of Isaac . . ."

He looks up and down as he reads from the page. Whenever he looks down he can hardly be heard. People walk in and out of the sanctuary through front doors and back. The congregation is full of parents and grandparents, though there are a few exceptions. Three teenage girls with hair pinned up, mascara, and exposed knees emerge through the door behind the pulpit and then turn suddenly and scurry out. Most of the congregation members will not fit in this tiny building, so they are crammed into the JCC gymnasium a mile away, where the rabbi is.

"There are several interpretations that are traditionally made of the Akeidah. The first, of course, is that the story shows Abraham's perfect faith in God's justice. When God asks the patriarch to sacrifice his son Isaac, he does not hesitate, but rather shows himself unflinchingly ready to perform what is required."

I pinch Becca's thigh and whisper snobbishly, "I have a bad feeling about this." She smiles, but barely tilts her head.

I survey the crowd again. All around I see men and women leaning forward with their hands joined and forearms resting on the pews in front of them. They tilt their heads left or right periodically to expose their ears, in their earnestness and respect. The traffic in and out continues to my surprise. In my annoyance I am newly sympathetic to the speaker, especially as his eyes move to the rear of the sanctuary where the door clicks loudly. He swallows some words to wet his throat.

"In Kant's reading of the Akeidah the patriarch mistakes the voice commanding him to sacrifice Isaac as belonging to God, for such a commandment cannot derive from God."

It is clear that this modest and serious man, an academic at the university, intends to rescue God *and* Abraham. I lean over to Becca.

"He's going to pull the old switcheroo," I say.

The couple in front of us gets up and advances one pew. The man now sitting directly in front of them uses what little flexibility remains in his neck to participate in the commotion.

"Stewart was going to have heatstroke sitting by that window," I hear the woman say.

"So open it up," the man says. He nudges the figure to his right, a bulky youth wearing a suit with shoulder pads. Half a minute elapses before he figures out how to use the pole-hook to jiggle the latch.

"Thank you," the woman says.

The rear door clicks again and I look back. It's Davey, Becca's brother. The speaker, looking out of the corner of his eyes without shifting his head, continues nervously with his intricate analysis. He is wrapping up.

"And so, we must believe that Abraham, far from being willing to sacrifice Isaac, has faith that God's justice will become manifest ultimately, and is inconsistent with murder."

"Strength be with you," the congregation responds lazily and without unity, like the sound of a stone skipping on water. He has not reached them.

After the service, most of the congregation still remaining quickly clears out. I mill with Becca's family and a couple of their close friends, whose children are also there. Davey comes over.

"Poor Isaac gets absolutely *worked* by God and Abraham," he smiles. "Don't you think?"

"Oh yeah," I laugh. "I bet he was thinking idol worship outside of Canaan sounded pretty good."

That night I call my family. My sister is home for high holidays.

"How were services?" my father says after hello. My mother and sister are also on the phone.

"Actually, I was surprised, but I found them even less satisfying than at Etz Chaim. But the sermon was interesting, though it was a bit like watching someone try to turn a caterpillar into a butterfly with an X-acto knife."

"What about you? How were services?"

"Makes you want to puke," my mother says. "Your sister's so funny. Tell your brother what you said."

"What's up, bro. The woman giving the sermon was a bit cuckoo. She kept flapping her arms like she thought she was some kind of angel, or something. At one point she says, 'Don't carry more than you can hold.' Evidently this woman never shopped in *machaneh yehudah*. So I said, 'Every time I go to the market I carry more than I can hold.' I should get one of those little old lady carts!"

"You would make the best little old lady," I say.

"Are you kidding? I'm going to kick ass as a senior citizen," Naomi says.

"When the woman told us to hold hands," my mother says, "I thought your father was going to kill her."

"Was that today, Mom? You went *both* days?" I say.

"Are you crazy? With my back?" she says. "I need two days with that crowd like I need a hole in the head. Your sister and your father, the two crazies, went today. They're the only idiots who walk in this heat halfway across the city."

"It was terrible," my father says. "Silverman gave the sermon today. He got from unconditional love to *really* listening, but I think he missed a couple of steps in between."

Before Silverman, the old rabbi posted signs at the entrance to the synagogue warning against lashon ha'ra, the evil tongue of gossip.

"Did I tell you about Merav?" my mother asks.

* * *

A couple of months into my Canadian adventure, I go to the beach with Becca. Pulling into the lot, I am surprised by a tailgater hounding me. I try to quickly locate an open space, but give up and slow down to let the guy pass. The car lurches out, revs its engine, and squeals forward into one of two adjacent openings. A man in formalwear and rimless glasses trots off holding something heavy in one hand. He disappears in a maple grove strangely overpopulated with squawking children on a weekday morning in September.

"So you Canadians aren't all sunbeams and daffodils, eh?" I say.

The elementary school cross-country meet means the pleasantly odd sight of hundreds of winded pre-pubescents chugging through dry, deep sand. Becca and I wander off, but then before going home stop by the finish line to watch the conclusion of a race.

"Suzie's out there right now, doin' great," I hear a man say. In one hand he holds a shiny metal thing, forefinger poised.

"Oh my god, that asshole in the parking lot was carrying a *video camera*! He was coming to film his kid!" I say.

"You sound disappointed," Becca laughs.

CABLES

Roberta Hill

For Jemiah Aitch

The weight of the black bag on her left shoulder made Penny Rooks stumble before she trudged down the second flight of stairs. She juggled the five books in her right arm, unlocked the door and shoved ass-first inside. Relieved no one was in the hall, she let the books topple on the desk. Two giant white boxes shrank the space. On the largest, *Intel Inside.* Beyond them the poster of goldfish fanning blue and purple water with their diaphanous tails and a nautilus shell with brown brush marks along the edge Sam bought her on their first anniversary. Ever since the divorce a year ago, she couldn't bear human closeness. Why did she smell crayons? She was in first grade again. The boxes pushed her to the wall.

Intel Inside. The computer and its companion took so much space she had no room to sit. She tried to lift one, grappling with holds on far sides of the box. Her arms didn't reach, spanning what felt like the distance between Chicago and Minneapolis. On the day of their divorce, Sam called from Chicago to tell her she was old, fat, ugly. All the Indians in Chicago knew she never learned how to treat a man. Soon after Indians around the Twin Cities heard their story, Sam's version. Every time he put her down, she burned until after fifteen years, smoke clouded everything. Why was it wrong to beat a dead horse? She wanted to remember all that went wrong. As a newly wed, she asked Sam what he loved about her. "You're functional," he said as a tease. She chased him and made him take it back, but truth was he meant it. The light fell from the basement window on her faded jeans and she looked at her thighs. These are the thighs of an Indian woman in graduate school she thought, then again the thighs of an angry woman who hates uncertainty, the thighs of Ziggy and Luna's mom.

Her mind? A blank space where an unseen hand was writing "Trachenburg" in neat script. Professor Simms grilled her on the readings. She couldn't move toward his viewpoint. Her marriage failed because she couldn't judge when to hold, when to fold, when to do laundry. Any curious gaze brought wind-burn to her heart. She had loved Sam intensely and believed he loved her too but when they split three years ago, she saw herself from another point of view and her mind broke. She went here and there, dragging her two kids along. Hard, bitter and moving. Then her older cousin told her to go to graduate school. She hugged herself and looked up at the squares of the sound-proof ceiling.

Her cousin Molly asked, "How can you get a Masters in counseling and shun people?" I'll open up some day, but not today. She rubbed the desk. It and two metal chairs were all that fit in the narrow room in the basement of Scott Hall. No air for research assistants. The ticking radiator cranked heat on the warm October day. Harmony unfolded among those whose who had time, where programs and curricula grew over centuries, where white students went along and weren't often asked puzzling questions like "Where you from? What you doing here? You not out panhandling? You from the Panhandle? Do you speak English?" Sunlight blossomed suddenly from the window on the top of the wall. She was suddenly underwater with kelp rising and fish trailing a fan of bubbles. Behind in research, behind in writing, behind in finding friends. *Intel inside.* A gift from her reservation. Shirley put in a requisition and had it shipped to Scott Hall. No one at the university cared where it came from. Penny couldn't believe the tribe sent it.

She pried open the nearest box. Cables, pieces of plastic, two manuals the size of novellas, blue-edged "Easy Directions," sandwich bags for what she'd have left over. Stuff to stump her. The 800 number another computer answered with strings of options. Four years ago she thought a cursor was someone who cursed. She closed the box and pulled open another. The monitor, an encased idol in foamy white molds. She wedged her hand inside and lifted but the foam held steady. She needed help.

Three days after asking around, standing in the entrance to the red brick building, she was at the windows watching wind push leaves and papers when Sharon Hurley from her wired kids seminar came inside. "Hey, I'm glad you're here," she said. She handed Penny a card and winked, "Call Eli. Pricey but worth every cent." Penny matched Sharon's stride as she continued through the foyer. "Get on his good side," she said, turning around and walking backwards. "He's in demand." Sharon turned and flew up the central stairs.

Penny looked at the eggshell-colored card. Eli Lawrence Hatch. Two email addresses, a phone and pager scrolled in sky blue. She phoned from her office and left her number, then she closed the door and settled into reading T. D. Myer's *Patterns in Research Protocols.* She dozed until the phone woke her. She didn't expect a voice hesitant and gentle. Yes, he'd meet her the next afternoon. *The set-up would take a few hours. I charge twenty an hour.* Penny didn't want it set up only to zap out as soon as the guy left. Computers meant change. She didn't want change, also called a paradigmatic shift. They were making a world of robot snakes and cockroaches. They designed swarms of robot flies to photograph people and what they did at night. Those at the top wanted the basic condition of a fascist state. The lonely are easy to manipulate. Instead she asked about his experience and training? *A computer science major in my last semester. Worked tech support in Central College, setting up machines, developing software, managing databases, troubleshooting.* What about linking it to the server? *Piece of cake. I've been building computers since junior high.* In computer science class years ago, she waited in line with her punch cards and shared stories. She hated diagrams pointing to yes/no squares. She hated yes/no. They'd meet at Dinky Dome.

The next afternoon, Penny fixed herself up before leaving for Dinky Dome. She brushed her long brown hair, twisted it into a mushroom at the back of her head and squashed it with the pick from her beaded rose barrette. Wasn't her face too broad? Weren't her eyes too far apart? In the year since her divorce, she looked younger, alive from simple curiosity. Her lips curved slightly downward. Be happy your cheeks are prominent. She wiped the eyebrow pencil smudge from underneath one lower lid. Are young eyes brighter? She got to Dinky Dome an hour early. The smell of Chinese food, fries and burgers, strawberry smoothies wafted through the hazy air. Friends meeting friends. The tall brown-haired guy with the red backpack? Nope. She looked up at the white dome, sunlight fell from the windows down to the second floor balcony where more folks were hunched over notebooks, eating sale-priced egg rolls. Laughter and high-pitched women's voices edged her through the building until she took the steps on the far end of the open court. She wanted to eat upstairs and look over the balcony railing at the crowd. Just in case he came in early. He probably wouldn't stay. Her kind of luck! No one looked mildly techy. Oh my god! He said outside the dome! She grabbed her bag, met the rush of students heading up the stairs, and twisting through, got outside. No one waited for anything.

She looked up the street. The dome clock jumped three minutes. The planned streets laid in squares, the students filling up the streets with chatter didn't settle the strange feeling of daylight moving on the earth while she sat on the steps. October and the end of warmth. Underneath the sky, the night went on working. Did she even give a damn? Clumps of talkers, solitudes, couples with a stupid glow around them. Among the students on bikes, a stately guy in a navy jacket pedaled slowly past on a bright green Mongoose. A few more bikes, then an athlete came speeding down University Avenue toward the dome. Not holding his handlebars, he pedaled a black mountain bike with bright green forks, a blue and black backpack snug against his shoulders. He glanced behind him, grabbed the handlebars, stood up, keeping up with a red Honda, swooped behind it, managing the two lanes of traffic before leaning into the corner and disappearing behind a building. He was a black guy, Middle Eastern. Judgments are easier than truth. For six weeks her professor believed she belonged to a Sephardim community in exile. He encouraged her not to hide her tragic past. She spoke of her tragic past but when she made it clear she was Dakota, Mohawk and French, he told her real Indian women were more subdued. Penny stood up from the steps and stretched. Give it up! Just as she turned to go, she heard the voice on the phone coming from the guy on the bike, now without one.

He spoke to a young white woman who chirruped into zesty air. She hated chirruping women. Penny swung her bag to her left shoulder and strolled over, listening hard. At thirty yards away, the traffic on University zooming, the woman's exuberant voice spoke about circuits. Was he? Penny waved, boldly trying to get his attention. She didn't want to wait any longer. The man's brown eyes caught her own. He lifted his eyebrows and chin as if to question her. She glanced around and pointed at him. Was he the guy? Yes? He glanced around. Was she the one? Contact. She nodded. The man stepped her way. The student leaned and rubbed her breasts against his arm. The current war there meant fewer available men, but were earlier generations so obviously physical? Free love goes with wars. That's the way life balances. Her odds of finding a single man about her age were five to one. She watched Eli exude patience. He backed away, smiled, but enjoyed the woman's attention.

He looked energetic and poised. A high, intelligent forehead. Zillions of black curls with hair cut into a cap from the top of his head to the nape of his neck, squared around his ears. His sideburns grew down his jaw and merged into a beard that covered the shadowy part of his cheeks. He wrinkled his forehead and stepped toward her to end the conversation. Finally, the woman left. Penny felt uneasy with so much magnetic energy. His beard didn't grow completely beneath his lips, except for a small patch. His lips were full with a precise bow. His complexion almost a bit darker than her warm chocolate taffy. His eyes were lighter, the color of chestnuts; hers, mahogany. A generous nose. Eli looked easy-going, confident, muscular, solid in his stride. She should run away, say she wasn't the person he looked for. She never expected him to be Arabic, Black, or whatever he was.

"Penny Rooks?" He rubbed his eye. Genuinely surprised he showed up, she held out her hand and he took it.

"Eli," she said. A warm, firm handshake. He looked up and down at the traffic, then explained he had just gotten out of a super tough class. They waited for the light. Eli didn't walk. He strode with each foot firmly on the ground. He made her feel calm, almost attractive. The way he carried himself caused her to straighten up. Doing so, she felt her shoulder bag less burdensome. They reached the curb and his upper arm bumped into her shoulder as he adjusted his backpack. A little electric pulse passed into her. A light beam jumping from one cell to another. He stopped, not knowing where her office was.

"Say, I went to class and then headed over here. You probably want me to get started, but I am soooo hungry." With one hand on his stomach, he scanned her over taking in every freckle, wrinkle and scar. Old, fat, ugly, she stopped at the curb. She thought of how impatient her twelve year old son Ziggy got when he was hungry. This man could be the same way. He'd rush through setting up her computer. So what if she hadn't eaten lunch with a man since she moved there. Food brought friendship.

"We could head over to April's Restaurant and get a quick bite. Then you won't faint while putting up my system."

"I can eat at any time and any place."

They walked through Dinky Town where the upwardly mobile met the frantic lost. Eli explained his mom was French and Irish, his dad, African-American and Cherokee. "I'm a mixed kid." A term he used to describe himself. She was mixed but remembered how in her neighborhood as she grew up being mixed meant being Mexican-Indian. They were walking along, shifting their backpacks, being regular students. Eli radiated sunshine. She was smiling inside when she realized Eli had asked about her.

"I'm Mohawk, Dakota, and French. I don't claim French, since the fur trader that married my great-grandmother sailed back to France and left her with four children. He earned wealth trading beaver pelts. Every Indian that came to trade brought his height in pelts. Whether he was 4 feet or 6 feet tall, the deal was the same: one gun each. It depleted the beaver in no time." Some family members claim French-Indian, some claim French. She didn't know why, but she erased the French trader because he deserved it. She claimed Indian. Her soul searching and the 1970s gave her that.

They sat in the booth at April's Burger Fantasy, talking and watching the folks coming in. He ordered hamburger with fries. She picked apart her salad. It was tough to complete a Computer Science major with two grizzly bear classes back to back. He couldn't always afford what he needed. He scrimped. His last semester. He started on his plate before she got half way through the salad. She paid for his food, because as he talked, he appealed to her maternal nature. He was the little brother she always wanted and never had the luck to get. As he talked, he twisted his beard in little circles. She remembered sitting in the back of the class in Grover Cleveland Elementary twirling her long hair into coils. Her mother brushed it harder than her sister Rainy's. She felt her long hair now, smoothed a curl over her ear, remembering how anxious school and classmates made her. Why did she decide to attend the university? He delighted in eating. Here and now was a man taking the time to enjoy his food, to chew it well, to drink well, to laugh and talk, completely at ease. She smiled, aware of how much she enjoyed the moment.

They didn't make men like him when she was young. She didn't see anyone like him back then. He looked at a small, blond woman burdened by books and lifted his eyebrows, like he was willing to help if she sent him a signal.

"I wished I had been alive in the 1960s and 70s," he said. "My parents lived through the riots. They met and fell in love in Haight Ashbury, then moved here. They were in the Civil Rights Movement. I wish I could've heard Jimi Hendrix in concert. His Star Spangled Banner says it all."

She found herself telling him more than she knew about herself. "When Jimi played that, his feelings went beneath our navels, deep into our dreams—that longing and pain for peace. Hundreds protesting war, wanting changes. The fifties were like living in a cell. Then Harrison played 'Here Comes the Sun.' I remember being in a commune north of San Francisco where people shared hugs, happiness and knew that beauty creates life. I danced for life and love, for change. Then, I moved on, ended up at Wounded Knee and felt our oppression, you know, like a collective awakening. Twilight carried sweetness and beauty in the eyes of the most burned-out people. We were all fragile, tender and warm." She laughed lightly and stabbed her salad. "I sound like a gushing romantic. I met Sam at a disco club in Chicago. The globe in the dark, the glittery dress, the whole romantic set-up. We were married for a long time. 'Never Can Say Good-bye' was my theme song!"

"When did you move here?" She noticed the freckles along his cheeks. His innocence disarmed her. He wasn't doing anything but asking. Sam kept her from her finding friends, corralling her like a thoroughbred cutting horse until her work for him was done.

"This year. I'm angry. Divorced. You don't want to know. I might blow up and toss my salad at the mirror." Maybe she said too much, but Eli nodded, his gaze still open. He listened. How unsettling to be heard.

"I'm angry with this semester." He said, burger in mid-air. "I use my focus to see where to place my anger. Most of it gets focused on doing the problem sets for classes. My girlfriend wants to quit beauty school and get married after I graduate. I mean, shouldn't we both agree to this?" He licked his lips and bit into the burger.

No, it was an advertising pitch to believe everyone found the right match. People pick and choose, get coerced or rejected. What was important—shared values, agreeing on what was important together. It takes negotiation and subterfuge. Months she never waited for because she was a romantic and made

Sam into someone he never was. Sam hated responsibilities: children, dental bills, anything that required action. She didn't know this until a year into the marriage. Eli left a tip for the waitress. It felt strange to be walking with a man who was attentive and kind, who didn't walk far ahead or keep her at his backside. They headed to Scott Hall.

The stuffy office oozed heat. Eli dug through boxes, starting with the computer, at ease as an otter in an ocean of kelp. Lifting the monitor as Styrofoam fell on each side like a ship coming out of a lock, he placed it on the desk. Penny watched him, feeling thrilled that at least her computer would make her office appear studious. Eli was absorbed, still chatting, aware of her. She felt energy in her body, watching him take out equipment, rummage for set-up discs, cables. Such steadiness, calmness, perseverance was new. His presence—muscular, strong, brought an ache into her soul. She felt relaxed, curious, and smelling crayons in the air, remembered the excitement she felt when she first started graduate school. Down to earth, good natured, patient, Eli's eyebrows and forehead wrinkled when he looked for a cable or picked through packaging. Life wasn't hard. It was easy! Figure out connections! Get connected, feel the Source pulsing through you. "There's far more energy in darkness than light," he explained, telling her about astronomy. A thimbleful of dark matter made a star and solar system! He leaned from the back of the monitor to the tower, hooking, bolting, screwing, checking as he went, his long fingers elegant in their movements, his perceptive mind watching where things went as his talking and sharing settled into the simple human activity they had been for millennia.

Penny watched him. He's beautiful she thought. I won't see him after I pay him, but we're sharing the most natural thing in the world. It's like watching a fancy dancer whirl and balance on the drum beats, a potter throw a lump on a wheel and with hands firm and fluid pulling up a teapot, like Jimi playing guitar. Could men and women speak so openly to each other? I must be so far beyond the age of glamour that he can speak freely. Were men reared to be kind and open-hearted, self-assured? She wanted to rear Ziggy to be that way.

Eli took the small pieces inside the plastic, fitting them, testing, adjusting, standing up and bending over to hook, unhook, re-hook cables. Penny felt herself easing into his atmosphere. Everything will work out fine, testing, oops, testing again. He likes sports with pomp and ritual. She doesn't do sports. He loves a situation where every physical sensation, arms, legs, hands, feet, breathing get synchronized and you get that sense of perception, that merging into the field of vision—you become one with the landscape. It's our sixth sense called priopropriation. She's felt that when she comes out of the office as the sun is setting and the yellow leaves go scattering across the still dark green grass, yes, and the feeling comes all by itself. She notices his hands again with sensitive fingertips where various tools appear—pliers unhinging into metal wedges, screwdrivers, a tool like an acrobat spinning through a thousand folds. He likes details, paying attention to details. She likes the big picture; if she bought a house someday it would be on a high hill and she'd be the hawk woman taking in the view. He'd find the right place at the right time, letting destiny work that way. When he's in doubt, he leans out. He liked doing favors for people to build good energies for the future. She liked working hard for things. She enjoyed holding on to grudges. The best defense is having nothing to defend he answered. Then she stopped speaking because the years she spent dreaming of a future that never occurred loomed in the dark basement windows.

Visions never are in sync with reality. That's why they're visions. How many dreams got lost? She couldn't speak of it. She needed space.

"Sometimes I get frustrated by the things I miss in the broader perspective," Penny said.

"I'm grateful for everything I get, no matter what it is," Eli said.

"I'm angry and so pissed off at life, I could blast stones into gravel," she said.

"Maybe you should work at a rock quarry this summer. Seriously, it'd do you good."

Her cables were all hooked up. He settled like a maestro into the chair before the screen, motioning for her to sit in a chair and pull it near him. He handled the keyboard like it was part of him. The way Jimi played guitar. Comfortably. Alert. Powerful. He sat so close her leg rubbed against him. In a blast of light, she wanted a man like him, wanted to feel more than she had ever felt before. Brushing Eli's legs made her body thrum with an energy she couldn't speak of. Being hooked up, wanting to be hooked up, feeling hooked up felt good. He scratched under his chin and began to explain how the computer thinks. It goes so fast but does one thing at a time. She's got a monster machine. No way! Oh yes. You got a big machine here. He tells her she could put libraries inside. He pulls out a little flat mirror-like thing, a palm pilot. Shows her how many bytes it has and how many her machine has.

She smells his sweat as his thigh brushes hers, as he talks. He sees her glance, catches its meaning and goes on. He tells her about his bike and how good it is for saving the earth, how more people should ride bikes. She wants to save the earth. She doesn't know what she wants other than to get over her divorce, stop being afraid of men, failure and the blank screen in her mind with Trachenburg written on it.

"Who?" he asks. She realizes then she wasn't talking to herself. She tries to explain that Ludwig wrote "Tractatus Logico-Philosophicus," something a professor went ballistic over. She felt it reduced what she was most interested in, but what she couldn't express—values, feelings, qualities in the human heart. No one in Counseling Psych listened. They agreed with Ludwig that "A new possibility cannot be discovered later."

She doesn't want a blank screen, to make mistakes. Oh god, she thinks, what is happening here? Eli breaks into a belly laugh, his eyes smiling at her. Mistakes are cool. You have to figure out what's a mistake, what's a glitch. Her body had potential, power, energy and she feels amazement, fear, then more amazement pouring from her as her intellect nosedives and curiosity pulls her toward him. Eli does all he can to increase awareness, to be alive.

How was your high school? I was an outsider in a place with race prejudice, my nose was too big, my hair too curly for an Indian. People thought I was proud and arrogant when I was scared as hell, she says. Tapping on keys to make various icons appear on the screen, Eli wonders why racial mixtures were considered an abomination. He didn't know what that meant as a child.

"No one wanted to date me. I was ugly all through high school," she says.

"You're far from ugly," he says, typing more codes to connect her to the server. She stops and looks at him. He's a fresh wind, typing the keyboard, watching the screen glowing green as it responds with boxes and buttons. He's not manipulating her. He's sending a cable into her soul, heart and head. What if she lost that bitter edge she's carried inside forever?

"Ever had a heart break, Eli?"

He twirls his beard and looks into her eyes as if he's right there, so close she sees the ochre in his pupils. She looks away. "Oh yes," he says, "but I still seek harmony and balance. So, sometimes when it doesn't work out, I hurt but I'm grateful for the change."

Then he takes her wrist lightly the way a butterfly lands on a flower petal and welcomes life. He brings his other hand toward hers to show how in judo you move with the force coming at you. Whatever comes at you gives you energy. So you take that energy and use it if you don't resist. You have to figure all energy coming at you comes from the Source of Life. His hand is warm as he moves hers with his into a full circle. The movement. Don't think resistance. Just let power flow through the cable. Let mistakes come. If you make the same mistake, you can fix it. If you can't make it again, it's a glitch and let it go.

He was aware he was touching her, that she was a woman, beautiful even and as alive as he was, that she wasn't an image or object. Eli may have worked with objects and people, but he felt the difference between flesh and plastic. He let go her hand as gently as he took it. "Judo is the study of balance. There's a great class on Tuesday nights."

He got up and looked at her. His radiant gaze made her laugh. Would she want to join the class? An image flashed into her of herself rolling on the floor and slapping the mat. She looked at her hand. She liked being a student. The machine blinked off and on, then started ticking as it loaded icons on the desk top. Each machine fits a person, conforms to that person as it falls into the groove of how one works with it. It was dark beyond the windows and the streetlight shone through. He rose and gathered his tools. She paid him. Then they walked outside together, climbing the steps and going out into the crisp air. She could learn. Wasn't that what first graders understood—that everybody learns? What a delicious night! Would he come by if she messed up? She'd buy him supper next time. He looked into her heart then up at oak leaves turning bronze and rustling in the dark under the streetlight. They walked toward Dinky Dome, laughing at some odd idea zooming through delightful autumn air.

THE CLOCHARD

Chester Himes

It is midnight warm and clear. A full moon shines on the beauty of the Seine. An American, exquisitely wined and dined, walks along the banks, smoking an after dinner cigar. Couples embrace in the shadows, campers sleep on the pavement. Suddenly, a cry for help breaks into the American's musings. Hysterical with anxiety, a ragged Clochard points towards a little dog struggling in the channel, and says in accented English: "My poor dog, he is drowning and I can not swim." Instantly the American strips off his coat and prepares to dive into the water. But the Clochard detains him for a moment, urging him to strip off the rest of his clothes, saying no one will take notice and that his little dog would never forgive himself if the gentleman ruined his fine clothes. Without a moment's hesitation, the American strips to his underwear and dives to the rescue. Whereupon the Clochard quickly gathers up the American's clothes and whistles to the dog which swims rapidly to the bank. Waving gaily to the chagrined swimmer, the Clochard runs up the ramp, followed by the dog, and goes to another part of the Seine where he bathes and shaves at a public hydrant. He then dons the stolen clothes, examines the loaded purse, and strolls along the boulevards as a rich American. On his orders the dog follows several paces behind so as not to appear to be together. Later he arrives among the hectic throngs in Montmartre: tourists, artists, detectives, ladies of the night. Finally he permits himself to be picked up, but he is careless, and the efficient lady robs him of his clothes for a sympathetic American she has befriended. She found her American lurking half nude on the banks of the Seine with a fantastic story about being robbed by an English speaking bum and a confidence dog.

WHO'S PASSING FOR WHO?

Langston Hughes

One of the great difficulties about being a member of a minority race is that so many kindhearted, well-meaning bores gather around to help. Usually, to tell the truth, they have nothing to help with, except their company which is often appallingly dull. Some members of the Negro race seem very well able to put up with it, though, in these uplifting years. Such was Caleb Johnson, colored social worker, who was always dragging around with him some nondescript white person or two, inviting them to dinner, showing them Harlem, ending up at the Savoy— much to the displeasure of whatever friends of his might be out that evening for fun, not sociology.

Friends are friends and, unfortunately, overearnest uplifters are uplifters—no matter what color they may be. If it were the white race that was ground down instead of Negroes, Caleb Johnson would be one of the first to offer Nordics the sympathy of his utterly inane society, under the impression that somehow he would be doing them a great deal of good.

You see, Caleb, and his white friends, too, were all bores. Or so we, who lived in Harlem's literary bohemia during the "Negro Renaissance" thought. We literary ones considered ourselves too broad-minded to be bothered with questions of color. We liked people of any race who smoked incessantly, drank liberally, wore complexion and morality as loose garments, and made fun of anyone who didn't do likewise. We snubbed and high-hatted any Negro or white luckless enough not to understand Gertrude Stein, Ulysses, Man Ray, the theremin, Jean Toomer, or George Antheil. By the end of the 1920's Caleb was just catching up to Dos Passos. He thought H. G. Wells good.

We met Caleb one night in Small's. He had three assorted white folks in tow. We would have passed him by with but a nod had he not hailed us enthusiastically, risen, and introduced us with great acclaim to his friends who turned out to be schoolteachers from Iowa, a woman and two men. They appeared amazed and delighted to meet all at once two Negro writers and a black painter in the flesh. They invited us to have a drink with them. Money being scarce with us, we deigned to sit down at their table.

The white lady said, "I've never met a Negro writer before."

The two men added, "Neither have we."

"Why, we know any number of *white* writers," we three dark bohemians declared with bored nonchalance.

"But Negro writers are much more rare," said the lady.

"There are plenty in Harlem," we said.

"But not in Iowa," said one of the men, shaking his mop of red hair.

"There are no good *white* writers in Iowa either, are there?" we asked superciliously.

"Oh, yes, Ruth Suckow came from there."

Whereupon we proceeded to light in upon Ruth Suckow as old hat and to annihilate her in favor of Kay Boyle. The way we flung names around seemed to impress both Caleb and his white guests. This, of course, delighted us, though we were too young and too proud to admit it.

The drinks came and everything was going well, all of us drinking, and we three showing off in a high-brow manner, when suddenly at the table just behind us a man got up and knocked down a woman. He was a brownskin man. The woman was blonde. As she rose he knocked her down again. Then the red-haired man from Iowa got up and knocked the colored man down.

He said, "Keep your hands off that white woman."

The man got up and said, "She's not a white woman. She's my wife."

One of the waiters added, "She's not white, sir, she's colored."

Whereupon the man from Iowa looked puzzled, dropped his fists, and said, "I'm sorry."

The colored man said, "What are you doing up here in Harlem anyway, interfering with my family affairs?"

The white man said, "I thought she was a white woman."

The woman who had been on the floor rose and said, "Well, I'm not a white woman, I'm colored, and you leave my husband alone."

Then they both lit in on the gentleman from Iowa. It took all of us and several waiters, too, to separate them. When it was over the manager requested us to kindly pay our bill and get out. He said we were disturbing the peace. So we all left. We went to a fish restaurant down the street. Caleb was terribly apologetic to his white friends. We artists were both mad and amused.

"Why did you say you were sorry," said the colored painter to the visitor from Iowa, "after you'd hit that man—and then found out it wasn't a white woman you were defending, but merely a light colored woman who looked white?"

"Well," answered the red-haired Iowan, "I didn't mean to be butting in if they were all the same race."

"Don't you think a woman needs defending from a brute, no matter what race she may be?" asked the painter.

"Yes, but I think it's up to you to defend your own women."

"Oh, so you'd divide up a brawl according to races, no matter who was right?"

"Well, I wouldn't say that."

"You mean you wouldn't defend a colored woman whose husband was knocking her down?" asked the poet.

Before the visitor had time to answer, the painter said, "No! You just got mad because you thought a black man was hitting a *white* woman."

"But she *looked* like a white woman," countered the man.

"Maybe she was just passing for colored," I said.

"Like some Negroes pass for white," Caleb interposed.

"Anyhow, I don't like it," said the colored painter, "the way you stopped defending her when you found out she wasn't white."

"No, we don't like it," we all agreed except Caleb. Caleb said in extenuation, "But Mr. Stubblefield is new to Harlem."

The red-haired white man said, "Yes, it's my first time here."

"Maybe Mr. Stubblefield ought to stay out of Harlem," we observed.

"I agree," Mr. Stubblefield said. "Good night."

He got up then and there and left the café. He stalked as he walked. His red head disappeared into the night.

"Oh, that's too bad," said the white couple who remained. "Stubby's temper just got the best of him. But explain to us, are many colored folks really as fair as that woman?"

"Sure, lots of them have more white blood than colored, and pass for white."

"Do they?" said the lady and gentleman from Iowa.

"You never read Nella Larsen?" we asked.

"She writes novels," Caleb explained. "She's part white herself."

"Read her," we advised. "Also read the *Autobiography of an Ex-colored Man*." Not that we had read it ourselves—because we paid but little attention to the older colored writers—but we knew it was about passing for white.

We all ordered fish and settled down comfortably to shocking our white friends with tales about how many Negroes there were passing for white all over America. We were determined to *épater le bourgeois* real good via this white couple we had cornered, when the woman leaned over the table in the midst of our dissertations and said, "Listen, gentlemen, you needn't spread the word, but me and my husband aren't white either. We've just been *passing* for white for the last fifteen years."

"What?"

"We're colored, too, just like you," said the husband. "But it's better passing for white because we make more money."

Well, that took the wind out of us. It took the wind out of Caleb, too. He thought all the time he was showing some fine white folks Harlem—and they were as colored as he was!

Caleb almost never cursed. But this time he said, "I'll be damned!"

Then everybody laughed. And laughed! We almost had hysterics. All at once we dropped our professionally self-conscious "Negro" manners, became natural, ate fish, and talked and kidded freely like colored folks do when there are no white folks around. We really had fun then, joking about that red-haired guy who mistook a fair colored woman for white. After the fish we went to two or three more night spots and drank until five o'clock in the morning.

Finally we put the light-colored people in a taxi heading downtown. They turned to shout a last good-by. The cab was just about to move off, when the woman called to the driver to stop.

She leaned out the window and said with a grin, "Listen, boys! I hate to confuse you again. But, to tell the truth, my husband and I aren't really colored at all. We're white. We just thought we'd kid you by passing for colored a little while—just as you said Negroes sometimes pass for white."

She laughed as they sped off toward Central Park, waving, "Good-by!"

We didn't say a thing. We just stood there on the corner in Harlem dumbfounded—not knowing now *which* way we'd been fooled. Were they really white—passing for colored? Or colored—passing for white?

Whatever race they were, they had had too much fun at our expense—even if they did pay for the drinks.

DEBUT

Kristin Hunter

"Hold *still*, Judy," Mrs. Simmons said around the spray of pins that protruded dangerously from her mouth. She gave the thirtieth tug to the tight sash at the waist of the dress. "Now walk over there and turn around slowly."

The dress, Judy's first long one, was white organdy over taffeta, with spaghetti straps that bared her round brown shoulders and a floating skirt and a wide sash that cascaded in a butterfly effect behind. It was a dream, but Judy was sick and tired of the endless fittings she had endured so that she might wear it at the Debutantes' Ball. Her thoughts leaped ahead to the Ball itself . . .

"*Slowly*, I said!" Mrs. Simmons' dark, angular face was always grim, but now it was screwed into an expression resembling a prune. Judy, starting nervously, began to revolve by moving her feet an inch at a time.

Her mother watched her critically. "No, it's still not right. I'll just have to rip out that waistline seam again."

"Oh, Mother!" Judy's impatience slipped out at last. "Nobody's going to notice all those little details."

"They will too. They'll be watching you every minute, hoping to see something wrong. You've got to be the *best*. Can't you get that through your head?" Mrs. Simmons gave a sigh of despair. "You better start noticin' 'all those little details' yourself. I can't do it for you all your life. Now turn around and stand up straight."

"Oh, Mother," Judy said, close to tears from being made to turn and pose while her feet itched to be dancing, "I can't stand it any more!"

"You can't stand it, huh? How do you think *I* feel?" Mrs. Simmons said in her harshest tone.

Judy was immediately ashamed, remembering the weeks her mother had spent at the sewing machine, pricking her already tattered fingers with needles and pins, and the great weight of sacrifice that had been borne on Mrs. Simmons' shoulders for the past two years so that Judy might bare hers at the Ball.

"All right, take it off," her mother said. "I'm going to take it up the street to Mrs. Luby and let her help me. It's got to be right or I won't let you leave the house."

"Can't we just leave it the way it is, Mother?" Judy pleaded without hope of success. "I think it's perfect."

"You would," Mrs. Simmons said tartly as she folded the dress and prepared to bear it out of the room. "Sometimes I think I'll never get it through your head. You got to look just right and act just right. That Rose Griffin and those other girls can afford to be careless, maybe, but you can't. You're gonna be the darkest, poorest one there."

Judy shivered in her new lace strapless bra and her old, childish knit snuggies. "You make it sound like a battle I'm going to instead of just a dance."

"It is a battle," her mother said firmly. "It starts tonight and it goes on for the rest of your life. The battle to hold your head up and get someplace and be somebody. We've done all we can for you, your father and I. Now you've got to start fighting some on your own." She gave Judy a slight smile, her voice softened a little. "You'll do all right, don't worry. Try and get some rest this afternoon. Just don't mess up your hair."

"All right, Mother," Judy said listlessly.

She did not really think her father had much to do with anything that happened to her. It was her mother who had ingratiated her way into the Gay Charmers two years ago, taking all sorts of humiliation from the better-dressed, better-off, lighter-skinned women, humbly making and mending their dresses, fixing food for their meetings, addressing more mail and selling more tickets than anyone else. The club had put it off as long as they could, but finally they had to admit Mrs. Simmons to membership because she worked so hard. And that meant, of course, that Judy would be on the list for this year's Ball.

Her father, a quiet carpenter who had given up any other ambitions years ago, did not think much of Negro society or his wife's fierce determination to launch Judy into it. "Just keep clean and be decent," he would say. "That's all anybody has to do."

Her mother always answered, "If that's all I did we'd still be on relief," and he would shut up with shame over the years when he had been laid off repeatedly and her days' work and sewing had kept them going. Now he had steady work but she refused to quit, as if she expected it to end at any moment. The intense energy that burned in Mrs. Simmons' large dark eyes had scorched her features into permanent irony. She worked day and night and spent her spare time scheming and planning. Whatever her personal ambitions had been, Judy knew she blamed Mr. Simmons for their failure; now all her schemes revolved around their only child.

Judy went to her mother's window and watched her stride down the street with the dress until she was hidden by the high brick wall that went around two sides of their house. Then she returned to her own room. She did not get dressed because she was afraid of pulling a sweater over her hair—her mother would notice the difference even if it looked all right to Judy—and because she was afraid that doing anything, even getting dressed, might precipitate her into the battle. She drew a stool up to her window and looked out. She had no real view, but she liked her room. The wall hid the crowded tenement houses beyond the alley, and from its cracks and bumps and depressions she could construct any imaginary landscape she chose. It was how she had spent most of the free hours of her dreamy adolescence.

"Hey, can I go?"

It was the voice of an invisible boy in the alley. As another boy chuckled, Judy recognized the familiar ritual; if you said yes, they said, "Can I go with you?" It had been tried on her dozens of times. She always walked past, head in the air, as if she had not heard. Her mother said that was the only thing to do; if they knew she was a lady, they wouldn't dare bother her. But this time a girl's voice, cool and assured, answered.

"If you think you're big enough," it said.

It was Lucy Mae Watkins; Judy could picture her standing there in a tight dress with bright, brazen eyes.

"I'm big enough to give you a baby," the boy answered.

Judy would die if a boy ever spoke to her like that, but she knew Lucy Mae could handle it. Lucy Mae could handle all the boys, even if they ganged up on her, because she had been born knowing something other girls had to learn.

"Aw, you ain't big enough to give me a shoe-shine," she told him.

"Come here and I'll show you how big I am," the boy said.

"Yeah, Lucy Mae, what's happenin'?" another, younger boy said. "Come here and tell us."

Lucy Mae laughed. "What I'm puttin' down is too strong for little boys like you."

"Come here a minute, baby," the first boy said. "I got a cigarette for you."

"Aw, I ain't studyin' your cigarettes," Lucy Mae answered. But her voice was closer, directly below Judy. There were the sounds of a scuffle and Lucy Mae's muffled laughter. When she spoke her voice sounded raw and cross. "Come on now, boy. Cut it out and give me the damn cigarette." There was more scuffling, and the sharp crack of a slap, and then Lucy Mae said, "Cut it out, I said. Just for that I'm gonna take 'em all." The clack of high heels rang down the sidewalk with a boy's clumsy shoes in pursuit.

Judy realized that there were three of them down there. "Let her go, Buster," one said. "You can't catch her now."

"Aw, hell, man, she took the whole damn pack," the one called Buster complained.

"That'll learn you!" Lucy Mae's voice mocked from down the street. "Don't mess with nothin' you can't handle."

"Hey, Lucy Mae. Hey, I heard Rudy Grant already gave you a baby," a second boy called out.

"Yeah. Is that true, Lucy Mae?" the youngest one yelled.

There was no answer. She must be a block away by now.

For a moment the hidden boys were silent; then one of them guffawed directly below Judy, and the other two joined in the secret male laughter that was oddly high-pitched and feminine.

"Aw, man, I don't know what you all laughin' about," Buster finally grumbled. "That girl took all my cigarettes. You got some, Leroy?"

"Naw," the second boy said.

"Me neither," the third one said.

"What we gonna do? I ain't got but fifteen cent. Hell, man, I want more than a feel for a pack of cigarettes." There was an unpleasant whine in Buster's voice. "Hell, for a pack of cigarettes I want a bitch to come across."

"She will next time, man," the boy called Leroy said.

"She better," Buster said. "You know she better. If she pass by here again, we gonna jump her, you hear?"

"Sure, man," Leroy said. "The three of us can grab her easy."

"Then we can all three of us have some fun. Oh, *yeah*, man," the youngest boy said. He sounded as if he might be about 14.

Leroy said, "We oughta get Roland and J. T. too. For a whole pack of cigarettes she oughta treat all five of us."

"Aw, man, why tell Roland and J. T.?" the youngest voice whined. "They ain't in it. Them was *our* cigarettes."

"They was *my* cigarettes, you mean," Buster said with authority. "You guys better quit it before I decide to cut you out."

"Oh, man, don't do that. We with you, you know that."

"Sure, Buster, we your aces, man."

"All right, that's better." There was a minute of silence.

Then, "What we gonna do with the girl, Buster?" the youngest one wanted to know.

"When she come back we gonna jump the bitch, man. We gonna jump her and grab her. Then we gonna turn her every way but loose." He went on, spinning a crude fantasy that got wilder each time he retold it, until it became so secretive that their voices dropped to a low indistinct murmur punctuated by guffaws. Now and then Judy could distinguish the word "girl" or the other word they used for it; these words always produced the loudest guffaws of all. She shook off her fear with the thought that Lucy Mae was too smart to pass there again today. She had heard them at their dirty talk in the alley before and had always been successful in ignoring it; it had nothing to do with her, the wall protected her from their kind. All the ugliness was on their side of it, and this side was hers to fill with beauty.

She turned on her radio to shut them out completely and began to weave her tapestry to its music. More for practice than anything else, she started by picturing the maps of the places to which she intended to travel, then went on to the faces of her friends. Rose Griffin's sharp, Indian profile appeared on the wall. Her coloring was like an Indian's too and her hair was straight and black and glossy. Judy's hair, naturally none of these things, had been "done" four days ago so that tonight it would be "old" enough to have a gloss as natural-looking as Rose's. But Rose, despite her handsome looks, was silly; her voice broke constantly into high-pitched giggles and she became even sillier and more nervous around boys.

Judy was not sure that she knew how to act around boys either. The sisters kept boys and girls apart at the Catholic high school where her parents sent her to keep her away from low-class kids. But she felt that she knew a secret; tonight, in that dress, with her hair in a sophisticated upsweep, she would be transformed into a poised princess. Tonight all the college boys her mother described so eagerly would rush to dance with her, and then from somewhere *the boy* would appear. She did not know his name; she neither knew nor cared whether he went to college, but she imagined that he would be as dark as she was, and that there would be awe and diffidence in his manner as he bent to kiss her hand . . .

A waltz swelled from the radio; the wall, turning blue in deepening twilight, came alive with whirling figures. Judy rose and began to go through the steps she had rehearsed for so many weeks. She swirled with a practiced smile on her face, holding an imaginary skirt at her side; turned, dipped, and flicked on her bedside lamp without missing a fraction of the beat. Faster and faster she danced with her imaginary partner, to an inner music that was better than the sounds on the radio.

She was "coming out," and tonight the world would discover what it had been waiting for all these years.

"Aw, git it, baby." She ignored it as she would ignore the crowds that lined the streets to watch her pass on her way to the Ball.

"Aw, do your number." She waltzed on, safe and secure on her side of the wall.

"Can I come up there and do it with you?"

At this she stopped, paralyzed. Somehow they had come over the wall or around it and into her room.

"Man, I sure like the view, from here," the youngest boy said. "How come we never tried this view before?"

She came to life, ran quickly to the lamp and turned it off, but not before Buster said, "Yeah, and the back view is fine, too."

"Aw, she turned off the light," a voice complained.

"Put it on again, baby, we don't mean no harm."

"Let us see you dance some more. I bet you can really do it."

"Yeah, I bet she can shimmy on down."

"You know it, man."

"Come on down here, baby," Buster's voice urged softly dangerously. "I got a cigarette for you."

"Yeah, and he got something else for you, too."

Judy, flattened against her closet door, gradually lost her urge to scream. She realized that she was shivering in her underwear. Taking a deep breath, she opened the closet door and found her robe. She thought of going to the window and yelling down, "You don't have a thing I want. Do you understand?" But she had more important things to do.

Wrapping her hair in protective plastic, she ran a full steaming tub and dumped in half a bottle of her mother's favorite cologne. At first she scrubbed herself furiously, irritating her skin. But finally she stopped, knowing she would never be able to get cleaner than this again. She could not wash away the thing they considered dirty, the thing that made them pronounce "girl" in the same way as the other four-letter words they wrote on the wall, in the alley; it was part of her, just as it was part of her mother and Rose Griffin and Lucy Mae. She relaxed then because it was true that the boys in the alley did not have a thing she wanted. She had what they wanted, and the knowledge replaced her shame with a strange, calm feeling of power.

After her bath she splashed on more cologne and spent 40 minutes on her makeup, erasing and retracing her eyebrows six times until she was satisfied. She went to her mother's room then and found the dress, finished and freshly pressed, on its hanger.

When Mrs. Simmons came upstairs to help her daughter she found her sitting on the bench before the vanity mirror as if it were a throne. She looked young and arrogant and beautiful and perfect and cold.

"Why, you're dressed already," Mrs. Simmons said in surprise. While she stared, Judy rose with perfect, icy grace and glided to the center of the room. She stood there motionless as a mannequin.

"I want you to fix the hem, Mother," she directed. "It's still uneven in back."

Her mother went down obediently on her knees muttering, "It looks all right to me." She put in a couple of pins. "That better?"

"Yes," Judy said with a brief glance at the mirror. "You'll have to sew it on me, Mother. I can't take it off now. I'd ruin my hair."

Mrs. Simmons went to fetch her sewing things, returned, and surveyed her daughter. "You sure did a good job on yourself, I must say," she admitted grudgingly. "Can't find a thing to complain about. You'll look as good as anybody there."

"Of course, Mother," Judy said as Mrs. Simmons knelt and sewed. "I don't know what you were so worried about." Her secret feeling of confidence had returned, stronger than ever, but the evening ahead was no longer the vague girlish fantasy she had pictured on the wall; it had hard, clear outlines leading up to a definite goal. She would be the belle of the Ball because she knew more than Rose Griffin and her silly friends; more than her mother; more, even, than Lucy Mae, because she knew better than to settle for a mere pack of cigarettes.

"There," her mother said, breaking the thread. She got up. "I never expected to get you ready this early. Ernest Lee won't be here for another hour."

"That silly Ernest Lee," Judy said, with a new contempt in her young voice. Until tonight she had been pleased by the thought of going to the dance with Ernest Lee; he was nice, she felt comfortable with him, and he might even be the awe-struck boy of her dream. He was a dark, serious neighborhood boy who could not afford to go to college; Mrs. Simmons had reluctantly selected him to take Judy to the dance because all the Gay Charmers' sons were spoken for. Now, with an undertone of excitement, Judy said, "I'm going to ditch him after the first dance, Mother. You'll see. I'm going to come home with one of the college boys."

"It's very nice, Ernest Lee," she told him an hour later when he handed her the white orchid, "but it's rather small. I'm going to wear it on my wrist, if you don't mind." And then, dazzling him with a smile of sweetest cruelty, she stepped back and waited while he fumbled with the door.

"You know, Edward, I'm not worried about her any more," Mrs. Simmons said to her husband after the children were gone. Her voice became harsh and grating. "Put down that paper and listen to me! Aren't you interested in your child?— That's better," she said as he complied meekly. "I was saying, I do believe she's learned what I've been trying to teach her, after all."

SWEAT

Zora Neale Hurston

I

It was eleven o'clock of a Spring night in Florida. It was Sunday. Any other night, Delia Jones would have been in bed for two hours by this time. But she was a washwoman, and Monday morning meant a great deal to her. So she collected the soiled clothes on Saturday when she returned the clean things. Sunday night after church, she sorted and put the white things to soak. It saved her almost a half-day's start. A great hamper in the bedroom held the clothes that she brought home. It was so much neater than a number of bundles lying around.

She squatted on the kitchen floor beside the great pile of clothes, sorting them into small heaps according to color, and humming a song in a mournful key, but wondering through it all where Sykes, her husband, had gone with her horse and buckboard.

Just then something long, round, limp and black fell upon her shoulders and slithered to the floor beside her. A great terror took hold of her. It softened her knees and dried her mouth so that it was a full minute before she could cry out or move. Then she saw that it was the big bull whip her husband liked to carry when he drove.

She lifted her eyes to the door and saw him standing there bent over with laughter at her fright. She screamed at him.

"Sykes, what you throw dat whip on me like dat? You know it would skeer me—looks just like a snake, an' you knows how skeered Ah is of snakes."

"Course Ah knowed it! That's how come Ah done it." He slapped his leg with his hand and almost rolled on the ground in his mirth. "If you such a big fool dat you got to have a fit over a earth worm or a string, Ah don't keer how bad Ah skeer you."

"You ain't got no business doing it. Gawd knows it's a sin. Some day Ah'm goin-tuh drop dead from some of yo' foolishness. 'Nother thing; where you been wid mah rig? Ah feeds dat pony. He ain't fuh you to be drivin' wid no bull whip."

"You sho' is one aggravatin' nigger woman!" he declared and stepped into the room. She resumed her work and did not answer him at once. "Ah done tole you time and again to keep them white folks' clothes outa dis house."

He picked up the whip and glared at her. Delia went on with her work. She went out into the yard and returned with a galvanized tub and set it on the wash-bench. She saw that Sykes had kicked all of the clothes together again, and now stood in her way truculently, his whole manner hoping, *praying*, for an argument. But she walked calmly around him and commenced to re-sort the things.

"Next time, Ah'm gointer kick 'em outdoors," he threatened as he struck a match along the leg of his corduroy breeches.

Delia never looked up from her work, and her thin, stooped shoulders sagged further.

"Ah ain't for no fuss t'night Sykes. Ah just come from taking sacrament at the church house."

He snorted scornfully. "Yeah, you just come from de church house on a Sunday night, but heah you is gone to work on them clothes. You ain't nothing but a hypocrite. One of them amen-corner Christians—sing, whoop, and shout, then come home and wash white folks' clothes on the Sabbath."

He stepped roughly upon the whitest pile of things, kicking them helter-skelter as he crossed the room. His wife gave a little scream of dismay, and quickly gathered them together again.

"Sykes, you quit grindin' dirt into these clothes! How can Ah git through by Sat'day if Ah don't start on Sunday?"

"Ah don't keer if you never git through. Anyhow, Ah done promised Gawd and a couple of other men, Ah ain't gointer have it in mah house. Don't gimme no lip neither, else Ah'll throw 'em out and put mah fist up side yo' head to boot."

Delia's habitual meekness seemed to slip from her shoulders like a blown scarf. She was on her feet; her poor little body, her bare knuckly hands bravely defying the strapping hulk before her.

"Looka heah, Sykes, you done gone too fur. Ah been married to you fur fifteen years, and Ah been takin' in washin' fur fifteen years. Sweat, sweat, sweat! Work and sweat, cry and sweat, pray and sweat!"

"What's that got to do with me?" he asked brutally.

"What's it got to do with you, Sykes? Mah tub of suds is filled yo belly with vittles more times than yo' hands is filled it. Mah sweat is done paid for this house and Ah reckon Ah kin keep on sweatin' in it."

She seized the iron skillet from the stove and struck a defensive pose, which act surprised him greatly, coming from her. It cowed him and he did not strike her as he usually did.

"Naw you won't," she panted, "that ole snaggle-toothed black woman you runnin' with ain't comin' heah to pile up on *mah* sweat and blood. You ain't paid for nothin' on this place, and Ah'm gointer stay right heah till Ah'm toted out foot foremost."

"Well, you better quit gittin' me riled up, else they'll be totin' you out sooner than you expect. Ah'm so tired of you Ah don't know whut to do. Gawd! How Ah hates skinny wimmen!"

A little awed by this new Delia, he sidled out of the door and slammed the back gate after him. He did not say where he had gone, but she knew too well. She knew very well that he would not return until nearly daybreak also. Her work over, she went on to bed but not to sleep at once. Things had come to a pretty pass!

She lay awake, gazing upon the debris that cluttered their matrimonial trail. Not an image left standing along the way. Anything like flowers had long ago been drowned in the salty stream that had been pressed from her heart. Her tears, her sweat, her blood. She had brought love to the union and he had brought a longing after the flesh. Two months after the wedding, he had given her the first brutal beating. She had the memory of his numerous trips to Orlando with all of his wages when he had returned to her penniless, even before the first year had passed. She was young and soft then, but now she thought of her knotty, muscled limbs, her harsh knuckly hands, and drew herself up into an unhappy little ball in the middle of the big feather bed. Too late now to hope for love, even if it were not Bertha it would be someone else. This case differed from the others only in that she was bolder than the others. Too late for everything except her little home. She had built it for her old days, and planted one by one the trees and flowers there. It was lovely to her, lovely.

Somehow, before sleep came, she found herself saying aloud: "Oh well, whatever goes over the Devil's back, is got to come under his belly. Sometime or ruther, Sykes, like everybody else, is gointer reap his sowing." After that she was able to build a spiritual earthworks against her husband. His shells could no longer reach her. AMEN. She went to sleep and slept until he announced his presence in bed by kicking her feet and rudely snatching the covers away.

"Gimme some kivah heah, an' git yo' damn foots over on yo' own side! Ah oughter mash you in yo' mouf fuh drawing dat skillet on me."

Delia went clear to the rail without answering him. A triumphant indifference to all that he was or did.

II

The week was as full of work for Delia as all other weeks, and Saturday found her behind her little pony, collecting and delivering clothes.

It was a hot, hot day near the end of July. The village men on Joe Clarke's porch even chewed cane listlessly. They did not hurl the cane-knots as usual. They let them dribble over the edge of the porch. Even conversation had collapsed under the heat.

"Heah come Delia Jones," Jim Merchant said, as the shaggy pony came 'round the bend of the road toward them. The rusty buckboard was heaped with baskets of crisp, clean laundry.

"Yep," Joe Lindsay agreed. "Hot or col', rain or shine, jes' ez reg'lar ez de weeks roll roun' Delia carries 'em an' fetches 'em on Sat'day."

"She better if she wanter eat," said Moss. "Syke Jones ain't wuth de shot an' powder hit would tek tuh kill 'em. Not to huh he ain't."

"He sho' ain't," Walter Thomas chimed in. "It's too bad, too, cause she wuz a right pretty li'l trick when he got huh. Ah'd uh mah'ied huh mahself if he hadnter beat me to it."

Delia nodded briefly at the men as she drove past.

"Too much knockin' will ruin *any* 'oman. He done beat huh 'nough tuh kill three women, let 'lone change they looks," said Elijah Moseley. "How Syke kin stommuck dat big black greasy Mogul he's layin' roun' wid, gits me. Ah swear dat eight-rock couldn't kiss a sardine can Ah done thowed out de back do' 'way las' yeah."

"Aw, she's fat, thass how come. He's allus been crazy 'bout fat women," put in Merchant. "He'd a' been tied up wid one long time ago if he could a' found one tuh have him. Did Ah tell yuh 'bout him come sidlin' roun' *mah* wife—bringin' her a basket uh peecan's outa his yard fuh a present? Yessir, mah wife! She tol' him tuh take 'em right straight back home, 'cause Delia works so hard ovah dat wash-tub she reckon everything on de place taste lak sweat an' soapsuds. Ah jus' wisht Ah'd a' caught 'im 'roun' dere! Ah'd a' made his hips ketch on fiah down dat shell road."

"Ah know he done it, too. Ah sees 'im grinnin' at every 'oman dat passes," Walter Thomas said. "But even so, he useter eat some mighty big hunks uh humble pie tuh git dat li'l 'oman he got. She wuz ez pritty ez a speckled pup! Dat wuz fifteen years ago. He useter be so skeered uh losin' huh, she could make him do some parts of a husband's duty. Dey never wuz de same in de mind."

"There oughter be a law about him," said Lindsay. "He ain't fit tuh carry guts tuh a bear."

Clarke spoke for the first time. "Tain't no law on earth dat kin make a man be decent if it ain't in 'im. There's plenty men dat takes a wife lak dey do a joint uh sugar-cane. It's round, juicy an' sweet when dey gits it. But dey squeeze an' grind, squeeze an' grind an' wring tell dey wring every drop uh pleasure dat's in 'em out. When dey's satisfied dat dey is wrung dry, dey treats 'em jes' lak dey do a cane-chew. Dey thows 'em away. Dey knows whut dey is doin' while dey is at it, an' hates theirselves fuh it but they keeps on hangin' after huh tell she's empty. Den dey hates huh fuh bein' a cane-chew an' in de way."

"We oughter take Syke an' dat stray 'oman uh his'n down in Lake Howell swamp an' lay on de rawhide till they cain't say Lawd a' mussy. He allus wuz uh ovahbearin' niggah, but since dat white 'oman from up north done teached 'im how to run a automobile, he done got too beggety to live—an' we oughter kill 'im,"—Old Man Anderson advised.

A grunt of approval went around the porch. But the heat was melting their civic virtue and Elijah Moseley began to bait Joe Clarke.

"Come on, Joe, git a melon outa dere an' slice it up for yo' customers. We'se all sufferin' wid de heat. De bear's done got *me*!"

"Thass right, Joe, a watermelon is jes' whut Ah needs tuh cure de eppizudicks," Walter Thomas joined forces with Moseley. "Come on dere, Joe. We all is steady customers an' you ain't set us up in a long time. Ah chooses dat long, bowlegged Floridy favorite."

"A god, an' be dough. You all gimme twenty cents and slice away," Clarke retorted. "Ah needs a col' slice m'self. Heah, everybody chip in. Ah'll lend y'all mah meat knife."

The money was all quickly subscribed and the huge melon brought forth. At that moment, Sykes and Bertha arrived. A determined silence fell on the porch and the melon was put away again.

Merchant snapped down the blade of his jackknife and moved toward the store door.

"Come on in, Joe, an' gimme a slab uh sow belly an' uh pound uh coffee—almost fuhgot 'twas Sat'day. Got to git on home." Most of the men left also.

Just then Delia drove past on her way home, as Sykes was ordering magnificently for Bertha. It pleased him for Delia to see.

"Git whutsoever yo' heart desires, Honey. Wait a minute, Joe. Give huh two bottles uh strawberry soda-water, uh quart parched groundpeas, an' a block uh chewin' gum."

With all this they left the store, with Sykes reminding Bertha that this was his town and she could have it if she wanted it.

The men returned soon after they left, and held their watermelon feast.

"Where did Syke Jones git da 'oman from nohow?" Lindsay asked.

"Ovah Apopka. Guess dey musta been cleanin' out de town when she lef'. She don't look lak a thing but a hunk uh liver wid hair on it."

"Well, she sho' kin squall," Dave Carter contributed. "When she gits ready tuh laff, she jes' opens huh mouf an' latches it back tuh de las' notch. No ole granpa alligator down in Lake Bell ain't got nothin' on huh."

III

Bertha had been in town three months now. Sykes was still paying her room-rent at Della Lewis'—the only house in town that would have taken her in. Sykes took her frequently to Winter Park to 'stomps'. He still assured her that he was the swellest man in the state.

"Sho' you kin have dat li'l ole house soon's Ah git dat 'oman outa dere. Everything b'longs tuh me an' you sho' kin have it. Ah sho' 'bominates uh skinny 'oman. Lawdy, you sho' is got one portly shape on you! You kin git *anything* you wants. Dis is *mah* town an' you sho' kin have it."

Delia's work-worn knees crawled over the earth in Gethsemane and up the rocks of Calvary many, many times during these months. She avoided the villagers and meeting places in her efforts to be blind and deaf. But Bertha nullified this to a degree, by coming to Delia's house to call Sykes out to her at the gate.

Delia and Sykes fought all the time now with no peaceful interludes. They slept and ate in silence. Two or three times Delia had attempted a timid friendliness, but she was repulsed each time. It was plain that the breaches must remain agape.

The sun had burned July to August. The heat streamed down like a million hot arrows, smiting all things living upon the earth. Grass withered, leaves browned, snakes went blind in shedding and men and dogs went mad. Dog days!

Delia came home one day and found Sykes there before her. She wondered, but started to go on into the house without speaking, even though he was standing in the kitchen door and she must either stoop under his arm or ask him to move. He made no room for her. She noticed a soap box beside the steps, but paid no particular attention to it, knowing that he must have brought it there. As she was stooping to pass under his outstretched arm, he suddenly pushed her backward, laughingly.

"Look in de box dere Delia, Ah done brung yuh somethin'!"

She nearly fell upon the box in her stumbling, and when she saw what it held, she all but fainted outright.

"Syke! Syke, mah Gawd! You take dat rattlesnake 'way from heah! You *gottuh*. Oh, Jesus, have mussy!"

"Ah ain't got tuh do nuthin' uh de kin'—fact is Ah ain't got tuh do nothin' but die. Tain't no use uh you puttin' on airs makin' out lak you skeered uh dat snake— he's gointer stay right heah tell he die. He wouldn't bite me cause Ah knows how tuh handle 'im. Nohow he wouldn't risk breakin' out his fangs 'gin *yo* skinny laigs."

"Naw, now Syke, don't keep dat thing 'round tryin' tuh skeer me tuh death. You knows Ah'm even feared uh earth worms. Thass de biggest snake Ah evah did see. Kill 'im Syke, please."

"Doan ast me tuh do nothin' fuh yuh. Goin' 'round tryin' tuh be so damn aster-perious. Naw, Ah ain't gonna kill it. Ah think uh damn sight mo' uh him dan you! Dat's a nice snake an' anybody doan lak 'im kin jes' hit de grit."

The village soon heard that Sykes had the snake, and came to see and ask questions.

"How de hen-fire did you ketch dat six-foot rattler, Syke?" Thomas asked.

"He's full uh frogs so he cin't hardly move, thass how Ah eased up on 'm. But Ah'm a snake charmer an' knows how tuh handle 'em. Shux, dat ain't nothin'. Ah could ketch one eve'y day if Ah so wanted tuh."

"Whut he needs is a heavy hick'ry club leaned real heavy on his head. Dat's de bes' way tuh charm a rattlesnake."

"Naw, Walt, y'all jes' don't understand dese diamon' backs lak Ah do," said Sykes in a superior tone of voice.

The village agreed with Walter, but the snake stayed on. His box remained by the kitchen door with its screen wire covering. Two or three days later it had digested its meal of frogs and literally came to life. It rattled at every movement in the kitchen or the yard. One day as Delia came down the kitchen steps she saw his chalky-white fangs curved like scimitars hung in the wire meshes. This time she did not run away with averted eyes as usual. She stood for a long time in the door-way in a red fury that grew bloodier for every second that she regarded the creature that was her torment.

That night she broached the subject as soon as Sykes sat down to the table.

"Syke, Ah wants you tuh take dat snake 'way fum heah. You done starved me an' Ah put up widcher, you done beat me and Ah took dat, but you done kilt all mah insides bringin' dat varmint heah."

Sykes poured out a saucer full of coffee and drank it deliberately before he answered her.

"A whole lot Ah keer 'bout how you feels inside uh out. Dat snake ain't goin' no damn wheah till Ah gits ready fuh 'im tuh go. So fur as beatin' is concerned, yuh ain't took near all dat you gointer take ef yuh stay 'round *me*."

Delia pushed back her plate and got up from the table. "Ah hates you, Syke," she said calmly. "Ah hates you tuh de same degree dat Ah useter love yuh. Ah done took an' took till mah belly is full up tuh mah neck. Dat's de reason Ah got mah letter fum de church an' moved mah membership tuh Woodbridge—so Ah don't haftuh take no sacrament wid yuh. Ah don't wantuh see yuh 'round me atall. Lay 'round wid dat 'oman all yuh wants tuh, but gwan 'way fum me an' mah house. Ah hates yuh lak uh suck-egg dog."

Sykes almost let the huge wad of corn bread and collard greens he was chewing fall out of his mouth in amazement. He had a hard time whipping himself up to the proper fury to try to answer Delia.

"Well, Ah'm glad you does hate me. Ah'm sho' tiahed uh you hangin' ontuh me. Ah don't want yuh. Look at yuh stringey ole neck! Yo' rawbony laigs an' arms is enough tuh cut uh man tuh death. You looks jes' lak de devvul's doll-baby tuh *me*. You cain't hate me no worse dan Ah hates you. Ah been hatin' *you* fuh years."

"Yo' ole black hide don't look lak nothin' tuh me, but uh passle uh wrinkled up rubber, wid yo' big ole yeahs flappin' on each side lak uh paih uh buzzard wings. Don't think Ah'm gointuh be run 'way fum mah house neither. Ah'm goin' tuh de white folks 'bout *you*, mah young man, de very nex' time you lay yo' han's on me. Mah cup is done run ovah." Delia said this with no signs of fear and Sykes departed from the house, threatening her, but made not the slightest move to carry out any of them.

That night he did not return at all, and the next day being Sunday, Delia was glad she did not have to quarrel before she hitched up her pony and drove the four miles to Woodbridge.

She stayed to the night service—"love feast"—which was very warm and full of spirit. In the emotional winds her domestic trials were borne far and wide so that she sang as she drove homeward,

> Jurden water, black an' col
> Chills de body, not de soul
> An' Ah wantah cross Jurden in uh calm time.

She came from the barn to the kitchen door and stopped.

"Whut's de mattah, ol' Satan, you ain't kickin' up yo' racket?" She addressed the snake's box. Complete silence. She went on into the house with a new hope in its birth struggles. Perhaps her threat to go to the white folks had frightened Sykes! Perhaps he was sorry! Fifteen years of misery and suppression had brought Delia to the place where she would hope *anything* that looked toward a way over or through her wall of inhibitions.

She felt in the match-safe behind the stove at once for a match. There was only one there.

"Dat niggah wouldn't fetch nothin' heah tuh save his rotten neck, but he kin run thew whut Ah brings quick enough. Now he done toted off nigh on tuh haff uh box uh matches. He done had dat 'oman heah in mah house, too."

Nobody but a woman could tell how she knew this even before she struck the match. But she did and it put her into a new fury.

Presently she brought in the tubs to put the white things to soak. This time she decided she need not bring the hamper out of the bedroom; she would go in there and do the sorting. She picked up the pot-bellied lamp and went in. The room was small and the hamper stood hard by the foot of the white iron bed. She could sit and reach through the bedposts—resting as she worked.

"Ah wantah cross Jurden in uh calm time." She was singing again. The mood of the "love feast" had returned. She threw back the lid of the basket almost gaily. Then, moved by both horror and terror, she sprang back toward the door. *There lay the snake in the basket!* He moved sluggishly at first, but even as she turned round and round, jumped up and down in an insanity of fear, he began to stir vigorously. She saw him pouring his awful beauty from the basket upon the bed, then she seized the lamp and ran as fast as she could to the kitchen. The wind from the open door blew out the light and the darkness added to her terror. She sped to the darkness of the yard, slamming the door after her before she thought to set down the lamp: She did not feel safe even on the ground, so she climbed up in the hay barn.

There for an hour or more she lay sprawled upon the hay a gibbering wreck.

Finally she grew quiet, and after that came coherent thought. With this stalked through her a cold, bloody rage. Hours of this. A period of introspection, a space of retrospection, then a mixture of both. Out of this an awful calm.

"Well, Ah done de bes' Ah could. If things ain't right, Gawd knows tain't mah fault."

She went to sleep—a twitch sleep—and woke up to a faint gray sky. There was a loud hollow sound below. She peered out. Sykes was at the wood-pile, demolishing a wire-covered box.

He hurried to the kitchen door, but hung outside there some minutes before he entered, and stood some minutes more inside before he closed it after him.

The gray in the sky was spreading. Delia descended without fear now, and crouched beneath the low bedroom window. The drawn shade shut out the dawn, shut in the night. But the thin walls held back no sound.

"Dat ol' scratch is woke up now!" She mused at the tremendous whirr inside, which every woodsman knows, is one of the sound illusions. The rattler is a ventriloquist. His whirr sounds to the right, to the left, straight ahead, behind, close under foot—everywhere but where it is. Woe to him who guesses wrong unless he is prepared to hold up his end of the argument! Sometimes he strikes without rattling at all.

Inside, Sykes heard nothing until he knocked a pot lid off the stove while trying to reach the match-safe in the dark. He had emptied his pockets at Bertha's.

The snake seemed to wake up under the stove and Sykes made a quick leap into the bedroom. In spite of the gin he had had, his head was clearing now.

"Mah Gawd!" he chattered, "ef Ah could on'y strack uh light!"

The rattling ceased for a moment as he stood paralyzed. He waited. It seemed that the snake waited also.

"Oh, fuh de light! Ah thought he'd be too sick"—Sykes was muttering to himself when the whirr began again, closer, right underfoot this time. Long before this, Sykes' ability to think had been flattened down to primitive instinct and he leaped—onto the bed.

Outside Delia heard a cry that might have come from a maddened chimpanzee, a stricken gorilla. All the terror, all the horror, all the rage that man possibly could express, without a recognizable human sound.

A tremendous stir inside there, another series of animal screams, the intermittent whirr of the reptile. The shade torn violently down from the window, letting in the red dawn, a huge brown hand seizing the window stick, great dull blows upon the wooden floor punctuating the gibberish of sound long after the rattle of the snake had abruptly subsided. All this Delia could see and hear from her place beneath the window, and it made her ill. She crept over to the four-o'clocks and stretched herself on the cool earth to recover.

She lay there. "Delia, Delia!" She could hear Sykes calling in a most despairing tone as one who expected no answer. The sun crept on up, and he called. Delia could not move—her legs had gone flabby. She never moved, he called, and the sun kept rising.

"Mah Gawd!" She heard him moan, "Mah Gawd fum Heben!" She heard him stumbling about and got up from her flower-bed. The sun was growing warm. As she approached the door she heard him call out hopefully, "Delia, is dat you Ah heah?"

She saw him on his hands and knees as soon as she reached the door. He crept an inch or two toward her—all that he was able, and she saw his horribly swollen neck and his one open eye shining with hope. A surge of pity too strong to support bore her away from that eye that must, could not, fail to see the tubs. He would see the lamp. Orlando with its doctors was too far. She could scarcely reach the chinaberry tree, where she waited in the growing heat while inside she knew the cold river was creeping up and up to extinguish that eye which must know by now that she knew.

THE FATHER AND THE SON

Yuri Kageyama

My father is a lump of meat. He was not always this way.

He is still big. The beige sauce that hangs in a plastic bag above his bed pours into his intestines through a hole in the side of his bulging abdomen, feeding him effortlessly without the gorging, smacking of lips that used to be his favorite pastime.

My father used to work for NASA. I used to be asked what my father did for a living. People would wonder why a person so physically Japanese would speak perfect English with a Southern accent. NASA engineers worked in Huntsville, Alabama. I went to high school there while my father helped send people to the moon.

More than once, my colleagues at The Tokyo Times, Japan's largest English-language newspaper, where I now work, would ask me in their characteristically patronizing tone: "Do you know what 'a rocket scientist' refers to when someone uses the expression: 'You don't have to be a rocket scientist'?"

I never found rockets particularly glamorous. I used to detest them. I used to dread going to see rockets on display in Florida during vacation, or having to sit in family gatherings in living rooms watching NASA videos of launches.

The rocket scientist is now speechless.

He cannot breathe any more than he can swallow. A hole in his throat keeps him breathing, although a nurse periodically must probe the hole with a suction tube to drain out mucous so he won't suffocate on his own phlegm.

His big appetite and his big voice used to dominate our family dinner table.

I used to hate the sound of his chewing.

Sometimes, things would get dramatically worse, and I got beaten.

He reached out and smacked me across the cheek. I would get thrown off my chair. I would see yellow stars circle in my head just like the Saturday morning cartoons. My cheek felt numb as though it had turned into rubber.

The causes for such outbursts have never been fully analyzed. I must have said the wrong thing, as young people tend to do, something too defiant, something too abrasive, something too honest.

Years later, after I got married, I had a chance to diplomatically ask my father why he was so angry back in those days.

He said he couldn't remember.

I guess sending people to the moon can get pretty stressful.

I was in first grade when I was called "Jap" for the first time.

A fat white boy taunted me from the street as I was looking out the window from my school bus.

"What's a Jap?" I asked my father.

I'd never forget the anger in his face.

"You must answer back," he said. "You must tell him, 'Yankee, go home!'"

It didn't make any sense. That's the slogan Japanese activists shouted against the U.S. Occupation. We weren't even in Japan anymore. We were in the Washington D.C. area then because my father was still working on his Ph.D.

I peer over the bed to look into his face. The stroke hasn't changed his chubby face, glowing with hardly a wrinkle.

He suddenly opens his eyes. They are slightly out of focus, comically cock-eyed, giving him a pathetic stunned, almost deranged, look.

A stench filters through the hole in his throat, and through his mouth he can't completely close, though he can't eat, breathe or speak.

"Otoosama," I say, using the "honorific" for "father."

He studies my face, slowly, like a digital camera waiting to focus its lens on a new unexpected object in its way.

His eyes open wider, sheer fear crossing over his crooked eyeballs.

Tears brim in my eyes.

"You don't have to be afraid," I tell him without speaking. "I am not going to hit you. I am not going to hit you."

I reach out and hold his hand, grasping his fingers in what ends up to be a power salute, although I'm not trying to give him the power salute.

His thumb moves erratically but with a force that's unmistakable. His thumb touches my thumb, playfully swishing about, caressing the sides of the skin, dodging, pushing, in "yubi-zumo," a "finger-wrestling" game that kids played when Japan wasn't modern and we didn't have all those Made-in-Japan, now Made-in-China, gadget toys.

The thumb that can push the other's thumb down in a hold for a count of 10 wins.

I let him win.

* * *

Some people said the professor—my father worked as a professor in Japan after retiring from his stint at NASA—was now "a vegetable."

This is inaccurate because my father was not unconscious. Some people said he was "brain dead," but that was totally inaccurate.

He kept his eyes closed much of time, but in the beginning he would try to talk, opening and closing his mouth like a goldfish gasping for air.

He could only make gurgling noises in his chest, and no one could understand a thing he was trying to say.

My teen-age son, who adored his grandfather, would even mimic his noises and laugh.

In a matter of weeks, the rocket scientist turned professor gave up, and stopped trying to talk.

If he had been a real vegetable or brain dead, then that would have in a way simplified things, as he wouldn't have really been there—at least not in the way we remembered him.

He wasn't there in the way we remembered him, exactly, either. But he was still there.

That was the problem.

But such problems have a way of giving way to other more pressing problems, like deadlines at The Tokyo Times.

My editors were the typical washed out "gaijin" who had stayed in Japan too long, gotten used to the special Occupation-style treatment they were doled out in Japan, this land of geisha and hot-spring massages, that before they knew it found themselves frightened by the sheer idea of going back and being judged in a free-market competition-rules all-men-are-created-equal land-of-opportunity America.

Their job constituted mainly of sitting around in a circle in the office, sorting through wire service copy and pretending to edit, while worrying more about their more lucrative jobs teaching English and book deals with publishers eager to ride on the "Japan is cool" fad.

As a reporter, I was busy, not only writing articles but also watching my back from sinister attacks from these editors with fragile egos.

Every reporter learns the art of self-defense against editors fairly quickly. The one-oh-one of journalism is to block it all out and focus on your own work.

Works of fiction are treated with respect. Editors ask your permission to change one word, to change a comma to a period.

Not so with articles.

Sometimes, you are lucky if you recognize anything that still speaks of yourself in the article after a stream of editors get done with putting in their two cents worth, their fingerprint, their value, their proof of a higher paycheck than yours well earned.

You want to scream after seeing what these editors do to stories.

Reporters I work with say, with a straight face, they spend more energy figuring out how each editor edits than on reporting, and writing in that style to protect their stories from weird changes.

Sadly, at The Tokyo Times, a reporter has nowhere to turn for poetic justice.

Still, these problems are just jokes compared to real heartbreak.

Heartbreak is the universal human experience of feeling an important organ shatter into a zillion pieces inside of you.

It is excruciating pain.

Historically, this expression has been used to describe unrequited love or breaking up in romantic relationships.

But heartbreak is what I ended up feeling when my son became lovers with an older woman at a PR agency, the Tokyo branch of a global company.

It seemed the perfect job for him while on summer vacation from college. It paid relatively well because of his bilingual skills.

No one had bargained for that female executive in her 30s, "career woman," as the Japanese call it, a new statistic amid the social changes in this nation, where people, both male and female, are staying single longer, rejecting the traditional role models of bread-winner husband and stay-at-home housewife.

Yoko, executive vice president, should have been the paragon of feminist virtue. Instead, she was a prowler, pouncing on a teen-ager, a sexual harasser. "Oh, Mom, she is so professional. She is so—so—together," he said purposely using a word from my generation to appease me.

"She knows all the Japanese ways of talking to clients, all those rules like how to win them over so they don't complain. She knows where everybody is supposed to sit according to the hierarchy at meetings, and all the proper phrasings and etiquette."

Age is not supposed to matter in love.

But I hated watching my son answer phone calls at 2 a.m. from Yoko, rush out of the house to see her. My son was also getting threatening calls from a Swede whom Yoko used to live with.

My son was not particularly worried about the Swede, although I was about to call the police, but he would call in a frenzied voice that I had to record a TV show he had promised to watch for Yoko, but had forgotten all about—some soap-operatic drama about a man's undying love for a woman dying of cancer.

He told me they had to sit around and have discussions about the show. He was in deep trouble if she found out he had missed an episode.

He also learned new names like Glenfiddich. He went on overnight business trips, playing mainly briefcase-carrier for Yoko.

I had an opportunity to meet Yoko at a hotel reception party for a major electronics company that her PR agency had a contract with and, it turned out, The Tokyo Times, wanted a story on.

She brought me a cup of tea. She held her own cup with both hands, demurely, a gracious thin smile constantly on her lips, and sipped on it without drinking.

"What are you thinking?" I asked abruptly in Japanese, not bothering with introductions and the obligatory business-card exchange. "He is just a kid. What do you think you are doing?"

She didn't blink. Her slant eyes stayed fixed on the tea cup. She had a bland Noh-mask face, except for flabby cheeks that made her face even more masklike. Perhaps this is Japanese beauty, I thought.

"I am extremely sorry for the concerns that this may have brought on you, Mother," she said.

I'm not your mother, I wanted to shout.

But I said: "What do you see in my son?"

"I realize you may see me as unworthy because of my age," she said, raising her tone half an octave in a characteristic yodeling throat trick of a Japanese "enka" singer. "I looked up, and your son was just there."

"Is this just a fling?" I asked, hoping it would be.

"I am not capable of flings," she said, giggling like a warbling geisha. My son found my behavior unacceptable.

He was moving out, he announced, to live with Yoko at her Roppongi apartment complex. He will finish college, he said, but he has made up his mind to marry Yoko.

I had tried to raise my son to be proud of his Japanese roots. But I was not prepared for this gaijin-inspired infatuation he was displaying of the stylized stereotype Japanese woman.

Instead of the dollish "kawaii" girls in Shibuya, dressed like maids and clowns, in frills and polka-dots, he had picked the kimono-clad shuffling woman of the

Edo Period, the one who knew how to walk three paces behind the samurai, the one well versed in the rules of the pecking order.

This was nothing other than self-hate—the manifestation of that perpetual mentality of racism that results in the rejection by the minority male of the minority female (or the minority female of the minority male) and enslaving worship of the majority race, so the ugliest member of the opposite sex of the majority race is by definition more attractive than the most beautiful member of the opposite sex of the minority race.

Except in this case, ironically, the race was the same—Asian.

My son was that ghetto boy, the American of Japanese ancestry, who was ashamed of how he wasn't a true proper Japanese—like Yoko so surely was.

"The value of an object is determined by the perceiver," my son wrote to me in a cell-phone e-mail after he moved out. "Is Yoko an old selfish hag? Or is she a beautiful Japanese woman?"

I felt my heart break inside of me. It crumbled. My chest pinched so tight as though every muscle there cramped tight like a fist, leaving just a giant hole there like the one in outer space where you drop endlessly forever and ever in your deepest dreams.

"I do not hate you," he wrote. "You are my mother and always will be."

This is heartbreak—when you can't love your own son.

* * *

Japanese funerals are rigid and proper like everything else Japanese.

Maybe the rules are there so people can forget their sorrows. There are so many rules it's impossible to be sad for long.

These days, the funeral has become a modern business. Companies charge a lot of money, but all you have to do is pick out everything in a catalogue, including the altar set-ups at the funeral hall, gifts for the guests, the lunch menu.

The bald-headed Buddhist priest in embroidered robes chants for about half an hour in some ancient language that not even Japanese understand, banging on a bell or another percussion instrument, allegedly for effect, but I suspect to prevent us from dozing off.

The most dramatic moment is when the mourners toss flowers into the coffin before it heads out to the nearby cremation facility.

It is practically obligatory for Japanese to weep at this final farewell.

But I never feel sad at such moments because I can't turn my emotions off and on like a faucet.

If anything, I have a hard time not bursting out laughing at Japanese funerals.

Some of the dumbest things feel irresistibly funny. The words of the priest's chants sound like an obscenity in English. Someone stumbles accidentally while walking up to offer incense at the altar. A distant relative has to make an impeccably sorrowful face that's so obnoxiously pretentious and fake.

The van for carrying the coffin is a station wagon with a garish glittery gold and black-lacquer miniature temple on top of its roof.

Family members must pay the priest a lot of money to have a post-mortem name for the deceased believed to guarantee entry into the after-life.

I do not know my father's religious name offhand. These are long names with difficult characters, as befitting the tens of thousands of yen paid to get it, not simple Baptism and Confirmation names like Magdalene or Peter.

I did not look into the coffin as I tossed in a handful of white chrysanthemums. It was sheer relief he had been released from that body.

I wanted to celebrate for my father.

But I kept quiet as we sat in a room, sipping tea and eating stale rice crackers, waiting for my father's body to get cooked in the giant oven at the cremation facility.

Japanese men get away with wearing a dark suit but women don't get off so easy.

Mourning clothes for women are sold in fancy department stores, the strangest dresses, based on Bette Davis movies probably, with no relevance to the realities of today, but worn always with a strand of pearls.

It's clear at first sight I am not properly dressed for this whole affair. I am wearing a black jacket and black pants, no pearls, my feeble attempt at mourning attire.

I have no time to contemplate this embarrassment as my son walks over and sits next to me.

He has broken up with Yoko, he tells me.

He neglected to tell me before, but every time he had tried to break up, she had threatened suicide. That was why he was running over there all the time at wee hours of the morning, he says matter of fact.

Yoko was taken to the hospital for a failed suicide attempt and is now on medication.

"Dealing with Yoko is very unpleasant," he says. "You can't imagine what it's been like."

* * *

The clockwork's stopping comes slowly. Hot flashes are reminders of what's no longer going to work. No more menstrual cycles, no more reproduction. No more that egg traveling in that burning red womb inside of you, waiting for that lowly sperm to come, swimming like puny pathetic tadpoles up the river, fractions of the size, or glamour, of jumping salmon going to their deaths, sometimes that fertilization unwanted, miscarrying or aborted, red bleeding blood red, but that time when birth is planned, desired, a gift, like Baby Jesus, crying out in the wilderness in the sterile hospital bed, red blood on his face, my son, with tiny hands and feet, moving, and he looks into my eyes, so wise, so perfect, and we have known each other for all eternity, red, those hot flashes tell you about that heat, burning, that place inside that never forgets.

Menopause sex is an affirmation of this legacy.

That is why it is human duty to perform this act regularly, like a religious ritual, in homage, in honor, to give thanks, no matter its futility in reproductory functionality.

My husband's arms still feel muscular and strong in the dark. His tongue and fingers against my breast and nipple feel warm, ticklish, as though the cells on my body are hyperactive, peeking from everywhere, waiting to rub against his cells, his prickly face, his biceps, his stomach against my stomach, his hardened penis. The skin is supposed to sag, wrinkle and shrivel with age, but everything instead feels taut and tight, so persistent and frantic, and we are young again, no, ageless, two people caught in time, waiting to die and be reborn and meet again, to have our son again, as the hot flashes explode in my abdomen in orgasm, popping red colors in my brain.

Someday, I'm going to build a house, my son once said when he was a toddler.

It's going to have music, books, and lots and lots of flowers, he said in that tiny voice children have that's so disarming and endearing like a kitten's meow.

Years later when he was in high school, my son told me a white schoolmate had laughed at him for wearing a Jimi Hendrix T-shirt. You don't even know who that is, you foreigner, the child had said.

"I grew up on Jimi Hendrix. My dad plays Jimi Hendrix solos, note for note," my son, the only Asian in his class, had said.

There is an old photo of my son, playing a toy guitar, standing knee-high next to my husband with his Fender. The boy has a strained look on his face, as though he is really sending that guitar wailing.

I see he has that same look on stage.

At a shabby cramped basement club in Koenji, where the smell of curry wafts everywhere, mixing with the beat of funky traps drumming, my son is playing blues guitar with other "freeter" Japanese youngsters in a band called Cigarette Box.

It was difficult finding the place, even with directions printed off the Internet. Except for a tiny sign, there is no clue above ground that this club exists like so many others scattered across Tokyo.

The crowd here appears to be mostly members of other bands waiting to play. They clap enthusiastically after every song as though they have been victims as misfit freaks of "ijime" bullying from more decent conformist Japanese while growing up and don't want to hurt anybody's feelings, if they can help it.

Huge warped pots of curry and rice sit on the counter, next to platefuls of fragrant pizza. It's all you can eat for a few hundred yen, complete with free drinks. I ask for tomato juice, and the boy behind the counter gives me a huge glass with ice cubes and a big straw.

They don't look around nervously as most Japanese do in crowds. Some are wearing funny hats. Their jeans are raggedy and have holes. They would fit right in, in Berkeley.

They sing about gratitude for compassion, memories of blowing bubbles in the air, their pet cat, rainbow clouds and flowers, hangovers, and lost love.

They squirm on stage, jump around, scream, banter with the crowd. People chuckle and shout back answers.

My son's new girlfriend Miu is the violinist for Cigarette Box.

She works at a record store in Akihabara but also plays with techno artists and a "world music" band.

She slaps me on the back when she sees me, in between sets.

My son doesn't like talking about this, but they met on the Internet. There are networking sites that help Japanese musicians find people to play with.

I found this out, rather accidentally from Miu, when we had lunch together at a pasta place in Shibuya on a weekend.

She said she took along the male harmonium player from her world music band, just in case, to the first jam session with my son. She figured meeting someone on the Net could be dangerous.

"But it was like I got sucked in, watching him play," she said as though mesmerized. "I couldn't play anything."

I bought a hat for Miu at the Shibuya 109 shopping complex because she looks good in hats.

She also looks good in mini-skirts, torn jeans, fake fur, dangling earrings, just about anything. She has a red blister on her neck from practicing her violin.

I hate to say this. After Yoko, anybody halfway normal was OK by me. But Miu is too good to be true. When she plays, I love her so much I feel like crying.

Bring out the violins—for real.

I am afraid, I tell Miu. I am getting old. My father is dead. As time passes, I will get older and older.

I don't know why I am telling her this.

She has barely been around on this planet for some 20 years, and she doesn't know a thing about getting old.

I don't know if I did the right thing.

My son is trying to play music instead of seeking a steady job at a PR firm. He is no more Jimi Hendrix than his father is, or ever will be, and I can't really help him because I am just a reporter.

We are mere insignificant dots on the cosmic map, even more difficult to find than this club was in the night backstreets of Tokyo. The only reason I am not too afraid now is because the music is so loud I can't think straight.

Things will work out. You will enter a new stage in life, Miu says.

There's a strange finality that's somehow reassuring.

Miu looks at me and then whispers into my ear: "The most important thing to know is that everything is going to be OK."

MOSES MAMA

William Melvin Kelley

I surprise people who don't know me very well by calling myself a feministicist. They wonder how an old bachelor literary historian can espouse such radical views as equal pay for equal work, and even equal pay for comparable work, though occasionally I have trouble with the comparable part. But I more surprise them by assuring them that my feministicism runs deeper than even money. I genuinely believe that in any way men care to define it, women bear half the responsibility for everything that humankind has destroyed or accomplished.

I didn't always feel that way. I had a good traditional education. So naturally I started out believing in the superiority of men and never thought to look behind any of the renowned men of history to see if any female lurked there, exerting strong influence. Now I know better. Whether or not we know their names, and even though they themselves don't always know it, women stand there behind or beside men, contributing equally to humankind's development.

I owe credit for sowing the first seeds of my feministicism to my paternal grand-mother, Nanny Eva Dunford, whom I met for the first time at seventeen years of age in 1952. We never had any hard evidence establishing her date of birth. She maintained that missionaries had brought her from Africa in 1866 at the age of four. But we always suspected that an 1872 birth date seemed more likely. Still she could have come from Africa. She seemed to have no European ancestry. Both my father (years ago) and myself (more recently) have searched unsuccessfully for record of her parents. And she did give us the name of the missionaries, a couple named Willson (with two L's). I had an exchange of letters with the Willson family, but they didn't give much help. All to say that Nanny Eva knew her Bible as well as any scholar. She knew it cold and hot, Pentateuch and Revelation. Quote a phrase from the Bible and she could cite chapter and verse. If it had multiple citations, she would know that too. "Isaiah quotin David, son," she would say, amazing me.

Nanny Eva Dunford lived with my uncle GL and his wife Rose in a near-mansion high up on a hill in New Marsails. Segregation and all! With little educa-tion but with an engaging personality, uncle GL had already made and lost three fortunes. In 1952, he owned a bar, a record store and a taxi service. So they lived well, even though they could not sip from certain drinking fountains. Irony.

A few days after my father and I had arrived from New York, Nanny Eva and I found ourselves out on the verandah overlooking New Marsails and the Gulf beyond. She looked clean and crisp, chocolate brown and shiny skinned with kinky white hair like a cloud framing her fierce-eyed face. I felt moved to take some photos of her with my little argoflex box camera. I excused myself and went inside to get it, then returned to the verandah.

"Now, son, Nanny don'want no pictures! Just take that box camera right back inside!"

I told her she looked extremely photogenic and begged her to let me take some pictures, thinking that I might not have too many more chances. She looked strong, but had lived at least eighty years.

"Don'want no pictures took I tell you." She pursed her lips, squinted. "Don'need none."

But I needed them, I insisted. Her two other grandchildren, my brother Peter and my sister Connie, had only one faded snapshot of her, taken in the 1930s. We needed something more recent.

"Might break yo camera," she warned. "Busted every camera ever took a picture o me. Ugly like mud. No Lena Vaughan. So less you don'plan on takin pictures afta this . . ." She held the s, hissing.

I promised her I'd only take a few, though I wanted to take a whole roll of twelve. I asked her to sit up straight and smooth her skirt over her knees.

She shot me a fiery glance. "Makin me look like a glamour girl? Easy to see you don'have no respect for no women cept as glamour girls."

I protested, asking her if I'd disrespected her since meeting her.

"Not me, you better not, but our kind, womankind. I done hear what you said last night afta supper. Didn'think Rose n me could hear, but we could hear you bold." Nanny Eva sucked her tongue. "Bout them five Jewish men startin everythin."

It hit me. After supper the night before, while the women cleared the table and washed the dishes, prettyfaced aunt Rose bustling, Nanny Eva doing what she could at slower pace, the men, uncle GL and my father and I sitting at the diningroom table, had conducted wide-ranging intrafamilial and intergenerational discussions, during the course of which the subject of the Jews came up. Uncle GL stood opposed. I doubt if he'd even met a Jew in his largely segregated life, but he blamed the Jews for the recent World War II. My father objected strenuously. He'd lived in New York City for a quarter century, coming to the conclusion that the Jews meant no harm, and occasionally helped Africamerica. Seventeen years old and snottynosed, I ventured an opinion expressed in the hallways of my private school by students if not faculty, that all Western Thought had evolved out of the philosophies of five Jewish men: Moses-Jesus-Marx-Freud-and-Einstein. Now Nanny Eva had taken offense.

"Five Jewish men startin everythin! Zif women didn'have no say in the world. What bout blessed Jesus Mama Mary? What the Catholics do widout her? Bet you never wonder why Creator God want to bring in Jesus by Mary, stead o just make him wid mud like he done Adam. Cos it done need a woman. And what bout Jokerbed?"

I had followed her until the last. Lost a moment, my nervous index finger had squeezed off a shot, the first of the roll, which developed slightly blurred, her eyes wide open and eyebrows raised.

"Moses Mama. Saved the world n didn'get no credit fo it. Know why?"

Some ideas take time to get through to me. Others come like lightning. Jokerbed (later I learned the correct spelling), Mother of Moses saved the world? Inwardly I scoffed as only a private school brat can scoff.

"Cos men write the story when it all said n done did. So they make it look like men save the day. Women steppin in when the goin get so bad only a woman can save it. Nobody thinkin bout writin it down when Hard Times holdin court. Everybody too busy scramblin. N women the best scramblers, eggs n otherwise. Cos women the first n best experimenters. Now put that box camera away n tell Nanny Eva what you want fo yo dinner!"

I tried to divert her, pointing out that I'd thought she wanted to tell me about Jochebed, the mother of Moses, unless perhaps Nanny Eva really had nothing worthwhile to say about this little-known woman.

Well I shouldn't have said that. The heat coming out of her eyes seemed to jelly the air between us. "Nothin worth sayin? Bout Moses Mama? Why son, what the most hard times you ever know?"

While I thought of an answer, I took a second shot, the old lady glaring at me, really the top of my head as I bent looking into the viewfinder.

"Ever been a slave? Well, I never did actually be one, but did know plenty was as a girl n they told me all bout it. First off they buyin n sellin you like bulls and cows. Workin a place twenty years n have some roots, a good man n some chilren, then the owner dyin on you n the greedy relations come swoopin down sayin, I want the strong one n I want the cook n I will take that little cutie over there. Now who you think done have the hardest time in slavery? Why the women, son. A man, cept fo the few has some backbone, just thinkin bout keepin self alive. A woman thinkin bout keepin chilren n self alive. Double duty n please her owner too!

"Folks talk bout the driver lash, but Nanny Eva consider the pain o the soul. Livin in the tornado n keepin yo fear n heat inside. Get beat but forbid to cry. Some folks raise they chilren that way. Bad business! Least when I done wail my chilren I let them wail." She fell silent, studying a spot on the verandah floor, her hands folded. I snapped photo no.three, an image I've treasured ever since.

The click broke her reverie. "Better pack that thing away." But a droll smile disrupted her stern face. "Got me good, didn'you?"

I wound forward to no.four, saying probably condescendingly that I found her analysis of slavery illuminating. Most commentators emphasized the abstract concept of freedom and the physical pain. But they would love slavery as a soul distorting experience in Ethics class at the Shaddy Bend School.

"I done miss some o that comin over in 1866 wid the Reverend Willson, but I done catch hell afta the Reconstruction. Not to say the Willsons didn'beat me regular, but like parents. Least they done say so n I believe them cos they give me Creator God n teach me to read n give me the Bible."

Her face went quiet and peaceful, her gaze tender under still black eyebrows, looking straight at me. I took photo no.four and wound forward to five.

"Sis Jochebed had Creator God too. Cos remember she be raise up in the tribe o Levi, tribe all the priests come from. Back befo Moses invent Hebrew n write anythin down, when the Hebrew chilren talkin they religion. Didn'have no time to read n write. Just be workin is all, makin n haulin brick fo the pyramids. Cos the Hebrew chilren be brought real low from Joseph time. Now Pharoah purely want to kill they boy babies. Even we didn'have it that bad in slavery times, when a baby boy o good stock worth much as sixty dollars. Killin boy babies the same like burnin money. So you see how desperate be those times fo the Hebrew chilren. Worth nothin!

"Now here be Jochebed wid two chilren n a new one comin. Already had a boy, Aaron workin at the pyramids. The girl Miriam safe fo now cos she hasn'reach breedin age yet. Now Jochebed pregnant n tryin not to look it, hidin her belly under dresses n skirts. Didn'want the Egyptian baby police to stop her on the street n give her a belly check. If they find she carryin they watch her n send somebody round to see if it come out a boy n kill it."

Her face looked grim as she leaned forward, whispering, conspiring with Jochebed and me to see the baby born and spared. I wanted to take photo no.five but didn't want the thunder of the shutter to break her spell.

"She give birth quiet like a cat, get the baby to cry, then get it to stop. Didn'want nobody to hear. She done have a midwife she could trust to keep her secret, probably old auntie Shiphrah known her from a girl. Wouldn'betray her no matta how much they pay. Look in they faces n flatout lie. No sir, I never hear bout no boy baby born down our lane. Anyway the Hebrew women has they babies n hide them befo we even get there."

Photo no.five captured the look of a righteous woman lying through her teeth, back straight, lips tight, above reproach.

"Then she had to hide him fo three months. Had a little crawl space she stuff him into whenever anybody she couldn'trust come to visit. Dress him like a girl when she has to take him out. Told his sister Miriam to call him Dinah afta Jacob daughter whenever anybody spicious come snoopin.

"When he reach three months old n start to gettin rambunctious, she had one of them dreams biblical folks has when Creator God want to tell them somethin. She dream she walkin down to the river Nile wid a load o clo'es fo washin when she come up on two women wid they feet danglin in the water. One she done know right away as Sarah wife o Abraham. Other one she didn'know at first. Well findin herself in the company o holy women, Jochebed fall on her knees n worship. But pretty quick they pull her up n make her sit down beside them, all three wid they feet in the water. Told her to cool her feet cos her line would do a heap o walkin. Then they tells her to build a little boat. Real fancy, painted colorful wid interestin designs all over it, the holy women say. Round this time Jochebed realize she dreamin, knowin how you know sometime n she say to herself, That sound ridiculous! Must be dreamin. O course you dreamin, Sarah say, how else you ever get to meet me? But you still needin a little boat. Take a little time wid it but you hasn'got much time. Jochebed couldn'make no sense o it. Why she needin a fancy little boat?"

Nanny Eva hardly noticed me squeezing off photo no.six, giving me an exasperated fleeting smile.

"Build it to see what'll happen, say the other holy woman, who Jochebed reco'nize as Mama Eve wife o Adam. Got to take a chance like Noah wife, specially when Hard Times holdin court. Sometimes even when you livin in Paradise. So build the boat n make it fancy. But then what? Jochebed aksin but wakin up befo Mama Eve n Sarah give a answer.

"So she commence to buildin a little boat, like a big covered basket, weavin it from grasses. Now the Bible say she done smear it wid slime, which could be mud or tar, to make it watertight. Then she paint it, red-yellow-blue-purple, rainbow colors n stud it wid pretty stones, so a body could see it glitterin n twinklin a long way off."

Her face turned thoughtful, a woman at her crafts, in the concentration of creation, deciding just where to put a stone or bit of glass; I squeezed off no.seven.

"But she still didn'know why she possess a fancy little boat n the baby police be getting mo spicious every day.

"Now Miriam big sister to Moses one o them wanderin chilren. No fence or chain keep them from wanderin. Had two such girls as that myself. Then they get marry n settle right down, never leave the house. Anyway in her wanderin, Miriam done go down to the river Nile, Main street to Eygpt in those times to watch the fishermen mendin they nets n sellin they fish n all the other activities on the river. Since no fence could keep her from wanderin where her heart want to wander, she have adventure through reeds to a beautiful cove where Pharoah daughter had a little swimmin pool builded right into the riverside n would swim butt nekid wid a gang o her girls.

"Miriam done get home late that evenin. Jochebed meetin her at the door wid a strap in her hand, aksin her where she been. Pretty quick Miriam tellin her mama all bout Pharoah daughter swimmin butt nekid in the river Nile n Jochebed forget whippin on her cos soon as she done hear bout Pharoah daughter, a whole plan come to her. Cos bout rich folks you can never get to see them less you work fo them. So she thankin the holy women o her dreams cos they done look into the future n give Jochebed a glimpse too."

Nanny Eva's face relaxed into the contentment of a woman who feels herself at one with universal forces. She hardly noticed or cared that I took photo no.eight.

"So now Moses Mama have a plan n the next day she start to make it real. She put her baby boy in his best little outfit, combin his hair n all. Then she take him n put him into the fancy little boat the holy women done have her build, tied him into it case it tip over. Then she took Miriam n tie a long leather tether to her wrist n tie the other end to the little boat. Miriam would steer it down the river Nile n into the cove where Pharoah daughter swimmin butt nekid.

"She kiss them both n bless them n send them down the river Nile, Miriam on the shore holdin the leather tether n the baby Moses in his fancy little boat. From the riverbank, Miriam coaxin the little boat into the cove where Pharoah daughter did her swimmin butt nekid. Then Miriam loose the leather tether n hide n watch the little boat drift into Pharoah daughter cove."

She fell silent, staring out at the Gulf. I took no.nine, and it did not disturb her. I leaned forward to see if she had fallen asleep.

"Plan went pretty well afta that. The glittery little boat done catch Pharoah daughter eye n she fetch it to her n see the baby Moses n fell right on in love. Even though she know by his little circumcise peepee that he come from the Hebrews. Must o been a cute healthy little baby boy, considerin what he to become. Dazzled her wid his big smile n bright face, Moses aft'all.

"Round this time in the general hustle n bustle made by the fancy boat n bright little boy, baby Moses get hungry n commence to cry. Miriam pop up n get him to quiet down n smile his big smile, which impressin Pharoah daughter. Right then n there, she offer Miriam a job takin care o her new adopted son. Jochebed had done told Miriam what to say next. Say she know a woman who just lost her child to the baby police n she still have milk n maybe she would wet nurse this baby til he old enough to eat solid food. Pharoah daughter like the plan."

She sat up straight and eager, the girl Miriam doing as her mother had instructed; I snapped no.ten.

"So Pharoah daughter send some palace guard wid Miriam to fetch sister Jochebed n bring her to the palace. Imagine how Moses mama heart be jumpin! Her plan workin but she still got to stay cool down cos she don'want to give herself away. Pharoah daughter command Moses mama to wetnurse her new little Hebrew son. At first, Jochebed pretend like she didn'want Pharoah daughter baby to suck the milk o the baby she lost to the baby police. But afta while, she give in. So home they all done go, the baby Moses, now Pharoah daughter son n Miriam n Jochebed along wid a wagonload o food n new clo'es. Right back home where they start out from that mornin!" She leaned back, laughed, and patted her thighs with her hands which seemed carved from baker's chocolate. I clicked no.eleven. "So if five Jewish men start everythin you got to put a Hebrew woman Jochebed in there wid them cos she begat Moses n save him a couple times, startin wid gettin him safe n protected inside Pharoah palace. Now what man would make up a plan like that?"

From that moment on, though I did not always know or act it, I surrendered to feministicism. Since then the concept of female historical equality has never strayed far from my consciousness, though in my personal relationships I've done as many jerky things as any man.

I took no.twelve, the last of the roll, the next day. Nanny Eva and I found ourselves on the verandah again. She had a lot of energy that morning and I ran to get my camera. When I returned she pointed her finger at me. "She save him another time when he kill that man. Had two such hotblooded sons as that myself. Shoot men over somethin foolish. But they yo boys n you got to save them. So how you think Moses get away afta he kill that man?" She raised her finger beside her twinkling eye; I clicked no.twelve and told her I did not know.

"Cos you didn'listen, son. Moses Mama dress him like a woman!"

GOD BLESS AMERICA

John O. Killens

Joe's dark eyes searched frantically for Cleo as he marched with the other Negro soldiers up the long thoroughfare towards the boat. Women were running out to the line of march, crying and laughing and kissing the men good-by. But where the hell was Cleo?

Beside him Luke Robinson, big and fat, nibbled from a carton of Baby Ruth candy as he walked. But Joe's eyes kept traveling up and down the line of civilians on either side of the street. She would be along here somewhere; any second now she would come calmly out of the throng and walk alongside him till they reached the boat. Joe's mind made a picture of her, and she looked the same as last night when he left her. As he had walked away, with the brisk California night air biting into his warm body, he had turned for one last glimpse of her in the doorway, tiny and smiling and waving good-by.

They had spent last night sitting in the little two-by-four room where they had lived for three months with hardly enough space to move around. He had rented it and sent for her when he came to California and learned that his outfit was training for immediate shipment to Korea, and they had lived there fiercely and desperately, like they were trying to live a whole lifetime. But last night they had sat on the side of the big iron bed, making conversation, half-listening to a portable radio, acting like it was just any night. Play-acting like in the movies.

It was late in the evening when he asked her, "How's little Joey acting lately?"

She looked down at herself. "Oh, pal Joey is having himself a ball." She smiled, took Joe's hand, and placed it on her belly; and he felt movement and life. His and her life, and he was going away from it and from her, maybe forever.

Cleo said, "He's trying to tell you good-by, darling." And she sat very still and seemed to ponder over her own words. And then all of a sudden she burst into tears.

She was in his arms and her shoulders shook. "It isn't fair! Why can't they take the ones that aren't married?"

He hugged her tight, feeling a great fullness in his throat. "Come on now, stop crying, hon. Cut it out, will you? I'll be back home before little Joey sees daylight."

"You may never come back. They're killing a lot of our boys over there. Oh, Joe, Joe, why did they have to go and start another war?"

In a gruff voice he said, "Don't you go worrying about Big Joey. He'll take care of himself. You just take care of little Joey and Cleo. That's what you do."

"Don't take any chances, Joe. Don't be a hero!"

He forced himself to laugh, and hugged her tighter. "Don't you worry about the mule going blind."

She made herself stop crying and wiped her face. "But I don't understand, Joe. I don't understand what colored soldiers have to fight for—especially against other colored people."

"Honey," said Joe gently, "we got to fight like anybody else. We can't just sit on the sidelines."

But she just looked at him and shook her head.

"Look," he said, "when I get back I'm going to finish college. I'm going to be a lawyer. That's what I'm fighting for."

She kept shaking her head as if she didn't hear him. "I don't know, Joe. Maybe it's because we were brought up kind of different, you and I. My father died when I was four. My mother worked all her life in white folks' kitchens. I just did make it through high school. You had it a whole lot better than most Negro boys." She went over to the box of Kleenex and blew her nose.

"I don't see where that has a thing to do with it."

He stared at her, angry with her for being so obstinate. Couldn't she see any progress at all? Look at Jackie Robinson. Look at Ralph Bunche. Goddamn it! They'd been over it all before. What did she want him to do about it anyway? Become a deserter?

She stood up over him. "Can't see it, Joe—just can't see it! I want you here, Joe. Here with me where you belong. Don't leave me, Joe! Please—" She was crying now. "Joe, Joe, what're we going to do? Maybe it would be better to get rid of little Joey—" Her brown eyes were wide with terror. "No, Joe, No! I didn't mean that! I didn't mean it, darling! Don't know what I'm saying . . ."

She sat down beside him, bent over, her face in her hands. It was terrible for him, seeing her this way. He got up and walked from one side of the little room to the other. He thought about what the white captain from Hattiesburg, Mississippi, had said. "Men, we have a job to do. Our outfit is just as damn important as any outfit in the United States Army, white or colored. And we're working towards complete integration. It's a long, hard pull, but I guarantee you every soldier will be treated equally and without discrimination. Remember, we're fighting for the dignity of the individual." Luke Robinson had looked at the tall, lanky captain with an arrogant smile.

Joe stopped in front of Cleo and made himself speak calmly. "Look, hon, it isn't like it used to be at all. Why can't you take my word for it? They're integrating colored soldiers now. And anyhow, what the hell's the use of getting all heated up about it? I *got* to go. That's all there is to it."

He sat down beside her again. He wanted fiercely to believe that things were really changing for his kind of people. Make it easier for him—make it much easier for him and Cleo, if they both believed that colored soldiers had a stake in fighting the war in Korea. Cleo wiped her eyes and blew her nose, and they changed the subject, talked about the baby, suppose it turned out to be a girl, what would her name be? A little after midnight he kissed her good-night and walked back to the barracks.

The soldiers were marching in full field dress, with packs on their backs, duffle-bags on their shoulders, and carbines and rifles. As they approached the big white ship, there was talking and joke-cracking and nervous laughter. They were the leading Negro outfit, immediately following the last of the white troops. Even at route step there was a certain uniform cadence in the sound of their feet striking the asphalt road as they moved forward under the midday sun, through a long funnel of people and palm trees and shrubbery. But Joe hadn't spotted Cleo yet, and he was getting sick from worry. Had anything happened?

Luke Robinson, beside him, was talking and laughing and grumbling. "Boy, I'm telling you, these peoples is a bitch on wheels. Say, Office Willie, what you reckon I read in your Harlem paper last night?" Office Willie was his nickname for Joe because Joe was the company clerk—a high-school graduate, two years in college, something special. "I read where some of your folks' leaders called on the President and demanded that colored soldiers be allowed to fight at the front instead of in quartermaster. Ain't that a damn shame?"

Joe's eyes shifted distractedly from the line of people to Luke, and back to the people again.

"Percy Johnson can have my uniform any day in the week," said Luke. "He want to fight so bad. Them goddamn Koreans ain't done me nothing. I ain't mad with a living ass."

Joe liked Luke Robinson, only he was so damn sensitive on the color question. Many times Joe had told him to take the chip off his shoulder and be somebody. But he had no time for Luke now. Seeing the ship plainly, and the white troops getting aboard, he felt a growing fear. Fear that maybe he had passed Cleo and they hadn't seen each other for looking so damn hard. Fear that he wouldn't get to see her at all—never-ever again. Maybe she was ill, with no way to let him know, too sick to move. He thought of what she had said last night, about little Joey. Maybe . . .

And then he saw her, up ahead, waving at him, with the widest and prettiest and most confident smile anybody ever smiled. He was so goddamn glad he could hardly move his lips to smile or laugh or anything else.

She ran right up to him. "Hello, soldier boy, where you think you're going?"

"Damn," he said finally in as calm a voice as he could manage. "I thought for a while you had forgotten what day it was. Thought you had forgotten to come to my going-away party."

"Now, how do you sound?" She laughed at the funny look on his face, and told him he looked cute with dark glasses on, needing a shave and with the pack on his back. She seemed so cheerful, he couldn't believe she was the same person who had completely broken down last night. He felt the tears rush out of his eyes and spill down his face.

She pretended not to notice, and walked with him till they reached the last block. The women were not allowed to go any further. Looking at her, he wished somehow that she would cry, just a little bit anyhow. But she didn't cry at all. She reached up and kissed him quickly. "Good-by, darling, take care of yourself. Little Joey and I will write every day, beginning this afternoon." And then she was gone.

The last of the white soldiers were boarding the beautiful white ship, and a band on board was playing *God Bless America*. He felt a chill, like an electric current, pass across his slight shoulders, and he wasn't sure whether it was from *God*

Bless America or from leaving Cleo behind. He hoped she could hear the music; maybe it would make her understand why Americans, no matter what their color, had to go and fight so many thousands of miles away from home.

They stopped in the middle of the block and stood waiting till the white regiment was all aboard. He wanted to look back for one last glimpse of Cleo, but he wouldn't let himself. Then they started again, marching toward the ship. And suddenly the band stopped playing *God Bless America* and jumped into another tune—*The Darktown Strutters' Ball* . . .

He didn't want to believe his ears. He looked up at the ship and saw some of the white soldiers on deck waving and smiling at the Negro soldiers, yelling "Yeah, Man!" and popping their fingers. A taste of gall crept up from his stomach into his mouth.

"Goddamn," he heard Luke say, "that the kind of music *I* like." The husky soldier cut a little step. "I guess Mr. Charlie want us to jitterbug onto his pretty white boat. Equal treatment. . . . We ain't no soldiers, we're a bunch of goddamn clowns."

Joe felt an awful heat growing inside his collar. He hoped fiercely that Cleo was too far away to hear.

Luke grinned at him. "What's the matter, good kid? Mad about something? Damn—that's what I hate about you colored folks. Take that goddamn chip off your shoulder. They just trying to make you people feel at home. Don't you recognize the Negro national anthem when you hear it?"

Joe didn't answer. He just felt his anger mounting and he wished he could walk right out of the line and to hell with everything. But with *The Darktown Strutters' Ball* ringing in his ears, he put his head up, threw his shoulders back, and kept on marching towards the big white boat.

VOL DE NUIT

Susanne Lee

It would take thirteen hours on Cathay Pacific to arrive in another universe. Leaving Kai Tak in Hong Kong was always a glorious adventure, especially on a night flight. With the runway jutting into the harbor, the craft's wings looking perilously like they might clip the buildings, the takeoff gave Kari a dizzying view of the neon and the glistening blue and white glass skyscrapers with the junks and container ships below.

Leaving Hong Kong; leaving San Francisco; leaving New York.

It seemed Kari's life was all about leaving.

She was on her way to London. The emperor was at Oxford, reading law. She felt giddy. He was three years older and they had known each other for ages; Kari had a predilection for tall smart boys. They were alike: a punky irreverent sense of humor, and a love of literature and adventure. Was she in love with this big brother?

She lit a Dunhill, Alex's favorite. She would miss that crazy Aussie woman. That lazy afternoon they hung out at the Intercontinental, smoking joints and ordering room service cakes and fries. Those many many nights dancing in clubs in Lan Kwai Fong, stumbling out onto the streets for smokes, fresh air and steaming bowls of wontons from a *daipaidong* before heading back to Alex's. Then there was Kari's own near-miss career as a bar hostess/posh escort.

* * *

Was it only three weeks ago when Alex called Kari to meet at Club Mercedes? Alex, of the "never leave home without mascara and lipstick" school, looked relaxed and tanned, her hair blonde with golden highlights. She wore a mauve linen jacket over a body-hugging dress of the same color, pearl earrings, high-heeled sandals and a gold man's watch. Kari wore a black rayon summer frock with spaghetti straps and matching black flats.

The girls were slinking in, in satin and silk dresses, variations of Alex's look, chic and expensive. Donna Summer's "Last Dance" was playing amid the chatter. In the front, the mama-san, a fortyish Chinese woman with an elaborate hairdo, greeted the early birds, a group of young Caucasian and Japanese businessmen, following the lead of a much savvier older gent, obviously a repeat visitor. A blonde ex-jock flashed a smile at Kari. *God, he thinks I'm one.*

Alex sat Kari down at the back tables, had two Campari and sodas brought over and signaled to the mama-san. Kari sensed the collusion. *Why the fuck am I here?* Alex lit up and passed Kari the red box; Kari took one.

"Kari, it's easy money. Work a few weeks and take off forever. No one knows." Alex smiled over Kari's shoulder at someone she knew.

"I don't like the idea of fucking old pasty pudgy guys. What does it say about the guy who has to buy it? Gross."

"It's an accepted part of the culture."

"Alex, don't pull 'It's Asia, it's different' bullshit with me." She surveyed the sumptuous room with its Vegas worthy chandeliers and the mix of older men and attractive women skilled in the art of flirtation. The few stray *gweilos*, Caucasians, stood out in this crowd.

"Fine, love. Just consider the option."

"I'd rather keep it simple." Kari ran her finger around the rim of her glass. "If I like a man, he doesn't even have to buy me a cup of coffee."

Alex flicked her cigarette dismissively into the ashtray. "Cheap of you."

"OK, for the sake of argument, Alex, how *do you* handle the ugly fogies?"

"Close your eyes, count and think of God or any man you desire. Right now, mine is the Robert Mitchum in *Out of the Past*."

Kari made a face of displeasure. "Sorry Alex. I have a penchant for good-looking boys. No business transactions and my choice."

Alex exhaled, putting a grin into the air worthy of the Cheshire Cat. "Just remember, Club Mercedes is always here."

* * *

The stewardess, a pretty prissy Chinese woman in a tailored uniform, shook Kari out of her reveries with her chirpy voice. Kari winked at her and took out a little metal box a merchant in Chungking Mansions had given her, deciding between a percocet or a Valium. She popped a couple.

The stewardess started the safety presentation in that clipped English-inflected tone of educated Hong Kong Chinese. Kari always watched; she was a prim marionette, but Kari wanted her very own Singapore girl. Fly me, baby. Damn, no JAL yuzu drunk tonight. She had taken a few too many planes recently. She put on her Wayfarers. No designer specs. She hid behind them, to avoid conversation and sleep through the film.

It had been a wild ten months. She was armed with admission to law school (the default fallback of every grad of her era) and to a PhD program in Comp Lit, but had taken a deferral and bought a round-the-world ticket: first stop: Hong Kong.

Next stop: London. She and the emperor were never lovers, but Kari was anxious to connect with this man, half a world away, whose photo booth photo she carried with her. She remembered the four a.m. talks they had on the roof of his apartment as they smoked joints, the drives they took speeding down 5 with the radio blasting.

Thinking about the Hong Kong she was leaving, Kari pictured the calm of Star Ferry, the elegant green and white vessels traversing the harbor, that fast food joint with the fresh papaya shakes. She wouldn't miss the smell of durian in August or being sworn at in Cantonese by a crabby old lady with a cigarette dangling from her lip.

She wore white, instead of her usual black, because it was what she'd just got back from the cleaners. The pills kicked in and Kari drifted.

White white white, the Foster's Freeze vanilla ice cream cones she grew up eating, the snow angels she obsessively made in parks and on roofs, sledding down hills, the lights of the city, the barely sweet flesh of mangosteens, the snowballs she heaved, the white sheets on Mongkok clotheslines.

Kari wore white ballet flats, hand-me-downs from Alex, white jeans, a tailored men's linen jacket from the San Francisco Goodwill, the pink silk pocket square, and the white cotton T she stole from Ryo, not because she kept mementos of her liaisons, but she happened to end up with this one and it reminded her of that entanglement.

Poor Ryo. The whole episode made her squirm. He was fun to be around, whether it was exploring the detail of some temple or staying out absorbing nocturnal Hong Kong, and she fucked things up. He was never the love of her life, but he didn't deserve the mix of her unintentional cruelty and her inability to commit to anything; it was Kari's pattern of running head-on into a relationship and then withdrawing once she sensed anything resembling intimacy.

Kari dozed off to a night of sound sleep punctuated with a chain of vivid dream images: her toes newly painted in the sand as the sea swirled around them; running breathlessly down Nathan Road, past a rainbow of Chinese signs and blurred faces of indeterminate age, race and sex; sliding off the wooden banister at the library; kissing a long-haired man with silver earrings under an awning during a monsoon; looking at the people in the train across her northbound to Shanghai, each meeting her gaze unblinking; eating a skewer of fresh grilled quail eggs at a bustling night market; a quiet wave washing up a motionless, peaceful-looking little dark-haired girl onto a crowded beach.

Waking for breakfast, her own vol de nuit, night flight, was over and unlike St. Exupery, who disappeared into the sea, she was safe. Kari sipped the thankfully strong black tea, as the South Asian man in the next seat chatted her up; her independence reminded him of his own daughter, he said. He gave her his card: Omar Bannerjee, barrister. She should call if she had any problem in London. Kari thanked him, full of suspicion, but it was not the first time she misread a man. Then there was the emperor. Had she misread him, too? She would call him later that afternoon.

She walked the aisle, stretched her arms and neck, came back and strapped herself in.

Landing. Bump. Welcome to Heathrow.

THIN

Minjon LeNoir-Irwin

Since the age of 25 years old, Andrea knew the benefits of exercise and the dangers of carbohydrates. She had been hanging on to that college freshman 15 pounds for far too long. Every time she looked in the mirror she saw rolls on top of rolls. Each time Andrea sat down, she felt as if she were sitting in an inner tube. With each step, it felt as if Jell-O was attached to various parts of her body. What happened to the 80's high school girl, the one who could eat two donuts for breakfast, McDonald's for lunch and Taco Bell for dinner on the same day and still fit into her biker shorts and tank tops the next day? She was long, long gone.

After Andrea had an intense argument with her best friend De'Nial, she let her win. So she set out to take control of her life. Andrea knew there was A LOT of work to be done, so she decided to join a gym. The first day she set foot into a gym she felt completely overweight and overwhelmed. There were several cardio machines, weight machines, free weights and people ranging from all sizes and shapes. Feeling intimidated and lacking any direction, Andrea decided to walk on the treadmill breaking a little sweat and then packed up shop. This continued for a few weeks, and although she saw some minor changes, it was going to take a lot more to become that girl.

What is that girl, one may ask. "That Girl" is those women at the gym that every female gym goer desires to look like, the one that wears the skimpy outfits with matching sneakers. The one with the six-pack abs, well defined biceps, triceps, quads and hamstrings. The girl who looks like she just stepped off the cover of *Shape* magazine. She was the girl Andrea wanted to be.

As Andrea began her quest to achieve bodily perfection, she ran out and bought every health and fitness magazine she could find and read them from cover to cover. Then she decided it was time to devise a plan. The first thing Andrea did was go out and buy a couple of cute girl workout outfits and some new sneakers, which matched of course. She figured if she looked the part then maybe she could transform into "That Girl." She learned how to calculate her BMI (Body Mass Index), RRH (Resting Heart Rate), and MHR (Maximum Heart Rate). It was as if Andrea should have been granted an honorary Ph.D. from ACE (American Counsel on Exercise).

During the first few weeks Andrea quickly learned that it was going to take a lot more than a cute black and white workout outfit, matching shoes, leg warmers and a headband to get a killer body. She was going to take self-control, discipline, and focus.

Andrea set her alarm clock to wake up at 5:30 am every morning to be at the gym by 5:45 am and to make it to work on time. She needed to leave the gym by 7:15 am. This would allow her one hour and thirty minutes a day to work on achieving "That Girl" status. During the first few weeks Andrea walked on the treadmill, rode the bike, and took the basic aerobics classes. After two months she began running three miles a day and within three months she was able to run six miles with ease. Andrea noticed some slight changes in the way her clothes fit, but still she needed more. The question Andrea then began to ask herself was, is there any truth to the old sayings "You are what you eat" or a "Moment on your lips forever on your hips." Knowing she had a decent start on a fitness regime, Andrea attempted and scrutinized every diet on the market: Jenny Craig, Slim Fast, Cabbage Soup, Binging and Purging, NutriSystems, and last but not least starvation. Her findings indicated the following:

Jenny Craig: Food expensive and not that great. Andrea felt as if she were eating cardboard and eventually the Chicken Picante tasted like Beef Wellington. After the first three days she gave into temptation and decided to forget it.

Slim Fast: Yea, a shake for breakfast, a shake for lunch, and a sensible dinner. By the time dinner came around, Andrea was everything but sensible. She was ravenous. Did she miss something? Were there supposed to be actual meals in between each shake?

Cabbage Soup: All Andrea could say was she did not eat cabbage for one year after a week on that diet.

Atkins: Meat, meat, and more meat. Andrea was weak, could not concentrate, and blacked out on two occasions.

Binging and laxatives: Tried it for a week. Ate all the cupcakes, pizza, fried chicken and biscuits she wanted and then inhaled 6 laxatives. All Andrea could say was hemorrhoids and bad breath. Enough said. Not cool.

NutriSystems: Okay, enough meals in a box for one month that can stay on the shelf for 4 weeks. Come on. Andrea requested a refund within the first three days.

Starvation: Andrea figured that if she ate an apple and a bowl of cereal for breakfast and drank plenty of water and did not eat anything else until the next day she would be fine. Little did she know that by 7:00 pm she was so hungry she would have killed someone for a French fry or eaten a small child if it were put in front of her with hot sauce on it. Starvation can only lead to erratic, bipolar, and highly dysfunctional behavior.

Andrea then decided to monitor what she put in her mouth by eating more fruits and vegetables and less cookies and fried foods. She consulted a nutritionist and they devised a plan that would allow her to intake a certain number of calories based on her desired weight. Findings indicated slow and steady results.

Andrea knew that if she were to lose the 15 pounds she had gained in college and turn an additional five into muscle then she would be well on her way to becoming the object of gym envy. Equipping herself with a plan, the knowledge and tools Andrea felt confident in her abilities to see this through to the end.

Four months into her program, Andrea had gone from 130 pounds to 110 pounds. She was definitely smaller but still flabby. Andrea had heard about a thing called a personal trainer and she decided to see what they were about. All she could say is ouch, ouch, ouch. She started off with two one hour sessions a week and after two months of not being able to sit on a toilet, Andrea saw something stick out of the side of her arm. It was called a tricep muscle. Something she didn't even know she had. Before long these things were popping out everywhere. Andrea was beginning to develop characteristics of "That Girl." She had triceps, biceps, traps, quads, calves, hamstrings, glutes, shoulders, and last but not least abs. Yes, the tubby girl who was merely walking at a rate of 3.5 on the treadmill had abs. Had Andrea become her?

In month six Andrea walked into the gym and she could see the glares of eyes on her nicely crafted physique. She got her certification in group fitness and began teaching kickboxing, step, and yoga. Women were asking Andrea; yes her, for pointers and tips on achieving desired results.

So eleven years and one child later, what has Andrea learned?

- Diets don't work
- Cute exercise apparel is not the answer
- Starvation, don't think so
- Just because you ate tamales at lunch it doesn't mean you have to run an extra 3 miles
- Border line insanity is eating enough food for an army and having chocolate laxatives for dessert
- Being "That Girl" in her twenties is much harder to maintain in your mid thirties
- You will not be any happier because the number on the scale is 5 pounds less than it was two months prior
- Eating healthy and following some sort of fitness routine has other benefits besides looking good in a bikini
- It's okay to miss a workout to stay in bed watching Barney with your children
- Eating macaroni and cheese, and yams on Thanksgiving is not going to kill you. Just don't take any home.

Goal setting with realistic expectations and accepting occasional setbacks is what this is all about. So, is Andrea still "That Girl"? Well . . . she weightlifted for an hour today and taught a step class. Sorry, she has to go because her big piece of Godiva Chocolate Cheesecake with extra whip cream is melting.

GEOGRAPHY ONE

Russell Charles Leong

Spring rains appeared as the month ended, heightening the tropical humidity that enabled me to sleep at night with only a thin covering. Still waking up alone in the small hours before dawn, as I had been doing all month, I decided to leave Los Angeles for a day. The empty cans I left scattered about my backyard had filled with tepid rainwater. Mosquito larvae were already beginning to hatch. I bought twenty tins of tuna fish from the Thrifty's Drugstore because they were fifty cents each. It was the easiest way to eat. I had pared my living habits down. Even the *Times* was stacked haphazardly on the steps: I did not bother to unfold the soggy papers or read the news.

In advance, I checked my car's highway map of Orange County, the region south between Los Angeles and San Diego. Fifty miles one way meant a daily commute for some people; for me, it was a rare journey, a hundred miles round-trip. I had never driven that many miles out of Los Angeles and recalled only the cross streets—Brookhaven and Katella—in Little Saigon. No address or phone number. Though Lac Hai and I had been to the temple twice, at the time I did not pay attention to the route. Today I would go there alone.

On the way home from work the night before, I had stopped by the Thai market in Hollywood and bought two large boxes of dried Chinese noodles for the Sifu of the temple. The market had escaped the burning of the riots here two weeks ago, but the block still held the acrid smell of other charred buildings, intensified by the May rains. I had placed two ten-dollar bills in a white envelope, scribbling my name and Hai's on the flap. The twin bills symbolized a kind of symmetry that I had hoped to achieve in my life. I placed a small framed photo he'd given me of himself into the shopping bag and put everything in my car trunk.

I needed to return to the place where I had felt at home, a stranger among fellow strangers. If Vietnamese had been refugees to America when they first arrived, I was, ironically, in this position now, a refugee to that house that served as temple, shelter, and garden for the Buddhist monk.

The Interstate 5 funneled my car smoothly past working-class industrial towns—Montebello, Commerce, Downey, Norwalk—southeast of downtown Los Angeles. The morning was warm, smudged with brown haze at the horizon. Sweat soaked my shirt. Billboard mirages of Las Vegas casino shows in the desert and sleek Japanese automobiles glittered between real palm trees and poplars. I held my speed at seventy miles an hour as my eyes focused on the towns ahead. Sante Fe Springs. Anaheim. La Palma. I drove on. The freeway sign said "22, Garden Grove Connector," which would lead me west to Little Saigon.

Housing on these suburban streets—Magnolia, Euclid, Beach—was arranged without regard for pedestrian life: one side of the street had fifteen-foot concrete sound barriers which backed middle-class housing developments. Directly across from them, older, single-family dwellings from the 1950s and '60s—the kind built on concrete slabs—faced the blank walls. Newer developments, built cheaply of beige stucco, segregated themselves from the older houses.

Finally, Brookhaven. My eyes searched its length for the simple tract home which served as the temple. The lush oriental arrangement of rose bushes, aloes, bodhi trees, sago palms, and the plaster statue of Quan Am—goddess of mercy—fronted the house. I stopped the car, took the shopping bag from the trunk, and walked across the street. A single pair of men's black shoes, not the usual row of a dozen pairs. The door was shut. I knocked once, then again. The window curtains were drawn. A black umbrella leaned against a windowsill. Hung outside the door was a talisman made of old copper Chinese coins laced up with red cotton string in the shape of a sword and a ceramic incense holder filled with burnt punk sticks. No answer. Ten o'clock. Maybe the Sifu was still asleep or out for the morning.

I resigned myself to waiting. The Sifu had cut the flowering bodhi tree down to almost half its original size. He said that the roots could spread under and beyond the house; in Vietnam they grew to gigantic dimensions. The smell of the roses he tended permeated the air. I paced up and down the narrow entrance way.

I rapped on the door again. Silence. In my anxious walking back and forth, I counted forty-five steps across the width of the house lot. A dirty blue Pontiac stopped beside me. An Asian man about my size got out, walked up to the door of the temple, and knocked. Turning toward me, he asked in Vietnamese if anyone was home. I answered in English. He smiled.

"I'm in trouble. I need three dollars for gas." I gave him three rumpled dollar bills.

"Thanks," he said, stuffing them into his shirt pocket. "I haven't been here in years. When I first came to this country ten years ago, I visited the temple. I had promised Buddha that if the boat made it to Thailand, and I ever got to America, that's what I would do. Sifu was kind, and rented me a room until I could settle down."

When I didn't respond, he continued.

"I'm a welder, but I got laid off yesterday. Maybe my wife will leave me—because I took her forty dollars last night to the Bicycle Club. I lost it all. I can't stop gambling."

He sat himself down on a rock under one of the two bodhi trees at the entry way. "Here, sit down," he motioned with his hand, "it's cooler in the shade." I sat next to him on the other flat rock, absorbed by the droning of bees and passing automobiles.

"These monks sleep late sometimes. They study old books at night," he said.

"Maybe he went shopping for food."

"If you see the monk, tell him I came by. I'll come back later." He stood up. We shook hands and he hurried off without telling me his name.

After waiting two hours I got into my car and drove around the block to the corner shopping mall. Lac Hai and I had walked through here, the last time we visited the temple together. He bought yellow mums and gladioli for the temple altar from the florist.

I returned to the temple but the door was still shut. I left the two boxes of noodles on the step. Should I leave the envelope with the money in the mailbox, in the plastic bag with the noodles, or slip it under the door? I decided that the door was safest, but retrieved the framed photo of Lac Hai from the bag. The sun's glare obscured the image of Hai pressed behind the glass, the small petulant mouth and dark eyes set obliquely into the pale face. On the surface of the finger-smudged glass, I could sense my own features reflected.

The rains had swollen the door tight and there was barely space underneath. I nudged the envelope in. Barking from behind the door—Phuc, the temple dog. He tugged at the envelope, and it disappeared under the door for good. I hoped he would give it to his master. "Phuc, Phuc," I shouted. Perhaps he would recognize my voice.

Once more, I drove off. I was hungry. At a Chinese-Vietnamese restaurant, I ate all of the squid-and-vegetable lunch plate. Returning to the temple, I saw that the package of noodles was still against the door. The man who had gambled away his luck and money had not come back. I would return to Los Angeles.

The night you left me you avoided my eyes. With my right index finger, I traced the printed image of the pink lotus framed in yellow: Tra Man Sen, Lotus Tea / 100 grams or 3.5 ounces. Red cardboard box, now emptied. Empty. I stirred the last of the green leaves into a cup of hot water. The monk, I recall, had served us such a tea at the temple. But that evening we did not drink anything.

Now my throat is dry, as are my eyes. I refuse to cry over this common affair between men. *Chuntzu chih chiao tan ju shui*—between gentlemen, friendship appears indifferent but is pure like water. That's about all I remember from studying Chinese, and that adage comes in handy now. More clarity: tacked on my kitchen wall, a torn newspaper clipping. On the paper, words by Aung San Suu Kyi, the Burmese leader under house arrest for her political speeches. She had written about coolness which lies beneath the shade of trees, of teachers, and of Buddha's teaching. I cut the article out of the paper and retyped it. I am not Buddhist, but I was moved because she had spoken her thoughts to thousands of people, whereas I have no one to speak to now.

I lock and unlock my hands, from fist to open palm, tracing the fate lines without caring whether they mean anything. Rub each fingertip. The tea is not strong enough, its bitterness turning to sweet aftertaste on the tongue. On the kitchen sideboard the bottle of Crown Royal that a friend gave me for Tet, the lunar New Year. I uncap it, sniffing up the fumes, but recap the bottle. I want to see you, Lac Hai, your face clearly in my eyes. For I am a Chinese man from America, left dry by a man of water who was born in the delta between the Red and Black rivers.

I spit on the tile floor. Why were you born? Where did you come from? I'm standing in the kitchen, I realize, staring at the fissured plaster walls. At you. Offspring of Lac Long Quan and Au Co, who, between them, produced one hundred eggs according to legend. Fifty of their children returned with their father to the seacoast; the others remained in the mountains with their mother. Those who went to the seas and the deltas became the Vietnamese.

So goes the tale. And thousands of years later you were born, Hai. How you came to America is your own story to tell. But how we met is mine. You thought you had the last word. No. My story is the last word, since you will never say "yes" to me.

Blue outdoor floodlights spot the palm trees and bougainvillea, linger on Spanish roof tiles and French doors that link the hillside deck to the garden. The literal truth comes out in clichés: Hollywood Hills, a circa 1920s neo-Italianate stucco mansion. A living room dressed for parties: gilded Indonesian wood carvings on Plexiglass bases; stuffed white couches. A hundred decorative Asian men—Thai, Chinese, Filipino, Japanese, Vietnamese—are dancing on the hardwood floor together with voracious Anglos who never look as young as the Asians, even if they really are younger. Double platters of fried chicken, lumpia, chow mein, lots of rice, and American pies: peach, apple, cherry. Two cut-glass punch bowls over-flowed with sangria and citrus rinds. You are a Gypsy floating about the room, a red bandanna around your shining brow, one silver earring, and a vest of dark leather. You never throw me a glance, but I follow your cheekbones and lips with my eyes as desire catches at my throat. Three days later, I telephone you.

The black Toyota pickup hurtles through the smog-white afternoon, heading south on the Interstate 5 toward Little Saigon, Orange County. You drive fast, sun-glasses framing the bridge of your nose, hands cleanly maneuvering the stick shift with long fingers. Following the curve of the freeway, you tell me how you've traveled the roads of the world and ended up here.

Ten years ago, at eighteen, you went from Buddhist temple to temple seeking the peace of mind that each monastery promised. You shaved your head. You meditated on your knees. You talked back and forth past midnight over tea with your monks, wore out pair after pair of sandals strolling the muddy fields of Taiwan, Thailand, Japan, France. Skinny chickens, heat and cold, and thick-walled buildings were the same in every country. Bare floors. Old books. A few compassionate monks. Most of them, who just followed rituals without risking heart or mind, disappointed you in the end.

You observed their teachings well enough, but could not quell other desires. That desire which still causes your body temperature to rise in fever. But neither meditation nor lovemaking could contain or release this heat, for your pleasure walks the same path as your pain.

"Just friends for today," you tell me. "Tomorrow is less certain than the past."

Traveling a route you know by heart, you seek the pure sky of a childhood that was never your own. From dawn to dusk, your sky was fractured with rockets and fragments of fuselage. For your wartime hunger, Catholic-orphanage nuns beat you with bamboo canes that bruised your child's skin. A stranger to your history, I am neither father, teacher, brother, nor lover. In the truck I touch your thigh but you draw back, not trusting me or anyone who touches you. Exit Little Saigon: we swerve past the green enameled sign onto Bolsa, a boulevard crammed with two-story strip malls—Vietnamese bakeries, banks, beauty parlors, stationery stores, coffee shops, bookstores. Snack on sweet rice cakes and drink iced concoctions of brown sugar, red dates, and seaweed. You drink and look away. I would have talked with you in a new language for me: Vietnamese. Now silence runs deeper between us, a blade dividing memory.

You want to stop at the temple to visit your Sifu, with whom you had studied for several months. First we buy flowers for the altar, pink, yellow, and white mums. Inside the truck, I bring the large bouquet to my face. The petals darken into fingers that gesture with a sudden life of their own, settling upon my eyelids and lips.

The conversation between you and the monk is all yours. You sit across from each other in a corner of the room. The monk does not look directly at you, and not to me at all. But I steal a look at him—at his face tanned from gardening and at his clean-shaved head and nape. Then I bow by the altar and leave the room, exiting the side door to the backyard. It's a derelict space that backdrops the temple, painted yellow and trimmed at the roof, eaves, and windows with red. For Vietnamese, as for Chinese, these colors must be auspicious.

The yard is large for a tract home. The diving board on which I sit overhangs the edge of the swimming pool drained of its water. A concrete kidney-shaped grave is swollen with the legs of odd chairs, cracked tables, and a hundred aloe plants in black plastic tubs.

Somewhere inside the temple the monk is chanting. His sutras seemed to unlock doors, lift windows and solid walls, sweeping past wooden eaves—and alighting upon the aloes in the yard. I sit in the midst of the debris, discarding another layer of my life. Last week a friend told me that seven of his buddies had died of AIDS. No one wanted to know. In Asian families, you just slowly disappear. Your family rents a small room for you. They feed you lunch. Dinner. Rice, fish, vegetables.

At my feet, aloes thrust green spikes upwards from black dirt, promise to heal wounds and burns, to restore the skin's luster. From this ground pure light would surely arise over suburban roofs and power lines, illuminating the path of green aloes by which I would return to the house.

Inside the temple the monk is already cutting cabbages for supper on the nicked Formica table. I find myself alone with him. You are gone to some other part of the house. Sound of sink water running down the drain.

From eastern deserts, Santa Ana winds blow inwards to Los Angeles. Sand submerges my feet, then rises and fills my eyes. The wind plays tricks. I am alone in bed, listening to it. Noises of branches and leaves rush against each other as arms and legs brush over mine. Burying me. My body is bloated with chrysanthemum leaves, like a Mexican birthday piñata, waiting for children to break it open with sticks. What will fall out? Flowers float on the Cuu Long—Mekong. Do white petals heed death or life? I do not know. Santa Ana winds blow through cheap condominium walls in the City of Angels, currents which sap the vines of my desire.

Dry throat, the night after you leave. Fifth gin and tonic. I am at The Bar, drowning in the shadows of Asian men half my age who gyrate on the dance floor. An Anglo man standing beside me named Doug or Eddie is talking. I listen, laugh, but do not turn my face to him. I wait for you to walk in with a new friend, for both of you to cast insinuating glances, like violets, at this roomful of men. Only after I have seen this with my own eyes will I leave. Dark petals unfurl, mocking me. Maybe it is the gin and tonic. I take black coffee, and after that, another gin.

I probably look younger than my thirty-seven years, in a white nylon windbreaker, snug Levis, black sneakers. Yet I detest the remnants of youth on myself. In the photograph, Hai, you are wearing a long-sleeved shirt that covers your arms, but it was not your concealed body or veiled spirit that most intrigued me. It was your journey that directed my imagination, as I have never ventured outside the country of my birth. China was a mental atlas of winding rivers and mountain ranges; Vietnam was still farther away in space and time. Beyond the black-and-white images of soldiers, helicopters, and villages captured on my television screen, that southern land was once the impassioned object of an antiwar demonstration that I had joined twenty years ago.

My stomach turns, entrails holding in rancid water, petals, leaves. The churning of Santa Ana air gathers momentum, drowning out the DJ. If I make it home tomorrow morning, the sky should clear from the wind. The bartender does not want to pour me another drink. I insist.

"I will give you a flower," I tell him. "Have you heard of *Flowers of Evil?* By a French poet. But I forget his name tonight."

The barman relents.

Around me, floors begin to crack and sway. Chrysanthemums fall apart, their ravaged petals plucking up stray insects. Even hands to my ears cannot shut out the wind. Stop.

The television blazes. We live in the heat of the desert, in jerry-built towns of plastic pipe and drywall. I long for waters past.

In the tenth century, Ngo Quyen defeated a Chinese armada in the Bach Dang river. He ordered huge timbers tipped with iron to be buried in the tidal shallows. At high tide these were hidden, and when Chinese troopships appeared, the lighter Vietnamese boats went out to meet them. The submerged timbers skewered the Chinese hulls. Then Vietnamese boats, their prows painted with lucky eyes, swiftly advanced and burned the Chinese ships.

Reaching the alluvial plains, between the brows of the Red and Black rivers, you can see the features of the land. Your face is flushed, sweating. Heat rises from your belly and chest. I press a cool white towel on you. More cold tea. You fall asleep in my arms. Maybe a fever, via these erratic winds, has seeped into your nostrils.

You get a haircut. It's almost like being home—mirrors and bicycles casually propped up below the banyan trees, and men, young and old, having a haircut and shave. Only in Little Saigon your haircut is indoors, under cool fluorescent lights. But the same extended conversations, the same jokes. Your black hair falls to the floor in dark wisps and you flirt with the Amerasian haircutter. You feel almost at home, but not quite. Even at my apartment, settled on the black leather-and-chrome couch with your Vietnamese martial-arts novels and cassette tapes, you're awkward with my domesticity—your long legs angled out in borrowed sweatpants.

When we go out to eat with friends you joke in Vietnamese. The most I can do is utter the dishes in Chinese syllables, but that is not enough. Your accent betrays a thousand uprisings: revolts against forebears and foreigners; against the Chinese, French, Japanese, Americans. When we get home one night you have not spoken with me at all: English has disappeared from your vocabulary. I ask what's wrong. You turn your head away from mine on the pillow, muttering: "If you want soap-opera dialogue then just turn on the TV, okay?"

"No soap opera—Chinese opera. How about *Taking Tiger Mountain by Strategy?*" I laugh, deflecting your sarcasm. "Don't forget I'm still Chinese."

"How would you know anything about taking? You never had your home taken away like I did. By Communists. In Saigon my stepfather had a three-story house, with a small ballroom on the top floor. A balcony, with blue tiles, that we danced or slept on during the summer . . ."

Not wanting to hear the same story again, yet still wanting you, I smother your face with the coverlet and crawl quickly underneath, bringing my face to your belly and pressing my lips farther down. I take you in my mouth until all I can hear is your breathing. Your body tosses and turns. Wordless. You come without touching me, your hands slackened against the pillow. So your silence is against me, a being who is both American and Chinese.

Ignorant, I do not share your dialect. I shave the shadow off my face in the morning. I learned that Vietnam lies in one time zone. That's all I remember from Geography One, junior high, about Vietnam.

But we lie awake in many zones. You speak to me across one time zone, and I speak to you in another. Your thoughts turn away earlier or my words tumble out later. Or, just the reverse. Zones which divide us.

Whenever you are alone you drive to Redondo Beach and watch the water. Hai: the name for "water," which is your real name. Water which takes you back, to the plains between the Red and Black rivers. One day you asked me the English name of the *mai* tree, with small yellow blossoms that open during Tet. I do not know the English name. On the kitchen table: the green plate from which you ate, the cup from which you drank. You may not return, but I leave them anyway, as I leave your sandals at the door.

I fall deeper into sleep under which everything becomes transparent. My hands search for mineral places we once crossed together—blue veins, black quartz. Your eyes travel farther back, to limestone hills above the river, dredging up timbers tipped with shining iron. Buried in river water. Hidden at high tide. Timber after timber, a forest of weapons. I stare at the deceptive calmness of the water.

I drop the teacup on the kitchen floor. It does not shatter, but remains whole. The cup holds departed kin, a spirit which wants to stay here. Neither libations nor liaisons could free me of it. Nonsense. Superstition. I, Miles Mak, am a college-educated Chinese American, after all, raised in Queens, New York, by way of Connecticut, Seattle, and, finally, Los Angeles.

Wash the night away. Rinse the plates and cups. Put them away, less the one in hand. Leaves, dark as sand or seeds, cleave to the bottom of my cup.

A truck lumbered past me, forcing me to steer my compact car against the next lane divider. Soon the glassy towers of downtown insurance and banking companies thrust their heads through the smog. The drive back up was faster than the ride down. When I reached Hollywood it was still the middle of the afternoon. I went to the Holiday Gym, a pink stucco exercise palace with pop music piped in from dawn to dusk. In the mid-afternoon it was almost deserted. Methodically, on the chrome and red vinyl-padded machines, I crossed from one to the other, flexing back and biceps, doing sit-ups and leg lifts to bury the time. Though I had not seen the Sifu I felt relieved even to have located the temple again. The steel-chromed bars rose up and down in front of my eyes. Sweat lined my face. I was imprisoned in my exertion of choice. I needed to sweat, whether it was under the sun or induced within this air-cooled environment. A few middle-aged Korean women with rubber head caps were swimming in the lap pool. Their pale heads and shoulders, bobbing up and down in the green water, took on the androgynous cast of fleshy sea creatures.

After showering, I went home, opened a can of tuna fish and a can of cream-of-mushroom soup, and poured all of it over leftover rice. The kitchen clock read 5:30 p.m. Dead heat of traffic. I could wait a while. Maybe I would drive back to the temple tonight. Rewrapping the picture of Hai in white paper, I put it beside the door, intending to bring it back with me.

Night on Interstate 5 released the day's torpor: automobile headlights turned upon each other, thousands of metallic bodies feeding heat and carbon exhaust to the hungry darkness. I drove slowly, without ambition, yielding to the cars already in front of me. I reached the Garden Grove freeway which connected to Little Saigon, but the sign said "West Connector Closed." Darkness. So I got off the East exit, opposite to where I wanted to go. The faceless buildings of a vast suburban shopping mall in the City of Orange surrounded me; it was fifteen minutes before I realized I was traveling in a circle, around the perimeter of the shopping center's department stores, now closed. I continued driving down the empty streets.

Irritated, I did not think to stop the car and check my map. Instead my eyes searched for Vietnamese shop signs, oriental mini-malls, and people. The pedestrians on the sidewalk had dark hair and were not tall. I squinted at them, hoping they were Asian. More auto body shops, Taco Bell signs, and liquor stores. This was not Little Saigon but a Latino barrio, part of Anaheim or Santa Ana.

I stopped at a red light and rolled down my window, catching the attention of the Asian driver in a gray Nissan sedan beside my car. "Bolsa," I yelled, the main street of Little Saigon. He pointed his finger in the opposite direction. I thanked him and made a U-turn at the next light. Residential blocks had the same concrete barriers which obscured my vision and direction. I found a gas station not yet closed. The Pakistani said, "Drive down for a couple of miles, you will pass Euclid, then Brookhaven, and make a right."

The temple might be shut for the night or the Sifu already asleep. Following the gas station attendant's directions, I found Brookhaven. I pulled my car up near the door next to the temple and got out. As I approached the door, the one light shining in a back window suddenly turned dark. I knocked softly. In an instant, the window lit up again. The door opened.

An unfamiliar face peered out at me. In the porch light I did not know whether the smooth face was a man's or a woman's. The person greeted me in Vietnamese. In the back room, I could see the Sifu adjusting his robe.

"Sifu," I called.

He asked me to come in and sit and introduced me to his assistant. Under the light, the young man looked all of fifteen, but he must have been at least ten years older. The monk explained that they had been separated twenty years by the war, but ran into each other in Los Angeles. As a child, the young man lived next door to the monk's house, south of Saigon. After the youth arrived in the U.S., he attended a year of junior college but had to drop out. He ended up here at the temple.

I hung my head, apologized for the late hour, and hoped that I had not disturbed them. I explained that I had come in the morning, but that the temple door was locked. The Sifu said, "Oh, I thought it was some traveling monks who had dropped by to visit and left us those boxes of noodles."

I unwrapped the photo and showed it to the monk. With a look of consternation, he handed it back to me. Glancing away from me, he focused his eyes past the carved brass candlesticks and fruit-laden platters, to a point beyond the image of the gold-leafed Buddha that occupied the center place on the altar table.

In English, he said: "You need not say more." Switching to Vietnamese, he paused between sentences to allow his assistant to translate. "A bird wants more than he can eat, so he flies into the trap. A fish wants more than he can eat, so he catches the hook. Know when you have enough." He pointed to the curtained windows.

"There, in the daytime, can you see the two trees at the entrance to this temple? When birds alight on the leaves, the trees do not show happiness. When the birds fly away, the trees do not reveal sadness. Be like these two trees."

The room enveloped the three of us, our knees and feet touching the felt carpet.

"Being born is unhappiness, as being sick is unhappiness. Old age or dying is also unhappiness. But still another form of unhappiness is happiness itself."

I could feel my hands go warm and pressed my palms onto the carpet beneath my legs. It was ten minutes, if that much. The Sifu's words resounded, as sound does, in the spaces within me.

"Go home and sleep."

I thrust the photograph of Lac Hai into his hands. "He does not belong to me," I said.

I stood up and thanked his assistant for helping. As I reached the door, the terrier, Phuc, barked at me, wagging his tail. I looked back at the monk, about to ask if the dog had retrieved the envelope with the money. Sifu nodded his head in the affirmative even before my asking.

"Next time you come," he said, "we'll cook some of the noodles for you."

I put my palms together, bowed, and backed out of the doorway. Someone switched off the porch light. My shoes were dampened with night dew and I put them on in the dark.

BLACK KOREA 2

Walter K. Lew

> *Or your little chop-suey ass will be a target . . . .*
> —Ice Cube

Last summer, four black cops arrested me because I was "dat Chinese man." You want proof? Get me the money I need for a lawyer—I'll pay you back extra after I win.

We do win.

* * *

EPISODE: After an afternoon of collecting quotations, diagrams, and photos for an essay on *DICTEE* (written by a Korean American murdered by a security guard in SoHo), I spend a night in the Library of Congress's basement video dungeon, two of First District's finest holding cages, and Central Cell Block.

For being "dat chinese man."

IN THE BASEMENT OF THE LIBRARY OF CONGRESS: Sat for two hours while cops tried to figure out forms and sign their names. "Do they want our weight or his?" "I don't know—that's a tough one. You better go ask the Captain." Don't they have to read me my rights or something? What are one's rights when there's no witness but four empowered gook-grillers? Twenty more minutes pass.

"Do we put in his birthdate or ours?"

"I don't know. That's a tough one."

"I guess I'll go ask the captain. Man, these are tough."

Then it's time for handcuffs and hauling me again for the ride to First District. Young admirer driving the cruiser coos to Captain, "Jeez, I didn't know you had it in you." *Badge no. 31 thirty-one, thirty-one, 7 p.m.* I repeat like a mantra. His name, too—Not mine.

AT FIRST DISTRICT: The squad congratulates itself, "This is good—it sets a precedent." Denied release on citation by Metro PD because "You mean dat chinese man? He hasn't been in the country long enough," despite my records, sister, and a reporter friend saying I was born & raised in Baltimore, 60 miles away, despite my Bawl'mer drawl. "Do we put in his birthplace or our birthplace?"

No ancestral pine and guardian-graced hillock in Baltimore, 100 mi away, quaked at all this. Sleep, grandfathers grandmothers: I know you sigh already from your own history.

TWO HOURS LATER, STILL AT FIRST DISTRICT: Captain and his crew shuffle out of station, smiling, assuring my sister and friend that I will be free in minutes. Just working for the public good, ma'am. *They have a dream! They have a dreee-am! Like the permed asshole with the citizen's achievement awards covering his left tit who got a hard-on-all-ovah-his-body whenever he pushed me around ("Stand behind me and put your thUMB out"): that even the lowly He and All the Righteous Rest may rejoice as they trample over fallen yellars and ba-baloneyans, always holding high the colors of our world-champion Killah-nation in the cause of of . . . Liberty and Freedom for All . . . No, I mean the NEW WORD ODOR! Hail to the . . . I have SEEN the glory of the*

Now solely Metro PD's meat, yours Truly, Lew.

Half-nelsoned and shoved away from my pleading sister and my friend scribbling down names and badge numbers. Dried blood-smears all over the cell's lemon brick.

FOLLOW THE YELLOW BRICK WALL: I look down at the steel bench and, after idly glancing along the scattered initials and dates there, discern in the dim fluorescent light that, near the middle, a few Korean letters have also been scratched into it. After fifteen minutes of staring and studying, I still cannot make them form a complete word. First syllable: *Mu*, probably meaning "non-," "without-," "not," or maybe it's the *mu* of "soldier, weapon, martial." Then a *ch* and *n*, but there is no vowel in between to make a full syllable. I conjecture that, since one cannot have anything in the cell except the minimum of clothing—even my shoelaces have been confiscated—maybe police came at that point and took the stylus or prisoner away.

Mu ch n

* * *

OFF TO CENTRAL CELL BLOCK: The whole airless paddywagon to myself, wire tight around the wrists, doubled through my belt loops, marking more flesh each time we bounce through a rut and I'm bumped around on the metal plank, window so small and dull I don't know where the hell I am, back-and-forth around the city cuz brainchild forgot my papers.

"You're spending the night here in CCB, no matter what you say." Three hours to frisk, photograph, and fingerprint me for the third time (I think—I've lost track), tortured by "Married with Children" and Arnold S.'s "Commando" on the one-finger-typing officer's tube, though I enjoy the scene where Arnoould's high-heeled sidekick blasts open a paddywagon with an anti-tank bazooka.

Some Latino and Black youngsters I'm being processed with complain about their treatment.

"So sue us, go ahead and sue the whole fuckin department," the sandwich-munching officer grins. "Do you know how HIGH the stack of cases waiting to be heard is?"

He lifts his free hand about four feet above the desk. (Me? I just want his fuckin sandwich.)

"Yeah, maybe you'll get heard 2 or 3 years from now. And you'd better have a good lawyer too—WE're the Federal government!"

Here we go. Just like a Bronson film. Big beautiful belaying pin switches to open and shut cages from a distance, brass showing through where the paint's chipped.

"Officer, put him in here with me, I'm LONEsome. . . ."

"Sorry—I don't assign the cells."

Mine is number 22, Jim Palmer's old number! The officer performs his most helpful service of the day: passing single cigarettes back and forth like lacing up a high-top as he walks along between the two rows of cages, 25¢ each.

* * *

IN CELL 22: To my surprise, I find my brothers of this evening in the many-throated, constantly thrusting and sighing conversation rolling like a wave up and down between the cages. A red bandanna'd gang member asks me ("He's a SCHOLAR!") into their banter, and I quickly conjoin my own solos of sympathetic cluck. They laugh and I laugh: we share our stories of false apprehending.

After a cup of Hi-C (orange color) for dinner, I lay down on a perforated metal frame (my bunk) in water and cigarette ash. For a night of conjuring poems—but for whom? I have no listening *volk*. For the bantering brothers here then, endlessly joking black boys and brown boys, all sad inside if you listen close enough, but most of all the invisible one with the Korean blade who drifted along with me from First District's yellow brick, forever laying the dark puzzle out before me like a scarred nameplate or gravestone so broad it blocks off the whole field of vision.

Mu ch__n

Answer this, s/he pleads, I too don know what I'm spelling out   Please complete it for me so I short bars of light flicker in the cigarette smoke free of this pain of writing what I don know that etches itself into bones of my arm my hand

mu ch n

* * *

MAYBE SINCE THEN I have passed a brother or sister on the street, that very pattern of scarring weight and need altering a bit the swing of his or her arm on one side, slowing by just the width-of-a-moment how a hand lifts or "warms itself around a cup of coffee"

MU CH N

I guess and gaze, present it to others
    Ajoshi, I kos-ul chom pwa chuseyo!
Still have not made up our mind.

REENA

Paule Marshall

Like most people with unpleasant childhoods, I am on constant guard against the past—the past being for me the people and places associated with the years I served out my girlhood in Brooklyn. The places no longer matter that much since most of them have vanished. The old grammar school, for instance, P.S. 35 ("Dirty 5's" we called it and with justification) has been replaced by a low, coldly functional arrangement of glass and Permastone which bears its name but has none of the feel of a school about it. The small, grudgingly lighted stores along Fulton Street, the soda parlor that was like a church with its stained-glass panels in the door and marble floor have given way to those impersonal emporiums, the supermarkets. Our house even, a brownstone relic whose halls smelled comfortingly of dust and lemon oil, the somnolent street upon which it stood, the tall, muscular trees which shaded it were leveled years ago to make way for a city housing project—a stark, graceless warren for the poor. So that now whenever I revisit that old section of Brooklyn and see these new and ugly forms, I feel nothing. I might as well be in a strange city.

But it is another matter with the people of my past, the faces that in their darkness were myriad reflections of mine. Whenever I encounter them at the funeral or wake, the wedding or christening—those ceremonies by which the past reaffirms its hold—my guard drops and memories banished to the rear of the mind rush forward to rout the present. I almost become the child again—anxious and angry, disgracefully diffident.

Reena was one of the people from that time, and a main contributor to my sense of ineffectualness then. She had not done this deliberately. It was just that whenever she talked about herself (and this was not as often as most people) she seemed to be talking about me also. She ruthlessly analyzed herself, sparing herself nothing. Her honesty was so absolute it was a kind of cruelty.

She had not changed, I was to discover in meeting her again after a separation of twenty years. Nor had I really. For although the years had altered our positions (she was no longer the lord and I the lackey) and I could even afford to forgive her now, she still had the ability to disturb me profoundly by dredging to the surface those aspects of myself that I kept buried. This time, as I listened to her talk over the stretch of one long night, she made vivid without knowing it what is perhaps the most critical fact of my existence—that definition of me, of her and millions like us, formulated by others to serve out their fantasies, a definition we have to combat at an unconscionable cost to the self and even use, at times, in order to survive; the cause of so much shame and rage as well as, oddly enough, a source of pride: simply, what it has meant, what it means, to be a black woman in America.

We met—Reena and myself—at the funeral of her aunt who had been my godmother and whom I had also called aunt, Aunt Vi, and loved, for she and her house had been, respectively, a source of understanding and a place of calm for me as a child. Reena entered the church where the funeral service was being held as though she, not the minister, were coming to officiate, sat down among the immediate family up front, and turned to inspect those behind her. I saw her face then.

It was a good copy of the original. The familiar mold was there, that is, and the configuration of bone beneath the skin was the same despite the slight fleshiness I had never seen there before; features had even retained their distinctive touches: the positive set to her mouth, the assertive lift to her nose, the same insistent, unsettling eyes which when she was angry became as black as her skin—and this was total, unnerving, and very beautiful. Yet something had happened to her face. It was different despite its sameness. Aging even while it remained enviably young. Time had sketched in, very lightly, the evidence of the twenty years.

As soon as the funeral service was over, I left, hurrying out of the church into the early November night. The wind, already at its winter strength, brought with it the smell of dead leaves and the image of Aunt Vi there in the church, as dead as the leaves—as well as the thought of Reena, whom I would see later at the wake.

Her real name had been Doreen, a standard for girls among West Indians (her mother, like my parents, was from Barbados), but she had changed it to Reena on her twelfth birthday—"As a present to myself"—and had enforced the change on her family by refusing to answer to the old name. "Reena. With two e's!" she would say and imprint those e's on your mind with the indelible black of her eyes and a thin threatening finger that was like a quill.

She and I had not been friends through our own choice. Rather, our mothers, who had known each other since childhood, had forced the relationship. And from the beginning, I had been at a disadvantage. For Reena, as early as the age of twelve, had had a quality that was unique, superior, and therefore dangerous. She seemed defined, even then, all of a piece, the raw edges of her adolescence smoothed over; indeed, she seemed to have escaped adolescence altogether and made one dazzling leap from childhood into the very arena of adult life. At thirteen, for instance, she was reading Zola, Hauptmann, Steinbeck, while I was still in the thrall of the Little Minister and Lorna Doone. When I could only barely conceive of the world beyond Brooklyn, she was talking of the Civil War in Spain, lynchings in the South, Hitler in Poland—and talking with the outrage and passion of a revolutionary. I would try, I remember, to console myself with the thought that she was really an adult masquerading as a child, which meant that I could not possibly be her match.

For her part, Reena put up with me and was, by turns, patronizing and impatient. I merely served as the audience before whom she rehearsed her ideas and the yardstick by which she measured her worldliness and knowledge.

"Do you realize that this stupid country supplied Japan with the scrap iron to make the weapons she's now using against it?" she had shouted at me once.

I had not known that.

Just as she overwhelmed me, she overwhelmed her family, with the result that despite a half dozen brothers and sisters who consumed quantities of bread and jam whenever they visited us, she behaved like an only child and got away with it. Her father, a gentle man with skin the color of dried tobacco and with the nose Reena had inherited jutting out like a crag from his nondescript face, had come from Georgia and was always making jokes about having married a foreigner—Reena's mother being from the West Indies. When not joking, he seemed slightly bewildered by his large family and so in awe of Reena that he avoided her. Reena's mother, a small, dry, formidably black woman, was less a person to me than the abstract principle of force, power, energy. She was alternately strict and indulgent with Reena and, despite the inconsistency, surprisingly effective.

They lived when I knew them in a cold-water railroad flat above a kosher butcher on Belmont Avenue in Brownsville, some distance from us—and this in itself added to Reena's exotic quality. For it was a place where Sunday became Saturday, with all the stores open and pushcarts piled with vegetables and yard goods lined up along the curb, a crowded place where people hawked and spat freely in the streaming gutters and the men looked as if they had just stepped from the pages of the Old Testament with their profuse beards and long, black, satin coats.

When Reena was fifteen her family moved to Jamaica in Queens and since, in those days, Jamaica was considered too far away for visiting, our families lost contact and I did not see Reena again until we were both in college and then only once and not to speak to . . .

* * *

I had walked some distance and by the time I got to the wake, which was being held at Aunt Vi's house, it was well under way. It was a good wake. Aunt Vi would have been pleased. There was plenty to drink, and more than enough to eat, including some Barbadian favorites: coconut bread, pone made with the cassava root, and the little crisp codfish cakes that are so hot with peppers they bring tears to the eyes as you bite into them.

I had missed the beginning, when everyone had probably sat around talking about Aunt Vi and recalling the few events that had distinguished her otherwise undistinguished life. (Someone, I'm sure, had told of the time she had missed the excursion boat to Atlantic City and had held her own private picnic—complete with pigeon peas and rice and fricassee chicken—on the pier at 42nd Street.) By the time I arrived, though, it would have been indiscreet to mention her name, for by then the wake had become—and this would also have pleased her—a celebration of life.

I had had two drinks, one right after the other, and was well into my third when Reena, who must have been upstairs, entered the basement kitchen where I was. She saw me before I had quite seen her, and with a cry that alerted the entire room to her presence and charged the air with her special force, she rushed toward me.

"Hey, I'm the one who was supposed to be the writer, not you! Do you know, I still can't believe it," she said, stepping back, her blackness heightened by a white mocking smile. "I read both your books over and over again and I can't really believe it. My Little Paulie!"

I did not mind. For there was respect and even wonder behind the patronizing words and in her eyes. The old imbalance between us had ended and I was suddenly glad to see her.

I told her so and we both began talking at once, but Reena's voice overpowered mine, so that all I could do after a time was listen while she discussed my books, and dutifully answer her questions about my personal life.

"And what about you?" I said, almost brutally, at the first chance I got. "What've you been up to all this time?"

She got up abruptly. "Good Lord, in here's noisy as hell. Come on, let's go upstairs."

We got fresh drinks and went up to Aunt Vi's bedroom, where in the soft light from the lamps, the huge Victorian bed and the pink satin bedspread with roses of the same material strewn over its surface looked as if they had never been used. And, in a way, this was true. Aunt Vi had seldom slept in her bed or, for that matter, lived in her house, because in order to pay for it, she had had to work at a sleeping-in job which gave her only Thursdays and every other Sunday off.

Reena sat on the bed, crushing the roses, and I sat on one of the numerous trunks which crowded the room. They contained every dress, coat, hat, and shoe that Aunt Vi had worn since coming to the United States. I again asked Reena what she had been doing over the years.

"Do you want a blow-by-blow account?" she said. But despite the flippancy, she was suddenly serious. And when she began it was clear that she had written out the narrative in her mind many times. The words came too easily; the events, the incidents had been ordered in time, and the meaning of her behavior and of the people with whom she had been involved had been painstakingly analyzed. She talked willingly, with desperation almost. And the words by themselves weren't enough. She used her hands to give them form and urgency. I became totally involved with her and all that she said. So much so that as the night wore on I was not certain at times whether it was she or I speaking.

* * *

From the time her family moved to Jamaica until she was nineteen or so, Reena's life sounded, from what she told me in the beginning, as ordinary as mine and most of the girls we knew. After high school she had gone on to one of the free city colleges, where she had majored in journalism, worked part time in the school library, and, surprisingly enough, joined a houseplan. (Even I hadn't gone that far.) It was an all-Negro club, since there was a tacit understanding that Negro and white girls did not join each other's houseplans. "Integration, northern style," she said, shrugging.

It seems that Reena had had a purpose and a plan in joining the group. "I thought," she said with a wry smile, "I could get those girls up off their complacent rumps and out doing something about social issues. . . . I couldn't get them to budge. I remember after the war when a Negro ex-soldier had his eyes gouged out by a bus driver down South I tried getting them to demonstrate on campus. I talked until I was hoarse, but to no avail. They were too busy planning the annual autumn frolic."

Her laugh was bitter but forgiving and it ended in a long, reflective silence. After which she said quietly, "It wasn't that they didn't give a damn. It was just, I suppose, that like most people they didn't want to get involved to the extent that they might have to stand up and be counted. If it ever came to that. Then another thing. They thought they were safe, special. After all, they had grown up in the North, most of them, and so had escaped the southern-style prejudice; their parents, like mine, were struggling to put them through college; they could look forward to being tidy little schoolteachers, social workers, and lab technicians. Oh, they were safe!" The sarcasm scored her voice and then abruptly gave way to pity. "Poor things, they weren't safe, you see, and would never be as long as millions like themselves in Harlem, on Chicago's South Side, down South, all over the place, were unsafe. I tried to tell them this—and they accused me of being oversensitive. They tried not to listen. But I would have held out and, I'm sure, even brought some of them around eventually if this other business with a silly boy hadn't happened at the same time. . . ."

Reena told me then about her first, brief, and apparently innocent affair with a boy she had met at one of the houseplan parties. It had ended, she said, when the boy's parents had met her. "That was it," she said and the flat of her hand cut into the air. "He was forbidden to see me. The reason? He couldn't bring himself to tell me, but I knew. I was too black.

"Naturally, it wasn't the first time something like that had happened. In fact, you might say that was the theme of my childhood. Because I was dark I was always being plastered with Vaseline so I wouldn't look ashy. Whenever I had my picture taken they would pile a whitish powder on my face and make the lights so bright I always came out looking ghostly. My mother stopped speaking to any number of people because they said I would have been pretty if I hadn't been so dark. Like nearly every little black girl, I had my share of dreams of waking up to find myself with long, blond curls, blue eyes, and skin like milk. So I should have been prepared. Besides, that boy's parents were really rejecting themselves in rejecting me.

"Take us"—and her hands, opening in front of my face as she suddenly leaned forward, seemed to offer me the whole of black humanity. "We live surrounded by white images, and white in this world is synonymous with the good, light, beauty, success, so that, despite ourselves sometimes, we run after that whiteness and deny our darkness, which has been made into the symbol of all that is evil and inferior. I wasn't a person to that boy's parents, but a symbol of the darkness they were in flight from, so that just as they—that boy, his parents, those silly girls in the houseplan—were running from, me, I started running from them . . ."

* * *

It must have been shortly after this happened when I saw Reena at a debate which was being held at my college. She did not see me, since she was one of the speakers and I was merely part of her audience in the crowded auditorium. The topic had something to do with intellectual freedom in the colleges (McCarthyism was coming into vogue then) and aside from a Jewish boy from City College, Reena was the most effective—sharp, provocative, her position the most radical. The others on the panel seemed intimidated not only by the strength and cogency of her argument but by the sheer impact of her blackness in their white midst.

Her color might have been a weapon she used to dazzle and disarm her opponents. And she had highlighted it with the clothes she was wearing: a white dress patterned with large blocks of primary colors I remember (it looked Mexican) and a pair of intricately wrought silver earrings—long and with many little parts which clashed like muted cymbals over the microphone each time she moved her head. She wore her hair cropped short like a boy's and it was not straightened like mine and the other Negro girls' in the audience, but left in its coarse natural state: a small forest under which her face emerged in its intense and startling handsomeness. I remember she left the auditorium in triumph that day, surrounded by a noisy entourage from her college—all of them white.

"We were very serious," she said now, describing the left-wing group she had belonged to then—and there was a defensiveness in her voice which sought to protect them from all censure. "We believed—because we were young, I suppose, and had nothing as yet to risk—that we could do something about the injustices which everyone around us seemed to take for granted. So we picketed and demonstrated and bombarded Washington with our protests, only to have our names added to the Attorney General's list for all our trouble. We were always standing on street corners handing out leaflets or getting people to sign petitions. We always seemed to pick the coldest days to do that." Her smile held long after the words had died.

"I, we all, had such a sense of purpose then," she said softly, and a sadness lay aslant the smile now, darkening it. "We were forever holding meetings, having endless discussions, arguing, shouting, theorizing. And we had fun. Those parties! There was always somebody with a guitar. We were always singing. . . ." Suddenly, she began singing—and her voice was sure, militant, and faintly self-mocking,

"But the banks are made of marble
With a guard at every door
And the vaults are stuffed with silver
That the workers sweated for . . ."

When she spoke again the words were a sad coda to the song. "Well, as you probably know, things came to an ugly head with McCarthy reigning in Washington, and I was one of the people temporarily suspended from school."

She broke off and we both waited, the ice in our glasses melted and the drinks gone flat.

"At first, I didn't mind," she said finally. "After all, we were right. The fact that they suspended us proved it. Besides, I was in the middle of an affair, a real one this time, and too busy with that to care about anything else." She paused again, frowning.

"He was white," she said quickly and glanced at me as though to surprise either shock or disapproval in my face. "We were very involved. At one point—I think just after we had been suspended and he started working—we even thought of getting married. Living in New York, moving in the crowd we did, we might have been able to manage it. But I couldn't. There were too many complex things going on beneath the surface," she said, her voice strained by the hopelessness she must have felt then, her hands shaping it in the air between us. "Neither one of us could really escape what our color had come to mean in this country. Let me explain. Bob was always, for some odd reason, talking about how much the Negro suffered, and although I would agree with him I would also try to get across that, you know, like all people we also had fun once in a while, loved our children, liked making love—that we were human beings, for God's sake. But he only wanted to hear about the suffering. It was as if this comforted him and eased his own suffering— and he did suffer because of any number of things: his own uncertainty, for one, his difficulties with his family, for another . . .

"Once, I remember, when his father came into New York, Bob insisted that I meet him. I don't know why I agreed to go with him. . . ." She took a deep breath and raised her head very high. "I'll never forget or forgive the look on that old man's face when he opened his hotel-room door and saw me. The horror. I might have been the personification of every evil in the world. His inability to believe that it was his son standing there holding my hand. His shock. I'm sure he never fully recovered. I know I never did. Nor can I forget Bob's laugh in the elevator afterwards, the way he kept repeating: 'Did you see his face when he saw you? Did you . . . ?' He had used me, you see. I had been the means, the instrument of his revenge.

"And I wasn't any better. I used him. I took every opportunity to treat him shabbily, trying, you see, through him, to get at that white world which had not only denied me, but had turned my own against me." Her eyes closed. "I went numb all over when I understood what we were doing to, and with, each other. I stayed numb for a long time."

As Reena described the events which followed—the break with Bob, her gradual withdrawal from the left-wing group ("I had had it with them too. I got tired of being 'their Negro,' their pet. Besides, they were just all talk, really. All theories and abstractions. I doubt that, with all their elaborate plans for the Negro and for the workers of the world, any of them had ever been near a factory or up to Harlem")—as she spoke about her reinstatement in school, her voice suggested the numbness she had felt then. It only stirred into life again when she talked of her graduation.

"You should have seen my parents. It was really their day. My mother was so proud she complained about everything: her seat, the heat, the speaker; and my father just sat there long after everybody had left, too awed to move. God, it meant so much to them. It was as if I had made up for the generations his people had picked cotton in Georgia and my mother's family had cut cane in the West Indies. It frightened me."

I asked her after a long wait what she had done after graduating.

"How do you mean, what I did. Looked for a job. Tell me, have you ever looked for work in this man's city?"

"I know," I said, holding up my hand. "Don't tell me."

We both looked at my raised hand which sought to waive the discussion, then at each other and suddenly we laughed, a laugh so loud and violent with pain and outrage it brought tears.

"Girl," Reena said, the tears silver against her blackness. "You could put me blindfolded right now at the Times Building on 42nd Street and I would be able to find my way to every newspaper office in town. But tell me, how come white folks is so *hard*?"

"Just bo'n hard."

We were laughing again and this time I nearly slid off the trunk and Reena fell back among the satin roses.

"I didn't know there were so many ways of saying 'no' without ever once using the word," she said, the laughter lodged in her throat, but her eyes had gone hard. "Sometimes I'd find myself in the elevator, on my way out, and smiling all over myself because I thought I had gotten the job, before it would hit me that they had really said no, not yes. Some of those people in personnel had so perfected their smiles they looked almost genuine. The ones who used to get me, though, were those who tried to make the interview into an intimate chat between friends. They'd put you in a comfortable chair, offer you a cigarette, and order coffee. How I hated that coffee. They didn't know it—or maybe they did—but it was like offering me hemlock. . . .

"You think Christ had it tough?" Her laughter rushed against the air which resisted it. "I was crucified five days a week and half-day on Saturday. I became almost paranoid. I began to think there might be something other than color wrong with me which everybody but me could see, some rare disease that had turned me into a monster.

"My parents suffered. And that bothered me most, because I felt I had failed them. My father didn't say anything but I knew because he avoided me more than usual. He was ashamed, I think, that he hadn't been able, as a man and as my father, to prevent this. My mother—well, you know her. In one breath she would try to comfort me by cursing them: 'But God blind them,'"—and Reena's voice captured her mother's aggressive accent—"'if you had come looking for a job mopping down their floors they would o' hire you, the brutes. But mark my words, their time goin' come, 'cause God don't love ugly and he ain't stuck on pretty.' And in the next breath she would curse me, 'Journalism! Journalism! Whoever heard of colored people taking up journalism. You must feel you's white or something so. The people is right to chuck you out their office. . . .' Poor thing, to make up for saying all that she would wash my white gloves every night and cook cereal for me in the morning as is I were a little girl again. Once she went out and bought me a suit she couldn't afford from Lord and Taylor's. I looked like a Smith girl in blackface in it. . . . So guess where I ended up?"

"As a social investigator for the Welfare Department. Where else?"

We were helpless with laughter again.

"You too?"

"No," I said, "I taught, but that was just as bad."

"No," she said, sobering abruptly. "Nothing's as bad as working for Welfare. Do you know what they really mean by a social investigator? A spy. Someone whose dirty job it is to snoop into the corners of the lives of the poor and make their poverty more vivid by taking from them the last shred of privacy. 'Mrs. Jones, is that a new dress you're wearing?' 'Mrs. Brown, this kerosene heater is not listed in the household items. Did you get an authorization for it?' 'Mrs. Smith, is that a tele-phone I hear ringing under the sofa?' I was utterly demoralized within a month.

"And another thing. I thought I knew about poverty. I mean, I remember, as a child, having to eat soup made with those white beans the government used to give out free for days running, sometimes, because there was nothing else. I had lived in Brownsville, among all the poor Jews and Poles and Irish there. But what I saw in Harlem, where I had my case load, was different somehow. Perhaps because it seemed so final. There didn't seem to be any way to escape from those dark hallways and dingy furnished rooms . . . All that defeat." Closing her eyes, she fin-ished the stale whiskey and soda in her glass.

"I remember a client of mine, a girl my age with three children already and no father for them and living in the expensive squalor of a rooming house. Her bewil-derment. Her resignation. Her anger. She could have pulled herself out of the mess she was in? People say that, you know, including some Negroes. But this girl didn't have a chance. She had been trapped from the day she was born in some small town down South.

"She became my reference. From then on and even now, whenever I hear people and groups coming up with all kinds of solutions to the quote Negro problem, I ask one question. What are they really doing for that girl, to save her or to save the children? . . . The answer isn't very encouraging."

* * *

It was some time before she continued, and then she told me that after Welfare she had gone to work for a private social-work agency, in their publicity department, and had started on her master's in journalism at Columbia. She also left home around this time.

"I had to. My mother started putting the pressure on me to get married. The hints, the remarks—and you know my mother was never the subtle type—her anxiety, which made me anxious about getting married after a while. Besides, it was time for me to be on my own."

In contrast to the unmistakably radical character of her late adolescence (her membership in the left-wing group, the affair with Bob, her suspension from college), Reena's life of this period sounded ordinary, standard—and she admitted it with a slightly self-deprecating, apologetic smile. It was similar to that of any number of unmarried professional Negro women in New York or Los Angeles or Washington: the job teaching or doing social work which brought in a fairly decent salary, the small apartment with kitchenette which they sometimes shared with a roommate; a car, some of them; membership in various political and social action organizations for the militant few like Reena; the vacations in Mexico, Europe, the West Indies, and now Africa; the occasional date. "The interesting men were invariably married," Reena said and then mentioned having had one affair during that time. She had found out he was married and had thought of her only as the perfect mistress. "The bastard," she said, but her smile forgave him.

"Women alone!" she cried, laughing sadly, and her raised opened arms, the empty glass she held in one hand made eloquent their aloneness. "Alone and lonely, and indulging themselves while they wait. The girls of the houseplan have reached their majority only to find that all those years they spent accumulating their degrees and finding the well-paying jobs in the hope that this would raise their stock have, instead, put them at a disadvantage. For the few eligible men around—those who are their intellectual and professional peers, whom they can respect (and there are very few of them)—don't necessarily marry them, but younger women without the degrees and the fat jobs, who are no threat, or they don't marry at all because they are either queer or mother-ridden. Or they marry white women. Now, intellectually I accept this. In fact, some of my best friends are white women . . ." And again our laughter—that loud, searing burst which we used to cauterize our hurt mounted into the unaccepting silence of the room. "After all, our goal is a fully integrated society. And perhaps, as some people believe, the only solution to the race problem is miscegenation. Besides, a man should be able to marry whomever he wishes. Emotionally, though, I am less kind and understanding, and I resent like hell the reasons some black men give for rejecting us for them."

"We're too middle-class-oriented," I said. "Conservative."

"Right. Even though, thank God, that doesn't apply to me."

"Too threatening . . . castrating . . ."

"Too independent and impatient with them for not being more ambitious . . . contemptuous . . ."

"Sexually inhibited and unimaginative . . ."

"And the old myth of the excessive sexuality of the black woman goes out the window," Reena cried.

"Not supportive, unwilling to submerge our interests for theirs . . ."

"Lacking in the subtle art of getting and keeping a man . . ."

We had recited the accusations in the form and tone of a litany, and in the silence which followed we shared a thin, hopeless smile.

"They condemn us," Reena said softly but with anger, "without taking history into account. We are still, most of us, the black woman who had to be almost frighteningly strong in order for us all to survive. For, after all, she was the one whom they left (and I don't hold this against them; I understand) with the children to raise, who had to *make* it somehow or the other. And we are still, so many of us, living that history.

"You would think that they would understand this, but few do. So it's up to us. We have got to understand them and save them for ourselves. How? By being, on one hand, persons in our own right and, on the other, fully the woman and the wife. . . . Christ, listen to who's talking! I had my chance. And I tried. Very hard. But it wasn't enough."

* * *

The festive sounds of the wake had died to a sober murmur beyond the bedroom. The crowd had gone, leaving only Reena and myself upstairs and the last of Aunt Vi's closest friends in the basement below. They were drinking coffee. I smelled it, felt its warmth and intimacy in the empty house, heard the distant tapping of the cups against the saucers and voices muted by grief. The wake had come full circle: they were again mourning Aunt Vi.

And Reena might have been mourning with them, sitting there amid the satin roses, framed by the massive headboard. Her hands lay as if they had been broken in her lap. Her eyes were like those of someone blind or dead. I got up to go and get some coffee for her.

"You met my husband," she said quickly, stopping me.

"Have I?" I said, sitting down again.

"Yes, before we were married even. At an autograph party for you. He was free-lancing—he's a photographer—and one of the Negro magazines had sent him to cover the party."

As she went on to describe him I remembered him vaguely, not his face, but his rather large body stretching and bending with a dancer's fluidity and grace as he took the pictures. I had heard him talking to a group of people about some issue on race relations very much in the news then and had been struck by his vehemence. For the moment I had found this almost odd, since he was so fair-skinned he could have passed for white.

They had met, Reena told me now, at a benefit show for a Harlem day nursery given by one of the progressive groups she belonged to, and had married a month afterward. From all that she said they had had a full and exciting life for a long time. Her words were so vivid that I could almost see them: she with her startling blackness and extraordinary force and he with his near-white skin and a militancy which matched hers; both of them moving among the disaffected in New York, their stand on political and social issues equally uncompromising, the line of their allegiance reaching directly to all those trapped in Harlem. And they had lived the meaning of this allegiance, so that even when they could have afforded a life among the black bourgeoisie of St. Albans or Teaneck, they had chosen to live if not in Harlem so close that there was no difference.

"I—we—were so happy I was frightened at times. Not that anything would change between us, but that someone or something in the world outside us would invade our private place and destroy us out of envy. Perhaps this is what did happen. . . ." She shrugged and even tried to smile but she could not manage it. "Something slipped in while we weren't looking and began its deadly work.

"Maybe it started when Dave took a job with a Negro magazine. I'm not sure. Anyway, in no time, he hated it: the routine, unimaginative pictures he had to take and the magazine itself, which dealt only in unrealities: the high-society world of the black bourgeoisie and the spectacular strides Negroes were making in all fields—you know the type. Yet Dave wouldn't leave. It wasn't the money, but a kind of safety which he had never experienced before which kept him there. He would talk about free-lancing again, about storming the gates of the white magazines downtown, of opening his own studio—but he never acted on any one of these things. You see, despite his talent—and he was very talented—he had a diffidence that was fatal.

"When I understood this I literally forced him to open the studio—and perhaps I should have been more subtle and indirect, but that's not my nature. Besides, I was frightened and desperate to help. Nothing happened for a time. Dave's work was too experimental to be commercial. Gradually, though, his photographs started appearing in the prestige camera magazines and money from various awards and exhibits and an occasional assignment started coming in.

"This wasn't enough somehow. Dave also wanted the big, gaudy commercial success that would dazzle and confound that white world downtown and force it to see him. And yet, as I said before, he couldn't bring himself to try—and this contradiction began to get to him after awhile.

"It was then, I think, that I began to fail him. I didn't know how to help, you see. I had never felt so inadequate before. And this was very strange and disturbing for someone like me. I was being submerged in his problems—and I began fighting against this.

"I started working again (I had stopped after the second baby). And I was lucky because I got back my old job. And unlucky because Dave saw it as my way of pointing up his deficiencies. I couldn't convince him otherwise: that I had to do it for my own sanity. He would accuse me of wanting to see him fail, of trapping him in all kinds of responsibilities. . . . After a time we both got caught up in this thing, and ugliness came between us, and I began to answer his anger with anger and to trade him insult for insult.

"Things fell apart very quickly after that. I couldn't bear the pain of living with him—the insults, our mutual despair, his mocking, the silence. I couldn't subject the children to it any longer. The divorce didn't take long. And thank God, because of the children, we are pleasant when we have to see each other. He's making out very well, I hear."

She said nothing more, but simply bowed her head as though waiting for me to pass judgment on her. I don't know how long we remained like this, but when Reena finally raised her head, the darkness at the window had vanished and dawn was a still, gray smoke against the pane.

"Do you know," she said, and her eyes were clear and a smile had won out over pain, "I enjoy being alone. I don't tell people this because they'll accuse me of either lying or deluding myself. But I do. Perhaps, as my mother tells me, it's only temporary. I don't think so, though. I feel I don't ever want to be involved again. It's not that I've lost interest in men. I go out occasionally, but it's never anything serious. You see, I have all that I want for now."

Her children first of all, she told me, and from her description they sounded intelligent and capable. She was a friend as well as a mother to them, it seemed. They were planning, the four of them, to spend the summer touring Canada. "I will feel that I have done well by them if I give them, if nothing more, a sense of themselves and their worth and importance as black people. Everything I do with them, for them, is to this end. I don't want them ever to be confused about this. They must have their identifications straight from the beginning. No white dolls for them!"

Then her job. She was working now as a researcher for a small progressive news magazine with the promise that once she completed her master's in journalism (she was working on the thesis now) she might get a chance to do some minor reporting. And like most people she hoped to write someday. "If I can ever stop talking away my substance," she said laughing.

And she was still active in any number of social action groups. In another week or so she would be heading a delegation of mothers down to City Hall "to give the Mayor a little hell about conditions in the schools in Harlem." She had started an organization that was carrying on an almost door-to-door campaign in her neighborhood to expose, as she put it, "the blood suckers: all those slum lords and storekeepers with their fixed scales, the finance companies that never tell you the real price of a thing, the petty salesmen that leech off the poor. . . ." In May she was taking her two older girls on a nationwide pilgrimage to Washington to urge for a more rapid implementation of the school-desegregation law.

"It's uncanny," she said and the laugh which accompanied the words was warm, soft with wonder at herself, girlish even and the air in the room which had refused her laughter before rushed to absorb this now. "Really uncanny. Here I am, practically middle-aged, with three children to raise by myself and with little or no money to do it and yet I feel, strangely enough, as though life is just beginning—that it's new and fresh with all kinds of possibilities. Maybe it's because I've been through my purgatory and I can't ever be overwhelmed again. I don't know. Anyway, you should see me on evenings after I put the children to bed. I sit alone in the living room (I've repainted it and changed all the furniture since Dave's gone, so that it would at least look different)—I sit there making plans and all of them seem possible. The most important plan right now is Africa. I've already started saving the fare."

I asked her whether she was planning to live there permanently and she said simply, "I want to live and work there. For how long, for a lifetime, I can't say. All I know is that I have to. For myself and for my children. It is important that they see black people who have truly a place and history of their own and who are building for a new and, hopefully, more sensible world. And I must see it, get close to it because I can never lose the sense of being a displaced person here in America because of my color. Oh, I know I should remain and fight not only for integration (even though, frankly, I question whether I want to be integrated into America as it stands now, with its complacency and materialism, its soullessness) but to help change the country into something better, sounder—if that is still possible. But I have to go to Africa. . . ."

"Poor Aunt Vi," she said after a long silence and straightened one of the roses she had crushed. "She never really got to enjoy her bed of roses what with only Thursdays and every other Sunday off. All that hard work. All her life . . . Our lives have got to make more sense, if only for her."

We got up to leave shortly afterwards. Reena was staying on to attend the burial later in the morning, but I was taking the subway to Manhattan. We parted with the usual promise to get together and exchanged telephone numbers. And Reena did phone a week or so later. I don't remember what we talked about though.

Some months later I invited her to a party I was giving before leaving the country. But she did not come.

GOLD COAST

James Alan McPherson

That spring, when I had a great deal of potential and no money at all, I took a job as a janitor. That was when I was still very young and spent money very freely, and when, almost every night, I drifted off to sleep lulled by sweet anticipation of that time when my potential would suddenly be realized and there would be capsule biographies of my life on dust jackets of many books, all proclaiming: ". . . He knew life on many levels. From shoeshine boy, free-lance waiter, 3rd cook, janitor, he rose to . . ." I had never been a janitor before, and I did not really have to be one, and that is why I did it. But now, much later, I think it might have been because it is possible to be a janitor without becoming one, and at parties or at mixers, when asked what it was I did for a living, it was pretty good to hook my thumbs in my vest pockets and say comfortably: "Why, I am an apprentice janitor." The hippies would think it degenerate and really dig me and people in Philosophy and Law and Business would feel uncomfortable trying to make me feel better about my station while wondering how the hell I had managed to crash the party.

"What's an apprentice janitor?" they would ask.

"I haven't got my card yet," I would reply. "Right now I'm just taking lessons. There's lots of complicated stuff you have to learn before you get your own card and your own building."

"What kind of stuff?"

"Human nature, for one thing. *Race* nature, for another."

"Why race?"

"Because," I would say in a low voice, looking around lest someone else should overhear, "you have to be able to spot Jews and Negroes who are passing."

"That's terrible," would surely be said then with a hint of indignation.

"It's an art," I would add masterfully.

After a good pause I would invariably be asked: "But you're a Negro yourself, how can you keep your own people out?"

At which point I would look terribly disappointed and say: "*I* don't keep them out. But if they get in it's my job to make their stay just as miserable as possible. Things are changing."

Now the speaker would just look at me in disbelief.

"It's Janitorial Objectivity," I would say to finish the thing as the speaker began to edge away. "Don't hate me," I would call after him to considerable embarrassment. "Somebody has to do it."

It was an old building near Harvard Square. Conrad Aiken had once lived there, and in the days of the Gold Coast, before Harvard built its great houses, it had been a very fine haven for the rich; but that was a world ago, and this building was one of the few monuments of that era which had survived. The lobby had a high ceiling with thick redwood beams, and it was replete with marble floor, fancy ironwork, and an old-fashioned house telephone which no longer worked. Each apartment had a small fireplace, and even the large bathtubs and chain toilets, when I was having my touch of nature, made me wonder what prominent personage of the past had worn away all the newness. And, being there, I felt a certain affinity toward the rich.

It was a funny building, because the people who lived there made it old. Conveniently placed as it was between the Houses and Harvard Yard, I expected to find it occupied by a company of hippies, hopeful working girls, and assorted graduate students. Instead, there was a majority of old maids, dowagers, asexual middle-aged men, homosexual young men, a few married couples, and a teacher. No one was shacking up there, and walking through the quiet halls in the early evening, I sometimes had the urge to knock on a door and expose myself just to hear someone breathe hard for once.

It was a Cambridge spring: down by the Charles happy students were making love while sad-eyed middle-aged men watched them from the bridge. It was a time of activity: Law students were busy sublimating, Business School people were making records of the money they would make, the Harvard Houses were clearing out, and in the Square bearded pot-pushers were setting up their restaurant tables in anticipation of the Summer School faithfuls. There was a change of season in the air, and to comply with its urgings, James Sullivan, the old superintendent, passed his three beaten garbage cans on to me with the charge that I should take up his daily rounds of the six floors, and with unflinching humility, gather whatever scraps the old-maid tenants had refused to husband.

I then became very rich, with my own apartment, a sensitive girl, a stereo, two speakers, one tattered chair, one fork, a job, and the urge to acquire. Having all this and youth besides made me pity Sullivan: he had been in that building thirty years and had its whole history recorded in the little folds of his mind, as his own life was recorded in the wrinkles of his face. All he had to show for his time there was a berserk dog, a wife almost as mad as the dog, three cats, bursitis, acute myopia, and a drinking problem. He was well over seventy and could hardly walk, and his weekly check of twenty-two dollars from the company that managed the building would not support anything. So, out of compromise, he was retired to superintendent of my labor.

My first day as janitor, while I skillfully lugged my three overflowing cans of garbage out of the building, he sat on his bench in the lobby, faded and old and smoking, in patched, loose blue pants. He watched me. He was a chain smoker, and I noticed right away that he very carefully dropped all of the ashes and butts on the floor and crushed them under his feet until there was a yellow and gray smear. Then he laboriously pushed the mess under the bench with his shoe, all the while eyeing me like a cat in silence as I hauled the many cans of muck out to the big disposal unit next to the building. When I had finished, he gave me two old plates to help stock my kitchen and his first piece of advice.

"Sit down, for Chrissake, and take a load off your feet," he told me.

I sat on the red bench next to him and accepted the wilted cigarette he offered me from the crushed package he kept in his sweater pocket.

"Now, I'll tell you something to help you get along in the building," he said.

I listened attentively.

"If any of these sons of bitches ever ask you to do something extra, be sure to charge them for it."

I assured him that I absolutely would.

"If they can afford to live here, they can afford to pay. The bastards."

"Undoubtedly," I assured him again.

"And another thing," he added. "Don't let any of these girls shove any cat shit under your nose. That ain't your job. You tell them to put it in a bag and take it out themselves."

I reminded him that I knew very well my station in life and that I was not about to haul cat shit or anything of that nature. He looked at me through his thick-lensed glasses for a long time. He looked like a cat himself. "That's right," he said at last. "And if they still try to sneak it in the trash be sure to make the bastards pay. They can afford it." He crushed his seventh butt on the floor and scattered the mess some more while he lit up another. "I never hauled out no cat shit in the thirty years I been here, and you don't do it either."

"I'm going up to wash my hands," I said.

"Remember," he called after me, "don't take no shit from any of them."

I protested once more that, upon my life, I would never, never do it, not even for the prettiest girl in the building. Going up in the elevator, I felt comfortably resolved that I would never do it. There were no pretty girls in the building.

I never found out what he had done before he came there, but I do know that being a janitor in that building was as high as he ever got in life. He had watched two generations of the rich pass the building on their way to the Yard, and he had seen many governors ride white horses into that same Yard to send sons and daughters of the rich out into life to produce, to acquire, to procreate, and to send back sons and daughters so that the cycle would continue. He had watched the cycle from when he had been able to haul the cans out for himself, and now he could not, and he was bitter.

He was Irish, of course, and he took pride in Irish accomplishments when he could have none of his own. He had known Frank O'Connor when that writer had been at Harvard. He told me on many occasions how O'Connor had stopped to talk every day on his way to the Yard. He had also known James Michael Curley, and his most colorful memory of the man was a long-ago day when he and James Curley sat in a Boston bar and one of Curley's runners had come in and said: "Hey, Jim, Sol Bernstein the Jew wants to see you." And Curley, in his deep, memorial voice, had said to James Sullivan: "Let us go forth and meet this Israelite Prince." These were his memories, and I would obediently put aside my garbage cans and laugh with him over the hundred or so colorful, insignificant little details which made up a whole lifetime of living in the basement of Harvard. And although they were of little value to me then, I knew that they were the reflections of a lifetime and the happiest moments he would ever have, being sold to me cheap, as youthful time is cheap, for as little time and interest as I wanted to spend. It was a buyer's market.

In those days I believed myself gifted with a boundless perception and attacked my daily garbage route with a gusto superenforced by the happy knowledge that behind each of the fifty or so doors in our building lived a story which could, if I chose to grace it with the magic of my pen, become immortal. I watched my tenants fanatically, noting their perversions, their visitors, and their eating habits. So intense was my search for material that I had to restrain myself from going through their refuse scrap by scrap; but at the topmost layers of muck, without too much hand soiling in the process, I set my perception to work. By late June, however, I had discovered only enough to put together a skimpy, rather naive Henry Miller novel, the most colorful discoveries being:

1. The lady in #24 was an alumnus of Paducah College
2. The couple in #55 made love at least 500 times a week, and the wife had not yet discovered the pill
3. The old lady in #36 was still having monthly inconvenience
4. The two fatsos in #56 consumed nightly an extraordinary amount of chili
5. The fat man in #54 had two dogs that were married to each other, but he was not married to anyone at all
6. The middle-aged single man in #63 threw out an awful lot of flowers

Disturbed by the snail's progress I was making, I confessed my futility to James one day as he sat on his bench chain-smoking and smearing butts on my newly waxed lobby floor. "So you want to know about the tenants?" he said, his cat's eyes flickering over me.

I nodded.

"Well, the first thing to notice is how many Jews there are."

"I haven't noticed any Jews," I said.

He eyed me in amazement.

"Well, a few," I said quickly to prevent my treasured perception from being dulled any further.

"A few, hell," he said. "There's more Jews here than anybody."

"How can you tell?"

He gave me that undecided look again. "Where do you think all that garbage comes from?" He nodded feebly toward my bulging cans. I looked just in time to prevent a stray noodle from slipping over the brim. "That's right," he continued. "Jews are the biggest eaters in the world. They eat the best too."

I confessed then that I was of the chicken-soup generation and believed that Jews ate only enough to muster strength for their daily trips to the bank.

"Not so!" he replied emphatically. "You never heard the expression: 'Let's get to the restaurant before the Jews get there'?"

I shook my head sadly.

"You don't know that in certain restaurants they take the free onions and pickles off the tables when they see Jews coming?"

I held my head down in shame over the bounteous heap.

He trudged over to my can and began to turn back the leaves of noodles and crumpled tissues from #47 with his hand. After a few seconds of digging, he unmucked an empty pâté can. "Look at that," he said triumphantly. "Gourmet stuff, no less."

"That's from #44," I said.

"What else?" he said, all-knowingly. "In 1946 a Swedish girl moved in up there and took a Jewish girl for her roommate. Then the Swedish girl moved out and there's been a Jewish Dynasty up there ever since."

I recalled that #44 was occupied by a couple that threw out a good number of S. S. Pierce cans, Chivas Regal bottles, assorted broken records, and back issues of *Evergreen* and the *Realist*.

"You're right," I said.

"Of course," he replied, as if there were never any doubt. "I can spot them anywhere, even when they think they're passing." He leaned closer and said in a you-and-me voice: "But don't ever say anything bad about them in public. The Anti-Defamation League will get you."

Just then his wife screamed for him from the second floor, and the dog joined her and beat against the door. He got into the elevator painfully and said: "Don't ever talk about them in public. You don't know who they are, and that Defamation League will take everything you got."

Sullivan did not really dislike Jews. He was just bitter toward anyone better off than himself. He lived with his wife on the second floor, and his apartment was very dirty because both of them were sick and old, and neither could move very well. His wife swept dirt out into the hall, and two hours after I had mopped and waxed their section of the floor, there was sure to be a layer of dirt, grease, and crushed-scattered tobacco from their door to the end of the hall. There was a smell of dogs and cats and age and death about their door, and I did not ever want to have to go in there for any reason because I feared something about it I cannot name.

Mrs. Sullivan, I found out, was from South Africa. She loved animals much more than people, and there was a great deal of pain in her face. She kept little cans of meat posted at strategic points about the building, and I often came across her in the early morning or late at night throwing scraps out of the second-floor window to stray cats. Once, when James was about to throttle a stray mouse in their apartment, she had screamed at him to give the mouse a sporting chance. Whenever she attempted to walk she had to balance herself against a wall or a rail, and she hated the building because it confined her. She also hated James and most of the tenants. On the other hand, she loved the "Johnny Carson Show," she loved to sit outside on the front steps (because she could go no further unassisted), and she loved to talk to anyone who would stop to listen. She never spoke coherently except when she was cursing James, and then she had a vocabulary like a drunken sailor. She had great, shrill lungs, and her screams, accompanied by the rabid barks of the dog, could be heard all over the building. She was never really clean, her teeth were bad, and the first most pathetic thing in the world was to see her sitting on the steps in the morning watching the world pass, in a stained smock and a fresh summer blue hat she kept just to wear downstairs, with no place in the world to go. James told me, on the many occasions of her screaming, that she was mentally disturbed and could not help herself. The admirable thing about him was that he never lost his temper with her, no matter how rough her curses became and no matter who heard them. And the second most pathetic thing in the world was to see them slowly making their way in Harvard Square, he supporting her, through the hurrying crowds of miniskirted summer girls, J-Pressed Ivy Leaguers, beatniks, and bused Japanese tourists, decked in cameras, who would take pictures of every inch of Harvard Square except them. Once a hippie had brushed past them and called back over his shoulder: "Don't break any track records, Mr. and Mrs. Speedy Molasses."

Also on the second floor lived Miss O'Hara, a spinster who hated Sullivan as only an old maid can hate an old man. Across from her lived a very nice, gentle celibate named Murphy, who had once served with Montgomery in North Africa and who was now spending the rest of his life cleaning his little apartment and gossiping with Miss O'Hara. It was an Irish floor.

I never found out just why Miss O'Hara hated the Sullivans with such a passion. Perhaps it was because they were so unkempt and she was so superciliously clean. Perhaps it was because Miss O'Hara had a great deal of Irish pride, and they were stereotyped Irish. Perhaps it was because she merely had no reason to like them. She was a fanatic about cleanliness and put out her little bit of garbage wrapped very neatly in yesterday's *Christian Science Monitor* and tied in a bow with a fresh piece of string. Collecting all those little neat packages, I would wonder where she got the string and imagined her at night breaking meat market locks with a hairpin and hobbling off with yards and yards of white cord concealed under the gray sweater she always wore. I could even imagine her back in her little apartment chuckling and rolling the cord into a great white ball by candlelight. Then she would stash it away in her bread box. Miss O'Hara kept her door slightly open until late at night, and I suspected that she heard everything that went on in the building. I had the feeling that I should never dare to make love with gusto for fear that she would overhear and write down all my happy-time phrases, to be maliciously recounted to me if she were ever provoked.

She had been in the building longer than Sullivan, and I suppose that her greatest ambition in life was to outlive him and then attend his wake with a knitting ball and needle. She had been trying to get him fired for twenty-five years or so, and did not know when to quit. On summer nights when I painfully mopped the second floor, she would offer me root beer, apples, or cupcakes while trying to pump me for evidence against him.

"He's just a filthy old man, Robert," she would declare in a little-old-lady whisper. "And don't think you have to clean up those dirty old butts of his. Just report him to the Company."

"Oh, I don't mind," I would tell her, gulping the root beer as fast as possible.

"Well, they're both a couple of lushes, if you ask me. They haven't been sober a day in twenty-five years."

"Well, she's sick too, you know."

"Ha!" She would throw up her hands in disgust. "She's only sick when he doesn't give her the booze."

I fought to keep down a burp. "How long have *you* been here?"

She motioned for me to step out of the hall and into her dark apartment. "Don't tell him"—she nodded toward Sullivan's door—"but I've been here thirty-four years." She waited for me to be taken aback. Then she added: "And it was a better building before those two lushes came."

She then offered me an apple, asked five times if the dog's barking bothered me, forced me to take a fudge brownie, said that the cats had wet the floor again last night, got me to dust the top of a large chest too high for her to reach, had me pick up the minute specks of dust which fell from my dustcloth, pressed another root beer on me, and then showed me her family album. As an afterthought, she had me take down a big old picture of her great-grandfather, also too high for her to reach, so that I could dust that too. Then together we picked up the dust from it which might have fallen to the floor. "He's really a filthy old man, Robert," she said in closing, "and don't be afraid to report him to the Property Manager anytime you want."

I assured her that I would do it at the slightest provocation from Sullivan, finally accepted an apple but refused the money she offered, and escaped back to my mopping. Even then she watched me, smiling, from her half-opened door.

"Why does Miss O'Hara hate you?" I asked James once.

He lifted his cigaretted hand and let the long ash fall elegantly to the floor. "That old bitch has been an albatross around my neck ever since I got here," he said. "Don't trust her, Robert. It was her kind that sat around singing hymns and watching them burn saints in this state."

In those days I had forgotten that I was first of all a black and I had a very lovely girl who was not first of all a black. It is quite possible that my ancestors rowed her ancestors across on the *Mayflower*, and she was very rich in that alone. We were both very young and optimistic then, and she believed with me in my potential and liked me partly because of it; and I was happy because she belonged to me and not to the race, which made her special. It made me special too because I did not have to wear a beard or hate or be especially hip or ultra Ivy Leagueish. I did not have to smoke pot or supply her with it, or be for any cause at all except myself. I only had to be myself, which pleased me; and I only had to produce, which pleased both of us. Like many of the artistically inclined rich, she wanted to own in someone else what she could not own in herself. But this I did not mind, and I forgave her for it because she forgave me moods and the constant smell of garbage and a great deal of latent hostility. She only minded James Sullivan, and all the valuable time I was wasting listening to him rattle on and on. His conversations, she thought, were useless, repetitious, and promised nothing of value to me. She was accustomed to the old-rich, whose conversations meandered around a leitmotiv of how well off they were and how much they would leave behind very soon. She was not at all cold, but she had been taught how to tolerate the old-poor and perhaps toss them a greeting in passing. But nothing more.

Sullivan did not like her when I first introduced them because he saw that she was not a beatnik and could not be dismissed. It is in the nature of things that liberal people will tolerate two interracial beatniks more than they will an intelligent, serious-minded mixed couple. The former liaison is easy to dismiss as the dregs of both races, deserving of each other and the contempt of both races; but the latter poses a threat because there is no immediacy of overpowering sensuality or "you-pick-my-fleas-I'll-pick-yours" apparent on the surface of things, and people, even the most publicly liberal, cannot dismiss it so easily.

"That girl is Irish, isn't she?" he had asked one day in my apartment soon after I had introduced them.

"No," I said definitely.

"What's her name?"

"Judy Smith," I said, which was not her name at all.

"Well, I can spot it," he said. "She's got Irish blood all right."

"Everybody's got a little Irish blood," I told him.

He looked at me cattily and craftily from behind his thick lenses. "Well, she's from a good family, I suppose."

"I suppose," I said.

He paused to let some ashes fall to the rug. "They say the Colonel's Lady and Nelly O'Grady are sisters under the skin." Then he added: "Rudyard Kipling."

"That's true," I said with equal innuendo, "that's why you have to maintain a distinction by marrying the Colonel's Lady."

An understanding passed between us then, and we never spoke more on the subject.

Almost every night the cats wet the second floor while Meg Sullivan watched the "Johnny Carson Show" and the dog howled and clawed the door. During commercials Meg would curse James to get out and stop dropping ashes on the floor or to take the dog out or something else, totally unintelligible to those of us on the fourth, fifth, and sixth floors. Even after the Carson show she would still curse him to get out, until finally he would go down to the basement and put away a bottle or two of wine. There was a steady stench of cat functions in the basement, and with all the grease and dirt, discarded trunks, beer bottles, chairs, old tools, and the filthy sofa on which he sometimes slept, seeing him there made me want to cry. He drank the cheapest sherry, the wino kind, straight from the bottle: and on many nights that summer at 2:00 A.M. my phone would ring me out of bed.

"Rob? Jimmy Sullivan here. What are you doing?"

There was nothing suitable to say.

"Come on down to the basement for a drink."

"I have to be at work at 8:30," I would protest.

"Can't you have just one drink?" he would say pathetically.

I would carry down my own glass so that I would not have to drink out of the bottle. Looking at him on the sofa, I could not be mad because now I had many records for my stereo, a story that was going well, a girl who believed in me and who belonged to me and not to the race, a new set of dishes, and a tomorrow morning with younger people.

"I don't want to burden you unduly," he would always preface.

I would force myself not to look at my watch and say: "Of course not."

"My Meg is not in the best health, you know," he would say, handing the bottle to me.

"She's just old."

"The doctors say she should be in an institution."

"That's no place to be."

"I'm a sick man myself, Rob. I can't take much more. She's crazy."

"Anybody who loves animals can't be crazy."

He took another long draw from the bottle. "I won't live another year. I'll be dead in a year."

"You don't know that."

He looked at me closely, without his glasses, so that I could see the desperation in his eyes. "I just hope Meg goes before I do. I don't want them to put her in an institution after I'm gone."

At 2:00 A.M., with the cat stench in my nose and a glass of bad sherry standing still in my hand because I refuse in my mind to touch it, and all my dreams of greatness are above him and the basement and the building itself, I did not know what to say. The only way I could keep from hating myself was to start him talking about the AMA or the Medicare program or beatniks. He was pure hell on all three. To him, the Medical Profession was "morally bankrupt," Medicare was a great farce which deprived oldsters like himself of their "rainy-day dollars," and beatniks were "dropouts from the human race." He could rage on and on in perfect phrases about all three of his major dislikes, and I had the feeling that because the sentences were so well constructed and well turned, he might have memorized them from something he had read. But then he was extremely well read, and it did not matter if he had borrowed a phrase or two from someone else. The ideas were still his own.

It would be 3:00 A.M. before I knew it, and then 3:30, and still he would go on. He hated politicians in general and liked to recount, at these times, his private catalog of political observations. By the time he got around to Civil Rights it would be 4:00 A.M., and I could not feel responsible for him at that hour. I would begin to yawn, and at first he would just ignore it. Then I would start to edge toward the door, and he would see that he could hold me no longer, not even by declaring that he wanted to be an honorary Negro because he loved the race so much.

"I hope I haven't burdened you unduly," he would say again.

"Of course not," I would say, because it was over then, and I could leave him and the smell of the cats there, and sometimes I would go out in the cool night and walk around the Yard and be thankful that I was only an assistant janitor, and a transient one at that. Walking in the early dawn and seeing the Summer School fellows sneak out of the girls' dormitories in the Yard gave me a good feeling, and I thought that tomorrow night it would be good to make love myself so that I could be busy when he called.

"Why don't you tell that old man your job doesn't include baby-sitting with him," Jean told me many times when she came over to visit during the day and found me sleeping.

I would look at her and think to myself about social forces and the pressures massing and poised, waiting to attack us. It was still July then. It was hot, and I was working good.

"He's just an old man," I said. "Who else would listen to him."

"You're too soft. As long as you do your work you don't have to be bothered with him."

"He could be a story if I listened long enough."

"There are too many stories about old people."

"No," I said, thinking about us again, "there are just too many people who have no stories."

Sometimes he would come up and she would be there, but I would let him come in anyway, and he would stand there looking dirty and uncomfortable, offering some invented reason for having intruded. At these times something silent would pass between them, something I cannot name, which would reduce him to exactly what he was: an old man, come out of his basement to intrude where he was not wanted. But all the time this was being communicated, there would be a surface, friendly conversation between them. And after five minutes or so of being unwelcome, he would apologize for having come, drop a few ashes on the rug, and back out the door. Downstairs we could hear his wife screaming.

We endured the aged and August was almost over. Inside the building the cats were still wetting, Meg was still screaming, the dog was getting madder, and Sullivan began to drink during the day. Outside it was hot and lush and green, and the Summer girls were wearing shorter miniskirts and no panties and the middle-aged men down by the Charles were going wild on their bridge. Everyone was restless for change, for August is the month when undone summer things must be finished or regretted all through the winter.

Being imaginative people, Jean and I played a number of original games. One of them we called "Social Forces," the object of which was to see which side could break us first. We played it with the unknown night riders who screamed obscenities from passing cars. And because that was her side I would look at her expectantly, but she would laugh and say: "No." We played it at parties with unaware blacks who attempted to enchant her with skillful dances and hip vocabularies, believing her to be community property. She would be polite and aloof, and much later, it then being my turn, she would look at me expectantly. And I would force a smile and say: "No." The last round was played while taking her home in a subway car, on a hot August night, when one side of the car was black and tense and hating and the other side was white and of the same mind. There was not enough room on either side for the two of us to sit and we would not separate; so we stood, holding on to a steel post through all the stops, feeling all of the eyes, between the two sides of the car and the two sides of the world. We aged. And getting off finally at the stop which was no longer ours, we looked at each other, again expectantly, and there was nothing left to say.

I began to avoid the old man, would not answer the door when I knew it was he who was knocking, and waited until very late at night, when he could not possibly be awake, to haul the trash down. I hated the building then; and I was really a janitor for the first time. I slept a lot and wrote very little. And I did not give a damn about Medicare, the AMA, the building, Meg, or the crazy dog. I began to consider moving out.

In that same week, Miss O'Hara finally succeeded in badgering Murphy, the celibate Irishman, and a few other tenants into signing a complaint about the dog. No doubt Murphy signed because he was a nice fellow and women like Miss O'Hara had always dominated him. He did not really mind the dog: he did not really mind anything. She called him "Frank Dear," and I had the feeling that when he came to that place, fresh from Montgomery's Campaign, he must have had a will of his own; but she had drained it all away, year by year, so that now he would do anything just to be agreeable.

One day soon after the complaint, the little chubby Property Manager came around to tell Sullivan that the dog had to be taken away. Miss O'Hara told me the good news later, when she finally got around to my door.

"Well, that crazy dog is gone now, Robert. Those two are enough."

"Where is the dog?" I asked.

"I don't know, but Albert Rustin made them get him out. You should have seen the old drunk's face," she said. "That dirty old useless man."

"You should be at peace now," I said.

"Almost," was her reply. "The best thing is to get rid of those two old boozers along with the dog."

I congratulated Miss O'Hara and went out. I knew that the old man would be drinking and would want to talk. But very late that evening he called on the telephone and caught me in.

"Rob?" he said. "James Sullivan here. Would you come down to my apartment like a good fellow? I want to ask you something important."

I had never been in his apartment before and did not want to go then. But I went down anyway.

They had three rooms, all grimy from corner to corner. There was a peculiar odor in that place I did not ever want to smell again, and his wife was dragging herself around the room talking in mumbles. When she saw me come in the door, she said: "I can't clean it up. I just can't. Look at that window. I can't reach it. I can't keep it clean." She threw up both her hands and held her head down and to the side. "The whole place is dirty, and I can't clean it up."

"What do you want?" I said to Sullivan.

"Sit down." He motioned me to a kitchen chair. "Have you changed that bulb on the fifth floor?"

"It's done."

He was silent for a while, drinking from a bottle of sherry, and he gave me some and a dirty glass. "You're the first person who's been in here in years," he said. "We couldn't have company because of the dog."

Somewhere in my mind was a note that I should never go into his apartment. But the dog had never been the reason. "Well, he's gone now," I said, fingering the dirty glass of sherry.

He began to cry. "They took my dog away," he said. "It was all I had. How can they take a man's dog away from him?"

There was nothing I could say.

"I couldn't do nothing," he continued. After a while he added: "But I know who it was. It was that old bitch O'Hara. Don't ever trust her, Rob. She smiles in your face, but it was her kind that laughed when they burned Joan of Arc in this state."

Seeing him there, crying and making me feel unmanly because I wanted to touch him or say something warm, also made me eager to be far away and running hard.

"Everybody's got problems," I said. "I don't have a girl now."

He brightened immediately, and for a while he looked almost happy in his old cat's eyes. Then he staggered over to my chair and held out his hand. I did not touch it, and he finally pulled it back. "I know how you feel," he said. "I know just how you feel."

"Sure," I said.

"But you're a young man, you have a future. But not me. I'll be dead inside of a year."

Just then his wife dragged herself in to offer me a cigar. They were being hospitable, and I forced myself to drink a little of the sherry.

"They took my dog away today," she mumbled. "That's all I had in the world, my dog."

I looked at the old man. He was drinking from the bottle.

During the first week of September one of the middle-aged men down by the Charles got tired of looking and tried to take a necking girl away from her boyfriend. The police hauled him off to jail, and the girl pulled down her dress tearfully. A few days later another man exposed himself near the same spot. And that same week a dead body was found on the banks of the Charles.

The miniskirted brigade had moved out of the Yard, and it was quiet and green and peaceful there. In our building another Jewish couple moved into #44. They did not eat gourmet stuff, and on occasion, threw out pork-and-beans cans. But I had lost interest in perception. I now had many records for my stereo, loads of S. S. Pierce stuff, and a small bottle of Chivas Regal which I never opened. I was working good again, and I did not miss other things as much; or at least I told myself that.

The old man was coming up steadily now, at least three times a day, and I had resigned myself to it. If I refused to let him in, he would always come back later with a missing bulb on the fifth floor. We had taken to buying cases of beer together, and when he had finished his half, which was very frequently, he would come up to polish off mine. I began to enjoy talking politics, the AMA, Medicare, beatniks, and listening to him recite from books he had read. I discovered that he was very well read in history, philosophy, literature, and law. He was extraordinarily fond of saying: "I am really a cut above being a building superintendent. Circumstances made me what I am." And even though he was drunk and dirty and it was very late at night, I believed him and liked him anyway because having him there was much better than being alone. After he had gone I could sleep, and I was not lonely in sleep; and it did not really matter how late I was at work the next morning because when I thought about it all, I discovered that nothing really matters except not being old and being alive and having potential to dream about, and not being alone.

THE DAY THEY WENT SHOPPING

Nancy Mercado

The day they went shopping, food shopping as on any other day when the sun was out and bright and the breeze seemed more like air conditioning than air streaming from an oven, nothing out of the ordinary was expected as they strolled through the brightly lit and polished supermarket aisles looking for the best buys, or, in her case, just looking for pleasure, just walking and daydreaming of how different life would be if she had the money to buy whatever she needed, if only she could become famous somehow, maybe as a singer, maybe a dancer, oh she already knew she had what it took in the *looks department* although her certainty was never revealed to friends, not to anyone for fear she'd be rejected, seen as a conceited young girl who in fact was quite insecure due to her mother's reprimanding, a constant censure that had not succeeded in making the girl bitter, as this long-haired olive-skinned beauty made her way up and down the sparkling aisles dreaming, if only she had money, she could get her parents and brothers out of that apartment situated in a crippled house that made weird noises and swayed with the ocean winds when it stormed, that apartment where one of them made the dining room his bedroom for years, cursing his meager living conditions to himself night after night just as he fell asleep, his resolve to live a better life as soon as possible coupled with being the ladies' man that he was, that had pushed him into abruptly marrying, quitting high school to get a job, and moving upstairs with his young bride, only to find himself drafted into the Vietnam War shortly after, forced to serve for several years, putting the family in a state of panic day after day during dinner time when the remaining members sat around the television set having dinner, watching the war rage on, wondering whether he was alive or dead or if his face would be the next close up taken in some battlefield, maybe in a makeshift infirmary thousands of miles away, or maybe the body was being flown back in a box just as the family finished their meal where they sat, on flowery plastic slip covered sofa chairs, except for one of them sitting at the dinner table eating where any normal human being would, away from the mayhem of the day where a bit of peace could be captured if only for the precious thirty minutes or so it took to chew up the food, longer if the food was chewed properly with care as he did, sitting there quietly gazing into space, patiently taking bite after bite, his jaws in slow motion, moving ever so delicately, with such tranquility, he seemed mesmerized after a hard day of labor in a restaurant kitchen, mixing concoctions in huge vats, sauces of every kind, working around ovens that were fiery mammoths capable of swallowing any person alive and whole, and perhaps it was his hard work, the reason why he, the bread winner of the house, sat in a meditative state, it was the only way of regaining his soul, of reclaiming his right to self determination, to freedom from a ten hour underpaid work day, because it was a way of making peace with himself and God, maybe it was his age that made it possible to accept this fate gracefully, to ward off his desires for more money, for a better life, to come to terms with an existence of borderline poverty and having to sacrifice the better part of productive years to sustain a family, to ensure that none of them would suffer, to make sure none would simply become homeless, and so this was the kind of person he was and for which she was eternally grateful as she served him dinner, jumping between the war on the tube and the rice, beans and stewing chicken in the kitchen, she worried about the son in the war who wasn't even her son but, in fact, his son from a previous marriage, but this didn't matter to her, she loved the boy just the same, and besides, she worried more often than not about one thing or the other, worried about the house swaying in the winter winds as she sat up all night in the dark, in that small linoleum covered living room alone, reciting the rosary, she was a murky figure slightly hunched over, convinced whispering this litany would not only ensure the structure's survival as well as those who slept there but would eventually grant the family a better apartment, a better life, and so she kept herself in that room until dawn, even though the storm's hostility rammed through every crack of the house, steadily dropping the temperature as the hours passed, she sat on that cold plastic slip covered sofa located in the corner of the room and must have counted the number of times she repeated the rosary before God answered, before the winds went silent, before a ray of sunlight would bounce off one of those plastic covers, bringing an end to that frigid obscurity, to that living nightmare she felt was hers alone, her nightmare that threatened to become the girl's nightmare also, the girl who was startled awake, had tiptoed into the living room and was now sitting nearby, staring into space, daydreaming again, only this time it was in the dark where her thoughts rolled like a movie as she remembered the good times spent during the summer, dressing up, stepping out with her sister-in-law to the boardwalk where the overweight sun having no restrictions placed on it, no buildings jetting into the heavens to cut off its expression, detailed every splinter that was the boardwalk, pronounced the outline of shops unmistakable, exaggerated the glare returned from steel amusement rides over and over as they circled packed with screaming passengers, magnified the splendor from ocean waves for miles, transformed sun bathers with luminous bronzed skin into museum statues, or, if vermilion in hue, into hot peppers from a distance, the whole mob of them hanging around the shops, enjoying a foot long or some ice cream, a wonderful display of humanity just having fun, no fights, no wars, no gloom, as the girls, grateful participants in this display, strolled down the boardwalk enjoying every minute with no worries to think of, the married one almost forgetting her young husband was on the other side of the world under a very different kind of sun, engaged in a terribly different display of humanity, this young married woman who could be mistaken for one of those exquisite bronze statues in her own night, of medium height, slim with black shoulder length hair that flicked skyward at its ends, possessed the whitest and most perfectly straight set of teeth, maybe these were the reasons he fell in love with her, because she owned such an unforgettable

smile capable of hypnotizing anyone within the range of its light, or was it just her
overall beauty, or perhaps he sensed she shared in his ambition to raise the standard
of their lives, to someday want for nothing in this world, or was it her outbursts of
jealousy that made him feel appreciated, those times when any item in their home,
anything reachable such as hanging pictures, a table clock, a dish or figurine would
do as a projectile, perhaps it was all of these attributes that, when summed up,
embodied the woman he desired, not to mention the kindnesses she extended
towards his family, like the times she bathed his sister, washing all the length of the
girl's hair, heartily scrubbing, conditioning, toweling it off and patiently setting the
heap into rollers strand by endless strand, or the occasions when she'd offer a nice
word to her mother-in-law's church friend, the frequent visitor who often wore a
green suit to Sunday Mass, a petite middle aged salt and pepper haired lady as
strict in her Catholic practice as the mother-in-law, they never wore make-up,
never wore pants and attended church at least two, sometimes three times a week,
the best of friends, they confided in each other for years in every way but one, the
little lady never spoke of her desire for an improved life, of how she secretly wished
for more money, just enough to make ends meet, just enough to enable her to shop
for the children's needs at a store on the Avenue for once, instead of the Salvation
Army, fearing this secret wish might be seen as ingratitude for the life God had
given her, she never spoke of this desire, but made her petition in silent prayers,
only to request forgiveness afterwards for emotions she was convinced were greed,
unlike her oldest son, a loving generous soul she believed was devoid of such feelings, the son who one day opted to leave the family for motives she surmised must
have had to do with her, her imperfect cooking, her nagging, her overbearing ways
which were most assuredly the reasons why this young man, a dedicated factory
worker who always shared the bit of money earned with them, had been frightened
away to the other side of the country, her caring son who in fact left in pursuit of a
dream recounted to him as a boy by his father, a dream of a desert measureless and
colorful at dawn and dusk, surely a glorious place and a better life to be lived were
the real grounds for his departure one night, leaving behind only a note stuffed
with some faded dollar bills folded neatly in half for the family, always kind and
caring like the times he cooked homemade desserts especially loved by his little
brothers, the times he watched over the boys, taking them to the local playground
where they'd spend hours on swings and seesaws while he challenged friends to a
game of checkers, his mother at church and father at work, or when he looked after his parents, preparing their baths, rubbing their worn and tired limbs, making
them tea, now he was sorely missed above all, by his mother who grieved his loss,
like her best friend grieved for the child in Vietnam who would also write a note,
this one arriving by mail one day before she'd return from shopping with daughter
and daughter-in-law, as they laid bags of groceries down, some on chairs, others on
the plastic-covered dining room table, the girl staying behind peeking into the
mailbox, snatching and reading the post card she found, running up the stairs
panting and waving the thing wildly between breaths, would tell them the son's
message the card held, a message his mother didn't believe until the wife read it
again, causing the old woman's knees to weaken and buckle as she dropped into a
chair praising God for the young man's release, the news, spinning off celebrations

in the weeks to come, the young wife upstairs preparing her home, preparing herself, cleaning, polishing, setting everything in its proper place, the hanging pictures, the flick of her hair, the figurines, the table clock unplugged on their bedroom night stand, her nails polished to perfection, her smile, luminous and downstairs, the cooking fest between both parents, their kitchen buzzing and warm, the table set for all, the good friend also there donning her stylish green suit helped to organize things with her conversation, spoke about the loving child she had not heard from, while the young girl sitting in the sun-drenched living room with the television set off and the plastic slip covers, dusted, gleaming, daydreamed about this day, "how would he appear, what hour would he arrive," dreamed into the future, of the fun times they would share on the boardwalk, their chance to become beautiful like works of art, like bronzed museum statues, her wish to become famous, to make money didn't cross her mind just then as she heard a knock coming from the door.

A WIFE'S STORY

Bharati Mukherjee

Imre says forget it, but I'm going to write David Mamet. So Patels are hard to sell
real estate to. You buy them a beer, whisper Glengarry Glen Ross, and they smell
swamp instead of sun and surf. They work hard, eat cheap, live ten to a room, stash
their savings under futons in Queens, and before you know it they own half of
Hoboken. You say, where's the sweet gullibility that made this nation great?

Polish jokes, Patel jokes: that's not why I want to write Mamet.

Seen their women?

Everybody laughs. Imre laughs. The dozing fat man with the Barnes & Noble
sack between his legs, the woman next to him, the usher, everybody. The theater
isn't so dark that they can't see me. In my red silk sari I'm conspicuous. Plump,
gold paisleys sparkle on my chest.

The actor is just warming up. *Seen their women?* He plays a salesman, he's had a
bad day and now he's in a Chinese restaurant trying to loosen up. His face is pink.
His wool-blend slacks are creased at the crotch. We bought our tickets at half-
price, we're sitting in the front row, but at the edge, and we see things we shouldn't
be seeing. At least I do, or think I do. Spittle, actors goosing each other, little
winks, streaks of makeup.

Maybe they're improvising dialogue too. Maybe Mamet's provided them with
insult kits, Thursdays for Chinese, Wednesdays for Hispanics, today for Indians.
Maybe they get together before curtain time, see an Indian woman settling in the
front row off to the side, and say to each other: "Hey, forget Friday. Let's get *her*
today. See if she cries. See if she walks out." Maybe, like the salesmen they play,
they have a little bet on.

Maybe I shouldn't feel betrayed.

Their women, he goes again. *They look like they've just been fucked by a dead cat.*

The fat man hoots so hard he nudges my elbow off our shared armrest.

"Imre. I'm going home." But Imre's hunched so far forward he doesn't hear.
English isn't his best language. A refugee from Budapest, he has to listen hard. "I
didn't pay eighteen dollars to be insulted."

I don't hate Mamet. It's the tyranny of the American dream that scares me: First,
you don't exist. Then you're invisible. Then you're funny. Then you're disgusting.
Insult, my American friends will tell me, is a kind of acceptance. No instant
dignity here. A play like this, back home, would cause riots. Communal, racist,
and antisocial. The actors wouldn't make it off stage. This play, and all these awful
feelings, would be safely locked up.

I long, at times, for clear-cut answers. Offer me instant dignity, today, and I'll take it.

"What?" Imre moves toward me without taking his eyes off the actor. "Come again?"

Tears come. I want to stand, scream, make an awful scene. I long for ugly, nasty rage.

The actor is ranting, flinging spittle. *Give me a chance. I'm not finished, I can get back on the board. I tell that asshole, give me a real lead. And what does that asshole give me? Patels. Nothing but Patels.*

This time Imre works an arm around my shoulders. "Panna, what is Patel? Why are you taking it all so personally?"

I shrink from his touch, but I don't walk out. Expensive girls' schools in Lausanne and Bombay have trained me to behave well. My manners are exquisite, my feelings are delicate, my gestures refined, my moods undetectable. They have seen me through riots, uprootings, separation, my son's death.

"I'm not taking it personally."

The fat man looks at us. The woman looks too, and shushes.

I stare back at the two of them. Then I stare, mean and cool, at the man's elbow. Under the bright blue polyester Hawaiian shirt sleeve, the elbow looks soft and runny. "Excuse me," I say. My voice has the effortless meanness of well-bred displaced Third World women, though my rhetoric has been learned elsewhere. "You're exploiting my space."

Startled, the man snatches his arm away from me. He cradles it against his breast. By the time he's ready with comebacks, I've turned my back on him. I've probably ruined the first act for him. I know I've ruined it for Imre.

It's not my fault; it's the *situation*. Old colonies wear down. Patels—the new pioneers—have to be suspicious. Idi Amin's lesson is permanent. AT&T wires move good advice from continent to continent. Keep all assets liquid. Get into 7–11s, get out of condos and motels. I know how both sides feel, that's the trouble. The Patel sniffing out scams, the sad salesmen on the stage: postcolonialism has made me their referee. It's hate I long for; simple, brutish, partisan hate.

After the show Imre and I make our way toward Broadway. Sometimes he holds my hand; it doesn't mean anything more than that crazies and drunks are crouched in doorways. Imre's been here over two years, but he's stayed very old-world, very courtly, openly protective of women. I met him in a seminar on special ed. last semester. His wife is a nurse somewhere in the Hungarian countryside. There are two sons, and miles of petitions for their emigration. My husband manages a mill two hundred miles north of Bombay. There are no children.

"You make things tough on yourself," Imre says. He assumed Patel was a Jewish name or maybe Hispanic; everything makes equal sense to him. He found the play tasteless, he worried about the effect of vulgar language on my sensitive ears. "You have to let go a bit." And as though to show me how to let go, he breaks away from me, bounds ahead with his head ducked tight, then dances on amazingly jerky legs. He's a Magyar, he often tells me, and deep down, he's an Asian too. I catch glimpses of it, knife-blade Attila cheekbones, despite the blondish hair. In his faded jeans and leather jacket, he's a rock video star. I watch MTV for hours in the apartment when Charity's working the evening shift at Macy's. I listen to WPLJ on Charity's earphones. Why should I be ashamed? Television in India is so uplifting.

Imre stops as suddenly as he'd started. People walk around us. The summer sidewalk is full of theatergoers in seersucker suits; Imre's year-round jacket is out of place. European. Cops in twos and threes huddle, lightly tap their thighs with night sticks and smile at me with benevolence. I want to wink at them, get us all in trouble, tell them the crazy dancing man is from the Warsaw Pact. I'm too shy to break into dance on Broadway. So I hug Imre instead.

The hug takes him by surprise. He wants me to let go, but he doesn't really expect me to let go. He staggers, though I weigh no more than 104 pounds, and with him, I pitch forward slightly. Then he catches me, and we walk arm in arm to the bus stop. My husband would never dance or hug a woman on Broadway. Nor would my brothers. They aren't stuffy people, but they went to Anglican boarding schools and they have a well-developed sense of what's silly.

"Imre." I squeeze his big, rough hand. "I'm sorry I ruined the evening for you."

"You did nothing of the kind." He sounds tired. "Let's not wait for the bus. Let's splurge and take a cab instead."

Imre always has unexpected funds. The Network, he calls it, Class of '56.

In the back of the cab, without even trying, I feel light, almost free. Memories of Indian destitutes mix with the hordes of New York street people, and they float free, like astronauts, inside my head. I've made it. I'm making something of my life. I've left home, my husband, to get a Ph.D. in special ed: I have a multiple-entry visa and a small scholarship for two years. After that, we'll see. My mother was beaten by her mother-in-law, my grandmother, when she'd registered for French lessons at the Alliance Française. My grandmother, the eldest daughter of a rich zamindar, was illiterate.

Imre and the cabdriver talk away in Russian. I keep my eyes closed. That way I can feel the floaters better. I'll write Mamet tonight. I feel strong, reckless. Maybe, I'll write Steven Spielberg too; tell him that Indians don't eat monkey brains.

We've made it. Patels must have made it. Mamet, Spielberg: they're not condescending to us. Maybe they're a little bit afraid.

Charity Chin, my roommate, is sitting on the floor drinking Chablis out of a plastic wineglass. She is five foot six, three inches taller than me, but weighs a kilo and a half less than I do. She is a "hands" model. Orientals are supposed to have a monopoly in the hands-modelling business, she says. She had her eyes fixed eight or nine months ago and out of gratitude sleeps with her plastic surgeon every third Wednesday.

"Oh, good," Charity says. "I'm glad you're back early. I need to talk."

She's been writing checks. MCI, Con Ed, Bonwit Teller. Envelopes, already stamped and sealed, form a pyramid between her shapely, knee-socked legs. The checkbook's cover is brown plastic, grained to look like cowhide. Each time Charity flips back the cover, white geese fly over sky-colored checks. She makes good money, but she's extravagant. The difference adds up to this shared, rent-controlled Chelsea one-bedroom.

"All right. Talk."

When I first moved in, she was seeing an analyst. Now she sees a nutritionist.

"Eric called: From Oregon."

"What did he want?"

"He wants me to pay half the rent on his loft for last spring. He asked me to move back, remember? He *begged* me."

Eric is Charity's estranged husband.

"What does your nutritionist say?" Eric now wears a red jumpsuit and tills the soil in Rajneeshpuram.

"You think Phil's a creep too, don't you? What else can he be when creeps are all I attract?"

Phil is a flutist with thinning hair. He's very touchy on the subject of *flautists* versus *flutists*. He's touchy on every subject, from music to books to foods to clothes. He teaches at a small college upstate, and Charity bought a used blue Datsun ("Nissan," Phil insists) last month so she could spend weekends with him. She returns every Sunday night, exhausted and exasperated. Phil and I don't have much to say to each other—he's the only musician I know; the men in my family are lawyers, engineers, or in business—but I like him. Around me, he loosens up. When he visits, he bakes us loaves of pumpernickel bread. He waxes our kitchen floor. Like many men in this country, he seems to me a displaced child, or even a woman, looking for something that passed him by, or for something that he can never have. If he thinks I'm not looking, he sneaks his hands under Charity's sweater, but there isn't too much there. Here, she's a model with high ambitions. In India, she'd be a flat-chested old maid.

I'm shy in front of the lovers. A darkness comes over me when I see them horsing around.

"It isn't the money," Charity says. Oh? I think. "He says he still loves me. Then he turns around and asks me for five hundred."

What's so strange about that, I want to ask. She still loves Eric, and Eric, red jumpsuit and all, is smart enough to know it. Love is a commodity, hoarded like any other. Mamet knows. But I say, "I'm not the person to ask about love." Charity knows that mine was a traditional Hindu marriage. My parents, with the help of a marriage broker, who was my mother's cousin, picked out a groom. All I had to do was get to know his taste in food.

It'll be a long evening, I'm afraid. Charity likes to confess. I unpleat my silk sari—it no longer looks too showy—wrap it in muslin cloth and put it away in a dresser drawer. Saris are hard to have laundered in Manhattan, though there's a good man in Jackson Heights. My next step will be to brew us a pot of chrysanthemum tea. It's a very special tea from the mainland. Charity's uncle gave it to us. I like him. He's a humpbacked, awkward, terrified man. He runs a gift store on Mott Street, and though he doesn't speak much English, he seems to have done well. Once upon a time he worked for the railways in Chengdu, Szechwan Province, and during the Wuchang Uprising, he was shot at. When I'm down, when I'm lonely for my husband, when I think of our son, or when I need to be held, I think of Charity's uncle. If I hadn't left home, I'd never have heard of the Wuchang Uprising. I've broadened my horizons.

Very late that night my husband calls me from Ahmadabad, a town of textile mills north of Bombay. My husband is a vice president at Lakshmi Cotton Mills. Lakshmi is the goddess of wealth, but LCM (Priv.), Ltd., is doing poorly. Lockouts, strikes, rock-throwings. My husband lives on digitalis, which he calls the food for our *yuga* of discontent.

"We had a bad mishap at the mill today." Then he says nothing for seconds.

The operator comes on. "Do you have the right party, sir? We're trying to reach Mrs. Butt."

"Bhatt," I insist. "*B* for Bombay, *H* for Haryana, *A* for Ahmadabad, double *T* for Tamil Nadu." It's a litany. "This is she."

"One of our lorries was firebombed today. Resulting in three deaths. The driver, old Karamchand, and his two children."

I know how my husband's eyes look this minute, how the eye rims sag and the yellow corneas shine and bulge with pain. He is not an emotional man—the Ahmadabad Institute of Management has trained him to cut losses, to look on the bright side of economic catastrophes—but tonight he's feeling low. I try to remember a driver named Karamchand, but can't. That part of my life is over, the way *trucks* have replaced *lorries* in my vocabulary, the way Charity Chin and her lurid love life have replaced inherited notions of marital duty. Tomorrow he'll come out of it. Soon he'll be eating again. He'll sleep like a baby. He's been trained to believe in turnovers. Every morning he rubs his scalp with cantharidine oil so his hair will grow back again.

"It could be your car next." Affection, love. Who can tell the difference in a traditional marriage in which a wife still doesn't call her husband by his first name?

"No. They know I'm a flunky, just like them. Well paid, maybe. No need for undue anxiety, please."

Then his voice breaks. He says he needs me, he misses me, he wants me to come to him damp from my evening shower, smelling of sandalwood soap, my braid decorated with jasmines.

"I need you too."

"Not to worry, please," he says. "I am coming in a fortnight's time. I have already made arrangements."

Outside my window, fire trucks whine, up Eighth Avenue. I wonder if he can hear them, what he thinks of a life like mine, led amid disorder.

"I am thinking it'll be like a honeymoon. More or less."

When I was in college, waiting to be married, I imagined honeymoons were only for the more fashionable girls, the girls who came from slightly racy families, smoked Sobranies in the dorm lavatories and put up posters of Kabir Bedi, who was supposed to have made it as a big star in the West. My husband wants us to go to Niagara. I'm not to worry about foreign exchange. He's arranged for extra dollars through the Gujarati Network, with a cousin in San Jose. And he's bought four hundred more on the black market. "Tell me you need me. Panna, please tell me again."

I change out of the cotton pants and shirt I've been wearing all day and put on a sari to meet my husband at JFK. I don't forget the jewelry; the marriage necklace of *mangalsutra*, gold drop earrings, heavy gold bangles. I don't wear them every day.

In this borough of vice and greed, who knows when, or whom, desire will over-whelm.

My husband spots me in the crowd and waves. He has lost weight, and changed his glasses. The arm, uplifted in a cheery wave, is bony, frail, almost opalescent.

In the Carey Coach, we hold hands. He strokes my fingers one by one. "How come you aren't wearing my mother's ring?"

"Because muggers know about Indian women," I say. They know with us it's 24-karat. His mother's ring is showy, in ghastly taste anywhere but India: a blood-red Burma ruby set in a gold frame of floral sprays. My mother-in-law got her guru to bless the ring before I left for the States.

He looks disconcerted. He's used to a different role. He's the knowing, suspicious one in the family. He seems to be sulking, and finally he comes out with it. "You've said nothing about my new glasses." I compliment him on the glasses, how chic and Western-executive they make him look. But I can't help the other things, necessities until he learns the ropes. I handle the money, buy the tickets. I don't know if this makes me unhappy.

* * *

Charity drives her Nissan upstate, so for two weeks we are to have the apartment to ourselves. This is more privacy than we ever had in India. No parents, no servants, to keep us modest. We play at housekeeping. Imre has lent us a hibachi, and I grill saffron chicken breasts. My husband marvels at the size of the Perdue hens. "They're big like peacocks, no? These Americans, they're really something!" He tries out pizzas, burgers, McNuggets. He chews. He explores. He judges. He loves it all, fears nothing, feels at home in the summer odors, the clutter of Manhattan streets. Since he thinks that the American palate is bland, he carries a bottle of red peppers in his pocket. I wheel a shopping cart down the aisles of the neighborhood Grand Union, and he follows, swiftly, greedily. He picks up hair rinses and high-protein diet powders. There's so much I already take for granted.

One night, Imre stops by. He wants us to go with him to a movie. In his work shirt and red leather tie, he looks arty or strung out. It's only been a week, but I feel as though I am really seeing him for the first time. The yellow hair worn very short at the sides, the wide, narrow lips. He's a good-looking man, but self-conscious, almost arrogant. He's picked the movie we should see. He always tells me what to see, what to read. He buys the *Voice*. He's a natural avant-gardist. For tonight he's chosen *Numéro Deux*.

"Is it a musical?" my husband asks. The Radio City Music Hall is on his list of sights to see. He's read up on the history of the Rockettes. He doesn't catch Imre's sympathetic wink.

Guilt, shame, loyalty. I long to be ungracious, not ingratiate myself with both men.

That night my husband calculates in rupees the money we've wasted on Godard. "That refugee fellow, Nagy, must have a screw loose in his head. I paid very steep price for dollars on the black market."

Some afternoons we go shopping. Back home we hated shopping, but now it is a lovers' project. My husband's shopping list startles me. I feel I am just getting to

298 | Bharati Mukherjee

know him. Maybe, like Imre, freed from the dignities of old-world culture, he too could get drunk and squirt Cheez Whiz on a guest. I watch him dart into stores in his gleaming leather shoes. Jockey shorts on sale in outdoor bins on Broadway entrance him. White tube socks with different bands of color delight him. He looks for microcassettes, for anything small and electronic and smuggleable. He needs a garment bag. He calls it a "wardrobe," and I have to translate.

"All of New York is having sales, no?"

My heart speeds watching him this happy. It's the third week in August, almost the end of summer, and the city smells ripe, it cannot bear more heat, more money, more energy.

"This is so smashing! The prices are so excellent!" Recklessly, my prudent husband signs away traveller's checks. How he intends to smuggle it all back I don't dare ask. With a microwave, he calculates, we could get rid of our cook.

This has to be love, I think. Charity, Eric, Phil: they may be experts on sex. My husband doesn't chase me around the sofa, but he pushes me down on Charity's battered cushions, and the man who has never entered the kitchen of our Ahmad-abad house now comes toward me with a dish tub of steamy water to massage away the pavement heat.

Ten days into his vacation my husband checks out brochures for sightseeing tours. Shortline, Grayline, Crossroads: his new vinyl briefcase is full of schedules and pamphlets. While I make pancakes out of a mix, he comparison shops. Tour number one costs $10.95 and will give us the World Trade Center, China-town, and the United Nations. Tour number three would take us both uptown *and* downtown for $14.95, but my husband is absolutely sure he doesn't want to see Harlem. We settle for tour number four: Downtown and the Dame. It's offered by a new tour company with a small, dirty office at Eighth and Forty-eighth.

The sidewalk outside the office is colorful with tourists. My husband sends me in to buy the tickets because he has come to feel Americans don't understand his accent.

The dark man, Lebanese probably, behind the counter comes on too friendly. "Come on, doll, make my day!" He won't say which tour is his. "Number four? Honey, no! Look, you've wrecked me! Say you'll change your mind." He takes two twenties and gives back change. He holds the tickets, forcing me to pull. He leans closer. "I'm off after lunch."

My husband must have been watching me from the sidewalk. "What was the chap saying?" he demands. "I told you not to wear pants. He thinks you are Puerto Rican. He thinks he can treat you with disrespect."

The bus is crowded and we have to sit across the aisle from each other. The tour guide begins his patter on Forty-sixth. He looks like an actor, his hair bleached and blow-dried. Up close he must look middle-aged, but from where I sit his skin is smooth and his cheeks faintly red.

"Welcome to the Big Apple, folks." The guide uses a microphone. "Big Apple. That's what we native Manhattan degenerates call our city. Today we have guests from fifteen foreign countries and six states from this U. S. of A. That makes the

Tourist Bureau real happy. And let me assure you that while we may be the richest city in the richest country in the world, it's okay to tip your charming and talented attendant." He laughs. Then he swings his hip out into the aisle and sings a song.

"And it's mighty fancy on old Delancey Street, you know. . . ."

My husband looks irritable. The guide is, as expected, a good singer. "The bloody man should be giving us histories of buildings we are passing, no?" I pat his hand, the mood passes. He cranes his neck. Our window seats have both gone to Japanese. It's the tour of his life. Next to this, the quick business trips to Manchester and Glasgow pale.

"And tell me what street compares to Mott Street, in July. . . ."

The guide wants applause. He manages a derisive laugh from the Americans up front. He's working the aisles now. "I coulda been somebody, right? I coulda been a star!" Two or three of us smile, those of us who recognize the parody. He catches my smile. The sun is on his harsh, bleached hair. "Right, your highness? Look, we gotta maharani with us! Couldn't I have been a star?"

"Right!" I say, my voice coming out a squeal. I've been trained to adapt; what else can I say?

We drive through traffic past landmark office buildings and churches. The guide flips his hands. "Art deco," he keeps saying. I hear him confide to one of the Americans: "Beats me. I went to a cheap guide's school." My husband wants to know more about this Art Deco, but the guide sings another song.

"We made a foolish choice," my husband grumbles. "We are sitting in the bus only. We're not going into famous buildings." He scrutinizes the pamphlets in his jacket pocket. I think, at least it's air-conditioned in here. I could sit here in the cool shadows of the city forever.

Only five of us appear to have opted for the "Downtown and the Dame" tour. The others will ride back uptown past the United Nations after we've been dropped off at the pier for the ferry to the Statue of Liberty.

An elderly European pulls a camera out of his wife's designer tote bag. He takes pictures of the boats in the harbor, the Japanese in kimonos eating popcorn, scavenging pigeons, me. Then, pushing his wife ahead of him, he climbs back on the bus and waves to us. For a second I feel terribly lost. I wish we were on the bus going back to the apartment. I know I'll not be able to describe any of this to Charity, or to Imre. I'm too proud to admit I went on a guided tour.

The view of the city from the Circle Line ferry is seductive, unreal. The skyline wavers out of reach, but never quite vanishes. The summer sun pushes through fluffy clouds and dapples the glass of office towers. My husband looks thrilled, even more than he had on the shopping trips down Broadway. Tourists and dreamers, we have spent our life's savings to see this skyline, this statue.

"Quick, take a picture of me!" my husband yells as he moves toward a gap of railings. A Japanese matron has given up her position in order to change film. "Before the Twin Towers disappear!"

I focus, I wait for a large Oriental family to walk out of my range. My husband holds his pose tight against the railing. He wants to look relaxed, an international businessman at home in all the financial markets.

A bearded man slides across the bench toward me. "Like this," he says and helps me get my husband in focus. "You want me to take the photo for you?" His name, he says, is Goran. He is Goran from Yugoslavia, as though that were enough for tracking him down. Imre from Hungary. Panna from India. He pulls the old Leica out of my hand, signaling the Orientals to beat it, and clicks away. "I'm a photographer," he says. He could have been a camera thief. That's what my husband would have assumed. Somehow, I trusted. "Get you a beer?" he asks.

"I don't. Drink, I mean. Thank you very much." I say those last words very loud, for everyone's benefit. The odd bottles of Soave with Imre don't count.

"Too bad." Goran gives back the camera.

"Take one more!" my husband shouts from the railing. "Just to be sure!"

The island itself disappoints. The Lady has brutal scaffolding holding her in. The museum is closed. The snack bar is dirty and expensive. My husband reads out the prices to me. He orders two french fries and two Cokes. We sit at picnic tables and wait for the ferry to take us back.

"What was that hippie chap saying?"

As if I could say. A day-care center has brought its kids, at least forty of them, to the island for the day. The kids, all wearing name tags, run around us. I can't help noticing how many are Indian. Even a Patel, probably a Bhatt if I looked hard enough. They toss hamburger bits at pigeons. They kick styrofoam cups. The pigeons are slow, greedy, persistent. I have to shoo one off the table top. I don't think my husband thinks about our son.

"What hippie?"

"The one on the boat. With the beard and the hair."

My husband doesn't look at me. He shakes out his paper napkin and tries to protect his french fries from pigeon feathers.

"Oh, him. He said he was from Dubrovnik." It isn't true, but I don't want trouble.

"What did he say about Dubrovnik?"

I know enough about Dubrovnik to get by. Imre's told me about it. And about Mostar and Zagreb. In Mostar white Muslims sing the call to prayer. I would like to see that before I die: white Muslims. Whole peoples have moved before me; they've adapted. The night Imre told me about Mostar was also the night I saw my first snow in Manhattan. We'd walked down to Chelsea from Columbia. We'd walked and talked and I hadn't felt tired at all.

"You're too innocent," my husband says. He reaches for my hand. "Panna," he cries with pain in his voice, and I am brought back from perfect, floating memories of snow, "I've come to take you back. I have seen how men watch you."

"What?"

"Come back, now. I have tickets. We have all the things we will ever need. I can't live without you."

A little girl with wiry braids kicks a bottle cap at his shoes. The pigeons wheel and scuttle around us. My husband covers his fries with spread-out fingers. "No kicking," he tells the girl. Her name, Beulah, is printed in green ink on a heart-shaped name tag. He forces a smile, and Beulah smiles back. Then she starts to flap her arms. She flaps, she hops. The pigeons go crazy for fries and scraps.

"Special ed. course is two years," I remind him. "I can't go back."

My husband picks up our trays and throws them into the garbage before I can stop him. He's carried disposability a little too far. "We've been taken," he says, moving toward the dock, though the ferry will not arrive for another twenty minutes. "The ferry costs only two dollars round-trip per person. We should have chosen tour number one for $10.95 instead of tour number four for $14.95."

With my Lebanese friend, I think. "But this way we don't have to worry about cabs. The bus will pick us up at the pier and take us back to midtown. Then we can walk home."

"New York is full of cheats and whatnot. Just like Bombay." He is not accusing me of infidelity. I feel dread all the same.

That night, after we've gone to bed, the phone rings. My husband listens, then hands the phone to me. "What is this woman saying?" He turns on the pink Macy's lamp by the bed. "I am not understanding these Negro people's accents."

The operator repeats the message. It's a cable from one of the directors of Lakshmi Cotton Mills. "Massive violent labor confrontation anticipated. Stop. Return posthaste. Stop. Cable flight details. Signed Kantilal Shah."

"It's not your factory," I say. "You're supposed to be on vacation."

"So, you are worrying about me? Yes? You reject my heartfelt wishes but you worry about me?" He pulls me close, slips the straps of my nightdress off my shoulder. "Wait a minute."

I wait, unclothed, for my husband to come back to me. The water is running in the bathroom. In the ten days he has been here he has learned American rites: deodorants, fragrances. Tomorrow morning he'll call Air India; tomorrow evening he'll be on his way back to Bombay. Tonight I should make up to him for my years away, the gutted trucks, the degree I'll never use in India. I want to pretend with him that nothing has changed.

In the mirror that hangs on the bathroom door, I watch my naked body turn, the breasts, the thighs glow. The body's beauty amazes. I stand here shameless, in ways he has never seen me. I am free, afloat, watching somebody else.

BOY ON A WOODEN HORSE

Alejandro Murguía

The end of August, 1956. A Saturday in Mexico City. In my black charro outfit bought especially for today's occasion, I go with La Guela to Mercado La Merced. La Guela is my tight-fisted grandmother under whose care I live. She grips my wrist with her claw of a hand and hauls me aboard the bus. "Sombras," by Javier Solís, the newest idol of the Mexican public, is blaring from the radio. We squeeze through the bus till a man with a hat gives us his seat, and I climb on La Guela's bony lap. She is taking me to have my photograph taken. With a puff on his cigarette, the driver forces the stick shift into gear and the bus lurches forward. He wipes the back of his neck with an oily handkerchief and looks at me through the oblong mirror that has a decal of a naked woman. A plastic Virgen de Guadalupe is glued to the dashboard. The red fringe across the windshield bobs up and down as the bus chugs through traffic, thick with cars and noisy claxons. The driver's cigarette and the diesel fumes make me dizzy, but I fight off the nausea by thinking of Mother.

I am Mundo, a six-year-old fierce capricho of a boy, a walking tantrum and a torment for La Guela. She threatens me when I don't behave, like this morning, when I rolled one calcetín over the other. She cried in frustration when she couldn't find the sock that was there all along. Then on our way out the door she pointed a crooked finger in my face, "After the mercado, watch out those robachicos don't snatch you." Her words shrivel me up. This morning La Guela said I could easily be lost in this city of a million strangers. The streets are danger-ous, teeming with robachicos, boogiemen who snatch children from buses then dig out their eyes, cut off their tongues, and force them to beg in the streets.

Every afternoon La Guela burns scented candles that make me cough while she kneels in the living room before chrome photos of her saints. She is so sinister in her holiness the cackle of her prayers scares me. Sometimes my sister Meche and I have to kneel on the tile floor and pray with her. La Guela says the Devil is the Prince of Darkness and our sins are to blame for everything. At night, my personal demons gather behind closet doors; brujas hide in every darkened corner; Satan himself lurks in the bathroom, ready to pounce on little boys. La Guela, this brittle woman dressed in black, with an eye cloudy as an oyster, an eye that looks at me without seeing, controls me with the power of fear.

On the bus, stiff on La Guela's lap, I close my eyes and pretend I am blind, that my hands are cut off, that I'm missing a leg. I imagine a world without light, a world without my sister's radiant eyes, a world without Mother, her beautiful face that gives meaning to life. I much prefer my sight. I am the pampered son of a future star of Mexican cinema whose glossy studio portraits adorn our house. I don't believe in saints; it's to Mother's photo I pray at night before falling asleep.

As we near the mercado the cries of street vendors offering tomatoes and chilis compete with the shouts of boys running alongside the bus selling newspapers— *"¡Excélsior! ¡El Excélsior!"* The monotonous windows of gray apartment houses, replicated a hundred times, reflect the cloudless sky. We pass a building under construction made entirely of glass and chrome. This is La Capital before the earthquake of 1957, before sanctioned greed picks clean the bones of its citizens, before pollution smothers the Ahuehuete trees in Chapultepec Park, turning them yellow as old tobacco. But on this Saturday, at least for the moment, Mexico City is a magnificent metropolis, the grandest city in the world, the Paris of the '20s, the Madrid of the '30s, the New York of the '40s, all blended together in its cafés and cinemas. It boasts of famous muralists, exotic painters, sensuous poets, legendary screen actors, and the most beautiful dusky women of this century, Dolores del Río, María Félix, Toña La Negra, the poetess Pita Amor, and the fashion model María Asúnsulo, mujeres muy hembras, capricious and arrogant. And also on this list because she is beautiful and berrinchuda—Mother, her light still reaching me, still illuminating the dark roads I travel.

La Guela and I have come across town to La Merced from Calle Niño Perdido. We share a crumbling colonial house with two other families, the Navarros and the Sendenios, and the paper-thin walls cannot hide the disaster of our lives. My parents are divorced, a major scandal in the Mexico of that era. Mother, strong-willed and intelligent, as well as beautiful, comes from New Mexico, the little town of Belén. Her mother—La Guela—lives in mourning, honoring her dead. La Guela birthed three sons, none of whom lived to see twenty. Her favorite and youngest, Severio, was killed in the early days of the war in the Pacific, in Corregidor in 1942. After this last tragedy La Guela flees, with her candles and her prayers, to Mexico City and to other sorrows.

As we reach our stop across from Mercado La Merced, the radio announcer breaks into the music with the news of another horrific accident. A bus has plunged off a curve, dragging a dozen citizens to their doom. The driver digs a brown scapular from under his shirt and kisses it. Last night a comet streaked over the city illuminating the sky with a bright orange tail that dripped fire. Panic-driven crowds rushed to the Basilica and prayed till dawn. Meche says it means the end of the world. And Meche never lies.

* * *

All my childhood memories unwind in black-and-white, as if my life was either light or shadows, without a middle ground. I recall those years like a series of cinematic dissolves and fade-outs, scenes that blend into each other, a montage of close-ups and quick cuts—Mother's perfect face as she lines her mouth with lipstick; Meche, with her big eyes, pretty as a hibiscus, singing rancheras; La Guela's wrinkled face, praying to her saints. I remember Mexico City as if I'm seeing it through an overhead shot from a helicopter: Avenida Reforma is a wide-angle shot, straight and lined with glass and chrome high-rises, the ancient trees arching over the dense traffic. The elegant avenue is intersected with glorietas and statues mounted on pedestals, heroic Cuauhtémoc, Columbus, El Caballito. My favorite is the golden Angel with outstretched wings at the entrance to Chapultepec Park, the glorious symbol of the city. To me, the Angel is the naive hope of my youth, the future we all dreamed would come with golden wings and lead us to paradise. The Mexico City of my childhood is a city of illusions, a city of dreams, where the loteria nacional turns homeless paupers into millionaires overnight. It is a glamorous city, and it fits Mother like a hundred-peso hat. She loves to relax in the mornings in her red robe, sipping her coffee, enjoying the view from our patio of Popo and Ixta, those eternal lovers, stunningly visible on the horizon. For lunch she likes Sanborn's, where she runs into movie stars like Arturo de Cordova and María Félix.

My father is an accountant for Pemex, a step up from his previous job in a shoe factory. He puts in thirteen-and fourteen-hour days trying to keep the books straight, but there's so much graft he is driven to despair. I often overhear him complain to Mother—How am I supposed to balance the Chief's accounts when he doesn't know how much he's stolen this month? Mother shrugs. She is preparing to abandon ship and the fortunes of Petroleos Mexicanos, the national oil company, mean nothing to her.

My sister Mercedes—all I ever call her is Meche—has big luminous eyes, eyes that see farther than other people, that look great on a virgin saint or a martyr. What is my first memory of Meche? She is in a park—La Alameda? Pedestrians are handing her coins because they think she is performing for her supper, but Meche is singing rancheras because she likes to shout, pegar gritos with all her heart. The Catholic school nuns say that Meche is a genius, that she has a remarkable memory able to recall after one reading the entire contents of Hardy's *Life of the Saints*. But Meche doesn't love saints, she loves Chabela Vargas, Lucha Reyes, and Lola Beltrán, and she knows all their sad songs. My parents call her La Divina, a divine angel. Every morning, La Guela plaits Meche's hair in a tight black braid that swings behind her like a rope tying her down to the Mexican earth.

Mother, movies, songs, all jumbled together, create my childhood memories. Meche and I are in the Cine Colonial; the audience is hushed while up on the big screen Pedro Infante sings "Mi nana Pancha." The movie is *Escuela de Vagabundos*, and behind Pedro Infante we can see Mother, who is wearing braids—which she never does at home—and a white blouse that makes her look poor, because she is an extra in this scene and Pedro Infante is playing a jobless vagabond. A beam of pure light projects Mother's face on the screen and the theater grows hushed before her radiant features. When the camera pans in for a close-up of Mother, my eyes fill with tears of joy. It is this image of Mother that is a freeze-frame in my memory. I stare lovingly at her beautiful face, the penciled brows, her fabulous eyes. Mother's face, the size of a movie screen, fades in and out of all my childhood memories, but the edges are always blurred, the image never clearly focused. When I picture Mother, I think of her as pure light, puritita luz. Meche is an angel, the lunar light that peers in through the Venetian blinds, playing on my face when I'm trying to sleep. Sometimes I think those years in Mexico City are really a movie I saw at the Cine Alamo or at the Cine Colonial. I'm confused by the illusion, but accept it as reality.

La Guela and I are going across town that Saturday to take my picture so it can be sent to Mother, who is spending a month in Acapulco. She has gone to the famous resort to film commercials, some of the first for Mexican television. I have seen her appear on the neighbor's TV set. She was holding a bottle of aspirin and saying something like "Nada mas que Cafiaspirina me quita el dolor de cabeza." Then she smiled. Meche and I are ecstatic when we see Mother on television but La Guela purses her lips and says nothing. Mother is an aspiring actress who has appeared in several productions as an extra, *Llevame en Tus Brazos*, with Ninón Sevilla, and the forgettable *Secretaria Peligrosa*, in which she actually has two lines: "Aquí esta su café. ¿No gusta algo mas?"

But she is being groomed to be a future star, already being touted as the next Dolores del Río. Mother is a stunning beauty, her hair smooth as obsidian, her eyes dark pools, big enough for every Mexican male to swim in. These commercials she is filming in Acapulco will open the doors to fame and riches for her, or so she hopes, or so we all hope.

* * *

At La Merced, the photographer places the wide sombrero at a rakish angle, revealing my smooth forehead. He fixes the lights on my round face and I stare at the camera with the sharp intensity of a six-year-old, dressed in his first charro outfit decorated with twisty white braids around the collar and along the arms and down the pant seams. I am mounted on a wooden horse painted with dots to resemble a pinto, but with no pretense at reality since in the photo can be seen quite clearly that the horse is mounted on a stand.

My left hand holds the horse's reins in the proper underhand manner, my right hand grips the handle of a big pistol buckled around the waist, a lariat hangs from the pommel. The edge of the backdrop is decorated with painted geraniums, maguey plants, and organ cactus, and in the center there's the two volcanoes, Popo and Ixta. A flock of swallows flies through the painted sky, above them white chubby clouds and a propeller plane with the markings of the Mexican flag.

An instant before the photographer snaps the picture and the flash fixes me forever on the wooden horse, my right shoelace unravels like a string on a top.

* * *

Mother celebrated her quinceañera in Mexico City with a white dress from El Palacio de Hierro. At the end of World War II she is a nineteen-year-old stenographer in the Department of Public Works. She goes to the movies every Saturday with her friends; they have coffee afterwards on Insurgentes, or go window shopping in La Zona Rosa. Then she meets my father, a galán in a pin-stripe suit with orchids on his tie.

They honeymoon in Vera Cruz and Meche is born the following year. Four years later, while they're on vacation in Hollywood, my father breaks his left leg in a car accident. Mother is eight months pregnant. They decide to stay till my father recuperates. That's why I am born in Hollywood, USA, in a small stucco hotel on Cahuenga Boulevard, a stone's throw from the Hollywood Walk of Fame. I will be the second and last child of this marriage, a native son of California but raised in Mexico, La Capital.

On their return to Mexico City, my father pays someone off and gets hired by Pemex, and their lives settle into the rich monotony of work and occasional nights out, until the afternoon a producer sees Mother having lunch at Sanborn's, in La Casa de Las Azulejas. He is Fernando de Fuentes, chief of production for Diana Films, and he offers Mother a role in a movie; the movie is *Escuela de Vagabundos*, the leading actor is the biggest star in Mexican cinema, Pedro Infante. Her first role lasts barely three minutes, but she is swept up in the glamour and make-believe of the movies. An avalanche of parties and gala dinners follows. My father feels uncomfortable around these Churubusco studio big shots, but he escorts her anyway. They attend the film opening at the Teatro Chapultepec. Later, when Mother talks about that magical evening, she will recall the fountain in the lobby bubbled pink champagne instead of water. I hear these stories from my father when I'm older, but I am too young to remember exactly when the movie premiered.

Her debut in *Escuela de Vagabundos* is followed by minor roles, promises and offers of bigger roles the following year. Fernando de Fuentes is having a script written for her and Mother decides to pursue a movie career, which leads to the big break up. My father admires everything from the United States; Mother strives to be more Mexican than the Mexicans. My father wants a typical middle-class life, but Mother wants everything, and she wants it now. These are the irreconcilable differences that rend them asunder.

When Mother announces her intention to change her name to Amelia Zea, our apartment on Calle Bucareli is the setting for angry scenes. I recall loud music on the radio, followed by lots of arguing and shouting while my father drinks one "jaibol" after the other.

"You're a married woman with two kids. Forget that tontería."

"I want my own life, something more than this."

"This isn't good enough for you? Have it your way. But I won't stick around."

"No one's asking you to."

Then my father packs a suitcase and leaves. For a while, Meche and I have ugly sibling fights because she supports our father, and I—I am in love with Mother. She is a goddess who can do no wrong, and I worship at her altar.

Soon we cannot afford the apartment on Calle Bucareli so we move to Niño Perdido where the rents are cheaper. This is the decaying house Meche calls "the swamp." The tiles are worn to the dirt, mold breeds in every crack, and paint curls away from the walls. La Guela complains about our neighbors she refers to as those "pelados." But through all this Mother dresses elegantly, wears white gloves and little hats with black veils like a model that just stepped out of a photograph.

We have no phone so Mother takes her calls at the corner pharmacy, and Dr. Martínez sends a boy to tell her when she's wanted. She is struggling to find work as an actress and seems to be always waiting for an important call. In the meantime she paints her nails, applying each stroke of the tiny brush with the precision of a surgeon. Or she sits before her vanity, trying on make-up, and lets me watch. I love it when she brings out her make-up, her nail polish, her blush, the mascara, the combs, the cut-glass atomizer, and goes through the ritual painting, spraying, and trying on different looks, different hair styles, five different shades of lipstick. It's like a game for me, watching her become all the different women she is. "What do you think of this color, amorcito? Do you think it makes me look too dark?"

I think she looks beautiful in every shade of red. She keeps the radio tuned to XEW and she adores the songs of María Luisa Landín, especially "Amor Perdido," which is all the current rage. At the end of this ritual that lasts for hours, Mother is gloriously transformed into Amelia Zea, future star of movies and television. Some days I haven't eaten a bite, but what do I care? Hunger only sharpens my senses to her beauty.

* * *

La Capital is a city of extremes. On Avenida de la Reforma I admire long sleek automobiles driven by chauffeurs in uniform. Through television and the movies I glimpse the lazy luxury of the rich. But I am overcome by a strange sadness the first time I see a trajinero, one of those desperate men who strap chairs to their backs and carry old people or invalids for a peso. We are saved from the stench of the open sewers outside the zaguán by the almond trees that bloom in the courtyard, drifting their fragrance into our house.

My refuge is the gnarled almond tree outside our door, where propped on its branches I snap pebbles at birds with my slingshot. My other toy is a yellow top with red stripes. I can make the top dance between my fingers, into my palm, where it spins happily; the lead point doesn't hurt but tickles like one of Meche's kisses.

On Fridays the man who sharpens knives comes around blowing a reed flute; the vegetable seller turns the corner in his red and yellow wagon; the camote seller hisses his presence with a steam whistle and a raspy voice that shouts, "¡C-a-a-a-a-m-o-o-tes! Tres por un peso!" The candy man Cayetano sets up his woodenbox of amber cone pirules and golosinas outside the iron-grilled door. The palomilla of chavalos who play in the courtyard is made up of Ñengo, whose eyes drip yellow tears, and his brother Chucho, who stutters. My best friend is La Liebre, who owns a thousand freckles, he is my mero nero. He is eight and doesn't know how to read, but he can count to a hundred.

Ñengo is our leader, stocky and tough as a pit bull. He brings us *Vodevil*, the macho magazine with drawings by Vargas and sepia photos of Tongolele, the striptease dancer, in garters and high heels. He's also good at stealing a handful of sweets as he runs by Cayetano, slivers of candied papaya, or squares of red and white coconut he shares with us behind the lavanderias where the women wash clothes. Cayetano's beard is linty and stained with coffee. His coat is covered with different colored patches. Sometimes he gives La Liebre and me a free candy, but then he tries to pinch our crotch, and says he wants *our* pírul. So we make fun of him and his straw hat.

One day La Liebre takes me to his house in another colonia. We walk for blocks then ride a bus then walk some more. The city is so huge that we wander the labyrinth streets by instinct and sense of touch. He leads me to an alley, smelly with urine. In the dark flooded passageway I hear rats grinding their teeth as they scurry around our shoes. La Liebre lives behind a yellow door, in an unlit, ominous hovel. The walls are made of cardboard nailed over wooden frames. He sleeps behind a dirty blanket hung on a string; his bed is a petate, a straw mat he shares with two brothers and a sister. The place feels abandoned, like no one has lived here in a hundred years. La Liebre discovers a cigarette butt in a pile of trash and we sit on the dirt floor while he takes a few puffs. He tells me about sex but I don't believe him. So he drops his pants and shows me his paloma, then makes it grow with his hand. It's something I know nothing about. He laughs. "You'll see your father screwing your mother one day," he says.

The words are barely out of his mouth when I shove him to the ground. He tries to get up but I shove him down again. I stand over him angry as a fire ant. "Take it back buey." He smiles with rotten teeth, his pinga still hanging out of his pants. "Don't be a cabrón," he says, and offers me the butt. I try his smoke. *¡Tos!* *¡Tos!* My head spins like the silver-winged horse in the merry-go-round of Chapultepec Park and Mother's face appears surrounded by kleig lights. I refuse to think of Mother as anything but a pure and perfect angel.

* * *

I much prefer the streets where I am free of La Guela's tyranny. Somehow my cuates, Ñengo, Chucho, La Liebre, and I escape drowning in the nearby river when we go swimming; somehow, we are not crushed by buses or the religious fears propping up heaven. At night, la palomilla comes to our apartment, and Meche adjusts the Bakelite knobs of our Phillips radio to "Cuentos de Misterio," and we stretch out on the floor, losing ourselves in the stories of Edgar Allan Poe, or we share the latest Jorge G. Cruz photonovelas of El Santo, the masked wrestler who is our idol. Of this palomilla I have forgotten their real names if I ever knew them. We will mature like in speeded-up film, we will become young men within the coming year. These memories blend into each other without set frames; in one I'm a six-year-old boy listening to the radio, the next minute I'm that same boy in an abandoned shack smoking cigarettes. The approaching months will tear our childhood from us, will maim and deform us, will leave us dazed and stunned.

* * *

As Mother becomes ever more busy with her career, La Guela takes over the task of raising me. She demands devotion to her saints, but her endless praying bores me. When I'm forced to kneel with her, I mix up the prayers so she becomes confused—Our Mother who art in heaven. . . . I don't need to cross the ocean to see fanatics. Every Sunday morning La Guela wraps a black rebozo over her head and follows the crowds to the Tepeyac where devotees of La Virgen de Guadalupe cross the stone plaza on their knees, leaving bloody trails on the lava bricks. I see women faint before the Virgen's candle-lit altar, grown men wipe tears from their mustaches. On Ash Wednesday I make a giant scene when the priest tries to mark my forehead with ashes. I scream and squirm till La Guela drags me out of church, angry as the devil, but I wipe the ash cross off my forehead, anyway.

La Guela says I am born in Los Unai. I am from the other side. "You're a Pocho," she says. "You aren't Mexican at all." I want to know what she means. But she loses herself in mumbled prayers and I forget what she has said. By now I believe she is completely crazy.

In counterpoint to La Guela, Mother allows me everything, even keeps me home from school. I'm a precocious boy, teaching myself to read at the age of four. Mother thinks this is charming and has me read to her friends, budding starlets who smile when I read aloud the society pages of *El Excélsior*. These young actresses are impeccably dressed, stylish women, their heads filled with stars, their bosoms with perfume, they plant kisses on my forehead that leave me spinning.

* * *

I am first conscious of desire one afternoon when Mother returns from the salon in Polanco where she has her hair done. She is stunningly beautiful that day, all manicured and perfumed, her hair in short curls; I am in awe of her. She stands at our door and says to me, "I told my hairdresser I couldn't pay him till next week. And you know what he said amorcito? 'Never mind. It's my pleasure.'"

Even then I know she has irresistible charm, a face to launch her to fame and stardom. She removes her high heels and curls up on the chenille bedspread for a nap. She is wearing a dark silk dress that clings to her hips, revealing her shapely legs the color of cognac. I watch her sleeping. I'm fascinated by the curve of her hips, the sheen of her nylons, her breasts rising and falling, her face in repose. A powerful and painful emotion strikes me: I am in love with Mother, and I will kill any man who hurts her. I'm sure of this—I want this slumbering angel to myself. At the same time I'm confused by my desire, I don't know what it means. I don't have the words to explain what I feel. How can I be worthy of an angel?

* * *

Months after we have moved to Calle Niño Perdido, my father appears one night and takes me to a boxing match at La Plaza de Toros. Eighty thousand screaming Mexicans are rooting for Ratón Macias. The cigar smoke and the heat make me nauseated. My father has to carry me outside, where he listens to the fight on the loud speakers. Then we go to Insurgentes and in the middle of the celebrating mobs, my father jumps on a car hood and, waving his hat, he shouts till he's hoarse, "¡Viva México! ¡Viva México!" It's the one and only time he is proud of being Mexican. Another time he takes Meche to the circus in Puebla and I have a tantrum only Mother can comfort. She holds me in her arms after my father leaves, and coddles me—her precioso. My face is covered with tears and her perfume, and I want to be forever sheltered in her arms.

Later that night, she has me help her get dressed. She keeps her silky underthings in drawers scented with dried gardenias. I unfold the nylon stockings she will roll over her beautiful legs, and I see how she snaps them in place with garters. I am the one who stands on a chair and zips her up. "Amorcito, you understand I have to go out don't you? I need to meet those big-shot producers. That's the only way a girl will get those good roles. And those are the only ones that count, precioso." Then she leaves with her actress friends and I'm alone with La Guela.

Once Mother goes out for the night, La Guela starts in. Her voice, shrill and bitter, hints of scandal and the fires of damnation. "What is this world coming to? Who can believe the way those women dress, if I didn't know better I'd say they were rameras, prostitutes. God will punish them because He sees everything we do."

I don't listen to La Guela; instead I stare at Mother's studio portrait on the wall, more beatific than Father Pio's. I fall asleep past midnight, curled asleep on the floor, waiting for Mother to come home. Mother doesn't appear till the next morning, by then La Guela's rage has simmered down to a smouldering ember. But I am so grateful when Mother returns that I rush to hug her and smother her face and hands with kisses.

Then a tall, handsome man with a mustache appears to comfort Mother. They spend many afternoons riding around the city in his white Chrysler convertible that is the talk of the colonia. She tells me they are just friends. "He's married," she confides, "but that doesn't make him a devil, does it amorcito?"

Mother has two great loves, the movies—and window-shopping. She spends hours in front of display windows admiring furniture; sometimes I think the nickel-plated living room set in the front window of Salinas y Rocha is ours. After one of these all day excursions with Mother and La Guela, we wind up in the palm-filled lobby of the Hotel Reforma, where the man with the mustache is waiting. I am not allowed in the heavily chromed Chrysler. Mother drives off with the handsome man leaving me with La Guela.

* * *

The photo of me on the wooden horse will be mailed to Mother in Acapulco. She will carry the photo in her suitcase along with her perfume—Schiaparelli's "Shocking" is her favorite—her silk stockings, her make-up, her beautiful dresses, a book of poems by Pita Amor, the script that has been written for her, "Las Mil Y Una Noches," a role that will later go to María Antonieta Pons, and a scarf in which she has wrapped a dried gardenia. Her boyfriend at the time—she has dumped the idol and is now seeing Alvaro Baena, a cinematographer—will pack her suitcase in the trunk of the pearl white 1954 MG convertible they will drive back to Mexico City. She will be madly in love with Alvaro when they leave Acapulco. It will be the last day she will be in love.

Amelia Zea, destined to be a star of Mexican cinema, will drive the sports car for the first hour; when the hairpin curves of the highway make her dizzy, they stop in front of a roadside restaurant. Alvaro buys her a 7-Up and takes over the driving. She will be sitting in the passenger seat, trailing a ribbon of smoke from a Casinos cigarette, her favorite brand. She'll have her long hair tied back with a silk scarf, a gift from an admirer. Her head will be filled with memories of Acapulco, the Hotel Guacamaya, drinking highballs at poolside, and whatever other fun she might have experienced with Alvaro. Perhaps her thoughts will touch on my father, or on one of her other lovers, perhaps they will touch on Meche or even on me. When she gets tired she rests her head on Alvaro's shoulder as he drives, so she will not see the truck that passes them on the left, that cuts too sharply in front of them and shakes her awake with the frightening sound of brakes screeching. The sudden bone-crushing force throws her forward into the windshield as the sports car collides with the cement-loaded truck and Alvaro is hurled from the vehicle to an instant and merciful death, while Mother is left broken in the crumpled interior of the MG.

When my father is notified of the accident, nearly twelve hours later, he rushes from his office in the Pemex building and hurries to her bedside in the hospital at

Taxco. She has suffered multiple injuries, internal hemorrhaging, cuts and abrasions on her face, but worst is the broken vertebra that leaves her paralyzed. She cannot move from the neck down, only her eyes hold any spark of life.

My father arranges for an ambulance to take her to the Hospital Inglés in Mexico City, and he rides with her, keeping watch over her now fragile beauty. Before he leaves Taxco, he goes to the site of the accident.

The MG is a twisted mess of steel pushed to the side of the road; the suitcases, her clothes and jewelery are all gone. He gathers from the roadside whatever belongings have not been scavenged and brings back pages of the script, the book of poems with the cover smudged with grease and dirt, and the photo of me on the wooden horse, crimped at one corner, as if someone had considered, then decided against taking it.

The next two days mother goes in and out of consciousness, in and out of deliriums in which she hallucinates herself as a young girl in the fields of Belén playing with her brothers. My father takes a twenty-four hour vigil at her bedside, sleeping on a cot, calling all over the country till he finally locates a specialist in Guadalajara, who agrees to come see her. Meche and I visit on the second day, and mother does not recognize us. Her face is purple with bruises; only her eyes, those dark stars, reveal the woman she is. I kiss her bruised forehead. When I leave my vision is blurry. I will never see her again. Before the specialist can arrive, she dies at three in the morning, my father at her side.

It rains on the day of Mother's funeral. Before we leave for the crematorium, Meche takes scissors to her braid and snip, snip, separates herself from her childhood. Amelia Zea's friends, the hopeful starlets all show up. Fernando de Fuentes, who discovered Mother in Sanborn's, says a few words. Delia Magaña, the first of their group to make it big, hires a ten-piece orchestra to play in the lobby of the crematorium, "Amor Perdido." There is no priest, no prayers, no absolution. Her ashes are sent to my father, La Guela will not have them.

Afterwards, they all come to our house and the grim Guela serves coffee. Mother's friends tell stories about her, they nibble on pan dulce, wipe the powdered sugar from their lips, and cry big trembling sobs into their scented hankies. They bid farewell to Amelia Zea in the name of the close-up, the wide-angle shot, and the Cinemascope.

* * *

After Mother's funeral the house in Niño Perdido turns into a bedlam of prayers and evil brujas that curse my life with La Guela. Darkness terrifies me. At night La Llorona hides in closets and I dream of buildings burning, with charred skulls and hands raining down on me. I spend most of my days with La Liebre. If before, La Guela instilled in me fear for the smoke-belching buses, now I ride the back bumpers, hopping on as they stop for lights on Pino Suarez. I turn insolent with La Guela; I curse her and stay out late, often coming home at midnight, sometimes later. I become a six-year-old impossible to control, angry at the world.

La Liebre is a street-wise kid, he hangs with the teporochos, steals from the mercaderas, and shows me how to smoke grifa. We twist the brown grifa into pitos with strips of *El Excélsior* and sneak into the Teatro Alamo to see movies of Tin Tan, or Resortes. From the mambo-dancing, caló-rapping zoot-suiter Tin Tan, I learn my first words of English—"oqaí," "guan momen," "whassamarer," "shaddup." When we don't have grifa we smoke cigarette butts scavenged from the gutters. Or I steal copper coins from blind newsellers, or La Liebre steals pesos from the candy man, and we drift off, smoking grifa and sipping coffee around trash-can fires, laughing at the billboard neon fireworks that light up the Mexico City nights. This is my age of childhood in a city that no longer exists. This is the world I travel sightless, aimless as a beggar, without hope or redemption, chingas o te chíngan.

Then La Liebre disappears without a trace, vanishes into the maze of the city; with Cayetano the candy man. I'm left to wander the streets alone. I come home only when I'm exhausted. If Meche is feeling better, there's merienda waiting for me, a snack of hot chocolate and pan dulce. Sometimes only a glass of milk. Sometimes nothing. La Guela no longer calls me Mundo, but my full name, Reymundo, as if I'm now grownup and must leave behind my childhood name.

Months go by. I'm now seven. I'm in Plaza Garibaldi waiting for a drunk to fall asleep on a bench so I can go through his pockets when a voice calls me over.

—Órale cuatacho.

I barely recognize La Liebre. He's covered with dirt from sleeping on the streets, or in worse places. He says he couldn't take it with the candy man anymore. I don't ask what it is he couldn't take—but La Liebre tells me what Cayetano did, and I cannot look my best friend in the eye. When he's finished, it's like he's someone I don't know anymore. We're like two kids on a sinking boat doomed to watch each other drown. So we hatch a plan to run away, maybe to Vera Cruz, or Merida, anywhere to get away from this nightmare.

I tell him, "Meet at my house in the morning, early, I'll take some pesos from La Guela, y nos largamos a la chíngada."

I cannot sleep all night. As soon as my lids close, devils appear with eyes like candles. Way before daybreak I crawl out of bed and sneak into La Guela's room. The creaking floorboards sound loud as thunder. She keeps her money in a coffee can hidden behind a statue of La Virgen. I reach in without disturbing her and withdraw a fistful of pesos. Then I look one last time at Meche, who is sleeping off some medication, and place a tender kiss on her forehead. The courtyard is empty, icy. A rooster-colored moon hangs over me as I make my way through the shadows to the zaguán where La Liebre is waiting for me. The silence is so heavy the city appears dead.

I cross the courtyard but I stall at the entrance of the zaguán. Something holds me back. I call for La Liebre, call again. I see someone or something moving in the shadows. Then out of the darkness Cayetano's bearded face appears. I suffocate when he puts his arm around my shoulder. His hand tightens around my neck, "I've been waiting for you," he says. His fingers smell of ether. I can't breathe; all I can do is whisper, "Don't hurt me." I can't tell if this is a dream, but just in case, I suddenly wail like a siren. At that same instant the earth starts trembling, the walls sway, a rumble rises from the bowels of the earth that rattles every bone in me. As I break free of Cayetano's grip and leap back into the courtyard, the zaguán crumbles with a terrific roar and an explosion of dust. I see our house swaying, then the apartment building next door collapses like a house of cards, and a powerful blast shakes the courtyard with such force that it knocks me down. A hundred screams splinter the night. I hear babies wailing. More screams, countless sirens, the world is coming to an end.

I wake up in the courtyard with La Guela and Meche hugging me, their faces wet with tears of terror. It's the morning of July 28, 1957. Smoke blots out the pale morning sun, the survivors gathered in the courtyard are delirious with total panic. Señora Senderuo, still in her robe, is stumbling around all dazed. One wall of our house is missing. Sirens pierce the sky. A powerful earthquake has destroyed the city. The golden Angel on La Reforma has fallen and lies shattered in pieces as if it were not made of bronze but of plaster. "Ay, Dios mío, dios mío, what will we do," La Guela screams. The city is without electricity or water. The ten-foot wall around our house is dust. Where the zaguán once stood there's a pyramid of bricks, rubble, and twisted rebars. Meche says I was sleepwalking; that's why they found me knocked out in the courtyard. La Guela thanks La Virgen for my safety. I don't say a word when the Green Cross medics come by asking about survivors trapped in the ruins.

The weeks that follow are a blur. The skyscrapers on La Reforma are abandoned, skeletal. A four-story retail store has collapsed like a limp balloon. Four blocks away, the ultra-modern pharmaceutical building is a mountain of broken glass. Everywhere the bones of the city are showing like some newly unearthed pre-Columbian ruins. The house where we lived is condemned and we move to my cousin Arturo's house in San Angel. Heavy rains follow the earthquake as if even the Virgen of Guadalupe had abandoned her children. In the outskirts of the city those without homes are drowned or washed away by the rampaging waters. In the Zócalo, furniture, sofas and TVs float out the doors of houses. After the rains, a hurricane wind rips tiles from roofs and knocks down trees in La Alameda. We hear rumors about plagues, thousands dead, whole colonias gone, and entire towns buried in the countryside. Frightened crowds mob the Tepeyac to pray for deliverance. But there is no deliverance, nowhere to hide.

Everyday La Guela tells us our father is going to take us to Los Unai, that he will save us. But at night we huddle in the park of San Angel and sleep beneath ominous stars that seem to mock our fate.

Several months after the earthquake, our plane tickets finally arrive. La Guela, who is coming with us, hires a taxi to the airport—Meche is dressed in white and I'm in a dark suit with tie, and black polished shoes. When we arrive at the airport, a huge four-prop plane modern as the country we are going to is revving its motors on the tarmac. Soon the line of people starts boarding the TWA plane and La Guela grabs Meche by the elbow and I take her hand and together we go up the metal staircase, into the whirlwind of the engines that suck us into another vortex. I am happy, we are leaving the ruins of the city of dreams.

I will not see Mexico City again till I am nineteen. By then the city will be a congested pit of decay and corruption, its wide avenues lined with human debris and portraits of El Presidente on every telephone pole and tree. I return just before the 1968 Olympics, when the army unleashed its fury against the students in Tlatelolco. I saw what was done and the lies to cover it up. But that's not the Mexico City that I knew, the city of my childhood.

A long time ago I promised myself there was no point in looking back. I never saw La Liebre again or heard what ever became of him. Ñengo and Chucho disappeared into the streets like phantoms. Years later I came across a photo in *Alarma!* of two brothers arrested for car theft, and I thought that it could be them. I have never been back to Niño Perdido. But sometimes I can't help but return to Mexico City in my memory, dig around in those ruins of my childhood for an overlooked scene that will explain who I am. When I sit at my desk and look at the photo of myself as a boy on a wooden horse, it reminds me of where I come from, and that fate unravels faster than a shoelace on a six-year-old's shoe. And with those memories burning vivid as the afternoon sun on the Victorian rooftops, I pick up a pencil and begin to write.

The end of August, 1956. A Saturday in Mexico City.

TALES LEFT UNTOLD

Aphrodite Désirée Navab

To my beloved, Richard Jochum

PROLOGUE

To tell a tale is all that's left, to those forbidden passage home. It's in the telling not the tale, that the untold pieces get re-sewn. To pick them up, one by one, and then throw them in the air. Is this storyteller's mad hope that one piece will make it there.

TALE #1

These are the bags I bring with me, suitcases burdened with memory. I'll put them down and open them. To let them breathe before they speak. To tell a tale that needs to be. To travel with these bags and me. Back in time, watching signs, marking, mapping who I am.

I am Iranian, Greek, American. Not just one, but all of them. How I've tried for consistency, to be one of them, complete. Just one of them, please. Just to make things neat. How I've tried all my life to be, no messy ambiguity, no ambivalent loyalty—to be one whole, one identity.

The flag of each nation, in me, stirs little sensation. No nationalism shouts loud in me. Even after living in all three. To see one flag burned in the other country; there's no going back for me. My people held my other people hostage. The weight of this I carry in my luggage. A criminal in reverse, hypocritical, perverse; over a blaming finger becomes a hollow gesture pointing at them, yet right back at me. Because them is me. I am all three, both the beauty and the blood they've shed, all three.

TALE #2

It is not fear of planes I feel. A different crash takes place in me. I thought that time would pass. And so would too, the suspicious eyes that sort me through. "How did you become American?" the interrogation begins. The airport official's eyes questioning me up and down. First, at me and then, at it. In my passport, in black ink, disclosing where it is I'm from: born in Esfahan, Iran.

Passport, all-American outside but a potential terrorist inside. Permitting them to terrorize me. Picking points to punish me.

I was fifteen with a group of girls on a trip from the U.S. to Canada. Please don't give me trouble in front of them all. Don't single me out away from them all. Don't hold me long. Remember that age? You want to belong. Don't stop me, search me, steal me. Why do the others all prance through? When my passport is just as blue? Official eagle, stamped and scaled, so much prejudice revealed.

"How did you become American?"

I sweat, I sweat, again that dread I've done nothing but what's in his head. "My mother is American. My father, sister, brothers, me, we were all born in Iran, see. That is it. That is why."

"No that's not right," he said. "Not at all. That's not right. Try again."

Here he makes me go again. "My mother is American. By birth she is, but I am not. By birth I am Iranian."

"That's not right," he said. "Not at all. You've got it wrong. Try again."

I sweat, I sweat, again that dread. I've done nothing but what's in his head. "I've told you all it is I know. That's all. I'm hiding nothing. Let me go. Check my body. Check my bags. Check my soul, just end this show."

Don't sneak around me here and there. Don't twist and turn me while they stare. I know where it is I'm from, and I can see where it is I've come.

"The correct answer," anger rising in his voice, impatient at my persistence, "You are American by your own birth, not your mother's or anyone else's. This is the only answer that's correct."

He stamped my passport, he let me go. Humiliated like this, I was never before.

Tale #3

"You have a nice tan."

But I was born with this skin.

"You have a nice tan."

But this is my own, my palest skin. No sun it's seen in seven months. No soap can wash this color off.

"They call this olive skin."

They do? I eat olives, yes I do. Like candy, it is true I do. Does that make me an olive too? I am not greasy. I am not green.

"Greasy hair and greasy skin."

Everyday I wash my skin. Everyday I wash my hair. Sometimes twice within one day, just to make it go away.

"They also call this sallow skin."

Sallow, shiny, greasy, green. Yellow, oily, dirty, mean. I scrub my forehead dry, inside. I rub it again and again, outside. I look both ways, though, before I do. You never know whom you'll run into. I cautiously raise the back of my hand, carefully gesturing with my hand. Pretending to be wiping sweat. Pretending the oily skin was wet.

A dot, a spot, a speck on the wall, anything not to stand out at all. Twenty years I've dealt with this. Twenty years I've rubbed it raw. Oily, olive, oily, skin oozing oil that burns within. I am not black. I am not white. And never, ever am I green. I am an unremarkable gray in between.

TALE #4

My tongue is twisted. My tongue is tied. My tongue is torn with all the lies. Each time I turn it this way and that, an unfamiliar sound spins its way out. One half screams for the other to come. The other half stands there completely numb. One half knows not what the other half speaks. One half scorns what the other half seeks.

My tongue, it trips me, leading me there. Trapping me in the storyteller's snare. One half leaves while the other half stays. One half sees what the other betrays. One half gestures in meaningless motions. The other half squints to make sense of these notions. But all she sees is spit in the air, from that storyteller standing ridiculous, there.

TALE #5

I am not a Persian carpet. You may not wipe your feet on me. You may not rest or lie on me. You may not sip your tea on me; with a cube of sugar between gold-teeth, hiding what is rotten, beneath.

I am not a Persian carpet. You may not do your prayers on me. You may not trade me, wheel or deal me. No embargoes can be placed on me. No children weave eyes blind for me. My value does not increase with age. No pattern can contain this rage. Rubbing your greedy hands. Imagining how to fill your land. Measuring with an abacus in hand. No sticks can beat the dust from me. No streams can wipe the stains from me. No sun can make my dampness clean.

I am not a Persian carpet. But for you that is all in Iran you see: an Oriental commodity, a decorative oddity, an object for your pleasure, at your leisure, never, ever, will I let you, make me.

TALE #6

At times I need to go away, deep within my memory. And travel to the land I've lost, my childhood there, completely. I cannot see. We cannot touch. We haven't talked in twenty years.

Across the sky, the night is hung. I toss, I turn. No longer dreaming in my native tongue. A stranger to my homeland, even if you should take my hand. Even if we should exchange sand, strangers we will be. The home you were, you are not now. The child I was I put away inside, all these years and years outside.

And with which tongue can I tell her tale? Of a revolution which came and went, tearing up her home. Forbidding passage to her father, sequestering him alone. That from her airplane window, she watched him, until she could see no more.

I pull these images out. Wrapping them around. Getting lost and then found. Defying time who's tapping his foot, waiting and wanting, me to forget.

TALE #7

There will always be time, to wonder why and where. There will always be time, to imagine ways of going there. There will never be a way, to make up time not spent together before death. There will never be a way to make up not seeing, not touching, not loving your parents before, during and after their death.

Because you could not mourn their death, Baba, I will mourn for you. Because you chose life for us, Baba, I choose this too for you. Because your exile has been death, Baba, I will travel there for you. I will kiss their eyes for you. I will beat my chest for you. I will tear my hair for you.

Walking in the funeral procession, that none of us did see. Singing songs of dispossession, that no one there did hear. An ululation, a lamentation, a scream released from its frustration, to do the things denied to you. Baba, this space here, I've made for you.

I've let it grow, to sweep the floors. My hair collects the exiled days.

It was through his back, I saw him crack. It was from behind, I saw him break. First stone, his father's death. Second stone, his mother's. Third stone, forbidden to honor them, trying to topple him, until I stepped in then.

I've let it grow, to sweep the floors. My hair wraps itself around the stones.

His silent suffering, not shown, not shared. He stood there staring out the window, at an Iran that was not there. He stood there, trembling out that window. This kind of grief I could not bear.

A silent shiver went down his spine—an aching, unaware, seen from behind.

I've let it grow, to sweep the floors. My hair hides eyes, too hurt to stare.

There will always be time, to wonder why and where. There will always be time, to imagine ways of going there. There will never be a way, to forget the aching of an exiled man. There will never be a way, to justify why for you, your father is that man.

An ululation, a lamentation, a scream released from its frustration, to do the things denied to you. Baba, this space here, is all I can do.

EPILOGUE

To tell a tale, when there's nothing more, is when meaning itself has shut its door. It is then that the uninvited guest comes in, breathing life into the rest. It is then that the untold tales begin, resurrecting that old quest.

GUILT PAYMENT

Ty Pak

"If I'd had the right teacher, I wouldn't have failed in the Western Regionals," says Mira bitterly.

"But you've won the Hawaii audition," I point out. "Look how many competitors you had to put behind to get that far. John Singleton's daughter, Mary, who everybody said had a heavenly voice, placed only third. You hold the crown here."

"I'm no tractable Polynesian lass to be content with an island title. I want to go all the way to the top. I want to sing at the Metropolitan. I want to show the whole world what a Korean-American girl can do."

"There is always next year, and besides you have to learn to be content . . ."

"With a thousand-dollar cash prize? And end up salesgirling or teaching a bunch of tone-deaf kids, occasionally singing on the side at churches and ceremonies for a pittance? I don't want any part of it. I must go to Florence and study under Maestro Vincenti."

"Isn't Florence where he comes from, that Italian snob hanging around you all the time, Peter, Petro, or whatever his blasted name is?"

"Piero. I haven't seen a man with a worse memory for names. I really don't see how you could have become a professor of English, which presumably takes a lot of memorizing. Well, after all, it's only the University of Hawaii you are a professor at."

"Young lady, we are discussing this Piero fellow and your fantastic scheme of going to his native town at a great cost for no purpose at all . . ."

"What've you got against him? Anyway, Piero has nothing to do with it. It's just a coincidence that the world-renowned maestro happens to reside now at the place where Piero was born."

"Where his parents and relatives live, no doubt."

"Will you or will you not make this little sacrifice? When I get the big roles, the money you are investing now will seem like nothing. I will pay you back every cent with interest. I simply have to go to Italy."

"But what have the Italians got that this great country of ours hasn't? Go back to Juilliard and take graduate courses or private lessons from Professor Bertram whom you used to think so highly of."

"He is old fashioned. Passe. Played out. He is old. Period. I have to breathe fresh air, learn new styles and techniques, receive new inspirations, get out of this old country."

"Since when has the U.S. become an old country?"

"Father, I respect your knowledge of English, but you know very little about musicianship, especially operatic singing and the training and discipline that go with it."

Haven't I paid full tuition for all her special lessons ever since she was three? But of course I hold my tongue.

"Trust my judgment, father. If it was avoidable, I wouldn't ask. This is the only way. I know Mother would see it my way if she were alive."

That vanquishes me for good. Oh, the burden of remorse and self-recrimination! It was quite by accident that Mira came by this infallible formula for neutralizing my resistance. She was about seven and wanted to go to a carnival at the other end of the island. She had been to a dozen already, and they were of course all such dreadful bores to me. Besides, I had an important paper to finish for a journal. I couldn't spare the time. Pettishly she remarked that her friend Joyce's mother was taking her children, adding that if she had a mother like everybody else, she would not be left at the mercy of a selfish father who did nothing for others and just read and read all day long. Life was no fun at this house of ours, she said. Her mother, whom she had never known, would see it her way, she was sure.

Silently, like a sleep-walker, I drove her 50 miles to the Haleiwa Beach Park carnival grounds. I had been her slave ever since. Not that she was reckless in the exercise of her power. Like a discerning monarch she let me, her subject, enjoy a degree of independence—even an illusion of sovereignty—in small things, but when it came to things that really mattered, matters of money and time, out came the mighty club to beat me flat. She must wonder at the efficacy of this weapon, for invariably she asked me, a smile twinkling in her eyes, what wicked thing I had done to her mother. But she never really gave me a chance to tell her, as she bolted away humming or singing merrily over the fresh reaffirmation of her supremacy. After all, when you have it good, why jinx it by looking into the whence and wherefore? But would I have told her if she really wanted to know? Not in a million years.

* * *

We had been married only eight months, Yoomi and I, when the war broke out, on Sunday, June 25, 1950. On Monday I went to the university as usual. We were to carry on our business as usual, Syngman Rhee told us over and over on the radio. The whole affair was nothing but a border skirmish, for which the provokers, rash North Korean communists, would be soundly thrashed by the South Korean army, backed by the U.S. with its atom bombs. The spring semester was winding to a close, and the finals were not too far off. The monsoon had started early and it rained dismally, incessantly. Neither the faculty nor the students could keep their minds on their books. I called on my class to translate some passages from Hardy but could not get their attention. When I called a student's name, he would look briefly at me with indifference, then turn away to resume his talk with his friends. There was no point in dragging on. When I came out of the classroom, I noticed the same restiveness had possessed all the other classes: students had poured out into the school yard, milling around like lost ants. The general assembly bell rang and the dean mounted the rostrum. The school was to go into recess indefinitely until further notice. I left for home, wondering whether the indefiniteness included the end of the month, pay day.

Hayhwa Avenue was filled with trucks of khaki-clad troops in netted helmets heading north up Miyari Pass. There was an intermittent distant boom like suppressed thunder, which got louder and more insistent by the minute. At night-fall cannon shells whirred overhead, freezing the blood. Shrapnel tore the rain-drenched, blacked-out air. Machine guns and rifles rattled. Grenades exploded. The terror-stricken populace, caught in the crossfire, ran blindly for shelter, getting maimed and mauled in the process. They had to get away, to run, no matter where. The artillery shells seemed to be aimed directly at their homes, the places they had known so long and well, and they sought refuge by running right into the hills where the shells pelted like hailstones. The next morning the sky opened and the indifferent sun shone, disclaiming all responsibility for the nightmare of the previous night. Russian tanks were already in town. Rhee had fled south after destroying the Han bridge, making sure that nobody, neither the invading army nor his trusting people, followed him.

A wave of mass arrests swept through the city. All those who had managed to make a decent living were counter-revolutionaries, enemies of the people. Their houses, their jobs were proof enough of their treachery. The dregs of society rose to the top and banded themselves into Youth Leagues, Women's Leagues, People's Leagues. Armed with fixed bayonets, the gift of the victors, these upstart self-decreed legislators and justices, flaunting their red headbands and armbands of authority, ferreted out the enemies of the people who had committed the colossal crime of supporting their families with all the diligence their training and aptitude afforded. The Soosong Elementary School, packed full to bursting with such undesirables, was posted with armed guards. Other public places also served as collection and detention points. A percentage of the prisoners were taken out at regular intervals and shot at public squares, where their bodies were left to be spat on and kicked at, to rot for days. First to go were all government employees, however lowly: office clerks, guards, even custodians. But top priority was given to the so-called power sectors, policemen, tax officials, and soldiers. There was a whole division of Rhee's soldiers, stragglers and wounded, who hadn't gotten away before the bridge fell.

I went into hiding and managed to elude the first searches. We had just moved to the house a few months before, and nobody in the neighborhood knew about my teaching position at the university. But they caught on soon enough, and Yoomi, nearing her time and anemic from malnutrition, had to go to the district office to account with browbeatings and threats for my absence. With the intensi-fying American air raids, which did not distinguish between military and civilian targets, it wasn't too uncommon to be reported missing, unless there were witnesses to the contrary. There was no food in the house, and Yoomi had to drag her heavy body laden with clothes, utensils, and other valuables for barter at the nearest open market, until we had nothing left. Even the bedding was gone, and we shivered at night.

The only news we had of the war was what the communists gave out. The fall of the Pusan perimeter was imminent, the last holdout of the American running dogs. They would he driven into the sea to drown, and the fatherland would at last be one. As the days lengthened into weeks, I wondered whether there was any point in my continued hiding, which meant overworking Yoomi to death. I con-templated seriously giving myself up, but Yoomi wouldn't have it. Sangjo Kim, the historian, Wongyong Chay, the criminologist, and all those we knew had been coralled and marched away God knew where.

One day after carrying home a sack of barley for the last of my winter clothing, she collapsed at the gate. Since I could not go out and help lest the neighbors should see, she crawled on all fours, undid the latch, and came into the house. Her labor had started. The placenta had burst. It was our first birth, but I had heard that this was an emergency. Her life was at stake, but when I made ready to run for the midwife who resided in the neighborhood, Yoomi clutched my ankles with an unbreakable grip. She would not let me go. I watched helplessly, biting my lip as the pangs tortured and twisted her. Mira was eventually born. Yoomi, delirious with fever, lay unconscious for days. I hated the bawling lump of flesh, the cause of the impending death of my beloved.

I made barley broth and fed it to the baby, but she rejected the food after a few sips. She raised hell, her face turning red and blotchy. In spite of her delirium Yoomi heard the child, hugged it close and fumbled about her breast. I offered no assistance; either the baby had to survive on barley broth or perish. It would not further endanger its mother's health by leeching. With an uncanny homing instinct the little brute deftly sought out the teats. Then, gathering her lips into a snout, she cupped them over one with a flopping sound and sucked away voraciously, draining her mother's life blood. She sucked and sucked, until the previously swollen sacs sagged and shriveled. Then she bawled for more.

I was furious and could have strangled her. Marveling at my unnatural disposition, I wondered what the poets who spewed ardently about parental affection could have meant. The crying, wetting, misshapen, grotesque bundle of newborn flesh did not inspire me with anything but loathing. I resented her untimely intrusion. Already her birth could be kept secret no more. The neighbors had heard her cries and came officiously to assist and give advice to my half-dead wife, while I had to scamper away to my perch under the roof, erasing all traces of my latest descent.

Miraculously Yoomi survived the days of fever, near starvation, and constant suction by the little vampire. She was back on her feet to feed all three of us, now carrying the baby on her back. We had sold the stereo and records, the clock and radio, the guitar and accordion, even the harmonica and cymbal. The time had come to part with our wedding gifts, her half-karat diamond ring and my Omega watch, which we had sworn never to sell. I again proposed to give myself up. Surely the communists must have use for an English professor. Maybe I could be their translator, intelligence decoder, or what not, but again Yoomi prevented me.

It was early September and the food from our wedding mementos had lasted only a week. Yoomi hired herself out as a kitchen maid at a neighbor's, Char somebody, who was some kind of a big wheel with the new regime. We had been smelling his barbecuing beef all through the summer. The place seemed a Mecca for the Communist cadres to congregate and celebrate, their drunken, raucous singing lasting through the night. These communists didn't seem to know choral singing at all and everybody always sang in unison. The repertoire was limited to the Red Flag, the Glorious Leader Ilsung Kim, and other Party and Army songs which they never seemed to tire of, which were too sacrosanct to allow accompaniment by any musical instrument other than their own vocal cords. Occasionally they tried some traditional folk songs. At this point some rank amateur banged down on our Baldwin grand, off key.

One of the first things every citizen had to do was report to the authorities special luxuries such as the piano. Yoomi volunteered and contributed it to the cause to forestall its inevitable discovery by the search parties, which might keep looking to find more. Perhaps such cooperation might mollify their suspicion and antagonism toward our house, if not quite win their favor. The piano was moved to Char's. Yoomi's father had bought it on her graduation from college with top honors in her piano class. She had brought it with her when she married me. We had planned a recital sometime in September at the Municipal Hall with the Seoul Philharmonic. Of course none of the Communists had kept up with the musical scene of the south and nobody knew her. To them she was just another miserable housewife, a reactionary's deserted wife, with an infant child to feed. But when they seemed to murder the good music and ruin the piano, I felt an urge to show to Char and comrades what a good musician like Yoomi could do with it. Even their musical travesty stopped altogether and the piano was never heard again. We learned later that the grand had been moved to some public hall for the Liberation Day ceremony on August 15, but the place was bombed and a piano was the farthest thing from anybody's mind.

Her pay was the burnt layer of rice scraped off the bottom of the pot and occasionally the leftover goodies from their tables. At that time, when a peck of rice was worth more than a piano, we had to consider this a generous remuneration. But the strain of work so soon after childbirth ruined her health despite the improved diet. She hemorrhaged continuously. Her shining eyes receded deeper and deeper into their bony sockets, and her skin grew sallow. Sweat stood on her forehead and dizzy spells forced her to steady herself by holding on to the wall or furniture. I told her to stop working; we could skimp, and the burnt rice, which we ate by soaking in water, would see us through a week. By then surely the Americans would be back. Witness the almost round-the-clock air raids by the American Air Force, completely paralyzing all daytime mobility of the People's Army.

But Yoomi wouldn't listen. She had to do it for her baby, who indeed prospered. Her cheeks filled out nicely, and her earlier formlessness gave way to a proportioned articulation of features. When she smiled and crooned in her contentment after a lengthy feeding at her mother's breast, there was even a hint of the innocence and beauty of the Raphaelite Christ child. While she was the epitome of health, her mother withered. I resented the little selfish creature and resisted my growing fondness for her.

September was drawing to a close, yet Seoul was still solidly in the hands of the Communists. The air raids seemed a mere surface irritation to the dug-in, deeply-entrenched ground forces. After what seemed to be a thorough devastation of anti-aircraft bunkers in a given area, the new formation of fighters and bombers the next day would be greeted with as vigorous salvos of flak as before from the same area. Time was said to be running out for the Communists. But it might run out for the Americans, too. After all, planes and bombs couldn't be inexhaustible. And time was definitely running out for us, our little microcosm of three, a nameless and lost speck in the vast macabre chessboard of indiscriminate death and destruction.

Whole streets were turning into honeycombs of pillboxes and bunkers. Naval bombardment had begun from American ships off Inchon, systematically erasing the city off the map. Fires broke out everywhere. A few houses down the block from ours got hit. What had been a sturdy concrete structure disintegrated, leaving a huge crater, while the ensuing fire spread and stopped just before our house. Yoomi and Mira had been moved out, and I was almost smoked out myself. We might absorb a direct hit ourselves at any minute. Wistfully I looked at the repapered walls of our main bedroom, how we had spent days looking for the right color and pattern, how upset we had been whenever a fly left a black spot and what meticulous care we had taken to remove the blemish without staining the rest of the paper.

Last-minute roundups of reactionaries were going on, which now included just about every civilian still left in the city who could not be positively identified as an activist in the new regime. As the first U.S. Marines crossed the Han, the detainees at various basements and temporary lockups, emaciated, bruised, mangled skeletons who had somehow survived the torture and interrogation without food, were led out and shot. Both banks of the Chonggay Drain were strewn with their bodies. Some were packed into abandoned air raid trenches and buried alive. Many were simply shot on the streets and left there to be trampled. Whole families, including the very young and old, were executed. The Communists became more vicious and wanton; if they were to die, they would leave no survivors to curse their memory and exult over their end. They killed anybody for no cause at all.

One night there came a loud knock at the gate. Our hearts were tight knots. Our legs wouldn't move. Mira started crying frantically, bringing us to our senses. Yoomi snatched her up and went to the door, at the same time motioning me to the attic. But there was no time for it. There seemed to be half a dozen of them and they were already through the gate, apparently having broken the latch. They were beaming their flashlights all over the house, especially toward the attic. One was going into the kitchen, another to the basement, a third to the back of the house. I had barely gotten into the outhouse latrine by the fence, when I realized one of them was coming toward it. In the three-by-five compartment I had no alternative but to jump into the tank, feet first, my hands pushing down the slippery sides. The thick mass on top closed over my head without a ripple. I was conscious of a flashlight overhead. The stamping feet on the creaky boards left and the door banged. I nevertheless stayed submerged as long as I could.

I heard Yoomi shriek. She thought they had found me in the attic when three of them vaulted into it through the access trap and turned over every piece of furniture stored there, poking into the corners with their bayonets. It was painful not to go out and reassure her of my safety. Mira went on screaming harder; probably Yoomi had dropped her. At one point I thought they were coming back to the latrine and was ready to duck again, but they didn't. About half an hour later, what seemed like an eternity, I issued out of the outhouse and ran to the inner courtyard. Hair disordered and face ashen, Yoomi was suckling Mira. She gave a start as if she had seen a ghost. She had passed out and regained consciousness only minutes before. She thought they had taken me away. Only then did we Thank God I had postponed installing the flush toilet. The cost of the new plumbing and septic tank system, there being no city sewage, had been prohibitive.

We had to leave the house. A shell had gouged a big hole on the street next to the stone fence, which had been blown off like dust. The roof had collapsed and we were squeezed between the sprung closet door frame and a fallen beam. A window slat dug into my calf, but Yoomi and Mira were unhurt. We had to get out fast. The dry wood had caught fire, and the smoke pierced and blinded our eyes. Shells were falling everywhere. The night sky was lit with a reddish glow that gave the illusion of soaking the whole city in blood. But the alleys were pitch dark, except for occasional flickerings through the openings.

Just as I turned a corner, with Yoomi and Mira close behind, rifle shots rang out. Instantly I drew back. Pressing close to the wall we retreated into the alley we had emerged from. A patrol of the People's Army passed. They paused briefly at the corner to peer into the darkness, but apparently more urgent business elsewhere didn't allow them to tarry. We came out of the alley, rounded the corner, and swiftly went along the other street. Dry plane leaves crackled at our feet, startling us. We kept walking fast, backtracking and detouring whenever a shell crashed near, a roadblock loomed ahead, or a patrol was audible. We were going in the general direction of the Han to the south, but the topography, jumbled beyond recognition by dugouts and shellings, was thoroughly confusing. To the south the sky was bright with flares, probably attesting to the American beachhead. Only the Americans would try to expel darkness, and we had agreed that our hope lay in getting through the Communist battle zone to the brighter sky.

Sudden tommy gun bursts were followed by the noise of people shouting and running.

"Stop or we'll shoot," a voice yelled. The tommy guns burped. Instinctively we had crouched flat to the ground. Shots whizzed past. Cannonade continued with their booms and crashes. A highrise down the block tottered and broke up. Whole walls and floors flew overhead and dumped all around us. We got out of the alley and suddenly came to the broad Namsan Avenue, pale with the shimmer of flares and fires and explosions. The avenue was full of enfilade. We had to get away from this highway of flying metal.

"Let's find a trench, an air raid shelter," I said.

"They say they're filled up with bodies," Yoomi said.

My spine crawled. I shuddered at the thought of what must have happened to the man who had been fleeing in our direction a minute before. A half circle of grey was fanning slowly in the eastern sky, eroding the redness of artificial illumination. The chilly morning breeze buffeted our noses with whiffs of rancid smoke, the overpowering compound of burning gunpowder, wood, paint, earth, concrete, and human flesh.

There was a flare right above our heads, disclosing our shapes. For the first time we looked at each other's face in the eerie light and were shocked at our skeletal haggardness, as if all the meat had evaporated. But we were not allowed the luxury of mutual scrutiny for long. A few feet from us lay a headless man's body, drenched in blood, still warm, kicking. The brains had spilt out of the bashed head a few feet away. Dark patches of blood stippled the whitewashed wall. Yoomi trembled and hid her face in my chest.

"Let's get into a trench before we get it ourselves," I said, pulling her behind me into an alley. There was a tearing explosion. The place we had just stood disappeared in a cloud of fiery smoke. More mortar shells rained upon the same spot. We could see fire spitting out of a machine gun emplacement a little distance away. Near South Gate we found and jumped into an unoccupied dugout, about four feet by ten feet. The floor was covered with a sheet of water. The walls were slimy. The smell of mildew, feces, and decay staggered us. Fresh pine trunks, their green-needled branches sticking up here and there, supported the ceiling of earth packed in straw bags. Where the bagging was torn, earth cascaded into the puddle of water on the floor with each ground-shaking explosion. Yoomi uncovered the flap of cloth she had put across Mira's face. She slept on soundly, quite unconcerned. One shell fell almost on top of the trench. The ceiling and walls shook, ready to cave in. The dust was suffocating. Instinctively Yoomi hid Mira's face against her bosom. The infant's nostrils fluttered, her eyelids quivered, her clenched hands waved uncertainly. Then she went back to sleep, her facial muscles relaxing, even hinting a smile. I was gripped with compunction. The little innocent life seemed the dearest thing in the world. I recalled how beastly my attitude had been toward this sublime being, free from taint and impurity. Her faint, still-lingering smile seemed the climax of all life, as if all previous generations had existed only to culminate in this perfection. So many lives had been plowed back into the soil to sprout this exquisite flower.

A hot puff of air, as if somebody had suddenly opened a heated oven, filled the trench, sizzling the wet floor. Flames darted into the trench from the opening. We gasped for breath. Our bodies were like burning brands. We doubled up and burrowed our heads into the ground, but the floor was aflame, too. Outside were rushing feet and loud voices.

"Napalms, napalms," shouted somebody running past our trench.

"Retreat to Position Two," another voice shouted, as the trotting feet scattered. Shortly afterward, there were other voices.

"Stop!" somebody yelled. Tommy guns clattered away, followed by screams. Cool air came into our trench and we could breathe. Mira let out a piercing cry. Her face was flushed like a ball of fire. Yoomi tried to comfort her but Mira kicked and thrashed, crying louder and louder. We heard footsteps approaching us. Yoomi bared her breast and tried to pacify Mira, but it did not work. The child dodged her head left or right, thrusting her hands mightily against her mother, and her face contorted with the effort, her cry growing louder. We didn't know what to do. Discovery by the Communist soldiers would be certain death. Anyone other than themselves on this battle line would be enemy agents or undesirables summarily to be executed. At that moment, just as the detachment of troops was almost above our trench, more napalms fell around our trench, and the footsteps ceased. Hot flames hissed past the entrance, and some leaped in, almost licking us. I pulled Yoomi to the other end of the trench, our feet sinking in the mud. Mira expressed her disapproval of the jolt by doubling the decibels of her cry.

"Help, good people. Help!" said a voice at the mouth of the trench. Our hair stood up and our breath stopped. A young man of about twenty was crawling into the trench. He dragged one leg, his torn flesh showing through gaping trousers. His entire face was sleek with blood.

"I heard you, good people," he said. "I knew you could not be bad. People with crying children can't be bad. Give me anything to tie up my wound with."

Yoomi tore a strip from her skirt before I had a chance to protest and handed it to the wounded man. He hurriedly tied up his thigh, stopping the bleeding in the leg. He stretched out his hand for more strips of cloth and Yoomi was about to oblige, which would have left her practically bare. I stopped her. The young man noticed it. He tore off his torn trouser leg, split it along the seam, and wiped his face. There was an ominous gash in his upper left forehead from which blood kept oozing. He bound his head above his eye and just below the wound, which seemed to stem the bleeding somewhat.

"Can't you stop the baby's crying?" he said, looking at us with annoyance. "They'll hear us for sure, just as I heard you, and we will be done for. They shoot any civilian. It is their last vengeance."

"Do they really?" I said incredulously.

"You'll find out soon enough if you let the child carry on," he said, urgently, imperatively. He made a lunge toward Mira but stopped short when Yoomi gathered Mira closer to her and shrank from him.

"Don't you hear them coming this way? I'll be damned if I'll get shot in this stinking hole because of a crying baby," he said, crawling out of the trench. A few seconds later, amid the crashes of artillery and mortar, we heard the nervous chatter of tommy guns and a long scream, which could have been the young man's, but we weren't sure. There were more feet, rushing back and forth, more explosions.

"He was right. We'll get caught if we stay here with her crying her head off like this. We've got to leave her and get out," I said.

"Leave her?"

"Yes. But we'll come back for her. They won't kill a baby."

Horrified, she backed away from me, holding Mira tightly.

"If you want to live so badly that you have to abandon your own child, then go away from us," Yoomi said in disgust.

"It's not a question of abandoning. It's a question of avoiding suicide. It's survival, survival of us, you and me."

"What about Mira?"

"A lump of flesh, hardly conscious of its own existence!"

"Why is she crying if she's not conscious?"

"That's precisely what I mean. If she was truly aware of her position, she wouldn't cry. We have perception, a fully developed adult consciousness, but hers is not even human yet. It's not much different from that of bugs. Besides, we made her. We can make many more like her."

I heard another detachment of troops approaching, their voices growing louder. Mira seemed to time her crying for a crescendo. In immediate reaction I put my hand across her mouth.

"Get away from her," Yoomi shrieked shrilly above Mira's crying, at the same time bending down and biting my hand so hard that a bone crunched. I jumped back in pain. The detachment was unmistakably coming directly toward us.

"Get out! Get out! I don't know you. We have no need of you," Yoomi was shouting. I had no time to think. I bounded out of the trench. Tommy guns burped behind me. A giant had grabbed me by the thigh. I fell down. Something warm suffused my leg. There was a loud thunder that completely deafened me and knocked out my senses.

The next time I noticed anything, it was broad daylight. I was lying before the gaunt remains of a building. Down the street, on both sides, I saw crumbling pillboxes and barricades with machine guns and dead soldiers slung across the sandbags. Farther down the street, around the Taypyongdong Rotary, a motorcade of American amphibious tanks, armored cars, and trucks was approaching, followed by thousands of Koreans waving flags and shouting hooray to the saviors. Where had they all been? I thought they had all been murdered or starved and no soul had been left alive in Seoul. In between the shouts and the rumble of the engines I heard a baby's subdued, hoarse whimpering. For the first time I remembered what had happened. I stood up and tried to run, but the big hand pulled me down. My left leg was a useless stump. It was the very same leg from whose calf a splinter had been extracted earlier. The bullet, entering at a small neat hole, had departed on the other side after wrenching out a big chunk of steak, bone and all. The rest of my leg hung by mere skin. How foolish the Korean saying that one doesn't get hurt twice in the same place!

I crawled across the street to the heap of earth from under which the sobbing of the baby continued intermittently, inaudibly. I started digging away frantically with my hands. Soon the nails broke off and the fingers bled. The crowd arrived. An American Marine walked up. To his surprise, I explained in English that my wife and baby were underneath. He had several of his buddies come with shovels. First came to sight a People's Army soldier with a broken back. Then, under a log, in a cubic foot of space, Mira was safe, although her legs were trapped in earth. The jagged end of a beam had rammed through Yoomi's chest.

* * *

"All right, Mira," I say. "I'll get the money ready tomorrow, and you can make the plane reservations and other preparations. But please write to me when you get to Florence."

"Oh, Dad, you are an angel," she says, hugging me. "I'll remember this always and pay you back, all of it and more. I know what kind of a sacrifice this is to you."

Does she? Perhaps. Strangely, she doesn't ask this time the usual question of what wicked thing I have done to her mother. Well, no matter. It boils down to the same thing, me picking up the tab, sweating and toiling to fulfill her big decisions. I'll have to withdraw from my Christmas Club savings, which I have intended for my next sabbatical trip to England. I'll be signing a note at the University Credit Union to pay back within three years. I thought I had finally gotten out of all those debts, those eternal monthly salary deductions, for the car, the TV, the stereo, the piano, everything except the house mortgage, but here I go again, accepting more installment payments. Mira may indeed go on to sing at La Scalla or the Metropolitan, but even if she doesn't, well, she won't bring her mother into the picture again, at least not for a while. But why do things have to be so tough for Americans now? I remember the times when an average American income commanded princely accommodations abroad. It is quite the other way around now. Damn Arabs, damn Japanese, damn Italians, damn Koreans with their exports and favorable trade balances!

GOODBYE AND GOOD LUCK

Grace Paley

I was popular in certain circles, says Aunt Rose. I wasn't no thinner then, only more stationary in the flesh. In time to come, Lillie, don't be surprised—change is a fact of God. From this no one is excused. Only a person like your mama stands on one foot, she don't notice how big her behind is getting and sings in the canary's ear for thirty years. Who's listening? Papa's in the shop. You and Seymour, thinking about yourself. So she waits in a spotless kitchen for a kind word and thinks—poor Rosie . . .

Poor Rosie! If there was more life in my little sister, she would know my heart is a regular college of feelings and there is such information between my corset and me that her whole married life is a kindergarten.

Nowadays you could find me any time in a hotel, uptown or downtown. Who needs an apartment to live like a maid with a dustrag in the hand, sneezing? I'm in very good with the busboys, it's more interesting than home, all kinds of people, everybody with a reason . . .

And my reason, Lillie, is a long time ago I said to the forelady, "Missus, if I can't sit by the window, I can't sit." "If you can't sit, girlie," she says politely, "go stand on the street corner." And that's how I got unemployed in novelty wear.

For my next job I answered an ad which said: "Refined young lady, medium salary, cultural organization." I went by trolley to the address, the Russian Art Theater of Second Avenue, where they played only the best Yiddish plays. They needed a ticket seller, someone like me, who likes the public but is very sharp on crooks. The man who interviewed me was the manager, a certain type.

Immediately he said: "Rosie Lieber, you surely got a build on you!"

"It takes all kinds, Mr. Krimberg."

"Don't misunderstand me, little girl," he said. "I appreciate, I appreciate. A young lady lacking fore and aft, her blood is so busy warming the toes and the fingertips, it don't have time to circulate where it's most required."

Everybody likes kindness. I said to him: "Only don't be fresh, Mr. Krimberg, and we'll make a good bargain."

We did: Nine dollars a week, a glass of tea every night, a free ticket once a week for Mama, and I could go watch rehearsals any time I want.

My first nine dollars was in the grocer's hands ready to move on already, when Krimberg said to me, "Rosie, here's a great gentleman, a member of this remarkable theater, wants to meet you, impressed no doubt by your big brown eyes."

And who was it, Lillie? Listen to me, before my very eyes was Volodya Vlashkin, called by the people of those days the Valentino of Second Avenue. I took one look, and I said to myself: Where did a Jewish boy grow up so big? "Just outside Kiev," he told me.

How? "My mama nursed me till I was six. I was the only boy in the village to have such health."

"My goodness, Vlashkin, six years old! She must have had shredded wheat there, not breasts, poor woman."

"My mother was beautiful," he said. "She had eyes like stars."

He had such a way of expressing himself, it brought tears.

To Krimberg, Vlashkin said after this introduction: "Who is responsible for hiding this wonderful young person in a cage?"

"That is where the ticket seller sells."

"So, David, go in there and sell tickets for a half hour. I have something in mind in regards to the future of this girl and this company. Go, David, be a good boy. And you, Miss Lieber, please, I suggest Feinberg's for a glass of tea. The rehearsals are long. I enjoy a quiet interlude with a friendly person."

So he took me there, Feinberg's, then around the corner, a place so full of Hungarians, it was deafening. In the back room was a table of honor for him. On the tablecloth embroidered by the lady of the house was *Here Vlashkin Eats*. We finished one glass of tea in quietness, out of thirst, when I finally made up my mind what to say.

"Mr. Vlashkin, I saw you a couple weeks ago, even before I started working here, in *The Sea Gull*. Believe me, if I was that girl, I wouldn't look even for a minute on the young bourgeois fellow. He could fall out of the play altogether. How Chekhov could put him in the same play as you, I can't understand."

"You liked me?" he asked, taking my hand and kindly patting it. "Well, well, young people still like me . . . so, and you like the theater too? Good. And you, Rose, you know you have such a nice hand, so warm to the touch, such a fine skin, tell me, why do you wear a scarf around your neck? You only hide your young, young throat. These are not olden times, my child, to live in shame."

"Who's ashamed?" I said, taking off the kerchief, but my hand right away went to the kerchief's place, because the truth is, it really was olden times, and I was still of a nature to melt with shame.

"Have some more tea, my dear."

"No, thank you, I am a samovar already."

"Dorfmann!" he hollered like a king. "Bring this child a seltzer with fresh ice!"

In weeks to follow I had the privilege to know him better and better as a person—also the opportunity to see him in his profession. The time was autumn; the theater full of coming and going. Rehearsing without end. After *The Sea Gull* flopped, *The Salesman from Istanbul* played, a great success.

Here the ladies went crazy. On the opening night, in the middle of the first scene, one missus—a widow or her husband worked too long hours—began to clap and sing out, "Oi, oi, Vlashkin." Soon there was such a tumult, the actors had to stop acting. Vlashkin stepped forward. Only not Vlashkin to the eyes . . . a younger man with pitch-black hair, lively on restless feet, his mouth clever. A half a century later at the end of the play he came out again, a gray philosopher, a student of life from only reading books, his hands as smooth as silk . . . I cried to think who I was—nothing—and such a man could look at me with interest.

Then I got a small raise, due to he kindly put in a good word for me, and also for fifty cents a night I was given the pleasure together with cousins, in-laws, and plain stage-struck kids to be part of a crowd scene and to see like he saw every single night: the hundreds of pale faces waiting for his feelings to make them laugh or bend down their heads in sorrow.

The sad day came, I kissed my mama goodbye. Vlashkin helped me to get a reasonable room near the theater to be more free. Also my outstanding friend would have a place to recline away from the noise of the dressing rooms. She cried and she cried. "This is a different way of living, Mama," I said. "Besides, I am driven by love."

"You! You, a nothing, a rotten hole in a piece of cheese, are you telling me what is life?" she screamed.

Very insulted, I went away from her. But I am good-natured—you know fat people are like that—kind, and I thought to myself, poor Mama . . . it is true she got more of an idea of life than me. She married who she didn't like, a sick man, his spirit already swallowed up by God. He never washed. He had an unhappy smell. His teeth fell out, his hair disappeared, he got smaller, shriveled up little by little, till goodbye and good luck he was gone and only came to Mama's mind when she went to the mailbox under the stairs to get the electric bill. In memory of him and out of respect for mankind, I decided to live for love.

Don't laugh, you ignorant girl.

Do you think it was easy for me? I had to give Mama a little something. Ruthie was saving up together with your papa for linens, a couple knives and forks. In the morning I had to do piecework if I wanted to keep by myself. So I made flowers. Before lunch time every day a whole garden grew on my table.

This was my independence, Lillie dear, blooming, but it didn't have no roots and its face was paper.

Meanwhile Krimberg went after me too. No doubt observing the success of Vlashkin, he thought, Aha, open sesame . . . Others in the company similar. After me in those years were the following: Krimberg I mentioned. Carl Zimmer, played innocent young fellows with a wig. Charlie Peel, a Christian who fell in the soup by accident, a creator of beautiful sets. "Color is his middle name," says Vlashkin, always to the point.

I put this in to show you your fat old aunt was not crazy out of loneliness. In those noisy years I had friends among interesting people who admired me for reasons of youth and that I was a first-class listener.

The actresses—Raisele, Marya, Esther Leopold—were only interested in tomorrow. After them was the rich men, producers, the whole garment center; their past is a pincushion, future the eye of a needle.

Finally the day came, I no longer could keep my tact in my mouth. I said: "Vlashkin, I hear by carrier pigeon you have a wife, children, the whole combination."

"True, I don't tell stories. I make no pretense."

"That isn't the question. What is this lady like? It hurts me to ask, but tell me, Vlashkin . . . a man's life is something I don't clearly see."

"Little girl, I have told you a hundred times, this small room is the convent of my troubled spirit. Here I come to your innocent shelter to refresh myself in the midst of an agonized life."

"Ach, Vlashkin, serious, serious, who is this lady?"

"Rosie, she is a fine woman of the middle classes, a good mother to my children, three in number, girls all, a good cook, in her youth handsome, now no longer young. You see, could I be more frank? I entrust you, dear, with my soul."

It was some few months later at the New Year's ball of the Russian Artists Club, I met Mrs. Vlashkin, a woman with black hair in a low bun, straight and too proud. She sat at a small table speaking in a deep voice to whoever stopped a moment to converse. Her Yiddish was perfect, each word cut like a special jewel. I looked at her. She noticed me like she noticed everybody, cold like Christmas morning. Then she got tired. Vlashkin called a taxi and I never saw her again. Poor woman, she did not know I was on the same stage with her. The poison I was to her role, she did not know.

Later on that night in front of my door I said to Vlashkin, "No more. This isn't for me. I am sick from it all. I am no home breaker."

"Girlie," he said, "don't be foolish."

"No, no, goodbye, good luck," I said. "I am sincere."

So I went and stayed with Mama for a week's vacation and cleaned up all the closets and scrubbed the walls till the paint came off. She was very grateful, all the same her hard life made her say, "Now we see the end. If you live like a bum, you are finally a lunatic."

After this few days I came back to my life. When we met, me and Vlashkin, we said only hello and goodbye, and, then for a few sad years, with the head we nodded as if to say, "Yes, Yes, I know who you are."

Meanwhile in the field was a whole new strategy. Your mama and your grandmama brought around—boys. Your own father had a brother, you never even seen him, Ruben. A serious fellow, his idealism was his hat and his coat. "Rosie, I offer you a big new free happy unusual life." How? "With me, we will raise up the sands of Palestine to make a nation. That is the land of tomorrow for us Jews." "Ha-ha, Ruben, I'll go tomorrow then." "Rosie!" says Ruben. "We need strong women like you, mothers and farmers." "You don't fool me, Ruben, what you need is dray horses. But for that you need more money." "I don't like your attitude, Rose." "In that case, go and multiply. Goodbye."

Another fellow: Yonkel Gurstein, a regular sport, dressed to kill, with such an excitable nature. In those days—it looks to me like yesterday—the youngest girls wore undergarments like Battle Creek, Michigan. To him it was a matter of seconds. Where did he practice, a Jewish boy? Nowadays I suppose it is easier, Lillie? My goodness, I ain't asking you nothing—touchy, touchy . . .

Well, by now you must know yourself, honey, whatever you do, life don't stop. It only sits a minute and dreams a dream.

While I was saying to all these silly youngsters "no, no, no," Vlashkin went to Europe and toured a few seasons . . . Moscow, Prague, London, even Berlin—already a pessimistic place. When he came back he wrote a book you could get from the library even today, *The Jewish Actor Abroad*. If someday you're interested enough in my lonesome years, you could read it. You could absorb a flavor of the man from the book. No, no, I am not mentioned. After all, who am I?

When the book came out I stopped him in the street to say congratulations. But I am not a liar, so I pointed out, too, the egotism of many parts—even the critics said something along such lines.

"Talk is cheap," Vlashkin answered me. "But who are the critics? Tell me, do they create? Not to mention," he continues, "there is a line in Shakespeare in one of the plays from the great history of England. It says, 'Self-loving is not so vile a sin, my liege, as self-neglecting.' This idea also appears in modern times in the moralistic followers of Freud . . . Rosie, are you listening? You asked a question. By the way, you look very well. How come no wedding ring?"

I walked away from this conversation in tears. But this talking in the street opened the happy road up for more discussions. In regard to many things . . . For instance, the management—very narrow-minded—wouldn't give him any more certain young men's parts. Fools. What youngest man knew enough about life to be as young as him?

"Rosie, Rosie," he said to me one day, "I see by the clock on your rosy, rosy face you must be thirty."

"The hands are slow, Vlashkin. On a week before Thursday I was thirty-four."

"Is that so? Rosie, I worry about you. It has been on my mind to talk to you. You are losing your time. Do you understand it? A woman should not lose her time."

"Oi, Vlashkin, if you are my friend, what is time?"

For this he had no answer, only looked at me surprised. We went instead, full of interest but not with our former speed, up to my new place on Ninety-fourth Street. The same pictures on the wall, all of Vlashkin, only now everything painted red and black, which was stylish, and new upholstery.

A few years ago there was a book by another member of that fine company, an actress, the one that learned English very good and went uptown—Marya Kavkaz, in which she says certain things regarding Vlashkin. Such as, he was her lover for eleven years, she's not ashamed to write this down. Without respect for him, his wife and children, or even others who also may have feelings in the matter.

Now, Lillie, don't be surprised. This is called a fact of life. An actor's soul must be like a diamond. The more faces it got the more shining is his name. Honey, you will no doubt love and marry one man and have a couple kids and be happy forever till you die tired. More than that, a person like us don't have to know. But a great artist like Volodya Vlashkin . . . in order to make a job on the stage, he's got to practice. I understand it now, to him life is like a rehearsal.

Myself, when I saw him in *The Father-in-Law*—an older man in love with a darling young girl, his son's wife, played by Raisele Maisel—I cried. What he said to this girl, how he whispered such sweetness, how all his hot feelings were on his face . . . Lillie, all this experience he had with me. The very words were the same. You can imagine how proud I was.

So the story creeps to an end.

I noticed it first on my mother's face, the rotten handwriting of time, scribbled up and down her cheeks, across her forehead back and forth—a child could read—

it said old, old, old. But it troubled my heart most to see these realities scratched on Vlashkin's wonderful expression.

First the company fell apart. The theater ended. Esther Leopold died from being very aged. Krimberg had a heart attack. Marya went to Broadway. Also Raisele changed her name to Roslyn and was a big comical hit in the movies. Vlashkin himself, no place to go, retired. It said in the paper, "An actor without peer, he will write his memoirs and spend his last years in the bosom of his family among his thriving grandchildren, the apple of his wife's doting eye."

This is journalism.

We made for him a great dinner of honor. At this dinner I said to him, for the last time, I thought, "Goodbye, dear friend, topic of my life, now we part." And to myself I said further: Finished. This is your lonesome bed. A lady what they call fat and fifty. You made it personally. From this lonesome bed you will finally fall to a bed not so lonesome, only crowded with a million bones.

And now comes? Lillie, guess.

Last week, washing my underwear in the basin, I get a buzz on the phone. "Excuse me, is this the Rose Lieber formerly connected with the Russian Art Theater?"

"It is."

"Well, well, how do you do, Rose? This is Vlashkin."

"Vlashkin! Volodya Vlashkin?"

"In fact. How are you, Rose?"

"Living, Vlashkin, thank you."

"You are all right? Really, Rose? Your health is good? You are working?"

"My health, considering the weight it must carry, is first-class. I am back for some years now where I started, in novelty wear."

"Very interesting."

"Listen, Vlashkin, tell me the truth, what's on your mind?"

"My mind? Rosie, I am looking up an old friend, an old warmhearted companion of more joyful days. My circumstances, by the way, are changed. I am retired, as you know. Also I am a free man."

"What? What do you mean?"

"Mrs. Vlashkin is divorcing me."

"What come over her? Did you start drinking or something from melancholy?"

"She is divorcing me for adultery."

"But, Vlashkin, you should excuse me, don't be insulted, but you got maybe seventeen, eighteen years on me, and even me, all this nonsense—this daydreams and nightmares—is mostly for the pleasure of conversation alone."

"I pointed all this out to her. My dear, I said, my time is past, my blood is as dry as my bones. The truth is, Rose, she isn't accustomed to have a man around all day, reading out loud from the papers the interesting events of our time, waiting for breakfast, waiting for lunch. So all day she gets madder and madder. By nighttime a furious old lady gives me my supper. She has information from the last fifty years to pepper my soup. Surely there was a Judas in that theater, saying every day, 'Vlashkin, Vlashkin, Vlashkin . . .' and while my heart was circulating with his smiles he was on the wire passing the dope to my wife."

"Such a foolish end, Volodya, to such a lively story. What is your plans?"

"First, could I ask you for dinner and the theater—uptown, of course? After this . . . we are old friends. I have money to burn. What your heart desires. Others are like grass, the north wind of time has cut out their heart. Of you, Rosie, I re-create only kindness. What a woman should be to a man, you were to me. Do you think, Rosie, a couple of old pals like us could have a few good times among the material things of this world?"

My answer, Lillie, in a minute was altogether, "Yes, yes, come up," I said. "Ask the room by the switchboard, let us talk."

So he came that night and every night in the week, we talked of his long life. Even at the end of time, a fascinating man. And like men are, too, till time's end, trying to get away in one piece.

"Listen, Rosie," he explains the other day. "I was married to my wife, do you realize, nearly half a century. What good was it? Look at the bitterness. The more I think of it, the more I think we would be fools to marry."

"Volodya Vlashkin," I told him straight, "when I was young I warmed your cold back many a night, no questions asked. You admit it, I didn't make no demands. I was softhearted. I didn't want to be called Rosie Lieber, a breaker up of homes. But now, Vlashkin, you are a free man. How could you ask me to go with you on trains to stay in strange hotels, among Americans, not your wife? Be ashamed."

So now, darling Lillie, tell this story to your mama from your young mouth. She don't listen to a word from me. She only screams, "I'll faint, I'll faint." Tell her after all I'll have a husband, which, as everybody knows, a woman should have at least one before the end of the story.

My goodness, I am already late. Give me a kiss. After all, I watched you grow from a plain seed. So give me a couple wishes on my wedding day. A long and happy life. Many years of love. Hug Mama, tell her from Aunt Rose, goodbye and good luck.

BUZZARDS CELEBRATE PREDATION'S END

Ishmael Reed

After the Great Deluge receded, life began a new. The world was once again pristine and it was agreed upon by those living creatures that had survived this calamity that the Creator was disappointed with the results of her handiwork. Lacking the knowledge of we moderns that there are most likely billions of earthlike planets in multi universes, and that the presence of life on one is infinitely insignificant despite all of the hullabaloo, and that regardless of the many creation stories whose intent is to ennoble the whole enterprise, life most likely originated from some cellular things that kept warm around volcanic spewing originating in the deep ocean a billion or so years ago. There was even speculation that life originated on Mars or that the human species is just another form of fungi, like the stuff you get on your toenails.

Before the Deluge there was constant preying and being preyed upon. And so at an international conference the preyed upon and predators met and decided to end this constant craving for flesh. They vowed to seek alternative forms of nutrition. Maybe Green Tea. All except the Buzzards and one other animal who felt that the conference was yet another triumph for political correctness. Among those in the animal Kingdom, the Buzzards were the most conservative.

Besides, these birds were of the kind that let others do the hard work of pursuit while they arrived after the killing to devour the spoils like relatives who show up for a visit and eat you out of house and home. Relatives whom you might find in the small hours of the morning rummaging about your refrigerator for the last scraps of last night's dinner. Relatives who take control of the remote so that you're unable to surf your favorite channels. Relatives who can't take a hint.

But without predation being the basis of animal activity animals were surviving longer and so animal remains were available infrequently. There was no room in this scheme for those whose survival depended upon a high fat diet. In fact, natural enemies like Cats and Dogs were now forming cooperatives and mutual aidesocieties. Lions and Lambs were enjoying each others' company at parties that sometimes lasted for days. Mongooses and Cobras were exchanging admiring letters. Whenever there was the possibility of a collision between sharks and their enemies, both parties would greet each other with profuse courtesies. The Shark would say, "After you, my beloved adversary," and the adversary would say, "My dear Shark, I wouldn't think of interrupting your daily swim. Please proceed." Leopards could be seen nurturing orphaned Baboons.

The Buzzards had a meeting. King Buzzard rose and spoke.

"We lack the initiative to hunt things down and are dependent upon others doing our work for us. Now that there seems to be some sort of commitment to go Vegan by the other animals, there has been a decrease in our food supply. I have such a craving for meat, why, why, I might eat one of you. Our diet is limited to animals that have perished from disease or died a natural death. This has become dull, dull, dull. We miss the thrill of the hunt. I mean somebody else's hunt."

A young Buzzard rose and proposed that the Buzzards go Vegan. He was shouted down by the rest of the Buzzards. One of the elder Buzzards, a Grandfather Buzzard, who was of wise council rose. All turned to him as he was very much respected.

"Since we have no hunting skills and are dependent upon others for meat, why don't we devise a plan to bring the animals to us. That way, we won't have to exert ourselves."

All of the Buzzards agreed with this plan, a plan that wouldn't require them to put out much effort. One Buzzard said, "Sounds simple enough, but how do we accomplish that? Get all of the animals to come to us? And once we get them here what do we do with them?"

Grandfather Buzzard rose again. "We will have to change our policy temporarily. We will kill them and eat them." The old Buzzard wasn't one to mincemeat his words so to speak. He was quite emphatic. Well his idea raised alarm among some of the more progressive Buzzards who were against killing; they threatened to walk out of the meeting until one of their own suggested that if they didn't go along with this new policy that would only be in practice, temporarily, they'd be accused of appeasement.

Predictably, the progressives gave in.

And so, after the meeting, they began sending out invitations to all factions of the animal, fish and bird communities. That the Buzzards were having a large gala to honor the cessation of hostilities between predator and prey.

Animals went onto chat rooms to let their feelings be known. Most thought it a good idea. There was, however, some dissent. The Crows and Ravens signed a group letter raising questions about the invitation. Why would carrion eaters all of a sudden show a gentle side? Why were they insisting that the animals, fish, and birds travel to Buzzard Land for the gala instead of holding it at some neutral place? Their thinking was dismissed by the others as pre-Deluge. They were called paranoid, cranky, irritable, grouchy, cross and of course, angry. Some of the song birds ridiculed their song. Calling it squawky, brittle, harsh and coarse. About as welcome to the ears as the screeching sound made by chalk being pushed across a blackboard.

Well the day arrived. Animals, birds and fish decked out in their finery made their way to Buzzard Land where they dined, danced, made love and ate a variety of fruit and vegetables. Then according to plan, the Buzzards sounded a warning of an approaching predator, one that was feared throughout the animal Kingdom, the only other animal that refused to sign the anti-predation treaty, and if it had would have violated it. The Buzzards knew the most terrifying cry of the animal world. From the top of their lungs the Buzzards shouted, "The Humans are coming. The Humans are coming." The animals scrambled and trampled one another in their attempt to exit the large hall in which the banquet was being held, but the Buzzards had locked the doors. During the ensuing panic, the animals tore at each other with ferocity until many of them were dead. The Buzzards then moved in and finished off the dying. They dined until they passed out. Bloated. Coma like. Having eaten so much, there were many explosions of gas and the windows were opened allowing some of those animals that had been playing possum an opportunity to escape.

After this disaster, recriminations began almost immediately and such quarrelling and paw pointing led to the pre Deluge situation of predation. The Buzzards were back in business.

And that's why while many bird species whose songs were much more beautiful, whose feathers were so gorgeous as to adorn the costumes of Monarchs, and who were much cuter have vanished. Crows still own the Marina, shooing Seagulls away and the Ravens rule Telegraph Hill. *Caw Caw Caw.*

MICE

Danny Romero

The noises were coming from down below again. There was always something going on down there in that garage ever since the old woman who owned the building died and her sisters started wrangling over the property and moving in their relatives. First it was with the Morton Town drug dealers with their knocking on the door going on at all hours of the day and night and the exchanges of baggies, bindles and balloons. Whispers.

Nicolas had been down there once before when he was talking to the tenant, Howard. He carried a forty-ounce bottle of Ranier Ale and swayed from side to side. "Eh, they aren't going to beat me up," he said, after knocking on the garage door late at night. Some of the other Morton Town hoods didn't know him or trust him and crouched in the darkness behind the bushes ready to pounce, but Howard told them Nicolas was all right, and the two of them stood there in the dark space, cluttered and smelling of dry dog shit and stale water. They shared a joint of marijuana while loud funk music drifted in from another part of the house.

He was half glad the Sheriffs came and closed down the operation. There were too many dope fiends at his doorstep and the traffic had become much too heavy. He was glad he wasn't home that day they kicked down the door. He knew he could always find some grass some place else.

Downstairs someone was banging on a pipe. The washing machine began with a loud moooooaaaaannnnnn. He could hear a child crying and things being jostled around down there. Intervals of almost silence were followed by barely audible slaps. Then the crying grew louder. More things were jostled around. Nicolas figured they were boxes or furniture. He didn't know for sure what all was down there these days.

There were children down there now. He knew that much. Nicolas saw the kids all the time out in front playing by the driveway. Sometimes he said hello when he passed them by. Sometimes they answered him. He yelled at them good one time, at the top of his lungs, when he found someone had opened his mail and thrown it in the back by the garbage cans. They all denied it, blaming another kid who they pointed out just down the street. Nicolas went and yelled at that kid too.

The phone rang waking him out of a light sleep. He figured it must have been two in the morning. He picked up the receiver. "Hello," he said. There was no answer. "Hello," he said again, expecting only the silence. He hung the phone up and slumped back onto his mattress. "Jesus Christ," he muttered, turning on his side. The washing machine began down below.

Saturday morning was clean-up day for Nicolas. He gathered up the paper bags filled with garbage and carried them down the stairs and out to the cans behind the house. He could hear yelling from an open window as he passed by. He tried to make as little noise as possible so as to be undetected.

Back upstairs he began his cleaning. The floor needed to be mopped. Ever since Charlie and Max had come by a couple of nights before it needed to be mopped. Nicolas shook his head. "That Charlie," he said to himself, "he's sure fuckin' crazy."

Charlie always fell asleep in a chair with a beer in his hand. You could never get him to put it down or go and lay down himself. He'd just mumble and snort, sometimes laugh. The other two would try and pry the can from his fingers, but there was no letting go for Charlie. He'd just sit there passed out until he spilled the beer on his pants and the floor. That would wake him.

Max wasn't any better though, never finishing his beer entirely, and putting his cigarettes out in the cans. Later when he stumbled out of the door he would always manage to kick a few over. And the food from Ollie's B-B-Q, over on Compton Avenue, didn't help matters either. Nicolas would have to mop up before the ants found their way to the drops of thick B-B-Q sauce on the floor. Ollie's was good food, but awful sloppy. And even more so when you're drunk.

Nicolas poured some Pine-Sol into a bucket of hot water. The fumes pinched at his nostrils. He took the bucket and mop into the living room. There were footsteps coming up the stairs. He opened the door before the person knocked.

"Is there a problem with the garbage cans," asked a woman. She was short, black and skinny. More scrawny than skinny with three front teeth missing. Nicolas thought she looked like an ostrich the way her nose and mouth were shaped.

"No problems with me," answered Nicolas. He looked down at the bottom of the stairs and saw the three children looking up at him. The little girl had curlers in her hair and clutched a black baby girl rag doll. She wore a bandage around her left knee. The oldest boy was fat. He ate graham crackers from out of a box. The other boy was not as fat. He just looked mean and carried a stick. Nicolas guessed they were in age from four to eight, the girl being the youngest.

"The landlady said I could use that can. I've been using it for weeks now," said Nicolas.

"Well now Mrs. Dawson is my grandmother," said the woman as if to impress Nicolas with the fact.

"Oh really," said Nicolas. "Well, I talked with the woman just the other day and asked if I was to use that can because the garbage men won't pick up the other. And she said to go right ahead and use it. Since I've been living here longer."

The woman looked at him. "Well, I'll have to check with her on that," she said. "I didn't mean to bother you." She smiled at Nicolas, trying to look sexy with a hole in her face where her missing teeth should have been.

"No problem," said Nicolas. He was about to close the door.

"Wha's your name anyway," the woman said. "My name's Sharon."

"Nicolas," he said, sitting down in the doorway.

"Pleased to meet you Nicolas."

"Pleased to meet you Sharon."

"Do you have a phone up here Nicolas," she asked.

"Yeah, I have one," he said, wondering what the hell she wanted to know for.

"Good," she said, "so do I an' . . . I was wondering . . ." She went on, "You know because my husband and I separated. It's just me an' my kids an' ah . . . you know . . . Here do me favor an' take my number down."

Nicolas went inside and got a pen and paper to humor her.

"It's 555–6758," she said. "All right . . . now Nicolas . . . could you call me if you hear me screaming." Nicolas swallowed. "You see my husband's getting out of county jail in a couple of weeks, an' I don't know what it'll be like. . . ."

"No problem," said Nicholas. He began folding the paper nervously.

She went on, "Because I've been seeing this other man . . . an' well you unnerstan' . . . you know a person gets lonely an' all . . . an' his family, grandmother an' all them . . . well the man's white an' they don't like him . . . an' . . ."

"No problem," said Nicolas, just wanting now to get her down the stairs and on her way. "Sure, I understand," he said.

"All right Nicolas," she said. "Thanks a lot . . . Nicolas, that's such a sweet name. I'll remember your name for sure now Nicolas."

"Sounds good," said Nicolas, standing to get her to move along a little quicker.

"I'll see you," she said, beginning down the stairs.

"Yeah sure," said Nicolas, closing the door.

"Oh Nicolas?" He groaned, sticking his head out only. "You having any trouble with mice up there now?"

"Mice?" said Nicolas. He stepped out onto the stairs. "No I haven't why?"

"Yessirree Nicolas. There's some in the garage and I found one in our apartment las' night. We think they're coming in through the heater. I don't let my kids in the garage no more because there's mice in there for sure." She turned and went down. "I'll see you." She smiled.

"Yeah all right, bye," said Nicolas. He went inside. "Mice. Jesus Christ. Mice." He went over to look at the heater. Some of the vents were bent out of shape. He wondered if a mouse could fit through there. He went and got a pair of pliers from out of the kitchen and bent the vents back into place as best he could. It would have to be a real tiny mouse to get through there he figured. He moved a chair up against the heater. He never used it anyway; gas was too expensive. He sat down in the chair a moment.

Sounds were coming up through the heater. It was the children. He moved a little closer and put his ear up against the steel.

"Come on Daniel let me hold it," said a girl's voice.

"Wait your turn, Felicia," came the answer.

"Give it to me," said the oldest boy. "I'm the one that found it out by the cans." There was hissing.

"Keep your hand on its tail, Tyrone," said Daniel.

"Ow you fucking cat," said Tyrone. "I'll fix your ass." The animal hissed.

"Take it outside. Take it outside," said Daniel.

Nicolas heard the children walk out of the garage and close the door. He moved over to the kitchen window looking down at them now in the driveway by the stairs to the apartment. The older boy held a cat over his head, grabbing it by the tail and swinging it, the cat howling and hissing and spitting and clawing at the air wildly as it went around and around in a circle over the boy's head. Nicolas went and opened the door and yelled down at them.

"Eh leave that fucking cat alone you asshole," he said. "What the hell you think you're doing anyway?"

The three kids looked up at him. "Put the fucking thing down," he said again.

The boy swung it one last time over his head and let it fly. The cat swirled over to the empty lot, going down with a thud on the ground before getting up and shooting off down the street.

"You asshole," said Nicolas. "What if someone did that to you? How would you like it, huh?" The three kids stood there silent looking up at him with varying expressions: the oldest's sort of dumb, the middle one's mean, and the youngest's babylike. "Get out of here now," he went on, walking back into his apartment. The children stood there for a moment, then walked off themselves.

Back inside Nicolas had himself a beer. Things were a drag like always with the tenants downstairs. "Who knows what the father's like," he wondered. "Probably some Shermed out blood, who's in and out of the joint. Jeezus."

He didn't make much money working part time at the public library as a page putting the books away, and he was thinking about taking some night classes next semester at East Los Angeles College. The rent here he could afford. Almost anyway. He was a little behind, but told the landlady that he had had some extra bills and that he was already in school. She gave him some slack on the rent, not charging him a late fee, and giving him some extra time to pay her off.

Later that night when he was laying in bed, watching the news on television he got up to take a "mean leakiaso." He was coming out of the bathroom with a glass in his hand when he heard the garage door open and close down below. He went over to the heater and listened through the vents. The children were talking. They sounded out of breath as if they had been out running around in the dark.

"Do you think we can get it, Tyrone? . . ."

"Yeah, I think so Daniel. Mama'll probably won't be home till late again tomorrow . . . So we can jus' go out like tonight. . . ."

"That kid always leaves it out," said the girl.

"We won't leave it out Felicia. Huh, Tyrone?"

"Hell no," he said. "We can keep it in here. Mama never looks around in here."

They were silent for a while. All Nicolas could hear was rummaging among what sounded like boxes. It sounded like dishes and papers were being looked through to him. He couldn't tell for sure. He turned in for the night when he heard the washing machine start up.

When he came home from work Monday evening he passed the children out in front of their door. "Hi," he said. They all just stood and looked at him. The girl made a small smile. Nicolas smiled long and large. It was a good day so far. He picked up the "especial" from La Mas Market on Florence on the way home. A twelve pack of Miller Beer for five dollars was okay with him. He was going to be mellow and not drink any Ranier Ale tonight. "Now what the fuck," he said as he approached his apartment.

There were magazines strewn all about the bottom of the stairs, in the driveway and even in the vacant lot. It looked to him as though the kids had spent the entire afternoon out there reading and looking through old magazines they found in the garage. Nicolas walked back over to the children and rounded them up. "Heeeeeey are those your magazines," he said.

"Yeah," said the oldest of the three as if everything in the world was okay and that Nicolas was only bothering him and taking up his time. He ate an ice cream bar, his face all covered with the chocolate.

"Go and clean that mess up over there," said Nicolas. "I don't want you leaving all your crap over in front of my apartment. I don't go and do that in front of your house. So I don't want you to do it in front of mine. Okay? Now go and clean up all those fucking magazines."

"We didn't do it," said the middle one.

"Come on now," said Nicolas. "I don't have time for all of that crap." He shifted his package from his right to his left arm. "You wouldn't like it if I did that to you. Your mother wouldn't like it that's for sure. So go and clean up that crap. Go on now."

"Sheeeeeeiiiiiiittttttt," said the middle one. The two others moved over reluctantly, dragging their feet and walking slowly.

"Come on Daniel," said the oldest boy.

"Sheeeeeeiiiiiiittttttt," said the boy again. He stood there for a while, looking mean, then finally joined his brother and sister walking over towards the mess.

"Fucking little assholes," Nicolas said to himself following.

The children walked and picked the magazines up as slowly as they possibly could, reaching down as if it was such an effort that they could barely make it. They dragged their feet walking behind the building to the trash can.

"You're not going to keep any of those," said Nicolas, trying to be friendly. "I didn't say you had to throw them away. Now." He shifted the package in his arms again.

The three continued at their pace. Nicolas put his bag down and started helping so they would get a move on. He didn't want to spend the next half hour watching them dragging their feet and grumbling. "Eh, I'll give you a hand," he said, "and we'll get it done a lot quicker. See if we all lend a hand . . ." The children remained silent doing as they had been all along, working as slowly as they possibly could.

Inside he had himself some dinner. He ate the tacos de carne asada he had left over from lunch. He bought them from a truck and couldn't finish all six that he had ordered. He saved some of the chili too, so he planned on having a feast all over again, cracking open one of the "meelers" and munching away in front of the television.

At work he always ate out these days, buying some tacos or a burrito from the truck across the street and going over to the carwash if there were no Sheriffs around. There he'd sit and have himself a couple of beers in a paper bag while he ate his lunch. The workers at the car wash never said anything, or at the library when he came in smelling like beer. He never had more than two or three so didn't risk acting all stupid while he was at work. Not like when he was still smoking the Sherm and he'd be all buzzbombed at work and they had to send him home early a couple of times because he didn't know what all was going on. He liked his job because his co-workers were nice guys and never said anything about his drinking or getting buzzbombed sometimes during his lunch hour.

He leafed through the Herald Examiner he picked up at La Mas while he ate. He read about the usual number of murders, assaults, robberies and drug busts in the greater L.A. area with little interest. The only thing that attracted his attention was an article about a sting operation conducted by the police in San Francisco. A bunch of people had been arrested because they had jumped bail and were out on the lam with warrants on their asses. They were lured by the police with the phony chance of getting Superbowl tickets for cheap. Consequently they were nabbed and sent back to the can. Nicolas didn't like those sting operations. He felt they were unconstitutional and the police a bunch of lousy crooks themselves anyway. He was always careful about maybe being caught in one of those operations, like when he was buying dope or something like a stolen television or stereo from someone he didn't know. But he was careful about things like that.

He put the paper aside and picked up a schedule of classes from off of the table. He went and lay down on the couch. The television was still on in the other room. He carried another bottle of "meeler" with him. He would have to decide what all he was going to take at E.L.A.C. now that he had decided that he was going to school. All he really wanted was to meet women, and Max had told him that was the place.

"The chicks on the eastside are hot," he had said. "That's why I'm going man."

"But you don't have a girlfriend," Nicolas had countered.

"Eh, that's 'cause I don't want one, man," said Max. "This way I can get all the boom-boom I want and not worry about some bitch trying to own me. Eh man, it's cool. No lie."

So Nicolas decided to give it a try. "Eh maybe I'll even learn something," he said to himself. The phone rang and he went and picked it up. There was no one on the other end. "Asshole," he said into the receiver and went back to his business.

The next day coming home from work Nicolas went through the park. He met Miguel and Killer, a couple of old homeboys from La Florencia, he knew from a long time ago.

They stood around and talked for a while drinking some Night Train wine. A little guy rode over to them on a ten speed bike. He had a beanie rolled way down almost past his eyes and his Pendleton buttoned all the way up and down and his khakis cleaned and pressed with sharp creases. He smelled like paint. It was in his eyes. They called him Peanut.

"Eh you wanna buy a bike," he asked Nicolas. "It's from South Gate. Twenty-five dollars."

Nicolas gave him fifteen dollars and half the sack of weed he got from Miguel. He took off for home on his new bike. It looked newly painted, but sloppily. "That dude, Peanut, had more paint up his nose than what's on this bike," he thought as he drove it.

At home he was sitting around feeling a little hammered from the wine. He wished his mother were still alive. He hadn't thought much about that lately, but Night Train had a way of doing that to him. It was almost a year now since she passed away. He thought about calling his sister, but didn't. "She'll probably want me to come over or something like that. Hassle me or something. Fuck it."

The kids were in the garage laughing. He heard them walk out and slam the door. He got up off the couch to see what they were doing outside this time. The three were out in the driveway. The oldest was standing away from the others poised to send a Coke bottle crashing against the pavement, his brother and sister looking away and shielding their eyes and smiling.

Nicolas opened the door. "Eh what the fuck are you doing? Quit that shit out," he said. "I'm getting sick and tired of your little asses dirtying things up around here." The boy stood there with the bottle still poised. "You guys better get your shit together," he went on from the top of the stairs, "or there's going to be some trouble. And your mother doesn't want that to happen, I know, because you might get thrown out and then where the hell you going to live?" The three just looked at him, standing there as they had been. "Eh and you kids better not have any ideas of going out at night and stealing other kids' bikes or whatever you gorillas are planning on doing either. Or I'll call the Sheriffs and they'll come around and haul your asses away." The children walked away, grumbling and cursing, and Nicolas went back inside, still thinking about his mother.

That night he heard them in the garage again. "I don't like that man at all that lives up there," said the oldest. Nicolas sat in a chair by the heater listening and drinking Ranier Ale. "What you think, Daniel?"

"Yeah," said Daniel, "I don't like him either. He's always yelling at us to clean things up around here and shit like that. He's worser than mom."

"Yeah. An' everytime we gonna do something he comes along and starts trouble."

"Yeah. Like that time we was gonna start that fire in the lot and he came over and cussed us out and told us not to do it," said Daniel.

"How did he know we was gonna do that," said the girl. "Hey mister long-hair . . ."

"Hey mister longhair," the oldest cut in, "How come you always coming along and spoiling our fun?"

"Yeah mister longhair," said Daniel, banging his stick on the concrete floor. "Who are you anyway," he said.

"Yeah," said the little girl. "Who are you anyway? Where are you from?"

Nicolas went and lay down on his mattress, barely able to hear them from there. He fell asleep listening to their whispers and cries of inquiry. The children kept on talking. "I know," said the oldest, "let's do something to that man. And then maybe he'll leave us alone . . ."

A few days later in the week Nicolas drove up on his bike after work a little wobbly after stopping off in the park again and digging the scene with the gangster lean with Miguel, Killer and someone they called TNT. They drank more Night Train. As he was driving up Morton Avenue he noticed there was more broken glass than usual along the street and all the way up to his driveway. He was careful not to run over any. The children were out in front and he told them to clean it the hell up fast or he was calling the Sheriffs to come and throw their asses in jail where they probably belonged anyway. "Now get your little black asses over there and clean up that shit," he said, "I know you little motherfuckers went and did all that crap."

"We didn't do nothing," said Tyrone.

"Yeah," said Daniel.

"The fuck you didn't do nothing," said Nicolas. "I'm tired of your rotten little asses. Get that fucking glass out of my driveway. Fuck the rest of the street goddammitt, at least you kids are gonna clean up that shit, you little monsters."

Nicolas ranted and raved and had them clean the glass up from out of the driveway while he paced back and forth by the stairs. "Forget about the rest of the goddam street. I know you did it, but fuck it," he sputtered. "I wish you kids would leave me the fucking alone with all your goddam bottle breaking and shit like starting fires and stealing bikes and torturing cats and who knows what the hell else you fucking do when I'm not around to find out."

That night he moved his whole bedroom around. He moved the mattress so that it was almost blocking the door to the living room, but was as close as he could get it to the heater without blocking the entire doorway or putting it in the living room. On this side of the room he was near the telephone. It was a cheap one from some discount electronics store. Max had left it behind one day and Nicolas hooked it up. It hung on the wall or lay on the floor. The ring was a low chirp he sometimes couldn't hear. And sometimes thought he heard when it wasn't ringing.

Here the mattress was away from the window, but in front of a large mirror on the opposite wall. He thought it might be interesting if he ever got another woman up to his apartment. He pushed the dresser over to the window and put a lamp next to the telephone. He was rolling himself up a "leno" when he heard the children down below.

"There he goes," Nicolas heard the little girl squeal. He was pleased that he was able to hear them clearly from his new vantage point.

"Get him Tyrone," the girl said again.

Things were moved around down there and it sounded like aluminum cans were being thrown, clanking off the walls and washer and dryer.

"I'll get him this time." What sounded like a dresser was pushed aside and boxes were knocked over. "Hey, there's more," said the boy.

"EEEEEEEEEEKKKKKKKKKK," said the girl, squealing louder.

"Get out the way Daniel." More cans clanked off walls. The three yelled and ran out of the garage.

Nicolas didn't hear or see them for several days after this and he was beginning to miss them. Even though he didn't like all the trouble they started and got into he got a charge out of yelling at them and listening to them at night or in the day when they were in the garage and knowing what they were up to and planning.

He had begun to enjoy coming home and finding them out in front playing, now that he knew what they had been saying to each other at night in the garage. He baffled the children who now wondered how Nicolas knew, it seemed, everything they thought or talked about. Nicolas enjoyed his little game, smiling secretively when he passed them in the yard and dropping a nonchalant comment about things he shouldn't have been privy to.

"Did you ever find that blue shirt you were looking for, Daniel?" he said once and Daniel stood there frowning at Nicolas and grunted in answer.

"Tyrone stuffed your doll behind the washer Felicia. If you look there I'm sure you'll find it," he told the girl once and she looked perplexed while her two brothers scowled. The three would look at him with squinting and inquisitive eyes, the oldest's now more serious, the middle one's meaner and the girl's having taken on a certain coolness.

The washing machine still ran almost all of the night, but no longer could Nicolas hear their voices carried by the reverberations of the machinery, walls and heater. Those few days he watched more television than before and until much later in the night usually falling asleep with it on and waking at three or four A.M. to a buzzing snow-filled screen.

It was a lonely weekend. Saturday Nicolas found a letter addressed to the children in care of their mother in his mailbox. He went over to their house and knocked on their door, but there was no answer. He slipped the letter into their mail slot and went back to his apartment.

The mail man was always mixing up their addresses and he sometimes found his mail left by his doorstep by the mother or one of her children. Not too long ago, right after they had first moved in, Nicolas found his phone bill had been opened. Everything was still intact, but still he didn't like it and was going to raise a fuss, but decided not to: unable to prove the children had opened it or that it had not simply opened during the mailing process. He thought about changing his phone number because of the crank calls he received on occasion. People calling and hanging up or staying on the line without saying a word.

Sunday night he heard them come home all noisy and yelling at each other as they clambered out of the car. Nicolas was watching The Fugitive on television. He liked that show. He liked the way the character was always on the run, but you knew that he was cool and innocent besides. The show was already going to end, it being almost eleven, and during the next commercial he put the television in the bedroom where he could watch it while he lay down. He grabbed a short six-pack of Ranier Ale and took that to bed with him also. The phone rang, but he wasn't going to answer it. "It's probably that asshole," he thought.

The news was on. There were some mean things going on in the city. A whole bunch of drive-by shootings off of Vernon Avenue and over in Compton. He was already passing out from the booze and the thirty milligrams of valium he had left over from his mother's stash of pills the doctor had given her when she was still alive, when he heard the garage door open and close. He kept an ear open for the children while the news continued. The washer started going almost immediately. He heard the door open and close several more times, people going in and out of the garage, but no children's voices. "They must be whispering or something," he thought.

He got out of bed and went into the kitchen, taking a glass out of the sink of dirty dishes and taking it into the bedroom. He put it up against the wood of the wall, hoping to amplify their voices. It didn't help much. He went into the living room and leaned it up against the heater vents and strained his hearing. He caught only snips of the conversation.

"I don't know about that . . ."

"Well . . . can't . . . if nothing . . ."

". . . so there . . . because . . ."

He couldn't make any sense of the conversation. The third one came back into the room. There was silence. Soon music drifted up through the heater vent.

"It's a Small World" was playing. Nicolas heard them close the door and leave while the music continued playing. It must have been a cassette because the song began over and over again. He turned the television on louder and opened another Ale. He didn't like that song no way. "Those little fuckers," thought Nicolas. It seemed all night long the tape kept playing and he thought he heard someone go into there once during the night and turn the tape over and again began the same stupid song.

Nicolas couldn't hear them with the music playing. And they now always had it playing while they were down there in the garage. A couple of days of this passed and Nicolas wasn't getting much sleep because they left the tape playing all night long and it was driving him out of his mind.

"I'm going to steal that fucking radio if it's the last thing I do," he decided one night. So the next day he called into work saying he would be late because of a dentist appointment. Afterwards he waited around his apartment for a while until he was sure no one was home down there. He grabbed the waste basket from out of the kitchen and walked down the stairs to the back of the building.

He planned on jimmying the window open like he had heard some of the Morton Town dope fiends do it once when he was upstairs with the lights out and getting his johnson stroked by some woman he didn't see anymore. He lingered outside the window, taking a screwdriver from out of his pocket and forcing it underneath the wood frame.

It didn't take much effort to get it open and he looked inside. He wasn't too keen on having to go in there with all the mice. "And who knows what all else is in there," he thought. It was dark and damp as he had remembered it being. And cluttered with boxes and trash.

He leaned inside the open window, trying as best he could not to touch the cobwebs all around him, and looked about. There was the washer and dryer over on his left next to a door leading into the apartment. There was a pile of newspapers still held together by rubber bands and a motocross bike. It looked new. Most of the rest of the space was cluttered with boxes, all of them squashed. Their contents fell out from them: old and broken toys and clothes. There were also a few mattresses leaning up against the other wall and next to them three milk crates and a table.

The table was covered with dust and empty candy wrappers and potato chip bags. Among them was a small cassette player. The cord led over to an outlet not too far from him. He stepped back out of the window and took one last look around him. No one was watching. He scooted his body up some and leaned far into the open window. He was just barely able to reach the cord and pulled on it, sending the cassette player crashing to the ground. He heard tiny animal sounds all around him.

Nicolas put his feet back on the ground and pulled the cord. The cassette player dragged along the concrete floor. He lifted it out of the window and opened it. The cassette was still inside. He took the whole thing and put it in the waste basket and took it to his apartment. Upstairs he collected some of the newspapers that were lying around and took them out to the trash, just in case anyone was watching him. He knew no questions would be asked about a simple B and E, especially when only a radio was taken so he didn't bother closing the window. "They're not going to call the fuzz anyway," he thought, going back up the stairs.

The children didn't like it. That night in the garage they were furious. "I know it was that man upstairs," Nicolas heard Tyrone say clearly.

"Yeah," the other two agreed.

"Man he makes me mad," said Daniel, slapping his stick against the wall.

Nicolas grinned at himself, sitting on the floor in the living room and looking through a box of old photographs and drawings of times gone by and pounding down the Ales.

"What we gonna do about him," said Felicia.

Nicolas made a sad face as she said this, looking like he was going to cry and then finished the 16 ouncer and popped open another. He moved over towards the heater and pressed his lips up against the vents and burped loudly, wondering if they could hear him. The cassette player was sitting in the other room and he was tempted to play their song for them, but didn't.

"Let's burn him," said Daniel. "I got matches. We could do the stairs or something."

"Yeah," said Felicia. "Maybe then he'll just stay up there and rot."

Nicolas was drunk in his confidence that his phone worked and that he couldn't be trapped. "Oh yeah," he said. "That's what you're gonna do little fuckers, huh?"

"Maybe we got some gasoline or something in here," said Tyrone. "I bet we do."

Nicolas perked up at that. He heard them moving things around down there. "EEEEEEEEEKKKKK," said the little girl. Things were knocked over and cans clanked off the walls. He was beginning to doze off from the sauce and boredom, but fought it off, taking another drink and still listening to things being thrown around and the grumbles and curses down below. He heard the door leading outside open and close and stood up and walked over to the kitchen. He stood there by the window with the lights all out and peeking behind the curtain, down at the stairs and driveway.

There was only black out there. He sat down at the kitchen table and waited, looking out the window and taking drinks from his Ale between dozing off. He would have stepped outside, but he only went out there at night if it was an emergency and there was still plenty to drink in the refrigerator. If they were going to burn the stairs down, he figured, he would be able to see it start from where he sat and then be able to act accordingly.

He thought for a moment he saw them out there, but couldn't be sure. They looked as though they were just across the way in the vacant lot and staring at him the way they did when he passed them in the afternoon and they were playing. He wasn't sure if they were out there or not and wasn't going to check. The night passed slowly.

Less frequently were the children out front when he came home. On the rare occasion that they were Nicolas would try and be friendly with them more than ever. "Hey, how are you doing today," he asked.

And the three would stand there silent.

"Nice day today, isn't it," he said. "How was school?"

And the children would just stand there, stopping their playing and standing there staring at him as he walked and talked. Later in the afternoon he heard them talking loudly, while he lay in bed with a hangover.

"Come on now, Tyrone, hurry up," said Daniel.

"Fuck you boy," said Tyrone. "I know."

"We're really gonna show that man, huh," said Felicia.

"Yeah. We got all these bottles and we're gonna break 'em all in the driveway. We're gonna fuck him up. And he's gonna get a flat tire on his cheap old bike," said Tyrone.

"Yeah we're gonna show him not to fuck with us, huh," said Felicia.

"You got 'em all," said Daniel.

There was a great sound of bottles clinking together down there. Nicolas listened. He was tired and his head was pounding, He sat up in bed. "Bold little fuckers," he thought. He dragged himself out of bed and went over to the kitchen window. He looked down at the driveway and saw their shadows stretching long and lean across the asphalt.

"Eh what do you think you're going to be doing," he said, opening the door and stepping out onto the stairs. The children had already run off. He went down and looked around a little, but couldn't find a sign. He went back up the stairs, running when the phone started ringing.

"Hello," he said, picking up the receiver. There was only silence on the other end. "You fucking dildo," he said into the phone. Outside a bottle crashed in the driveway.

Nicolas hung up the phone and slumped back down onto the mattress. He found an open can of Ale and drank from it. It had been sitting there all day and was warm. He looked around the room and found a small pile of loose coins. He counted it up to see if he could buy at least another quart. He thought he'd fix some Top Ramen Noodles later on for dinner, because it was easy enough and there wasn't much else in the house. Monday was payday and still two days off. He planned on calling his sister later on in the evening and maybe going to visit her so he could get a meal and borrow a few dollars to hold him over.

He took the can with him outside and finished it off. He had a little more than three dollars in change. Enough for a couple of quarts if they let him slide on a few cents until later. "I'll call Vicki when I get back and tell her I'm coming over." He walked around the pile of glass in the driveway and went to talk with the children's mother.

"Your kids are in the garage at night. I can hear them," he said when the woman answered the door.

"Oh no," said Sharon. "Those are the mice I tol' you about. My children aren't allowed in the garage in the day time, let alone at night time. I won't let them in there."

"Well maybe," said Nicolas. "But I'm pretty sure your children are down in there also." He saw Tyrone over his mother's shoulder, peeking around a corner.

Sharon didn't like the way Nicolas looked that afternoon. "Like some long-haired fag," she thought. She took a swallow from the glass in her hand. "No they're not mister," she said. "I raised my children right. If I tell 'em not to do something they don't do it. They listen to me. And who the hell you think you are anyway, telling me how to raise my children or that they don't listen to me. Jus' who the hell you think you are." She swayed a little, spilling some wine on her nightgown.

"I didn't mean to imply any of that," said Nicolas. His stomach turned and he felt like he was going to shit in his pants at any moment. "I'm sorry," he said. His butt cheeks quivered and he sucked them in. "I'm sorry," he went on. "I was only saying that I think that maybe they are down there. I mean I know what I hear. Right?"

"Well I don't care what the hell you thought mister. I think you been drinking too much of that Ranier Ale—what do they call it—that green death stuff—I see you going back and forth to the store for those big forty ounce bottles. Don't think I'm blind mister." She took a drink, some of it dribbling down her chin. Her stare was cold. "So now, who the hell you—some old wino like you—you think you are tellin' me stuff about my kids. When I know damn well it's that green death you be drinking that's creating all those sounds you be hearing."

"I didn't mean to upset you," said Nicolas. "I'm sorry. That's not what I meant . . ." The door slammed in his face.

Back upstairs he took a long gulp out of the quart bottle. His skin felt all itchy and hot. "Fuck that bitch," he said. He farted a wet one and laughed. He sat down on his mattress and picked up the phone. He was going to call his sister, but put it down when he heard the children once again down below.

"I saw mama yelling at mister longhair," said Tyrone. He ate handfuls of fritos from out of a large bowl. "I thought mama was gonna hit him the way she was yelling."

"Why was mama yelling at you mister longhair," said Felicia, looking up at the ceiling. "Why was mama yelling at you the way Tyrone says she was?"

"'Cause he was ratting on us, I bet," said Daniel, banging his stick on the concrete. "Ratting on us about being in here I bet."

Nicolas picked the cassette player up and pressed the play button. The scratchy sound came out of it after a while. He kept the volume down low and drank from the bottle, listening.

"Hey mister longhair," said Tyrone, "our mama doesn't know that we're in here. She's not as smart as us. She won't believe you." They all three laughed.

"When I get that longhair," said Daniel. "I'm gonna poke out his eyes, like this." He gestured like he was stabbing at someone where right then and there was only air.

Nicolas pressed the stop button. "Fuck you," he said. He threw the cassette player across the room and lit a cigarette. It banged against the wall, leaving a black mark, then skidded across the wooden floor. The phone rang. Nicolas wasn't going to pick it up. He drank some more and listened.

"Wha's mama doing now," asked Felicia.

"I don't know," said Tyrone. "She's on the phone." He stuffed his mouth with fritos, some of them falling onto the ground to be carried away by mice.

"Daddy's supposed to be coming back tomarra," he said. Nicolas walked over to the heater to hear more. "He's an ex-con now," said Tyrone. They all smiled. "What you gonna be when you grow up Daniel," he asked.

Daniel stepped out into the open. He planted his feet firmly on the ground, his legs slightly apart, his weight perfectly balanced on both sides as best his six-year-old mind could coordinate. He raised his stick as if for combat and swung it. All three laughed the sound echoing up through the heater.

THE FUNERAL

Corie Rosen

That morning the air was clean and bright, full of the sounds of the kinds of birds that nest in the eaves of suburban neighborhoods. Through the open door Adam could see the spring day that hovered just beyond the narrow coffin room. The room itself was filled with whispering guests and Adam, turning his attention from what he considered the inappropriately temperate weather, strained to make sense of the conversation.

"Poor dear," said one of the heavy women in black.

"The death of a child. So unnatural," said another.

"Her only girl too," sighed a third.

"Only seventeen. Such a tender age," said a fourth.

"At least her suffering is over," a male voice said.

Turning away from them, Adam straightened his lapels as his father had taught him. He was almost thirteen, but had not yet developed the stature of a man and the height of the women left him standing in shadows. He moved toward the doorway, near the side of the room and out of the way of the many pairs of feet. In the morning light the coffin was matter-of-fact and not at all frightening as it had seemed in the night. He made eye contact with his reflection in the box's glossy side panels and breathed deeply. Anna is in the box, he thought.

"My sister is in the box," he whispered, unbelieving. Then he drew in another long breath.

The night before he had awakened screaming in the dark. He had dreamed of coffins, yawning cavernous things with eyes like wolves and teeth like tigers that had come pounding after him in the night, chasing him into a thicket where darkness had given way only to more darkness and the noise of his pursuers was thunderous and wild. It was the sound of his own crying that had awakened him. His father had come into his room, turned on the light and sat on the end of the bed, talking until Adam felt sleep come to him again. He knew he should have been embarrassed to cry in front of his father, but the weight of his relief was so great that his heart could accommodate no other feeling and nestling into his comforter he fell into a guiltless sleep.

Then, in the early morning hours, there were more dreams. He saw his sister in her coffin, then back in the hospital, thin and weak in her cotton nightgown, doctors laboring over her, whispering the cancer secrets that only they knew. Then he was on the beach with Anna, a vacation to the coast that the family had taken many summers before. She had his hand in hers and was leading him down to the water. They had just turned to face the brilliant blue of the wide waving ocean when he woke up again. His father's voice was calling him in to breakfast.

That was hours before the people began to arrive, before they piled into cars and went back to the graveyard and the coffin room. During the ceremony, some nearby sprinklers were running and he kept himself busy counting the tick, tick, tick of their rotations, watching the wet sprays dampen the grass and the shoes of the late comers who invariably arrived holding bundles of flowers. The ceremony lasted either five-hundred and nine sprinkler tick's or four-hundred and nine. He had lost count once when his fat old aunt, Mirabelle, had started to cry and had clasped him to her sticky, makeup-streaked face.

At home, his mother locked herself behind the oak door of the downstairs bedroom, cried all day, saw no one, and would not be consoled. Old fat Mirabelle stayed and spent most of her time watching dull television shows about older single women who meet wonderful executives in drycleaners or elevators or at their sister-in-law's divorce hearing. Adam discovered her choice of programming accidentally when he wandered into Mirabelle's line of sight and he was forced to spend an entire morning watching a movie about a young secretary who falls in love with her boss and loses fifteen pounds in the process.

"Adam, where are you off to now?" She asked as he scrambled out of the room.

"Be right back."

He was escaping down the hallway, happy to have evaded his aunt, when he noticed that Anna's bedroom door had fallen open. His mother had pointedly asked that the door to that room be kept closed, but the springs in the handle were unreliable and the door had a way of drifting open all on its own. Beyond the wayward door lay the neat room, where everything was just as she had left it. He sat on her bed, admired her pictures, then opened her closet and examined her neatly hung clothes, her pink flip-flops, her collection of high topped tennis shoes. He took out her old tennis racket and swung a few times, but the racket was too heavy and he placed it back in its corner of the closet, careful to restore it to the exact position in which it had been left. He sat down next to the low pink book-shelf where Anna had collected her stories. They were mostly short picture books that she had saved from childhood, the kind with large pictures that thrill young children. They were simple and easy to understand, but he opened them anyway. One by one he entered them, caressing their glossy pages and quickly disappearing into the Grimm Fairy Tales, English gardens, Ancient Greece, places that Anna had been before him.

He read through the afternoon and into the evening and that night his dreams were vivid and full of the shapes and colors he had seen in the wide books' glossy pages. Witches and wizards visited him and once he woke up with a start, surprised to find his face wet with briney tears. But the dreams came again and within the dreams again the picture books. He read stacks of them on the beach and together he and Anna walked into the water carrying armloads of text that floated before them like foam on the crest of a wave.

There were hundreds of old books on her shelf, and the next day, while his mother cried, his father greeted guests and the television blared, he read. It went on like that for two days. And each night when he slept he found Anna, a stack of picture books and the wild brilliant sea.

On the morning of the third day, his father came into his room. His mother's crying had ceased and the television too had fallen silent. The guests had stopped coming and the house was still with too much quiet.

"Hey Bud," his father said, patting him on the head, "we've got some work to do today."

Adam stifled a groan, "All right. In a minute."

"Your mother and your aunt went over to the neighbors'. And we've got to clean some things out of Anna's room."

"Really?" Adam asked, sitting upright, abandoning his dream on the edge of his pillow. He had been visiting her on the beach again.

"It's up to us, as the men of the house, to take care of this."

Adam pursed his lips.

"I don't want to do it any more than you do. But it's too much for your mother just now. You understand. We've got to be strong for her. It's our job."

"Today," his father added.

The room was easy enough to empty. Yellow and white clothes came out of dresser drawers and went quickly into boxes. Blue jeans fell from closet hangers like leaves in autumn, making sad heaps on the floor before they too were added to the boxed inventory. Bedding was folded and laid away and a window blind was pulled, letting sunlight stream into the room where it made a narrow pool of light on the bare carpet, like a long finger pointing cruelly toward the vacant space. Bare walls and closets yawned with emptiness, showing yellowed paint and cracked moldings and scattered heart shaped stickers. The only thing left to empty was the long low bookcase where Anna had kept her stories.

One by one Adam and his father placed them in boxes, stacking them neatly together and banishing them from their pink ledges. On the shelves the books had seemed lively, promising, worlds waiting to be discovered. But stacked in their cardboard cubes, the books seemed old and tattered, tired messengers eager for rest. The image struck Adam and he sat down on the carpet, clutched a small stack of flat books to his chest and began to sob, quietly at first, then with increasing fervor until he was wailing violently, like a woman wracked with grief.

"Don't cry. Don't cry. It will be all right. I promise." His father began, but Adam was beyond the cast of speech, shaking with the force of his lament, his face red and puffy.

"We've got to do something," he managed to heave through his tears.

"Okay, Bud. Anything you want. Let's do something."

"But there isn't anything we can do," he howled.

"It's hard. It's really hard. This is hard for us all. But it's going to be all right."

Adam wiped his nose on the sleeve of his shirt and glared at his father.

That night they all ate dinner in silence. The chicken stew and pie had been brought to the house by a neighbor and had the foreign taste of restaurant food. Mirabelle generously allowed herself a third helping and Adam noticed that her lipstick left a red smudge on the edge of her water glass. After dinner, his mother and father went into their room and closed the oak door and Mirabelle returned to the small living room and its big television. Adam was still in the kitchen. When he heard his aunt snoring loudly, her face half buried in one of the plaid sofa cushions, he stood up and slipped down the hall into Anna's old room, now empty except for an unwieldy stack of cardboard cubes. The picture books were easy to find and he carried one box, then another, down the dark hallway, into the kitchen, and out of the sliding glass door into the dark, cool yard.

In the kitchen he opened drawer after drawer, careful not to wake his aunt. From the drawer next to the oven he withdrew a slim matchbook which he clasped tightly as he hurried outside. Standing over the books, he looked down at their stained and softened corners and he struck the first match. It ignited with a startling pop and he dropped it quickly onto the books where it smoldered and hissed against the back of a slick cover. Then he lit another, and another. With the fourth he fumbled and nearly burned himself, but the books were already burning, the sides of the boxes hosting a curlicue of flames whose tendrils grew longer and longer, reaching like desperate fingers into the night sky. The odor of destruction wafted into the house and the kitchen door flew open.

"What on earth are you doing?" his father asked.

Adam looked back at him and said nothing.

Moving quickly, his father turned on the spigot attached to the garden hose and began to douse the books.

The flames receded a little, but the fire remained. They stood there like that, Adam silently watching, his father holding the long green hose, until the last reluctant flame died into the black, watery mess.

Adam met his father's eyes, said nothing, turned, and went inside. Later, while he slept, he searched for Anna in his dreams, looked for their beach and her sickbed, her thin face and her pale nightgown, but he could not find them. The compartments of his mind were empty like the darkened room down the hall. That night he slept soundly, dreamed nothing and was quiet.

MANNY

Floyd Salas

Steam billowed from a locomotive smoke stack, frayed into nothing under the roof of the yellow wooden platform. Manny, Manny, I chanted silently as soldier after soldier suddenly took shape at the top of the steep iron steps, gripped the handrail, then dropped down into the crowd of family and friends below them. I wanted each one of them to be Manny.

Each time a brown uniform appeared in the doorway, I held my breath, hoping it was him, a shine of excitement in my eyes as bright as a sheen of tears, sure he'd finally found a way to come home when he got my letter.

Dad, a small, satisfied smile on his face, draped in a loose-fitting suit picked out by Dora to make him look younger, deep blue and solemn enough to show mourning, but no black, except for his tie, was a jolly mass of solid bulk. Dora looked like a picture in a magazine in a dress suit that captured her mood: a soft green, trim and tailored as her sweet manner, modest and simple and yet stunning as her long brown hair, the sweet beauty of her features. Even though I was just a boy and she was my older sister, I knew this. Even girls looked at her when we walked by on the way to church. Unlike Mom whom I never thought of as attractive. Not that she wasn't, I guess, but I just felt the warmth of her. She was the center of all my existence and I felt secure and contented around her and now she was gone. That's all I knew, but now I was happy because at least Manny was coming back home.

"There he is!"

Manny appeared in the doorway, cap pushed back on his head, the cap brim rounding his face, brown eyes wondering for the second he scanned the crowd. Then he saw us, waved from the doorway with a smile of recognition, glancing at each one of us as if to see who was there, then jerked the brim of his cap down and stepped down into the crowd clustered around the doorway.

I couldn't even see his brown cap for a few moments until he stepped full bodied in his uniform out of the circle of people around the steps, and walked toward us, broad shouldered, suitcase in one hand, gym bag in the other. I got the chills I felt so good. Yet, though his lip still curled with a big grin, he stared hard at me with his brows notched together under his cap brim.

I stepped forward to meet him in my cotton windbreaker jacket, cheeks warm with joy, legs bent and springy. Manny was home again.

Manny put both his bags down, looped a long right hand out and hooked it around my neck and pulled me to him, pressed my crewcut head hard against his chest, and kept it there.

I looked up and he looked down for a few seconds, capbrim covering his eyes, a flesh fold under his tucked-in chin.

Dora leaned over my head and kissed Manny's cheek. Dad squeezed his free hand and patted his shoulder.

Manny kept one hand on my bristly, crewcut head and pressed my face against his chest, even when he picked up his suitcase, and looked around. I held onto Manny and he kept his arm around me. I picked up the gym bag with the boxing gear with my free hand, smiling.

He held onto me when we began to walk—the suitcase in his left hand and his right arm hooked around my shoulders—down the gray wooden floor of the platform, past the sun-yellowed clapboard walls and the weathered wooden pillars.

He never let go even when we turned down the ramp into the main building, the sound of our footsteps rising from the hardwood floor, a half-stepped, marching sound, because we walked in time together, a distinct sound different from the sound of all the other footsteps, the depot noises. I could almost see it ripple our shadow, skimming the floor ahead of us.

And he didn't let go when we had to walk through a cloud of cigar stink and around the two old men who had caused it and who talked together in the middle of the aisle, either, and all the rest of us wrinkled up our noses, nor when we had to walk through and around the clusters of suitcases and dufflebags scattered all the way down the aisle to the glass doors at the end, and he didn't let go when we got to the doors either, just bumped one with his left shoulder muscle and pushed it wide open, and kept it open, facing the glass with me, his suitcase flattened against it by his knees, for all of us to pass through, before he weaved back like slipping a punch and let go and the door swung closed, but he still didn't let go of me then or I let go of him all the way across the parking lot or while sidestepping through some parked cars to get to the back of the blue Studebaker, though he had to let go of me there in order to open the trunk and put the bags in.

I stood behind him, shoulders hunched, hands bunched in my windbreaker pockets as he lifted up the trunk lid, then bent my head and blinked my eyes when he picked up the suitcase, then made a hissing sound like a tire leak through my front teeth.

Manny's head spun around, one eye looking over his shoulder at me. Dora started toward me from the rear door. Dad shook his car keys. "What's wrong? What's the matter with you? Stop that! Stop that!"

I stood there, hands bunched in my jacket pockets, shoulders hunched, head down, and stepped back away from Dora when she tried to touch me, shaking my head back and forth to insist that there was nothing wrong, trying to smile.

* * *

I followed Manny all over the house: upstairs to the bedroom to put his bags away, then waited in the hall while he took a leak, then followed him downstairs into the kitchen, then stood up against the wall as neighbor men and male cousins came over and everybody crowded in the kitchen and drank coffee and smoked cigarettes.

"All these big guys marching down the road, taking long steps, and I can't let them beat me, so I stretch my legs and hit the pace hard and all my running and training pays off, and after ten miles, they've all slowed down but me and one tall guy who's been to college and run long distance, and the Sergeant says, 'What the hell's the matter with you sonofabitches up there? A bunch of bastards can't keep up with a little man like Serrano. He's the toughest man in the whole fucking troop, Goddamnit! March!'"

Everyone laughed, but I was astounded at the way he cussed for the first time ever in the house. Dad only grinned. There were no women around. Dora was upstairs with her baby, Cousin Rachel was upstairs in her room, and Mom was dead.

"Boyd. Get Dad's shotgun and your .22 out of the closet," Manny said, "and I'll show you how they teach us to fight with bayonets."

There I was with a rifle in my hand, learning how to jab and parry with the barrel, then cross with the butt to the head. All the men murmured at how quickly I picked it up.

Then he taught me to stand at attention and salute arms, snapping that rifle up in two slapping movements, "Hup, one, two!" then down to his side again in two more, "Hup, one, two!"

Manny was serious. Dad was serious. All the men were serious. I was learning how to handle a gun, to salute arms, to become a soldier, to save our country. I felt like I could save my country. I felt like I could leave the empty house and go to war like my brothers and fight good and become a hero like Manny and save the world from the Unholy Trio, Tojo and Hitler and Mussolini: "Hup, hup! One, two, three! Hup, hup! One, two, three!"

* * *

"Boyd, go up and get my boxing bag for me. I want to show some of my boxing medals to Dad!" Manny said, and I ran upstairs and into his bedroom as fast as I could and grabbed the bag and ran downstairs again.

I was panting when I got back to the kitchen and handed the bag to Manny. I watched, longing to win one of those gold medals, or one of those chrome fighters mounted on a pedestal, or have my picture in the paper like that, and have the men all admire it and me. I longed to be like Manny, as big as Manny, look like Manny, be as strong as Manny. I loved Manny. I ran up and down the stairs all day doing things for Manny, running errands for Manny, and loving every bit of it, all of it, wishing I could do it all day, every day, for the rest of my life.

* * *

After dinner when all the guys had gone, Dad pulled a chair up to the kitchen table, turned it around and sat in it backwards, using its backrest for an armrest, his belly big as a pillow against it, his tie flapping over his folded arms, and asked, "Had many fights since you went back to camp?"

"Two bouts, Dad, and won both by knockouts."

Dad's face glowed like the golden gloves nuggets that hung by a tiny gold chain from the tieclasp Manny had given him. My face glowed too, though I stood now against the clothes chute in the corner of the kitchen, with a fine red line forking across one eye, a reminder that I'd cried only a couple of hours before.

"How is it that you were able to get a furlough so soon again, Manny? You were here for two weeks only a couple of months ago." Rachel, Mom's old maid cousin, made a sour face.

She sat by the kitchen door with an insinuating smirk on her twisted mouth, glassy pop eyes, pale flesh so bloodless and transparent that the blue of her bones seemed to show through her hands.

Manny got a blank look on his face, his upper lip heavy with shadow. "Guys in the special services like me, who entertain the troops, aren't subject to the restrictions of most GIs," he said. His voice sharpened. "Got it?"

"I think I do," she said.

Manny stared at her for a few seconds and it was as if whatever was seething in Rachel had seeped like a poisonous odor out of her pulpy pores and floated over the room. Even Dad, with his flapping tie touching the chrome rungs of the backrest, had a dense look to his brown eyes, and a long finger of shadow reached from his loose lower lip to his sagging chin. For a whole minute there must not have been a single word or motion made by any of us.

Then Manny barked, "Let's go to the dance tonight, Boyd. I saw a poster at the SP depot and Lionel Hampton's at the auditorium."

I pushed off the doorframe in seconds, a grin on my face, but got caught by a couple of body punches, tiny digs to the gut, that didn't hurt much but knocked the breath out of me, buckled me up at the beltline. "Hey!"

"Get dressed," Manny said. "Let's go have some fun. That's what I came home for."

A grin on my face I felt so good. I was getting to go hear one of the greatest jitterbug bands going. I couldn't sit down or stand still while I waited for him to finish with his bath upstairs, and I didn't want to wrinkle my tweed sportcoat and my gabardine brown slacks either. Kept walking back and forth between the rooms on the first floor: out the kitchen, through the dining room, into the double size front room, over to the front window, where Dad always sat now, staring out past the knotted curtain to the street, mourning Mom and listening to the Red River Valley about "the cowboy who loved you so true."

Manny whistled at me from the open, sliding dining room doors, then grinned. I grinned back, yet noticed that there wasn't any curl to his lip, no cupid's bow, more like a tightened knot in a stretched string when his lips spread, and though there was a glad shine to his deep-set eyes, there was still a damp tone to his voice all the time he was talking on the way there in the car, as if the heavy bay dew had come in with the middle of winter to dampen it, bringing the deep sound out, giving a heavy timbre to it, instead of leaving it high and dry and light like it was in the summer. I wondered if he was worrying about me. It seemed that there was something bothering him, but I didn't want to ruin the great fun by thinking about it too much.

I grinned when he made me squeal at the way he swerved to the right and around a car at a stop sign in front of us, then shot across the street without stopping at all. But when he parked the car and when he asked for the tickets at the box office, he spoke in that same deep tone.

* * *

I caught my breath. The bandstand looked a block away. Bright. About five thousand sailors in blue, soldiers in khaki brown, and girls and guys in civvies out on the dance floor.

Up close by the bandstand, Hamp was blowing vibes, furry balled sticks fluttering over the keys like a hundred moths, sweat on his brown face, smiling down.

The shiny mouths of the brass horns behind him blew out a hot chorus and swung back and forth in rhythm to the base hum and the drum beat, and some people in the crowd cried out, "Yeah! Yeah!" and the dancers swung with style, too.

Manny swayed from side to side with short boxer's steps, ridges of his neck muscles branching into his muscular back even in his brown uniform, big brow like a banner above his handsome face.

I followed him around the fringes of the floor, along a few rows of spectators' seats, elevated like a box circle. Manny started greeting guys and girls he knew from around the neighborhood and from all over Oakland, because he was a boxing champion and in the papers. It made me proud to be with him, the way he looked, wavy-haired and husky, with a neat drop of his tailored gabardine slacks down to his military shoes, the oxblood polish below his cuffless pant legs, yet with a polite, thoughtful mood, not smiling.

"Hey, Manny! How come back so soon?" one guy asked, with a smile and a handshake.

But Manny didn't smile, his chin came right up and his back arched and his chest puffed out, and he answered, "Got pull," and pulled his hand free from the guy, then turned away made me hurry through the crowd to catch up with him.

"What about him?" I asked, by the bandstand, trying to keep up.

"Talks too much," Manny answered, and kept working his way around people out into the hall to the closest bar, which was only a cubby hole in the wall spread out barely long enough for six bartenders to hustle in. I wondered what was up when Manny ordered two beers and a coke in a low voice, then started chug-a-lugging the first beer while the bartender was filling the second.

The old guy noticed and stared at him with a pair of whiskey-yellowed eyes with wrinkled booze pouches beneath them that looked like basted eggs.

Manny smacked his lips when he brought the cup down and saw the old guy looking at him, as if to show that he didn't care what the guy thought.

But the old guy was a rounder as sharp as his thin mustache, knew where the action was, even I could tell. When he put the second beer down and got my coke and picked up the dollar bill, he didn't look at Manny again until he had turned around to the cash register to make change, where he watched Manny in the bar mirror without being seen.

I watched him as he watched Manny kill the whole cup without bringing it down from his mouth a second time, then picked up the second beer without wiping his lips or even waiting for the bubbles in his belly to settle and started on that one, too. He didn't seem to see the bartender at all until he lifted up his finger to signal for another beer, saw the guy in the mirror looking at him and then poked at the cup for another one like he still didn't care.

When he got back his change, he said, "It's good for a guy to drink once a while, Boyd."

I took a swallow of my coke so as not to have to look at him, or the bartender, who grinned crookedly, while I waited for Manny to finish off the second beer. He looked like he really needed it, a full paper cup in one hand and the other tipped bottom up and draining. I had to walk slow behind him as he gulped big swallows of the third one with every step he took all the way back down the hall to the dance floor.

* * *

He'd almost killed the cup when a drunken sailor hit against me with his hip and knocked me to the side with a grunt.

"Hey, Yo-yo! What do you think you're doing?" Manny said, grabbing me and holding me up on my feet.

"What 'a you care, Doggie?" said another sailor, bigger, tougher, an Okie, with red wrinkles on his neck.

"You make the move and find out, yo-yo!" Manny said and spread his legs to fight just as the drunk sailor threw a flying block at his chest, but hardly touched it with his shoulder before he got hit by a flicking left hook uppercut, inside and up like a pure reflex on Manny's part, that licked on the underside of the guy's chin and dropped him down to the floor which made the tough sailor cock a right hand throw it overhand at Manny like it was a baseball instead of a fist.

Manny easily bobbed to his left below it, then swung right back on a heel and toe to his right with a left hook and caught the sailor with a crack of knuckles that carried him two feet through the air, slanted sidewise, before he dropped. He'd flattened both of them.

"Watch yourself, Boyd!" Manny shouted, then crouched, teeth showing in a tiny smirk, and a doubled fist by each flexed jaw muscle, to meet the charge of the red-necked sailor, who'd staggered to his feet, and all his friends. Then with his head down so that he only caught the punches that touched him on the back of his head and shoulders, he started banging to their bodies with both hands, blasting every sailor that got close to him with a crippling blow to the gut, caving each guy in, and getting the rest of them so excited that they got in each other's way and hit each other by mistake and hit other people in the watching crowd, too, who got mad and hit back, while Manny, who backed up as he punched, bumped into the people behind him, who were pushing forward to see the big fight, who bumped into guys behind them, who got mad and started punching at them, and pretty quick there were about four or five other fights going on between sailors and civilians, and sailors and sailors, and civilians and civilians, too, while the cops were trying to beat their way into the center of the riot with their billyclubs to the bang of the drum, the blare of the trumpets, the curses of the sailors, the screams of the girls, who stampeded with fright and scared everybody around them, and got them wild with fright, too, and they stampeded, too, and many people fell and nearly everyone around got trapped in the huge, tussling, scuffling, punching, kicking, milling crowd, that kept revolving and revolving with such increasing momentum that it suddenly broke loose and surged down the dance floor like a huge wave, catching everybody on the floor up in it, sucking everybody along.

* * *

Dancers and cops were knocked around by the smashing force of the screaming, stampeding crowd. Dancers lost their partners, and the cops their clubs. Manny got spun around in a circle like he was caught in a whirlpool, a stiff-featured set to his face, not even thinking of fighting anymore, only concerned with somehow keeping his hold on me now, one hand on the back of my coat collar, the other on my arm, to keep me from getting knocked down and stomped to death beneath all those metal-plated shoes and dagger-sharp high heels, and I had only one thought myself and that was to hold onto Manny's wrist for life or death, too scared to even scream. Then Manny got swept down the floor and lost his grip on me.

Stretched out and battered by the bodies of people in the crowd like a small flag in a bad wind, I had the luck to grab hold of an iron railing which fenced in the spectators' seats. I pulled myself up onto the elevated platform, then stood up on a seat and watched the tidal wave of people sort of batter itself down the dance floor with a rumbling roar that reverberated way up in the gallery, where it echoed and re-echoed like an unbroken barrage of cannon fire, against the ominous back-ground sound of the band, punctuated by the man yells and the girl screams and the hoarse shouts for help of people who had got knocked down and trampled over, then left sprawled behind by, the huge crowd that kept surging in a big circle like a whirlpool that went all the way around the floor and back to the bandstand where it had started from and where it came to a crushing, grunting halt with an interlocking of arms and legs, breasts and backs, shoulders and hips just as Hamp brought his arm down with the last beat of the half-time piece and stopped the band.

* * *

For just a few seconds there was almost absolute quiet and almost absolute stillness in the big arena, only a shuffling of feet and a rippling of heads as the whole mob seemed to set like jello, stick together so close that I could only see a bubble of blue uniforms below me, white caps like ducks at sea, and lipstick spots and pompadours where girls stood, and I could have never found Manny, though I kept looking for him.

But in those moments of silence so utter and so out of place after what had just happened, Hamp suddenly woke up and saw what was facing him, that the riot had stopped for just a second and he straightened up like a soldier, looked down at the crowd again, then spun around, shouted, "Gin for Christmas," whipped his hand around to wind up his band fast, stamped his foot down, "Bam-bam-bam!" to start them off on the right beat, to hit it and hop right to it, and help him capture that mob before it got loose again.

His body movements seemed to crackle like fire. I could hear the rustle of his clothes when he swung his wrist around, then whipped his whole arm wide for the rhythm section to take it away as the stamps of his foot cracked like pistol shots just before the horns came in with a blasting chorus, as exciting as a marching band, and the rippling of heads and the shuffling of feet came to a complete stop as every face in the crowd looked up and looked long, as every guy and girl got caught up and swept along by the pulsing beat, the rousing chorus, then began to bob their heads after the first couple of bars, then sway in time with the groups around them, and the groups themselves to cause dips and swells like waves or heads in the middle of the human sea, because everybody was with it, and stayed with it.

Hamp had them and he kept them, and as soon as he knew he had them, he leaped over to his drums and picked up his sticks and started to rat-a-tat-tat for them, and everybody in the band grinned and hustled to help him, from the base man humped over his big-bodied baby to the horn men with their pursed mouths curled up at the corners, and grins began to flicker up like foam flecks from the crowd below, which made Hamp feel so good that he began to grunt to the chord sounds that the base made, and people in the crowd picked up and liked it and joined him, and pretty quick there was one big chorus of "Uh-uh-uh-uh-uh-uh!" and he kept tom-toming away until he was sure that they were hypnotized, hung up with him, then he stopped drumming and stepped out in front again, and stopped grunting, and spun back around to his band and twirled his drum stick up high and then down like a baton and brought the band right down to a quick blaring finish of the short piece, then twirled back around to face the crowd, and, sweating so hard that he gleamed, he threw up his arms and bowed low from the waist.

The whole gigantic crowd busted up in a great big shout for Hamp and his boys, a prolonged applause that was pierced by whistles and punctuated by stamping feet, and more yells and more whistles and more clapping for two or three more minutes because everybody realized that Hamp had saved the scene, had made them feel good when they had felt bad and had flipped out.

Then the whole crowd seemed to crack apart all at once like a honeycomb, when the applause finally began to quiet down, and the people headed for the exits, to hit that hallway and have a drink and come back down to normal once again.

As the masses of people flowed on by me, still standing up on the seat in the box section by the exit, and thinned out on the floor, I caught sight of Manny, about ten feet from the bandstand, and I waved my arm until he finally saw me up high, waved back, then started toward me.

I took a good look at him as he drew slowly near to me, then reached out and grabbed my hand and helped me down to the dance floor, where he squeezed both of my shoulders, then, resting his hand lightly on my shoulder, walked into the hall with me.

* * *

I got to be with Manny all the time for over a week, went everywhere with him, cut school, and even hung out in the neighborhood bars with him. And when I found a twenty dollar bill on the floor next to a bar stool in the Green Spot on Sixteenth Street and gave it to Manny, Manny said, "We'll split it. Ten for you and ten for me, like real buddies."

And when we walked down the block, all the neighbors leaned out and waved and said hello to my handsome soldier brother, and my big brother waved with one hand and put his other hand on my shoulder and held it there as we walked down the street in the sunshine, everything shining, my brother and me shining. I had my big brother with me. I was not alone. I was happy again, I got to be . . . with Manny.

* * *

From the top of the stairs, I saw the red light of an MP jeep down in the darkened street. I watched it change colors and blur through the stained glass of the hall window as I went down to answer the door bell from the bedroom where I had been sparring with Manny, the glove smacks and bouncing sounds of our feet still fresh in my mind.

I landed by the door with a springing jump from the hall stairs, my sweaty T-shirt all marked with rusty glove burns from body punches, I opened the door using both gloves.

"How many military men in this house?" the big MP barked. He was over six feet, his overseas cap pointed as a widow's peak in the middle of his frowning brow, freckles dotted emphatically across his thick nose.

"What?" I asked.

"Give me the names of the servicemen in this house!" he said and glared at me down below him, all of the features on his face corkscrewed round his hard blue eye.

"What's wrong?" I asked with a flushed face, my boxing gloves as big as bar bells on my thin arms, covering them nearly all the way to the elbows.

"Awwww, shit! Isn't there anybody of age in this goddamned house?" The MP's snarl came from deep down in his gut. He stamped into the hallway with his big boots, wrinkling up his blue eye.

Dora slid the front room door open. "What's wrong?"

"Names of all the military men in this house," the MP demanded.

"There *are* no military men in this house," she said.

"But, Dora, Man—" I said, but she stated again, this time sharply: "There are none!" and stepped between the MP and me.

"Hey!" the MP said, looking at me. "Why's that kid wearing boxing gloves? Isn't Manny Serrano a boxer?"

Dora colored darkly in the hall light. "Go up to your room, Boyd," and I took the stairs two at a time and ran down the hall, bursting into the bedroom just as Manny was clamping a glove between his knees to pull his hand free.

"Don't go down, Manny!" I said. "There's an MP's down there!"

But Manny only glanced up as he pulled the last glove off and grabbed for his tailored shirt without even pausing to answer me, though he did say as he moved: "Put my gloves in my boxing bag and get my suitcase out of the closet, Boyd," and started tucking his shirt-tails in.

I had his pair of gloves in that bag with the rest of his equipment by the time he had finished tucking in his shirt when Manny suddenly stopped, with both hands on his belt, and stared at me. Waves of curly hair spit-curled down on his forehead from sweat, and regret that I had to find out showed in the sagging lines of his handsome face. Finally, he cinched his belt to buckle it and said, "Boyd . . . I had to go over the hill to come and see you after you wrote that letter to me about

Mom. About how you were going crazy with grief and seeing ghosts and Dad sitting down there every night listening to those cowboy songs. I had to do it this way because I didn't have a furlough coming again until after the new year. Do you understand? AWOL. Absent Without Leave. Do you see why I did it? Do you know why the MP's here now?"

But when I just stood there with my mouth open, Manny squeezed my arm and said, "Didn't we have fun, Boyd? Didn't we?" And when I nodded for an answer because I still couldn't talk, Manny said, "Then don't feel bad. I'll only get restricted to the base or something. Maybe thirty days in the guardhouse at worst. My CO needs me to win fights for him, son."

But when I still stood there with my mouth shut and sullen, Manny dropped his hand and sighed and said, "No use running now. It'll only make things worse. They'll just watch the house and catch me anyway. I better go with the MP now that everybody knows I'm AWOL and get a free ride back to base. Do you see that I've got to go back now, Boyd? Do you?"

When I nodded again, Manny said, "Good boy! Now pick up my bag," and lifted his own suitcase out of the closet.

I stuffed the glove down in the gym bag with the rest of the equipment and snapped the bag shut and followed Manny out of the room and down the hall, where he shouted from the top of the stairs: "I'm Serrano, soldier, the guy you're looking for," and stopped the argument that was still going on down by the front door between Dora and the MP.

He then slipped his coat on and started down the stairs, fixing his tie with one hand, and had finished buttoning his coat too by the bottom step, where he held his hands out for the MP's cuffs and winked over his shoulder at me when the MP snapped them on with a clash of metal that sounded loud as a handclap to me. And the big guy felt so good about getting him finally that he even wrinkled up his blue eyes and nodded at Dora to let her know who was boss now.

But her eyes had already turned wet with tears, glistening drops on her lashes. She reached out and pressed her hand on Manny's chest, as if she could still stop him from being taken away. Manny lifted his hand-cuffed hands, sort of flexed his muscles to do it, and touched her hand with the backs of his thumbs once, lightly, said, "I'll write," then reached down and grabbed his suitcase with his cuffed hands and pushed past her and the MP, without glancing back at me.

I followed my brother down the porch stairs, holding the gym bag up high by my waist with both hands so I wouldn't trip on the steps, and walked out to the double-parked jeep, its red light still shining, where I handed the bag to the MP to put in the jeep with the suitcase.

Manny winked at me again, but, lips trembling, I couldn't wink back.

The jeep moved away, Manny turning around on his seat to look at me. Then he smiled, raised his arms and shook his hand-cuffed hands over his head.

A sob bubbled out from between my lips as his head blurred into a dark blob in the Plexiglas rear window, finally vanishing from sight altogether as the jeep turned the corner with a blink of its tail-lights. Manny still shaking his hands overhead like a victor at the end of a bout.

LYNCHING FOR PROFIT

George S. Schuyler

(Address of Hon. I. M. A. Sapp, prominent advertising man of Moronville, Georgia, delivered to a group of up-and-coming men of vision assembled in the metropolis of that great state.)

Gentlemen: The great money-making possibilities of lynching have been overlooked. All of you will agree that these outbreaks of righteous indignation are necessary to protect our women (our *white* women, if you please) and maintain forever inviolate the supremacy of the white race. Even among the black leaders of a certain type there is a tendency to condone what others call a "crime" because a cessation of lynching would mean monetary loss to them. Since lynching will probably exist for some time to come, why not control and direct it into profitable channels? It is about the only activity in the United States that is not carefully organized and planned with an eye to financial return, yet we have neglected to organize it all these years.

And how can we do this? Well, you all know that the news of a lynching to be held always draws a large audience of white people. They will come from miles around to see that justice is done, and perhaps to carry a souvenir back home. I have known hangings and burnings in this state that have drawn spontaneous gatherings of as high as 2,000 people.

Now if it is possible to bring together that many people to witness lynching with only by-word-of-mouth advertising, why isn't it possible to bring 50,000 people from all parts of the state by inaugurating the same advertising methods we have found so potent in the sale of soap, underwear, cigarettes, and overalls? Why can't we do it? Why can't we make this practice more profitable? Why can't we inject the spirit of Service into it? That's the word, gentlemen—Service!

Just think of it, friends! Fifty thousand visitors! What does this mean to the railroads, the hotels, the garages, the restaurants, the street cars, the storekeepers, the merchants? Think it over! Fifty thousand people with good money in their pockets! Fifty thousand people imbued with the holiday spirit! Fifty thousand people unmindful of the morrow! Here is a golden opportunity. We have lynched 500 blacks in Georgia since 1882 in defense of our ideals, and while it is a record of which we are very proud, I think we should deplore the fact that we have not made it yield us direct returns.

I am not theorizing, gentlemen. We did this very thing in Moronville a few weeks ago and the results were exceedingly gratifying. At a meeting of the solid and substantial business men of the city, I brought up this matter and it was enthusiastically endorsed by all. Everybody promised to cooperate and a fund of $1,000 was raised to finance the advertising. Then we went to work.

The editor of the Moronville Gazette printed a news article about a white woman being insulted by a big, burly, black brute. He worked that assiduously every day for a week in his news and editorial columns. The local Klavern of the K. K. K. bought thousands of copies and distributed them throughout our section. On Sunday the preachers delivered strong sermons against the menace of lecherous brutes. Then the Sheriff announced that he had not yet been able to locate the culprits but promised an arrest soon. Several white women wrote letters to the editor claiming to have been insulted. The white people began to clamor for action. Finally the Sheriff arrested a troublesome darkey on suspicion and put him in the county jail. Everything was all set then, so we ran a half page advertisement in the Moronville Gazette and the Klan distributed copies free for fifty miles around.

Let me pause here to read a copy of the advertisement:

NEGRO TO BE BURNED AT STAKE

In Moronville, Ga.
At the Cretin County Fairgrounds
Come One! Come All!

Bring the Family and Spend a Pleasant Day.
Plenty of Refreshments Served.

———

Excursions from All Neighboring Towns at Half Price.
Street Cars Will Take You Directly to the Fairgrounds.

———

COME AND SEE THE GHASTLY SIGHT!

HEAR THE BLACK VILLAIN SCREAM!

SMELL THE ROASTING FLESH!

TAKE HOME A KNUCKLE OR RIB!

The Biggest Lynching Ever Staged!

———

ADMISSION ONE DOLLAR

Including War Tax.

A Seat for Every Man, Woman and Child.
Come and Be Comfortable—No Rowdyism.

Perfect Order Will Be Maintained by
THE MORONVILLE POLICE DEPARTMENT.

The results, gentlemen, far exceeded our expectations. We made more money in one day than we had made in the previous week. During the excitement we easily persuaded a wealthy old darkey to sell out a valuable piece of ground we had been trying to get for many years. The cotton mill owners were able to reduce wages 5 cents an hour without a clamor by subscribing $1,000 to the local K. K. K. The Negro ministers reported increased collections, the darkies became much more polite than formerly, and their leaders drew up a resolution expressing confidence in the *good* white people of the town and condemning the Negro criminal element. Insurance collections leaped from 60 per cent to 99 per cent in the next two weeks. Our white churches reported that contributions for foreign missionary work broke all previous records. The number of Negro migrants was small and were mostly from the more assertive element that seems to have difficulty in knowing its place, especially since the late War for Democracy. Even the better type of Negroes were glad to see them go because it was felt that they disturbed the cordial relations existing between the races. In the North, we learned the Negro agitational organizations increased revenues by 25 per cent and the principal Negro newspapers all reported leaps in circulation.

You can see, therefore, with what great possibilities this project is pregnant. We have in our favor the easily stirred indignation of our white people (b) an almost inexhaustible supply of Negroes, (c) the support of all business interests, the K. K. K., and the white and black clergy. There is no danger that the Negro leaders will attempt to stir up their people except to religious ecstasy, and experience has shown that we need not fear the interference of the Federal Government. Moreover, even if some politician in Washington should protest, we can easily show our increase in income tax payments and that will quell the outburst of any politician.

It is unnecessary and unsound to lynch many Negroes—one a month will be sufficient to bring the desired results, and at the same time will keep our lynching record low enough to appease the tender-hearted. All the police chiefs have privately promised to cooperate, the Klan will furnish ushers at $5 a head, the sawmills will supply fuel, and the railroads will give 5 per cent of their excursion revenue for the erection of health clinics and schools for Negroes. Thus the success of this project is assured in every way.

With the enthusiasm of our hard-headed business men and the support of almost all elements of the population, this new venture can be made a marvelous success and a credit to our business acumen. (Prolonged and deafening applause.)

THE MULATTO

Victor Séjour

I

The first rays of dawn were just beginning to light the black mountaintops when I left the Cape for Saint-Marc, a small town in St. Domingue, now known as Haiti. I had seen so many exquisite landscapes and thick, tall forests that, truth to tell, I had begun to believe myself indifferent to these virile beauties of creation. But at the sight of this town, with its picturesque vegetation, its bizarre and novel nature, I was stunned; I stood dumbstruck before the sublime diversity of God's works. The moment I arrived, I was accosted by an old negro, at least seventy years of age; his step was firm, his head held high, his form imposing and vigorous; save the remarkable whiteness of his curly hair, nothing betrayed his age. As is common in that country, he wore a large straw hat and was dressed in trousers of coarse gray linen, with a kind of jacket made from plain batiste.

"Good day, Master," he said, tipping his hat when he saw me.

"Ah! There you are . . .," and I offered him my hand, which he shook in return.

"Master," he said, "that's quite noble-hearted of you. . . . But you know, do you not, that a negro's as vile as a dog; society rejects him; men detest him; the laws curse him. . . . Yes, he's a most unhappy being, who hasn't even the consolation of always being virtuous. . . . He may be born good, noble, and generous; God may grant him a great and loyal soul; but despite all that, he often goes to his grave with bloodstained hands, and a heart hungering after yet more vengeance. For how many times has he seen the dreams of his youth destroyed? How many times has experience taught him that his good deeds count for nothing, and that he should love neither his wife nor his son; for one day the former will be seduced by the master; and his own flesh and blood will be sold and transported away despite his despair. What, then, can you expect him to become? Shall he smash his skull against the paving stones? Shall he kill his torturer? Or do you believe the human heart can find a way to bear such misfortune?"

The old negro fell silent a moment, as if awaiting my response.

"You'd have to be mad to believe that," he continued, heatedly. "If he continues to live, it can only be for vengeance; for soon he shall rise . . . and, from the day he shakes off his servility, the master would do better to have a starving tiger raging beside him than to meet that man face to face." While the old man spoke, his face lit up, his eyes sparkled, and his heart pounded forcefully. I would not have believed one could discover that much life and power beneath such an aged exterior. Taking advantage of this moment of excitement, I said to him: "Antoine, you promised you'd tell me the story of your friend Georges."

"Do you want to hear it now?"

"Certainly . . ." We sat down, he on my trunk, myself on my valise. Here is what he told me:

"Do you see this edifice that rises so graciously toward the sky and whose reflection seems to rise from the sea; this edifice that in its peculiarity resembles a temple and in its pretense a palace? This is the house of Saint-M* * *. Each day, in one of this building's rooms, one finds an assemblage of hangers-on, men of independent means, and the great plantation owners. The first two groups play billiards or smoke the delicious cigars of Havana, while the third purchases negroes; that is, free men who have been torn from their country by ruse or by force, and who have become, by violence, the goods, the property of their fellow men. . . . Over here we have the husband without the wife; there, the sister without the brother; farther on, the mother without the children. This makes you shudder? Yet this loathsome commerce goes on continuously. Soon, in any case, the offering is a young Senegalese woman, so beautiful that from every mouth leaps the exclamation: 'How pretty!' Everyone there wants her for his mistress, but not one of them dares dispute the prize with the young Alfred, now twenty-one years old and one of the richest planters in the country.

"'How much do you want for this woman?'

"'Fifteen hundred piasters,' replied the auctioneer.

"'Fifteen hundred piasters,' Alfred rejoined dryly.

"'Yes indeed, Sir.'

"'That's your price?'

"'That's my price.'

"'That's awfully expensive.'

"'Expensive?' replied the auctioneer, with an air of surprise. 'But surely you see how pretty she is; how clear her skin is, how firm her flesh is. She's eighteen years old at the most. . . .' Even as he spoke, he ran his shameless hands all over the ample and half-naked form of the beautiful African.

"'Is she guaranteed?' asked Alfred, after a moment of reflection.

"'As pure as the morning dew,' the auctioneer responded. 'But, for that matter, you yourself can. . . .'

"'No no, there's no need,' said Alfred, interrupting him. 'I trust you.'

"'I've never sold a single piece of bad merchandise,' replied the vendor, twirling his whiskers with a triumphant air. When the bill of sale had been signed and all formalities resolved, the auctioneer approached the young slave.

"'This man is now your master,' he said, pointing toward Alfred.

"'I know it,' the negress answered coldly.

"'Are you content?'

"'What does it matter to me . . . him or some other. . . .'

"'But surely . . .' stammered the auctioneer, searching for some answer.

"'But surely what?' said the African, with some humor. 'And if he doesn't suit me?'

"'My word, that would be unfortunate, for everything is finished. . . .'

"'Well then, I'll keep my thoughts to myself.'

"Ten minutes later, Alfred's new slave stepped into a carriage that set off along the *chemin des quepes*, a well-made road that leads out into those delicious fields that surround Saint-Marc like young virgins at the foot of the altar. A somber melancholy enveloped her soul, and she began to weep. The driver understood only too well what was going on inside her, and thus made no attempt to distract her. But when he saw Alfred's white house appear in the distance, he involuntarily leaned down toward the unfortunate girl and, with a voice full of tears, said to her: 'Sister, what's your name?'

"'Laïsa,' she answered, without raising her head.

"At the sound of this name, the driver shivered. Then, gaining control of his emotions, he asked: 'Your mother?'

"'She's dead. . . .'

"'Your father?'

"'He's dead. . . .'

"'Poor child,' he murmured. 'What country are you from, Laïsa?'

"'From Senegal. . . .'

"Tears rose in his eyes; she was a fellow countrywoman.

"'Sister,' he said, wiping his eyes, 'perhaps you know old Chambo and his daughter. . . .'

"'Why?' answered the girl, raising her head quickly.

"'Why?' continued the driver, in obvious discomfort, 'well, old Chambo is my father, and . . .'

"'My God,' cried out the orphan, cutting off the driver before he could finish. 'You are?'

"'Jacques Chambo.'

"'You're my brother!'

"'Laïsa!'

"They threw themselves into each other's arms. They were still embracing when the carriage passed through the main entrance to Alfred's property. The overseer was waiting. . . . 'What's this I see,' he shouted, uncoiling an immense whip that he always carried on his belt; 'Jacques kissing the new arrival before my very eyes. . . . What impertinence!' With this, lashes began to fall on the unhappy man, and spurts of blood leaped from his face."

II

"Alfred may have been a decent man, humane and loyal with his equals, but you can be certain he was a hard, cruel man toward his slaves. I won't tell you everything he did in order to possess Laïsa; for in the end she was virtually raped. For almost a year, she shared her master's bed. But Alfred was already beginning to tire of her; he found her ugly, cold, and insolent. About this time the poor woman gave birth to a boy and gave him the name Georges. Alfred refused to recognize him, drove the mother from his presence, and relegated her to the most miserable hut on his lands, despite the fact that he knew very well, as well as one can, that he was the child's father.

"Georges grew up without ever hearing the name of his father; and when, at times, he attempted to penetrate the mystery surrounding his birth, his mother remained inflexible, never yielding to his entreaties. On one occasion only, she said to him: 'My son, you shall learn your name only when you reach twenty-five, for then you will be a man; you will be better able to guard its secret. You don't realize that he has forbidden me to speak to you about him and threatens you if I do . . . . And Georges, don't you see, this man's hatred would be your death.'

"'What does that matter,' Georges shouted impetuously. 'At least I could reproach him for his unspeakable conduct.'

"'Hush. . . . Hush, Georges. The walls have ears and someone will talk,' moaned the poor mother as she trembled.

"A few years later this unhappy woman died, leaving to Georges, her only son, as his entire inheritance, a small leather pouch containing a portrait of the boy's father. But she exacted a promise that the pouch not be opened until his twenty-fifth year; then she kissed him, and her head fell back onto the pillow. . . . She was dead. The painful cries that escaped the orphan drew the other slaves around him. . . . They all set to crying, they beat their chests, they tore their hair in agony. Following these gestures of suffering, they bathed the dead woman's body and laid it out on a kind of long table, raised on wooden supports. The dead woman is placed on her back, her face turned to the East, dressed in her finest clothing, with her hands folded on her chest. At her feet is a bowl filled with holy water, in which a sprig of jasmine is floating; and, finally, at the four corners of this funereal bed; the flames of torches rise up. . . . Each of them, having blessed the remains of the deceased, kneels and prays; for most of the negro races, despite their fetishism, have profound faith in the existence of God. When this first ceremony is finished, another one, no less singular, commences. . . . There are shouts, tears, songs, and then funeral dances!"

III

"Georges had all the talents necessary for becoming a well-regarded gentleman; yet he was possessed of a haughty, tenacious, willful nature; he had one of those oriental sorts of dispositions, the kind that, once pushed far enough from the path of virtue, will stride boldly down the path of crime. He would have given ten years of his life to know the name of his father, but he dared not violate the solemn oath he had made to his dying mother. It was as if nature pushed him toward Alfred; he liked him, as much as one can like a man; and Alfred esteemed him, but with that esteem that the horseman bears for the most handsome and vigorous of his chargers. In those days, a band of thieves was spreading desolation through the region; already several of the settlers had fallen victim to them. One night, by what chance I know not, Georges learned of their plans. They had sworn to murder Alfred. The slave ran immediately to his master's side.

"'Master, master,' he shouted. . . . 'In heaven's name, follow me.'

"Alfred raised his eyebrows.

"'Please! come, come, master,' the mulatto insisted passionately.

"'Good God,' Alfred replied, 'I believe you're commanding me.'

"'Forgive me, master . . . forgive me . . . I'm beside myself . . . I don't know what I'm saying . . . but in heaven's name, come, follow me, because. . . .'

"'Explain yourself,' said Alfred, in an angry tone. . . .

"The mulatto hesitated.

"'At once; I order you,' continued Alfred, as he rose menacingly.

"'Master, you're to be murdered tonight.'

"'By the Virgin, you're lying. . . .'

"'Master, they mean to take your life.'

"'Who?'

"'The bandits.'

"'Who told you this?'

"'Master, that's my secret . . .' said the mulatto in a submissive voice.

"'Do you have weapons?' rejoined Alfred, after a moment of silence.

"The mulatto pulled back a few of the rags that covered him, revealing an axe and a pair of pistols.

"'Good,' said Alfred, hastily arming himself.

"'Master, are you ready?'

"'Let's go. . . .'

"'Let's go,' repeated the mulatto as he stepped toward the door.

Alfred held him back by the arm.

"'But where to?'

"'To your closest friend, Monsieur Arthur.'

"As they were about to leave the room, there was a ferocious pounding at the door.

"'The devil,' exclaimed the mulatto, 'it's too late. . . .'

"'What say you?'

"'They're here,' replied Georges, pointing at the door. . . .

"'Ah!'

"'Master, what's wrong?'

"'Nothing . . . a sudden pain. . . .'

"'Don't worry, master, they'll have to walk over my body before they get to you,' said the slave with a calm and resigned air.

"This calm, this noble devotion, were calculated to reassure the most cowardly of men. Yet at these last words, Alfred trembled even more, overwhelmed by a horrible thought. He reckoned that Georges, despite his generosity, was an accomplice of the murderers. Such is the tyrant: he believes all other men incapable of elevated sentiments or selfless dedication, for they must be small-minded, perfidious souls. . . . Their souls are but uncultivated ground, where nothing grows but thorns and weeds. The door shook violently. At this point, Alfred could no longer control his fears; he had just seen the mulatto smiling, whether from joy or anger he knew not.

"'Scoundrel!' he shouted, dashing into the next room; 'you're trying to have me murdered, but your plot will fail'—upon which he disappeared. Georges bit his lips in rage, but had no time to think, for the door flew open and four men stood in the threshold. Like a flash of lightning, the mulatto drew his pistols and pressed his back to the wall, crying out in a deep voice:

"'Wretches! What do you want?'

"'We want to have a talk with you,' rejoined one of them, firing a bullet at Georges from point-blank range.

"'A fine shot,' muttered Georges, shaking.

"The bullet had broken his left arm. Georges let off a shot. The brigand whirled three times about and fell stone dead. A second followed instantly. At this point, like a furious lion tormented by hunters, Georges, with his axe in his fist and his dagger in his teeth, threw himself upon his adversaries. . . . A hideous struggle ensues. . . . The combatants grapple . . . collide again . . . they seem bound together. . . . The axe blade glistens. . . . The dagger, faithful to the hand that guides it, works its way into the enemy's breast. . . . But never a shout, not a word . . . not a whisper escapes the mouths of these three men, wallowing among the cadavers as if at the heart of some intoxicating orgy. . . . To see them thus, pale and blood-spattered, silent and full of desperation, one must imagine three phantoms throwing themselves against each other, tearing themselves to pieces, in the depths of a grave. . . . Meanwhile Georges is covered with wounds; he can barely hold himself up. . . . Oh! the intrepid mulatto has reached his end; the severing axe is lifted above his head. . . . Suddenly two explosions are heard, and the two brigands slump to the floor, blaspheming God as they drop. At the same moment, Alfred returns, followed by a young negro. He has the wounded man carried to his hut, and instructs his doctor to attend to him. Now, how is it that Georges was saved by the same man who had just accused him of treachery? As he ran off, Alfred heard the sound of a gun, and the clash of steel; blushing at his own cowardice, he awoke his valet de chambre and flew to the aid of his liberator. Ah, I've forgotten to tell you that Georges had a wife, by the name Zelia, whom he loved with every fiber of his being; she was a mulatto about eighteen or twenty years old, standing very straight and tall, with black hair and a gaze full of tenderness and love. Georges lay for twelve days somewhere between life and death. Alfred visited him often; and, driven on by some fateful chance, he became enamored of Zelia. But, unfortunately for him, she was not one of these women who sell their favors or use them to pay tribute to their master. She repelled Alfred's propositions with humble dignity; for she never forgot that this was a master speaking to a slave. Instead of being moved by this display of a virtue that is so rare among women, above all among those who, like Zelia, are slaves, and who, every day, see their shameless companions prostitute themselves to the colonists, thereby only feeding more licentiousness; instead of being moved, as I said, Alfred flew into a rage. . . . What!—him, the despot, the Bey, the Sultan of the Antilles, being spurned by a slave . . . how ironic! Thus he swore he would possess her. . . . A few days before Georges was recovered, Alfred summoned Zelia to his chamber. Then, attending to nothing but his criminal desires, he threw his arms around her and planted a burning kiss on her face. The young slave begged, pleaded, resisted; but all in vain. . . . Already he draws her toward the adulterous bed; already. . . . Then, the young slave, filled with a noble indignation, repulses him with one final effort, but one so sudden, so powerful, that Alfred lost his balance and struck his head as he fell. . . . At this sight, Zelia began to tear her hair in despair, crying tears of rage; for she understood perfectly, the unhappy girl, that death was her fate for having drawn the blood of a being so vile. After crying for some time, she left to be at her husband's side. He must have been dreaming about her, for there was a smile on his lips.

"'Georges . . . Georges . . .' she cried out in agony.

"The mulatto opened his eyes; and his first impulse was to smile at the sight of his beloved. Zelia recounted for him everything that had happened. He didn't want to believe it, but soon he was convinced of his misfortune; for some men entered his hut and tied up his wife while she stood sobbing. . . . Georges made an effort to rise up; but, still weakened, he fell back onto his bed, his eyes haggard, his hands clenched, his mouth gasping for air."

IV

"Ten days later, two white creole children were playing in the street.

"'Charles,' one said to the other: 'is it true that the mulatto woman who wanted to kill her master is to be hung tomorrow?'

"'At eight o'clock,' answered the other.

"'Will you go?'

"'Oh yes, certainly.'

"'Won't that be fine, to see her pirouetting between the earth and the sky,' rejoined the first, laughing as they walked off.

"Does it surprise you to hear two children, at ten years of age, conversing so gayly on the death of another? This is, perhaps, an inevitable consequence of their education. From their earliest days, they have heard it ceaselessly repeated, that we were born to serve them, that we were created to attend to their whims, and that they need have no more or less consideration for us than for a dog. . . . Indeed, what is our agony and suffering to them? Have they not, just as often, seen their best horses die? They don't weep for them, for they're rich, and tomorrow they'll buy others. . . . While these two children were speaking, Georges was at the feet of his master.

"'Master, have mercy . . . mercy . . .' he cried out, weeping. . . . 'Have pity on her . . . Master, pardon her. . . . Oh! yes, pardon her, it is in your power . . . oh! speak . . . you have only to say the word . . . just one word . . . and she will live.'

"Alfred made no answer.

"'Oh! for pity's sake . . . master . . . for pity's sake, tell me you pardon her . . . oh! Speak . . . answer me, master . . . won't you pardon her. . . .' The unhappy man was bent double with pain. . . .

"Alfred remained impassive, turning his head aside. . . .

"'Oh!' continued Georges, begging, 'please answer . . . just one word . . . please say something; you see how your silence is tearing my heart in two . . . it's killing me. . . .'

"'There's nothing I can do,' Alfred finally answered, in an icy tone.

"The mulatto dried his tears, and raised himself to his full height.

"'Master,' he continued in a hollow voice, 'do you remember what you said to me, as I lay twisting in agony on my bed?'

"'No. . . .'

"'Well! I can remember . . . the master said to the slave: you saved my life; what can I grant you in return? Do you want your freedom? 'Master,' answered the slave, 'I can never be free, while my son and my wife are slaves.' To which the master replied: 'If ever you ask me, I swear that your wishes shall be granted'; and the slave did not ask, for he was content that he had saved his master's life . . . but today, today when he knows that, in eighteen hours, his wife will no longer be among the living, he flies to throw himself at your feet, and to call out to you: master, in God's name, save my wife.' And the mulatto, his hands clasped, with a supplicating gaze, fell to his knees and began to cry, his tears falling like rain. . . .

"Alfred turned his head away. . . .

"'Master . . . master . . . for pity, give me an answer. . . . Oh! say that you want her to live . . . in God's name . . . in your mother's name . . . mercy . . . have mercy upon us. . . .' and the mulatto kissed the dust at his feet.

"Alfred stood silent.

"'But speak, at least, to this poor man who begs you,' he said, sobbing.

"Alfred said nothing.

"'My God . . . my God! how miserable I am . . .' and he rolled on the floor, pulling at his hair in torment.

"Finally, Alfred decided to speak: 'I have already told you that it is no longer up to me to pardon her.'

"'Master,' murmured Georges, still crying, 'she will probably be condemned; for only you and I know that she is innocent.'

"At these words from the mulatto, the blood rose to Alfred's face, and fury to his heart. . . .

"Georges understood that it was no longer time to beg, for he had raised the veil that covered his master's crime; thus he stood up resolutely.

"'Leave . . . get out,' Alfred shouted at him.

"Instead of leaving; the mulatto crossed his arms on his chest and, with a fierce look, eyed his master scornfully from head to foot.

"'Get out! get out, I say,' continued Alfred, more and more angrily.

"'I'm not leaving,' answered Georges.

"'This is defiance, you wretch.' He made a motion to strike him, but his hand remained at his side, so full of pride and hatred was George's gaze. . . .

"'What! you can leave her to be killed, to have her throat cut, to be murdered,' said the mulatto, 'when you know her to be innocent . . . when, like a coward, you wanted to seduce her?'

"'Insolent! What are you saying?'

"'I'm saying that it would be an infamous deed to let her die. . . .'

"'Georges . . . Georges. . . .'

"'I am saying that you're a scoundrel,' screamed Georges, giving full rein to his anger, and seizing Alfred by the arm . . . 'ah! she'll die . . . she will die because she didn't prostitute herself to you . . . because you're white . . . because you're her master . . . you lying coward.'

"'Careful, Georges,' replied Alfred, trying to take a tone of assurance. 'Be careful that instead of one victim tomorrow, the executioner does not find two.'

"'You talk of victim and executioner, wretch,' shouted Georges. . . . 'So that means she dies . . . her . . . my Zelia . . . but you should know that her life is linked to your own.'

"'Georges!'

"'You should know that your head will remain on your shoulders only so long as she lives.'

"'Georges . . . Georges!'

"'You should know that I will kill you, that I'll drink your blood, if even a hair on her head is harmed.'

"During all this time, the mulatto was shaking Alfred with all his strength.

"'Let me go,' cried Alfred.

"'Ah! she's dying . . . she's dying' . . . the mulatto screamed deliriously.

"'Georges, let me go!'

"'Shut your mouth . . . shut it, you scoundrel . . . ah! she's dying . . . well then, should the executioner put an end to my wife . . .' he continued with a hideous smile.

"Alfred was so agitated he didn't even know that Georges had left. He went directly to his hut, where his child of two years was sleeping in a light cradle made from lianas; taking up the child, he slipped away. In order to understand what follows, you must know that there was only a small river to cross from Alfred's home before one arrives in the midst of those thick forests that seem to hold the new world in their arms.

"For six long hours, Georges walked without a rest; at last he stopped, a few steps from a hut built in the deepest heart of the forest; you'll understand the joy that shone in his eyes when you realize that this tiny hut, isolated as it is, is the camp of the Maroons; that is, of slaves who have fled the tyranny of their masters. At this moment the hut was filled with murmurs, for a rustling had been heard in the forest, and the leader, swearing that the noise was not that of any animal, had taken his rifle and gone out. . . . Suddenly the underbrush parted before him and he found himself face to face with a stranger.

"'By my freedom,' he cried, looking over the newcomer, 'you found our recess all too easily.'

"'Africa and freedom,' Georges replied calmly, as he pushed aside the barrel of the rifle. . . . 'I'm one of you.'

"'Your name.'

"'Georges, slave of Alfred.'

"They shook hands and embraced.

"The next day the crowd clamored round a scaffold, from which hung the body of a young mulatto woman. . . . When she had expired, the executioner let her corpse down into a pine coffin and, ten minutes later, body and coffin were thrown into a ditch that was opened at the edge of the forest.

"Thus this woman, for having been too virtuous, died the kind of death meted out to the vilest criminal. Would this alone not suffice to render the gentlest of men dangerous and bloodthirsty?"

V

"Three years had passed since the death of the virtuous Zelia. For a time, Alfred was in extreme torment; by day, he seemed to see a vengeful hand descending toward his head; he trembled at night because the darkness brought him hideous, frightful dreams. Soon, however, he banished from his thoughts both the painful memory of the martyr and the terrible threat Georges had made; he married and became a father. . . . Oh! how gratified he felt, when he was told that his prayers were answered, he who had humbly kissed the church floor each evening, beseeching the Virgin of Sorrows to grant him a son.

"For Georges also, there was happiness in this child's arrival. For if he had hoped for three years without attempting to strike back at his wife's executioner; if he had lain sleepless so many nights, with fury in his heart and a hand on his dagger, it was because he was waiting for Alfred to find himself, like Georges, with a wife and a son. It was because he wished to kill him only when dear and precious bonds linked him to this world. . . . Georges had always maintained close ties with one of Alfred's slaves; indeed, he visited him each week; and that slave had never given Georges any news more important than that of the newborn's arrival. . . . He immediately set out for the house of his enemy. On his way he met a negress who was bringing a cup of broth to Madame Alfred; he stopped her, exchanged a few insignificant words, and went on. . . . After many difficulties, he managed to slip his way, like a snake, into Alfred's rooms; once there, hidden in the space between the bed and the wall, he awaited his master. . . . A moment later, Alfred entered the room, humming a tune; he opened his secretary and took out a superb jewel box, set with diamonds, that he had promised his wife, should she give him a son; but, filled with joy and happiness, he sat down and put his head between his hands, like a man who can't believe his unexpected good fortune. Then, on raising his head, he saw before him a kind of motionless shadow, with arms crossed on its breast and two burning eyes that possessed all the ferocity of a tiger preparing to tear its prey to pieces. Alfred made a motion to stand, but a powerful arm held him down in his chair.

"'What do you want with me,' Alfred whispered, in a trembling voice.

"'To compliment you on the birth of your child,' answered a voice that seemed to emerge from the tomb.

"Alfred shook from head to toe, his hair stood on end, and a cold sweat poured over his limbs.

"'I don't know you,' Alfred muttered weakly. . . .

"'Georges is the name.'

"'You. . . .'

"'You thought I was dead, I suppose,' said the mulatto with a convulsive laugh.

"'Help . . . help,' cried Alfred.

"'Who will help you,' rejoined the mulatto . . . 'haven't you dismissed your servants, haven't you closed your doors, to be alone with your wife . . . so you see, your cries are useless . . . you should commend your soul to God.'

"Alfred had begun to rise from his chair, but at these last words he fell back, pale and trembling.

"'Oh! have pity, Georges . . . don't kill me, not today.'

"Georges shrugged his shoulders. 'Master, isn't it horrible to die when you're happy; to lie down in the grave at the moment you see your fondest dreams coming true . . . oh! it's horrible, isn't it,' said the mulatto with an infernal laugh. . . .

"'Mercy, Georges. . . .'

"'And yet,' he continued, 'such is your destiny . . . you shall die today, this hour, this minute, without giving your wife your last farewell. . . .'

"'Have pity . . . pity. . . .'

"'Without kissing your newborn son a second time. . . .'

"'Oh! mercy . . . mercy.'

"'I think my vengeance is worthy of your own . . . I would have sold my soul to the Devil, had he promised me this moment.'

"'Oh! mercy . . . please take pity on me,' said Alfred, throwing himself at the feet of the mulatto.

"Georges shrugged his shoulders and raised his axe.

"'Oh! one more hour of life!'

"'To embrace your wife, is that it?'

"'One minute. . . .'

"'To see your son again, right?'

"'Oh! have pity. . . .'

"'You might as well plead with the starving tiger to let go his prey.'

"'In God's name, Georges.'

"'I don't believe in that any longer.'

"'In the name of your father. . . .'

"At this, Georges's fury subsided.

"'My father . . . my father,' repeated the mulatto, tears in his eyes. 'Do you know him . . . oh! tell me his name. . . . What's his name . . . oh! tell me, tell me his name . . . I'll pardon you . . . I'll bless you.'

"And the mulatto nearly fell on his knees before his master. But suddenly, sharp cries were heard. . . .

"'Good heavens . . . that's my wife's voice,' cried Alfred, dashing toward the sounds. . . .

"As if he were coming back to his senses, the mulatto remembered that he had come to the house of his master, not to learn the name of his father, but to settle accounts with him for his wife's blood. Holding Alfred back, he told him with a hideous grin: 'Hold on, master; it's nothing.'

"'Jesus and Mary . . . don't you hear her calling for help.'

"'It's nothing, I tell you.'

"'Let me go . . . let me go . . . it's my wife's voice.'

"'No, it's the gasps of a dying woman.'

"'Wretch, you're lying. . . .'

"'I poisoned her. . . .'

"'Oh!'

"'Do you hear those cries . . . they're hers.'

"'The Devil. . . .'

"'Do you hear those screams . . . they're hers.'

"'A curse. . . .'

"During all this time, Alfred had been trying to shake free of the mulatto's grip; but he held him fast, tighter and tighter. As he did, his head rose higher, his heart beat fiercely, he steadied himself for his awful task.

"'Alfred . . . help . . . water . . . I'm suffocating,' shouted a woman, as she threw herself into the middle of the room. She was pale and disheveled, her eyes were starting out of her head, her hair was in wild disarray.

"'Alfred, Alfred for heaven's sake, help me . . . some water . . . I need water . . . my blood is boiling . . . my heart is twitching . . . oh! water, water. . . .'

"Alfred struggled mightily to help her, but Georges held him fast with an iron hand. Laughing like one of the damned, he cried out: 'No, master . . . I'm afraid not . . . I want your wife to die . . . right there . . . before your eyes . . . right in front of you . . . do you understand, master; right in front of you, asking you for water, for air, while you can do nothing to help her.'

"'Damnation . . . may you be damned,' howled Alfred, as he struggled like a madman.

"'You can curse and blaspheme all you want,' answered the mulatto . . . 'this is the way it's going to be. . . .'

"'Alfred,' the dying woman moaned again, 'good-bye . . . good-bye . . . I'm dying. . . .'

"'Look well,' responded the mulatto, still laughing. . . . 'Look . . . she's gasping . . . goodness! a single drop of this water would restore her to life.' He showed him a small vial.

"'My entire fortune for that drop of water. . . .' cried Alfred.

"'Have you gone mad, master. . . .'

"'Ah! that water . . . that water . . . don't you see she's dying . . . give it to me . . . please give it to me. . . .'

"'Here . . .' and the mulatto flung the vial against the wall.

"'Accursed,' screamed Alfred, seizing Georges by the neck. 'Oh! my entire life, my soul, for a dagger. . . .'

"Georges released Alfred's hands.

"'Now that she's dead, it's your turn, master,' he said as he lifted his axe.

"'Strike, executioner . . . strike . . . after poisoning her, you might as well kill your own fa—.' The ax fell, and Alfred's head rolled across the floor, but, as it rolled, the head distinctly pronounced the final syllable, '—ther. . . .' Georges at first believed he had misheard, but the word *father*, like a funeral knell, rang in his ears. To be certain, he opened the fateful pouch. . . . 'Ah!' he cried out, 'I'm cursed. . . .' An explosion was heard; and the next day, near the corpse of Alfred, was discovered the corpse of the unhappy Georges. . . ."

aw, babee, you so pretty

Ntozake Shange

not only waz she without a tan, but she held her purse close to her hip like a new yorker or someone who rode the Paris metro. she waz not from here, but from there.

There some coloureds, negroes, blacks, cd make a living big enough to leave there to come here: but no one went there much any more for all sorts of reasons. the big reason being immigration restrictions & unemployment. nowadays, immigration restrictions of every kind apply to any non-european persons who want to go there from here. just like unemployment applies to most non-european persons without titles of nobility or north american university training. some who want to go there from here risk fetching trouble with the customs authority there. or later with the police, who, can tell who's not from there cuz the shoes are pointed & laced strange/the pants be for august & yet it's january/the accent is patterned for port-au-prince, but working in crown heights. what makes a person comfortably ordinary here cd make him dangerously conspicuous there.

so some go to london or amsterdam or paris, where they are so many no one tries to tell who is from where. still the far right wing of every there prints lil pamphlets that say everyone from here shd leave there & go back where they came from.

anyway the yng woman i waz discussing waz from there & she was alone. that waz good. cuz if a man had no big brother in groningen. no aunt in rouen. no sponsor in chicago. this brown woman from there might be a good idea. everybody knows that rich white girls are hard to find. some of them joined the weather underground, some the baader-meinhof gang. a whole bunch of them gave up men entirely. so the exotic-lover-in-the-sun routine becomes more difficult to swing/if she wants to talk abt plastic explosives & the resistance of the black masses to socialism insteada giving head as the tide slips in or lending money just for the next few days. is hard to find a rich white girl who is so dumb, too.

anyway, the whole world knows, european & non-european alike, the whole world knows that nobody loves the black woman like they love farrah fawcett-majors. the whole world dont turn out for a dead black woman like they did for marilyn monroe. (actually, the demise of josephine baker waz an international event, but she waz also a war hero) the worldwide un-beloved black woman is a good idea, if she is from there & one is a yng man with gd looks, piercing eyes, knowledge of several romantic languages, the best dancing spots, the hill where one can see the entire bay at twilight, the beach where the seals & pelicans run free, the hidden "local" restaurants; or in paris. a métro map. in mexico city the young man might know where salsa is played, not that the Jalisco folklorico is not beautiful. but if she is from there & black she might want to dance a dance more familiar. such a yng man with such information exists in great numbers everywhere. he stops a yng woman with her bag on her hip, demanding she come to his house for dinner that night. (they are very hospitable) when the black woman from there says she must go to antwerp at 6:00/he says, then, when she comes back. his friends agree. (they are persistent) he asks, as he forces his number into her palm, are you alone. this is important. for the yng man from here with designs on a yng woman from there respects the territorial rights of another man, if he's in the country.

that is how the approach to the black woman works in the street. "aw babee/you so pretty" begins often in the lobby of hotels where the bright handsome yng men wd be loiterers were they not needed to tend the needs of the black women from there. tourists are usually white people or asians who didnt come all this way to meet a black woman who isnt even foreign. so the hotel managers wink an eye at the yng men in the lobby or by the bar who wd be loitering, but they are going to help her have a gd time. maybe help themselves, too.

everybody in the world, everybody knows the black woman from there is not created as a princess, as a jewel, a cherished lover. that's not how sapphire got her reputation, nor how mrs. jefferson perceives the world. "you know/babee/you dont act like them. aw babee/you so pretty."

the yng man in the hotel watches the yng black woman sit & sit & sit, while the european tourists dance with one another & the dapper local fellas mambo frenetically with secretaries from arizona. in search of the missing rich white girl. so our girl sits & sits & sits & sits. maybe she is courageous & taps her foot. maybe she is bold & enjoys the music, smiling, shaking shoulders. let her sit & know she is un-wanted. she is not white and she is not from here. let her know she is not pretty enough to dance the next merengue. then appear, mysteriously, in the comer of the bar. stare at her. just stare. when stevie wonder's song "isn't she lovely" blares thru the red-tinted light, ask her to dance & hold her as tyrone power wda. hold her & stare. dance yr ass off. she has been discovered by the non-european fred astaire. let her know she is a surprise . . . an event. by the look on yr face you've never seen any-one like this. black woman from there. you say, "aw/you not from here?" totally as-tonished. she murmurs that she is from there. as if to apologize for her unfortunate place of birth, you say, "aw babee/you so pretty." & it's all over.

a night in a pension near the sorbonne. pick her up from the mattress. throw her gainst the wall in a show of exotic temper & passion: *"maintenant, tu es ma femme. nous nous sommes mariés."* unions of this sort are common wherever the yng black women travel alone. a woman travelling alone is an affront to the non-european man, who is known the world over, to european & non-european alike, for his way with women, his sense of romance, how he can say "aw babee/you so pretty" & even a beautiful woman will believe no one else ever recognized her loveliness, till he came along.

he comes to a café in willemstad in the height of the sunset. an able-bodied, sinewy yng man who wants to buy one beer for the yng woman. after the first round, he discovers he has run out of money. so she must buy the next round, when he discovers what beautiful legs she has, how her mouth is like the breath of tiger lilies. the taxi driver doesnt speak english, but he knows to drop his countryman off before he takes the yng woman to her hotel. the tab is hers.

but hers are, also, the cheeks that grandma pinches, if the yng man has honorable intentions. all the family will meet the yng black woman from there. the family has been worried abt this yng man for a while. non-european families dont encourage bachelors. bachelorhood is a career we associate with the white people: dandies on the order of errol flynn, robert de niro. the non-european men have women. some women they marry & stay with forever. get chicken on sunday (chicken fricassee, arroz con pollo, poulet grillee, smothered chicken, depending on what kinda black woman she is & whether she is from here or there). then some women they just are with for years or a day. but our families do expect a yng man to waltz in with somebody at sometime. & if she's from there, the family's very excited. they tell the yng woman abt where they are from & how she cd almost be from the same place, except she is from there. but more rousing than coincidental genealogical traits the torrid declaration: "we shall make love in the . . .how you call it/yes in the earth, in the dirt. i will have you . . . in my . . . how you say . . . where things grow . . . aw/yes. i will have you in the soil." probably under the stars & smelling of wine an unforgettable international affair can be consummated.

at 11:30 one evening i waz at the port authority, new york, united states, myself. now i was there & i spoke english & i waz holding approximately $7 american currency, when a yng man from there came up to me from the front of the line of people waiting for the princeton new jersey united states local bus. i mean to say, he gave up his chance for a good seat to come say to me: "i never saw a black woman reading nietzsche." i waz demure enough, i said i had to for a philosophy class. but as the night went on i noticed this yng man waz so much like the yng men from here who use their bodies as bait & their smiles as passport alternatives. anyway the night did go on. we were snuggled together in the rear of the bus going down the jersey turnpike. he told me in english/which he had spoken all his life in st. louis/where he waz raised/that he had wanted all his life to meet someone like me/he wanted me to meet his family, who hadnt seen him in a long time, since he left missouri looking for opportunity/opportunity to sculpt. he had been every-place, he said, & i waznt like any black woman he had ever met anywhere. there or here. he had come back to new york cuz of immigration restrictions & high unem-ployment among black american sculptors abroad.

just as we got to princeton, he picked my face up from his shoulder where i had been fantasizing like mad & said: "aw babee/you so pretty." i believe that night i must have looked beautiful for a black woman from there. though a black woman from anywhere cd be asked at any moment to tour the universe. to climb a six-story walk-up with a brilliant & starving painter. to share kadushi. to meet mama. to getta kiss each time the swing falls toward the willow branch. to imag-ine where he say he from. & more/she cd/she cd have all of it/she cd not be taken long as she dont let a stranger be the first to say: "aw babee/you so pretty." after all, immigration restrictions & unemployment cd drive a man to drink or to lie. so if you know yr beautiful & bright & cherishable awready. when he say, in whatever language, "aw babee/you so pretty," you cd say, "i know, thank you." & then when he asks yr name again cuz yr answer was inaudible. you cd say: "diffi-cult." then he'll smile. & you'll smile. he'll say: "what nice legs you have." you can say: "yes. they run in the family."

"aw babee/i've never met any one like you."

"that's strange. there are millions of us."

DECOY

Ray Smith

Felix Overmeyer, the Chief Buyer for Stein Brothers department store and Assistant Manager in charge of public image, was busy hurrying about in his usual apprehensive manner, and wondering if everything would be in order. Each department's displays would be inspected by him in keeping with his private notion that he alone possessed that rare combination of aesthetic judgment and practical wisdom sufficient to make the final evaluation. He hoped one day to be in charge of store-wide security.

At the Jewelry Department he looked through the glass of the display case and scanned the items being arranged in neat patterns on the shelves and in velvet lined boxes. He barely heard the scurrying of other busy people throughout the store, preparing their own racks and counters, anticipating the ten o'clock opening.

"Very satisfactory Miss Johnson, as always." "Thank you Mr. Overmeyer. Hope we have a good day." She smiled, attempting to mask her true feeling. His presence always affected her studied composure although he never directly gave cause for concern. Her work was more than satisfactory. She knew that. But he always seemed to linger longer than necessary. Overmeyer tapped the glass counter-top near her folded brown hands with his frosty pink fingernails. She wore a lavender smock and a white kerchief tied in a loose fold about her neck, the prescribed uniform of the jewelry department.

Overmeyer checked his watch before moving to the hosiery section and its kelly green costumes. In twenty minute he needed to complete the inspection of all the remaining departments, but as always, he knew he would finish in time.

Ten minutes after opening the store became a maze of humanity in motion: every department hummed with activity. Overmeyer stationed himself near the front entrance and observed each patron as they entered, confident of his ability to evaluate each in terms of important qualities that determine character, substance, and illusive intangibles he chose to call inner worthiness. In his mind he analytically coded those who attracted his attention.

The matronly lady in the stylish straw hat and carrying an alligator purse was quality for sure. The young mother in the fashionable linen suites, wearing a pearl necklace with matching earrings was a spender without question.

The ruddy-faced man with the gray mustache: a rich aroma of smoke coming from a black Havana cigar, revealed substance. Not a college man but well off. The watch chain with the solid gold Kiwanis key draped across his vest settled any doubt.

Even the young man, fingering the center button on his brown flannel suit, displayed his worth to the knowing eye of Mr. Overmeyer—short blond hair, clean shaven, pleasantly intense, reflecting ambition, a future account to be cultivated.

Suddenly Overmeyer was cut short in his evaluations as he saw, coming through the front entrance, a young black male wearing in place of a shirt, a yellow and green striped, loose fitting garment. He walked straight up to Overmeyer who felt a compelling surge of apprehension.

"Say, my man, where's the men's department?" His tone was almost friendly.

"Why—a—it's on the second floor. Is there anything I can help you with? Something in particular you're looking for?"

"That's okay man, I know what I want. I can find it myself."

He made some sort of a parting gesture with his hand, a kind of half waving salute-like movement, flamboyant and exaggerated, as if it were the distorted remnant of some long forgotten ritual of leave taking.

The figure boarded the escalator. Overmeyer followed at the proper distance required for professional observing. His analytical mechanism registered trouble.

On the second floor the young man headed for the furniture department. Overmeyer followed and noticed he was also wearing a multi-colored skullcap made of brocade or knitted material and carried a large suede bag with a woven strap slung across his shoulder. He wondered what it contained. Bones? Tools? Political literature? Merchandise pilfered from another store?

Overmeyer saw visions of jungle treachery. Dusty shadows and ivory caches being secreted away at darkest night. Images of exotic costumes and heathen principles, incorrect and out of place.

"Forget the speculation! Keep your mind on your works. Don't let yourself get distracted!" Overmeyer often had to caution himself about drifting into reveries and deserting reality in times of stress, and when faced with an unpleasant situation.

The skullcap lingered in the china department examining stem wear and a milk glass cream and sugar set. Overmeyer thought he saw him fingering the brass latch on the suede bag while the other hand continued to inspect various items. He considered the logic of moving closer, the better to observe.

Before he could decide the figure was moving again through the notions department, turned left at men's clothing and headed straight to the rack of expensive leather coats.

Overmeyer's apprehension grew to panic proportions and what he did was walk too fast, almost revealing his concern. But the busy figure didn't notice.

Backing away slowly to a suitable distance, Overmeyer regained control of himself. He wondered if it was possible to put a leather coat in the suede bag.

The figure seemed to be checking the sleeve length of a black leather coat by holding the cuff with one hand and pinching the shoulder with the other. Then he stepped back and, looking from end to end, viewed the entire arrangement as if coming to a decision. Finally he turned and walked in the direction of Overmeyer who stepped aside to the nearest counter as if making some necessary adjustments to merchandise.

"You ain't got my size man. See you later." He boarded the escalator; Overmeyer followed only to see him head straight out the door.

A properly grateful Overmeyer returned to his station to enjoy a relief so magnificent that he hardly noticed the departure of the young executive in the brown suit.

The blond young man, holding tightly to an attache case, crossed the street and proceeded to a nearby corner where yellow shirt was leaning against the side of a building and smoking a pipe.

Seeing him the blue-eyed, brown suited gentleman broke into a pseudo walk, dipping his right shoulder with each step and holding his right arm slightly extended to the rear with the hand curved.

When he reached the corner he extended his hand, palm up for the brotherly greeting. Yellow shirt responded by slapping the palm and then extended his hand for the return slap.

"How'd we make out Bee Bee?"

Bee Bee glanced cautiously about before opening the case containing pocket calculators, tape recorders, and cameras.

"Look-a-here J.C.! Man we cleaned up! This case is damn near full."

"Not bad my man, but them calculators ain't worth much. You can buy them anywhere for about eighteen dollars, which means we can't get more than ten, unless we luck up on a dummy."

"What you mean cheap? Look at them price tags. Don't that say thirty-nine dollars and ninety-five cents? I can read you know." An indignant Bee Bee pointed an accusing finger at J.C.

"Don't be knocking my score man! You wouldn't be trying to cheat me would you?"

"Listen man, can't I teach you nothing? That tag's just for suckers. The fake price. It don't mean nothing." J.C. shoved the tag up in Bee Bee's face.

"Here's the real price, them numbers in the corner. Can't you remember what I told you?"

"Oh Yea, I forgot about that."

With Blue Eyes becoming sorrowful, J.C. relented.

"Don't worry about it man. These other items is real groovy stuff. Four Canon cameras wow! At least two hundred, and these tape recorders, another hundred. Not bad for a half hours work. So with our usual split that's about two hundred for me and one hundred for you. OK?"

"OK J.C. but I still don't see why we can't split fifty-fifty." Now it was J.C.'s turn to get upset.

"You know damn well why, Honkie! Cause I been arrested for loitering and trespassing and charged and tried and acquitted three times in the last two months and you ain't so much as gotten spoken to! That's why! Cause I got to spend time going through all them court hearings and getting cleared of trumped up charges while you home sleeping. That's why! Remember this partnership was your idea, seeing as how you understand the Caucasian mentality better than I do."

"Don't go getting your Indian blood up brother man." Bee Bee attempted conciliation.

"Ain't no harm in asking. The split's OK, just lost my head for a minute."

J.C. cooled. "Better close the brief case before somebody figures out what's happening. Let's get out of here and go see the fence."

Looking like lawyer and client on their way to court Bee Bee and J.C. were hardly considered an unusual pair on the downtown streets. Even the conversation that passed between them aroused little suspicion. Bee Bee was making small talk about going hunting with his father and how an artificial bird could be placed on the water in order to attract the real game. In spite of the lack of natural movement, it always seemed to work.

Meanwhile Mr. Overmeyer, back at the store, continued patrolling the aisles with an air of contentment; surrounded by a warmth very much like the feeling of putting on fresh socks. This was his terrain, his world and he was completely in change. He looked forward to the end of the day and having a quiet dinner at his favorite restaurant. What would it be—roast beef with fresh green beans and tomato salad; Oyster Benedict?

As he approached the camera department he heard a scream. "They're gone! My cameras are missing!"

Turning toward the agitated voice he could tell that Mrs. Joyce Krowanski was seriously upset, opening cabinets and searching through boxes.

"What's missing, Mrs. Krowanski? Did you say cameras?"

"Yes, yes, and some other stuff."

"Calm down, we'll look together. Where were they when you last saw them?"

"Right here on top of the counter." She paused long enough to press a button that sent an alarm throughout the store. Guards rushed to the front entrance. The store manager left his office on the second floor to see what was the problem; customers thought the bell was a fire alarm and were trying to leave. The manager got the details from Mrs. Krowanski and became angry.

"This wouldn't have happened Overmeyer if that new scanning system had been installed. Nothing could get past the entrance without setting off an alarm; but you convinced me it wasn't necessary. Now see what happened!"

Overmeyer tried to explain but the manager was already on his way back to his office. "We'll begin installation immediately after closing."

That evening Mr. Overmeyer didn't enjoy his dinner. He wondered about his future.

Within a month he was moved to a new position—Vice President in charge of fashion changes. He enjoyed his new situation, (which was more like being kicked upstairs) but he missed being amongst the customers, on the floor, supervising the sales crew.

When the new system went into operation shoplifters were caught at the door, a buzzing sound alerting the guards. Replaced by an electronic device no bigger than a nickel, Overmeyer gave up his ambition of being in charge of security.

Most puzzling was the type of persons being nabbed, quality customers who would have gone unnoticed if he were still on the job. He could only conclude that times had changed and class was more difficult to determine; in his new position, only changes in fashion were his concern.

But he continues to believe his methods were sound and one day he decided to see if he could pass his own test by shoplifting at a nearby store. He would take nothing of great value—only a small concealable item. He slipped a bottle of cologne in his pocket one was only thirty feet away when he heard a demanding voice.

"Hey you, I need to see what's in your pocket!"

"What pocket? What are you talking about? Can't you see who I am?"

"I know what you are, buddy-boy; just another well dressed shoplifter, that's what."

Overmeyer reached into his back pocket and pulled out his wallet. "Look at what I have in there. Do you think I need to steal?"

"That's what they all say; stealing is like some kind of game for you people. Come on, give it up."

"That's all it was, a game. I was only testing your security system."

"Maybe so, but it looks like the system passed and you failed."

"But I didn't hear any bell or buzzer."

"That's the beauty of it; we have a silent system; no bells, just a flashing light. Come along now; let's get this over with."

Overmeyer was not arrested because the object's value was so small. He was however, ordered to stay out of the store (unless accompanied by his mother). He wasn't use to being made fun of and left the store puzzled and dejected.

Later at an office party, with everyone feeling the effect of alcohol, he told of the incident but no one believed him.

"Overmeyer you've had too much to drink, concocting a story like that. Got any more tall tales?"

Feeling lightheaded and giddy, Overmeyer joined in and laughed along with the other disbelieving revelers. The more he wondered about the incident the more hilarious it became. What was he thinking of and how was he discovered? Were there clues, some indicators of which he was unaware? Was there really a silent button or was it something else that gave him away? He never would have suspected anyone with his cultured demeanor of being a petty thief.

Overmeyer walked home in a cloud of confusion as if the world, his world at least, had turned very much around leaving him dumbfounded.

But it wouldn't last. Things have a way of righting themselves. Those who count will retain their status; the others would continue to be obvious and easy to recognize.

MISS FURR AND MISS SKEENE

Gertrude Stein

Helen Furr had quite a pleasant home. Mrs Furr was quite a pleasant woman. Mr Furr was quite a pleasant man. Helen Furr had quite a pleasant voice a voice quite worth cultivating. She did not mind working. She worked to cultivate her voice. She did not find it gay living in the same place where she had always been living. She went to a place where some were cultivating something, voices and other things needing cultivating. She met Georgine Skeene there who was cultivating her voice which some thought was quite a pleasant one. Helen Furr and Georgine Skeene lived together then. Georgine Skeene liked travelling. Helen Furr did not care about travelling, she liked to stay in one place and be gay there. They were together then and travelled to another place and stayed there and were gay there.

They stayed there and were gay there, not very gay there, just gay there. They were both gay there, they were regularly working there both of them cultivating their voices there, they were both gay there. Georgine Skeene was gay there and she was regular, regular in being gay, regular in not being gay, regular in being a gay one who was not being gay longer than was needed to be one being quite a gay one. They were both gay then there and both working there then.

They were in a way both gay there where there were many cultivating something. They were both regular in being gay there. Helen Furr was gay there, she was gayer and gayer there and really she was just gay there, she was gayer and gayer there, that is to say she found ways of being gay there that she was using in being gay there. She was gay there, not gayer and gayer, just gay there, that is to say she was not gayer by using the things she found there that were gay things, she was gay there, always she was gay there.

They were quite regularly gay there, Helen Furr and Georgine Skeene, they were regularly gay there where they were gay. They were very regularly gay.

To be regularly gay was to do every day the gay thing that they did every day. To be regularly gay was to end every day at the same time after they had been regularly gay. They were regularly gay. They were gay every day. They ended every day in the same way, at the same time, and they had been every day regularly gay.

The voice Helen Furr was cultivating was quite a pleasant one. The voice Georgine Skeene was cultivating was, some said, a better one. The voice Helen Furr was cultivating she cultivated and it was quite completely a pleasant enough one then, a cultivated enough one then. The voice Georgine Skeene was cultivating she did not cultivate too much. She cultivated it quite some. She cultivated and she would sometime go on cultivating it and it was not then an unpleasant one, it would not be then an unpleasant one, it would be a quite richly enough cultivated one, it would be quite richly enough to be a pleasant enough one.

They were gay where there were many cultivating something. The two were gay there, were regularly gay there. Georgine Skeene would have liked to do more travelling. They did some travelling, not very much travelling, Georgine Skeene would have liked to do more travelling, Helen Furr did not care about doing travelling, she liked to stay in a place and be gay there.

They stayed in a place and were gay there, both of them stayed there, they stayed together there, they were gay there, they were regularly gay there.

They went quite often, not very often, but they did go back to where Helen Furr had a pleasant enough home and then Georgine Skeene went to a place where her brother had quite some distinction. They both went, every few years, went visiting to where Helen Furr had quite a pleasant home. Certainly Helen Furr would not find it gay to stay, she did not find it gay, she said she would not stay, she said she did not find it gay, she said she would not stay where she did not find it gay, she said she found it gay where she did stay and she did stay there where very many were cultivating something. She did stay there. She always did find it gay there.

She went to see them where she had always been living and where she did not find it gay. She had a pleasant home there, Mrs Furr was a pleasant enough woman, Mr Furr was a pleasant enough man, Helen told them and they were not worrying, that she did not find it gay living where she had always been living.

Georgine Skeene and Helen Furr were living where they were both cultivating their voices and they were gay there. They visited where Helen Furr had come from and then they went to where they were living where they were then regularly living.

There were some dark and heavy men there then. There were some who were not so heavy and some who were not so dark. Helen Furr and Georgine Skeene sat regularly with them. They sat regularly with the ones who were dark and heavy. They sat regularly with the ones who were not so dark. They sat regularly with the ones that were not so heavy. They sat with them regularly, sat with some of them. They went with them regularly went with them. They were regular then, they were gay then, they were where they wanted to be then where it was gay to be then, they were regularly gay then. There were men there then who were dark and heavy and they sat with them with Helen Furr and Georgine Skeene and they went with them with Miss Furr and Miss Skeene, and they went with the heavy and dark men Miss Furr and Miss Skeene went with them, and they sat with them, Miss Furr and Miss Skeene sat with them, and there were other men, some were not heavy men and they sat with Miss Furr and Miss Skeene and Miss Furr and Miss Skeene sat with them, and there were other men who were not dark men and they sat with Miss Furr and Miss Skeene and Miss Furr and Miss Skeene sat with them. Miss Furr and Miss Skeene went with them and they went with Miss Furr and Miss Skeene, some who were not heavy men, some who were not dark men. Miss Furr and Miss Skeene sat regularly, then sat with some men. Miss Furr and Miss Skeene went and there were some men with them. There were men and Miss Furr and Miss Skeene went with them, went somewhere with them, went with some of them.

Helen Furr and Georgine Skeene were regularly living where very many were living and cultivating in themselves something. Helen Furr and Georgine Skeene were living very regularly then, being very regular then in being gay then. They did then learn many ways to be gay and they were then being gay quite regular in being gay, being gay and they were learning little things, little things in ways of being gay, they were very regular then, they were learning very many little things in ways of being gay, they were being gay and using these little things they were learning to have to be gay with regularly gay with then and they were gay the same amount they had been gay. They were quite gay, they were quite regular, they were learning little things, gay little things, they were gay inside them and the same amount they had been gay, they were gay the same length of time they had been gay every day.

They were regular in being gay, they learned little things that are things in being gay, they learned many little things that are things in being gay, they were gay every day, they were regular, they were gay, they were gay the same length of time every day, they were gay, they were quite regularly gay.

Georgine Skeene went away to stay two months with her brother. Helen Furr did not go then to stay with her father and her mother. Helen Furr stayed there where they had been regularly living the two of them and she would then certainly not be lonesome, she would go on being gay. She did go on being gay. She was not any more gay but she was gay longer every day than they had been being gay when they were together being gay. She was gay then quite exactly the same way. She learned a few more little ways of being in being gay. She was quite gay and in the same way, the same way she had been gay and she was gay a little longer in the day, more of each day she was gay. She was gay longer every day than when the two of them had been being gay. She was gay quite in the way they had been gay, quite in the same way.

She was not lonesome then, she was not at all feeling any need of having Georgine Skeene. She was not astonished at this thing. She would have been a little astonished by this thing but she knew she was not astonished at anything and so she was not astonished at this thing not astonished at not feeling any need of having Georgine Skeene.

Helen Furr had quite a completely pleasant voice and it was quite well enough cultivated and she could use it and she did use it but then there was not any way of working at cultivating a completely pleasant voice when it has become a quite completely well enough cultivated one, and there was not much use in using it when one was not wanting it to be helping to make one a gay one. Helen Furr was not needing using her voice to be a gay one. She was gay then and sometimes she used her voice and she was not using it very often. It was quite completely enough cultivated and it was quite completely a pleasant one and she did not use it very often. She was then, she was quite exactly as gay as she had been, she was gay a little longer in the day than she had been.

She was gay exactly the same way. She was never tired of being gay that way. She had learned very many little ways to use in being gay. Very many were telling about using other ways in being gay. She was gay enough, she was always gay exactly the same way, she was always learning little things to use in being gay, she was telling about using other ways in being gay, she was telling about learning other ways in being gay, she was learning other ways in being gay, she would be using other ways in being gay, she would always be gay in the same way, when Georgine Skeene was there not so long each day as when Georgine Skeene was away.

She came to using many ways in being gay, she came to use every way in being gay. She went on living where many were cultivating something and she was gay, she had used every way to be gay.

They did not live together then Helen Furr and Georgine Skeene. Helen Furr lived there the longer where they had been living regularly together. Then neither of them were living there any longer. Helen Furr was living somewhere else then and telling some about being gay and she was gay then and she was living quite regularly then. She was regularly gay then. She was quite regular in being gay then. She remembered all the little ways of being gay. She used all the little ways of being gay. She was quite regularly gay. She told many then the way of being gay, she taught very many then little ways they could use in being gay. She was living very well, she was gay then, she went on living then, she was regular in being gay, she always was living very well and was gay very well and was telling about little ways one could be learning to use in being gay, and later was telling them quite often, telling them again and again.

THE SOMBRERO

Leon Surmelian

All that summer—my first American summer—I gloried in my suntan as I worked on the experimental farms, stripped down to my waist. I soaked up the sun, being a sun worshipper, but in July the sun got unbearably hot and I thought I'd better buy a straw hat to protect my head. Cutting and bailing alfalfa hay was an operation of epic proportions, and I drove a tractor, and hoed the weeds, and had a real love affair with the American earth. At the same time I worked as a milker in the University's dairy barns, and took a couple of courses in summer school. I was in charge of a special group of high producers, all conforming to the ideal dairy type, and I could almost see the corn silage and beet pulp and grain mixture and alfalfa hay I fed them at each milking churned into milk in their mighty barrels. I slept in the barn, and the cows slept in the pasture. I was roughing it, and felt more American by doing so.

One of my beautiful Ayrshires reacted positively to the tuberculin test and had to be removed from the herd. I loved my cows and the Ayrshires made me feel like the King of Scotland. My friend Scotty and I drove His Majesty's Favorite Pet to Grand Island in a truck. My first trip to another town. Combines drawn by tractors were harvesting the wheat. I liked these powerful earth smells mixed with the smells of food processing plants and of dehydrated alfalfa in the Platte River Valley. I felt once a man breathes the pure prairie air he would always want to come back as to a fountain of youth. On both sides of the highway spread out, in huge geometric patterns, and in perfect squares and rectangles, fields planted to wheat and corn and oats and alfalfa and sugar beets and sorghum and potatoes and soybean, and there was no end to the steady march of the sunflowers by the roadside.

The earth of Nebraska had a sensuous, physical appeal for me. I remembered that as a young boy of seven or eight I used to dig a hole in the earth, insert my penis in it, and lie as though in the arms of a loving woman.

A freight train almost a mile long steadily pounded away with a tremendous rattle and rumble of wheels, and red beef cattle with white faces, Herefords, Scotty said, were being taken to the stockyards of Chicago, Omaha, or Grand Island to be slaughtered. There were also refrigerator cars. Union Pacific. Missouri Pacific. Chicago Burlington & Quincy. Chicago and Northwestern. Rock Island. Chicago Great Western. Santa Fe. Illinois Central. Denver & Rio Grande. A second locomotive pushed from behind with short rhythmic blasts of its funnel. Buses went in both directions at 70 miles an hour, and I watched the license plates of automobiles: Idaho, Potato State; Kansas, Wheat State; New Mexico, Land of Enchantment. New Jersey, the Garden State. All boosting their states. In this country people drove two or three thousand miles to go fishing.

Grand Island had a busy metropolitan air about it. The atmosphere was different here, in a more thickly populated and greener part of the state. The largest city after Omaha and Lincoln, but it had only 25,000 people. Looked bigger. The world's greatest inland livestock market.

Scotty signed some papers, and we turned our cow over to a man who appraised it. I patted her on the back and said goodbye. I hated to think jello would be made from her skin, tendons and ligaments; her bones would be powdered into cleaning agents for scouring sinks and kitchen utensils. Nothing was wasted in packing plants. We drove next to a feed store and loaded our truck with sacks of beet pulp from a local sugar factory.

Scotty wanted to visit a friend before we went back to the University, and I said I'd just walk around and see the town, buy a straw hat, and get a haircut. "You need it," he said. I had not had a haircut for two months. We agreed to meet again before the county courthouse, which had a handsome nineteenth-century European look about it and was not of the strictly utilitarian type. Grand Island had European touches in its architecture. There was a large Roman Catholic cathedral here.

I strolled along the streets, with a cowboy gait, proud of the overalls I wore: my American uniform. Instead of buying an ordinary straw hat I bought a sombrero, a high-crowned hat with a very wide brim rolled at the edges and with a string that went under the chin. And wearing my sombrero I paused to watch a group of Mexican laborers repaving a street in the center of the town. The Spanish they spoke had a sweet European sound in Nebraska. Their foreman, the sheriff type, big, ruddy, kept a sharp eye on them and gave orders. Machines laid out the liquid asphalt, which had a pleasant bituminous smell, and the Mexicans spread it out to the proper thickness before heavy rollers tamped it down. These machines were like flame-throwers in the broiling heat, with the temperature 105° in the shade, and probably only Mexicans could do this kind of work in summer. I noticed the sign on a hamburger and cold drink stand: "For whites only. We do not cater to Mexicans." These earth-colored men, looking so docile and glad to have their jobs, could not even have a coke or a hamburger where they worked. I shook my head and walked away, thinking I'd rather have equality before this hamburger stand than equality before the law.

These Mexicans were probably paid ten times the wages they could expect to earn in Mexico, yet I wondered, is it worth it? No immigration quotas for them, they were needed in Nebraska and did much of the backbreaking field work for the sugar and grain barons: Were they allowed to enter the Grand Island cathedral these barons built and say a Hail Mary in Spanish? Mexico: Europe's bastard spawned by a squaw. A Latin failure beside Anglo-Saxon success. Men in sombreros, uprooted from their own land and rootless in Nebraska.

No use being so sentimental about the pioneers, I thought, as I walked on. They had their merits and were, yes, a heroic breed, but most of them were businessmen after all. Trade opened up the West. The trader came first. Others followed. No wonder the businessman occupied such an exalted position in Nebraska. The Spanish were here long before the real traders got in with their Bibles and rifles—and their violence. Coronado was a damn fool, Don Quixote in the Missouri Valley. He sought a mythical kingdom where even the poor ate from gold plates, and overlooked the real gold that lay in the land.

I strode jauntily into a barbershop and before I could say "Howdy folks" the barber, a short fat man with sagging jowls, wearing rimless glasses, frowned at me while giving a haircut.

"What you want?"

"I want a haircut."

He shook his jowls.

I looked at him, puzzled. Wasn't this a barbershop?

"Haircut," I said, gesturing with my fingers, as though holding a pair of scissors myself.

"We don't cut Mexicans' hair in this shop. You came to the wrong place, señor."

And maybe to the wrong country. I wanted to tell him I was not a Mexican, but I was too shocked to say a word. There were two other men in the shop who glanced at me and said nothing. The customers looked more civilized than the barber, and had the appearance of successful business or professional men. Couldn't they see I wasn't a Mexican? I felt betrayed by my own class.

"You heard me, get out. This shop's only for whites."

I wanted to shout at him, "Don't you talk to me like that! I am not a Mexican." I stood glaring at him, which a Mexican wasn't likely to do. But again, I could not say a word. I did not want to tell him—and these other men—my nationality. I did not want this barber to touch me, I recoiled from him, just as he found me untouchable himself. He had a phony professional look with his glasses, in his white coat, as if he were a surgeon, and was so very proud of being a white man in Grand Island, and a hundred per cent American. He had my blood boiling, and I did not care what happened to me if I struck him. I could have killed this barber. But I realized I could *never strike an American*. It would be like striking at America, slapping Uncle Sam in the face, smashing a dream, a vision, I knew I would never give up.

I turned on my heel and walked out of the shop, pondering on a discovery I just made about myself, that it was impossible for me to strike an American.

I stopped and watched the Mexicans again. The machines belched their hell-fire in the blaze of noon and the Mexicans toiled for their American masters, their faces and bodies smeared and blackened with asphalt. God pity them. I glanced at that sign again on the hamburger stand and thought these dark earthmen might prevail in the end, the USA and the USSR might burn each other out in nuclear war and the Mexican pop up from behind a cactus grinning under his sombrero and throwing his serape over his shoulder, Olé!

I put my sombrero away in the truck and entered another barbershop with a panicky feeling inside me. What would I do if this barber also took me for a Mexican and refused to cut my hair? By God, I'd go to Mexico and start a revolution of my own. But I was not untouchable here, thank Heaven. I did not speak a word for fear my accent would give me away, and I had turned so pale that I was a few shades lighter when I looked in the mirror.

"Medium?" asked the barber, tying the white hair cloth around my neck, over a strip of gauze, as sanitary laws required. I nodded, pretending to be absorbed in the magazine I was reading, an old copy of *Life* I had already read. "Clippers all around?" I nodded. "Trim the eyebrows?" I nodded. I did not let him stick his scissors into my nose, though. There was no sanitary law against this abominable practice, a good way of spreading colds. I said "Thank you" when he finished, got off the high chair, took out my wallet and handed him a $5 bill. He rang up the cash register and returned the change. I tipped him 25 cents; he was worth it. I was a gentleman and I hoped a white man once more. A close shave, though.

When we were driving back to the University, Scotty asked me, "Why so quiet?" "Just thinking," I said.

I could not tell him there are moments that destroy a world.

***

I wrote a new poem, in Sycamore Creek, which was my retreat, my private sanctuary in Nebraska, and comforted me even more than the library. Here I felt rested, unburdened, renewed. Nature had this soothing, healing power over me, and its harmonies seemed to straighten out my own twisted thinking. I sat under the same apple tree, now bearing apples, turning red, like my girl's cheeks, and the brook gleamed through the thick willow-green. I heard a woodpecker drilling, and listened to the flute-like notes of the blackbirds. The place was alive with birds, butterflies and ladybugs. My cows grazed in the pasture behind the barns or rested in the shade, chewing the cud.

I see wheatfields that are in heat
Soak up the Platte, and in their need
Swollen so big with the sun's seed
Kiss the rough hands, dancing bare feet
And tomahawks of bronze-skinned gods
For it's their joy to have all men
Feed upon them, to be just wheat.

I became aware of the fact that my anxiety, which never left me despite my euphoria on this campus, lessened, and I felt better and freer when I wrote a poem—and at the same time, I felt more American too. Poetry might well heal the inner split and bring my two disparate selves together and make me whole again. This was my basic problem: how to be whole again. A poem necessarily expressed an emotion— and I was trying to abolish my emotions in America and to be all utilitarian logic and iron will. The commissar of common sense. Emotions were messy affairs, explosions of irrational dark forces within us, sheer anarchy, but the point was that the heart took over when I wrote a poem, and try as I would I could not abolish my heart.

Suddenly clouds gathered out of nowhere and the sun disappeared as in an eclipse. A flash of lightning, then a cracking roll of thunder, the first I heard in Nebraska, and sounding like the chariot God rode in the skies of my childhood. Or was this a thunderbolt of the Indian gods crashing over Nebraska? I watched a dark sheet of slanting rain move toward the campus, and the first drops struck the ground like bullets and splashed against my eager face. The rain scared away a swarm of sparrows. I ran to a giant oak for cover as the rain came down in cataracts. I could see in the pasture the cows huddled under the trees and against the fences in that awkward way of theirs. The rain beat down the blackberry and raspberry bushes and the flaming purple crowns of bull-thistles. It shook a loquat tree, which by some miracle grew in this soil. It was exactly like the summer showers of my childhood in Greece.

I leaped with joy and ran from tree to tree and jumped over to the other side of the muddied creek that boiled over and swirled along with willow leaves. With wild goat cries I danced into the wood, entering a kingdom I knew of old and where the earliest memories of man, and of my own, came back. The rain swept into the wood, too, driving leaves, twigs, bits of moss before it. I let the wet branches brush against my face and licked the sky-sweet drops with the tip of my tongue. Every opening through the trees was like a magic casement through which I saw green castles where goblins dwelled and my own face as a child flattened out against a window pane, watching the wonders of the rain.

I sat down under a canopy of branches in a dry spot and rubbed my hands gleefully. The wood was small, just a bower of oak and sycamore and hickory and basswood and cottonwood, but I had the sensation of being in the boundless aboriginal forests of America and at the same time—that was the wonderful thing about this summer shower—in the woods of my childhood. I could hear the drumming and thrashing of the rain in a cottage in a summer camp for homeless children, where I built houses with playing cards and staged cavalry battles with horses I modeled in a village clay pit and which had matchsticks for their legs and tails.

A dreamy lassitude gradually overcame me, and closing my eyes I leaned my head on the spicy moss of a rock. I could smell the tobacco leaves strung on the frames before each house in a village close by the Turkish border in Thrace. I breathed in the fragrance of basil and dill and verbena, of mountain mint and thyme, pungent with the aromatic foliage of Byzantine chapels. I sniffed at the heavy tantalizing odors of walnut trees and citrons soaked in the rain; the sharp delicate fragrance of little lemons we called limonakia; of stolen apples and pears gleaming with raindrops and sweeter because of them.

Sheep bells that rang in Macedonian meadows tinkle-tinkled on the tympanum of my memory. Shepherd pipes bubbled through the morning blue. The sound of the ax was bandied back and forth by the rocks. I listened to the drip-drip of water trickling down the walls of rock-hewn monasteries and heard a mountain torrent dashing against the walls of a narrow gorge passable only for the devil, and the roaring surf of Greek shores rang in my ears.

I thought the rain makes children of all of us.

This shower ended as abruptly as it began. The sun came out and lighted the lattice-work of the underbrush. The birds and rabbits came out of their hidings and pecked at the ground or nibbled at the grass and leaves. I crawled out of the wood, holding my verses under my T-shirt, and looking up, I saw a rainbow, somehow my first in America, and looking like Christ spreading his arms over Nebraska.

I was wet, but it did not matter. Maybe this summer shower was my baptism as an American, and it washed out the barbershop in Grand Island. Standing under the rainbow I no longer felt like a stranger in a strange land, no longer an alien. If there are moments that destroy a world, there are also moments that remake it.

NAAHOLOOYAH

Mary TallMountain

Nobody's hands were quite like Mamma's. They were narrow with long thin fingers, and thumbs that bent out at the ends. The nails were scarred with nicks from the cutting of Salmon. In fish time they had rims of black, which had faded by winter till they were their usual pink-brown color. The hands acted as if they knew just what they were doing. When Mamma rested they folded, one on top of the other, and it seemed as if they were sleeping, but they were always ready to jump up. When they did, the turned-out thumbs gave them a busy air. The skin of her hands was both soft and rough. She thought about Mamma's hands coming toward her and Michael, usually holding things. It made her drowsy and comfortable.

At fish camp she had spent hours watching those hands work.

The right hand sailed clear up over the mother Salmon's big grey and pink body to her head, where it made two short strong chops with the sharp *toeeaamaas* that made Salmon's head slide away on the slippery table. From then on, how fast it moved! Every move was important. First, the two upper fins were flipped away and the lower one was sheared off low on the pearly breast over the sweeping fan of the tail. Next, Mamma's hand lifted and *toeeaamaas* drew a long red stroke that opened Salmon's belly. There in her silver lining were the perfect little jelly-red eggs. Ever so slowly, the right hand pried out the clump of eggs. Not much else was there, because Salmon ate hardly anything when she was going home with her eggs, which Mamma said were baby Salmon. Now the right hand ran *toeeaamaas* in another quick red line along the ivory-colored backbone. Both hands pressed the two halves out flat. They picked up *toeeaamaas* again and made slanting slices out from the thick inner body almost to the thin outer edges. These cuts were so fine that the skin was still all whole and was one skin, and its inside was red velvet. There was the fresh smell of new fish, the smell that Lidwynne thought she had always remembered from some dark place inside. It was a good smell and made her saliva bubble up. She thought she would like to taste a piece of that beautiful red velvet, right now.

When Mamma cut Salmon, the hands acted more careful than they ever did. It took both of them to dip Salmon into the tub of water and hoist the two halves up to hang over the drying rack. Lidwynne kept thinking now about the full racks of red king salmon, and the taste buds puckered more strongly. She could almost taste the sweet, smoky fish, the oil that was being heated out by the sun. How heavy *toeeaamaas* was, how Salmon's body pushed back at the sharp blade, but always gave and divided under it. Someday, she intended to cut Salmon herself. By the time she got to be ten, maybe even nine, Mamma would let her do it. Her hands would be big enough then, but now they were too small. Most Salmon were as big as she was. Much bigger than Michael, she thought.

He was grinning at her, with one tooth missing. It made him look wild and cockeyed. A blue sweater peeked out under his wadded and patched overalls that had once belonged to Lidwynne. "Where *eenaa*?" he asked. The wind gently rumpled his curls.

"In the house, Michael." She looked up at the window. Nobody was there. She had been upset, these days. Mamma and Daddy Clem had talked a lot, secretly. She was sleepy and lazy now because she'd lain awake so long trying to hear what they said. Mamma was very tired, too. Scary things had happened yesterday: first the soldiers fighting here in the yard, then Sister coming to see Mamma, her heavy black veil over her face that frowned. It seemed that all over the village, people were mad.

Mamma came outdoors. It was the first time since lunch that she had been out to see what was going on. Lidwynne was kneeling by *naaholooyah* now. There was a row of three, each with its little skin roof. The clay dirt had got dry, and the flaked mounds of the walls were pale brown, the color of pancakes. She pointed. "Look at *naaholooyah*!"

"*Snaa'*, you make dandy winter houses." Mamma sat down with her on the hard-packed ground.

"Maybe we go to Kaiyuh this winter and live in *naaholooyah*," Lidwynne said, excited inside at the thought. She had never been to Kaiyuh to winter camp. Sometimes Mamma and Grandpa and uncle and aunt and their children went out there to the old hunting grounds. It was supposed to be a wonderful place.

"Mmm-hmm." Mamma's face had gotten serious.

"But you said we could!" Lidwynne cried.

"I said maybe, you little dickens!" Mamma grabbed her and carried her over to the boardwalk. Michael was rolling around on it, giggling. Suddenly he tumbled off into the soft grass. Mamma gave a big laugh and picked him up so he wouldn't get scared, but he squirmed and squealed, unusually cross.

Lidwynne complained, "Why didn't you come see *naaholooyah*? I called but you didn't listen."

Mamma's lips moved against her cheek. "There's no time. Too much visiting." She yawned.

"Why do they all come here and visit?" Lidwynne frowned.

"It's just one of those times." Mamma carried them into the cabin and put them down. When she poured milk into a pan to heat, Michael wrinkled up to cry. She laid him slanty on her lap and pried open his mouth. "There's a new tooth coming," she said. Lidwynne craned her neck. "*Baghoo'*," Mamma said, showing her the new tooth poking up.

"*Baghoo'*," Lidwynne repeated. "When I was four did I have those growing too?"

"Sure, and you were cranky too, like he is right now."

"I was?"

"Oh, you're a cranky little girl." Mamma grinned into her eyes. "You're just like Grandpa. Look there."

Lidwynne stared at herself in the looking glass. She didn't think she looked at all like Grandpa. She was so short and he was so tall.

"See? Short and wide, like him. And you sure have got his temper." Mamma's dimple showed.

Michael sucked loudly at his bottle. "He's not mad any more. Look at that. He was plenty mad today, though. He bawled a lot." Lidwynne patted his warm little forehead. Now that he's four, she thought, he ought to eat regular food like I do. Not just that milk. Doctor Harry got mad when she wouldn't drink milk. She didn't like it at all. Maybe if she ever went Outside, she would get to drink real cow's milk. Now they just drank canned Carnation milk, mixed with water. Mamma and Nellie had to talk real hard to get her to drink it at all, but Michael never got tired of it. His face smoothed out now, and his eyelids kept shutting. His arms dropped back and his mouth slipped off the bottle. Mamma laid him in *ts'ibi*. "You can cover him up," she said.

Ts'ibi was a shallow pouch of heavy, well-worn canvas a yard square, hung from the ceiling by four solidly braided ropes passed through a fat gray coil spring and made into a ball-shaped knot, from which they splayed out to the corners of the frame and looped under the hard wide lip of wood over the edge of which the canvas curved up tightly; precisely spaced, the ropes wrapped around and under the lip and were nailed with the edge of the canvas to the smooth bottom. It was a sturdy smooth bowl deep enough to hold Michael safely. A nudge of the hand set the spring dancing lightly to put him to sleep; a harder one set it bouncing fast enough to awaken him without frightening him. Uncle Obal had made it. Lidwynne was going to have one too, when she had babies herself. She never missed a chance to watch Michael sleeping. Then she gently rocked him in *ts'ibi*. But she was too excited to sit still today. She pulled up the marten fur blanket and tucked it solidly around him.

Mamma sat down in her rocking chair by the window. "Hand me my thimble," she said. It was a regular thing they did, and Lidwynne gave her the thimble, which was a piece of caribou horn, shaved thin and curled to fit Mamma's thumb. Mamma threaded a needle with the papery thin *tl'aah* made of reindeer sinew she used for sewing hides. The *tl'aah* was tough, all right. Those hides were strong. Lidwynne watched her mother intently. Piles of *yoo'yoo'*, pink, silver, and blood-colored, gleamed in the fat sunbeam that dangled across the room. Those long fingers picked up a pink bead on the very end of the needle and stitched it to the piece of moosehide in her lap.

"Some day Lidwynne's going to do that." She leaned on the arm of the rocker. "That's going to be mittens," she announced. "Mittens for Lidwynne this winter."

"Yes," Mamma sighed. That thinking look was in her face again. "For Lidwynne this winter."

"What's the matter?" Lidwynne looked into Mamma's face that was bent over the beads, so bright in her brown hands.

Mamma looked at her. "*Snaa'*," she said, lingering over the word. There was something different in the tone of her voice today. "I have to take you and Michael to stay with Doctor and Nellie."

"What for?" Lidwynne thought: Again? it must be a joke.

"I'm going to be too busy to keep you this week."

"What you have to do?"

"I have to be ready if Grandpa calls me to council meeting."

Lidwynne's face brightened. She wasn't going away this time.

"Council meetings are about you and Michael."

"Why? What did we do?"

"Nellie and Doctor asked me if they could adopt you. You know that."

Oh, that crazy adoption stuff, again. "That what Grandpa was so mad about yesterday?"

"Mm-hmm."

"You mean you want to give Michael and me to them?"

Mamma looked out the window. The wind had started to blow in the grass, and the river was all rough. "Yes," she said.

Lidwynne's eyes got hot and trembly. "Why do you want to do that, Mamma?"

"Oh, *snaa'*, I don't want to." The last two words sounded heavy through her nose. But she went on talking in that funny sounding voice. "It's because I'm sick. That's the reason I have to let them keep you kids so much. They can take care of you better."

It wasn't a joke at all, then. Suddenly Lidwynne remembered Mamma coughing this summer, even when it was hot weather. And how when she laid her cheek on Mamma's chest she heard little whispers in there. She had thought before that it was just the way she breathed. Was that part of this sickness she was talking about? "They want to keep us all the time? At night and everything?"

"Yes, that's right." Mamma kept her face down looking at *yoo'yoo'*. Why won't she look at me? Lidwynne thought, putting her hands on Mamma's face. She turned around then to look out of the window, and it felt like she'd gone a long way off.

Real fast, Lidwynne hugged her. "You love me?"

Mamma made a deep chest sound and began to cough. Lidwynne got one of her big white handkerchiefs and Mamma blew her nose. She stared into Lidwynne's eyes, and now she was back from wherever she'd gone. "Of course I love you, foolish little one. I don't want you to go away. But if you do, I know you'll have a nice life, the way Doctor and Nellie do."

"Grandpa won't let them have us."

"He hasn't got anything to say about it. He just makes sure council does everything right. They have to decide. He stays with them till they do." Mamma snipped off a little thread close to the knot she'd made in back of the mitten. She put the skins away and closed the box. Everything in the room got clear and sharp like Lidwynne's reflection in the mirror. She would never forget *yoo'yoo'* burning like fire in the sunbeam.

She flung her arms around Mamma. She wanted to hold her so hard that she couldn't get away from her, ever. "I don't want to go any place, not even with Michael. I want to stay here."

"Ah," Mamma said to herself. She nuzzled her face into Lidwynne's neck. Her breath was warm on Lidwynne's skin, and her words made puffs of damp air, tight against the little wrinkles of fat under her chin. "I want you to stay, too."

"But why do we have to leave you? Can't we just visit them like we visit Auntie Madeline?" Lidwynne moved away and stared into Mamma's huge eyes, the color of shining blackberries.

"Now, I told you I'm sick. We can't help that. It's just lucky the Merricks are here. You've already told me you like them. If you don't, why do you want to go there visiting all the time?" Mamma's words sounded like echoes of themselves in a big dark cave.

Lidwynne knew her lower lip was beginning to stick out. It was getting colder in here. It must be the wind. She kept silent.

"They're good to you. They love you, Lidwynne. Don't you see, after a while I'll get sicker." Her rough hands came up and held Lidwynne's cheeks tight, and she saw her own reflections like dark still twins in Mamma's eyes.

"You're never going to get well?" Tears jumped out of her own eyes. Mamma wiped them. Then her face was buried in Mamma's apron and the hands were on her hair, patting, patting.

"Lidwynne, remember this word. Consumption. Your mamma has consumption, and she can't get well."

"It's terrible, to hurt you," Lidwynne sobbed, throwing her arms around Mamma's legs, hugging. The hands kept patting. Mamma rocked gently, and it was quiet in the room except for the little squeak of the rocker.

"Hey, *snaa'*, remember how mad Grandpa was yesterday, jumping all around?" Mamma was shaking a little. She must be laughing. Lidwynne peeked. Mamma was all dimpled up and her eyes were squeezed shut. She hollered, "Hoh, hoh! that funny Grandpa!" Lidwynne started to think of Grandpa and how he had looked. His face was red, his eyebrows were squeezed down into a white fringe so you couldn't see his pupils, and oh how mad he was, just yelling and yelling. Pretty soon she was laughing too, and they laughed till they were so tired they couldn't laugh anymore, and they were hugging and kissing, and Mamma wiped their faces and rocked her a while. Squeak, squeak, that's all that you could hear, and the two of them there warm and cozy in the quiet place.

Suddenly Lidwynne sat straight up. "Why can't we live at the barracks with Daddy?"

"He works for Uncle Sam, and he's got to go to Fort Gibbon pretty soon because Uncle Sam needs him there."

"Oh, that Uncle Sam!" Lidwynne filled the granite dipper at the water pail. She gulped the fresh river water, trying to swallow something that seemed to have gotten stuck in her throat.

She stared out the window. The wind had grown so strong it roared around the trees, stirring them up as if it had a spoon as big as a cloud. It whined over the roof and down the stovepipe and teased the fire so it flickered fast as red devils back of the little flower-shaped vents in the firebox of the stove. Its voice was like lots of people singing, far away.

It had blown *naaholooyah* away. There were only three small brown circles left on the ground.

THE WAR PRAYER

Mark Twain

It was a time of great and exalting excitement. The country was up in arms, the war was on, in every breast burned the holy fire of patriotism; the drums were beating, the bands playing, the toy pistols popping, the bunched firecrackers hissing and spluttering; on every hand and far down the receding and fading spread of roofs and balconies a fluttering wilderness of flags flashed in the sun; daily the young volunteers marched down the wide avenue gay and fine in their new uniforms, the proud fathers and mothers and sisters and sweethearts cheering them with voices choked with happy emotion as they swung by; nightly the packed mass meetings listened, panting, to patriot oratory which stirred the deepest deeps of their hearts, and which they interrupted at briefest intervals with cyclones of applause, the tears running down their cheeks the while; in the churches the pastors preached devotion to flag and country, and invoked the God of Battles beseeching His aid in our good cause in outpourings of fervid eloquence which moved every listener. It was indeed a glad and gracious time, and the half dozen rash spirits that ventured to disapprove of the war and cast a doubt upon its righteousness straightway got such a stern and angry warning that for their personal safety's sake they quickly shrank out of sight and offended no more in that way.

Sunday morning came—next day the battalions would leave for the front; the church was filled; the volunteers were there, their young faces alight with martial dreams—visions of the stern advance, the gathering momentum, the rushing charge, the flashing sabers, the flight of the foe, the tumult, the enveloping smoke, the fierce pursuit, the surrender! Then home from the war, bronzed heroes, welcomed, adored, submerged in golden seas of glory! With the volunteers sat their dear ones, proud, happy, and envied by the neighbors and friends who had no sons and brothers to send forth to the field of honor, there to win for the flag, or, failing, die the noblest of noble deaths. The service proceeded; a war chapter from the Old Testament was read; the first prayer was said; it was followed by an organ burst that shook the building, and with one impulse the house rose, with glowing eyes and beating hearts, and poured out that tremendous invocation

God the all-terrible! Thou who ordainest! Thunder thy clarion and lightning thy sword!

Then came the "long" prayer. None could remember the like of it for passionate pleading and moving and beautiful language. The burden of its supplication was, that an ever-merciful and benignant Father of us all would watch over our noble young soldiers, and aid, comfort, and encourage them in their patriotic work; bless them, shield them in the day of battle and the hour of peril, bear them in His mighty hand, make them strong and confident, invincible in the bloody onset; help them to crush the foe, grant to them and to their flag and country imperishable honor and glory—

An aged stranger entered and moved with slow and noiseless step up the main aisle, his eyes fixed upon the minister, his long body clothed in a robe that reached to his feet, his head bare, his white hair descending in a frothy cataract to his shoulders, his seamy face unnaturally pale, pale even to ghastliness. With all eyes following him and wondering, he made his silent way; without pausing, he ascended to the preacher's side and stood there waiting. With shut lids the preacher, unconscious of his presence, continued with his moving prayer, and at last finished it with the words, uttered in fervent appeal, "Bless our arms, grant us the victory, O Lord our God, Father and Protector of our land and flag!"

The stranger touched his arm, motioned him to step aside—which the startled minister did—and took his place. During some moments he surveyed the spellbound audience with solemn eyes, in which burned an uncanny light; then in a deep voice he said:

"I come from the Throne—bearing a message from Almighty God!" The words smote the house with a shock; if the stranger perceived it he gave no attention. "He has heard the prayer of His servant your shepherd, and will grant it if such shall be your desire after I, His messenger, shall have explained to you its import—that is to say, its full import. For it is like unto many of the prayers of men, in that it asks for more than he who utters it is aware of—except he pause and think.

"God's servant and yours has prayed his prayer. Has he paused and taken thought? Is it one prayer? No, it is two—one uttered, the other not. Both have reached the ear of Him Who heareth all supplications, the spoken and the unspoken. Ponder this—keep it in mind. If you would beseech a blessing upon yourself, beware! lest without intent you invoke a curse upon a neighbor at the same time. If you pray for the blessing of rain upon your crop which needs it, by that act you are possibly praying for a curse upon some neighbor's crop which may not need rain and can be injured by it.

"You have heard your servant's prayer—the uttered part of it. I am commissioned of God to put into words the other part of it—that part which the pastor—and also you in your hearts—fervently prayed silently. And ignorantly and unthinkingly? God grant that it was so! You heard these words: 'Grant us the victory, O Lord our God!' That is sufficient. *The whole* of the uttered prayer is compact into those pregnant words. Elaborations were not necessary. When you have prayed for victory you have prayed for many unmentioned results which follow victory—*must* follow it, cannot help but follow it. Upon the listening spirit of God fell also the unspoken part of the prayer. He commandeth me to put it into words. Listen!

"O Lord our Father, our young patriots, idols of our hearts, go forth to battle—be Thou near them! With them—in spirit—we also go forth from the sweet peace of our beloved firesides to smite the foe. O Lord our God, help us to tear their soldiers to bloody shreds with our shells; help us to cover their smiling fields with the pale forms of their patriot dead; help us to drown the thunder of the guns with the shrieks of their wounded, writhing in pain; help us to lay waste their humble homes with a hurricane of fire; help us to wring the hearts of their unoffending widows with unavailing grief; help us to turn them out roofless with little children to wander unfriended the wastes of their desolated land in rags and hunger and thirst, sports of the sun flames of summer and the icy winds of winter, broken in spirit, worn with travail, imploring Thee for the refuge of the grave and denied it—for our sakes who adore Thee, Lord, blast their hopes, blight their lives, protract their bitter pilgrimage, make heavy their steps, water their way with their tears, stain the white snow with the blood of their wounded feet! We ask it, in the spirit of love, of Him Who is the Source of Love, and Who is the ever-faithful refuge and friend of all that are sore beset and seek His aid with humble and contrite hearts. Amen.

(*After a pause.*) "Ye have prayed it; if ye still desire it, speak! The messenger of the Most High waits!"

It was believed afterward that the man was a lunatic, because there was no sense in what he said.

HAROLD BALL

E. Donald Two-Rivers

As you can well imagine, living in Chicago you get to meet a lot of characters. Like this guy I met named Harold who struck me as kind of odd. I saw the man go through changes and I hope he became a better person because of them. Well, to tell you the truth, I know the bastard did. There's a few things about Harold I need to tell you up front. The first is that Harold Ball felt cheated by life, plain and simple.

He wasn't a big guy, but he looked solid. He didn't have a sense of rhythm but that never did make any difference to the people who cared about him. Nevertheless, he liked to point that out. He was also probably the most intolerant black person I or anybody else will ever meet—at least that's what he'd tell you. He's something of a legend on the North Side because he once talked a despondent Arab out of committing suicide on his bus. Of course Harold claimed it was because he didn't want to have to go to court to testify. The city gave him some kind of medal for it. Harold said he threw it away. His wife said he has it hanging on his mirror in their bedroom. I'll bet his wife was telling the truth. Finally, he was so full of contradictions it was hard to figure out sometimes if you liked the son-of-a-bitch or hated him. Sometimes I just wanted to stay away from him, but that was hard to do because he showed up at the oddest of times. The man's favorite word was *hate*—at least to hear him tell it. He claimed he wasn't biased because he hated everybody the same.

Harold drove a bus for his living. He claimed to hate his job. He hated noisy teenagers, especially black girls and Mexicans. Didn't love his wife but didn't hate her. He hated the things she had done. Her friends all felt sorry for her because she was married to Harold. He hated most of them. He hated the *Chicago Sun-Times* because of its conservative writing, yet he read it every day without fail. He also hated the *Chicago Tribune* because of the way it was folded. He read it every day as well. You'll notice a lot of CTA (Chicago Transit Authority) bus drivers do that. They like to stay informed, I guess. There they'll be, kicked back and reading a paper while your mother is waiting for a goddamned bus on the corner with the wind blowing and goofy-looking dudes driving by blowing their horns at her. Yeah, Harold claimed to hate both rags but he read them like the Bible. He even read the ads. But that was typical of Harold—contradictions seemed to be a part of his life.

He wouldn't go to church. In fact, he proudly informed everyone who would listen that he hadn't been in one since he'd gotten married. He once said he thought his wife was having an affair with her church's preacher. Harold was drunk when he said it so no one paid him much mind. I met his wife twice. He was a lucky bastard to have her, as far as most of his friends were concerned.

Harold's bus route was the 151 Sheridan, second shift. He hadn't missed a day in fifteen years. He was a working man and prided himself on that fact. He'd driven that route for fifteen years, four-thirty to twelve, every day. Rain, shine, or snow, he drove that route and he knew every bump and pothole. Harold was sitting with Oliver, another bus driver, in a restaurant at Foster and Sheridan, waiting to take over his bus. He knew he would hate tonight's traffic.

"So Jesse Jackson says that 'poor people are not black or brown, they are white, they are female, and two-thirds are children.' Ain't that something?" said Oliver, as he read the newspaper spread out on the table. It was the start of their shift.

"He be bullshittin' too," Harold answered dryly.

"It says it right here," Oliver answered, pointing at the newspaper.

"I read it, I know what it says. But he ain't said shit. What makes him so right-eous? Out there always talking about this and that. I don't like no peoples like that."

"It's the message brother, not the messenger. The message is good. The dude's right on track."

"Anyway, who the hell made him the spokesman for every nigger in this coun-try? He did, that's who! Where's he live at anyway?" Harold asked. "I bet in some fancy suburb. He ain't never ridden on my bus."

Oliver ignored him.

"I really liked the part about what he calls the higher realm. He be talking right on, man. Character, brother! That's what we need to be looking for. We need to be looking past the goddamned color of skin and be seeing into each other's hearts. We need to see each other's character. Hell, when I was in Nam and the shit was coming down, do you think I cared about color or culture? Hell, when Charlie got to laying down his law on us, I couldn't give a damn about the color of the soldier next to me as long as he had on the same uniform. At that point, I'll tell you, when you be in a war, peoples just forgets about color. We was all Americans together. The other shit was forgotten about. I didn't care where the next guy was from. Didn't mean shit to me—or him either. I had a white guy save my ass once. That's why I don't pay no mind to that racial shit. Mostly idle talk. When things get really bad, then the real deal comes down. I'm here to tell you, race don't mean shit then." Oliver got up to get another cup of coffee.

"Take the receipt. She'll give you a free refill," Harold reminded his friend. As Oliver walked away Harold peered down Sheridan Road to the south. He was looking for the bus whose driver he would relieve. I hope she's running late, he thought. She needs to be written up. I don't know why no woman wants to be driving no bus. She should be home tending to her babies. As Oliver sat back down, Harold told him how he felt about woman bus drivers in general and the day driver in particular.

"Oh shit, man. You sound like some kind of caveman grunting around when you talk like that. This is 1997, boy. Wake up and smell the coffee. You got to admit she holds her own. She don't take no shit. Not even from you. You got to admire that."

"I don't got to do nothing but pay taxes and die. Don't be telling me what I got to do. I think she's one of them there bulldaggers the way she be so anti-man."

"Oh, man!" Oliver laughed. "She's got three kids."

"Why ain't she got no man?"

"She got a man. Remember that Oriental fellow? Don't you remember last year at the Christmas party? That was her man," Oliver explained.

"That ain't saying nothing about her. Not really. Look how she be the rest of the time," Harold countered.

"They got three beautiful kids together. He's a machinist somewhere. I think he said Elk Grove Village up north. Hell bro, he makes his. They be doing pretty good. They're trying anyway."

"Then how come she be so damned uppity with men?"

"You mean with you, right?" Oliver said as he stirred his coffee.

"Okay, then, tell me why she got to marry a Chink? She should be married to a nigger. Isn't that what she is?"

"I don't know about you sometime. Hell, this is 1997."

"So what it's 1997? Why don't she marry her own kind?"

"You know she's half-Indian too. I heard her tell you that one time," Oliver said.

"I don't believe that." Harold reached in his shirt pocket and continued. "Why would anyone want to be saying they be Indian? White man done took care of his ass. Why hell, them there Indians ought to just stay on the reservations and admit they be lucky to be alive. They all be a bunch of drunks."

"Don't even go there," Oliver warned. "My momma is half-Indian."

"Why all these niggers be saying they be part-Indian?"

"Jesus Christ, man, you are really a work of art. I'm going to bring you a book by this dude William Katz. It's called *Black Indians*. It tells a part of history that you never going to learn in school. Hell, you probably got some Indian in you too. Most people in this country do. It's just not mentioned in the history books."

"Here comes my bus. I got to go." Harold began gathering up his gear.

"See you at Laurie's for a quick one, okay? I'm buying."

"Maybe. I don't know. Yeah, okay. I'll be there." Oliver shook his head and laughed.

Harold's first run went without incident. Mostly working folks wanting to get their square asses home, he thought to himself as he pulled the bus up to a stop sign. Now he was heading south, his second time around. The riders had all changed. They were mostly young people heading out for the evening. A lot of them were students heading to night school.

As he drove, he recalled the words in the *Sun-Times* article that reported Jackson's speech at an all white school, about young black males and jails. "They come out of jail sicker and slicker and conditioned to recycle their pain," he had said.

Recycle their pain is right. Recycle it right back on other poor folks, Harold thought. There's more black-on-black crime in this city than needs to be, but according to Jackson it's the poor white women who are victimized the most. Then how come there's so much black-on-black crime? I be willing to bet most of those black-assed criminals ain't never robbed a white person. Harold smiled to himself at the thought. Those bad-assed niggers be robbing their own kind. It don't take no social scientist to figure these things out. Screw them, he thought, they ought to be locked up. Harold had a lot of misgivings about life, and crime was one area where he had definite concerns. His feelings about these guys, which he realized were partially irrational, were based on the fact that he had once been the victim of an armed robbery carried out by some young guys, one black and the others white. Recalling that humiliating night, he pulled the bus over roughly at Sheridan and Argyle where a young couple with two small children waved him down. The bus rocked as he screeched to a halt.

"Get on if you're getting on," he called out loudly. Look like Spanish to me, he thought. Both of them walked onto the bus with a child in their arms. They walked past the fare box and neither of them paid.

"Hey!" Harold called out sharply. "You got to pay." Wonder who the hell he thinks he is? Showing off for his woman. Harold didn't have a lot of patience when it came to what he referred to as "them foreigners." "They just take American jobs," he always said. Here we got nearly a million niggers ain't working and these folks come marching in here willing to work for near nothing. They be coming in here from Mexico, Poland, and even from Ireland. No wonder the Honky wants to hire him, he thought as he looked into the rearview mirror. The young man was putting his wife and kids into a seat.

"Hey, you! Amigo, you didn't pay. Ain't no one rides for free on my bus."

The young man looked up and nodded to Harold. Harold glared and pointed at the fare box. The young man looked at Harold intently, embarrassed by the implication. He stuck up his index finger to indicate he'd be right there. That son-of-a-bitch, Harold thought as his blood pressure went up two notches. He tapped on the fare box impatiently.

He glanced at a young, professional-looking black woman who had a pile of books on her lap. She'd gotten on at Berwyn and Sheridan. Harold knew she was heading for Truman College. She looked at Harold. Her large brown eyes snapped away sharply. Harold let his gaze slide down her body as he admired her Coke-bottle figure. She noticed him, snapped her legs tightly together, and looked out the window. What's wrong with her? Thinks she's hot shit, Harold concluded as he glanced back at the young man who was making his way to the front of the bus to pay.

"Ain't no one rides for free, Amigo!"

"I'm not your Amigo there, pal. I wasn't trying to ride for free. I was merely making sure my family was okay." The young man checked Harold with his flawless English. It made Harold look at him more closely.

The first thing Harold noticed was his shoes. They were Stacey Adams. He noticed that because they were his favorite brand. Then he saw the expensive black silk shirt and slightly faded, black Levi's jeans. Harold noticed that the young man wore a faded—or bleached—Levi's jacket with beadwork on it. He had long black hair neatly braided into a ponytail. Harold noticed a blue-and-white bone choker around the man's neck. He was digging in his pocket for the fare. Their eyes met and Harold glared at him defiantly. He didn't understand it, but he was going through some kind of emotional change. So I was wrong—he ain't no Mexican. But the sucker sure is an arrogant fellow. The young man returned his glare. Not blinking or yielding, he stared straight back into Harold's eyes. Harold blinked and looked away to check the road. The young man smiled.

"Rough night?" he asked in a soft but confident voice.

"And it's still early." Harold grunted by way of an answer. He looked at the young man who was smiling sympathetically. Harold felt less threatened—or whatever it was that he'd formerly been feeling.

"Yeah, I bet it's tough out here. I don't think I could deal with it myself."

At that moment, Harold noticed a car half a block away. He instinctively focused his attention on his driving. Probably going to pull out. Got to watch the son-of-a-bitch. People always in such a rush to get nowhere. His instincts proved correct. The car shot across the lane, heading in the opposite direction. Harold touched the brake and he tensed, ready to swerve if necessary. "Asshole," he said as he held the bus under control, avoiding hitting the car broadside.

"Nice driving," the young man commented.

"Thanks. I got to be on my toes all the time out here," Harold answered.

"Got to be tiring."

"Oh man, if you only knew," Harold laughed, almost bitterly. The young Indian man finished paying the fare and returned to his family. Harold watched them in his rearview mirror. The man's two-year-old son climbed on his lap, excited about the sights.

"Look at that! Look at that!" the child exclaimed. The little boy reminded Harold of his own kids, now fully grown and out of the house. He smiled as he thought of his kids. They didn't turn out half bad, he thought, as a feeling of contentment began to spread through his body. At Wilson, the pretty young woman pulled the stop cord.

"Have a nice night," Harold remarked as she stepped off the bus. She didn't reply or acknowledge him in any way. Screw you too, Harold said softly to himself. He pulled into traffic and forgot about the stuck-up woman.

At Sheridan and Montrose a small crowd of riders waited. It had just started to rain lightly. Not much more than a slight drizzle, but Harold knew what it would do to traffic. People just can't drive in rain or snow, he thought. He pulled the bus over with a jerk. Three young teenage girls, one black and two white, boarded. They were talking and laughing. Harold stiffened. He glanced in the rearview mirror and noticed several of the riders shifting uncomfortably. He shut the door and pulled away a little quicker than he had intended to. He didn't like teenagers like these ones. They ought to be in their houses doing their homework, he thought. Probably going to the Century Mall at Clark and Diversey to look at boys and who knows what else. As the bus jerked into the traffic, the girls let out a scream and one of them swore.

"Shit!" she said, "Can't you drive a little more careful?"

"What did you say?" Harold asked.

"Nothing!" she answered curtly.

"You keep on using foul language and I'll put you off this bus. You understand, young lady?"

The girls made their way toward the back of the bus. Harold cursed at the way they were dressed. Damned pants could fit me, he thought. They dress like a bunch of bums. A young girl should try to look pretty and sophisticated. Those baggy pants with the butt hanging below her knees look totally silly. The belt line was below her hips, revealing a pair of boxer underpants with spots on them. Harold looked back again to see if he was really seeing what he thought he was seeing. Those are boys' underwear she got on. What the hell is that all about? And that hair, he thought, got so much gel in it. Must be two gallons of axle grease on that head. The girls sat down and immediately began chattering and snapping their bubble gum. One of them started making funny faces at the Indian baby. The baby squealed with delight and cooed. Harold cursed under his breath and thought about telling them to leave the other riders alone. The Indian parents were smiling and began talking with the girls. The girl reached over and the woman handed her the baby. She began tickling it. Everyone was smiling. As he drove, Harold watched the scene. He wondered how come they were all so friendly.

Marine Drive was all torn up so Harold had to make a scheduled detour down Pine Grove to Addison, then over to Broadway as far south as Belmont. It added an extra fifteen minutes to his trip but he didn't mind because he got to see the sights on that street. What a bunch of liberal freaks, he thought as he expertly wheeled the bus through the congested traffic. At Broadway and Belmont two gay men got on his bus. They made him feel uncomfortable. Oliver often teased him and said gays made Harold uncomfortable because he was a latent homosexual. A closet queen, Oliver had said. Harold sometimes had questions about Oliver himself. Like with the Oriental guy, the husband of his day driver. As far as Harold was concerned, Oliver was just too damned accepting of others. A bleeding liberal of some sort.

Harold wondered how the hell Oliver could be so supportive of the couple when just a few years ago he'd served in Viet Nam and was paid to kill guys that looked just like him. When he asked Oliver about it, the friendly-natured bus driver had laughed.

"Ain't nobody wanted to be in the war. We was all in the same boat. It wasn't my war. I got drafted." That answer hadn't satisfied Harold. It seemed too pat and shallow.

"Would you let us know when we get to the water tower?" one of the gay guys asked.

"It'll be on the right. You can't miss it."

"Well, sir, we're strangers here."

You ain't kidding, Harold thought, stranger than hell if you ask me.

"Well?" the gay guy asked.

"Well, what?" Harold shot back. His body stiffened and he gripped the steering wheel tighter.

"I want you to announce when we get to the water tower. It's your job, isn't it?"

"My job is to drive this bus. I'm not a tour guide. Would you take a seat?"

"God, what an attitude! You should take a course in public relations. You don't have to bite my head off."

"Just take a seat or I'll have to ask you to leave this bus," Harold responded somewhat impatiently. Then in a low voice, he added, "Goddamned faggot."

"What did you say? What did you just call me?"

"I didn't call you nothing. Now take a seat."

"You called my friend a faggot," the second guy spoke up. "You are not allowed to say stuff like that."

"Would you please take a seat?" Harold had lowered his voice. Several of the riders were leaning forward to hear the exchange.

The second gay guy stood up. "I'm calling the bus company about you. What's your badge number? Get the name off his tag," he said to his friend.

"I'm going to have to ask you to leave this bus," Harold said as he pulled over at Sheridan and Diversey.

"I am not going anywhere. I paid and you insulted me by calling me a derogatory name," the first gay man said.

"You don't get off this bus, I'll kick your ass." Harold hadn't meant to threaten him, but it slipped out. He was getting enraged.

"And how do you think you're going to do that?" the guy asked with a laugh.

Harold looked closely at him. A well-built guy, he didn't flinch.

"Look, old man, you know and I know you can't kick my ass, so why don't you just drive the bus and I'll forget this whole ugly affair."

Harold glared at the guy. He didn't budge. Harold felt an agonized pang pass through him. Son-of-a-bitch, he thought. He's right, I probably can't kick his ass.

"Well, if you'll take a seat I'll drive."

"I'll do that as soon as you apologize."

Goddamned militant faggot. "Okay, okay. I'm sorry. I'll tell you when we get to the water tower. You get off at Chicago Avenue."

The gay guy stood his ground a minute more. His friend was urging him to sit down.

"Come on, just let it slide. He's an old guy."

"Like I'm getting sick of this shit. I have rights too."

Harold heard the two talking but was not able to respond even though they were calling him an old fart and several other things he didn't particularly care to hear. His mind was racing about a thousand miles an hour as he tried to concentrate on his driving.

He recalled a time he'd gone to the lake early in the morning to think. Some young guys walked up to him and asked for a cigarette. There were three of them. Harold handed one guy his pack and the guy put it in his pocket.

"Hey dude, what's up with you?" Harold asked.

"What do you mean?" the young guy said with a cocky grin on his face.

"You got my cigarettes in your pocket."

"You gave them to me. Made a donation to my cause. Right?"

Harold looked at the three of them. Petty-ass punks. They're going to take my cigarettes? No way! Harold considered grabbing the guy by the throat. He hesitated for a moment and the leader laughed.

"Old man, I wouldn't even think about it. You'll get your ass kicked. Why don't you just get on out of this park?" The smirk on his face irritated Harold. "I said get on out of this park before we decide to take everything you got."

Harold noted that one of the guys had edged over to the left where he picked up a good-sized stick. It was about the size of a baseball bat. The other guy moved to the right and took off his belt.

"So, what are you going to do old man?" the punk with the cigarettes asked.

Harold started backing away. The guy with the stick started to advance. The one who had removed his belt stepped further to the right and moved toward Harold. The leader stood his ground and smirked at Harold.

"You better get on out of here before we hurt you bad, old man. Get your old ass on out of here."

"You just going to take my cigarettes?" Harold asked.

"That's right, old man. I done took them."

Harold put up his hands and started to walk away. The punk grinned and relaxed. The other two, his sidekicks, stopped their advance toward Harold.

"Yeah, old man. Get out of here like he said," the one holding the stick recommended.

Harold walked away. Inside he was steaming and his face felt flushed. What is this? he wondered. This is the first time I've ever been victimized. What is it? Am I getting soft? Why didn't I just grab that punk and beat the shit out of him. It's what I would have done in the past. I must be getting old. My age must be showing.

Suddenly Harold slammed on the brakes and pulled hard on the steering wheel of the bus.

"Shit!" he said as he just missed a car that had turned sharply in front of him. "Goddamned assholes."

"Hey, why don't you take it easy? Don't you know how to drive?" It was the gay guy.

Harold turned and looked long and hard at the guy. He returned Harold's glare with his own.

"Okay. You want to try me, punk?" Harold said as he stood up and stepped away from the driver's seat. "Come on then."

"What are you doing, old man? You're going to get yourself beat into a heart attack, that's what." Both of the gay guys stood up threateningly.

Suddenly the young girl who had been holding the baby spoke up. "Sit down you sissies. He's an elder. Ain't you learned no respect for elders?" She got up and walked toward the front of the bus.

The young Indian man had handed his child over to his wife. The baby slept on the seat. He also stood up and walked to the front of the bus. "Come on guys, take it easy. We don't need this, do we?"

"I can handle this," Harold said.

"But you don't have to, guy. Does he, fellows?" he asked as he turned to the two gay men.

"Well, he should learn some respect. We paid to ride. Look how he's driving."

"Hey, it's not his fault traffic is so heavy, now is it, guys? Why don't you just sit back down and relax? Okay?"

The gay guy stared at the Indian for a long time, trying to decide what to do. When he made up his mind he spoke.

"No. No, it's not okay. Come on Jerry." He said to his friend, "Let's just catch a cab. I've had enough of these ethnics. See how they stick together. Grease balls."

"Look, guys, this isn't about color. Why you have to bring up ethnics is beyond me," the young Indian said.

"The hell it isn't!" one of the gay guys responded.

He turned to the young girl and said, "Bitch!"

"Faggot!" she shot back as she snapped her bubble gum.

Several of the riders started to laugh.

"Tell him, honey," someone spoke up.

"That's not necessary," the young Indian guy said to the girl.

"Well, he started it," she replied, but turned to go back to her seat.

"Come on, Jerry, I've had enough of this. Let's catch a cab. Let me off of this bus."

Harold opened the door and the two gay guys got off. Both cussed at Harold as they jumped down from the bus.

"You okay?" the Indian asked Harold.

"You could have whipped the both of them if you had to." It was the young girl. She looked out the window and stuck up her finger at the two men. They returned her gesture, plus some. Another night, Harold sighed.

"Yeah. I'm all right. I'll be okay." He turned to the other riders and offered his apology. No one said anything as Harold sat back down and put the bus in gear. Harold noticed that his hands were shaking. His knees felt weak. Two more months and I can retire, he thought. He and his friends were planning a big party at Laurie's on Broadway and Foster. A lot of bus drivers hung out there.

Once I retire, I'm getting my ass out of Chicago, I can tell you that much. I hate it here. Harold stopped for a moment and rethought his last thought. No I don't. All these years I thought I did, but really I don't. In fact, I kind of like it. He remembered the words in the article about Jesse Jackson's speech to a bunch of white kids. Too bad they couldn't have had this experience that we all just went through. You know, maybe Jackson's got a point, Harold thought to himself, maybe he's got a point. Character. That's where it's at. The Indian got character and that young white girl too. If that ain't character, I don't know what is, he thought. Respect your elders. Now that's character, he thought, despite the baggy pants and her daddy's underwear. Even those two gay guys. They was willing to stand up for what they believed in and get their gay asses whipped if they had to or, maybe, whip some old foolish ass. The last thought made Harold just a bit uncomfortable, but he dismissed it with a smile. They had character as well. Hell, everybody got character. We just need to see it, that's all. This whole city's full of people with character. Just got to be looking for it.

He started whistling. He looked into the rearview mirror at his customers. A bunch of nice people, he thought to himself. The three girls were gabbing excitedly and snapping their gum as they eyed young boys walking down Michigan Avenue. The Indian held his baby and rocked him gently. His other child, the two-year-old, sat on his mother's lap and looked out the window.

"Look at that! Look at that! Mommy, what's that?"

"It's life, boy!" Harold whispered in answer to the child's innocent question. He decided then and there to invite everyone on the bus to his retirement party. They might even come, he thought to himself.

I remember Harold's retirement party. Everyone was there. For an old guy who claimed to hate everyone, he sure turned out a good crowd. The small bar was full of people from every race. It was a multicultural event, the kind that some social scientist might spend big bucks to create, and it was all about old Harold.

Oliver and the woman bus driver were laughing about a time when Harold had gone off on her about some nearly forgotten incident. The Arab guy whom Harold had saved was uncovering a large tray of dolmas, which are rice and hamburger wrapped in olive leaves or something, that his wife had made. A Mexican with a CTA uniform was helping out the bar maid. I was sitting at the bar with my date telling her about how Harold always bitched about everything I ever wrote and said I was a dreamer. Harold, well, Harold was at the other end of the bar being all sentimental and slobbery. His wife and the preacher were cutting a cake with a bus on top of it. The three young girls and the Indian couple were sitting at a table laughing about the time Harold had stood down the mean-assed gay guys. I listened to the sound of everyone recounting their experiences with old Harold. It was a happy sound. I looked over at him. He was hugging Oliver and handing him an envelope.

"What's this?" Oliver asked.

"It's that there newspaper article that changed my life," Harold answered. "Let me read it to everyone."

"Listen up everyone." Oliver yelled, "Old Harold's going to read something to us." Well, Harold started reading but he never got to finish because when he got to his favorite part, he started crying. The joint was absolutely silent. The only sound that could be heard was the traffic on the street. Oliver took the article and finished the part that Harold couldn't. He read out loud. "—A higher realm, and that's character." Harold blew his nose noisily and someone started singing,

"For he's a jolly good fellow, for he's a jolly good fellow." I looked over at Harold and the son-of-a-bitch was grinning and crying at the same time. His wife had her arm around him. For he's a jolly good fellow all right, I thought to myself, as I wiped a tear from my eye. My date leaned over and whispered a promise I won't repeat here, but for all you guys, sometimes it's good to let the opposite sex see your softer side. Harold leaned over and kissed his wife, then looked at me and winked. That's the last time I seen him but when I do see him again and I show him this story, I bet he'll say he hates it. But I know what he'll do: he'll fold it away and put it in his wallet. That's Harold, the retired 151 Sheridan CTA bus driver for ya.

PANIC PORTAGE

Gerald Vizenor

Maybe we don't love life enough? Have you noticed that death alone awakens our feelings? How we love the friends who have just left us? How we admire those of our teachers who have ceased to speak, their mouths filled with earth! Then the expression of admiration springs forth naturally, that admiration they were perhaps expecting from us all their lives. But do you know why we are always more just and more generous toward the dead? The reason is simple. With them there is no obligation. They leave us free and we can take our time, fit the testimonial in between a cocktail party and a nice little mistress, in our spare time, in short.

—ALBERT CAMUS, *The Fall*

MAYAGI ASHANDIWIN:

Please excuse my intrusion, *madame,* but are you by chance dining alone tonight? I ask only because this is the best table in the restaurant to see the sunset, a spectacular sight at this time of the year. The very hues and traces of creation, as you can see, waver on the horizon. The marvelous breaks of light inspire the heart and poetry. There, across the bay, the mighty red pines bow to each other, always to each other, grateful and ready to dance in the dash and remains of light, light, light.

I presume you are not here to gamble. Truly, your hands are so gentle, such lovely, nimble fingers, apparently not toned to the tedious motion of slot machines, and your eyes are honest, much too generous to feign a hand of poker. Forgive my gaze, *madame,* but my compliments are not mere cause of flattery. Casinos, you might say, enervate the mind and weaken the heart and hands, the very ruins of native sense, vision, and sovereignty, but this is a four star restaurant, a natural reason to drive more than a hundred miles for dinner on the reservation. Rightly so, the attribution of four stars is rather curious if not exceptional. The Michelin Guide awards one to three stars. The Canoe Rib Voyageur, *waaginaa,* a new tourist enterprise, created four stars for native casino restaurants.

My apologies for being so eager, as you rightly notice, but perhaps you would allow me to translate the menu, as the principal chef decided to use native words for the entrées. The customers seem to appreciate the exotic custom and they learn a few words of *anishinaabe* at the same time.

Chippewa, you are correct, *madame,* is the name of the *anishinaabe* in English. The dictionary name, as you know, is an uncertain transcription, a simulation, that comes to natives by way of an empire nomination. American Indian is another dominion simulation. I use the word native in my stories. English is obsessed with empire sanctions, a language of simulations, transitive tenets, and cultural impunities, and the very dominance of ordinary dictionaries makes it very difficult to otherwise evince a native word. There, you have my nominal lecture. Yes, you are doubly correct, my selection and reign of words are precise.

Thank you, *madame,* for inviting me to join you for dinner. The waiters know me here, as you can see, and they treat me with deference, a certain tease of distinction, savoir faire, or, you might say, native familiarity. I sit at this very table three or four times a week to watch the sunset, meet visitors to the casino, strangers to the *anishinaabe* menu, and pursue my stories about this parvenu reservation, but never on weekends.

The restaurant, you see, is overrun by seasons of hunters in designer camouflage, snowmobilers in noisy insulated suits, men and women of sport and mockery, the sounds of wild weekenders. Shrewdly, the casino manager corners these holiday hunters, preys on their sentiments of chance, animal, fowl, and material fatigue, and that, *madame,* covers the actual cost of this exotic restaurant.

Thank you, the waiters know exactly my tastes and what to concoct for me. Hendrick's Gin over clear, thick slivers of ice, tonic, and a slice of cucumber, always. My curious customs create a sense of presence, a singular native presence in the midst of situational losers at the casino, and the comeback stories are memorable. Haute Médoc Red Bordeaux for *madame,* a wine of cultural tributes, and for me a distinctive gin infused with Bulgarian Rose. I am a habitué, as you might imagine, of the Mayagi Ashandiwin Casino Restaurant.

A toast to your good health, my friend, and may we share memorable stories over dinner. Yes, the waiters are curious about our conversation. They notice our eyes and hands, already we are laughing as friends. You are very sensible to wonder about my countenance and conventions. Yes, my shirts are custom tailored by Turnbull and Asser on Jermyn Street in London. I see you wear silk and linen, natural and worldly. Yet, *madame,* we are surrounded by synthetics. Decadence, would you agree, is a pretentious, weary indulgence, not the mere distance of paucity and tailored clothes. My taste for distinctive clothes came very slowly, as you can imagine, starting on the reservation with only one flannel shirt at a time, and two pair of thick socks, the incredible conversion of a threadbare altar boy to a cosmopolitan journalist. I retired a few years ago and built a cabin near the mission, eight times larger than the one my father built more than sixty years ago. I have solar panels now, we had plastic sheets over the windows then.

You bear my intrusive manner with humor, but my way is not the same every night, and certainly this is not my needy side. I eat alone at least once a week, at this very table, but not by choice. The nightly diners, even at the sunset window, are not always a pleasant chance. Stray hunters invade the restaurant once or twice a week. They loudly toast and boast, and propagate the cruel separation of humans and animals, never storiers of natural reason. The hunters are poseurs in bulky camouflage and they have no tragic wisdom or sense of irony. A hunter without irony is a monotheist by dominion, crosier in hand, almost dead, and without a trace of grace. Dylan Thomas comes to mind, *madame,* the turns of ironic mercy in one of his poems, Death shall have no dominion. The devotion is recast, in part, from Romans, Knowing as we do that Christ, once raised from the dead, is never to die again. He is no longer under the dominion of death.

You must be familiar, then, with the history of the woodland fur trade? The French and *anishinaabe* were rapacious trappers, hunters, carnal woodland lovers, of course, and brought the otter, beaver, muskrat, martin, and other animals close to an unnatural extinction. Would you agree, the fur trade was a crime of genocide? Yes, of course, monotheistic, species genocide. The Chinese silk trade, a mere turn to silkworm fashions, saved the beaver from extinction by irony. Severe, indeed, *madame,* and the fur trade names of the waiters are an ironic appeasement for that genocide, the traces of breath, heart, and memory of woodland animals.

The waiters, as you can see, are dressed for the postmodern trade, or at least the notions of métis culture. The waistbands and hats are jaunty, couture. The waiters were actually trained for a few weeks at a tourist restaurant in Paris. They have assumed old trade names, once a practice of natives at the fur posts because their nicknames were uncommon and outsiders could not easily pronounce or transcribe the sounds. Michel Cadotte is our waiter, and even the women take the names of male traders. Peter Vezina, over there, she tends the bar. Basile Hudon dit Beaulieu is the maître d'hôtel who seated you at my sunset window. She was a lecturer in anthropology at the university for many years but decided there were more distinctive characters on the reservation, the Good Cheer Casino, and at the Mayagi Ashandiwin Restaurant.

True, the salaries are much better at the restaurant than at the university, and you are very perceptive, that some women writers assumed a masculine nom de plume to find a publisher, and nuns once espoused the names of men, the saints, an unbearable, ironic collusion of monotheistic and matrimonial servitude to Jesus Christ. Surely, *madame,* you would agree, and inquire with me, who were the ring bearers in such a perverse crusade?

Please accept my apologies for that profuse and rather insistent, cryptic irony. I would not want to abuse or depreciate your religious sentiments or signatures. The fur trade, you see, was at the verge of a new world of monotheistic contravention, derision, greed, and animal genocide. The state mandated the fashion economy of the fur trade and church missions were wicked conspirators in the separation, dominance, and animal genocide. Native communities have never been the same for the ratty priests sent to convert natives on reservations. I was an altar boy for a wicked mission priest. Since then, *madame,* the creators hear more irony in my censure of the Roman Catholic Church.

Catholic schools? Really? Now that is a severe, disciplinary education that never ends. Perhaps you are a lawyer because of the strict reign of parochial schools. My dubious tuition was at a mission church on the reservation. Severe, to be sure, and the pedagogy was a nightmare. I was an altar boy, now a server, for a wicked priest on the reservation. Not far from here, near Wiindigoo Lake. Father Meme was a depraved and loathsome mission priest. We gave him the nickname *meme,* a red headed woodpecker in *anishinaabe,* because of his bright mound of red hair, not the meme of biology.

How would you respond to the abuses, the actual curses of sleazy priests? My mother and a few tricky elders told me to respect the mission, honor the priests, and, by the secrecy of confessions, bear the burdens of penitence, and forgive the abuses of others, especially priests. Father Meme, however, was truly an evil presence with rosy cheeks, a cold and nasty bleeder, and he abused the altar boys, and our ancestors buried near the mission. That priest was cursed by ravens and might have brought down the mercy of the church by his confessions. He was sacrificed, the common justice of natural reason, not forgiven. Only the actual sacrifice of that priest is forgivable.

I am relieved, frankly, that you are no longer persuaded by the patriarchs and hierarchy of the church. I am doubly pleased because your censure of the priests invites me to be more descriptive and demonstrative in my stories about the depravity of priests on the reservation.

I am curious, of course, and must ask what brings you to the reservation? The Good Cheer Casino and, of course, the exotic menu at the Mayagi Ashandiwin Restaurant. Actually, the best reason is to see the great rush of sunsets over Leech Lake. Michel Cadotte, our waiter, told me you are a lawyer and historian from France.

Chippewa Constitution? Now that, *ma chère madame,* is very unusual, an extraordinary reason to travel thousands of miles to inquire about native rights and sovereignty. Native rights by birth, blood, breach, and bane, the alliteration of bigotry. I appreciate your dedication to consider mixed race natives, or crossbloods, and the racial enticements of separatism by the federal government. Some treaties were written that way but never endorsed. Cherokee separatism, of course, and by historical comparison to other tribal constitutions. Yes, there were similar sentiments here, moves to separate the crossbloods from tribal enrollment, but the racial notions of federal agents have not been taken seriously. The Cherokee, as you know, were slavers, and then, five or six generations later they voted to deny the rights to almost three thousand freedmen, but racial separatism is never an exoneration for the shame of slavery. Now we hear the blues of the native slavers, once we had some color. The Cherokee benefited from the labor, culture, and color of their slaves. The recent plebiscite of racial separatism was motivated by greed, dominance, and racial hatred. Pedigree separatism is not a practice of native sovereignty, and should never represent natural reason or the common interests of native cultures.

You are absolutely right, *madame,* the *anishinaabe* have never been slavers. The French fur trade was the primary source of our cultural union with outsiders and empires, and the *anishinaabe* were loyal to the Union in the Civil War. Now, any bloodthirsty separatist referenda might exclude the entire tribe by skin hues and strains of progenitor bounty. The government on this reservation, however, proscribes the use of the word race, the cruel arithmetic quantum of bloody genes, to determine a native presence and rightful residence.

The narrator in *The Fall,* a novel by your esteemed compatriot Albert Camus, inquired if it might be better for those who cannot do without slaves to nominate them free men? The point of the query is a good conscience, and that is certainly ironic. Natives were never the best slaves, and so they would never be freedmen. Native rights would always be the ironic strain of sovereignty. Would you agree that past slaves and freedmen are owed compensation?

Leech Lake shimmers by slants of curious light on the waves, waves, waves. Look, the sun bounces over the bay. You can see the eternal blaze of sunsets every autumn night from this very window. The air is clear, clean, and bright, more inspired by the sudden, cold turn of seasons. There, near the dock, the ravens march on the shoreline and catch the common shine. And we catch the sun, the same dance of light that rouses the ravens, red pine, and birch, wavers in your red wine, and there, brightly in the slivers of magical ice in my gin.

Do you sense the eternal melancholy of the sunset? The first emotive states of creation, the mental conditions of animals, birds, humans, come to this moment on the horizon. We share the sunsets forever with our ancestors. The waves shimmer and bear evermore the ancestral wounds of natives, the wounds caused by the fur trade, the duplicity of federal agents and priestly missions. See, my hands hold this late sun and my heart is almost healed by the last traces of the day. The bloody horizon gathers the memories of the night.

I promised you, *madame*, a translation of the menu before dark. You must be hungry after a long drive from the city. So, start at the top of the menu, and repeat after me. Not really, only a gentle tease. I am not a native speaker of *anishinaabemowin*, the language of the *anishinaabe*, but the words, tags, and phrases are eternal traces to that marvelous league of nature, natives, and nations. There, the first word *miijun*, or food, is rather ordinary on the reservation, but exotic to outsiders because the *giigoonh* fish, *mayagi bine*, pheasant, and other prosaic entrées on the menu are wild, fresh from the woodland border lakes. Yes, you are very perceptive, *mayagi* means exotic or foreign, as in the name of the restaurant and the novel preparation of the entrées, and *bine* is the word for partridge. So, the pheasant is an exotic partridge from the Old World. Yes, the fish and fowl are always fresh, caught or raised, and sometimes by native songs, in the northern woodland and lakes. The entrées are never frozen, and for that obvious reason the menu is printed for the day.

Pierre Hertel de Beaubassin, the principal chef, has personal contacts with natives who provide fresh *ogaa*, walleye, and *ginoozhe*, northern pike, from Lake Namakan, rainbow smelt in the spring, and *adikameg*, whitefish, from Chequamegon Bay in Lake Superior. Pierre is not explicitly connected to the fur trade. Rather, he selected a nom de guerre, the distinguished name of an eighteenth century French Commander at La Pointe on Madeline Island, Wisconsin.

Pierre, then, is the *mayagi* chef, and the preparations of his entrées are made even more exotic by the sauces and condiments. Really, you would like me to order? *Madame*, your tastes are exotic. I would, however, rather describe my favorite entrées and then you can decide on one or more. So, my favorite in the autumn is *miinan mayagi bine*, or blue pheasant. Pierre roasts the pheasant with wild blueberries and serves the blue breast on a mound of *manoomin*, wild rice. The color is peculiar, to be sure, but natural, the sea, sky, and jays. Some of my friends find this tender, *nookiz*, blue breast of pheasant closer to an abstract expressionist painting than dinner.

You might enjoy *akakanzhebwe waabooz*, a snowshoe hare, actually a baby rabbit, braised and stuffed with the heart and other organs, and then seasoned with *bagaani bimide*, peanut butter, *zhigaagawanzh*, onion, and *wiisagi jiisens*, or radish. Yes, *lapin de garenne*, wild, baby rabbits gently caught by natives every other day near Waboose Bay. The word *zhigaagawanzh* is related to *zhigaag*, skunk, and the name Chicago. The *waaboozwaaboo*, rabbit soup, is seasoned with peanut butter, radish, and *gichi aniibiish*, or cabbage. The word *gichi* means great, and *aniibish* means leaf, or a great leafy vegetable. And the word *bagaani* means nut or peanut, and *bimide*, oil or grease.

So, are you with me for the next entrée on the menu? Another favorite of mine is the fish soup, *giigoonhwaaboo*, seasoned with *mishiimin*, apple, *giikanaamozigan*, bacon, *mandaamin*, corn, *begesaan*, plum, yes plum, and *okaadaak*, carrot, *ookwemin*, black cherry, *manoominaaboo*, wild rice broth, and, at last, *giizhik*, white cedar ashes. Believe me, that is a very tasty fish soup. You might start with a small bowl. Basile, the maître d'hôtel, boasts that the fish soup cures nausea and seasickness. Pierre, the chef, naturally has the last word. Here, at the end of the menu, above his signature, he wrote *bakadekaazo*, the *anishinaabe* word means, to pretend to be hungry.

SON IN THE AFTERNOON

John A. Williams

It was hot. I tend to be a bitch when it's hot. I goosed the little Ford over Sepulveda Boulevard toward Santa Monica until I got stuck in the traffic that pours from L.A. into the surrounding towns. I'd had a very lousy day at the studio.

I was—still am—a writer, and this studio had hired me to check scripts and films with Negroes in them to make sure the Negro moviegoer wouldn't be offended. The signs were already clear one day the whole of American industry would be racing pell-mell to get a Negro, showcase a spade. I was kind of a pioneer. I'm a *Negro* writer, you see. The day had been tough because of a couple of verbs— slink and walk. One of those Hollywood hippies had done a script calling for a Negro waiter to slink away from the table where a dinner party was glaring at him. I said the waiter should walk, not slink, because later on he becomes a hero. The Hollywood hippie, who understood it all because he had some colored friends, said it was essential to the plot that the waiter slink. I said you don't slink one minute and become a hero the next; there has to be some consistency. The Negro actor I was standing up for said nothing either way. He had played Uncle Tom roles so long that he had become Uncle Tom. But the director agreed with me.

Anyway . . . hear me out now. I was on my way to Santa Monica to pick up my mother, Nora. It was a long haul for such a hot day. I had planned a quiet evening: a nice shower, fresh clothes, and then I would have dinner at the Watkins and talk with some of the musicians on the scene for a quick taste before they cut to their gigs. After, I was going to the Pigalle down on Figueroa and catch Earl Grant at the organ, and still later, if nothing exciting happened, I'd pick up Scottie and make it to the Lighthouse on the Beach or to the Strollers and listen to some of the white boys play. I liked the long drive, especially while listening to Sleepy Stein's show on the radio. Later, much later of course, it would be home, back to Watts.

So you see, this picking up Nora was a little inconvenient. My mother was a maid for the Couchmans. Ronald Couchman was an architect, a good one I understood from Nora, who has a fine sense for this sort of thing; you don't work in some hundred-odd houses during your life without getting some idea of the way a house should be laid out. Couchman's wife, Kay, was a playgirl who drove a white Jaguar from one party to another. My mother didn't like her too much; she didn't seem to care much for her son, Ronald junior. There's something wrong with a parent who can't really love her own child, Nora thought. The Couchmans lived in a real fine residential section, of course. A number of actors lived nearby, character actors, not really big stars.

Somehow it is very funny. I mean that the maids and butlers knew everything about these people, and these people knew nothing at all about the help. Through

Nora and her friends I knew who was laying whose wife, who had money and who *really* had money; I knew about the wild parties hours before the police, and who smoked marijuana, when, and where they got it.

To get to the Couchmans' driveway I had to go three blocks up one side of a palm-planted center strip and back down the other. The driveway bent gently, then swept back out of sight of the main road. The house, sheltered by slim palms, looked like a transplanted New England Colonial. I parked and walked to the kitchen door, skirting the growling Great Dane who was tied to a tree. That was the route to the kitchen door.

I don't like kitchen doors. Entering people's houses by them, I mean. I'd done this thing most of my life when I called at places where Nora worked to pick up the patched or worn sheets or the half-eaten roasts, the battered, tarnished silver— the fringe benefits of a housemaid. As a teenager I'd told Nora I was through with that crap; I was not going through anyone's kitchen door. She only laughed and said I'd learn. One day soon after, I called for her and without knocking walked right through the front door of this house and right on through the living room. I was almost out of the room when I saw feet behind the couch. I leaned over and there was Mr. Jorgensen and his wife making out like crazy. I guess they thought Nora had gone and it must have hit them sort of suddenly and they went at it like the hell bomb was due to drop any minute. I've been that way too, mostly in the spring. Of course, when Mr. Jorgensen looked over his shoulder and saw me, you know what happened. I was thrown out and Nora right behind me. It was the middle of winter, the old man was sick, and the coal bill three months overdue. Nora was right about those kitchen doors: I learned.

My mother saw me before I could ring the bell. She opened the door. "Hello," she said. She was breathing hard, like she'd been running or something. "Come in and sit down. I don't know *where* that Kay is. Little Ronald is sick, and she's probably out gettin' drunk again." She left me then and trotted back through the house, I guess to be with Ronnie. I hated the combination of her white nylon uniform, her dark brown face, and the wide streaks of gray in her hair. Nora had married this guy from Texas a few years after the old man had died. He was all right. He made out okay. Nora didn't have to work, but she just couldn't be still; she always had to be doing something. I suggested she quit work, but I had as much luck as her husband. I used to tease her about liking to be around those white folks. It would have been good for her to take an extended trip around the country visiting my brothers and sisters. Once she got to Philadelphia, she could go right out to the cemetery and sit awhile with the old man.

I walked through the Couchman home. I liked the library. I thought if I knew Couchman I'd like him. The room made me feel like that. I left it and went into the big living room. You could tell that Couchman had let his wife do that. Everything in it was fast, dartlike, with no sense of ease. But on the walls were several of Coachman's conceptions of buildings and homes. I guess he was a disciple of Wright. My mother walked rapidly through the room without looking at me and said, "Just be patient, Wendell. She should be here real soon."

"Yeah," I said, "with a snootful." I had turned back to the drawings when Ronnie scampered into the room, his face twisted with rage.

"Nora!" he tried to roar, perhaps the way he'd seen the parents of some of his friends roar at their maids. I'm quite sure Kay didn't shout at Nora, and I don't think Couchman would. But then no one shouts at Nora. "Nora, you come right back here this minute!" The little bastard shouted and stamped and pointed to a spot on the floor where Nora was supposed to come to roost. I have a nasty temper. Sometimes it lies dormant for ages, and at other times, like when the weather is hot and nothing seems to be going right, it's bubbling and ready to explode. "Don't talk to *my* mother like that, you little—!" I said sharply, breaking off just before I cursed. I wanted him to be large enough for me to strike. "How'd you like for me to talk to *your* mother like that?"

The nine-year-old looked up at me in surprise and confusion. He hadn't expected me to say anything. I was just another piece of furniture. Tears rose in his eyes and spilled out onto his pale cheeks. He put his hands behind him, twisted them. He moved backwards, away from me. He looked at my mother with a "Nora, come help me" look. And sure enough, there was Nora, speeding back across the room, gathering the kid in her arms, tucking his robe together. I was too angry to feel hatred for myself.

Ronnie was the Couchmans' only kid. Nora loved him. I suppose that was the trouble. Couchman was gone ten, twelve hours a day. Kay didn't stay around the house any longer than she had to. So Ronnie had only my mother. I think kids should have someone to love, and Nora wasn't a bad sort. But somehow when the six of us, her own children, were growing up we never had her. She was gone, out scuffling to get those crumbs to put into our mouths and shoes for our feet and praying for something to happen so that all the space in between would be taken care of. Nora's affection for us took the form of rushing out into the morning's five o'clock blackness to wake some silly bitch and get her coffee; took form in her trudging five miles home every night instead of taking the streetcar to save money to buy tablets for us, to use at school, we said. But the truth was that all of us liked to draw and we went through a writing tablet in a couple of hours every day. Can you imagine? There's not a goddamn artist among us. We never had the physical affection, the pat on the head, the quick, smiling kiss, the "gimme a hug" routine. All of this Ronnie was getting.

Now he buried his little blond head in Nora's breast and sobbed. "There, there now," Nora said. "Don't you cry, Ronnie. Ol' Wendell is just jealous, and he hasn't much sense either. He didn't mean nuthin'."

I left the room. Nora had hit it, of course, hit it and passed on. I looked back. It didn't look so incongruous, the white and black together, I mean. Ronnie was still sobbing. His head bobbed gently on Nora's shoulder. The only time I ever got that close to her was when she trapped me with a bear hug so she could whale the daylights out of me after I put a snowball through Mrs. Grant's window. I walked outside and lit a cigarette. When Ronnie was in the hospital the month before, Nora got me to run her way over to Hollywood every night to see him. I didn't like that worth a damn. All right, I'll admit it: it did upset me. All that affection I didn't get, nor my brothers and sisters, going to that little white boy who, without a doubt, when away from her called her the names he'd learned from adults. Can you imagine a nine-year-old kid calling Nora a "girl," "our girl"? I spat at the Great

Dane. He snarled and then I bounced a rock off his fanny. "Lay down, you bastard," I muttered. It was a good thing he was tied up.

I heard the low cough of the Jaguar slapping against the road. The car was throttled down, and with a muted roar it swung into the driveway. The woman aimed it for me. I was evil enough not to move. I was tired of playing with these people. At the last moment, grinning, she swung the wheel over and braked. She bounded out of the car like a tennis player vaulting over a net.

"Hi," she said, tugging at her shorts.

"Hello."

"You're Nora's boy?"

"I'm Nora's son." Hell, I was as old as she was; besides, I can't stand "boy."

"Nora tells us you're working in Hollywood. Like it?"

"It's all right."

"You must be pretty talented."

We stood looking at each other while the dog whined for her attention. Kay had a nice body and it was well tanned. She was high; boy, was she high. Looking at her, I could feel myself going into my sexy bastard routine; sometimes I can swing it great. Maybe it all had to do with the business inside.

Kay took off her sunglasses and took a good look at me. "Do you have a cigarette?"

I gave her one and lit it. "Nice tan," I said. Most white people I know think it's a great big deal if a Negro compliments them on their tans. It's a large laugh. You have all this volleyball about color, and come summer you can't hold the white folks back from the beaches, anyplace where they can get some sun. And of course the blacker they get, the more pleased they are. Crazy. If there is ever a Negro revolt, it will come during the summer and Negroes will descend upon the beaches around the nation and paralyze the country. You can't conceal cattle prods and bombs and pistols and police dogs when you're showing your birthday suit to the sun.

"You like it?" she asked. She was pleased. She placed her arm next to mine. "Almost the same color," she said.

"Ronnie isn't feeling well," I said.

"Oh, the poor kid. I'm so glad we have Nora. She's such a charm. I'll run right in and look at him. Do have a drink in the bar. Fix me one too, will you?" Kay skipped inside and I went to the bar and poured out two strong drinks. I made hers stronger than mine. She was back soon. "Nora was trying to put him to sleep and she made me stay out." She giggled. She quickly tossed off her drink. "Another, please?" While I was fixing her drink she was saying how amazing it was for Nora to have such a talented son. What she was really saying was that it was amazing for a servant to have a son who was not also a servant. "Anything can happen in a democracy," I said. "Servants' sons drink with madames and so on."

"Oh, Nora isn't a servant," Kay said. "She's part of the family."

Yeah, I thought. Where and how many times had I heard *that* before?

In the ensuing silence, she started to admire her tan again. "You think it's pretty good, do you? You don't know how hard I worked to get it." I moved close to her and held her arm. I placed my other arm around her. She pretended not to see or feel it, but she wasn't trying to get away either. In fact she was pressing closer and the register in my brain that tells me at the precise moment when I'm in, went off. Kay was *very* high. I put both arms around her and she put both hers around me. When I kissed her, she responded completely.

"Mom!"

"Ronnie, come back to bed," I heard Nora shout from the other room. We could hear Ronnie running over the rug in the outer room. Kay tried to get away from me, push me to one side, because we could tell that Ronnie knew where to look for his mom; he was running right for the bar, where we were. "Oh please," she said, "don't let him see us." I wouldn't let her push me away "Stop!" she hissed. "He'll *see* us!" We stopped struggling just for an instant and we listened to the echoes of the word *see*. She gritted her teeth and renewed her efforts to get away.

Me? I had the scene laid right out. The kid breaks into the room, see, and sees his mother in this real wriggly clinch with this colored guy who's just shouted at him, see, and no matter how his mother explains it away, the kid has the image—the colored guy and his mother—for the rest of his life, see?

That's the way it happened. The kid's mother hissed under her breath, *"You're crazy!"* and she looked at me as though she were seeing me or something about me for the very first time. I'd released her as soon as Ronnie, romping into the bar, saw us and came to a full, open-mouthed halt. Kay went to him. He looked first at me, then at his mother. Kay turned to me, but she couldn't speak.

Outside in the living room my mother called, "Wendell, where are you? We can go now."

I started to move past Kay and Ronnie. I felt many things, but I made myself think mostly, *There, you little bastard, there.*

My mother thrust her face inside the door and said, "Good-bye, Mrs. Couchman. See you tomorrow. 'Bye, Ronnie."

"Yes," Kay said, sort of stunned. "Tomorrow." She was reaching for Ronnie's hand as we left, but the kid was slapping her hand away. I hurried quickly after Nora, hating the long drive back to Watts.

MY BROTHER AT
THE CANADIAN BORDER

Sholeh Wolpé

For Omid

On their way to Canada in a red Mazda, my brother and his friend, PhDs and little sense, stopped at the border and the guard leaned forward, asked: *Where you boys heading?* My brother, *Welcome to Canada* poster in his eyes replied: *Mexico.* The guard blinked, stepped back then forward, said: *Sir, this is the Canadian border.* My brother turned to his friend, grabbed the map from his hands, slammed it on his shaved head. *You stupid idiot,* he yelled, *you've been holding the map upside down.*

In the interrogation room full of metal desks and chairs with wheels that squeaked and fluorescent light humming, bombarded with questions, and finally: *Race?* Stymied, my brother confessed: *I really don't know, my parents never said,* and the woman behind the desk widened her blue eyes to take in my brother's olive skin, hazel eyes, the blonde fur that covered his arms and legs. Disappearing behind a plastic partition, she returned with a dusty book, thick as War and Peace, said: *This will tell us your race. Where was your father born?* She asked, putting on her horn-rimmed glasses. *Persia,* he said. *Do you mean I-ran?*

I ran, you ran, we all ran, he smiled. *Where's your mother from?* Voice cold as a gun. *Russia,* he replied. She put one finger on a word above a chart in the book, the other on a word at the bottom of the page, brought them together looking like a mad mathematician bent on solving the crimes of zero times zero divided by one. Her fingers stopped on a word. Declared: *You are white.*

My brother stumbled back, a hand on his chest, eyes wide, mouth in an O as in *O my God! All these years and I did not know.* Then to the room, to the woman and the guards: *I am white. I can go anywhere. Do anything. I can go to Canada and pretend it's Mexico. At last, I am white and you have no reason to keep me here.*

A NEW DAY

Charles Wright

"I'm caught. Between the devil and the deep blue sea." Lee Mosely laughed and made a V for victory sign and closed the front door against a potpourri of family voices, shouting good wishes and tokens of warning.

The late, sharp March air was refreshing and helped cool his nervous excitement but his large hands were tight fists in his raincoat pockets. All morning he had been socking one fist into the other, running around the crowded, small living room like an impatient man waiting for a train, and had even screamed at his mother, who had recoiled as if he had sliced her heart with a knife. Andy, his brother-in-law, with his whine of advice. "Consider . . . Brother . . . "

Consider your five stair-step children. Consider the sweet, brown babe switching down the subway steps ahead of me. What would she say? Lee wondered.

Of course, deep down in his heart, he wanted the job, wanted it desperately. The job seemed to hold so much promise, and really he was getting nowhere fast, not a God damn place in the year and seven weeks that he had been shipping clerk at French-American Hats. But that job, too, in the beginning had held such promise. He remembered how everyone had been proud of him.

Lee Mosely was a twenty-five-year-old Negro, whose greatest achievement had been the fact that he had graduated twenty-fourth in his high school class of one hundred and twenty-seven. This new job that he was applying for promised the world, at least as much of the world as he expected to get in one hustling lifetime. But he wouldn't wear his Ivy League suits and unloosen his tie at ten in the morning for coffee and doughnuts. He would have to wear a uniform, and mouth a grave Yes mam and No mam. What was worse, his future boss was a Southern white woman, and he had never said one word to a Southern white woman in his life, had never expected to either.

"It's honest work, ain't it?" his mother had said. "Mrs. Davies ain't exactly a stranger. All our people down home worked for her people. They were mighty good to us and you should be proud to work for her. Why, you'll even be going overseas and none of us ain't been overseas except Joe and that was during the big war. Lord knows, Mrs. Davies pays well."

Lee had seen her picture once in the *Daily News*, leaving the opera, furred and bejeweled, a waxen little woman with huge, gleaming eyes, who faced the camera with pouting lips as if she were on the verge of spitting. He had laughed because it seemed strange to see a society woman posing as if she were on her way to jail.

Remembering, he laughed now and rushed up the subway steps at Columbus Circle.

Mrs. Maude T. Davies had taken a suite in a hotel on Central Park South for the spring, a spring that might well be two weeks or a year. Lee's Aunt Ella in South Carolina had arranged the job, a very easy job. Morning and afternoon drives around Central Park. The hotel's room service would supply the meals, and Lee would personally serve them. The salary was one hundred and fifty dollars a week, and it was understood that Lee could have the old, custom-built Packard on days off.

"Lord," Lee moaned audibly and sprinted into the servant's entrance of the hotel.

Before ringing the doorbell, he carefully wiped his face with a handkerchief that his mother had ironed last night and inspected his fingernails, cleared his throat, and stole a quick glance around the silent, silk-walled corridor.

He rang the doorbell, whispered "damnit," because the buzzing sound seemed as loud as the sea in his ears.

"Come in," a husky female voice shouted and Lee's heart exploded in his ears. His armpits began to drip.

But he opened the door manfully, and entered like a boy who was reluctant to accept a gift, his highly polished black shoes sinking into layers of apple-green carpet.

He raised his head slowly and saw Mrs. Davies sitting in a yellow satin wing chair, bundled in a mink coat and wearing white gloves. A flowered scarf was tied neatly around her small, oval head.

"I'm Lee Mosely. Sarah's boy. I came to see about a job."

Mrs. Davies looked at him coldly and then turned toward the bedroom.

"Muffie," she called, and then sat up stiffly, clasping her gloved hands. "You go down to the garage and get the car. Muffie and I will meet you in the lobby."

"Yes mam," Lee said, executing a nod that he prayed would serve as a polite bow. He turned smartly like a soldier and started for the door.

Muffie, a Yorkshire terrier bowed in yellow satin, trotted from the bedroom and darted between Lee's legs. His bark was like an old man coughing. Lee moaned, "Lord," and noiselessly closed the door.

He parked the beige Packard ever so carefully and hopped out of the car as Mrs. Davies emerged from the hotel lobby.

Extending his arm, he assisted Mrs. Davies from the curb.

"Thank you," she said sweetly. "Now, I expect you to open and close the car door but I'm no invalid. Do you understand?"

"Yes mam. I'm sorry."

"Drive me through the park."

Muffie barked. Lee closed the door and then they drove off as the sun skirted from behind dark clouds.

There were many people in the park and it was like a spring day except for the chilled air.

"We haven't had any snow in a long time," Lee said, making conversation. "Guess spring's just around the corner."

"I know that," Mrs. Davies said curtly.

And that was the end of their conversation until they returned to the hotel, twenty minutes later.

"Put the car away," Mrs. Davies commanded. "Don't linger in the garage. The waiter will bring up lunch shortly and you must receive him."

Would the waiter ever come? Lee wondered, pacing the yellow and white tiled serving pantry. Should he or Mrs. Davies phone down to the restaurant? The silence and waiting was unbearable. Even Muffie seemed to be barking impatiently.

The servant entrance bell rang and Mrs. Davies screamed, "Lee!" and he opened the door quickly and smiled at the pale, blue-veined waiter, who did not return the smile. He had eyes like a dead fish, Lee thought, rolling in the white covered tables. There was a hastily scrawled note which read: "Miss Davies food on top. Yours on bottom."

Grinning, Lee took his tray from under the bottom shelf, and was surprised to see two bottles of German beer. He set his tray on the pantry counter and took a quick peep at Mrs. Davies's tossed salad, one baby lamp chop. There was a split of champagne in a small iced bucket.

"Lord," he marveled, and rolled the white covered table into the living room.

"Where are you eating, mam?" Lee asked, pleased because his voice sounded so professional.

"Where?" Mrs. Davies boomed. "In this room, boy!"

"But don't you have a special place?" Lee asked, relieved to see a faint smile on the thin lips.

"Over by the window. I like the view. It's almost as pretty as South Carolina. Put the yellow wing over there too. I shall always dine by the window unless I decide otherwise. Understand?"

"Yes mam." Lee bowed and rolled the table in front of the floor-to-ceiling wall of windows. Then he rushed over and picked up the wing chair as if it were a loaf of bread.

He seated Mrs. Davies and asked gravely: "Will that be all, mam?"

"Of course!"

Exiting quickly, Lee remembered what his uncle Joe had said about V-day. "Man. When they tell us the war is over, I just sat down in the foxhole and shook my head."

And Lee Mosely shook his head and entered the serving pantry, took a deep breath of relief which might well have been a prayer.

He pulled up a leather-covered fruitwood stool to the pantry counter and began eating his lunch of fried chicken, mashed potatoes, gravy and tossed salad. He marveled at the silver domes covering the hot, tasty food, amused at his distorted reflection in the domes. He thanked God for the food and the good job. True, Mrs. Davies was sharp-tongued, a little funny, but she was nothing like the Southern women he had seen in the movies and on television and had read about in magazines and newspapers. She was not a part of Negro legends, of plots, deeds, and mockery. She was a wealthy woman named Mrs. Maude T. Davies.

Yeah, that's it, Lee mused in the quiet and luxury and warmth of the serving pantry.

He bit into a succulent chicken leg and took a long drink of the rich, clear-tasting German beer.

And then he belched. Mrs. Maude T. Davies screamed: "Nigger!"

I still have half a chicken leg left, Lee thought. He continued eating, chewing very slowly, but it was difficult to swallow. The chicken seemed to set on the valley of his tongue like glue.

So there was not only the pain of digesting but the quicksand sense of rage and frustration, and something else, a nameless something that had always started ruefully at the top of his skull like a windmill.

He knew he had heard *that* word, although the second lever of his mind kept insisting loudly that he was mistaken.

So he continued eating with difficulty his good lunch.

"Nigger boy!" Mrs. Davies repeated, a shrill command, strangely hot and tingling like the telephone wire of the imagination, the words entering through the paneled pantry door like a human being.

Lee Mosely sweated very hard summer and winter. Now, he felt his blood congeal, freeze, although his anger, hot and dry came bubbling to the surface. Saliva doubled in his mouth and his eyes smarted. The soggy chicken was still wedged on his tongue and he couldn't swallow it nor spit it out. He had never cried since becoming a man and thought very little of men who cried. But for the love of God, what could he do to check his rage, helplessness?

"Nigger!" Mrs. Davies screamed again, and he knew that some evil, white trick had come at last to castrate him. He had lived with this feeling for a long time and it was only natural that his stomach and bowels grumbled as if in protest.

And then like the clammy fear that evaporates at the crack of day, Lee's trembling left hand picked up the bottle of beer and he brought it to his lips and drank. He sopped the bread in the cold gravy. He lit a cigarette and drank the other bottle of German beer.

A few minutes later, he got up and went into the living room.

Mrs. Davies was sitting very erect and elegant in the satin chair, and had that snotty *Daily News* photograph expression, Lee thought bitterly.

"Mrs. Davies," he said politely, clearly, "did you call me?"

"Yes," Mrs. Maude T. Davies replied, like a jaded, professional actress. Her smile was warm, pleased, amused. "Lee, you and I are going to get along very well together. I like people who think before they answer."

SHIRLEY TEMPLE, HOTCHA-CHA

Wakako Yamauchi

I met Jobo Endo at Kazawa, a winter resort near Karuizawa, the vacation spa of Japan. I had already been in Japan two years. I'd left Heber, California, at fourteen to further my education in my parents' homeland. It was the winter of 1939. Jobo had also come from America, from an obscure place called Inglewood on the outskirts of Los Angeles. His family were farmers like mine, and they had struck a good year and sent their only son to Japan. It was common practice with the Japanese living in America, to send their more promising children to Japan for an education. Because of the prevailing racial discrimination, the future of Japanese in America was pretty bleak.

I am one of two girls. My sister Momo is three years younger.

I was then boarding at Keisen, an all-girl high school in Tokyo, and spending summer and winter holidays in Shizuoka with the Kodamas. They were *tokoro-no-mono*, people from the same prefecture, and although we had been family friends for a long time, the Kodamas were city people in America and Mr. Kodama, an insurance man, had made a killing in something or other and had retired in Japan with a substantial income. They were childless, and I suspect I had become a surrogate daughter because they bought all my clothes and books, and they had selected the school I attended, and bought me gifts my father could not afford. They'd always prefaced these gifts with oblique references to my father, but I knew he was not as clever as Mr. Kodama; our life in America was always one of poverty. At first I tried to believe that my father finally drew money from that desert farm, but letters from home made it clear that nothing had changed.

It was hard for me in Japan. I'd been thrown into a class of my peers, first year in high school, and I had a lot of catching up to do. I had to wrestle with the language, the written and spoken word, plus the courses themselves, and all those ideograms that a stroke displaced meant a whole different thing. I spent all my time studying; I read everything: newspapers, novels, want ads, labels . . . everything.

That winter I had come back to Shizuoka wan and worn, and Mrs. Kodama suggested the trip to the snow country to take my mind off of studies. The Kodamas were somewhat different from the average Japanese couple; maybe because they'd spent so much time in America, maybe because they had no children of their own, they were closer than most. If, as I'd heard later, Mr. Kodama had kept a mistress in Tokyo, I would not have guessed it. I loved them in a way not unlike the way I loved my parents, but of course, my mother was special and not replaced for all her manipulations and obsessive frugality. I was always made to feel guilty about the Kodama gifts. Poor Momo did not enjoy such luxuries, my mother said, and she herself had not bought a pair of shoes in six years.

The Kodamas had taken me to the snows. I remember clearly how it happened. As it is everywhere in Japan, there was a crowd of people milling around in bright snow clothes. Looking at them—rich daughters in Paris outfits, handsome young men in turtlenecks—one wouldn't guess there was a poor working class in Japan or that there was a war going on with China. It could have been a resort in America except for the language. But I was bored. I'd come with two elderly people who spent most of their time in the inn. Also I did not ski.

Jobo was standing outside the lodge attending to his gear when I brushed by and nearly tripped over his skis. His friend—he'd come with three or four colleagues—gave me a cross look, and Jobo said, "Hey, watch it!"

I was startled because he'd spoken to me in English, and I thought I passed for a native Japanese.

"How did you know I spoke English?" I asked.

"You can't walk like *that* and expect to pass for a Japanese girl," he said. He smiled and winked. "These skis are my magic carpet. They take me away from . . . ," he waved his hand, "everything." I knew then that he too studied hard to keep up. But I could tell he was more a survivor than I. His friends looked annoyed by my intrusion, and as he slowly and meticulously waxed his skis, they grumbled and went up the slope without him.

We spent the afternoon together. I watched as his red snow cap, among hundreds like it, skimmed in and out against the green pines and white snow. He was magnificent.

It was the best winter I'd had. I hadn't used my English for two years, but as we talked, I could feel the language return to me, rolling on my tongue and moving through my throat. It was like renewing ties with a long-lost friend. The carefree language released feelings from deeper still and bound me to Jobo with delight and intimacy. It was like sharing a secret from all of Japan.

The Kodamas liked him too. In those days, boy and girl relationships were discouraged, but they indulged us. I was seventeen and Jobo, twenty-one.

We exchanged addresses. He was attending Waseda University, also in Tokyo, and he suggested we meet again, away from school, away from the Kodamas.

Although I didn't know it then, Japan, already into the Sino-Japanese war, was preparing for the bigger one. I was so involved in studying and becoming a native, I was unaware of what was happening in the country. Jobo was the light of that winter; he gave purpose to everything.

It was the Christmas my mother sent the Shirley Temple doll. All my childhood on that barren farm, I wanted a Shirley Temple doll. I wished for her on every Christmas, every birthday, but she never showed up. For that long time, Shirley Temple was a symbol of the American world: ruffles, bows, straight legs, large eyes, curly hair, Jell-O for dessert, the pursuit of happiness, all those things that separated me from white America. Now at seventeen, when I was too old for her, after I left the American me behind, she came to me.

My mother wrote: "Mie-chan, you've always wanted a Shirley Temple doll and though you're a little old for it now, I've prevailed upon your father to buy one for you." Implicit, another year without new shoes; something else put off.

I cried when I opened the package. Mrs. Kodama said I was too old for dolls. Mr. Kodama said, "If I had known, I'd have bought one long ago."

Shirley became my dearest friend. She sat at my desk, her knowing eyes reminded me of a secret love that sent my heart leaping. Sometimes when frustration and fatigue gnawed at my brain, her smile turned warm and, in a voice remarkably like my mother's, she called my name: "Mieko, Mieko. . . ." Her unflagging smile assured me of a serene and confident future.

Jobo graduated the following spring. In his last year at Waseda his parents cut back his allowance. I knew this when our Saturday meetings changed from teahouses and noodle shops to a lamppost on the street, a stone bench in a park. Most of the time I took along my homework which Jobo helped me finish, and we would spend endless hours walking through gravel parkways, crowded department stores, never daring to touch except when jostled against each other by the crowd. His arm reached out to steady me then, and I felt the keen pleasure and security of his strong body.

On his graduation Jobo's parents sent a token gift, a small check, and a letter of congratulations and apology saying they knew he worked hard and they were very proud but could not afford more. He showed me a tiny gold tie clasp. "I guess I'm on my own now," he said and returned the clasp to his pocket.

Shortly after, he found a cheap apartment on the second floor, one room where he could sleep and cook his meals, and he got a job with the Japanese government translating letters and documents. After considerable hesitation ("I won't hurt you, Mie," he'd said), I consented to meet him at his apartment, and we left the inconvenience of park benches behind. I studied there, ate the meals he cooked, talked with him, and (it was the night he told me of his grave fear for the future) made love with him.

"Mie," he said, "if we're to see America again, we must go now."

That was in October. I still had another year in school, and neither of us had the fare. I started to cry. Jobo then said I should talk to the Kodamas and arrange for a loan, and we should take the necessary steps to leave Japan.

"Together?" I asked.

"We'll marry first, of course," he said.

"You'd marry me just to get back to America?"

"I'd marry you for any reason. You know I love you, don't you?" he said.

When I returned to Shizuoka that winter, I spoke to the Kodamas about Jobo's plan. They were shocked, but in their restrained way, they said they'd thought Jobo was a bit of an opportunist and that I should not make too much over this man. After all, what did we know of his background? And besides, Mrs. Kodama said, they already had a young man, a relative, a grandnephew, in mind for me, and they had planned to work out arrangements for a family meeting after I graduated. Mr. Kodama hastily pointed out that because they had no children of their own, they hoped this nephew and I would marry, come to live with them, and take over the family interests.

"I've already committed myself to Jobo," I said.

Mrs. Kodama grew quite agitated. "Mieko," she said, "these things are not determined on personal whim. We already have an understanding with your parents. Why do you think you came to live with us?"

"I see," I said, "I've been sold."

"Not true," Mr. Kodama said and went on to recommend we talk about it later when we were all more calm. Whatever, there was no hurry since spring was still a winter away, and as for returning to America, well, that would certainly have to wait until then.

Later I heard them whispering, Mr. Kodama saying, "*Shikata ga nai.* Love is love." Then, "Maybe it'll wear off by spring."

My mother wrote saying she could hardly believe that just last winter she had sent a doll to the same girl who spoke of marriage today and that I should remember I was still on the edge of childhood, emotions rampant, not ready to make such a serious decision, and that I should also not forget that the good Kodamas had my best interest in mind. "They've always loved you, Mieko," she wrote. No mention of contract; implicit, my obligations. In any case I should wait until after graduating before thinking of returning to America.

When I told Jobo all this, he grew very quiet. "It will be too late then," he said.

In spring the Kodamas gave me a small wedding reception in Shizuoka, replete with two sham *baishakunin*, matchmakers. At the time I wasn't sure I was pregnant, but I told them anyway, and they hastened to arrange this small wedding. It so happened I wasn't; I later explained this as a miscarriage because already I felt a coolness from them. Well, I can't complain. They gave me a wedding and let me go. True, under pressure, but they did let me go and with a certain grace.

Jobo and I started housekeeping in his second-floor apartment. And he was right, it was too late. With his salary, saving for fare back to America was impossible, and because of what I did to the Kodamas, I couldn't ask for money again. That didn't matter to me; I was happy with Jobo, playing his young wife (I was nineteen), still with my Shirley doll, who watched from the dresser as we made love on the tatami.

Jobo continued skiing when he could, but because of the increasing strain of war, traveling was curtailed and finally prohibited. Food was rationed from the beginning, and the rations grew smaller; there was hardly any place to go for recreation, and our first winter together, on the first snowfall of the season, Jobo simply sat at home and waxed his skis.

"We won't be going to the snows for a while, Jobo," I said.

"Someday, when this is over, we'll go back to Kazawa," he said.

That December Japan sent her planes to bomb the U.S. fleet in Pearl Harbor. All Jobo's fears had come to pass. We wept together the night we heard the news. We talked about our families in America; I held my Shirley, and the three of us went to bed. We clung together and Jobo said, "At least we have each other."

"And Shirley," I was thinking of my mother.

"Hotcha-cha," he said.

When I look back on those days, my mind blocks out the physical deprivation. And too, that was nothing compared to what was yet to come, and later when things got really bad, we spoke of those earlier days as "the good old days." In spite of short rations, the lack of everything imaginable, we were together and that was good. We'd heard of the awful things that were happening to our families in America, that all Japanese had been imprisoned behind barbed wire, and we began to speak of them as though they were already dead. "My mother was . . . ," I said. Jobo talked about his sisters Kiku and the younger Mary in the past tense too. We made a pact to survive. "We will live through this," we vowed, "and we will return to America and walk that good earth again."

Jobo, whose father's farm had apricot and fig trees, and five acres of berries, told me endless stories of how he would one day pick strawberries for me and drown them in fresh cream from the dairy not a quarter mile away. I saw the red berries bleeding into the white cream and tasted its fragrance. He spoke of the two eggs he'd always had for breakfast like two old friends he'd lost in the war. He said that when he returned, he would have those two eggs again, with bacon that crumbled to the touch, or a piece of pink ham maybe left over from dinner the night before. We spoke of food constantly—while rereading old letters from America we found casual references to food; while recycling a moth-eaten sweater, Jobo remarked it was the color of a ripe pear. I was knitting the yarn for a baby shawl. I was pregnant. I wondered how we would keep this baby alive, but Jobo said we must take only one day at a time.

That was in 1944. Japan was losing badly and soon the bombers came from America. Already we were required to limit the use of gas and electricity during certain hours of the day, but when the bombs fell, both services were shut off immediately. Coal and firewood were unavailable except through black market. The streets were picked clean of everything, every shred of burnable material for these emergency cookouts for our meager rations. Day after day we ate rice gruel with bits of potato or carrot, sometimes without the vegetables, sometimes without the rice. But we were still luckier than some.

One night incendiary bombs were dropped in a circle around Asakusa, fencing in the industrial center with a ring of fire. I was in my fourth month. When the alert sounded, I ran to the window. Explosions tore the sky and lit it an angry red. Heat from the fires struck my face. Sirens shrieked. In spite of the warning to keep inside, residents poured into the streets, crying for their trapped families. I thought of Jobo and panicked. Was he there on an official mission? My back gave out and I fell to the floor. My body turned numb. I remembered that Jobo had said if the bombs should strike our house while he was away, I should walk north and he would find me. My mind went cold and blank. I remained on the floor until Jobo came home.

I lost my baby that night. Jobo paid the doctor with his ration of rice.

While convalescing, an old neighbor who had clucked her tongue when she first heard of my pregnancy, and continued to cluck as I grew larger, came to help. Mrs. Domoto didn't look as underfed as the rest of us; her clothes were not as mean. All the neighbors remarked about this—these things came to our attention at the time. When Jobo brought her to see me she said, clucking again, "Better this way, Mie-san. Better. Too hard for children in this world."

In spite of her kindness, there was a cunning about Mrs. Domoto that made me uneasy, but I was unable to get on my feet, and she brought her own rice, and sometimes a little extra for us. Twice she brought some tiny pieces of salt fish. "You must get well," she said.

When I remember Mrs. Domoto, I get a weird feeling because there was something uncanny about her coming to us at a time when we needed help so desperately, and then moving on to Hiroshima almost immediately after.

She came for eight days. For three days she admired my Shirley. She stroked her fine legs and ran a dry wrinkled finger over her blue eyes. She touched the organdy tissue of her dress and felt the velvet polka dots. Her eyes turned upward as though she were recalling a dream. The fourth day, Mrs. Domoto offered a pound of rice for Shirley. I smiled weakly. On the fifth day she brought the first salt fish and made another offer. I shook my head. "Shirley is my contact with my mother," I explained.

"Mie-san," Mrs. Domoto said, "you must learn to survive. After all, this is only a doll. There's no more rice in the bin."

"Jobo will bring some home tonight."

"Your husband is growing very thin," she said. "I will bring you five pounds."

On the eighth day she came with the rice and the second fish, and when Jobo returned from work, she took my Shirley, wrapped her carefully in a *furoshiki*, bowed, and left. Neighbors told me later she went to join her daughter in Hiroshima. Jobo said he would make it up to me someday.

The city was bombed again the following day. The gas and electricity were shut off, and because I was too weak to go scavenging for firewood, we had nothing to cook with. And our apartment was bare. Piece by piece with each bombing we had burned everything we could spare. We were very hungry.

Jobo pretended to look for something to burn.

"There's nothing left," I said, and tried not to look at the skis that were leaning against a doorless cupboard. Jobo walked around the room once more and stopped in front of them. He ran his hand along the waxed surfaces. He started to laugh. We both laughed. We laughed so hard we cried. With all the waxing, the skis burned beautifully, and for the first time in years, we went to bed with our stomachs full.

About two weeks later, Mr. Kodama came to take me away from the city. He said he'd heard I was ill with a pregnancy, and it would be safer for me in Shizuoka. For the baby's sake, he said. I had to tell him once more that I'd lost the child. Tears came to his eyes then. He cried where I could not. "Ah, Mie-chan, *unn ga nai. . . .*" He meant I had no luck.

He took me back with him, and there I never lacked for food even though the national condition worsened. Mr. Kodama had *unn*. And except for brief meetings, Jobo and I were separated until the end of the war.

Once near the end of the war, Mrs. Kodama packed a lunch and some supplies for Jobo, and I took a train to Tokyo. The Kodamas provided these treats for us maybe twice a year; they took care of everything: fare, a few tins of food, and some small items—a bar of soap, a used shirt, a *tenugui*, a washcloth.

It was a particularly muggy day and Jobo looked tired. The apartment was depressing; I had forgotten how small and dark and hot it was. I asked Jobo if we couldn't take our lunch to the park where we used to meet. He said it wasn't the same anymore; everything had changed.

"We'll pretend it's the same," I said. "We'll pretend there is no war and we're young and in love."

I hadn't realized what had happened while I'd been away. The plants and trees—stems burned by heat from the bombs, foliage picked clean by residents—struggled for life like the rest of us. Ragged children with bloated bellies lay listlessly on the dry grass. The scrappier ones lurked in the leafless shrubs and eyed us carefully.

"Who are they? Don't they belong to someone?" I asked.

Jobo shrugged. "They're all over the place. Orphans, I guess. People get killed in wars and a lot of them are parents," he said. He unwrapped our lunch and began to eat.

"Jobo, how can you?" I asked.

"What? How can I what?"

"Eat . . . with those hungry kids looking at you."

"Everyone in the country's hungry," he said and continued eating. "I can; same as you can behind the Kodama walls," he said.

While we talked, one little fellow sprinted forward, and snatched a rice ball.

"Now, you see?" Jobo said sullenly. "We should have stayed home."

The other children salivated and groaned as the bold one gulped down the stolen rice ball. I divided the lunch in half; rewrapped Jobo's portion and set my half on the bench.

Jobo said, "It's no use, Mie. It's too big. You can't fix it with a couple of rice balls."

I knew that, but at that moment I remembered my own lost baby and some other feelings rushed at me. The Jobo I didn't know frightened me, and I started to cry.

Jobo stalked away. We walked home in silence.

That night when I went to lay out the bed, I found a hairpin in the futon. My body went cold like the time of the Asakusa bombing. When you reach a certain level of despair, feelings become more or less the same. Later I was to find still another level, but at that time the same cold blankness squeezed my brain. I couldn't function; I couldn't talk. Jobo thought the children in the park had upset me, and he tried hard to make me forget, but toward the end of the evening he grew quite peeved. He said, "You come for one visit in six months, and you turn it into a wake."

The Kodamas were concerned because I spent a lot of time crying. Finally I had to confess what had happened, and Mr. Kodama said I should be realistic—after all, except for a few visits, Jobo had been without me for almost two years. I should understand that. Tokyo is full of beautiful hungry women, he said. With all that hunger and loneliness and the political chaos, who could be blamed? War was the culprit. Mrs. Kodama thought we should stop giving things to Jobo, but Mr. Kodama quickly said no, we couldn't do that. He advised me not to think of it as a betrayal—men were that way . . . different from women—and I shouldn't blame the other woman because while I had enough to eat here, there were many who didn't, and when there's nothing left to barter and perhaps children to feed, well, I should try to understand that too.

The war ended in August with Hiroshima, Nagasaki, and the atom bomb. I can't talk about that bomb because everytime I think about it, something happens to me, and if it's true that nothing goes to waste, I must wonder what this experience was for, what my own life is for, and confront all those thoughts that make the silent hours of our lives so unbearable. I want to cry then, the same tears I shed for Shirley, the same I shed over the hairpin in the futon, and it doesn't make sense.

After the war, the food situation got worse—if you can imagine that. Tokyo was closed to the refugees because of this and the housing shortage. I stayed for a while longer in Shizuoka, maybe not quite a year, then Jobo found an apartment, again on the second floor, in Hayama, a fishing village not far from Tokyo.

By that time we got word from our families in America. My father had died in an internment camp; my mother and Momo had relocated to Chicago, where my sister attended the university. My mother worked in a candy factory. She sent us candy bars and small items that were good for bartering.

In the evenings I stood by our window facing the sea and waited for the fishing boats to come in. Those of us whose men worked in the city rushed out to meet the boats and tried to buy fish. The fishermen were prohibited from selling outside the markets so that the full catch could reach the starving urban residents. I would take my candy bar, or a cup of sugar, or a small tin of meat, and the men pushed to wait on me.

Jobo's parents had relocated to Cleveland. His father worked in maintenance, janitorial work, and his two sisters, Kiku and Mary, had cushy office jobs. They sent us things my mother could not afford—clothes, towels, bedding, food. I was pregnant again, and Jobo's dad wrote concerned letters on what I should eat. He prescribed a diet for me: proteins, beef, chicken, fish—pork is not important, he said—vegetables, yellow and green, milk, cheese—leave out the sweets. Jobo is his line to immortality, he said. I took the Endo gifts to the city for trading.

At the railroad station, signs of the occupation were everywhere. Apple-cheeked soldiers with neat haircuts and snappy uniforms (it was incredible that these laughing men had won that terrible war) were always present, often carrying with them family treasures, a sword, an ancient urn, a daughter. *Pan-pan* girls with brightly painted lips in dance-hall dresses lay in wait for them there, their conversation dripping sweet in broken English, like shards of a wind chime trying to make sounds in stagnant air. When I first saw them, the hairpin in the futon came to mind. And Mr. Kodama's advice. Would love ever be the same for them? After a while I stopped thinking about it.

This pregnancy also miscarried, and I had to believe something in me was to blame. Jobo and I didn't talk about it, but I knew he knew too. The economic situation improved, and we moved back to Tokyo. I never got pregnant again.

During the five years there, I often thought of the Kodamas. I wanted to ask Mrs. Kodama how she managed to survive those childless years and the possible infidelity. I supposed there were moments of unspeakable distress for her. I supposed that if I could hang in there, our marriage would reach a more gratifying state, and maybe we too would find someone to carry on Jobo's name. They had found a wife for the grandnephew.

Once I suggested we adopt a war orphan.

"I don't want nobody else's kid," Jobo said.

My mother had a coronary in the candy factory. She'd worked there through the thick and thin of getting Momo through school. She was proud; I can see her discreetly mentioning her psychologist daughter to her candy buddies. A claim to fame. Momo married a white fellow psychologist.

After her stroke, my mother told Momo she must see that I returned to America. She said they owed me that. So Momo sent us money, and Jobo and I applied for permanent residency—I'd always kept my American citizenship—and we left Japan.

It didn't go well in Chicago. My mother and I had traveled too far, too long on different roads to meet again on the same ground. For days on end, my mother, confined to a wheelchair, spoke of the indignities of the camp experience, the inadequate medical facilities, my father's dying there, the awful food, the gossiping, and when she went full circle, she started from the top again, as though her life would end if she stopped. Once she paused long enough to ask if we suffered much in Japan. I said yes. But it was past. I did not care to bring back the pain—or inflict it.

It didn't go well. Jobo with his Waseda diploma would not work in a factory. He said we simply had to move on.

We went to Cleveland. Jobo's father still worked in maintenance, but Kiku had a great job as a legal secretary. Mary had married and left the family. Mother Endo stayed home.

Jobo hired in at a realtor's on commission, so we lived on the Endo charity, and it didn't work. There was too much tension with three women in the house—Kiku, sophisticated and patronizing; Mother, sly and insinuating; and myself, slow, unable to cope with mechanized housekeeping, unable to speak up for my feelings, always on the edge of hysteria. Dad was all right, but his constant talk of babies and pregnancies was perhaps the most devastating of all.

It was my turn. I asked to move on, but Jobo was unwilling.

"Give me a chance to get started. I'm tired of moving," he said.

"I want to go back to California. I want to feel that sun again; I want to be free. I want my own house."

"That's nonsense," he said. "We have no money. Besides, Dad wants us all to be together."

"Together? They hate me!" I screamed.

But it was nothing I could prove. There was always this cloying politeness covering the barbs, and Jobo only saw the candy coating. He said I was paranoid. He said it was my own insecurity. It was the old Chinese water torture.

I took too long to think about it, and by the time I'd borrowed money from Momo, the whole of Cleveland wasn't big enough for us Endo women. Jobo, caught in the middle, defended Kiku, defended his mother, and sometimes even defended me. It was a miserable place to be, yet he would have stayed but for my determination to leave Cleveland, taking Jobo with me—my final revenge on the Endos.

I told him that in California, near a Japanese community, there would be plenty of opportunities for a smart bilingual man, especially in real estate. It would be a chance to help our Japanese-speaking people, I said. I could go to work, wait tables, anything, and maybe together we could buy a piece of property with fruit trees. I reminded him of our dream back in Japan during the terrible war years. I said we could have children.

Jobo told an elaborate lie about a fantastic job offer in Los Angeles, and the Endos, pretending to believe, let us go.

The lie became a reality. Jobo happened in on a real-estate boom; he sold from the start. Before the first year was up, we bought a modest frame house. I couldn't believe it. But I was hardly through furnishing it—sewing curtains, hunting bargains—when Jobo bought a larger house, and I no more got used to living in those surroundings when he bought a still larger and more beautiful house.

Now there was no longer need for me to select furnishings. There were people for that—decorators and landscapers—people for everything but my loneliness. I asked Jobo why we didn't ever buy that place in Inglewood, his old hometown, and he said, "No resale value. A noisy airport there . . . the place is changed. Everything changes. Keep up with the times, girl."

And we changed. Jobo was a super salesman. He became more and more occupied with work and related activities, the lunches, dinners, the clubs, the drinking; he often stayed out late, sometimes returning in the morning.

"Had too much to drink and slept it off in the car," he said then.

We quarreled a lot—bitterly. We bickered over every detail of our lives, what to buy, where to go, what to eat. After a while it got so ridiculous, I stopped snapping at every lead.

Momo came to visit us two springs after we moved into the fancy house. In spite of Jobo's noisy welcome, she immediately sniffed out trouble, and with quiet restraint she asked if I planned to spend the rest of my life knitting afghans and waiting for Jobo.

"What else is there for me?" I asked.

"You'll have to find your own alternatives," she said.

"Forty-five is too old to start a new life," I said.

"That's your choice," she said.

That summer I enrolled in a typing class, and before the season was over, I found work in an insurance office. It seemed unfair to take this job with so many women really needing the work, but it was a matter of survival for me too. I had decided to let go; to leave Jobo alone until, on his own, he returned to our marriage, and I couldn't stay idle all that painful time.

There were almost five more years of clothes, cars, parties, late hours, and further estrangement.

Well, I guess I gave him too much rope. All that affluence finally attracted a smart woman who outwitted Jobo. She got herself pregnant. She was from Japan, divorced from a white sailor, a hostess in one of the restaurants in town. Jobo said he hadn't meant the affair to go so far, but now he wanted a divorce. He wanted a new life. He wanted this child.

He came home one morning while I was having my coffee and preparing for work. He said he wanted to talk to me and casually tossed a paper bag on the table. "Brought you something," he said.

I looked in the bag and found a battered Shirley Temple doll. I held back my tears. Somewhere in his new lifestyle he had kept the memory of that time when we were so young, so poor, so close.

I said, "I owe you one, Jobo. A pair of skis . . . I owe you a pair of skis. . . . "

"You owe me nothing," he said. "I want to talk to you. I want a divorce."

The treachery, the betrayal! My anger came spewing out. "Is that why you brought me the doll? You set me up for this! You brought the doll and meant to bomb me with her!" I screamed.

"No," he said. "I found the doll months ago . . . three or four months ago in a junk shop. I saw it and I thought of you. I left it in the trunk of my car and forgot about it. Mie, I want a divorce. I got a girl pregnant and I have to marry her."

"Three or four months? In the trunk of your car? Oh, Jobo, why didn't you bring her to me then?"

"I forgot, I told you. Mie, don't you hear me? I said I want a divorce."

We didn't quarrel then. I cried a little; I asked him if he loved her. He thought so. I asked if she loved him. He thought so. It was hard for me to believe that this woman—young and beautiful, I supposed—could love an old rich man who'd grown pompous, obese, and unyielding. It was not so easy for me to love him, even remembering the hard-muscled skier he once was, the sweet vulnerable man who wept with me long ago.

"I'm sorry, Mie," he said. And an era passed.

It's been three years since that day. In the first year following, I found that deeper level of pain I spoke about earlier. Sometimes at night, memories of the old days came at me: the terror, the hunger, the sweet intimacy of early love, *pan-pan* girls walking through my room, their voices tinkling, a cup of sugar dropped from my trembling hand, dissolving into the beach sand, swarms of fish in the cool gray of a Hayama twilight, dying at my feet, and Jobo coming to me, once again young, once again loving, warming my blood once again. Those kind of dreams.

Awake, there were other confrontations: What was the reason for surviving the war, to come to this? What is the purpose of heartbreak? And if it all dies with me, what indeed was the use of it? Am I only a segment of a larger drama? Is there still another act?

I wonder sometimes if Jobo thinks of these things too. But I suppose with the new family, more immediate problems occupy him, putting off the day of reckoning. Maybe there is no such day. Maybe he will die happy, the answer in his grasp. Maybe love is the answer. Maybe neither of us loved enough.

Well, you can go on like this until the sun sets, but some truths simply will not be hurried to reveal themselves. And after a while, even pain gets boring, and one has to get on with it. Get on with life. And that—life—does not stop just because you'd like to jump off here and hop on somewhere else later. You go on, and somehow some of the old vitality returns.

My Shirley doll sits on my dresser now. I bought her a new wig and made a fancy nylon dress for her. She smiles at me. Her lips are cracked, she's a bit sallow, the luster is gone from her blue eyes. She's not what she used to be. But she's been around a long time now.

THE HOMECOMING
Frank Yerby

The train stretched itself out long and low against the tracks and ran very fast and smooth. The drive rods flashed out of the big pistons like blades of light, and the huge counter-weighted wheels were blurred solid with the speed. Out of the throat of the stack, the white smoke blasted up in stiff, hard pants, straight up for a yard; then the backward rushing mass of air caught it, trailing it out over the cars like a veil.

In the Jim Crow coach, just back of the mail car, Sergeant Willie Jackson pushed the window up a notch higher. The heat came blasting in the window in solid waves, bringing the dust with it, and the cinders. Willie mopped his face with his handkerchief. It came away stained with the dust and sweat.

"Damn," he said without heat, and looked out at the parched fields that were spinning backward past his window. Up on the edge of the skyline, a man stopped his plowing to wave at the passing train.

"How come we always do that?" Willie speculated idly. "Don't know a soul on this train—not a soul—but he got to wave. Oh, well . . ."

The train was bending itself around a curve, and the soft, long, lost, lonesome wail of the whistle cried out twice. Willie stirred in his seat, watching the cabins with the whitewash peeling off spinning backward past the train, lost in the immensity of sun-blasted fields under a pale, yellowish white sky, the blue washed out by the sun swath, and no cloud showing.

Up ahead, the water tower was rushing toward the train. Willie grinned. He had played under that tower as a boy. Water was always leaking out of it, enough water to cool a hard, skinny, little black body even in the heat of summer. The creek was off somewhere to the south, green and clear under the willows, making a little laughing sound over the rocks. He could see the trees that hid it now, the lone clump standing up abruptly in the brown and naked expanse of the fields.

Now the houses began to thicken, separated by only a few hundred yards instead of by miles. The train slowed, snorting tiredly into another curve. Across the diagonal of the bend, Willie could see the town, all of it—a few dozen buildings clustered around the Confederate Monument, bisected by a single paved street. The heat was pushing down on it like a gigantic hand, flattening it against the rust-brown earth.

Now the train was grinding to a stop. Willie swung down from the car, carefully keeping his left leg off the ground, taking the weight on his right. Nobody else got off the train.

The heat struck him in the face like a physical blow. The sunlight brought great drops of sweat out on his forehead, making his black face glisten. He stood there in the full glare, the light pointing up the little strips of colored ribbon on his tunic. One of them was purple, with two white ends. Then there was a yellow one with thin red, white, and blue stripes in the middle and red and white stripes near the two ends. Another was red with three white stripes near the ends. Willie wore his collar loose, and his uniform was faded, but he still stood erect, with his chest out and his belly sucked in.

He started across the street toward the Monument, throwing one leg a little stiffly. The white men who always sat around it on the little iron benches looked at him curiously. He came on until he stood in the shadow of the shaft. He looked up at the statue of the Confederate soldier, complete with knapsack and holding the musket with the little needle-type bayonet ready for the charge. At the foot of the shaft there was an inscription carved in stone. Willie spelled out the words:

"No nation rose so white and pure; none fell so free of stain."

He stood there, letting the words sink into his brain.

One of the tall loungers took a sliver of wood out of his mouth and grinned. He nudged his companion.

"What do it say, boy?" he asked.

Willie looked past him at the dusty, unpaved streets straggling out from the Monument.

"I ask you a question, boy." The white man's voice was very quiet.

"You talking to me?" Willie said softly.

"You know Goddamn well I'm talking to you. You got ears, ain't you?"

"You said boy," Willie said. "I didn't know you was talking to me."

"Who the hell else could I been talking to, nigger?" the white man demanded.

"I don't know," Willie said. "I didn't see no boys around."

The two white men got up.

"Ain't you forgetting something, nigger?" one of them asked, walking toward Willie.

"Not that I knows of," Willie declared.

"Ain't nobody ever told you to say sir to a white man?"

"Yes," Willie said. "They told me that."

"Yes what?" the white man prompted.

"Yes nothing." Willie said quietly. "Jus plain yes. And I don't think you better come any closer, white man."

"Nigger, do you know where you're at?"

"Yes," Willie said. "Yes, I knows. And I knows you can have me killed. But I don't care about that. Long time now I don't care. So please don't come no closer, white man. I'm asking you kindly."

The two men hesitated. Willie started toward them, walking very slowly. They stood very still, watching him come. Then at the last moment, they stood aside and let him pass. He limped across the street and went into the town's lone Five and Ten Cent Store.

"How come I come in here?" he muttered. "Ain't got nobody to buy nothing for." He stood still a moment, frowning. "Reckon I'll get some post cards to send the boys," he decided. He walked over to the rack and made his selections carefully: the new Post Office Building, the Memorial Bridge, the Confederate Monument. "Make this look like a real town," he said. "Keep that one hoss outa sight." Then he was limping over to the counter, the cards and the quarter in his hand. The salesgirl started toward him, her hand outstretched to take the money. But just before she reached him, a white woman came toward the counter, so the girl went on past Willie, smiling sweetly, saying, "Can I help you?"

"Look a here, girl," Willie said sharply. "I was here first."

The salesgirl and the woman both turned toward him, their mouths dropping open.

"My money the same color as hers," Willie said. He stuffed the cards in his pocket. Then deliberately he tossed the quarter on the counter and walked out the door.

"Well, I never!" the white woman gasped.

When Willie came out on the sidewalk, a little knot of men had gathered around the Monument. Willie could see the two men in the center talking to the others. Then they all stopped talking at once and looked at him. He limped on down the block and turned the corner.

At the next corner he turned again, and again at the next. Then he slowed. Nobody was following him.

The houses thinned out again. There were no trees shading the dirt road, powder-dry under the hammer blows of the sun. Willie limped on, the sweat pouring down his black face, soaking his collar. Then at last he was turning into a flagstone driveway curving toward a large, very old house, set well back from the road in a clump of pine trees. He went up on the broad, sweeping veranda, and rang the bell.

A very old black man opened the door. He looked at Willie with a puzzled expression, squinting his red, mottled old eyes against the light.

"Don't you remember me, Uncle Ben?" Willie said.

"Willie!" the old man said. "The Colonel sure be glad to see you! I go call him—right now!" Then he was off, trotting down the hall. Willie stood still, waiting.

The Colonel came out of the study, his hand outstretched.

"Willie," he said. "You little black scoundrel! Damn! You aren't little any more, are you?"

"No," Willie said. "I done growed."

"So I see! So I see! Come on back in the kitchen, boy. I want to talk to you."

Willie followed the lean, bent figure of the old white man through the house. In the kitchen Martha, the cook, gave a squeal of pleasure.

"Willie! My, my, how fine you's looking ! Sit down! Where you find him, Colonel Bob?"

"I just dropped by," Willie said.

"Fix him something to eat, Martha," the Colonel said, "while I pry some military information out of him."

Martha scurried off, her white teeth gleaming in a pleased smile.

"You've got a mighty heap of ribbons, Willie," the Colonel said. "What are they for?"

"This here purple one is the Purple Heart," Willie explained. "That was for my leg."

"Bad?" the Colonel demanded.

"Hand grenade. They had to take it off. This here leg's a fake."

"Well, I'll be damned! I never would have known it."

"They make them good now. And they teaches you before you leaves the hospital."

"What are the others for?"

"The yellow one means Pacific Theater of War," Willie said. "And the red one is the Good Conduct Medal."

"I knew you'd get that one," the Colonel declared. "You always were a good boy, Willie."

"Thank you," Willie said.

Martha was back now with coffee and cake. "Dinner be ready in a little," she said. "You're out for good, aren't you, Willie?"

"Yes."

"Good. I'll give you your old job back. I need an extra man on the place."

"Begging your pardon, Colonel Bob," Willie said, "I ain't staying here. I'm going North."

"What! What the clinking ding dang ever gave you such an idea?"

"I can't stay here, Colonel Bob. I ain't suited for here no more."

"The North is no place for niggers, Willie. Why, those dang-blasted Yankees would let you starve to death. Down here a good boy like you always got a white man to look after him. Any time you get hungry you can always come up to most anybody's back door and they'll feed you."

"Yes," Willie said. "They feed me all right. They say that's Colonel Bob's boy, Willie, and they give me a swell meal. That's how come I got to go."

"Now you're talking riddles, Willie."

"No, Colonel Bob, I ain't talking riddles. I seen men killed. My friends. I done growed inside, too, Colonel Bob."

"What's that got to do with your staying here?"

Martha came over to the table, bearing the steaming food on the tray. She stood there holding the tray, looking at Willie. He looked past her out the doorway where the big pines were shredding the sunlight.

"I done forgot too many things," he said slowly. "I done forgot how to scratch my head and shuffle my feet and grin when I don't feel like grinning."

"Willie!" Martha said. 'Don't talk like that! Don't you know you can't talk like that?"

Colonel Bob silenced her with a lifted hand.

"Somebody's been talking to you," he declared, "teaching you the wrong things."

"No. Just had a lot of time for thinking. Thought it up all by myself. I done fought and been most killed and now I'm a man. Can't be a boy no more. Nobody's boy. Not even yours, Colonel Bob."

"Willie!" Martha moaned.

"Got to be a man. My own man. Can't let my kids cut a buck and wing on the sidewalk for pennies. Can't ask for handouts round the back door. Got to come in the front door. Got to git it myself. Can't git it, then I starves proud, Colonel Bob."

Martha's mouth was working, forming the words, but no sound came out of it, no sound at all.

"Do you think it's right," Colonel Bob asked evenly, "for you to talk to a white man like this—any white man—even me?"

"I don't know. All I know is I got to go. I can't even say yessir no more. Ever time I do, it choke up in my throat like black vomit. Ain't coming to no more back doors. And when I gits old, folks going to say Mister Jackson—not no Uncle Willie."

"You're right, Willie," Colonel Bob said. "You better go. In fact, you'd better go right now."

Willie stood up and adjusted his overseas cap.

"Thank you, Colonel Bob," he said. "You been awful good to me. Now I reckon I be going."

Colonel Bob did not answer. Instead he got up and held the screen door open. Willie went past him out the door. On the steps he stopped.

"Good-by, Colonel Bob," he said softly.

The old white man looked at Willie as though he were going to say something, but then he thought better of it and closed his jaw down tight.

Willie turned away to go, but Uncle Ben was scurrying through the kitchen like an ancient rabbit.

"Colonel Bob!" he croaked. "There's trouble up in town. Man want you on the phone right now! Say they's after some colored soldier. Lawdy!"

"Yes," Willie said. "Maybe they after me."

"You stay right there," Colonel Bob growled, "and don't move a muscle! I'll be back in a minute." He turned and walked rapidly toward the front of the house.

Willie stood very still, looking up through a break in the trees at the pale, whitish blue sky. It was very high and empty. And in the trees, no bird sang. But Colonel Bob was coming back now, his face very red, and knotted into hard lines.

"Willie," he said, "did you tell two white men you'd kill them if they came nigh you?"

"Yes. I didn't say that, but that's what I meant."

"And did you have some kind of an argument with a white *woman*?"

"Yes, Colonel Bob."

"My God!"

"He crazy, Colonel Bob," Martha wailed. "He done gone plum outa his mind!"

"You better not go back to town," the Colonel said. "You better stay here until I can get you out after dark."

Willie smiled a little.

"I'm gonna ketch me a train," he said. "Two o'clock today, I'm gonna ketch it."

"You be kilt!" Martha declared. "They kill you sure!"

"We done run too much, Martha," Willie said slowly. "We done ran and hid and anyhow we done got caught. And then we goes down on our knees and begs. I ain't running. Done forgot how. Don't know how to run. Don't know how to beg. Just knows how to fight, that's all, Martha."

"Oh, Jesus, he crazy! Told you he crazy, Colonel Bob!"

Colonel Bob was looking at Willie, a slow, thoughtful look.

"Can't sneak off in the dark, Colonel Bob. Can't steal away to Jesus. Got to go marching. And don't a man better touch me." He turned and went down the steps. "Good-by Colonel Bob," he called.

"Crazy," Martha wept. "Out of his mind!"

"Stop your blubbering!" Colonel Bob snapped. "Willie's no more crazy than I am. Maybe it's the world that's crazy. I don't know. I thought I did, but I don't." His blue eyes looked after the retreating figure. "Three hundred years of wounded pride," he mused. "Three centuries of hurt dignity. Going down the road marching. What would happen if we let them—no, it's Goddamned impossible. . . ."

"Looney!" Martha sobbed. "Plum tetched!"

"They'll kill him," Colonel Bob said. "And they'll do it in the meanest damned way they can think of. His leg won't make any difference. Not all the dang blasted ribbons in the world. Crazy thing. Willie, a soldier of the republic—wounded, and this thing to happen. Crazy." He stopped suddenly, his blue eyes widening in his pale, old face, "Crazy!" he roared. "That's it! If I can make them think—That's it, that's it, by God!"

Then he was racing through the house toward the telephone.

Willie had gone on around the house toward the dirt road, where the heat was a visible thing, and turned his face in the direction of town.

When he neared the one paved street, the heat was lessening. He walked very slowly, turning off the old country road into Lee Avenue, the main street of the town. Then he was moving toward the station. There were many people in the street, he noticed, far more than usual. The sidewalk was almost blocked with men with eyes of blue ice, and a long, slow slouch to their walk. He went on quietly, paying no attention to them. He walked in an absolutely straight line, turning neither to the right nor the left, and each time they opened up their ranks to let him pass through. But afterwards came the sound of their footsteps falling in behind him, each man that he passed swelling the number until the sound of them walking was loud in the silent street.

He did not look back. He limped on his artificial leg making a scraping rustle on the sidewalk, and behind him, steadily, beat upon beat, not in perfect time, a little ragged, moving slowly, steadily, no faster nor slower than he was going, the white men came. They went down the street until they had almost reached the station. Then, moving his lips in prayer that had no words, Willie turned and faced them. They swung out into a broad semicircle, without hastening their steps, moving in toward him in the thick hot silence.

Willie opened his mouth to shriek at them, curse them, goad them into haste, but before his voice could rush past his dried and thickened tongue, the stillness was split from top to bottom by the wail of a siren. They all turned then, looking down the road, to where the khaki-colored truck was pounding up a billowing wall of dust, hurling straight toward them.

Then it was upon them, screeching to a stop, the great red crosses gleaming on its sides. The two soldiers were out of it almost before it was still, grabbing Willie by the arms, dragging him toward the ambulance. Then the young officer with the single silver bar on his cap was climbing down, and with him an old man with white hair.

"This the man, Colonel?" the young officer demanded.

Colonel Bob nodded.

"All right," the officer said. "We'll take over now. This man is a combat fatigue case—not responsible for his actions."

"But I got to go!" Willie said. "Got to ketch that train. Got to go North where I can be free, where I can be a man. You hear me, lieutenant, I got to go!"

The young officer jerked his head in the direction of the ambulance.

"Let me go!" Willie wept. "Let me go!"

But the soldiers were moving forward now, dragging the slim form with them, with one leg sticking out very stiffly, the heavy heel drawing a line through the heat-softened asphalt as they went.

GOING FOR THE MOON

Al Young

The first time it happened, I figured, well, chalk it up to coincidence. We'd been talking so much in science class about the connection between how you think and what actually happens to you that I figured that maybe subconsciously, like Mr. Cleveland's always saying, I might've been hallucinating or projecting or something.

I mean, when I got home and Edrick told me somebody'd actually heaved a brick in the window of the bar downstairs, I went to laughing and coughing so hard he got scared and, for a skinny minute there, musta thought I might be needing some professional attention. I even put on my coat and went down to see for myself the hole the brick'd made.

Naturally, I didn't stand right in fronta the Ivory Coast where Nate and June, the dippy bartenders, could see me. I had sense enough to go across the street. I was impressed. Whoever did it'd done a clean, righteous job. Nate and June had boarded the window up temporarily so business could go on as usual, but deep down I knew this was gonna put a hurting on those suckers. Yet and still, something about it was disturbing.

"Zee," said Edrick, "you don't seem all that happy about this."

"When did it happen?" I asked.

"Before I got up. So it musta been in broad daylight. I woke up to this big commotion down on the street. The police came out and stood around, and June was out there with her fat self, talking all loud and bad. I thought it was great!"

"I'll have to think about it," I told my brother.

"What's there to think about?"

"Don't know," I said. "It just makes me feel kinda creepy the way it all went down."

"But Zee, you yourself told me you'd been concentrating on shaking 'em up, didn't you? Or maybe I've just been imagining and making all this stuff up since you moved in?"

"No, it's true. I did sit and picture a lotta stuff, including a brick smashing out their window. That image came up a lot, I must admit."

"So now that it's popped out for real, Zee, how come you're acting so weird?"

It took a full minute for me to think through that one. I'm not into violence. At least I don't believe I ever was.

Out of all the missed sleep and raw nerves the Ivory Coast had caused us with that loud-ass jukebox of theirs, it was the bass that got to me. The damn thing pounded right under my bed like it was the Tell-Tale Heart or something. The minute my head hit the pillow, it was *boom-bip/boom-boom-bip*! I'm talking about every night of the week. And nights when I had some heavy studying to do for school or some paper or a short story to write, look like it got twice as loud.

Of course I'd call up and ask 'em to turn the music down. Usually, if it was Nate answering the phone, he'd just say something like: "Yeah, well, okay, it must be pretty rough on you, up there gotta go to school in the morning and here we are down here, rattling you all around in your bed. We'll see what we can do."

But June, she was mean, man! Cold! She'd say stuff like: "Listen, don't you think it's kinda weird, in the first place, to be living up over a bar? How come you don't move? This is a business we got going here."

"Now, wait a minute," I'd say. "What's that suppose to mean? Me and Edrick ain't running no business, so we don't count, right? Just so happens we like it here."

"Well, we do, too, and our customers got a right to be entertained."

That's the kinda changes the Ivory Coast'd been putting us through, only it was rougher on me than it was on Edrick because he worked between midnight and eight, the graveyard shift at Safeway. Why any supermarket thinks it's gotta be open twenty-four hours a day is still beyond me, but that's the way it was. Neither one of us wanted to have anything to do with the cops, so we never called 'em.

Also, the apartment, even though it was on the small side, was nice and got a lotta sun. Edrick had dragged home so many potted plants from the Safeway until the window side of the dining room was starting to look like Golden Gate Park. Okay, I'm exaggerating a little, but you know what I mean. I'm not exaggerating, though, when I tell you the rent was right. In other words we put up with all that racket and hurt feelings and hassle with the Ivory Coast because we liked being where we were, out there on Geary near Golden Gate Park.

The flip side, you understand, was being able to come home from school and there Edrick would be, usually just getting up and showering and shaving. So even with my little part-time bookstore job, which Miz Perlstein at Last Chance High had helped me get through Community Outreach Program, my brother and me still had time to hang out together.

I really like Edrick. After I got outta detention and Moms started leaning on that vodka again, the only solution was for me to go stay with him. I never knew our father. And as much as Moms and me fought and didn't get along, especially when she was juicing *and* smoking that stuff, I still missed her something terrible. Sometime in the middle of the afternoon, while I'd be working at the bookstore or in the middle of some class, I'd remember how Moms'd spoken to me inside a dream I'd forgot I had the night before. I worried about her, and wondered how long she was gonna stay down in Texas, drying out. Even though Edrick wasn't but twenty-two, that was old enough for him to be my legal guardian.

When I told Mr. Cleveland before class about what'd gone down at the Ivory Coast, he said: "I wouldn't feel too bad about that brick through the window, Zephyr. Just because the thought rolled round in your head, that doesn't necessarily mean you endorse that sort of thing."

"But I thought about it a lot," I told him. "And the night before it happened, I sat there on the edge of the bed, waiting to hear the glass go to shattering."

I liked talking with Mr. Cleveland in his office. He asked me to call him Wayne, which I would only do very once in a while. It never felt right. I mean, the brother was straight out of the sixties, the way he talked and thought. Even that big afro he wore and the dashikis he'd come in wearing sometime woulda looked corny on anybody else. But with Mr. Cleveland, there was something okay about that. I liked him. Somehow he automatically made you wanna show some respect.

I mean, he wasn't tryna force you into no mold or pretend like he was your buddy, like some of the people at the juvenile authority do. He was just tryna get me to do more of my own thinking for a change. Mosta the time anyway. I must admit there were days when Mr. Cleveland didn't make much sense with all that positive stuff he liked to talk. I mean, all the depressing stuff happening all around me was enough to make anybody negative.

"So you know what that means?" Mr. Cleveland was saying. "It means you weren't the only one in the building who's been bothered by the noise level of that bar. The possibility of that brick going through that window has probably been hanging out there in space in the form of a thought for a long time. It's a thought form that's been waiting for somebody to pick it up and act on it, that's all."

"You think so?" I said.

"I'd be willing to bet anything that's what occurred."

And when I looked at Mr. Cleveland, at the way the late spring sunlight was angling in through the dirty window by his desk and falling on his face, that's when I understood how much he himself believed in what he was telling me. I could tell by his eyes how excited he was.

"So," I said, "all this you're telling us about thought waves isn't just another theory?"

"Absolutely not, Zephyr. Thoughts are as real as microwaves or TV waves or radio or radiation."

It wasn't hard to see that Mr. Cleveland knew I still wasn't quite ready to buy all of this, even though we'd been kicking it around—along with atoms and biology and the universe and other mind-blowing stuff—since I got into his general science class and made it into one of my hyphenates last winter when I first came to Last Chance. A hyphenated class is when you take a regular class—like science or accounting or history or whatever—only you can make it, say, a creative writing class, too. That's what I've done with Mr. Cleveland's class.

And that's what I liked about Last Chance High. It wasn't just another alternative education deal tryna help you save face; it's saving my butt. I'm learning how giving is more important than to all the time be taking and receiving.

"The mind is a sending and receiving mechanism," Mr. Cleveland went on. "You still have a problem with that, don't you?"

"Yeah."

"And what is it?"

"Well," I said, "if it really works that way, then how come we mostly go through negative experiences?"

You'd have to have your nose cut clean off to keep from smelling all through the room that strong peppermint tea Mr. Cleveland liked to sip on. "Is that how life feels to you?" he said. "Mostly negative?"

"Sure, that's the way the world is, don't you think?"

"I used to think that way," he said.

Mr. Cleveland always leaves his door cracked, maybe so the next person in line to see him could see he was already busy with somebody, so I caught a little glimpse of Marlessa Washington out there in the hall. It was just enough to make my belly go to tingling. She was sitting out there, listening to her Walkman, kinda flipping through our textbook.

"What you've got to understand," Mr. Cleveland was saying, "is that the subconscious mind doesn't know how to take no for an answer."

"How do you mean?"

"Yes is the only answer it recognizes. It only knows how to carry out whatever instructions we give it. It's like we saw in class with seeds and what happens when you plant them in dark, fertile soil, then water and look after them. Up above ground, it might not look like much is happening. But down underneath, down below surface, there's plenty going on. Next thing you know—*bam!* Up comes the beginning of some flower or plant. It's like magic. That's what thinking is, Zephyr—magic. It's like a magic seed you plant in your subconscious, which is like soil. Then all you have to do is keep watering and fertilizing it. That's what we're doing all the time without realizing it."

"That's the part I don't get, Mr. Cleveland—I mean, Wayne."

He smiled and said, "All it means is this: A good deal of the time we're planting negative seeds of thought, negative suggestions in our subconscious without even realizing it."

"How do we do that?"

"We're unconscious of our thinking. We forget that thoughts are real, that thinking itself is real. It isn't a fantasy or something we imagine. Thought waves are real waves traveling out into the environment, the same as any other signals. They go out and get picked up on frequencies, or wavelengths. This room right now is full of voices and music and pictures passing clean through us, or maybe bouncing off us. All we have to do to pick them up is snap on a radio or television and tune it to the right frequency."

"Whoa!" I said. "That's more than I can handle!"

"No, it isn't, Zephyr. You've been waiting to hear all this for a long time now. I only happen to be the one you've okayed to put it to you straight and clear."

"I'll still have to think about it," I said.

Mr. Cleveland stood up with a big grin on his face and said, "And check out *how* you think about it."

"Well," I said, getting up from my chair, "right now I gotta go rock and roll with a test in Miss Santiago's current affairs class."

"Last Chance might be the last of the alternative high schools," Mr. Cleveland said, "but even here T.C.B. is still in style."

And even though the way he talked sounded funny and outta date sometime, Mr. Cleveland had that one right. I did have to take care of business in Santiago's class. Either that, or lose some units. Like everybody else who'd either been kicked out of or dropped out of some other high school, I liked Last Chance. And I wanted to get high school behind me and get on with it, whatever that meant.

The second time it happened, Marlessa was with me and I, for one, got pretty shook up again, even though we both tried to make out like what'd happened wasn't any big thing.

I'd finally got up the nerve to ask her out, so that Saturday night we were just crawling up to the toll booth on the Bay Bridge on the way back from a Run-DMC concert in Oakland. Marlessa was driving her mother's car, a raggedy old Rabbit. I handed her some quarters.

Marlessa squinched her face up and said, "No, Zephyr, I got enough for the toll."

"But if you're gonna drive," I said, "the least I can do is pay for this."

"But you've already paid for the concert tickets and our refreshments."

"So?"

"So that's enough. Besides, at the rate we're moving, I figure it's costing us about a penny a minute on this bridge to get to San Francisco. And with my luck, there won't be no parking place around our building after we get there."

"You still live at home?" I asked.

"Sure," said Marlessa. "If it wasn't for my mother and her friend baby-sitting for Little David, I don't know what I'd do. Don't you stay at home?"

"Nope. Well, not exactly."

She didn't say anything.

What I like most about Marlessa is she doesn't come right out and poke and pry around in your business. It's the same as when she looks at you. It's never direct or, I guess you could say, without your permission. She always looks like she's peeking at you through a slat in a venetian blind or out the corner of a curtain. I go for that. I suppose what I'm tryna say is that she's kinda shy, but she's also, you know, respectful.

After a while she said, "Little David, after I had him, both my parents said I was gonna have to support him my own self. That's why I dropped outta school for a year and a half. But then Mama got to where she loved Little David so, she said I needed to go back to school. I thought so, too. So that's how I wound up at Last Chance, where I could make my own schedule and really do courses that did *me* some good."

"You thought much yet about what you might wanna get into?"

"Yeah, I wanna either go to Contra Costa Community College or else to the University of San Francisco."

I was amazed. I mean, it sounded like Marlessa kinda had her act together. I still didn't have even the shakiest idea of what I wanted to do. I was starting to try to think about it, though.

"But how'd you get it narrowed down to those two?" I asked.

"They both have good restaurant management training programs," she said, "and that's what I wanna do."

"You mean, like, manage a Church's Chicken or a Burger King or a McDonald's?"

Marlessa laughed.

"No, Zephyr," she said. "You don't need no schooling to run a fast food joint. One day I'd like to open up a place of my own. Something with style, you know, where food from different kindsa cultures could come together."

"Like what?"

"Like, oh, we'd have a little soul food, but I'd be careful to pick which dishes we'd do because a lotta that Southern stuff'll kill you, you know. All that grease and high cholesterol. Then maybe some Guatemalan dishes and maybe some Samoan or Chinese food. You know, it'd be like a little tastebud sampling of San Francisco, all available in one place."

I said, "I can see you've been thinking about this."

"I dream a lot," Marlessa said. "I don't think it's anything wrong with that, do you?"

"Mr. Cleveland wouldn't think so."

Marlessa rolled up the window to shut out the booming rhythm and rap the car in the next lane was blasting us with. I looked over, sure it was gonna be a car fulla brothers and sisters, but it turned out to be a bunch of wild-looking Chinese kids. The girls had Technicolor streaks in their hair, and the dudes all had 'em an earring.

Marlessa laughed again. "On second thought," she turned to me and said, "change what I said to Vietnamese food."

I was tryna picture what such a restaurant would look like; how the tables would be spaced and how the menu would look. I even thought about what Marlessa might have on the walls and how the waiters or the waitresses would dress, and what the kitchen would look like. But it wasn't easy to picture. All I knew about restaurants was from the summer I worked at a McDonald's on Market Street, so all I could imagine was funk and commotion.

"Zephyr," she asked me all of a sudden, "are you still on probation?"

"No," I said, a little surprised that Marlessa would come right out and ask anything that personal. I tried to joke to smooth over the wrinkled-up feeling I had.

"No," I went on. "You won't catch me stealing *nothing* else again."

"What'd they actually nail you for, Zephyr?"

"Oh, I had this scam. It was beautiful."

"Please don't feel you gotta tell me about it."

"Okay," I said, glad to hear Marlessa say that. "But we thought it was pretty slick. We'd go in these big stores, ask the clerk for empty boxes for moving, and wind up looting 'em blind before we came out."

"Were you doing it for money, or what?"

"No, for fun mostly. Sure, we'd sell some of the stuff on the street, but mainly it was what me and my buddies did. I used to . . . Oh, I used to cop a lotta liquor that way."

"Were you one of those teenage alcoholics, too?"

"No," I said, feeling sad again. "No, I was getting it for my mother."

For a long time Marlessa fell back into her silent thing, acting like she was concentrating on making her exit from the bridge.

"You seen much of your mom lately?" Marlessa asked.

"No, just a postcard sometime. She don't call me or my brother much. Nowhere near enough, even though we tell her it's okay for her to call collect. Sometimes it really gets to me."

"Well," said Marlessa, "I see far too much of my mother. So what we got here is a situation that needs balancing. You need to see more of yours and I need to see less of mine."

I didn't think what Marlessa said was funny, but I kinda faked a weak chuckle anyway just to let her know how much I appreciated her interest.

"Uh-uh!" she said. "Now, here's where the problem comes up."

"What problem?"

"The parking problem. If you don't get over here where I live before nine o'-clock at night, ain't no way in the world these people are gonna leave you a parking space. Makes me sick!"

"Wait," I said. "Don't even think like that."

"Then what should I do, then?"

"Just picture that you're gonna get a parking place, just the right space for nobody else's car but yours. Tell you what, let's picture it together and see what happens."

"Aw, Zephyr, here you go again with all that Mr. Cleveland stuff."

"Here, let's just try it and see what happens, okay?"

While Marlessa headed up Hayes toward her place, right there across from Alamo Park, I went to picturing a big fat space right out in fronta her house almost. At first, I was scared to try to be too specific and was ready to settle for any kinda puny parking place at all. Then something inside me said no, that since it was only a mental exercise or game I was trying out, then, hell, I might as well up and go for the moon.

Before I knew it, Marlessa was driving right up to the house. I could feel all those let-down juices settling in my stomach. All that talking and picturing we'd been doing, and we might as well've been in some kinda oil painting. I mean, wasn't nothing moving!

Marlessa's jaws were starting to get tight as she circled the block. It looked to me like people were even parked bumper to bumper in red zones and by fire hydrants and in places where it was illegal for cars to be. "What's going on?" she asked. "This is worse than usual."

"Maybe somebody's having a party," I said.

"I don't hear no music," she said, "do you?"

"Are you still picturing that perfect space?" I asked Marlessa as she rounded the block a third time.

"I'd be lying to you, Zephyr, if I said I was."

"Well, I still am," I said. "And I'm going for the big one."

"What you mean, the big one?"

"I mean right out there in fronta your house."

It was so nice to hear Marlessa laughing again until suddenly it didn't seem to matter whether we ever found another parking space or not.

"I'm gonna drive over a coupla blocks," she said.

"No, no! Marlessa, let's just give it one more try. Go around the block again."

It caused her to do a lotta sighing, but Marlessa finally chugged around the block and eased up toward her apartment house again.

"See," she said, "this is getting old pretty fast, Zephyr."

And just when she said that, a big old van parked right in fronta her place started signaling to pull out from the curb. And that's not all. At the same time, people had suddenly popped out onto the street from outta nowhere and standing at their car doors with the keys in their hands.

"I don't believe this!" Marlessa said. "This isn't something you and some of your slick buddies set up, is it?"

The trouble was, I didn't believe it either. I didn't know what to say. All I did was grunt and shake my head the whole time Marlessa was parking the car.

Then we both got to giggling.

"Zephyr," she said, "that was something. We're gonna have to tell Mr. Cleveland about this. He likes all this strange synchronicity stuff."

"Yeah, but . . . I was so busy concentrating on this parking space . . . we forgot something."

"What?"

"How do *I* get home?"

Marlessa leaned across the seat and gave me a friendly little lipstick smack on the jaw.

"Well," she said, "I guess now we'd better get busy and start picturing some transportation for you, hunh?"

"What!"

"I'm only playing with you, Zephyr," she said. "Would you like to come up and meet Little David?"

"But, uh, it's kinda late. Won't your folks mind?"

"Folk."

"Hunh?"

"My father doesn't live with us anymore. And Mama rode up to Sacramento with my cousin to visit my grandmama."

"Your mother's gone?"

"Yeah, but that doesn't mean you can come up there and show out on me."

"Then who's minding your baby?"

"Zephyr," she said, "you ever hear tella baby-sitters? I'll drop you off when I drive the baby-sitter home."

And that's exactly what Marlessa did. She let me peep in at her little boy. He was a cute little joker, too. Looked mostly like Marlessa, but he musta favored his daddy some. I still can't get over her having a kid and still a kid herself.

But when we got upstairs and Mrs. Jackson pointed to the crib where the baby was sleeping, Marlessa went over, leaned down and kissed Little David. She kissed him in a way that was real different but sorta the same way she'd kissed on me back there in the car. Watching her do this, something clicked, and for a second, I flashed on how it used to be, a long time ago, when Dad and Moms were still together and they'd tuck me in bed for the night. That cozy feeling. You know. With a nice sleepiness pulled up around it all tight and snug like fresh-washed sheets and warm covers.

Marlessa drove Mrs. Jackson home, and I realized she only lived a few blocks from me. I sat in the back, holding the baby. He was all cute and blanketed down and everything, and it was an okay thing to do. But it still made me feel funny. I sure wasn't ready to be a father yet.

When Marlessa dropped me off, I said, "Let's do this again sometime."

"You tell me when."

"Is next Saturday too soon?"

"I'll tell you at school."

I said, "We have a telephone, you know."

She said, "Maybe the best thing would be to send you a telepathic message."

"We can try that, too," I said.

I honestly can't remember when the third time was. I mean, after that, I kinda lost count. Maybe a better way to put it would be to say I quit keeping track of my thoughts turning out to be for real. And I think that might be because my whole way of thinking is beginning to get changed around. Little by little, this idea about thoughts being magic isn't such a big, humongous thing anymore; it's just the way things are.

More and more I'm looking hard at what goes on inside my mind and how I feel about it. I'm starting to pick and choose my thoughts, the same as you'd pick a cassette to pop in the Walkman. I like being in charge of the kinda thoughts I play in my mind.

If Edrick and his sometime-girlfriend Rosie have a fight, and he starts sending out all those bummed-out feelings, well, that's Edrick. I mean, I can be sympathetic, but now I know I don't have to buy into his trip. Or if down at the bookstore I'm unpacking some newspaper like the *Enquirer* or the *Globe*, and the front-page story is about how everybody on earth, by the year 2055, is gonna to be dying from AIDS, I know I got a least two choices. I can either freeze on a headline such as that and stay hung up on it, or else I can stack that information up against other things we're learning about epidemics and disease.

Fifteen, twenty times a day somebody will be tryna sell me some crack, and I'll stop and think about what smoking it is gonna do to my mind, to this thought player of mine. I already know what weed and vodka used to do to Moms, and I see what dope is doing to other people I know, so I don't have to think too hard. Every few weeks, look like, somebody at Last Chance or one of my running buddies from the old neighborhood, over in Western Addition, would burn theirself out or catch some disease or just up and die all of a sudden.

I still felt like living for a long time, and I wish I could say there was a happy ending to this story, but I'm still living it out.

All I can report for sure right now—since mosta this is still so new to me—is that if the city keeps cutting back Last Chance's budget, pretty soon it won't exist no more. And this joint is too good a thing to lose. Mr. Cleveland keeps me up on all such as that.

"So what can we do about it?" I asked him.

"All you can do, Zephyr, is pass on anything good you think you might've picked up here. You know that rhyme of mine—'Hold on to what's alive and forget the other jive.'"

The other day when I got home, the Ivory Coast was all boarded up. Not just the window; the whole place! There was a sign pasted on that very window the brick'd sailed through. The Board of Health was shutting 'em down. Probably for being too nasty, I guess.

As I stood out there on Geary in the rain and read it, every word on the notice was like an M&M melting on your tongue, or maybe even like sitting in the movies and chewing on a Jujyfruit. I swear, I didn't have a thing to do with that. Still, I couldn't wait till Edrick got home to see it.

It's no accident, though, that Marlessa's starting to test out some of these mind games, or whatever you wanna call 'em. Now, since so much interesting stuff has been happening to me, Edrick and his girlfriend Rosie are sort of testing it out. Last week Edrick told me Safeway was finally gonna move him out of that grave-yard slot, where he's mainly been stocking shelves all night, and put him on the day shift as an apprentice checker.

When I asked Edrick how he felt about this, he said: "Well, I have been wanting a change for a long time. But I'm not sure I can make the switch all that easy. It's so peaceful there at night."

"Maybe," I said, just to get his goat, "this is the result of something Rosie's been concentrating on. She never was crazy about the hours you worked."

"Hmmm," said Edrick. "I don't know about all this brainwashing stuff."

"Let's just keep on sending Moms them good thoughts," I told him.

For the last couple of weeks, every night before I fall asleep, I been picturing Moms hard, imagining her getting well down there in Texas. I started doing this after I noticed how often somebody would either call me when I thought about 'em deep, or else I'd run into 'em. Some kinda way they'd show up. Me and Marlessa, we've been getting outrageous with it.

Guess what?

Moms called long distance from Houston this morning just when I was rushing out of the house to catch the bus to school.

"Hey, Moms," I said, all outta breath from dashing back up the steps, praying I could pick it up before that last ring.

"Hi, Zee," she said, all staticky. It wasn't the best connection in the world.

"What's going on? Is anything wrong?"

"No, are you and Edrick all right?"

"We're doing just fine. You get that last money order we sent?"

"Yeah, Zee, yeah, I got it. You're the best two boys a mother could wish for."

When she said that, I froze up a little. Moms never talked that way much, not that I can remember.

"Moms, you sound different."

"Different? How?"

"You sound better."

Even through all that long distance static and space, I could hear the little sniffling and funny breathing she was doing at the other end. So I wasn't a bit surprised when she came back on in this choked-up voice.

"Zee," she said.

"Yes, Moms."

"I'm sorry it's had to be like this. But I'll make it up to you two . . . somehow. I haven't had nothing to drink in so long, I've forgotten what it tastes like."

I didn't know what to say to this. Moms had told me and Edrick this so many times before, I wasn't sure how to react. But you know what? This time I didn't care.

"I'm into some new stuff, Moms."

"Like what?"

"Oh, just thinking more than I use to."

"Well, you never were what I'd call slow; just hard-headed like your father. Going by your letters, it sounds like you kinda like that school you're in. This teacher of yours, this Mr. Cleveland sounds like he's on the ball."

"It's the best thing ever happened to me, Moms. I'm writing a story about it."

"Yeah?"

"Well, never mind. When you coming home?"

"Zee?" she said, like all of a sudden the connection'd gotten so bad she couldn't hear me. "Zee? Baby, you still there?"

"Yeah, Moms, I'm right here."

"Oh, there you are. I can hear you now. Zee, there's something I have to tell you."

"What is it, Moms?"

"I love you."

"I love you, too, Moms. You coming home soon?"

She didn't say nothing for a long time. I stood there, looking down at the street where the #34 bus was just then creaking up.

"Pretty soon," she said finally. "I figured maybe right after school lets out might be the best time to come back up there and get resettled."

"Oh, that's good news."

"You and Edrick are gonna have to help me find a place to stay, though."

"Don't worry about that. You can stay here with us for a while if you have to. It'll be tight, but—"

"And Zee . . ."

"Yes, Moms."

"I even stopped smoking grass, too. But I haven't been able to cut out cigarettes yet. I'm gonna try, though."

"Don't worry about that, Moms. One thing at a time."

"I finally joined this outfit that helps drunks like me."

"Are you gonna let 'em help you, for a change?"

"Yes . . . yes, I am."

It took all the willpower I had to keep from blurting out all the stuff about thinking and thoughts Mr. Cleveland has been dropping on us. But something tells me Moms wasn't jiving this time. There was so much life in her voice, and I swear, this time I can almost feel deep down in my own gut how she wasn't as scared as she used to be. I knew there was a lotta thinking and concentrating to be done, but I was glad just the same.

"Moms," I cleared my throat and said, "me and Edrick can't wait."

THE LAST DREAM

Edgardo Vega Yunqué

The place, as she called it, was a spacious, high-ceilinged Upper West Side apartment on Riverside Drive. They were lucky back then to find one so large. Eventually they had run out of children before they ran out of rooms for them, she often thought now. She had always marveled at the view of the park with the river below and the Jersey palisades beyond it, the sun going down behind them each day as if it was her very own pleasure; each season bringing something new; watching the snow drift slowly down from the darkness above or seeing the sky streaked yellow with lightning, the thunder exploding so close and the rain swirling madly so that it made her think of castle and vampire movies, and she laughed and told the children stories by candlelight.

Their perch, high above the sounds and smells of the city, had given her a sense of achieved grandness. It was their home, a canyon dwelling, free like an eagle's aerie from which she had seen the children fly, going farther out each year, learning and being frightened but returning to be fed and to cry and to complain and laugh through countless birthdays, each celebrated with the middle-class decorum of written invitations, favors for the invited, and a propriety which established a tradition, until soon now they'd be gone and the two of them would be left alone to do she knew not what.

"Dan, would you like more coffee?" she asked.

"Yes, please," he said, looking up from the sports section. The rest of the Sunday *Times* was strewn about at his feet. Their Sunday breakfast ritual, late and heavy, had been over an hour ago, and as soon as he finished the paper, predictably, he'd suggest a walk in the park.

She returned with the coffee and placed it on a small table next to him. Without looking up he thanked her.

"Dan, I had a dream last night," she said, retrieving the books section.

"What kind of dream?" he asked, absently.

"I'll tell you after you're finished with the paper," she said.

"I'll only be another minute," he said.

Two years ago the exchange would've turned into a long, involved argument. Why had she brought it up if she was willing to wait until he was finished? And it would go on from there until he exhausted her and she went off to lick her wounds and question her intelligence, even though her intellectual capacity had been validated in degrees and in published academic papers of relative importance. Then something had happened and suddenly there were no more arguments.

The change had left her lonely and wanting, feeling as if she'd eventually be forced to look elsewhere again and would hate herself because she couldn't relax completely with anyone but him. And then she had begun to understand what had happened, so that the last two years had brought her a freedom she'd never known. But with the freedom came new responsibilities and the old dread that one day things would be over between them. The change had come about gradually, balancing the relationship without the carefully arranged agreements from which they had suffered throughout their marriage. She began sensing the honesty around that time.

But it wasn't honesty in the old way, with every sexual fantasy or past infidelity dissected and every ounce of pleasure rendered empty of meaning so that the people, the rivals, their lean bodies and quick intelligence had withered and died and not even their ghosts dared trespass anymore. And it wasn't honesty in the simulated life-death adolescence of long-faded encounter groups which had caused her more pain than she thought possible to bear and forced him to adopt greater control over his emotions than he needed. It was a different type of honesty, akin, she suspected, to a code of honor, some chivalrous set of rules which had somehow filtered through the books or movies to find them while they were unguarded.

There was no longer suspicion between them, the one knowing that if the other lied he or she would have to live with the lie. They had both learned they could exist without guilt. And slowly, tentatively, mutually, they had given the new life form. This rebirth of their marriage had been accomplished less by analysis than by deeds until the deeds were like posted signs that said "Ladies" or "Exit" or "Dairy." Except that their signs said things like "Inveterate Romantic," "Amateur Painter," "College Graduate with Degree in Fine Arts," "Member of New York State Bar Association." And people began calling again to visit, and there were dinner parties and laughter once more.

"It's like the French," he'd said, one similar weekend morning after a small party last year. They had been lounging, trying to make up their minds how to start putting the house back in order. She'd asked, how like the French, and he'd said, abstracted from the conversation as if he were thinking out loud, "You know. Whatever a person does is his own affair, but not really, because one wouldn't take a chance lying. It wouldn't mean anything to the other. A confession would be bad manners."

"You don't sound French," she'd said. "You sound British. Cricket and all that," and had said the latter with what sounded to her like an English accent.

"Maybe that's what it's all about," he'd said. "Maybe we've finally caught up. It's all a matter of language."

"Caught up? Oh, Dan, if your clients heard you they'd strip you of your liberal standing. Your Kunstler rating would dip considerably." She'd ignored the sign that said, "Careful—Socially Conscious Lawyer with Love of American Literature." She wanted to wound him but knew before she'd finished that he wouldn't respond and instead would be saying something like, "Advantage, Mr. Cartagena."

A thread of anger had passed quickly through her. She was momentarily back in Dr. Lehrman's richly carpeted, soundproof living room, screaming vile things at Dan, trying to free herself of constraints and inhibitions, but watching herself so that she didn't use those forbidden words—words like *cabrón, maricón, hijo de la gran puta, mamalón, mierda*, which would give her away; she almost gave in one time when he called her a common whore, wishing to shame him by revealing that even though he had grown up in relative luxury and his own father had been a lawyer, she had grown up in the shadow of La Marqueta, and both of them had been raised speaking "Puertorican," as most of their friends said; her insides screaming with the rage of wanting to announce that she was one of those dreaded Puerto Ricans; cringing whenever the papers or television made the distinction between Blacks, Whites, and Puerto Ricans; wanting to state that there were white Puerto Ricans and instead keeping to safe ground and always announcing that they were Spanish, the children absolutely convinced of this fact.

She was immediately back to that time, the color coming on quickly; the other members of the group, watching, their faces contorted. And then the picture faded once again into the late winter weekend morning with the Hudson River wearing gray, dying, and she not the least bit concerned about ecology, that too having passed from their lives, along with health foods and cooperatives, baby-sitting pools, encounters, politics, the women's movement, the Thalia Theater art films, jazz, and even the Vietnam War—their very own war, like World War II had been their parents' war. All of it had faded and they still "endured," so that the word no longer belonged to Faulkner but had become their own. She was sure Dan would've liked that.

"I don't think what influences people is the spoken language," she'd said finally. "Spoken language is too fleeting to make a lasting impression. What really influences people is in the literature. The good stuff with real people struggling with themselves."

"Mailer and his cynicism?" he'd asked, amused by her sudden seriousness.

"Yes, even Mailer."

And she'd watched him pull back, ashamed because in agreeing to include Mailer she had truly conceded graciously after years of bitterness about her brief and innocent romantic episode with Marion Danzig; poor Marion who aspired to being a writer and who had stated at a small dinner party that she had known Mailer and that, besides being an egomaniac, he would go down in history as a minor twentieth-century writer. Big, bad Dan Cartagena toying with Marion's emotions, intimidating her with his superior knowledge of literature until he had eventually chased Marion away. She, Frances Elizabeth Cartagena, née Cabrera, who did not fit the role of the dumb spic any more than he did, understood more than he'd hoped, and he had no right to ridicule her or demean himself by doing so.

"I'm sorry," he'd said. "I shouldn't have brought all that up."

"It's okay," she'd answered. "It's all pretty funny, anyway. The Dallas Orgasmic Repository."

"The what?" he said, hurt, as if he'd been left out of a private joke.

She'd repeated the phrase and laughed, tossing back her long black hair away from her face.

"That's where it all went. All the wasted love. Not lost out there in the vastness of the universe but stored in that book place and released in anger."

She'd tried sounding poetic and it made her laugh harder. She had finally rolled off the couch onto the carpeted floor and under the grand piano. He'd watched her curves fall slowly, her small, full body curling up fetally, her faded jeans and her New York University sweatshirt, the motto "Perstare et Praestare" all but gone from the seal; her body bare underneath; white; too white and vulnerable from winter and the cerebral existence of life on the Upper West Side.

He counted again and, like yesterday, in two years he would be fifty and she forty-six. Michael was nearly twenty-two and ready to enter law school; extremely serious, and as far as he knew hadn't touched drugs. Debby was eighteen and ready to enter college. She had the same luminescent skin, and from the rear he couldn't tell her and her mother apart, both bodies diminutive and incredibly beautifully shaped; discussing sexual issues with her friends, boys as well as girls, with ease; all of them worried sick about AIDS and relationships and he wondering what had happened to romance and afraid to ask.

"Fran, get up, for God's sake," he'd said.

She'd looked up from beneath the piano and her eyes mischievous, the gray green flashing in the winter sunlight, making her look younger than her years.

"I'm sorry," she'd said and got up. "Do you want something to eat? We can clean up later."

He'd looked at her and then she touched his face; the hand feeling unusually tender on his skin. He'd stood up and, placing a hand on her arm, steered her out of the living room, not with force but as a parody of someone being arrested or removed. Still smiling, she'd walked ahead of him, knowing what awaited her, down the hall in their bedroom; dark and warm, used to their arguments, a tired bedroom; unmade bed and reread books and clothes dangling like resting marionettes, not discarded in anger anymore but left there out of mutual respect because to pick up after the other was to insult.

"What are you doing?" she'd asked once they were inside the room and he'd closed the door, not feeling the excitement well up but knowing once they began she'd be totally for herself like he'd been these many years.

He didn't answer her but began undressing and she did the same. She waited for him, feeling his once lithe body search for her until he was there and she could join him, chase him, and, catching up to him, burst from consciousness; not romantically but like the son-of-a-bitch No. 2 Express roaring between Ninety-sixth and Seventy-second Streets when it races as if chased by demons so that it bounces and for a second seems to be airborne, floating free of the constraints of gravity, the rails a mere insinuation, flying without derailing as if the motorman, who was the conductor, loved and trusted the steel beneath him, talking Black to it: "Here we go, baby, one more time. God, yes." And when the train moved that way, the people bounced, their feet going up off the floor in that split second and down again, and it was enough New York thrills for one day because no matter how crazy they were and how starved for attention or tired of their anonymity, nobody wanted to be an "Eyewitness News" casualty. And, oh, yes, Dan, but without saying the words, sucking on her own fingers when she couldn't reach his mouth, bursting all at once so that the second up off the tracks went on and on and left her outside of herself with no regrets, and if it wasn't love, then all right.

It had happened again two months later and a few more times in between, without the intensity and slowly, tenderly, for old times' sake, and then they both knew about the honesty and it was like a game. The rules were clear and were never discussed and it was boring to cheat, to break the rules overtly without intelligence, so that the challenge was gone. She knew now what it was about and no longer had to ask him to explain. It was like he'd said it was with sports and games and everything else. The rules created a framework, a set of parameters, and nothing really happened outside those boundaries, except that which went unseen or unproven, which everyone did and it wasn't really cheating.

And then one day in spring, of all times, with Riverside Park greening, cast anew with Columbia students and Haitian and Central American soccer players, and Dominicans and Cubans still resentful if thought to be Puerto Ricans, the park filled with new mothers and their English perambulators and English sheepdogs tied to them—God knew why they affected the damn things—he'd grown tired. Not old, she'd thought, but simply tired of the fight. She watched him closely, knowing in advance he was gone, the fire dampened, the spirit broken, and she was once again the trophy, mounted, dusted, and seldom admired. And she needed him more now than in the past twenty-five years. She never thought of divorce anymore. Not because she couldn't find someone else, but because she'd fought and won her own battle with herself and now that she understood, he didn't want to play.

She stepped away from her reverie, stood up, and placed the books section atop the piano. She watched him as he stood up and crossed the room to fill his pipe.

"Dan?"

"Yes, Fran," he said, without turning around.

"I had a dream last night," she said, making it sound like she was bringing it up for the first time. "Do you want to hear about it?"

"Yes, of course," he said. He held a lighter to the pipe and blew a large cloud of glittering smoke which drifted slowly through the sunlight. He returned to his soft, worn leather chair. It was his father's law office chair and he had insisted on keeping it after the old man's death. "Tell me about it."

"Well, we were on an airplane," she said, kneeling up on the couch across from him. "An old airplane. There was a young blond girl on it. You know, with her hair curly and soft and a beautiful body and she was wearing a jumpsuit and goggles. Well, she went out on the wing of the plane and did stunts and waved to you and you waved back and clapped. And then when we landed she came up and draped herself all over you and told you how glad she was to see you again. I was furious, Dan. I walked up to her and asked her how come she didn't say hello to me. And sort of offhand, bitchy like, she said, 'Oh, hi,' and hugged you and you kissed her. Not on the cheek but with your mouths open, and then the two of you walked off and left me standing there. When I woke up I was in a jealous rage."

By the time she had finished speaking he was laughing out loud. He set his pipe down and leaped to his feet, suddenly athletic and full of pep.

"That's quite a dream," he said.

"Please don't laugh, Dan," she said. "It was very real."

She described the girl to the last detail. "She must've been twenty-three or four and she had those incredibly pert breasts that don't need support, her body taut but full."

"And you were jealous?"

"Furious."

He looked at her and the fire had returned to his eyes, she thought. He took her hand and led her to the bedroom. But there was no express roaring beneath Broadway, no first time at his parents' home in Rockaway Beach when his family had left the city and he was studying for his senior exams. Back then she had been in love with life and intelligence and felt lucky to have found someone like him, whose Puertoricanness was not worn as a battlefield ribbon; someone who was going to be a lawyer.

There was a honeymoon in Europe and incredible summer nights on the Adriatic coast when they would make love over and over. They could not stop talking to each other about their lives and their dreams, and the memories still remained vividly with her after all those years; traveling through the canals of Amsterdam and letting her mind float back as she imagined Vermeer ambling through the city in the 1700s; forgetting that their parents had come from a small, poverty-stricken Caribbean island full of self-important people; walking the cobblestoned streets of Nürnberg, stopping off to visit Albrecht Dürer's house, which dated back to the sixteenth century and had survived the Allied bombing, and then stopping off at a biergarten to take long, cold draughts of wheat beer that made her feel as if she were washing away the squalor of her childhood; making their way westward on a train through the Swiss Alps to France and then across the Pyrenees to Cataluña, spending the night in Barcelona and then going on to Madrid and the beauty of El Prado museum; the grand architecture of the capital putting her in touch with her true roots.

What was wrong with their saying they were Spanish; why was being Puerto Rican such a big deal? Why did they feel such pride? Why? Why couldn't they leave it alone? She was American. Dan was American. Their children were American. They were Spanish-American. There was no such thing as a Puerto Rican American. It was too long. It didn't make sense. Puerto Ricans couldn't be Something-Americans.

When it was over and he lay beside her, his breathing labored, she cried softly to herself and for herself and cursed the blond girl with the curly hair, wishing that she had truly dreamed her.

ACKNOWLEDGMENTS

We wish to first of all express our thanks to all the contributors to this anthology, and those agents, publishers, and executors of literary estates who represent some of the most famous authors in the United States, any one of whom could have depleted our entire permission budget, but accepted the same honorarium as little-known authors of excellent talent, as well as members of a younger generation of rising writers, in order that we could assemble this representative sample of American literature.

Our gratitude is due to the writers and agents who advised us of where to find great short fiction in various areas of the country and in particular communities in which they are expert, and also those who provided us with stories, reference materials and the most-essential contact information, including Lesley Himes for her kind offer of an unpublished work by Chester Himes, and Chester Himes's agent, Roslyn Targ, for making the negotiation complete; and Rudolfo Anaya, Faith Childs, Lucha Corpi, Joy Harjo, Persis M. Karim, Russell Leong, Nancy Mercado, Richard Peek, Craig Tenney, Lori and John Williams, Gerald Vizenor, Al Young, and especially our consultants Hillel Heinstein and Ishmael Hope.

We also wish to acknowledge the help of all the editors who were part of the long evolution of how this book came to be, starting with Lisa Moore, who in the early 1990s asked for this anthology when she was at HarperCollins College; Will Balliett, who got it moving again in 2006, at Thunder's Mouth Press, an imprint of Avalon, and who carried it over to Da Capo Press at Perseus Books when Avalon was folded into Perseus; and which continued to be shepherded by Will Balliett's former assistant Shaun Dillon and editor-at-large Bill Strachan, who took over when Will moved to another press; and finally, Ben Schafer and his assistant, Adelaide Docx, who saw the manuscript through to this publication.

We greatly appreciated the excellent service of Inderpal Singh and his assistants Sue Jin Park and Namrata Khadka at FastImaging in Berkeley, for making it possible to assemble the final manuscript in digital format—a process we could have never accomplished without their careful help.

And lastly, we especially thank Tennessee Reed, who has served as assistant to both of us throughout this anthology's history.

—Ishmael Reed and Carla Blank

CONTRIBUTORS

WAJAHAT ALI (b. 1980) is a Muslim American of Pakistani descent who was born and raised in Fremont, California, near the Silicon Valley area. He has been writing, producing and directing plays, films, and comedy sketches since he was a child, enlisting friends to be actors and crew. A short story writing assignment from Ishmael Reed's UC Berkeley creative writing class, with his encouragement, was transformed into a two-act family kitchen drama, *The Domestic Crusaders*. From 2004–2005, the play was performed by a cast drawn from the San Francisco Bay area's South Asian community, and, directed by Carla Blank, was presented in various Bay area venues in staged readings and in two showcase productions mounted at the Thrust Theatre of Berkeley Repertory Theatre and the San Jose State University Theater, receiving international attention. Now a lawyer, while completing law school at UC Davis (2007), he enlisted his fellow law students and professors to be actors in staged readings of his second play, *The Unwholly Warriors*, which was written to fulfill a course requirement. Ali is currently writing a two-part prequel/sequel of *The Domestic Crusaders*, short fiction, and posting his essays and interviews on online news sites including counterpunch.com and altmuslim.org.

JIMMY SANTIAGO BACA (b. 1952) was born in Santa Fe, New Mexico, of In-dio-Mexican descent. At first raised by his grandmother and later sent to an or-phanage, he became a runaway at age 13. After Baca was sentenced to five years in a maximum security prison on charges of drug possession, he began to turn his life around: he learned to read and write and discovered he had a passion for writing poetry. In 1979, he was released from prison, earned his GED, and had his poetry published in *Mother Jones* magazine and collected in his own New Directions pub-lication, *Immigrants in Our Own Land* (1979, 1991). Twelve more Baca poetry collections have followed since, the most recent of which is *Spring Poems Along the Rio Grande* (2007). Other publications include Baca's short story collection, *The Importance of a Piece of Paper* (2004); a collections of stories and essays, *Working in the Dark: Reflections of a Poet of the Barrio* (1992); a film script, *Bound by Honor* (for Disney Productions, 1992; released by Hollywood Pictures, 1993); and a play, *Los tres hijos de Julia* (1991). Among Baca's honors are a 1988 Pushcart Prize; a 1989 American Book Award for his semi-autobiographical novel in verse, *Martin and Meditations on the South Valley*; a 1990 International Hispanic Heritage Award; first place winner of the 1996 and 1997 World Champion Poetry Bout at

Taos; and the 2001 International Award for his memoir, *A Place to Stand*. In 2005, Baca created Cedar Tree Inc., a nonprofit foundation, to give people of all walks of life the opportunity to become educated and improve their lives. Providing free instruction, books, writing materials and scholarships, the foundation conducts writing workshops in prisons and community centers, besides offering an Internship program with live-in quarters located in Albuquerque, New Mexico. He lives with his family outside Albuquerque.

RUSSELL BANKS (b. 1940) was raised in New Hampshire and eastern Massachusetts. The eldest of four children in a working-class family, he was the first in his family to attend college. Banks has won O. Henry and Best American Short Story Awards, and his short story collections include *Searching for Survivors, The New World, Trailerpark* (1981), *Success Stories* (1986), and *The Angel on the Roof* (2000). His novels, which have been translated and published in Europe and Asia, include *The Book of Jamaica* (1980); *Continental Drift* (1985); *Rule of the Bone* (1996); *Cloudsplitter* (1998); *The Darling* (2004); and *The Reserve* (2008). Two other novels were made into feature-length films: *Affliction* (1990), directed by Paul Schrader; and *The Sweet Hereafter* (1992), Grand Jury Prize winner at the 1998 Cannes Film Festival, directed by Atom Egoyan, in which he appears with one of his four daughters, Caerthan Banks. Among his many other honors, Banks has received Guggenheim and NEA Fellowships, the John Dos Passos Prize, and the Literature Award from the American Academy of Arts and Letters, and he is a member of both the American Academy of Arts and Sciences and the American Academy of Arts and Letters. He has also served as president of the International Parliament of Writers and is founding president of Cities of Refuge North America, an organization of writers offering North American safe havens to writers worldwide who are being persecuted or silenced in their native countries, so they can continue to write without fear of reprisal. Banks lives in upstate New York and is the New York State Author.

MITCH BERMAN (b. 1956) was raised in California and Oregon. A graduate of the University of California at Berkeley and the writing program at Columbia University, he has taught creative writing at the University of Texas, the University of Colorado, and San Jose State University, where he also directed the Center for Literary Arts. Mitch Berman's short fiction has been nominated for five Pushcart Prizes, receiving special mention from the Pushcarts and a distinguished story of the year from *Best American Short Stories*. His writing has appeared in the periodicals *The New Yorker, Esquire, Playboy, The Nation, The Village Voice, TriQuarterly, Antioch Review, Gettysburg Review, Chicago Review, Boulevard, Witness, Conjunctions, Descant, Konch,* and *Agni*. His novel, *Time Capsule* (1987), was nominated by Putnam for the PEN/Hemingway Award and the Pulitzer Prize. He lives in New York City with his wife, Susanne Lee, and their son Kofi, who are also writers.

CECIL BROWN (b. 1943) was born in Bolton, North Carolina, to tobacco sharecropping parents. Resolved to leave the agrarian world of his ancestors, he received degrees in literature at Columbia University and the University of Chicago, and a

Ph.D. in folklore from the University of California, Berkeley. Brown's novels include *The Life and Loves of Mr. Jiveass Nigger* (1969), *Days without Weather* (1983), which won a 1984 American Book Award, and *I, Stagolee* (2007), based on the mythic ballad, as is his nonfiction book, *Stagolee Shot Billy* (2003), which provides the historical and social underpinnings of the myth. His other nonfiction books are *Dude, Where Is My Black Studies Department?* (2007), which discusses how Black Studies departments in universities have changed since their beginnings in the 1960s and 70s; and his autobiography, *Coming Up Down Home* (1993). Brown was a scriptwriter for the film *Which Way Is Up?* and has also written and directed his own films, most recently *Two-Fer.* He makes his home in the San Francisco Bay Area.

NASH CANDELARIA (b. 1928) was born in Los Angeles, into a family who traces their roots back about 13 generations in New Mexican history. They were among the first settlers of New Mexico, the refugees of the 1680 Pueblo Revolt, and the founders of the city of Albuquerque in 1706. One ancestor, Juan Candelaria, dictated a history of the New Mexico Territory in 1776. Nash Candelaria grew up in a Catholic-Anglo section of Los Angeles and after graduating from UCLA (1948, B.S. in Chemistry) began working for a pharmaceutical company in Glendale, California, while writing on the side. He wrote his first novel while serving in the U.S. Air Force during the Korean War. Upon his return to civilian life, he became a science writer-editor with a company that produced nuclear reactors and later worked in science advertising and sales promotions. Nash Candelaria's creative writing includes two short story collections, *The Day the Cisco Kid Shot John Wayne* (1982) and *Uncivil Rights and Other Short Stories* (1998); his four historical novels of the Rafa family cycle are *Memories of Alhambra* (1977), followed by *Not by the Sword* (1982), winner of a 1983 American Book Award, *Inheritance of Strangers* (1985), and *Leonor Park* (1997). He and his wife currently live in Santa Fe, New Mexico.

WANDA COLEMAN (b. 1946) was born in Watts and raised in South Central, both communities of Los Angeles. She has worked as a medical secretary, magazine editor, journalist, scriptwriter, and occasionally as a waitress or bartender to support herself as a writer. She has presented national and international readings of her works, and her electrifying performance style has earned her the title, "L.A. Blueswoman." *Art in the Court of the Blue Fag,* her first collection of poetry, appeared in 1977 from Black Sparrow Press (now Black Sparrow Books), beginning a thirty-year association with the press, which has produced eighteen books of her poetry and prose. Her most recent titles are a nonfiction prose work, *The Riot Inside Me: More Trials and Tremors* (2006), and a collection of thirteen short stories, *Jazz and Twelve O'Clock Tales* (2008). Her many literary honors include fellowships from the National Endowment for the Arts, the Guggenheim Foundation, and the California Arts Council. In 1999, her poetry collection *Bathwater Wine* received a Lenore Marshall Poetry Prize from the Academy of American Poets, *The Nation,* and the New Hope Foundation. Her poetry collection *Mercurochrome* (2001) was a bronze-medal finalist for the 2001 National Book Awards in Poetry and a 2002 finalist for the Paterson Poetry Prize. In 2003, she became the first literary artist to receive a C.O.L.A. Fellowship from the Los Angeles Department of Cultural Affairs. She currently resides in Southern California with her husband, Austin Straus, and family.

CONYUS lives in San Francisco next to the Pacific Ocean where he watches the Humpback Whales migrate down and up the California coast at sunset. His work has been published in various anthologies over the last four decades including: *The American Poetry Anthology*; *Califia, the California Poetry*; and *The Garden Thrives, Twentieth-Century African-American Poetry*. He is the recipient of a National Endowment for the Arts Creative Writing Fellowship.

ROBERT COOVER (b. 1932) was born in Charles City, Iowa, and received his B.A. in Slavic Studies in 1953 from Indiana University and his M.A. from the University of Chicago in General Studies in the Humanities in 1965, after service in the U.S. Navy from 1953 to 1957. His first novel, *Origin of the Brunists*, won the 1966 William Faulkner Award. His other novels include: *A Public Burning* (1977), which received a nomination for a National Book Award; *Spanking the Maid* (1982); *Gerald's Party* (1986); *Pinocchio in Venice* (1991); *John's Wife* (1991); *Briar Rose* (1997); *Ghost Town* (1998); *The Grand Hotels (of Joseph Cornel)* (2002); *The Adventures of Lucky Pierre* (2002); and *Stepmother* (2004). His poetry, plays, translations, and short fiction have been widely anthologized, and some of his short fiction appears in his collections *Pricksongs & Descants* (1969), *In Bed One Night and Other Brief Encounters* (1983), *Aesop's Forest and The Plot of the Mice* (1986 [with Brian Swann]), *Baseball and the Game of Life: Stories for the Thinking Fan* (1990), and *A Child Again* (2005). Throughout his writing career, Coover has presented his work and ideas in international forums and has taught at various colleges and universities, including Brown University, where he has been a member of the English Department since 1980, presently teaching courses in electronic writing and mixed media as well as standard writing workshops. Coover's many honors include two Guggenheim Fellowships, a National Endowment for the Arts Fellowship (1985), a DAAD Fellowship in Berlin (1990), three Obie Awards for an American Place Theater production of his play, "The Kid" (1972–1973), election to the American Academy of Arts and Letters in 1976, and a 1987 REA award for his lifetime contribution to the short story.

LUCHA CORPI (b. 1945) was born in the small town of Jáltipan in the state of Veracruz, Mexico, and came to Berkeley, California, as a young wife in 1964. Her son Arturo was born in Berkeley in 1967. Corpi graduated from UC Berkeley (B.A. Comparative Literature), where she served as a student member of the newly established Chicano Studies' Executive Committee on campus; as a volunteer dental assistant at the Clínica de La Raza, a Fruitvale Health Initiative established by UC students and faculty; and as a parent member of the Comité Popular de La Raza, a grass roots organization credited for establishing the first bilingual preschool and elementary school programs in the Oakland Public Schools. She was also a founding member of Aztlán Cultural, an arts service organization, and of Centro Chicano de

Escritores (Chicano Center for Writers). Both organizations merged and she served as the first president of the new center. She earned her master's degree in World and Comparative Literature from San Francisco State. Primarily known as a poet who writes in Spanish translated into English, she is also author of five novels written in English, four of which are mysteries featuring Brown Angel Investigations and Gloria Damasco, the first Chicana detective in American literature. Her novels include *Delia's Song* (1984), *Eulogy for a Brown Angel* (1992, 2002), which won the PEN Oakland Josephine Miles Award and the Multicultural Publisher's Exchange award for best fiction in 1992, *Cactus Blood* (1995), *Black Widow's Wardrobe* (1999) and *Crimson Moon* (2004). Her poetry is collected in *Variaciones sobre una tempestad/Variations on a Storm* (1990) and *Palabras de mediodia/Noon Words* (2001), with English translations by Catherine Rodríguez Nieto. Recently recovered from having lost her home and all of her writing in a fire, she lives in Oakland, California, where she was a tenured teacher in the Oakland Public Schools Neighborhood Centers Program for thirty years.

STANLEY CROUCH (b. 1945) was born and raised in Los Angeles, where, encouraged by his mother, he was writing by the age of eight. In the mid-1960s, he participated in Studio Watts drama workshops led by Jayne Cortez, as an actor and playwright, and taught drama, the history of jazz, and literature at Claremont College from 1968 to 1975. After moving to NYC in 1975, Crouch worked as a staff writer for *The Village Voice* from 1979 to 1988. His writing also began to appear in mainstream magazines such as *The New Yorker*, *Esquire*, and *New Republic*, where he is a contributing editor, and *New York Daily News*, where he is a columnist. He published a novel, *Don't the Moon Look Lonesome* (2000). His nonfiction books include the collected essays *Notes of a Hanging Judge* (1990), *The All-American Skin Game; or, The Decoy of Race: The Long and Short of It, 1990–1994* (1995), *Always in Pursuit: Fresh American Perspectives, 1995–1997* (1998), *Reconsidering the Souls of Black Folks* (2003, co-written with Playthell Benjamin), *The Artificial White Man: Essays on Authenticity* (2004), and *Considering Genius: Writings on Jazz* (2006). Stanley Crouch makes frequent appearances as a television commentator and lives in New York City where, since 1987, he has served as an artistic consultant at Lincoln Center, co-founding the department known as Jazz at Lincoln Center.

FIELDING DAWSON (1930–2002), visual artist and author of twenty-three books, was born in New York City. His father was a journalist and he grew up in Florida, Pennsylvania, and from the age of eight, lived in his mother's hometown of Kirkwood, Missouri, near St. Louis. At age fifteen his mother presented him with a typewriter, saying "we could use a new Saroyan." Dawson's life was profoundly influenced by his experiences at the experimental community of teachers and writers, Black Mountain College in North Carolina, where, beginning in 1949, he studied painting under Franz Kline and writing under Charles Olson. His work was often identified with that school, along with that of his fellow writers, including Robert Creeley, Robert Duncan, Joel Oppenheimer, and Ed Dorn. After he was drafted as a conscientious objector in 1953 and served as a cook at a military hospital, he returned to NYC where his writing and illustrations soon were appearing in various small press journals such as *Kulchur, Jargon, Mulch*, and *El Corno Emplumado*. Once Dawson gained recognition from the publication of *An Emotional Memoir of Franz Kline* (1967), he was able to concentrate on writing, design, and teaching. From 1984, for seventeen years, he taught writing workshops in prisons and also taught at-risk teenagers in alternative high schools, besides serving as chair of PEN's Prison Writing Committee and director of the PEN Prison Writing Workshop Program. *No Man's Land* (2000) is a fictionalized account of his prison experiences. He wrote essays and a *Penny Lane* trilogy of novels but mostly concentrated on short fiction, including the collections *Krazy Kat / The Unveiling and Other Stories 1951–1968; The Man Who Changed Overnight and Other Stories & Dreams 1970–1974* (1976); *Virginia Dare, Stories 1976–1981; Will She Understand?, New Short Stories 1982–1987;* and *Land of Milk and Honey* (2001). Dawson died suddenly, in New York City, after returning home from being fitted for a pacemaker. His literary archives are placed at the Dodd Research Center at the University of Connecticut at Storrs.

VIVIAN DEMUTH (b. 1958) is the author of the ecological novel *Eyes of the Forest* (Smoky Peace Press, 2007) and a poetry collection, *Breathing Nose Mountain* (Long Shot, 2004). Her short fiction and poetry have been published in journals in Canada, the United States, and Europe. She is currently working on a novel entitled *Bear War(den)*.

PAUL LAURENCE DUNBAR (1872–1906) was born the son of former Kentucky plantation slaves, in Dayton, Ohio, where he attended public schools, graduating from high school in 1891. Dunbar derived much of his writing style from oral storytelling traditions of Southern blacks, transmitted through his parents, who shared their stories of life before Emancipation. Taking out a loan to cover publication costs, he published *Oak and Ivy*, his first of eleven poetry volumes in 1893; the first of four short story collections, *Folks from Dixie* (1898), was followed by *The Strength of Gideon and Other Stories* (1900), *In Old Plantation Days* (1903), and *The Heart of Happy Hollow* (1904); his first of four novels, *The Uncalled*, appeared in 1898. Dunbar's fourth novel, *The Sport of the Gods* (1902), has been called the first major protest novel by a black American writer, and the first to portray black life in Harlem. Dunbar died young, at thirty-three, from the combined effects of tuberculosis, alcoholism, and periodic poverty that continued throughout his writing career even though Dunbar, renowned both nationally and internationally, achieved unusual popularity for an African American writing in his time and was honored with an appointment to a clerkship at the U.S. Library of Congress. Booker T. Washington called Dunbar the "Poet Laureate of the Negro Race," and the late scholar and writer Calvin Hernton called Dunbar "the pioneer and developer of black short fiction." His *Complete Poems*, published posthumously in 1913, was reissued as *The Collected Poetry of Paul Laurence Dunbar*, also appearing in 1994 with sixty additional poems. A general sampler, edited by Jay Martin and Gossie H. Hudson, was published as *The Paul Laurence Dunbar Reader* (1973).

ALICE DUNBAR-NELSON (1875–1935) was born Alice Ruth Moore in New Orleans, Louisiana. She graduated from Straight College (now Dillard University) and continued her education at the University of Pennsylvania, Cornell University, and the School of Industrial Arts, Philadelphia. Her first collection of poetry, sketches, and short stories was *Violets and Other Tales* (1895). One of her poems and her photograph, published in the Boston *Monthly Review*, caught the attention of Paul Laurence Dunbar, the most famous African American poet of that time, and they married in 1898. After P. L. Dunbar's early death in 1902, Dunbar-Nelson moved to Wilmington, Delaware, where she taught at Howard High School. In 1916, Dunbar-Nelson married Robert John Nelson, publisher of the *Wilmington Advocate*, a newspaper geared towards the advancement of African Americans. A writer and activist on political and social causes throughout her life, Dunbar-Nelson was fired from Howard High School in 1920 for attending a social justice conference in Marion, Ohio, convened by then-Republican presidential candidate Warren G. Harding, because school district employees were not supposed to engage in political activities. She became associate editor for the *Wilmington Advocate*, which she co-owned and operated with her husband, and associate editor of the *A.M.E. Church Review*. In 1923 she began writing a weekly column in the *Washington Eagle*, and her column also appeared in *The Pittsburgh Courier*, *New York Sun*, and *The Chicago Daily News*. A resident of Philadelphia at the time of her death from a heart ailment, she left manuscripts of novels and screenplays, and a diary.

STANLEY ELKIN (1930–1995) was born in New York City and grew up in Chicago. He earned three degrees from the University of Illinois, and in 1960, became a member of the English faculty at Washington University in St. Louis, the city where he lived with his wife, Joan Marion Jacobson, and where they raised three daughters. He authored more than a dozen works of fiction, beginning with his first novel, *Boswell: A Modern Comedy* (1964, 1999), and including *A Bad Man* (1967), *The Dick Gibson Show* (1971, 2000), *The Franchiser* (1976), *The Living End: A Triptych* (1977, 1978, 1979), and *The Magic Kingdom* (Dalkey edition, 2000); the short fiction collections *Criers and Kibitzers, Kibitzers and Criers* (1966, 2000), and *Early Elkin* (1985); and the novella collections *Searches and Seizures* (1973) and *Van Gogh's Room at Arles* (1993, 2002). He was a member of the American Academy and Institute of Arts and Letters and was recipient of numerous honors, including *The Paris Review* Humor Prize, Guggenheim and Rockefeller Foundation Fellowships, and two National Book Critics Circle Awards, for *George Mills* in 1982 and for his posthumously published last novel, *Mrs. Ted Bliss* (1995). Elkin, who lived with multiple sclerosis for most of his adult life, died of a heart attack. His manuscripts and papers are archived at Olin Library of Washington University in St. Louis.

JAMES T. FARRELL (1904–1979) was born and raised in Chicago, Illinois. His realistic writing style was grounded in his experiences growing up in his Irish American Catholic working-class family, surrounded by the Irish American community of Chicago's South Side. He participated in Trotskyite politics, joined the Socialist Workers Party (SWP) until 1946 when he joined the Workers Party, and then in the 1960s rejoined the SWP, because of their involvement with the civil rights and anti-Vietnam War movements. He attended the University of Chicago, although he was mostly self-taught as a writer. He began writing at the age of twenty-one, and when about twenty-five, published his first short story, "Slob." He persisted in writing as he believed, even after his work was censored in 1948 because of his radical politics, and his popularity and income continued to decline. This integrity helped endear him to many prominent writers who celebrated a "Salute to James T. Farrell," upon publication of his fiftieth book, *The Dunne Family* (1976), among whom were Ann Douglas, Pete Hamill, Arthur Schlesinger, Jr., and Norman Mailer, who once wrote that after reading Farrell in his freshman year at Harvard, "It changed my life . . . I wanted to write." He published 17 short story collections, including *Can All This Grandeur Perish? And Other Stories* (1937), *French Girls Are Vicious and Other Stories* (1955), *Side Street and Other Stories* (1961), and the posthumously published *Eight Short, Short Stories* (1981); twenty-five novels, including a series known as the Studs Lonigan trilogy, beginning with *Young Lonigan* (1932), *The Young Manhood of Studs Lonigan* (1934), and *Judgment Day* (1935), which was made into a film (1960) and a TV mini-series (1979), and another series based on a character in the Studs Lonigan novels, the Danny O'Neill pentalogy: *A World I Never Made* (1936), *No Star Is Lost* (1938), *Father and Son* (1940), *My Days of Anger* (1943), and *The Face of Time* (1953). At the time of his death, in New York City, he had completed ten volumes of what he intended to be a twenty-five volume cycle, *A Universe of Time*.

BENJAMIN FRANKLIN (1706–1790) was born in Boston, the tenth son of a soap maker. At age twelve, because his father could not afford to continue his education, he was apprenticed to his brother James, a printer. James began *The New England Courant*, called Boston's first "newspaper," when Benjamin was fifteen and where he finagled his first publication, under the pseudonym Silence Dogood. He continued to work as an apprentice printer until able to set himself up in the printing business and became so successful he began to secure government contracts and established franchise printing partnerships in other cities in the colonies. In 1729 he bought the *Pennsylvania Gazette*, which he made into the colonies' most successful newspaper. He continued to be its publisher, printer and contributor (often under aliases) until 1748. From 1733 to 1737, he published *Poor Richard's Almanack*, which was popular, most famously for his witty aphorisms, such as "A penny saved is a penny earned." In 1849, Franklin retired from business to concentrate on scientific experiments and inventions, and by the early 1750s was conducting experiments with electricity. By the 1770s, he had become one of the country's most distinguished statesmen and was the only person to sign four great documents of this time: the Declaration of Independence, to which he was a major contributor while serving as one of the five delegates on the drafting committee during the Second Continental Congress (1776); the Treaty of

Alliance with France (1778); the Treaty of Paris with Britain (1783); and the U.S. Constitution (1787). In 1789, as one of his last public acts, he wrote "Sidi Mehemet Ibrahim on the Slave Trade," an anti-slavery treatise.

ELLEN GEIST's fiction has been published in numerous magazines including *Konch Magazine, Big Bridge, River Styx,* and *Commentary.* She has been a recipient of residency fellowships at Yaddo and the Virginia Center for the Creative Arts. She has recently completed a memoir titled *Blue Zone.* Ellen received a B.A. from Antioch College, earned an M.Ed from University of Cincinnati, and attended NYU's Graduate Program in Creative Writing. She was born in Haifa, Israel, grew up in Allentown, Pennsylvania, and currently lives with her husband in New York City.

ANNA NELSON HARRY (1906–1982), a storyteller, was one of the last survivors of the Eyak nation and one of the last speakers of the Eyak language. She was born in Cordova, Alaska, the year the town began, and her birthplace became the location where the last Eyak community survived. (Historically, the Eyak people lived along the Gulf of Alaska coast, approximately from modern Yakutat to modern Cordova.) Cordova was site of one of four American salmon cannery operations begun in 1889, to which Chinese and white male crews were imported during every summer's operating season. The crews disrupted the town, bringing disease, uncontrolled vice and violence, and in this seasonal chaos, Anna Harry witnessed the murder of her mother when she was still a young child. In 1918, at the age of twelve, she married Galushia Nelson, a fluent Eyak and English speaker who had been educated in the lower mainland states. Together they served as the major informants to a joint expedition of American and Danish anthropologists during the 1930s, and those recordings became important source materials for linguistic study of the Eyak cultural heritage and language, a branch of the Athabascan-Eyak-Tlingit language family. (By 1933, the Cordova Eyak community totaled thirty-some people; only fifteen spoke Eyak.) After Galushia died in 1939, Anna Harry fled Cordova and settled in Yakutat, where she married Sampson Harry, a member of the Yakutat Tlingit community. She had four sons, who preceded her in death. Anna Nelson Harry learned the Eyaks' traditional tales and history from an elder identified as Old Chief Joe. Michael E. Krauss, translator of Anna Nelson Harry's stories, says "Her long, hard life spanned the unutterably tragic final chapter of the living history of her people. Anna had the gift of the Eyak language, to tell the stories of her people. . . ." Her expressions of about sixty texts, either transcribed in the 1930s, or tape recorded by Krauss in the 1960s and 1970s, sometimes differ in details small or significant, revealing how her creative process filtered her understanding of Eyak history and culture through her personal life experiences and feelings. (This biography is based on the Introduction to *In Honor of Eyak: The Art of Anna Nelson Harry,* compiled and edited by Michael E. Krauss. Fairbanks, AK: Alaska Native Language Center, University of Alaska, 1982.) (Also see entry on Michael E. Krauss.)

ROBERT HASS (b. 1941) was born and raised in San Francisco. He earned his B.A. at St. Mary's College in Moraga, California, and his M.A. and Ph.D. from Stanford University. At the beginning of his teaching career, he entered and won the Yale Younger Poets competition with his first book, *Field Guide*. Other poetry collections include, *Praise* (1979), which won the William Carlos Williams Award of the Poetry Society of America; *Human Wishes* (1989), which won the Common-wealth Club of California Medal for Poetry; *Sun Under Wood* (1996) which won the National Book Critics Circle Award; and his most recently published poetry collection, *Time and Materials, Poems 1997–2005* (2007), winner of a 2007 National Book Award and 2008 Pulitzer Prize. While serving as Poet Laureate Consultant in Poetry at the Library of Congress from 1995 to1997, he sponsored a weeklong celebration of American nature writing called "Watershed." Out of this event, Hass founded the nonprofit organization River of Words to promote poetry among young people and bring awareness to environmental issues, as exemplified by its annual Watershed readings featuring appearances by well-known poets with participants in River of Words. Among his many honors, Mr. Hass is a chancellor of the Academy of American Poets. He currently teaches in the English Department of UC Berkeley, and he and his wife, poet Brenda Hillman, make their home in San Francisco's East Bay area.

HILLEL HEINSTEIN was born in Jerusalem to a Moroccan-Israeli mother and Jewish-American father and grew up in Berkeley, California. He obtained his bachelor's degree in Biology from Cornell University, and his master's degree in English Literature from San Francisco State University. He wrote his master's thesis on the philosophical skepticism of Joseph Conrad. He currently resides with his partner in Toronto, where he teaches high school English, Creative Writing, and Biology.

ROBERTA HILL (b. 1947), who has published under the name of Roberta Hill Whiteman, is an Oneida poet, fiction writer, essayist, and scholar. A professor of English and American Indian Studies at the University of Wisconsin–Madison, she has written two collections of poetry, *Star Quilt* (1984, 2001) and *Philadelphia Flowers* (1996). A biography of her grandmother, Dr. Lillie Rosa Minoka-Hill, the second American Indian woman doctor, has been accepted for publication by the University of Nebraska Press. Her poetry, essays, and short fiction have appeared in numerous literary journals, magazines, and anthologies, including: *That's What She Said: Contemporary Poetry and Fiction by Native American Women*, edited by Rayna Green (1984); and *Reinventing the Enemy's Language: Contemporary Native Women's Writing of North America*, edited by Joy Harjo and Gloria Bird (1997). Recent poetry appears in *The American Indian Culture and Research Journal, The Beloit Poetry Journal, Luna*, and *Prairie Schooner*. Recent short fiction includes "Heartbreak," in *Crossing Waters, Crossing Worlds: The African Diaspora Indian Country*, edited by Tiya Miles and Sharon Holland (2006), and "Start Getting Up," in the magazine, *The Deadly Writers Patrol* (December 2007).

CHESTER HIMES (1909–1984) was born in Cleveland, Ohio. His father was a university professor and his mother a schoolteacher. At nineteen years of age, he was sentenced to a twenty-five-year term in federal prison for armed robbery, serving until 1936 at the Ohio State Penitentiary. A prolific writer, his first published short story, "Crazy in the Stir" (1934), appeared in *Esquire* with his prison number, 59623, as the author byline. His first novel, *If He Hollers Let Him Go* (1945), was followed by *Cast the First Stone* (1952), *The Third Generation* (1954), and *The Primitive* (1955). Although generally critical successes, these novels did not bring financial security, and after the critics rejected and the publisher abandoned his novel *Lonely Crusade* (1947), Chester Himes moved to Paris, France, where he enjoyed more acclaim than in the United States. In 1965 he moved to Spain, where he lived as an expatriate for the remainder of his life. Himes began writing his nine mystery/detective novels, set in 1950s and 1960s Harlem, while in Europe, including: *For Love of Imabelle* (1957), made into the film *A Rage in Harlem* (1991); *The Crazy Kill* (1959); *The Real Cool Killers* (1959); *The Big Gold Dream* (1960); *All Shot Up* (1960); *Cotton Comes to Harlem* (1965), made into a film with the same title (1970); *The Heat's On* (1966), which became the film *Come Back Charleston Blue* (1972); *Run Man Run* (1966); and *Blind Man with a Pistol* (1969). During his lifetime, Himes also published two other novels, *Pinktoes* (1961) and *A Case of Rape* (1980); the collection *Black on Black: Baby Sister and Selected Writings* (1973); and a two-volume autobiography, *The Quality of Hurt: The Early Years* (1972) and *My Life in Absurdity: The Later Years* (1976). The Before Columbus Foundation honored Himes with a Lifetime Achievement Award in 1982. He died in November 1984 in Moraira, Alicante, Spain, where he was living with his wife, Lesley. Posthumous publications include the collection, *The Collected Stories of Chester Himes* (Thunder's Mouth, 1990), with 61 stories written between 1933 and 1979, and *Plan B* (1993), an unfinished novel edited by Michel Fabre and Robert E. Skinner. His archives are available in New Orleans, at the Amistad Research Centre of Tulane University.

LANGSTON HUGHES (1902–1967) was born in Joplin, Missouri. He mainly grew up in Lawrence, Kansas, while also living in Illinois, Ohio, besides two years in Mexico with his father. He graduated from Central High School in Cleveland, Ohio, and worked a variety of jobs in Cleveland until he moved to New York City, where, even before he enrolled for one year of study at Columbia University in 1922, he had published his poem, "The Negro Speaks of Rivers," in *Crisis* magazine, edited by W. E. B. Du Bois. Perhaps the best-known artist in the Harlem Renaissance, before he had published his first book of poems, *The Weary Blues* (1926), Hughes had received from Carl Van Vechten the title of "the Negro Poet Laureate." Hughes was a prolific writer of novels, plays, autobiography, song lyrics, essays, histories, children's books, and short stories. His short story collections include *The Ways of White Folks* (1934), *Laughing to Keep from Crying* (1952), *Something in Common and Other Stories* (1963), and several collections of his stories about an urban folk hero, Jesse B. Semple or "Simple," which first appeared in the *Chicago Defender*. In 2002, the University of Missouri Press published *The Short Stories (Collected Works of Langston Hughes)*. Hughes also edited many important literary anthologies where he sought to give younger writers a helpful start to their careers, and he was the first to publish this book's editor, Ishmael Reed. Hughes continued writing throughout his life. His last volume of verse, *The Panther and the Lash*, was published posthumously, the year of his death in 1967. In 1990 Hughes's ashes were interred in a specially designed container and sealed under the floor of the Schomburg Center, under a floor cosmogram entitled "Rivers," and a ceremony at the Schomburg Center celebrated the return of Hughes's remains to Harlem on the eve of his birthday January 1, 1991.

KRISTIN HUNTER (b. 1931) was born in Philadelphia and raised in New Jersey. Her father was an elementary school principal and her mother was a teacher, until a New Jersey state law forbidding teachers to be mothers caused her early retirement. By the age of fourteen she was writing a regular column on teenage life for a widely distributed black newspaper, the *Pittsburgh Courier*. She continued writing for the *Courier* while attending the University of Pennsylvania, from which she graduated in 1951 with a degree in education, and where she also became a research assistant in the School of Social Work in 1961. She has authored many novels including: *God Bless the Child* (1964); *The Landlord* (1966), which in 1970 became the first novel by a black woman to be made into a film; *The Survivors* (1975); *The Lakestown Rebellion* (1978); *Kinfolks* (1996); *Do Unto Others* (2000); and *Breaking Away* (2003); and has achieved popular success with her writing for young adults, including the novel *Soul Brothers and Sister Lou* (1968) and a short story collection, *Guests in the Promised Land* (1973). Recipient of many awards, including the Moonstone Black Writing Celebration Lifetime Achievement Award, she continued to use Kristin Hunter as her pen name after marrying John Lattany in 1968. She retired from the University of Pennsylvania in 1995 after twenty-three years of teaching and currently lives in New Jersey.

ZORA NEALE HURSTON (1891–1960), an American writer, folklorist, and anthropologist, was born in Eatonville, Florida, one of the nation's first all-black incorporated townships. At fourteen she got her first job, as a maid traveling with a Gilbert and Sullivan theatrical troupe. In 1923 Hurston attended Howard University where she published short stories in *Stylus*, the university's literary magazine, and studied with Alain Locke, who in 1925 would publish the defining anthology of the Harlem Renaissance, *The New Negro*. When her short story "Drenched in Light" was published in *Opportunity*, the New York–based monthly magazine of the National Urban League, which was a primary outlet for writers associated with the Harlem Renaissance, she moved to Harlem in 1925 to pursue a literary career. She attended Barnard College, where she studied with anthropologist Franz Boas, graduating in 1927. At the same time she began to publish short stories with many writers identified with the Harlem Renaissance, although she had ongoing differences with the male intellectual leaders associated with that movement, and she became known for her storytelling performances, where she presented stories based on the lives of residents of her hometown of Eatonville. In 1927 she received a fellowship to return to Florida to study the oral traditions of her hometown, and she continued to travel in the South, in Alabama and Louisiana, before returning to Florida in 1931 where she lived with sharecroppers and migrant workers who were housed in labor camps. Her novel *Jonah's Gourd Vine* (1934) was followed in 1935 by *Mules and Men,* a collection of writing about her experiences in academia and the Florida field trips. During her two-year trip to the Caribbean on a Guggenheim Fellowship, Hurston wrote her most famous work, the novel *Their Eyes Were Watching God* (1937). The last book published during her lifetime was her autobiography, *Dust Tracks on the Road* (1942). All of her books were out of print at the time of her death in 1960, in Florida, where she was so poor she sought work as a maid. Beginning in 1977, interest in Hurston's work revived and her books were reissued, including two volumes by The Library of America: *Novels and Other Stories* (1995); and *Folklore, Memoirs, and Other Writings* (1995). In 2004, her hometown of Eatonville opened a Zora Neal Hurston Library (their spelling) and now hosts a yearly Zora Neale Hurston Festival.

YURI KAGEYAMA is a poet, writer, and journalist. She has written a book of poems, *Peeling* (I. Reed Press), and her works are published in more than a dozen literary publications. She has lived on both sides of the Pacific and sees herself as both American and Japanese. She is a magna cum laude graduate of Cornell University and has an M.A. in Sociology from the University of California, Berkeley. She is married and now works in Tokyo as a correspondent for a major wire service. Her San Francisco–born son, Isaku Kageyama, is a drummer with the *taiko* group Amanojaku in Tokyo.

WILLIAM MELVIN KELLEY (b. 1937) grew up in the Bronx, New York, where he attended Fieldston School on full scholarship. At Harvard College, he studied with John Hawkes and Archibald MacLeish, winning the Dana Read Prize in 1960 for the best piece of writing in any Harvard undergraduate publication. Kelley has lived in Boston, Rome, Ibiza, Paris, and for nine years Jamaica, teaching at the University of the West Indies from 1969–1971. His novels include *A Different Drummer* (1962), winner of the Richard and Hinda Rosenthal Foundation Award of the National Institute of Arts and Letters; *A Drop of Patience* (1965); *dem* (1967); and *Dunfords Travels Everywheres* (1970). Besides his uncollected short stories, which have appeared in *The Saturday Evening Post, The New Yorker, The Negro Digest, Quilt,* and many anthologies, he has a short story collection, *Dancers on the Shore* (1965), winner of *The Transatlantic Review* award. Other honors include a Whitney grant (1963), a Rockefeller Foundation grant, and the Black Academy of Arts and Letters Award (1970). He currently teaches at Sarah Lawrence College and makes his home with his wife, the visual artist Aiki, and four generations of family in Harlem USA.

JOHN O. KILLENS (1916–1987) was born in Macon, Georgia, and educated in schools on both sides of the Mason-Dixon line. Early drafts of his first novel, *Youngblood* (1954), were read to a group of New York City writers who, with Killens, formed the Harlem Writers Guild, for which he later served as chairman. His other novels include: *And Then We Heard the Thunder* (1963), based in part upon his World War II service in the amphibian forces in the South Pacific; *'Sippi*

(1967); *The Cotillion, or One Good Bull Is Half the Herd* (1971); *A Man Ain't Noth-in' but a Man* (1975); and *The Great Black Russian*, based on the life of Alexander Pushkin, the Russian writer of African descent. In addition, he authored a book of essays, *Black Man's Burden* (1965), and wrote for motion pictures and television, including the script for the film *Odds Against Tomorrow*, which starred Harry Belafonte. Killens, who served on the National Labor Relations Board before and after World War II, and taught at many universities, was living in Brooklyn at the time of death.

MICHAEL KRAUSS (b. 1934) is a linguist and student of Alaska Native Languages. He is also the founder of the Alaska Native Language Center (1972–2000), with which he is no longer associated. Krauss is a specialist in the Na-Dené language family; since the 1960s he has worked to document the Eyak language, a little-known Alaskan language, in addition to other Athabaskan and Eskimo-Aleut languages. Widely published in linguistic journals, he has also published *Eyak Texts* (1970) and *Eyak Dictionary* (1970), and he compiled, edited, wrote the introduction, and provided translations for *In Honor of Eyak: The Art of Anna Nelson Harry* (1982). Krauss says the changing versions of Anna Nelson Harry's stories revealed her experience of her "own Eyak people struggling to survive beside larger nations, Tlingit and Aleut, and [she] has seen those in turn now threatened by a still more giant one." Krauss now works to bring attention to the endangered language crisis. The Eyak language became extinct in January 2008. Krauss says Eyak is "the first Alaskan language to go. Who's next? There's always a bigger fish." (See entry on Anna Nelson Harry.)

SUSANNE LEE was born in Los Angeles and was educated at the University of California at Berkeley and Harvard. She has lived in Hong Kong, Mount Pleasant, Michigan, and Burgos, Spain. Her nonfiction on such diverse subjects as Hong Kong cinema, surrealism and blood sausage in Spain, rail travel in China, mixed-race children in the United States, and *mehndi* in Delhi has appeared in *The Village Voice*, *The Nation*, *Konch*, *A Gathering of the Tribes*, *SLAM*, and *Giant Robot*, and on WNYE-FM.

MINJON LENOIR-IRWIN (b. 1971) was born in San Diego and raised in Oakland, California, where she was educated in Catholic schools. She graduated from Howard University with a B.A. and a M.ED. and is currently an assistant principal of a public middle school in Oakland, where she lives with her husband, Matthew Irwin and their daughter, Madison. This is her first published story.

RUSSELL CHARLES LEONG (b. 1950) is a writer of poetry, fiction, essays, and memoir, and he is also a documentary filmmaker, visual artist, and taichiquan instructor. He was born and raised in San Francisco's Chinatown, where he attended local American and Chinese schools, and was a member of the original Kearny Street Asian-American Writers Workshop. A graduate of San Francisco State College (BA, 1972) and UCLA (MFA Theater, Film, Television, 1990), he attended National Taiwan University's Department of Chinese Languages and

Literature from 1974 to 1975. His poetry collection, *The Country of Dreams and Dust* (1993), received the PEN Josephine Miles Award in Literature. His short fiction from the 1970s through the 1990s are collected in *Phoenix Eyes and Other Stories* (2000), which won a 2001 American Book Award. His writing has been published in Shanghai and Taipei and has been widely anthologized in the United States, including *Aiiieeeee! An Anthology of Asian American Writers*, edited by Jeffrey Paul Chan, Frank Chin, Lawson Inada, and Shawn Wong (1974); *The Open Boat: Poems from Asian America* (1993), edited by Garrett Hongo; and *Charlie Chan Is Dead, An Anthology of Contemporary Asian American Fiction*, edited by Jessica Hagedorn (1993). He is author of a children's book, *My Chinatown A to Z* (1966), and was featured as one of fifty poets on the PBS series *The United States of Poetry*. Leong has served as the editor of *Amerasia Journal* since 1977 and is managing editor of the UCLA Asian American Studies Center publications. He also served as editor of *Asian American Sexualities: Dimensions of the Gay and Lesbian Experience* and *Moving the Image*, the first book on Asian American film and video.

WALTER K. LEW is the author of *Excerpts from: ΔIKTH DIKTE, for DICTEE (1982)* (1992); *Treadwinds: Poems & Intermedia Texts* (2002), winner of the Sixth Annual 2003 Literary Award of the Asian American Writers' Workshop and a fnalist for the PEN Center USA 2003 Literary Award in Poetry; and *The Ga-guhm Poems* (forthcoming). Lew has worked as associate producer of award-winning documentary films broadcast by CBS, PBS, and NHK-Japan, among others, and staged multimedia "movietelling" performances at international film festivals since 1982. His translations and scholarship in Korean and Asian American literature and film have been published widely. Founding editor of the Asian/diasporic press Kaya, Lew has also edited the foremost anthology of Asian North American poetry, *Premonitions* (1995); *Muae 1* (1995); *Crazy Melon and Chinese Apple: The Poems of Frances Chung* (2000); and, with Heinz Insu Fenkl, co-edited *Kôri: The Beacon Anthology of Korean American Fiction* (2001). Among the honors Lew has received are fellowships and grants from the National Endowment for the Arts, New York State Council on the Arts, Association for Asian Studies, 'A'A Arts, and the Korean Foundation for the Arts. Lew teaches in the Department of English of the University of Miami in Florida. His current projects include new movietelling pieces and translating the selected works of the Korean experimental modernist Yi Sang (1910–1937).

PAULE MARSHALL (b. 1929) was born Valenza Pauline Burke in Brooklyn, New York, to parents who had immigrated to the United States from Barbados in 1919. She grew up in Brooklyn, in a bi-cultural world of African Americans and African Caribbeans. She credits the aesthetic foundation of her writing to the times she listened, as a young girl, to kitchen table talk of her mother, her mother's West Indian neighbor-friends, and her six-month stay in Barbados with her grandmother, whom she visited at the age of nine. She married psychologist Kenneth Marshall in 1950 and graduated cum laude from Brooklyn College (1953). To make ends meet, she worked as a librarian for a short time before becoming the only woman working for *Our World*, an influential 1950s African American magazine, first as a researcher, and then as a staff writer. Separated from her husband in 1957, she gave birth to her son, Evan-Keith Marshall, the same year *Brown Girl, Brownstones* (1959), her first novel, was published, which *The Norton Anthology of African American Literature* called "the novel that most black feminist critics consider to be the beginning of contemporary African American women's writing." She was divorced in 1963 and remarried Nourry Menard, a Haitian businessman, in 1970. She also authored the novels *The Chosen Place, the Timeless People* (1969); *Praisesong for the Widow* (1983), which received a Before Columbus American Book Award; *Daughters* (1991); and *The Fisher King* (2000). Her two collections of short fiction are *Soul Clap Hands and Sing* (1961), which received the National Institute of Arts Award, and *Reena and Other Stories* (1983; also published as *Merle: A Novella and Other Stories*, 1984). Ms. Marshall has taught creative writing at Yale, Cornell, Columbia, the University of Iowa's Writers' Workshop, and UC Berkeley and was Distinguished Professor of English and Creative Writing at New York University. Among her many other honors are Guggenheim (1960) and National Endowment for the Arts Fellowships, a John Dos Passos Award for Literature, a 1992 MacArthur Fellows Award, and a Literary Lion from the New York Public Library in 1994.

JAMES ALAN MCPHERSON (b. 1943) was born and raised in Savannah, Georgia, in "a lower-class black community," as he describes in his essay, "On Becoming an American Writer" (*The Atlantic*, December 1978), where he attended segregated public schools. To help pay for his college education he worked various jobs, starting with the summer of 1962 when he was a dining car waiter on the Great Northern Railroad, the source material for his short story, "On Trains," that John Henrik Clarke anthologized in *A Century of the Best Black American Short Stories* (1966, 1993). His second short story, "Gold Coast," won the first prize in a 1965 *Atlantic Monthly* fiction contest, while he was in his second year of Harvard University Law School, and it was selected by John Updike for his collection, *Best American Short Stories of the Century* (2000). After completing law school, he received an M.F.A. from the University of Iowa's Writers' Workshop in 1969. McPherson is the author of two short story collections: *Hue and Cry* (1968) and *Elbow Room* (1977), for which he was awarded a 1978 Pulitzer Prize; *Crabcakes, a Memoir* (1998) covering the years from 1976 and including his experiences teaching in Japan; and a collection of essays, *A Region Not Home* (2000). His essays and short stories are widely published in mainstream magazines and literary periodicals such as *The New York Times Magazine, Esquire, Ploughshares*, and *The Iowa Review* and anthologies such as volumes of *The Best American Short Stories, The Best American Essays*, and *O. Henry Prize Stories*. With poet Miller Williams, he co-edited *Railroad: Trains and Train People* (1976), and in association with DeWitt Henry, founding editor of *Ploughshares*, he compiled and edited *Confronting Racial Difference* (1990) and *Fathering Daughters: Reflections by Men* (1998). Among his many honors are a 1970 National Institute of Arts and Letters grant, a Rockefeller grant, a Guggenheim Fellowship, and a MacArthur Foundation Award (1981). He has taught at the University of California, Santa Cruz, and Harvard, and he is presently a professor of English at the Iowa Writers' Workshop in Iowa City.

NANCY MERCADO (b. 1959) was born of Puerto Rican parents in Atlantic City, New Jersey. She came into prominence in 1980, after reading at the Nuyorican Poets Café in New York City, and has continued to present her work throughout the United States, Europe, and in Canada as a featured poet and conference panelist. She is the author of *It Concerns the Madness* (Long Shot Productions, 2000) and the forthcoming *Rooms for the Living: New York Poems,* with an introduction written by Ishmael Reed. She was also Contributing Editor and Writer for *Letras Femeninas* Volumen 31, Número 1: *The Journal of the Asociación de Literatura Femenina Hispánica* of Arizona State University and editor of *if the world were mine,* a children's anthology published by the New Jersey Performing Arts Center. Her work has appeared in many literary magazines and is widely anthologized, including: *Bowery Women Poems* (YBK Publishing); *In the Arms of Words: Poems for Tsunami Relief* (Foothills Publishing and Sherman Asher Press); *From Totems to Hip-Hop: A Multicultural Anthology of Poetry Across the Americas, 1900–2002* edited by Ishmael Reed (Thunder's Mouth Press); *Poetry After 911: An Anthology of New York Poets* (Melville House Publishers, 2002); *Bum Rush the Page: A Def Poetry Jam* (Crown Publishing, 2001); and *ALOUD: Voices from the Nuyorican Poets Café* (Henry Holt, 1994). She served, for eleven years, as an editor of *Long Shot,* www.longshot.org, and as the publication's editor-in-chief for one of those years. Nancy Mercado has a doctoral degree from Binghamton University–SUNY.

BHARATI MUKHERJEE (b. 1940) was born and raised in Calcutta, India, the daughter of a successful businessman. By the age of ten, she had authored many short stories and already knew she wanted to be a writer. After earning her B.A. from the University of Calcutta (1959) and M.A. in English and Ancient Indian Culture from the University of Baroda (1961), she came to the United States in 1961, where she earned an M.F.A. in Creative Writing (1963) and a Ph.D. in English and Comparative Literature (1969) at the University of Iowa's Writers' Workshop. At the Iowa Writers' Workshop she met a fellow student, Clark Blaise, and after a two-week courtship, they were married in 1963. Now a U.S. citizen, Mukherjee has described herself as "an American writer of Indian origin. . . . I write in the tradition of immigrant experience rather than nostalgia and expatriation." Her publications include the short story collections *Darkness* (1985) and *The Middleman and Other Stories* (1988), which received the National Book Critics Circle Award for fiction; the novels *The Tiger's Daughter* (1972), *Wife* (1975), *Jasmine* (1989), *The Holder of the World* (1993), *Leave It to Me* (1997), *Desirable Daughters* (2002), and *The Tree Bride* (2004); and the nonfiction *Days and Nights in Calcutta* (1977, a memoir co-authored with Clark Blaise), *The Sorrow and the Terror: The Haunting Legacy of the Air India Tragedy* (1987, co-authored with Clark Blaise), *Political Culture and Leadership in India* (1991), and *Regionalism in Indian Perspective* (1992). Among her many honors, she is a member of the American Academy of Arts and Sciences. A professor in the English Department at the University of California, Berkeley, Ms. Mukherjee has taught, lectured, and given readings at universities and colleges throughout the United States and Canada, and she and her husband frequently participate in national and international literary workshops and conferences. They maintain a home in San Francisco.

ALEJANDRO MURGUÍA (b. 1949) is a writer of fiction, poetry, memoir, and essays. His short story collections include *Farewell to the Coast* (1990), *Southern Front* (1990), and *This War Called Love* (2003), winner of a Before Columbus Foundation American Book Award. His other publications include his novel *Tres Rosas;* a memoir, *The Medicine of Memory: A Mexican Clan in California*, which was called "creative fiction" by Murguía and was nominated for the Victor Turner Prize in Ethnographic Writing. He is a founding member and first director of the Mission Cultural Center for Latino Arts in San Francisco and a founding editor of *Tin Tan*, published during the 1970s, which was the first Chicano magazine to have an international perspective. Murguía makes his home in San Francisco and is currently Writing Specialist in Raza Studies at San Francisco State University.

APHRODITE DÉSIRÉE NAVAB (b. 1971, Iran) is an Iranian-Greek-American artist and writer who uses visual art and writing to investigate transnational issues in art, education, cultural studies, and women's studies. She was Assistant Professor of Art at the College of Fine Arts, University of Florida. In 2004 she completed an Ed.D. in Art and Art Education at Teachers College, Columbia University, where she received the M.A. and Ed.M. degrees in 2000. She received her B.A. magna cum laude in Visual and Environmental Studies from Harvard University in 1993. Navab's art has been featured in over seventy exhibitions/film screenings around the world and is included in a number of permanent collections. She recently had a solo exhibition, *Super East-West Woman: Living on the Axis Fighting Evil Everywhere* (October–November 2007) at the Rhonda Schaller Studio in Chelsea, NYC. Navab has published several interdisciplinary scholarly journal articles concerning contemporary art. "Tales Left Untold" was published as a poem in the anthology *Let Me Tell You Where I've Been: New Writing by Women of the Iranian Diaspora* (2006), edited by Persis Karim and Parisa Milani. Navab's essay "What Is Home after Exile? An Iranian Greek American Homecoming" appears in *Homelands; Women's Journeys across Race, Place and Time* (2007), edited by Jenesha de Rivera and Patricia Justine Tumang.

TY PAK (b. 1938) was born in Korea and lived through his country's liberation from Japan in 1945, its division under U.S. and Soviet occupation, and the trauma of the Korean War, 1950–1953, during which his father died. After getting his law degree at Seoul National University in 1961, he worked as a reporter for the English dailies *Korean Republic* and *Korea Times*, until 1965 when he came to the United States and got his Ph.D. in English at Bowling Green State University in Ohio (1969). After a year's postdoctoral work at UC Berkeley, he taught in the English Department, University of Hawaii (1970 to 1987), when he took early retirement to devote himself to writing. A collection of thirteen stories, *Guilt Payment* (1983), was critically acclaimed and widely adopted as a textbook at many U.S. college campuses. His most recent books are *Cry Korea Cry* (1999), a novel, and *Moonbay* (1999), a collection of seven short stories previously published in various journals. Ty Pak has also widely lectured and published articles on the subjects of linguistics and Korean American and Asian American literature. Now a U.S. citizen, he is married, with three children, and lives in Honolulu.

GRACE PALEY (1922–2007) was born Grace Goodside in New York City, the third and youngest child of a family of socialist Russian Jews. (When the family arrived in the United States the name was changed from Gutseit.) She grew up in the Bronx, in a neighborhood "so dense with Jews I thought we were the great imposing majority." At nineteen, after one year at Hunter College, she married Jess Paley, a film cameraman. They had a son and daughter and later divorced; in 1972 she married Robert Nichols, a writer with whom she collaborated on a collection of their poems and stories, *Here and Somewhere Else* (2007). Paley concentrated on being a mother and was writing poetry until she was in her 30s, when she started writing about four dozen compact short stories, collected in the volumes *The Little Disturbances of Man* (1959), *Enormous Changes at the Last Minute* (1974), and *Later the Same Day* (1985), with some also appearing in *Long Walks and Intimate Talks* (1991). In a PEN American Center interview she explained: "People learn to write by doing various things. . . . My fiction teacher was poetry. . . . in writing poetry I wanted to address the world. . . . But writing stories, I wanted the world to explain itself to me, to speak to me." A founder of the Teachers & Writers Collaborative in New York City in 1967, Paley was elected to the National Academy of Arts and Letters in 1980. Among her other honors were an REA Award for the Short Story in 1993 and a 1994 nomination for both the Pulitzer Prize and National Book Award for *The Collected Stories* (1994, 2007). In a 1978 *New York Times* interview, she said, "I'm not writing a history of famous people, I am interested in a history of everyday life." In her everyday life she resided in Greenwich Village and taught at Sarah Lawrence College, the City College of New York, and Columbia and Syracuse Universities. A founder of the Greenwich Village Peace Center in 1961, she described herself as a "somewhat combative pacifist and cooperative anarchist." She was jailed several times for protesting the Vietnam War, lobbied for women's rights and against nuclear proliferation, and continued to protest the war in Iraq, even while sick with the cancer from which she died, at her Thetford Hill, Vermont, home, survived by her husband, two children, and three grandchildren.

DANNY ROMERO (b. 1961) was born and raised in Los Angeles, where he attended Catholic schools. He has degrees from University of California, Berkeley (BA, 1988), and Temple University (MA, 1993) in Philadelphia, where he taught writing (part-time) for many years. He currently teaches at Sacramento City College. Romero's poetry and short fiction have been published in literary journals and anthologies, including *West of the West: Imagining California* (1989), *Pieces of the Heart: New Chicano Fiction* (1993), *Under the Fifth Sun: Latino Literature from California* (2003), and *Latinos in Lotusland: An Anthology of Contemporary Southern California Literature* (2008). He is the author of the novel *Calle 10* (1996) and two chapbooks of poetry. A bilingual poetry collection is forthcoming from Bilingual Review Press. He lives with his wife and son in Sacramento, California.

CORIE ROSEN (b. 1980) was born in the suburbs of Los Angeles. She is the great niece of Holocaust survivors and the great granddaughter of Russian immigrants. She currently lives in Arizona. Her poem appears in *From Totems to Hip-Hop:*

A Multicultural Anthology of Poetry Across the Americas, 1900–2002, edited by Ishmael Reed (2003).

FLOYD SALAS (b. 1931) writes fiction, poetry, essays, and memoirs and has taught creative writing at San Francisco State University, University of California, Berkeley, University of San Francisco, Sonoma State University, and Foothill College, as well as at San Quentin, Folsom, Vacaville, and other correctional institutions. He is president of PEN Oakland and a former boxing coach for University of California, Berkeley. In addition to a recently completed novel in manuscript about 1940s Oakland, entitled *Dirty Boogie*, Salas has published four novels: *Tattoo the Wicked Cross* (1967), winner of the Joseph Henry Jackson Award, a Eugene F. Saxton Fellowship, and ranked in the Western 100 List of Best 20th Century Fiction by the *San Francisco Chronicle*; *What Now My Love* (1970); *Lay My Body on the Line* (1978), written and published by Ishmael Reed and Al Young's Y'Bird Press on National Endowment for the Arts Literary Fellowships; and *State of Emergency* (1996), awarded the 1997 PEN Oakland Literary Censorship Award. His memoir, *Buffalo Nickel* (1992), earned him a California Arts Council Literary Fellowship. His two volumes of poetry are *Color of My Living Heart* (1996) and *Love Bites: Poetry in Celebration of Dogs and Cats* (2006). Salas is editor of *Stories and Poems from Close to Home* (1986) and other anthologies of San Francisco Bay Area writing and was a staff writer for the NBC drama *Kingpin*, released in February 2003. A long-time resident of Berkeley, his archives are housed in the Bancroft Library, University of California, Berkeley.

GEORGE S. SCHUYLER (1895–1977), a writer of satiric fiction, plays, essays, and journalism, was born in Providence, Rhode Island, into a family whose ancestry included free blacks as far back in historical records as could be traced, with two great-grandfathers who fought on opposing sides in the American Revolution. He was raised in Syracuse, New York, and educated in public schools until he enlisted in the U.S. Army in 1912. For seven years he served in the racially segregated 25th U.S. Infantry Regiment, achieving the rank of first lieutenant by his discharge. He settled in New York City in 1922, where he became associated with the black Socialist group, Friends of Negro Freedom, headed by A. Philip Randolph and Chandler Owen. He served on the editorial board and wrote for their official monthly journal, *The Messenger*, from 1923 to 1928. During the 1920s he also contributed a column, "Views and Reviews," to the *Pittsburgh Courier*, a major black weekly newspaper, where, using the pseudonym Samuel I. Brooks, he published *Black Empire* in serial form. In 1932 the NAACP published a leaflet, *Mississippi River Slavery—1932*, that resulted from investigations by Schuyler and Roy Wilkins into working conditions on a federal flood-control project. A 1933 Senate investigation into their findings led to legislation setting U.S. government standards on minimum wages and working conditions for all workers. By the 1950s, Schuyler had become an anti-Communist, so aligned with right-wing positions he supported Senator Joseph McCarthy and his anti-Communist activities. As he expressed increasingly radical conservative viewpoints in his *Pittsburgh Courier* column, it became more controversial with the majority of the black community and the column was ended in 1966. In 1967, Schuyler began to write for William Loeb's ultraconservative *Union Leader*. In this same year he suffered the loss of his daughter, Phillipa Duke Schuyler, a child prodigy, with a widely publicized career as a classic concert pianist and composer, who was killed during a *Union Leader* assignment in Vietnam. Among Schuyler's publications are the satirical fantasy novel *Black No More; Being an Account of the Strange and Wonderful Workings of Science in the Land of the Free a. d. 1933–1940* (1931) and a historical novel, *Slaves Today, a Story of Liberia* (1931), based on five months of investigative research in Liberia; and nonfiction, most famously the essay, "The Negro-Art Hokum" (1926), which appeared with Langston Hughes' response, *The Negro Artist and the Racial Mountain*, in the June 1926 issue of the *Nation*; the two 1947 publications from the Catholic Information Society: *The Communist Conspiracy Against the Negro* and *The Red Drive in the Colonies*; and his autobiography, *Black and Conservative: The Autobiography of George S. Schuyler* (1966).

VICTOR SÉJOUR (1817–1874), author of fiction, poetry, essays, and plays, was born in New Orleans, Louisiana, to a free black father from Santo Domingo and a mixed-race mother from New Orleans. He was educated at private schools and, to avoid the difficulties encountered daily because of his race in the antebellum South, was sent by his parents to Paris at nineteen to continue his education, as was the custom among New Orleans's free blacks of sufficient means. He remained an expatriate writer in Paris, the first of many African American writers who would make this choice. Writing in French, Séjour authored plays in the forms of melodramas, comedies, and histories. His first play, *Diegareas,* a historical verse drama located in fifteenth-century Spain, was produced by the French national theater, Le Théâtre-Français, in 1844, launching a career in which he would reign as one of the most successful playwrights produced in nineteenth-century Paris. His most popular play, *Richard III* (1852), was among three of his dramas staged in New Orleans. *The Norton Anthology of African American Literature* identifies "*Le Mulâtre* (The Mulatto)" as "the earliest known work of African American fiction," and also "a remarkable precedent for the tradition of African American antislavery protest fiction." It was first published in French, in 1837, in a Parisian journal, *La Revue des Colonies*, sponsored by a society of men of color, which included Cyrille Bisette, an abolitionist who was the editor, and prominent French novelist Alexandre Dumas, *père*.

NTOZAKE SHANGE (b. 1948) was born Paulette Williams in Trenton, New Jersey, and from the age of eight, grew up in St. Louis, Missouri. Her father, a physician, and her mother, a psychiatric social worker, exposed her to art, music, and culture, and she began writing short stories and poetry as a child. She gave her first poetry reading while attending Barnard College (B.A. in American Studies, 1970), and with some of her friends, put together an anthology, *Fat Mama*, which she called her first "feminist experience." While in graduate school at the University of Southern California (M.A. in American Studies, 1973), she changed her name to Ntozake Shange (which in Zulu means "she who comes with her own things" and "she who walks like a lion"). She quickly garnered national critical success with her first theater work, *for colored girls who have considered suicide / when the rainbow is enuf* (1974–1976), which she called a "choreopoem." It evolved during workshop performances in a women's bar in Berkeley, California, in which she would read her poems accompanied by music and dance, and it traveled to Off-Off Broadway, and then Off-Broadway, and then moved to Broadway in 1976, winning 1977 Obie, Outer Critics Circle, Audelco, and *Mademoiselle* Awards and an Emmy nomination. In 1979, scripts of three other choreopoems, *Spell #7, A Photograph: Lovers in Motion,* and *Boogie Woogie Landscapes,* were published in the collection *Three Pieces,* which won the *Los Angeles Times* Book Prize for Poetry. She won a second Obie for her adaptation and direction of Brecht's *Mother Courage and Her Children* (1981). Shange fiction publications include *Sassafras: A Novella* (1977), which was expanded into the novel *Sassafras, Cypress and Indigo* (1982), *Betsy Brown: A Novel* (1985), and *Liliane: Resurrection of the Daughter* (1994); her poetry collections include *Nappy Edges* (1978), *Ridin' the Moon in Texas* (1989), and *I Live in Music* (1994); her essay collections include *See No Evil: Prefaces Essays and Accounts, 1976–1983* (1984). Her most recent books include two for children, *Float Like a Butterfly: Muhammad Ali* (2002) and *Daddy Says* (2003), and the forthcoming *How I Come by This Cryin' Song.* Ntozake Shange currently lives in Brooklyn, New york.

RAY SMITH (b. 1928) was born in Niagara Falls, New York. He graduated from the University of Buffalo with a degree in Anthropology and Sociology, and also attended University of Buffalo Law School. One of the founding members of Buffalo's African American Cultural Center, he participates in community theater projects as an actor and writer, with a special interest in developing short café-type musical presentations in theater supper clubs. He has been employed as a law clerk, probation officer, director of a community housing program and has been a teacher in the Buffalo schools since 1989. He poured his twenty years of experience as a single parent into his first short story collection, *The Color of Hope: and Other Short Stories* (2006), and is currently working on a second short story collection among other writing projects.

GERTRUDE STEIN (1874–1946) was born in Allegheny, Pennsylvania, the youngest of seven children in a wealthy, educated German Jewish American family. When she was a young child, the family lived in Vienna and Paris from 1875–1879 and then settled in Oakland, California. After her mother died in 1888 and her father in 1891, she and her brother Leo went to live with maternal relatives in Baltimore, and their inheritance was administered by their oldest brother, Michael. She joined Leo at Harvard, as a special student at the Annex (later Radcliffe College), where she studied with philosopher George Santayana and psychologist William James. She followed Leo to Johns Hopkins, while he studied biology and she studied medicine, but soon "bored," she intentionally failed out in 1904, influenced by her interest in writing, her intense affair with two women, and her brother Leo's departure for Paris to pursue his interests in art. Together in Paris, the Steins became major patrons of European and American impressionist and postimpressionist artists including Cézanne, Rousseau, Dove,

Demuth, Matisse, Picasso, and Braque, and their Saturday salons were attended by expatriate Americans and international writers and painters of the avant-garde, many of whom later became famous if not already famous. Her first published stories, *Three Lives* (1909), were written around the time she sat for her portrait by Picasso. Many volumes of experiments in poetry, fiction, and dramatic forms followed, besides the eight volumes of poetry, prose, fiction, portraits, and miscellany in *The Yale Edition of the Unpublished Writings of Gertrude Stein* edited by Carl Van Vechten (1951–1958). As famous for her exotic character as for her writing, during her lifetime her most famous works were *Autobiography of Alice B. Toklas* (1933), a bestseller; and the opera collaboration with composer Virgil Thomsom, *Four Saints in Three Acts* (1927), which toured the United States and England with an all-black cast in the 1930s. Among Stein's other publications are the collections *Tender Buttons* (1914) and *Geography and Plays* (1922), which includes "The Wedding," *Lectures in America* (1935), *Everybody's Autobiography* (1937), and *Wars I Have Seen* (1945). Stein remained in France during World War II with her lifelong companion, Alice B. Toklas, leaving Paris for their summer home in a small village where they lived without harassment by the Germans or the Vichy French government, protected by villagers and a friend with links to Pétain. They returned to Paris after the war, opening their apartment to American GIs. She completed her last work, *The Mother of Us All* (1945), an opera about Susan B. Anthony, shortly before her death from cancer, at the American Hospital. She is buried in Paris at the cemetery of Pére-Lachaise, joined by Alice B. Toklas twenty-one years later.

LEON SURMELIAN (1907–1995) was a writer of short stories, novels, poetry, memoir, and essays and translator of Armenian fables and folklore. He was born in Trebizond, Armenia. During the Armenian Genocide he escaped, and was raised in the Essayan orphanage in Constantinople. His first book, a volume of Armenian poetry titled *Louys Zvart (Joyful Light)* (1924), was published when he was a sixteen-year-old student at the Armenian Central Lycee. At seventeen he immigrated to the United States, intending to study agriculture, and graduated from Kansas State University. His bestselling memoir, *I Ask You Ladies and Gentlemen* (1945), recalling his childhood during the years of the Genocide, was translated into many languages. His extremely useful manual, *Techniques of Fiction Writing: Measure and Madness* (1968), evolved over years of teaching writing courses at the California State University at Los Angeles and the University of California Extension Division, and remains a standard reference. Surmelian published numerous short stories; a novel *98.6* (1950); and two volumes for UNESCO: the translations for *The Daredevils of Sassoun: The Armenian National Epic* (1964) and *Apples of Immortality: Folktales of Armenia* (1968).

MARY TALLMOUNTAIN (1910–1994) was born Mary Demoski in Nulato, Alaska, a village on the Yukon River, one hundred miles south of the Artic circle. Of mixed Russian, Scots-Irish, and Athabaskan ancestry, after her mother died of tuberculosis and she was orphaned at six, she was adopted by a non-Native couple. TallMountain worked as a legal secretary for many years. She began writing in her fifties, after developing a friendship with Paula Gunn Allen, a Native American scholar, writer, and editor, when for eighteen Months TallMountain wrote sixteen hours a, day and met with Allen once a week. Her published works over the next twenty-something years were mainly inspired by her early life experiences in Alaska during the 1920s, and include: *Nine Poems* (1977); *There Is No Word for Goodbye* (1981); *Matrilineal Cycle* (1988); *The Light on the Tent Wall* (1990); *A Quick Brush of Wings* (1991); and the posthumously published volumes *Listen to the Night: Poems to the Animal Spirits of Mother Earth* (1995) and *Haiku and Other Poetic Forms* (1996). For many years a resident of San Francisco's Tenderloin District, in her later years she returned to Alaska to teach in schools and give readings, there and throughout California. She was one of the poets featured on Bill Moyers's PBS series *The Power of the Word*. The Rasmussen Library at the University of Alaska in Fairbanks houses an archival collection of TallMountain's published and unpublished works. The TallMountain Circle, a nonprofit foundation she founded to benefit promising authors, which grants awards to writers from inner-city San Francisco and those of Native American heritage, also preserves and administers her literary estate.

MARK TWAIN (1835–1910) was born Samuel Langhorne Clemens in Missouri and was raised in the town of Hannibal, on the Mississippi River. After his father died when he was eleven years old, he apprenticed in a printing shop and traveled for four years as a journeyman printer. He then worked as a riverboat pilot until the Civil War began, when he briefly served with a Confederate unit, until, after joining his brother who had been appointed secretary of the Nevada Territory, he tried his hand at mining. Writing since childhood, by the age of sixteen he became a published author when a piece appeared in a Boston magazine. He assumed his pen name of Mark Twain (a term borrowed from a river leadsmen's call to alert when the depth of water was two fathoms) at the time he was hired as a reporter for the Virginia City *Territorial Enterprise*. His literary works, many of which continue to be standard texts for high school and college-level American literature courses, include the novels *Roughing It* (1872), *The Gilded Age* (1873), *The Adventures of Tom Sawyer* (1876), *The Prince and the Pauper* (1882), *Adventures of Huckleberry Finn* (1885), *A Connecticut Yankee in King Arthur's Court* (1889), and *The Tragedy of Pudd'nhead Wilson and the Comedy of Those Extraordinary Twins* (1894); and his nonfiction works include *The Innocents Abroad* (1869), *Life on the Mississippi* (1883), *Following the Equator* (1897), and his posthumously published *Autobiography* (1924).

E. DONALD TWO-RIVERS (b. 1945), a poet, playwright, and short story writer, is a full-blood Ojibwa who grew up in Sapawe, Ontario, and now makes his home in Chicago. Also a performance artist, he is the Founding Artistic Director of the Red Path Theater Company in Chicago, Illinois. His short stories are collected in *Survivor's Medicine* (1998), which won an American Book Award from Before Columbus Foundation in 1999. Other publications include *Briefcase Warriors: Stories for the Stage* (2000), a poetry collection, *a Dozen Cold Ones* (1992), and *Chili Corn*, the etext of a poem, part of a Web site for the play by the same name, http://www.studioz.org/ chili/poem.html.

GERALD VIZENOR (b. 1934) was born in Minneapolis, Minnesota. His father was from the White Earth Reservation (Anishinaabe) and his mother from the city, the granddaughter of immigrants. He grew up in a crowded tenement in Minneapolis, while living with his grandmother after his father was murdered, and later, in foster homes. His short stories have appeared in many anthologies and were collected in *Landfill Meditation: Crossblood Stories* (1991). He has authored five books of haiku, a form of poetry that he realized, while serving in the military in Japan, has similarities to native dream songs, and has also published studies of Anishinaabe dream songs and stories, *Summer in the Spring: Anishinaabe Lyric Poems and Stories* (1993). *Bearheart: The Heirship Chronicles* (1978) was his first novel; his second novel, *Griever: An American Monkey King in China*, won an American Book Award in 1988. An editor of many anthologies, they include *Narrative Chance: Postmodern Discourse on Native American Indian Literatures* (1989) and the HarperCollins College Mosaic Series' *Native American Literature, a Brief Introduction and Anthology* (1995), which won a PEN Oakland Josephine Miles Award. He has received two Lifetime Achievement Awards: The Native Writer's Circle of the Americas (2001) and the Western Literature Association (2005). He serves as Series Editor for *American Indian Literature and Critical Studies* at the University of Oklahoma Press; and is on the Editorial Boards of the Smithsonian Institution Press's series, *Studies in Native American Literature* and the *American Indian Lives* autobiography series at the University of Nebraska. Now a Professor Emeritus, Ethnic Studies, UC Berkeley, Vizenor lives in Albuquerque with his wife, Laura Hall, where he is Professor of American Studies at the University of New Mexico. His most recent novel, *Father Meme*, is forthcoming in 2008 from the University of New Mexico Press.

JOHN A. WILLIAMS (b. 1925) was born in Hinds County, Mississippi, and grew up in Syracuse, New York. After serving in the navy during World War II, where he began to write poetry, he finished high school and graduated from Syracuse University. Forced to leave graduate school for lack of funds, Williams began to be published in popular magazines while employed at a variety of jobs as a social worker, foundry operator, grocery clerk, and insurance company worker, besides working for CBS, NBC, and *Newsweek*, *Jet*, and *Ebony* magazines. These experiences proved useful to Williams when writing his novels, which include: *One for New York* (1960), *Night Song* (1961), *Sissie* (1963), *The Man Who Cried I Am* (1967), *Sons of Darkness, Sons of Light* (1969), *Captain Blackman* (1972), *Mothersill and the Foxes* (1975), and *!Click Song* (1982), winner of an American Book Award in 1983. He is also a prolific author of poetry, nonfiction, and an opera libretto, *Clifford's Blues* (1999). Williams taught many years at various colleges and universities, receiving the Lindback Award for Distinguished Teaching from Rutgers University (1982), and was inducted into both the National Institute of Arts and Letters (1982) and the National Literary Hall of Fame (1998). Williams recently assembled a publication of his correspondence with the writer Chester Himes, which they steadily maintained during the 1960s and 1970s (2008). He lives with his wife, Lori, in Teaneck, New Jersey.

SHOLEH WOLPÉ (b. 1961) was born in Iran and spent most of her teen years in the Caribbean and Europe, ending up in the United States, where she pursued master's degrees in Radio-TV-Film (Northwestern University) and Public Health (Johns Hopkins University). She is the author of *Rooftops of Tehran* (forthcoming, 2009), *Sin—Selected Poems of Forugh Farrokhzad* (2007), *The Scar Saloon* (2004), *Shame* (a three-act play that was first staged in Los Angeles in September, /2007) and a poetry CD (Refuge Studios). She is also associate editor of *The Norton Anthology of Modern Literature from the Muslim World* (forthcoming, 2009) and the guest editor of *Atlanta Review* (forthcoming 2009, Iran issue). Her poems, translations, essays, and reviews have appeared in scores of literary journals, periodicals, and anthologies worldwide, and have been translated into several languages. Ms. Wolpé currently lives in Los Angeles.

CHARLES WRIGHT (1932–2008) was born in New Franklin, Missouri, and at the age of eighteen attended the James Jones & Lowney Turner Handy Writer's Colony in Marshall, Illinois. A former columnist for the *Village Voice*, he also wrote for *Vogue* and *The New York Times*. Wright authored the auto biographical of the novels *The Messenger* (1963) and *The Wig* (1966) and a "journal-novel" *Absolutely Nothing to Get Alarmed About* (1973). The three volumes were reissued together in 1993 as *Absolutely Nothing to Get Alarmed About: The Complete Novels of Charles Wright*. Although he is frequently omitted from canon-establishing anthologies and bibliographies, Ishmael Reed commented in his introduction to a 2003 reissue of *The Wig:* "Charles Wright's novel marked a change in African-American fiction. . . . All of us who wanted to 'experiment,' as we were seeing our painter and musician friends experiment, used it as a model." Charles Wright lives in New York City where he is at work on a new book.

WAKAKO YAMAUCHI (b. 1924), a writer and a painter, was born Wakako Nakamura in Westmorland, California, to parents who were first-generation immigrants from Shizuoka Prefecture in Japan. She was raised in Southern California's Imperial Valley, where her parents moved the family from town to town as tenant farmers (California's Alien Land Law forbade Japanese landownership) and where they later owned a hotel catering to itinerant Japanese farmworkers, from which the family was evacuated under President Roosevelt's 1942 Executive Order. While interned for a year and a half at the Poston Relocation Center in Arizona, she worked on the camp's newspaper, the *Poston Chronicle,* where she met and became friends with fellow staff worker Hisaye Yamamoto. After the war she eventually resettled in Los Angeles, married Chester Yamauchi, and raised their daughter, Joy Yamauchi. In Garrett Hongo's introduction to her collected volume of stories, plays and memoir, *Songs My Mother Taught Me* (1994), she says "I was a Nisei housewife who did a story a year for the *Rafu Shimpo* [a bilingual English-Japanese daily] from 1960 until about 1974, when Frank Chin and the *Aiiieeee!* Boys found me and things changed." She divorced in 1975 and was writing full-time when Mako, the director of the East-West Players in Los Angeles, suggested she adapt into play form "And the Soul Shall Dance," a story published in *Aiiieeee!* Under a Rockefeller playwright-in-residence grant, she expanded the story into a play that was presented by

East-West Players and honored with a nationally televised PBS production in 1977–1978. Continuing to focus on playwriting, her plays have appeared in major venues including New York, where in 1980, her second play, *The Music Lessons* (based on her short story "In Heaven and Earth") was produced by Joseph Papp's New York Public Theater; New Haven, where Yale Repertory Theater staged *The Memento* (1987); and Los Angeles, where UCLA produced *12–1-A* (1992). Since 1965, she has lived in Gardena, California, and she continues to contribute to *Rafu Shimpo.*

FRANK YERBY (1916–1991) was born in Augusta, Georgia, and raised in the South. At the age of seventeen he became a published poet, with poems appearing in various magazines. Yerby moved back and forth between the South and North for his education and jobs. In 1938 he went to Chicago to study at the University of Chicago, where he became involved with the Federal Writers Project of the WPA and met fellow writers Arna Bontemps, Margaret Walker, and Richard Wright. One of his earliest short stories, "Health Card," won the O. Henry Memorial Award in 1944, the year it first appeared in *Harper's.* Yerby's first published novel, *The Foxes of Harrow* (1946), sold more than 55 million copies and was adapted into a popular film, as were his novels *The Golden Hawk* (1948) and *The Saracen Blade* (1952). Yerby authored a total of eighteen popular novels, which were translated into almost a dozen languages and sold over 21 million copies. In 1955 Yerby moved to Madrid, Spain, where he lived as an expatriate for the next thirty-five years of his life.

AL YOUNG (b. 1939) was born in Ocean Springs, Mississippi, on the Gulf Coast near Biloxi, and grew up in the South and Detroit, Michigan. He began writing as a child, publishing poems, stories, and articles by his early teens. To date Young has authored more than twenty books, including the novels *Snakes* (1970), *Who Is Angelina?* (1975), *Sitting Pretty* (1976), and *Seduction by Light*; the poetry collections *Dancing* (1969), *The Song Turning Back into Itself* (1971), *Geography of the Near Past* (1976), *The Blues Don't Change* (1982), *Heaven: Collected Poems 1956–1990* (1992), *The Sound of Dreams Remembered: Poems 1990–2000*, which received an American Book Award (2002), and *Something About the Blues* (2008); and the musical memoirs *Bodies & Soul* (1981), *Things Ain't What They Used to Be* (1987), and *Drowning in the Sea of Love* (1996), which received a PEN/USA Award for best non-fiction book of the year. He has adapted his own works for film and also written film scripts for Bill Cosby, Sidney Poitier, and Richard Pryor. Young has edited many anthologies including *African American Literature: A Brief Introduction and Anthology* and co-edited *Yardbird Lives!* (1995), with Ishmael Reed, and *The Literature of California*, with Jack Hicks, James D. Houston, and Maxine Hong Kingston. His many honors include a Wallace Stegner Writing Fellowship at Stanford; Guggenheim, Fulbright and NEA Fellowships; the 2007 Richard Wright Literary Excellence Award, and the Northern California Booksellers' 2008 Fred Cody Lifetime Achievement Award. Young has taught and been in-residence at many colleges and universities and has traveled extensively throughout the United States and internationally, giving lectures and readings that frequently include collaborations with musicians. He has been a board member of the Squaw Valley Community of Writers since 1995 and is a member of PEN Oakland. Honored as the state of California's Poet Laureate since 2005, he has made his home in the San Francisco Bay Area since 1961.

EDGARDO VEGA YUNQUÉ (b. 1936), a novelist and short story writer who has also published under the name Ed Vega, was born in the town of Cidra, Puerto Rico. He began living in New York City in 1949, at the age of twelve, after his Baptist minister father was appointed head of a Spanish-speaking congregation in the South Bronx. After high school he joined the air force, where he was trained as a radio operator and was stationed in the Azores and Athens, Greece. When his tour of duty was completed, he attended college in Santa Monica and NYU, where he majored in Latin American literature and met his future wife. After JFK's assassination Yunqué stopped school and began working as a War on Poverty community organizer in East Harlem. In 1977, his first short story, "Wild Horses," was published in the magazine *Nuestro*. Yunqué, who is widely anthologized, has to date authored three short fiction collections, including *Mendoza's Dreams* (1987) and *Casualty Report* (1991); and fourteen novels, including *The Comeback* (1985), *No Matter How Much You Promise to Cook or Pay the Rent You Blew It Cause Bill Bailey Ain't Never Coming Home Again* (2003), winner of a 2004 Josephine Myles PEN Oakland Award, *Blood Fugues* (2005), and *Rebecca Horowitz, Puerto Rican Sex Freak* (2008).

PERMISSIONS

ABOUT THE EDITORS

ISHMAEL REED (b. 1938), was born in Chattanooga, Tennessee, and from about age four, was raised in Buffalo, New York. His *New and Collected Poems, 1964–2006* (2006) was listed as one of the four best books of poetry published in 2006 by *The New York Times Book Review*, and in June, 2007, when issued in paperback edition as *New and Collected Poems, 1964–2007* (2007), it was awarded the California Gold Medal in Poetry by the Commonwealth Club. In 2008 his essay collection *Mixing It Up: Taking on the Media Bullies & Other Reflections* was published by Da Capo Press, and due in 2009 is his nonfiction work on Muhammad Ali, *Bigger Than Boxing* (Random House). Three books written or edited by Reed were published in 2003: *From Totems to Hip-Hop: A Multicultural Anthology of Poetry Across the Americas, 1900–2002*; *Another Day at the Front*; and *Blues City: A Walk in Oakland*. *The Reed Reader* (2000) includes excerpts from his nine published novels, selected essays, poetry, and two of his six plays, *Hubba City* and *The Preacher and the Rapper*. Other popular anthologies he has edited include *MultiAmerica: Essays in Cultural War and Cultural Peace* (1997), and the four-volume HarperCollinsCollege Literary Mosaic Series (1995–1996). Other Reed publications include the novels *Japanese by Spring, The Terrible Twos, The Terrible Threes, Reckless Eyeballing, Mumbo Jumbo,* (which Harold Bloom designated as one of the 500 important books of the Western canon), *The Last Days of Louisiana Red, Flight to Canada, Yellow-Back Radio Broke-Down,* and *The Free-Lance Pallbearers;* and collected essays *Another Day at the Front, Airing Dirty Laundry* and *Writin' Is Fightin'.* Two of his books have been nominated for National Book Awards, and a book of poetry, *Conjure*, was nominated for a Pulitzer Prize. Ishmael Reed founded the Before Columbus Foundation, which yearly presents its American Book Awards; the Oakland chapter of PEN; and There City Cinema. His online literary magazine, *Konch*, featuring poetry, essays, and fiction, can be found at *www.ishmaelreedpub.com.* Other honors include Guggenheim and National Endowment for the Arts Fellowships; the Langston Hughes Medal, awarded by City College of New York (1995); the Lila Wallace Reader's Digest Award (1997); a MacArthur Foundation Fellowship award (1998); a Fred Cody Award from the Bay Area Book Reviewers Association (1999); and induction into Chicago State University's National Literary Hall of Fame of Writers of African Descent. Reed makes his home in Oakland, California, where he is block captain of his neighborhood Home Alert program.

CARLA BLANK (b. 1941), co-editor of this anthology, was born and raised in Pittsburgh, Pennsylvania. A writer, editor, director, and teacher, her teaching materials from an art history course titled "Across Disciplines: 20th Century Art Forms," which she developed and taught at University of California, Berkeley, from 1994 to 1999, led to the creation of a cross-disciplinary historical reference book, *Rediscovering America: The Making of Multicultural America 1900–2000* (2003). Her experiences as a choreographer, performer, director, and teacher of dance and theater for forty years are shared in *Live OnStage!*, an anthology of performing arts techniques and styles co-authored with Jody Roberts (1997) that continues to be a resource for schools throughout the United States Most recently she has been director and dramaturg of new plays by Wajahat Ali, whose short story appears in this anthology. As editorial director of the Ishmael Reed Publishing Company, she edits and supervises production of its poetry and prose publications. She assembled 142 poets' biographies in Ishmael Reed's *From Totems to Hip-Hop: A Multicultural Anthology of Poetry Across the Americas, 1900–2002* (Thunder's Mouth Press, 2003) and was a contributing editor on the seminal anthology of California poetry, *Califia* (Y'Bird Books, 1979). Her current research and writing projects concern American women who became architects during the nineteenth century, and a nineteenth-century chronology similar in ambition to *Rediscovering America*. Her collaboration with Robert Wilson, entitled "Kool: Suzushi Hanayagi, a Moving Life," will premiere at New York City's Guggenheim Museum in 2009. Since 1979, she has lived in Oakland, California, with her family of writers, Ishmael Reed and Tennessee Reed.